FILIPINO POPULAR TALES

COLLECTED AND EDITED, WITH
COMPARATIVE NOTES,
BY DEAN S. FANSLER, PH.D.

PREFACE.

THE folk-tales in this volume, which were collected in the Philippines during the years from 1908 to 1914, have not appeared in print before. They are given to the public now in the hope that they will be no mean or uninteresting addition to the volumes of Oriental *Märchen* already in existence. The Philippine archipelago, from the very nature of its geographical position and its political history, cannot but be a significant field to the student of popular stories. Lying as it does at the very doors of China and Japan, connected as it is ethnically with the Malayan and Indian civilizations, Occidentalized as it has been for three centuries and more, it stands at the junction of East and West. It is therefore from this point of view that these tales have been put into a form convenient for reference. Their importance consists in their relationship to the body of world fiction.

The language in which these stories are presented is the language in which they were collected and written down, — English. Perhaps no apology is required for not printing the vernacular herewith; nevertheless an explanation might be made. In the first place, the object in recording these tales has been a literary one, not a linguistic one. In the second place, the number of distinctly different languages represented by the originals might be baffling even to the reader interested in linguistics, especially as our method of approach has been from the point of view of cycles of stories, and not from the point of view of the separate tribes telling them. In the third place, the form of prose tales among the Filipinos is not stereotyped; and there is likely to be no less variation between two Visayan versions of the same story, or between a Tagalog and a Visayan, than between the native form and the English rendering. Clearly Spanish would not be a better medium than English: for to-day there is more English than Spanish spoken in the Islands; besides, Spanish never penetrated into the very lives of the peasants, as English penetrates to-day by way of the school-house. I have endeavored to offset the disadvantages of the foreign medium by judicious and painstaking directions to my informants in the writing-down of the tales. Only in very rare cases was there any modification of the original version by the teller, as a concession to Occidental standards. Whatever substitutions I have been able to detect I have removed. In practically every case, not only to show that these are *bona fide* native stories, but also to indicate their geographical distribution, I have given the name of the narrator, his native town, and his province. In many cases I have given, in addition, the source of his information. I am firmly convinced that all the tales recorded here represent genuine Filipino tradition so far as the narrators are concerned, and that nothing has been "manufactured" consciously.

But what is "native," and what is "derived"? The folklore of the wild tribes — Negritos, Bagobos, Igorots — is in its way no more "uncontaminated" than that of the Tagalogs, Pampangans, Zambals, Pangasinans, Ilocanos, Bicols, and Visayans. The traditions of these Christianized tribes present as survivals, adaptations, modifications, fully as many puzzling and fascinating problems as the popular lore of the Pagan peoples. It should be remembered, that, no matter how wild and savage and isolated a tribe may be, it is impossible to prove that there has been no contact of that tribe with the outside civilized world. Conquest is not necessary to the introduction of a story or belief. The crew of a Portuguese trading-vessel with a genial narrator on board might conceivably be a much more successful transmitting-medium than a thousand *praos* full of brown warriors come to stay. Clearly the problem of analyzing and tracing the story-literature of the Christianized tribes differs only in degree from that connected with the Pagan tribes. In this volume I have treated the problem entirely from the former point of view, since there has been hitherto a tendency to neglect as of small value the stories of the Christianized peoples. However, for illustrative material I have drawn freely on works dealing with the non-Christian tribes, particularly in the case of stories that appear to be native; and I shall use the term "native" to mean merely "existent in the Islands before the Spaniards went there."

In the notes, I have attempted to answer for some of the tales the question as to what is native and what imported. I have not been able to reach a decision in the case of all, because of a lack of sufficient evidence. While the most obvious sources of importation from the Occident have been Spain and Portugal, the possibility of the introduction of French, Italian, and even Belgian stories through the medium of priests of those nationalities must not be overlooked. Furthermore, there is a no inconsiderable number of Basque sailors to be found on the small inter-island steamers that connect one end of the archipelago with the other. Even a very cursory glance at the tales in this collection reveals the fact that many of them are more or less close variants and analogues of tales distributed throughout the world. How or when this material reached the Philippines is hard to say. The importation of Arabian stories, for example, might have been made over many routes. The Hindoo beast-tales, too, might have quite circled the globe in their progress from east to west, and thus have been introduced to the Filipinos by the Spaniards and Portuguese. Again, the germs of a number of widespread *Märchen* may have existed in the archipelago long before the arrival of the Europeans, and, upon the introduction of Occidental civilization and culture, have undergone a development entirely consistent with the development that took place in Europe, giving us as a result remarkably close analogues of the Western tales. This I suspect to have been the case of some of our stories where, parallel with the localized popular versions, exist printed romances (in the vernacular) with the mediæval flavor and setting of chivalry. To give a specific case: the Visayans, Bicols, and Tagalogs in the coast towns feared the raids of Mindanao Mussulmans long before white feet trod the shores of the Islands, and many traditions of conflicts with these pirates are embedded in their legends. The Spaniard came in the sixteenth century, bringing with him stories of wars between Christians and Saracens in Europe. One result of this close analogy of actual historical situation was, I believe, a general tendency to levelling: that is, native traditions of such struggles took on the color of the Spanish romances; Spanish romances, on the other hand, which were popularized in the Islands, were very likely to be "localized." A maximum of caution and a minimum of dogmatism, then, are imperative, if one is to treat at all scientifically the relationship of the stories of a composite people like the Filipinos to the stories of the rest of the world.

A word might be added as to the nature of the tales. I have included only "hero tales, serious and droll," beast stories and fables, and *pourquoi* or "just-so" stories. Myths, legends, and fairy-tales (including all kinds of spirit and demon stories) I have purposely excluded, in order to keep the size of the volume within reasonable limits. I have, however, occasionally drawn upon my manuscript collection of these types to illustrate a native superstition or custom.

COLUMBIA UNIVERSITY,
    May, 1918.

CONTENTS.

FILIPINO STORIES GIVEN IN THE NOTES.

[Only stories from my own manuscript collection are listed here. Titles of those given in full are printed in Roman; of those given merely in abstract, in Italics. A "(C)" after a title indicates that the story is taken from one of the native *corridos*, or metrical romances printed in the vernacular.]

BIBLIOGRAPHY.

[The following list includes only such works as are referred to in abbreviated form in the notes throughout the volume.]

AARNE, ANTTI. Vergleichende Märchenforschungen. Helsingfors, 1908.

Arabian Nights' Entertainments. Translated by Sir RICHARD BURTON. 10 vols., 1885. Supplemental Nights, 6 vols., 1886–88.

Bahar-i-Danush. Translated from the Persian by JONATHAN SCOTT. 3 vols. Shrewsbury, 1799.

BAIN, R. NISBET. Russian Fairy Tales. From the Skazki of Polevoi. New York, N.D.

BASILE, G. Pentamerone. Translated by Sir RICHARD BURTON. 2 vols. London, 1893.

BATEMAN, G. W. Zanzibar Tales. Chicago, 1901.

BENFEY, THEODOR. Pantschatantra: fünf Bücher indischer Fabeln, Märchen und Erzählungen. Aus dem Sanskrit übersetzt, mit Einleitung und Anmerkungen. 2 vols. Leipzig, 1859.

BLUMENTRITT, FERDINAND. Diccionario mitológico (in Retana's Archivo del bibliófilo filipino, Vol. 2, Madrid, 1896).

BOLTE (JOHANNES) UND POLÍVKA (GEORG). Anmerkungen zu den Kinder- und Hausmärchen der Brüder Grimm. 2 vols. Leipzig, 1913, 1915. (Cited Bolte-Polívka.)

BOMPAS, C. H. Folklore of the Santal Parganas. London, 1909.

BURTON, Sir RICHARD. See *Arabian Nights' Entertainments*, and *Basile*.

(BUSK.) Sagas from the Far East; or Kalmouk and Mongolian Traditionary Tales. London, 1873. (Compiled by RACHEL HARRIETTE BUSK.)

CABALLERO, FERNAN. Cuentos y poesias populares Andaluces. Leipzig, 1866. See also *Ingram*.

CAMPBELL, A. Santal Folk-Tales. Pokhuria, India, 1891.

CAMPBELL, J. F. Popular Tales of the West Highlands. 4 vols. 1890.

CAMPBELL, KILLIS. The Seven Sages of Rome. Boston, 1907.

CHILD, FRANCIS J. English and Scottish Popular Ballads. 5 vols. in 10 parts. Boston, 1882–98.

CLOUSTON, W. A. Book of Noodles. London, 1888. (Cited Clouston 1.)

— A Group of Eastern Romances. 1889. Privately printed. (Cited Clouston 2.)

CLOUSTON, W. A. Popular Tales and Fictions. 2 vols. London, 1888. (Cited Clouston 3.)

COLE, FAY-COOPER. Traditions of the Tinguian. Chicago, 1915. (Cited Cole.)

COLE, MABEL COOK. Philippine Folk Tales. Chicago, 1916. (Cited M. C. Cole.)

COMPARETTI, D. Novelline Popolari Italiane. Rome, 1875.

COSQUIN, EMMANUEL. Contes Populaires de Lorraine. 2 vols. Paris (1887).

CRANE, THOMAS F. Italian Popular Tales. Boston, 1885.

CROOKE, W. Religion and Folklore of Northern India. 2 vols. Westminster, 1896.

DÄHNHARDT, OSKAR. Natursagen. Eine Sammlung naturdeutender Sagen, Märchen, Fabeln und Legenden. 4 vols. Leipzig, 1907-12.

DASENT, G. W. Popular Tales from the Norse. London, N.D. (The London Library.)

DAYRELL, ELPHINSTONE. Folk Stories from Southern Nigeria, West Africa. London, 1910.

DRACOTT, ALICE E. Simla Village Tales. London, 1906.

DUNLOP, JOHN COLIN. History of Fiction. Edited by H. WILSON. 2 vols. London, 1896.

EVANS, IVOR H. N. Folk Stories of the Tempassuk and Tuaran Districts, British North Borneo (in the Journal of the Royal Anthropological Institute of Great Britain and Ireland, 43 [1913]: 422-479). (Cited Evans.)

FANSLER, HARRIOTT E. Types of Prose Narratives. Chicago, 1911.

FLEESON, KATHERINE NEVILLE. Laos Folk-Lore of Farther India. Chicago, 1899.

Folk-Lore Journal. Folk-Lore Society. 7 vols. London, 1883-89. (Cited FLJ.)

Folk-Lore: A Quarterly Review, current since 1890. (Cited FL.)

FRERE, M. Old Deccan Days, or Hindoo Fairy Legends Current in Southern India. London, 1868.

GEROULD, G. H. The Grateful Dead. (Folk-Lore Society.) London, 1907.

Gesta Romanorum. Translated by the Rev. CHARLES SWAN. Revised edition. London, 1906.

GONZENBACH, LAURA. Sicilianische Märchen. 2 vols. Leipzig, 1870.

GRIMM, THE BROTHERS. Household Tales: with the Author's Notes. Translated from the German, and edited by M. Hunt. With an Introduction by Andrew Lang. 2 vols. London, 1884.

GROOME, F. H. Gypsy Folk Tales. London, 1899.

HAHN, J. G. VON. Griechische und albanesische Märchen. 2 vols. Leipzig, 1864.

HARTLAND, E. S. Science of Fairy Tales. London, 1891.

HONEŸ, JAMES A. South African Folk Tales. New York, 1910.

HOSE (CHARLES) and McDOUGALL (WILLIAM). The Pagan Tribes of Borneo. 2 vols. London, 1912. (Cited Hose-McDougall.)

Indian Antiquary — A Journal of Oriental Research in Archaeology, History, Literature, Languages, Philosophy, Religion, etc. Bombay (current).

INGRAM, J. H. Spanish Fairy Tales. Translated from Fernan Caballero. New York, N.D.

JACOBS, JOSEPH. Indian Fairy Tales. New York and London, 1913. (Cited Jacobs 1.)

— The Fables of Æsop. I. History of the Æsopic Fable. London, 1889. (Cited Jacobs 2.)

Jātaka, or Stories of the Buddha's Former Births. Translated from the Pāli by various hands. Edited by E. B. COWELL. 6 vols. Cambridge, V.D.

Journal of American Folk-Lore. (Cited JAFL.)

— Bayliss, Clara K., Tagalog Folk-Tales (JAFL 21 : 46–53).

— Benedict, Laura W., Bagobo Myths (JAFL 26 : 13–63).

— Chamberlain, A. F., Notes on Tagal Folk-Lore (JAFL 15 : 196–198).

— Gardner, Fletcher, Tagalog Folk-Tales (JAFL 20 : 104–116, 300–310).

— Maxfield, B. L., and Millington, W. H., Visayan Folk-Tales (JAFL 19:97–112; 20:89–103, 311–318).

Journal of Philology.

Journal of the Royal Asiatic Society of Bengal, N.S. (Cited JRASB.)

Kathā-sarit-sāgara. See *Somadeva.*

KINGSCOTE, Mrs. HOWARD. Tales of the Sun, or Folklore of Southern India. London, 1890.

KITTREDGE, GEORGE L. Arthur and Gorlagon (in Harvard Studies and Notes in Philology and Literature).

KNOWLES, the Rev. J. H. Folk-Tales of Kashmir. 2d ed. London, 1893.

KÖHLER, REINHOLD. Kleinere Schriften. I. Zur Märchenforschung. Edited by J. BOLTE. Weimar, 1898. (Cited Köhler-Bolte.)

LAL BEHARI DAY. Folk-Tales of Bengal. London, 1883.

LANG, ANDREW. Custom and Myth. 2d ed. London, 1885.

LEGRAND, E. Recueil de contes populaires grecs. Paris, 1881.

MACCULLOCH, J. A. The Childhood of Fiction: A Study of Folk Tales and Primitive Thought. London, 1905.

McCULLOCH, WILLIAM. Bengali Household Tales. London, 1912.

MEIER, E. Deutsche Volksmärchen aus Schwaben. Stuttgart, 1852.

METELERKAMP, SANNI. Outa Karel's Stories: South African Folk-Lore Tales. London, 1914.

MIJATOVIES, Mme. Serbian Folk-Lore. London, 1874.

Orient und Occident, insbesondere in ihren gegenwärtigen Beziehungen, etc. 3 vols. Göttingen, 1860–64.

Pantschatantra. See *Benfey*.

PANZER, FRIEDRICH. Studien zur germanischen Sagengeschichte. I. Beowulf. München, 1910.

Persian Tales: The 1001 Days. Translated by AMBROSE PHILLIPS. 2 vols. London, 1722. (References are to the 6th edition.)

PITRÈ, G. Fiabe, Novelline e Racconti Popolari Siciliane. 4 vols. Palermo, 1875.

PRÖHLE, H. Kinder- und Volksmärchen. Leipzig, 1853.

RADLOFF, W. Proben der Volkslitteratur der Turkischen Stämme Sud-Sibiriens. 6 vols. St. Petersburg, 1866–86.

RALSTON, W. R. S. Russian Folk Tales. London, 1873. (Cited Ralston 1.)

— Tibetan Tales. London, 1882. (Cited Ralston 2.)

RETANA, WENCESLAO. Aparato Bibliográfico. 3 vols. Madrid, 1906.

RITTERSHAUS, ADELINE. Die Neuisländischen Volksmärchen. Halle, 1902.

RIVIERE, J. Recueil de contes populaires de la Kabylie. Paris, 1882.

Romancero General. 2 vols. Ed. DURAN.

Romania: Recueil trimestriel. Ed. par P. MEYER et G. PARIS. Paris, current since 1872.

Rondallayre. Lo Rondallayre. Quentos populars catalans, colleccionats per Fr. Maspons y Labros. Barcelona, 1875.

ROTH, H. LING. The Natives of Sarawak and British North Borneo. 2 vols. London, 1896.

ROUSE, W. H. D. The Talking Thrush and Other Tales from India. London, 1899.

SCHIEFNER, ANTON VON. See *Tibetan Tales*.

SCHLEICHER, AUGUST. Litauische Märchen, Sprichworte, Rätsel und Lieder. Weimar, 1857.

SCHNELLER, C. Märchen und Sagen aus Wälschtirol. Innsbruck, 1867.

SCHOTT, ARTHUR und ALBERT. Walachische Maerchen. Stuttgart, 1845.

SCOTT, JONATHAN. See *Bahar-i-Danush*.

SELLERS, C. Tales from the Land of Nuts and Grapes. London, 1888.

SKEAT, W. W. Fables and Folk-Tales from an Eastern Forest. Cambridge, 1901. (Cited Skeat 1.)

SKEAT, W. W. Malay Magic. London, 1900. (Cited Skeat 2.)

SOMADEVA. Kathā-sarit-sāgara. Translated into English by C. H. TAWNEY. 2 vols. Calcutta, 1880, 1884.

STEEL (F. A.) and TEMPLE (R. C.). Wideawake Stories = Tales of the Punjab. London, 1894. (Cited Steel-Temple.)

STEERE, E. Swahili Tales. London, 1870.

STOKES, MAIVE. Indian Fairy Tales. London, 1880.

STRAPAROLA, GIOVAN F. Tredici piacevoli Notti. The Nights, now first translated into English by W. G. WATERS. 2 vols. London, 1894.

TAWNEY, C. H. See *Somadeva.*

THORNHILL, MARK. Indian Fairy Tales. London, 1888.

THORPE, B. Yule-Tide Stories. London, 1853.

Thousand and One Nights. See *Arabian Nights' Entertainment.*

Tibetan Tales. Translated from the Tibetan of the Kah-Gyur by F. ANTON VON SCHIEFNER. Done into English from the German, with an Introduction, by W. R. S. RALSTON. London, 1882. (Cited Ralston 2.)

Tootinameh; or Tales of a Parrot. Persian text with English translation. Calcutta, 1792.

WALDAU, A. Böhmisches Märchenbuch. Prag, 1860.

WARDROP, M. Georgian Folk Tales. London, 1894.

WEBSTER, WENTWORTH. Basque Legends. London (2d ed.), 1879.

WRATISLAW, A. H. Sixty Slavonic Folk-Tales. Boston, 1890.

WUK. Volksmärchen der Serben. Berlin, 1854.

FILIPINO POPULAR TALES.

I. HERO TALES AND DROLLS.

1. (a) SUAN'S GOOD LUCK.[1]

THERE was once an old woman who had an only son named
Suan.[2] Suan was a clever, sharp-witted boy. His mother
sent him to school. Instead of going to school, however,
Suan climbed up the tree that stood by the roadside. As soon
as his mother had passed by from the market, Suan hurried
home ahead of her. When she reached home, he cried, "Mother,
I know what you bought in the market to-day." He then told
her, article by article. This same thing happened so repeatedly,
that his mother began to believe in his skill as a diviner.

One day the ring of the datu's[3] daughter disappeared. All
the people in the locality searched for it, but in vain. The
datu called for volunteers to find the lost ring, and he offered
his daughter's hand as a prize to the one who should succeed.
Suan's mother heard of the proclamation. So she went to
the palace and presented Suan to the datu.

"Well, Suan, to-morrow tell me where the ring is," said the datu.

"Yes, my lord, I will tell you, if you will give your soldiers
over to me for to-night," Suan replied.

"You shall have everything you need," said the datu.

That evening Suan ordered the soldiers to stand around him in
a semicircle. When all were ready, Suan pointed at each one
of them, and said, "The ring is here, and nowhere else." It
so happened that Suan fixed his eyes on the guilty soldier, who
trembled and became pale. "I know who has it," said Suan.
Then he ordered them to retire.

Late in the night this soldier came to Suan, and said, "I will
get the ring you are in search of, and will give it to you if you
will promise me my safety."

"Give it to me, and you shall be safe," said Suan.

---

[1] Narrated by Macaria Garcia. The story is popular among the Pampangans.
[2] A common nickname for "Juan," equivalent to the English "Jack."
[3] *Datu*, old native name for "village chieftain."

I

Very early the next morning Suan came to the palace with a turkey in his arms. "Where is the ring?" the datu demanded.

"Why, sir, it is in this turkey's intestines," Suan replied. The turkey was then killed, and the ring was found inside it.

"You have done very well, Suan. Now you shall have my daughter's hand," said the datu. So Suan became the princess's husband.

One day the datu proposed a bet with any one who wished to prove Suan's skill. Accordingly another datu came. He offered to bet seven cascos [1] of treasure that Suan could not tell the number of seeds that were in his orange. Suan did not know what to do. At midnight he went secretly to the cascos. Here he heard their conversation, and from it he learned the number of seeds in the orange.

In the morning Suan said boastfully, "I tell you, your orange has nine seeds." Thus Suan won the whole treasure.

Hoping to recover his loss, the datu came again. This time he had with him fourteen cascos full of gold. He asked Suan to tell him what was inside his golden ball. Suan did not know what to say. So in the dead of night he went out to the cascos, but he could learn nothing there.

The next morning Suan was summoned into the presence of the two datus. He had no idea whatever as to what was in the ball; so he said scornfully, "Nonsense!"

"That is right, that is right!" shouted a man. "The ball contains nine cents." Consequently Suan won the fourteen cascos full of gold. From now on, nobody doubted Suan's merit.

(b) SUAN EKET. [2]

Many years ago there lived in the country of Campao a boy named Suan. While this boy was studying in a private school, it was said that he could not pronounce the letter x very well: he called it "eket." So his schoolmates nick-named him "Suan Eket."

Finally Suan left school, because, whenever he went there, the other pupils always shouted at him, "Eket, eket, eket!" He went home, and told his mother to buy him a pencil and a pad of paper. "I am the wisest boy in our town now," said he.

---

[1] *Casco*, a commodious wooden cargo-boat commonly used in rivers and propelled by poling.

[2] Narrated by Manuel Reyes, a Tagalog from Rizal province. He heard the story from his grandfather.

One night Suan stole his father's plough, and hid it in a creek near their house. The next morning his father could not find his plough.

"What are you looking for?" said Suan.

"My plough," answered his father.

"Come here, father! I will guess where it is." Suan took his pencil and a piece of paper. On the paper he wrote figures of various shapes. He then looked up, and said, —

"Ararokes, ararokes,
Na na nakawes
Ay na s'imburnales," —

which meant that the plough had been stolen by a neighbor and hidden in a creek. Suan's father looked for it in the creek near their house, and found it. In great wonder he said, "My son is truly the wisest boy in the town." News spread that Suan was a good guesser.

One day as Suan was up in a guava-tree, he saw his uncle Pedro ploughing. At noon Pedro went home to eat his dinner, leaving the plough and the carabao [1] in the field. Suan got down from the tree and climbed up on the carabao's back. He guided it to a very secret place in the mountains and hid it there. When Pedro came back, he could not find his carabao. A man who was passing by said, "Pedro, what are you looking for?"

"I am looking for my carabao. Somebody must have stolen it."

"Go to Suan, your nephew," said the man. "He can tell you who stole your carabao." So Pedro went to Suan's house, and told him to guess who had taken his carabao.

Suan took his pencil and a piece of paper. On the paper he wrote some round figures. He then looked up, and said, —

"Carabaues, carabaues,
Na nanakawes
Ay na sa bundokes," —

which meant that the carabao was stolen by a neighbor and was hidden in the mountain. For many days Pedro looked for it in the mountain. At last he found it in a very secret place. He then went to Suan's house, and told him that the carabao was truly in the mountain. In great wonder he said, "My nephew is surely a good guesser."

---

[1] *Carabao*, a gray water-buffalo used throughout the Archipelago as a draught-animal.

One Sunday a proclamation of the king was read. It was as follows: "The princess's ring is lost. Whoever can tell who stole it shall have my daughter for his wife; but he who tries and fails, loses his head."

When Suan's mother heard it, she immediately went to the palace, and said, "King, my son can tell you who stole your daughter's ring."

"Very well," said the king, "I will send my carriage for your son to ride to the palace in."

In great joy the woman went home. She was only ascending the ladder[1] when she shouted, "Suan, Suan, my fortunate son!"

"What is it, mother?" said Suan.

"I told the king that you could tell him who stole the princess's ring."

"Foolish mother, do you want me to die?" said Suan, trembling.

Suan had scarcely spoken these words when the king's carriage came. The coachman was a courtier. This man was really the one who had stolen the princess's ring. When Suan was in the carriage, he exclaimed in great sorrow, "Death is at hand!" Then he blasphemed, and said aloud to himself, "You will lose your life now."

The coachman thought that Suan was addressing him. He said to himself, "I once heard that this man is a good guesser. He must know that it was I who stole the ring, because he said that my death is at hand." So he knelt before Suan, and said, "Pity me! Don't tell the king that it was I who stole the ring!"

Suan was surprised at what the coachman said. After thinking for a moment, he asked, "Where is the ring?"

"Here it is."

"All right! Listen, and I will tell you what you must do in order that you may not be punished by the king. You must catch one of the king's geese to-night, and make it swallow the ring."

The coachman did what Suan had told him to do. He caught a goose and opened its mouth. He then dropped the ring into it, and pressed the bird's throat until it swallowed the ring.

[1] The usual means of getting into a native grass house is a bamboo ladder.

The next morning the king called Suan, and said, "Tell me now who stole my daughter's ring."

"May I have a candle? I cannot guess right if I have no candle," said Suan.

The king gave him one. He lighted it and put it on a round table. He then looked up and down. He went around the table several times, uttering Latin words. Lastly he said in a loud voice, "Mi domine!"

"Where is the ring?" said the king.

Suan replied, —

"Singsing na nawala
Ninakao ang akala
Ay nas' 'big ng gansa," —

which meant that the ring was not stolen, but had been swallowed by a goose. The king ordered all the geese to be killed. In the crop of one of them they found the ring. In great joy the king patted Suan on the back, and said, "You are truly the wisest boy in the world."

The next day there was a great entertainment, and Suan and the princess were married.

In a country on the other side of the sea was living a rich man named Mayabong. This man heard that the King of Campao had a son-in-law who was a good guesser. So he filled one of his cascos with gold and silver, and sailed to Campao. He went to the palace, and said, "King, is it true that your son-in-law is a good guesser?"

"Yes," said the king.

"Should you like to have a contest with me? If your son-in-law can tell how many seeds these melons I have brought here contain, I will give you that casco filled with gold and silver on the sea; but if he fails, you are to give me the same amount of money as I have brought."

The king agreed. Mayabong told him that they would meet at the public square the next day.

When Mayabong had gone away, the king called Suan, and said, "Mayabong has challenged me to a contest. You are to guess how many seeds the melons he has contain. Can you do it?" Suan was ashamed to refuse; so, even though he knew that he could not tell how many seeds a melon contained, he answered, "Yes."

When night came, Suan could not sleep. He was wondering what to do. At last he decided to drown himself in the sea. So he went to the shore and got into a tub. "I must drown myself far out, so that no one may find my body. If they see it, they will say that I was not truly a good guesser," he said to himself. He rowed and rowed until he was very tired. It so happened that he reached the place where Mayabong's casco was anchored. There he heard somebody talking. "How many seeds has the green melon?" said one. "Five," answered another. "How many seeds has the yellow one?" — "Six."

When Suan heard how many seeds each melon contained, he immediately rowed back to shore and went home.

The next morning Suan met Mayabong at the public square, as agreed. Mayabong held up a green melon, and said, "How many seeds does this melon contain?"

"Five seeds," answered Suan, after uttering some Latin words.

The melon was cut, and was found to contain five seeds. The king shouted, "We are right!"

Mayabong then held up another melon, and said, "How many does this one contain?"

Seeing that it was the yellow melon, Suan said, "It contains six."

When the melon was cut, it was found that Suan was right again. So he won the contest.

Now, Mayabong wanted to win his money back again. So he took a bottle and filled it with dung, and covered it tightly. He challenged the king again to a contest. But when Suan refused this time, because he had no idea as to what was in the bottle, the king said, "I let you marry my daughter, because I thought that you were a good guesser. Now you must prove that you are. If you refuse, you will lose your life."

When Mayabong asked what the bottle contained, Suan, filled with rage, picked it up and hurled it down on the floor, saying, "I consider that you are all waste to me." [1] When the bottle was broken, it was found to contain waste, or dung. In great joy the king crowned Suan to succeed him. Thus Suan lived happily the rest of his life with his wife the princess.

---

[1] This is a common Tagalog expression, and means, "I consider that you are all inferior to me in every respect."

NOTES.

Two other printed variants are —

(*c*) "Juan the Guesser" (in H. E. Fansler's Types of Prose Narratives [Chicago, 1911], pp. 73–77).
(*d*) "Juan Pusong" (JAFL 19: 107–108).

This story seems to be fairly widespread among the Filipinos: there is no doubt of its popularity. The distinguishing incidents of the type are as follows: —

A¹ Lazy son decides that he will go to school no longer, and (A²) with his ABC book or a pencil and pad of paper, he has no trouble in making his parents think him wise. (A³) He tells his mother that he has learned to be a prophet and can discover hidden things. (A⁴) He spies on his mother, and then "guesses" what she has prepared for supper.
B He hides his father's plough (cattle), and then finds it for him. (B¹) Plays similar trick on his uncle, thereby establishing his reputation as a diviner.
C King's daughter loses ring, and the king sends for Juan to find it under penalty of death if he fails, or (C¹) his mother volunteers her son's services. (C²) He accidentally discovers the thief by an ejaculation of sorrow, or (C³) shrewdly picks out the guilty one from among the soldiers.

    In either case he causes the ring to be hid in a secret place or swallowed by a goose (turkey), in whose body it is found the next day.
D Juan marries the princess.
E By overhearing a conversation, Juan is able to tell the number of seeds in an orange (melon), and to win large sum of money from a neighboring king who has come to bet with hero's father-in-law.
F Hero required to accept another bet, as to the contents of three jars. (Method as in E, — swimming out to neighboring king's casco and overhearing conversation.)
G Ejaculation guess as to contents of golden ball (bottle).
Ħ Afraid of being called on for further demonstration of his skill, hero burns his "magic" book.

These incidents are distributed among the four forms of the story as follows: —

Version *a* . . . . A¹A⁴C¹C²DEG
Version *b* . . . . A¹A²BB¹C¹C²DEG
Version *c*. . . . . A¹A²BCC²DE(accidentally hears answer)FH
Version *d* . . . . A¹A³A⁴EB

A concluding adventure is sometimes added to version *c*, "Juan the Guesser." King and queen of another country visit palace of Juan's father-in-law and want their newly-born child baptized. Juan is selected to be godfather. When called upon to sign the baptism certificate, he instantly dies of shame, pen in hand: he cannot write even his own name.

A connection between our story and Europe at once suggests itself. "Dr. Knowall" (Grimm, No. 98) is perhaps the best-known, though by no means the fullest, Western version. Bolte and Polívka (2 [1915]:402) give the skeleton of the cycle as follows: —

A¹ A peasant with the name of Crab (Cricket, Rat), who buys a physician's costume and calls himself Dr. Knowall, or (A²) who would like to satiate himself once with three days' eating, (B) discovers the thieves who have stolen from a distinguished gentleman a ring (treasure), by calling out upon the entrance of the servants (or at the end of the three days), "That is the first (second, third)!" (C) He also guesses what is in the covered dish (or closed hand) while commiserating himself, "Poor Crab (Cricket, Rat)!" (D¹) Through a purgative he by chance helps to find a stolen horse, or (D²) he discovers the horse that has previously been concealed by him. (E) He gets a living among the peasants, upon whom he has made an impression with a short or unintelligible sermon or through the crashing-down of the pulpit, which has previously been sawed through by him.

Bolte lists over a hundred and fifty stories containing one or more incidents of this cycle. The discovery of the ring inside a domestic fowl (sometimes animal) is found in most of the European versions, as is likewise the "ejaculation guess" (our C² and G).

These two details, however, are also found in Oriental forms of the story, which, as a whole, have some peculiarly distinctive traits. These (see Bolte-Polívka, 2:407) are (1) the rôle of the wife, (2) the collapsing of the room, (3) the burning of the magic book. The appearance in the Philippine versions of two of these *motifs* (one in modified form), together with a third (the betting-contest between the two kings, which is undoubtedly Eastern in origin), leads us to believe that our story of "Juan the Guesser" is in large measure descended directly from Oriental tradition, though it may owe something to Occidental influence.

In two of our variants it is the mother who in her fond pride places her son in jeopardy of losing his head. As the hero is a young bachelor when the story opens, the exploitation of his prowess would naturally devolve upon his mother. The burning of the magic book is found in version *c*, though the incident of the collapsing of the room or house is lacking in all our variants. The most characteristic episode, however, in the Philippine members of this cycle, is the betting-contest between the two kings. It is introduced five times into the four tales. Its only other occurrence that I know of in this cycle is in an Arabian story cited by Cosquin (2 : 192), which follows.

One day, when the king was boasting of his conjurer before some other kings, they said to him, "We too have some diviners. Let us compare their wits with the wisdom of your man." The kings then buried three pots, — one filled with milk, another with honey, and the third with pitch. The conjurers of the other kings could not say what was in the pots. Then Asfour (the hero) was called. He turned to his wife, and said, "All this (trouble) comes of you. We could have left the country. The first (time) it was milk; the second, honey; the third, pitch." The kings were dumfounded. "He has named the milk, the honey, and the pitch without hesitation," they said, and they gave him a pension.

The close resemblance between this detail and the corresponding one (F) in "Juan the Guesser" is immediately evident. The fact that the difficulty in Juan's career is overcome, not by an "ejaculation guess," but by a providential accident (much the same thing, however), does not decrease the significance of the two passages.

That the betting-contest between the two kings is an Oriental conception (very likely based on actual early custom) is further borne out by its appearance in a remarkable group of Eastern stories of the "Clever Lass" type (see Child, English and Scottish Ballads, I : II). "The gist of these narratives," writes Professor Child, "is that one king propounds tasks to another; in the earlier ones, with the intent to discover whether his brother-monarch enjoys the aid of such counsellors as will make an attack on him dangerous; in the later, with the demand that he shall acquit himself satisfactorily, or suffer a forfeit: and the king is delivered from a serious strait by the sagacity either of a minister . . . or of the daughter of his minister, who came to her father's assistance. . . . These tasks are always such as require ingenuity of one kind or another, whether in devising practical experiments, in contriving subterfuges, in solving riddles, or even in constructing compliments."

One other Oriental variant of this story may be cited because of its similarity to two of our tales (cf. our episodes C and C²). This is an Anamese version, printed in the "Chrestomathie cochin-chinoise" (Paris, 1872), I : 30: —

There was once a man who, being qualified for nothing, and not knowing how to earn a living, made up his mind one day to become a diviner. As luck had many times served him, the public came to believe in his oracles. . . . He amassed a good round sum, and day by day his success made him more bold and boastful. Once a golden tortoise disappeared from the palace of the king. As all searches for it resulted in nothing, some one mentioned the diviner to the king, and begged permission to summon him. The king ordered his litter prepared, the escort and the umbrellas of honor, and sent to have the conjurer fetched. When the conjurer learned what was the matter, he was very much disturbed, but he could not resist the commands of the king. Accordingly he dressed himself, entered the litter, and set out. Along the road the poor diviner continually bemoaned his fate. Finally he cried out, "What is the use of groaning? The stomach (*bung*) has caused it all; the belly (*da*) will suffer for it" (an Anamese proverb). Now, it happened that the two litter-bearers were named Bung and Da, and it was they who had stolen the king's gold tortoise. When they heard the exclamation of the diviner, they believed that they had been discovered. They begged him to have pity on them; they confessed that they had stolen the tortoise and had hidden it in the gutter. "Very well," said the diviner, "I will spare you; I will say nothing; reassure yourselves." When he reached the palace, he went through some magical performances, found the tortoise, and was overwhelmed by the king with rewards and honors. — COSQUIN, 2 : 192.

It is entirely possible that this story and our two stories containing the same situation are connected. Trading between Manila and Indo-China has been going on for centuries.

The history of the Philippine story has probably been something like this: To an early narrative about a wager between two neighboring kings or datus, in which the winner was aided by the shrewdness of an advisor (originally having a considerable amount of real ability), were added other adventures showing how the advisor came to have his post of honor. The germ of this story doubtless came from India *via* the Malay migrations; the additional details possibly belong to a much later period.

It is, moreover, not impossible that this whole cycle of the lucky "anti-hero" grew up as a conscious antithesis to the earlier cycle of the genuinely "Clever Lass" (see No. 7 in this collection).

In conclusion I might call attention to Benfey's treatment of this droll in "Orient und Occident" (1 : 371 *et seq.*). Benfey traces the story from the Orient, but considers that its fullest form is that given in Schleicher's Lithuanian legends. The tale is also found in "Somadeva," Chapter XXX (Tawney, 1 : 272–274).

2. THE CHARCOAL-MAKER WHO BECAME KING.[1]

Once upon a time there lived a king who had one beautiful daughter. When she was old enough to be married, her father, as was the custom in ancient times, made a proclamation throughout his kingdom thus: "Whosoever shall be able to bring me ten car-loads of money for ten successive days shall have the hand of my beautiful daughter and also my crown. If, however, any one undertakes and fails, he shall be put to death."

A boy, the only son of a poor charcoal-maker, heard this announcement in his little town. He hurried home to his mother, and said that he wanted to marry the beautiful princess

[1] Narrated by José R. Perez, a Tagalog living in Manila, who heard the story when a boy from his nurse.

and to be king of their country. The mother, however, paid no attention to what her foolish son had said, for she well knew that they had very little money.

The next day the boy, as usual, took his hatchet and went to the forest to cut wood. He started to cut down a very huge tree, which would take him several days to finish. While he was busy with his hatchet, he seemed to hear a voice saying, "Cut this tree no more. Dip your hand into the hole of the trunk, and you will find a purse which will give you all the money you wish." At first he did not pay any attention to the voice, but finally he obeyed it. To his surprise, he got the purse, but found it empty. Disappointed, he angrily threw it away; but as the purse hit the ground, silver money rolled merrily out of it. The youth quickly gathered up the coins; then, picking up the purse, he started for home, filled with happiness.

When he reached the house, he spread *petates* [1] over the floor of their little hut, called his mother, and began shaking the purse. The old woman was amazed and delighted when she saw dollars coming out in what seemed to be an inexhaustible stream. She did not ask her son where he had found the purse, but was now thoroughly convinced that he could marry the beautiful princess and be king afterwards.

The next morning she ordered her son to go to the palace to inform his Majesty that he would bring him the money he demanded in exchange for his daughter and his crown. The guard of the palace, however, thought that the youth was crazy; for he was poorly dressed and had rude manners. Therefore he refused to let him in. But their talk was overheard by the king, who ordered the guard to present the youth before him. The king read the announcement, emphasizing the part which said that in case of failure the contestant would be put to death. To this condition the charcoal-maker agreed. Then he asked the king to let him have a talk with his daughter. The meeting was granted, and the youth was extremely pleased with the beauty and vivacity of the princess.

After he had bidden her good-by, he told the king to send the cars with him to get the first ten car-loads of money. The cars were sent with guards. The drivers and the guards of the convoy were astonished when they saw the poor charcoal-maker fill the ten cars with bright new silver dollars. The

---

[1] *Petate* (Sp.-Mexican), a sleeping-mat made of woven straw.

princess, too, at first was very much pleased with such a large sum of money.

Five days went by, and the youth had not failed to send the amount of money required. "Five days more, and I shall surely be married!" said the princess to herself. "Married? Yes, married life is like music without words. But will it be in my case? My future husband is ugly, unrefined, and of low descent. But — he is rich. Yes, rich; but what are riches if I am going to be wretched? No, I will not marry him for all the world. I will play a trick on him."

The next day the guard informed her that the riches of the young man were inexhaustible, for the purse from which he got his money seemed to be magical. When she heard this, she commanded the guard to tell the young man that she wished to see him alone. Filled with joy because of this sign of her favor, the youth hastened to the palace, conducted by the guard. The princess entertained him regally, and tried all sorts of tricks to get possession of the magical purse. At last she succeeded in inducing him to go to sleep. While he was unconscious, the deceitful princess stole the purse and left him alone in the chamber.

When he awoke, he saw that the princess had deserted him and that his purse was gone. "Surely I am doomed to die if I don't leave this kingdom at once," said he to himself. "My purse is gone, and I cannot now fulfil my contract." He at once hurried home, told his parents to abandon their home and town, and he himself started on a journey for another kingdom. After much travelling, he reached mountainous places, and had eaten but little for many a day.

By good luck he came across a tree heavily laden with fruits. The tree was strange to him; but the delicious appearance of its fruit, and his hunger, tempted him to try some. While he was eating, he was terrified to find that two horns had appeared on his forehead. He tried his best to pull them off, but in vain. The next day he saw another tree, whose fruit appeared even more tempting. He climbed it, picked some fruits, and ate them. To his surprise, his horns immediately fell off. He wrapped some of this fruit up in his handkerchief, and then went back to find the tree whose fruit he had eaten the day before. He again ate some of its fruit, and again two horns grew out of his head. Then he ate some of the other kind, and the horns fell off. Confident now that he had a means of recovering his purse, he gathered some of the horn-producing fruits, wrapped them in his shirt, and started home. By this time he had been travelling for nearly two years, and his face had so changed that he could not be recognized by his own parents, or by his town-mates who had been hired by the king to search for him for execution.

When he reached his town, he decided to place himself in the king's palace as a helper of the royal cook. As he was willing to work without pay, he easily came to terms with the cook. One of the conditions of their agreement was that the cook would tell him whatever the king or the king's family were talking about. After a few months the charcoal-maker proved himself to be an excellent cook. In fact, he was now doing all the cooking in the palace; for the chief cook spent most of his time somewhere else, coming home only at meal times.

Now comes the fun of the story. One day while the cook was gone, the youth ground up the two kinds of fruit. He mixed the kind that produced horns with the king's food: the other kind, which caused the horns to fall off, he mixed with water and put into a jar. The cook arrived, and everything was ready. The table was prepared, and the king and his family were called to eat. The queen and the king and the beautiful princess, who were used to wearing golden crowns set with diamonds and other precious stones, were then to be seen with sharp ugly horns on their heads. When the king discovered that they all had horns, he summoned the cook at once, and asked, "What kind of food did you give us?"

"The same food that your Highness ate a week ago," replied the cook, who was terrified to see the royal family with horns.

"Cook, go and find a doctor. Don't tell him or any one else that we have horns. Tell the doctor that the king wants him to perform an operation," ordered the king.

The cook set out immediately to find a doctor; but he was intercepted by the charcoal-maker, who was eager to hear the king's order. "Where are you going? Say, cook, why are you in such a hurry? What is the matter?"

"Don't bother me!" said the cook. "I am going to find a doctor. The king and his family have horns on their heads, and I am ordered to find a doctor who can take them off."

"I can make those horns fall off. You needn't bother to

find a doctor. Here, try some of this food, cook!" said the helper, giving him some of the same food he had prepared for the king. The cook tried it, and it was good; but, to his alarm, he felt two horns on his head. To prevent rumors from reaching the ears of the king, the youth then gave the cook a glass of the water he had prepared, and the horns fell off. While the charcoal-maker was playing this trick on the cook, he related the story of his magical purse, and how he had lost it.

"Change your clothes, then, and get ready, and I will present you to the king as the doctor," said the cook.

The helper then dressed himself just like a doctor of surgery, and was conducted by the cook into the king's presence.

"Doctor, I want you to do all you can, and use the best of your wisdom, to take off these horns from our heads. But before doing it, promise me first that you will not unfold the matter to the people; for my queen, my daughter, and I would rather die than be known to have lived with horns. If you succeed in taking them off, you shall inherit one-half of my kingdom and have the hand of my fair daughter," said the king.

"I do promise. But listen, O king! In order to get rid of those horns, you must undergo the severest treatment, which may cause your death," replied the doctor.

"It is no matter. If we should die, we would rather die hornless than live with horns," said the king.

After the agreement was written out, the doctor ordered the treatment. The king and the queen were to be whipped until they bled, while the princess was to dance with the doctor until she became exhausted. These were the remedies given by the doctor.

While the king and queen were being whipped, the doctor — who, we must remember, was the cook's helper — went to the kitchen to get the jar of water which he had prepared. The cruel servants who were scourging the king and the queen took much delight in their task, and did not quit until the king and queen were almost lifeless. The doctor forgot the royal couple while he was dancing with the princess, and found them just about to die. He succeeded, however, in giving them some of the fruit-water he had made ready, and the horns fell off. The princess, exhausted, also asked for a drink when she stopped dancing, and the horns fell off her head too.

A few days afterwards the king and the queen died, and the doctor succeeded to the throne, with the beautiful princess as his wife. Then the doctor told her that he was the poor charcoal-maker who had owned the magic purse that she had stolen from him. As soon as he was seated on the throne, he made his friend the cook one of his courtiers. Although the new king was uneducated and unrefined, he welcomed all wise men to his palace as his counsellors, and his kingdom prospered as it had never done under its previous rulers.

NOTES.

Another Tagalog version, called "Pedro's Fortunes" and narrated by Facundo Esquivel of Nueva Ecija, represents the hero as inheriting the inexhaustible purse from his father.

Pedro, with his wealth, soon attracts the notice of the princess, who slyly wheedles his purse away from him. Bent on revenge, he sets out travelling. Hunger soon drives him to eat some beautiful blossoms he finds on a strange tree in the mountains. No sooner has he eaten, however, than horns grow out of his forehead. At first in despair, but later becoming philosophical, he eats some of the leaves of the tree. Horns disappear. Taking blossoms and leaves with him, he goes on. He finds another tree with blossoms similar to the first. He eats: fangs from upper jaw. Eats leaves from the same tree: fangs disappear. Takes with him specimens of both flowers and leaves. Third tree: blossoms tail-producing. When he reaches home, he makes a decoction of the three kinds of flowers, then goes to the palace and sells "lemonade from Paradise." King, queen, and princess drink: horns, fangs, tails. All efforts to remove them vain. Proclamation that princess's hand will be given to whoever can cure the royal family. Disguised as a doctor, Pedro cures king, queen, and princess with a decoction of the three kinds of leaves, first, however, demanding and getting back his purse. Pedro is married to princess.

These two stories (No. 2 and the variant) belong to the type in which the hero loses a magic article (or three magic articles) through the trickery of a princess, but recovers it (them) again by the aid of fruits (blossoms) which, if eaten, cause bodily deformity, — leprosy, horns, a tail, a long nose, transformation into an animal, or the like. The princess, a victim of one of these fruits, which the hero causes her to eat unwittingly, can be restored to her former beauty only by eating of another fruit which the hero, disguised as a physician, supplies on condition that the magic articles first stolen be given up. A detailed study of this cycle has been made by Antti Aarne (pp. 85–142). Aarne names the cycle "The Three Magic Articles and the Wonderful Fruit." After an examination of some hundred and forty-five variants of the story, all but four of which are European, he concludes that the tale arose among the Celts (British Isles and France) and spread eastward

(p. 135), and that the farther we go from these two lands, the more freely are the original details of the story handled (p. 137).

The prototype of this folk-tale Aarne reconstructs as follows (pp. 124–125): —

There are three brothers, soldiers. Each comes into the possession of a specific magic article. One obtains a purse which is never empty; the second, a horn which when blown raises an army; and the third, a mantle which transports its owner wherever he commands it to go. (The owner of the purse begins to lead such a luxurious life, that he becomes acquainted with the king and his family.) The king's daughter deprives the hero of his magic purse. He gets from his brother the second magic article, but the same thing happens again: the princess steals the horn likewise. A third time the hero goes to the princess, taking the mantle given him by his brother. With the help of this, the hero succeeds in punishing the princess by transporting her to a distant island. But she cheats him again. In the magic mantle she wishes herself home, leaving him on the island. He happens upon an apple-tree. He eats some of the fruit, but notices with dismay that horns have grown from his head. After a time he finds other apples; and when he has eaten them, the horns disappear, and he regains his original form. Unrecognized, the youth sets out to sell to the king's daughter some of the first apples. Without suspecting any evil, she eats them, and horns appear on her head. No one is able to cure her. Then the hero appears as a foreign physician at the court of the king, and makes ready his cure. He gives the princess enough of the good apple to cause the horns to decrease in size. In this way he compels her to give him back the stolen articles.

The Tagalog versions of the story differ considerably from this archetype. No brothers of the hero are mentioned. There is but one magic object, an inexhaustible purse: hence there is no magic flight to an island. In none of Aarne's variants do we find blossoms producing horns which may be removed only by leaves from the same tree, as in our variant. The tail-producing fruit is found in nine European versions (five Finnish, two Russian, two Italian), but the fang-producing blossom is peculiar only to our variant; likewise the "lemonade from Paradise" method of dispensing the extract. In thirty-five of the Finnish and Russian forms of the story the hero whips the princess to make her give up the stolen articles, or introduces whipping as a part of the cure (cf. No. 2). Both Filipino versions end with the marriage of the hero to the princess, a detail often lacking in the other versions.

It is impossible to say when or whence this tale reached the Philippines. The fact that the story does not seem to be widespread in the Islands suggests that its introduction was recent, while the separate incidents point to some Finnish or Russian version as source. The only crystallized elements found in the Philippines are the poor hero's obtaining a magic purse, his aspiring to the hand of the princess, her theft of the magic object, and its recovery by means of horn-producing fruits. The complete story (2) seems to be more native and less "manufactured" than the variant.

Besides Aarne, for a general discussion of this cycle see Cosquin, 1 : 123–132; R. Köhler's notes to Gonzenbach's No. 31, and his variants of this story in Zeitschrift des Vereins für Volkskunde (1896); Von Hahn, 2 : 246–247; Grimm, notes to No. 122, "Donkey Cabbages" (in Tales [ed. Hunt], 2 : 419–423). F. H. Groome's "The Seer" (No. 23), a part of which resembles very closely the literary form of the story in the Gesta Romanorum (ch. 120), seems to have been overlooked by Aarne.

3. THE STORY OF CARANCAL.[1]

Once upon a time there lived a couple who had long been married, but had no child. Every Sunday they went to church and begged God to give them a son. They even asked the witches in their town why God would not give them a child. The witches told them that they would have one after a year, but that when born he would be no longer than a span. Nevertheless the couple gave thanks.

After a year a son was born to them. He was very small, as the witches had foretold, but he was stronger than any one would expect such a small child to be. "It is strange," said a neighbor. "Why, he eats more food than his stomach can hold." The boy grew larger and larger, and the amount of food he ate became greater and greater. When he became four feet tall, his daily requirements were a *cavan* [2] of rice and twenty-five pounds of meat and fish. "I can't imagine how so small a person can eat so much food," said his mother to her husband. "He is like a grasshopper: he eats all the time."

Carancal, as the boy was called, was very strong and very kind-hearted. He was the leader of the other boys of the town, for he could beat all of them in wrestling.

After a few years the family's property had all been sold to buy food for the boy. Day after day they became poorer and poorer, for Carancal's father had no other business but fishing. So one day when Carancal was away playing, the wife said to her husband, "What shall we do with Carancal? He will make us as poor as rats. It is better for us to tell him to go earn his living, for he is old enough to work."

---

[1] Narrated by José P. Caedo, a Tagalog from Batangas, Batangas.

[2] *Cavan*, a dry measure used in the Philippines, equal to about 75 quarts.

"No, it is a shame to send him off," said the father, "for we asked God for him. I will take him to the forest and there kill him; and if the neighbors ask how he died, we will say that an accident befell him while cutting trees."

Early the next morning his father led Carancal to the forest, and they began to cut down a very big tree. When the tree was about to fall, Carancal's father ordered the son to stand where the tree inclined; so that when it fell, Carancal was entirely buried. The father immediately went home, thinking that his son had surely been killed; but when he and his wife were talking, Carancal came home with the big tree on his shoulders.

"Father, father, why did you leave me alone in the forest?" said the obedient boy.

The father could not move or speak, for shame of himself. He only helped his son unload the heavy burden. The mother could not speak either, for fear Carancal might suspect their bad intentions toward him. Accordingly she and her husband planned another scheme.

The next day Carancal was invited by his father to go fishing. They rowed and rowed until they were far out into the blue sea. Then they put their net into the water. "Carancal, dive down and see that our net is sound," said the father. Carancal obeyed. In about a minute the water became red and began to foam. This made the old man think that his son had been devoured by a big fish, so he rowed homeward. When he reached home, his wife anxiously asked if Carancal was dead; and the husband said, "Yes." They then cooked their meal and began to eat. But their supper was not half finished when Carancal came in, carrying a big alligator. He again asked his father why he had left him alone to bring such a big load. The father said, "I thought you had been killed by a large fish." Carancal then asked his mother to cook him a *cavan* of rice, for he was tired from swimming such a long distance.

The couple were now discouraged; they could not think of any way by which to get rid of Carancal. At last the impatient woman said, "Carancal, you had better go out into the world to see what you can do toward earning your own living. You know that we are becoming poorer and poorer." . . .

"Mother," interrupted the boy, "I really did not wish to go away from you; but, now that you drive me as if I were not your son, I cannot stay." He paused for a moment to wipe the tears from his cheeks. "You know that I love you; but you, in turn, hate me. What shall I do? I am your son, and so I must not disobey you. But before I depart, father and mother, please give me a bolo,[1] a big bolo, to protect myself in case of danger."

The parents willingly promised that he should have one. and after two days an enormous bolo five yards long was finished. Carancal took it, kissed the hands of his parents,[2] and then went away with a heavy heart.

When he had left his little village behind, he did not know which way to go. He was like a ship without a rudder. He walked and walked until he came to a forest, where he met Bugtongpalasan.[3] Carancal asked him where he was going; and Bugtongpalasan said, "I am wandering, but I do not know where to go. I have lost my parents, and they have left me nothing to inherit."

"Do you want to go with me?" said Carancal.

"Yes," said Bugtongpalasan.

"Let us wrestle first, and the loser will carry my bolo," said Carancal as a challenge. They wrestled; and Bugtongpalasan was defeated, so he had to carry the big bolo.

Then they continued their journey until they met Tunkod-bola,[4] whom Carancal also challenged to a wrestling-match. Tunkodbola laughed at Carancal, and said, "Look at this!" He twisted up a tree near by, and hurled it out of sight.

"That is all right. Let us wrestle, and we will see if you can twist me," said Carancal scornfully. So they wrestled. The earth trembled, trees were uprooted, large stones rolled about; but Tunkodbola was defeated.

"Here, take this bolo and carry it!" said Carancal triumphantly; and they continued their journey.

When they reached the top of a mountain, they saw a big man. This was Macabuhalbundok.[5] Carancal challenged him; but Macabuhalbundok only laughed, and pushed up a hill. As

---

[1] *Bolo*, a cutlass-like knife used by the natives either for agricultural or war purposes.

[2] The usual Filipino salute of respect for parents or grandparents.

[3] This name literally means, "only one *palasan* [a large plant of llana]." The hero was so called because he was the strongest man in his town.

[4] So called because he used as a cane (Tag. *tungkod*) the large cylindrical piece of iron used for crushing sugar-cane (Tag. *bolo*).

[5] Literally, "one who can overturn a mountain."

the hill fell, he said, "Look at this hill! I gave it only a little push, and it was overthrown."

"Well, I am not a hill," said Carancal. "I can balance my-self." They wrestled together, and Carancal was once more the winner.

The four companions now walked on together. They were all wandering about, not knowing where to go. When they were in the midst of a thick wood, they became hungry; so Carancal, their captain, ordered one of them to climb a tall tree and see if any house was nigh. Bugtongpalasan did so, and he saw a big house near the edge of the forest. They all went to the house to see if they might not beg some food.

It was a very large house; but all the windows were closed, and it seemed to be uninhabited. They knocked at the door, but no one answered. Then they went in, and found a table covered with delicious food; and as they were almost famished, they lost no time in devouring what seemed to have been prepared for them. After all had eaten, three of them went hunting, leaving Bugtongpalasan behind to cook more food for them against their return.

While Bugtongpalasan was cooking, he felt the earth tremble, and in a short time he saw a big giant ascending the stairs of the house, saying, *"Ho, bajo tao cainco,"* [1] which means "I smell a man whom I will eat." Bugtongpalasan faced him, but what could a man do to a big giant? The monster pulled a hair out of his head and tied Bugtongpalasan to a post. Then he cooked his own meal. After eating, he went away, leaving his prisoner in the house.

When the three arrived, they were very angry with Bug-tongpalasan because no food had been prepared for them; but they untied him, and made him get the meal. Tunkodbola was the next one left behind as cook while the others went hunting, but he had the same experience as Bugtongpalasan. Then Macabuhalbondok; but the same thing happened to him too.

It was now the turn of Carancal to try his wit, strength, and luck. Before the three left, he had them shave his head. When the giant came and saw that Carancal's head was white, he laughed. "It is a very fine thing to have a white head," said the giant. "Make my head white, too."

---

[1] For the "Fee-fi-fo-fum" phrase in folk-tales, see Bolte-Polívka, 1 : 289–292.

"Your head must be shaved to be white," said Carancal, "and it is a very difficult thing to shave a head."

"Never mind that! I want to have my head shaved," said the giant impatiently.

Carancal then got some ropes and wax. He tied the giant tightly to a post, and then smeared his body with wax. He next took a match and set the giant's body on fire. Thus the giant was destroyed, and the four lived in the house as if it were their own.

Not long afterwards a rumor reached their ears. It was to this effect: that in a certain kingdom on the other side of the sea lived a king who wanted to have a huge stone removed from its place. This stone was so big that it covered much ground. The prize that would be given to the one who could remove it was the hand of the king's prettiest daughter.

The four set out to try their strength. At that time there were no boats for them to sail on, so they had to swim. After three weeks' swimming, they landed on an island-like place in the sea, to rest. It was smooth and slippery, which made them wonder what it could be. Carancal, accordingly, drew his bolo and thrust it into the island. How fast the island moved after the stroke! It was not really an island, but a very big fish. Fortunately the fish carried the travellers near the shores of the kingdom they were seeking.

When the four arrived, they immediately presented themselves to the king, and told him that they would try to move the stone. The king ordered one of his soldiers to show them the stone. There a big crowd of people collected to watch the four strong men.

The first to try was Bugtongpalasan. He could hardly budge it. Then Tunkodbola tried, but moved it only a few yards. When Macabuhalbundok's turn came, he moved the great stone half a mile; but the king said that it was not satisfactory. Carancal then took hold of the rope tied to the stone, and gave a swing. In a minute the great stone was out of sight.

The king was very much pleased, and asked Carancal to choose a princess for his wife. "I am not old enough to marry, my lord," said Carancal sadly (*sic!*). "I will marry one of my companions to your daughter, however, if you are willing."

The king agreed, and Bugtongpalasan was made a prince.

The three unmarried men lived with Bugtongpalasan. By this time they were known not only throughout the whole kingdom where they were, but also in other countries. They had not enjoyed a year's hospitality in Bugtongpalasan's home when a letter addressed to the four men came. It was as follows: —

I have heard that you have superhuman strength, which I now greatly need. About a week ago a monster fish floated up to the shore of my town. It is decaying, and has a most offensive odor. My men in vain have tried to drag the fish out into the middle of the sea. I write to inform you that if you can rid us of it, I will let one of you marry my prettiest daughter.

KING WALANGTACUT.[1]

After Carancal had read the letter, he instantly remembered the fish that had helped them in travelling. The three companions made themselves ready, bade Bugtongpalasan good-by, and set out for Walangtacut's kingdom. They travelled on foot, for the place was not very far away.

In every town they passed through, the people cried, "Hurrah for the strong men!" The king received them with a banquet, and all the houses of the town were decorated with flags. In a word, every one welcomed them.

After the banquet was over, the three men marched with the king and all his counsellors, knights, dukes, and the common people to where the decaying fish lay. In this test, too, Carancal was the only successful one. Again he refused to marry; but as the princess was very anxious to have a strong man for her husband, Tunkodbola was chosen by Carancal, and he became her husband.

The fame of the strong men was now nearly universal. All the surrounding kings sent congratulations. The heroes received offers of marriage from many beautiful ladies of the neighboring kingdoms.

One day when Carancal and Macabuhalbundok were talking together, one of them suggested that they go on another journey. The other agreed, and both of them made preparations. But when they were about to start, a letter from another king came, addressed to Carancal. The king said in his letter that a great stone had fallen in his park. "It is so big that I thought

---

[1] Literally, "without fear, fearless."

it was the sky that fell," he wrote. "I am willing to marry you to my youngest daughter if you can remove it from its present place," said the king.

The two friends accepted the invitation, and immediately began their journey. They travelled by land and sea for many a day. At last they reached the place. There they found the same stone which they had removed before. As he knew that he could not move it far enough, Macabuhalbundok did not make any attempt: Carancal was again the one who did the work.

Once more Carancal refused to marry. "I am too young yet to marry," he said to the king. "In my place I will put my companion." So Macabuhalbundok was married.

Carancal remained a bachelor, for he did not wish to have a wife. The three princes considered him as their father, though he was younger than any of them. For a long time Carancal lived with each of them a year in rotation. Not long after the marriage of Macabuhalbundok, the father-in-law of Bugtongpalasan died, and so Bugtongpalasan became the king. Then the following year Tunkodbola's father-in-law died, and Tunkodbola became also a king. After many years the father-in-law of Macabuhalbundok died, and Macabuhalbundok succeeded to the throne. Thus Carancal was the benefactor of three kings.

One day Carancal thought of visiting his cruel parents and of living with them. So he set out, carrying with him plenty of money, which the three kings had given him. This time his parents did not drive him away, for he had much wealth. Carancal lived once more with his parents, and had three kings under him.

NOTES.

Of this story I have eight variants, as follows: —

(a) "Pusong" (Visayan), narrated by Fermin Torralba.
(b) "Cabagboc" (Bicol), narrated by Pacifico Buenconsejo.
(c) "Sandapal" (Tagalog), narrated by Pilar Ejercito.
(d) "Sandangcal" (Pampangan), narrated by Anastacia Villegas.
(e) "Greedy Juan" (Pampangan), narrated by Wenceslao Vitug.
(f) "Juan Tapon" (Ilocano), narrated by C. Gironella.
(g) "Dangandangan" (Ilocano), narrated by Salvador Reyes.
(h) "Tangarangan" (Ibanag), narrated by Candido Morales.

The incidents of this cycle may be tabulated thus.

A The hero, when born, is only a span in length, and never grows taller
than four feet. He early develops an enormous appetite, and by the
time he is twelve years old he has eaten his parents out of everything.

B Attempts of parents (or uncle) to get rid of the hero: (B¹) by letting
a tree fall on him, (B²) by throwing him into a deep well and then
stoning him, (B³) by commanding him to dive into river to repair
fishing-net, (B⁴) by persuading him to enter wrestling-match with
the king's champion, (B⁵) by pushing him into the sea or by pushing
rocks on him at the seashore.

C Hero's first exploits: (C¹) carrying tree home on his shoulders, (C²)
killing crocodile in river, or king of fishes in the sea, (C³) escape from
the well, (C⁴) defeating champion.

D The hero now decides to leave home, (D¹) taking with him a strong
club, an enormous bolo, or an enormous top, sword, and sheath.

E On his travels he meets two (three) strong men, whom he surpasses
in strength-tests; or (E¹) three men, whom he hires. They all
journey along together, seeking adventures.

F Tasks of the companions: (F¹) killing of troublesome giant by the hero
after the monster has worsted the two other strong men, (F²) removal of large stone from king's grounds, (F³) removal of enormous
decaying fish, (F⁴) killing of two giants, (F⁵) killing seven-headed
man, (F⁶) battering, blowing, and running contest with king's
strong men.

G Hero marries off his companions, but remains single himself, and (G¹)
returns home to live with his parents, either for good or for only
a short time.

These incidents are distributed among the different versions thus: —

No. 3 . . . . AB¹B²C¹C³DD¹EF¹F²F³GG¹
Version *a* . . . . AB¹B²D
Version *b* . . . . .C¹DD¹EF²F⁴F⁵GG¹
Version *c* . . . . AB³B¹B⁴C¹C²C⁴
Version *d* . . . . AB¹B²C¹C³DE¹F⁶
Version *e* . . . . AB¹B²C¹C²DG¹
Version *f* . . . . AB⁴B¹C¹C⁴
Version *g* . . . . AB¹B²C¹C³D¹DD¹EF⁴G
Version *h* . . . . AB¹B²C¹C³DD¹

Up to the point where the hero leaves home, these various Filipino
stories agree in the main: i.e., the hero is a dwarf of superhuman
strength and extraordinary eating-capacity; his parents (or guardian)
are driven by poverty to attempt to kill him (usually twice, sometimes
thrice), but their efforts are vain; he finally determines to leave home,
often taking with him some mighty weapon. From this point on, the
narratives differ widely. All are alike in this respect, however: the
hero never marries. Obviously this group of stories is connected with
two well-known European cycles of folk-tales, — "Strong Hans"
and "John the Bear." The points of resemblance will be indicated

below in an analysis of the incidents found in the members of our group. (Variants are referred to by italicized lower-case letters thus: *a* [Pusong], *b* [Cabagboc], etc. No. 3 refers to our complete story of "Carancal.")

A Hero is born as result of childless couple's unceasing petitions to Heaven (3, *a*, *f*, *g*), and is only a span in length when born (*c*, *d*, *g*). Three of the tales do not mention anything definite about the hero's birth (*b*, *e*, *h*). In all, however, his name is significant, indicating the fact that he is either a dwarf, or wonderfully strong, or a glutton (3 Carancal, from Tag. *dangkal*, "a palm;" [*a*] Pusong, from Vis. *puso*, "paunch, belly;" [*b*] Cabagboc, from Bicol, "strong;" [*c*] Sandapal, from Tag. *dapal*, "a span;" [*d*] Sandangcal, from Pampangan *dangkal* = Tag.; [*f*] Tapon, Ilocano for "short;" [*g*] and [*h*] Tangarangan and Dangandangan, from Ilocano *dangan*, "a span"). *a* describes the hero as having "a big head and large stomach," but as being "very, very strong, he ate a sack of corn or rice every day." In *b* the hero "had great strength even when an infant." Sandangcal (*d*) required a carabao-liver every meal. In *e* the hero's voracious appetite is mentioned. The hero in *c* "would eat everything in the house, leaving no food for his parents." Juan Tapon (*f*), when three years old, "used to eat daily half a *ganta* of rice and a pound of meat, besides fish and vegetables;" the quantity of food he required increased steadily until, when he was fourteen, his parents could no longer support him. However, he never grew taller than a six-year-old boy. Dangandangan (*g*) could walk and talk the day he was born. He could eat one *cavan* of rice and one carabao daily. The hero of *h* was so greedy that by the time he was a "young man" his father could no longer support him. He is described as a "dwarf." In *c* and *d* there is nothing to indicate that the hero was not always a Tom Thumb in size.

Nearly all these details may be found duplicated in *Märchen* of the "John the Bear" and "Strong Hans" types. For analogues, see Friedrich Panzer's Beowulf, pp. 28–33, 47–48, 50–52. In Grimm's story of the "Young Giant" (No. 90) the hero, when born, was only as big as a thumb, and for several years did not grow one hair's breadth. But a giant got hold of him and suckled him for six years, during which time he grew tall and strong, after the manner of giants. It is interesting to note that none of the nine Filipino versions make any reference to an animal parentage or extraordinary source of nourishment of the hero.

B The poverty of the parents is the motive for their attempts on his life in *a*, *c*, *d*, *e*, *f*, *h*. In *a* the mother proposes the scheme; in *h*, the father; in *g* it is the boy's uncle, by whom he had been adopted when his parents died. This "unnatural parents" *motif* is lacking in the European variants.

B¹⁻⁵ With the various attempts to destroy the hero may be discussed his escapes (C¹⁻⁵). The "falling-tree" episode occurs in all the stories but one (*b*). The events of this incident are conducted in various ways. In *a*, *c*, *h*, the hero is told to "catch the tree when it falls," so that he can carry it home (in *c* the hero is pushed clear into the ground by the weight of the tree). In *d* the father directs his son to stand in a certain place, "so that the tree will not fall on him;" but when Sandangcal sees that he is about to be crushed, he nimbly jumps aside unobserved by his father, who thinks him killed. In *f* the tree is made to fall on the body of the sleeping hero. In *g* Darangdarang is told to stand beside the tree being cut: it falls on him. In all the stories but *d* the hero performs the feat of carrying home a tree on his shoulders (C^1). This episode is not uncommon in the European versions (see Panzer, *op. cit.*, p. 35), but there the hero performs it while out at service. By the process of contamination these two incidents (B^1C^1) have worked their way into another Filipino story not of our cycle, — the Visayan story of "Juan the Student" (see JAFL 19 : 104).

B^2 Of the other methods of putting an end to the hero's life, the "well" episode is the most common. In *d* and *h* father and son go to dig a well. When it is several metres deep, the father rains stones on the boy, who is working at the bottom, and leaves him for dead. In *g* the hero is sent down a well to find a lost ring; and while he is there, stones and rocks are thrown on him by his treacherous uncle. In all three the hero escapes, wiser, but none the worse, for his adventure (C^2). This incident is very common in European members of the cycle. Bolte and Polívka (2 : 288–292) note its occurrence in twenty-five different stories.

B^3 In our story of "Carancal," as has been remarked, and in *e*, the father commands his son to dive into deep water to see if the fishing-net is intact. Seeing blood and foam appear on the surface of the water, the father goes home, confident that he is rid of his son at last; but not long afterward, when the parents are eating, the hero appears, carrying on his shoulder a huge crocodile he has killed (C^3). Analogous to this exploit is Sandapal's capture of the king of the fishes, after his father has faithlessly pushed him overboard into the deep sea (*c*). The hero's fight under water with a monstrous fish or crocodile, the blood and foam telling the story of a desperate struggle going on, reminds one strongly of Beowulf's fight with Grendel's dam.

B^4 In *c*, as a last resort, the father takes his son to the king, and has the best royal warrior fight the small boy. Sandapal conquers in five minutes. In *f* the father persuades his son to enter a wrestling-match held by the king. Juan easily throws all his opponents. With this incident compare the Middle-English "Tale of Gamelyn" (ll. 183–270) and Shakespeare's "As You Like It" (act i, sc. ii).

B^5 In *a* the father, at the instigation of his wife, pushes large rocks from a cliff down upon his son by the seashore; but the son returns home later, rolling an immense bowlder that threatens to crush the house.

D, D^1 Satisfied that he is no longer wanted at home, the hero sets out on adventures (*a, g, h*), taking along with him as a weapon a bolo five yards long (3), or a mighty bolo his father had given him, — such a one that none but the hero could wield it (*g*), or a short stout club (*h*). In *b* the parents are not cruel to their son. The hero leaves home with the kindest of feeling for his father. He carries along with him an enormous top, so heavy that four persons could not lift it, and which, when spun, could be heard for miles; a long sword made by a black-smith; and a wooden sheath for it made by the father. In the European versions of the story the weapons of the hero play an important part (see Panzer, 39–43). In *c* the story ends with the sale of Sandapal to the king. In *d*, after Sandangcal has escaped from the well, he comes home at night, and, finding his parents asleep, shakes the house. Thinking it is an earthquake, they jump from the windows in terror,. and are killed. (This incident is also told as a separate story; see JAFL 20 : 305, No. 17.) After the hero has eaten up all the livestock he had inherited by their death, he sells his property and sets out on his travels. In *e* the father sells his greedy son to merchants. In *f* the parents finally give up attempts on their son's life, and he goes away to join the army.

E The companions — Carancal (3), Cabagboc (*b*), Sandangcal (*d*), and Dangandangan (*g*) — meet with extraordinary men, who accompany them on their travels. Cabagboc surpasses Cabual ("Breaker") and Cagabot ("Uprooter") in a contest of skill, and they agree to go with him as his servants. Dangandangan meets two strong men, — Paridis, who uproots forests with his hands; and Aolo,[1] the mighty fisher for sharks, whose net is so large that weights as big as mortars are needed to sink it. But neither of these two can turn the hero's bolo over, hence they become his servants. Sandangcal (*d*), who nowhere in the story displays any great strength, rather only crafti-ness and greed, meets one at a time three strong fellows, whom he persuades to go with him by promising to double the sum they had been working for. These men are Mountain-Destroyer, who could destroy a mountain with one blow of his club; Blower, who could refresh the whole world with his breath; and Messenger, whose steps were one hundred leagues apart. This story, which seems to be far removed from the other tales of the group, has obviously been influenced by stories of the "Skilful Companions" cycle (see No. 11), where the hero merely directs his servants, doing none of the work himself. On the other hand, in 3, *b*, *g*, the wonderful companions are more or less *impedimenta:* the hero himself does all the hard work; they are merely his foil. For the "Genossen" in other *Märchen* of "John the Bear" type, see Panzer, 66–74; Cosquin, 1 : 9, 23–27.

F[1] The adventure with the demon in the house in the forest, related in 3, is not found in the other Filipino versions of the tale. It is found in the Islands, however, in the form of a separate story, two widely dif-ferent variants of which are printed below (4, [*a*] and [*b*]). This incident occurs in nearly all the folk-tales of the "John the Bear"

---

[1] Paridis may possibly be identified with Paderes, the strong man whom Rodrigo de Villas (the Cid) meets in the woods, who uproots a huge tree with which to fight the hero, but who is finally overcome. Paderes and Rodrigo become fast friends. This character occupies a prominent place in the metrical romance entitled "Rodrigo de Villas," which has been printed in the Pampango, Ilocano, Tagalog, and Bicol dialects. Aolo may be a corruption of Añgalo, represented in Ilocano saga as a great fisherman. Many legends told to-day by the Ilocanos in connection with the Abra River, in northern Luzon, centre about the heroic Añgalo.

type. Bolte and Polívka, in their notes to Grimm, No. 91 (2 : 301–315), indicate its appearance in one hundred and eighty-three Western and Eastern stories. As Panzer has shown (p. 77) that the mistreatment of the companions by the demon in the woods usually takes place while the one left behind is cooking food for the others out on the hunt, this *motif* might more exactly be called the "interrupted-cooking" episode than "Der Dämon im Waldhaus" (Panzer's name for it). For Mexican and American Indian variants, see JAFL 25 : 244–254, 255. Spanish and Hindoo versions are cited by Bolte and Polívka (2 : 305, 314).

It is pretty clear that the episode as narrated in our stories 3 and 4 owes nothing to the Spanish variants mentioned by Bolte.

F^{2-5} The removal of an enormous stone is a task that Carancal has to perform twice. This exhibition of superhuman strength is of a piece with the strong hero's other exploits, and has nothing in common with the transplanting of mountains by means of magic. (F^3) The removal of a monstrous decaying fish is found in *b* as well as in 3. Cabagboc catches up the fish on the end of his sword, and hurls the carcass into the middle of the ocean. These exploits of the rock and the fish are not unlike the feat of the Santal hero Gumda, who throws the king's elephant over seven seas (Campbell, 59). (F^4) In *b* the task of slaying the man-eating giant falls upon Cabagboc, and his companion Uprooter, as the other comrade, Breaker, has been married to the king's daughter. The giants are finally despatched by the hero, who cuts off their heads with his sword. In *g* the two strong men Paridis and Aolo are about to be slain by the man-eating giant against whom they have been sent by the hero to fight, when the hero suddenly appears and cuts off the monster's head with his mighty bolo. (F^5) The killing of a seven-headed dragon is a commonplace in folk-tales; a seven-headed man is not so usual. Cabagboc, after both of his comrades have been given royal wives, journeys alone. He comes to a river guarded by a seven-headed man who proves invulnerable for a whole day. Then a mysterious voice tells the hero to strike the monster in the middle of the forehead, as this is the only place in which it can be mortally wounded. Cabagboc does so and conquers. (F^6) The hero's wagering his strong men against a king's strong men will be discussed in the notes to No. 11. The task of Pusong (*a*) has not been mentioned yet. After Pusong leaves home, he journeys by himself, and finally comes to a place where the inhabitants are feverishly building fortifications against the Moros, who are threatening the island. By lending his phenomenal strength, Pusong enables the people to finish their forts in one night. Out of gratitude they later make him their leader. Months later, when the Moros make their raid, they are defeated by Pusong, and captured with all their slaves. Among the wounded slaves are the parents of Pusong. On recognizing their son, they instantly die of shame for their past cruelty to him. Nor can the hero bear the shock any better than they: he too falls dead.

ADDITIONAL NOTES. — The three weeks' swim in 3 suggests Beowulf's swim of a week and his fight with the sea-monsters (Beowulf 535 ff.). The mistaking of a monster fish for an island seems to be an Oriental notion. It occurs in the "1001 Nights" ("First Voyage of Sindbad the Sailor;" see Lane's note 8 to this story).

G The *denouement.* Cabagboc finally reaches home, and spends the rest of his life with his parents (*b*); Sandapal (*c*) is bought by the king, and amuses the court lords and ladies by his feats of strength; Sandangcal (*d*) distributes ten billion pesos among his three helpers, and lives the rest of his days feasting on carabao-livers; Greedy Juan (*e*) comes back home with a magic money-producing goat, which he leaves to his parents, while he by chance finds a wonderful house in the forest with plenty to eat, and there he remains; Juan Tapon (*f*) joins the king's army to fight a neighboring monarch; Dangan-dangan (*g*) becomes a general in the king's army; Tangarangan (*h*) performs marvellous deeds abroad, but never returns home again.

Two other variants remain to be noticed briefly. One of these I have only in abstract, the other is avowedly a confusion of two stories by the narrator. Both are Ilocano tales. The hero's name in both is Kakarangkang (from *kaka*, a term of respect given to either a senior or a junior; and *dangkang*, "a span"). In both, the hero is a great eater and prodigiously strong. The only adventure of Kakarangkang recorded in the abstract is an adventure with a crocodile. Kakarang-kang goes fishing and hooks a crocodile; but, while trying to draw it to shore, he is thrown into the air, falls into the reptile's mouth, and is swallowed. He manages, however, to cut his way out. In the other story, besides some incidents properly belonging to the story of "The Monkey and the Turtle" (cf. also 4 [*b*]), we find this same adventure with the crocodile, the slaying of a seven-headed giant (F⁵), and the removal of an enormous decaying fish (F³). The diminutive hero receives the hand of the king's daughter in return for this last service, — an honor which the heroes of our other versions decline. The incident of the small hero being swallowed by an animal and ulti-mately emerging into the light of day alive, at once suggests Tom Thumb's adventure in the cow and the wolf. For "swallow" tales in general, see Macculloch, 47–51; Bolte-Polívka, 1 : 395–398; Cos-quin, 2 : 150–155. The combination of the "interrupted-cooking" episode (F¹), which properly belongs to the "John the Bear" cycle, with *motifs* from "The Monkey and the Turtle" and "The Monkey and the Crocodile" stories, will be discussed in the notes to Nos. 4, 55, and 56.

4. (*a*) SUAC AND HIS ADVENTURES.[1]

Once upon a time, in a certain town in Pampanga, there lived a boy named Suac. In order to try his fortune, one day he went a-hunting with Sunga and Sacu in Mount Telapayong.

[1] Narrated by Anastacia Villegas of Arayat, Pampanga, who heard the story from her grandmother.

When they reached the mountain, they spread their nets, and made their dogs ready for the chase, to see if any wild animals would come to that place. Not long afterwards they captured a large hog. They took it under a large tree and killed it. Then Sunga and Suac went out into the forest again.

Sacu was left to prepare their food. While he was busy cooking, he heard a voice saying, "Ha, ha! what a nice meal you are preparing! Hurry up! I am hungry." On looking up, Sacu saw on the top of the tree a horrible creature, — a very large black man with a long beard. This was Pugut.

Sacu said to him, "*Aba!*¹ I am not cooking this food for you. My companions and I are hungry."

"Well, let us see who shall have it, then," said Pugut as he came down the tree. At first Sacu did not want to give him the food; but Pugut knocked the hunter down, and before he had time to recover had eaten up all the food. Then he climbed the tree again. When Sunga and Suac came back, Sunga said to Sacu, "Is the food ready? Here is a deer that we have caught."

Sacu answered, "When the food was ready, Pugut came and ate it all. I tried to prevent him, but in vain: I could not resist him."

"Well," said Sunga, "let me be the cook while you and Suac are the hunters." Then Sacu and Suac went out, and Sunga was left to cook. The food was no sooner ready than Pugut came again, and ate it all as before. So when the hunters returned, bringing a hog with them, they still had nothing to eat.

Accordingly Suac was left to cook, and his companions went away to hunt again. Suac roasted the hog. Pugut smelled it. He looked down, and said, "Ha, ha! I have another cook; hurry up! boy, I am hungry."

"I pray you, please do not deprive us of this food too," said Suac.

"I must have it, for I am hungry," said Pugut. "Otherwise I shall eat you up." When the hog was roasted a nice brown, Pugut came down the tree. But Suac placed the food near the fire and stood by it; and when Pugut tried to seize it, the boy pushed him into the fire. Pugut's beard was burnt, and it became kinky.² The boy then ran to a deep pit. He covered

¹ *Aba!* a very common exclamation of surprise. It sometimes expresses disgust.

² We seem here to have a myth element explaining why the Negrito's hair is kinky. See notes for definition of *pugut*.

it on the top with grass. Pugut did not stay to eat the food, but followed Suac. Suac was very cunning. He stood on the opposite side of the pit, and said, "I pray you, do not step on my grass!"

"I am going to eat you up," said Pugut angrily, as he stepped on the grass and fell into the pit. The boy covered the pit with stones and earth, thinking that Pugut would perish there; but he was mistaken. Suac had not gone far when he saw Pugut following him; but just then he saw, too, a crocodile. He stopped and resolutely waited for Pugut, whom he gave a blow and pushed into the mouth of the crocodile. Thus Pugut was destroyed.

Suac then took his victim's club, and returned under the tree. After a while his companions came back. He related to them how he had overcome Pugut, and then they ate. The next day they returned to town.

Suac, on hearing that there was a giant who came every night into the neighborhood to devour people, went one night to encounter the giant. When the giant came, he said, "You are just the thing for me to eat." But Suac gave him a deadly blow with Pugut's club, and the giant tumbled down dead.

Later Suac rid the islands of all the wild monsters, and became the ruler over his people.

(*b*) THE THREE FRIENDS, — THE MONKEY, THE DOG, AND THE CARABAO.[1]

Once there lived three friends, — a monkey, a dog, and a carabao. They were getting tired of city life, so they decided to go to the country to hunt. They took along with them rice, meat, and some kitchen utensils.

The first day the carabao was left at home to cook the food, so that his two companions might have something to eat when they returned from the hunt. After the monkey and the dog had departed, the carabao began to fry the meat. Unfortunately the noise of the frying was heard by the Buñgisñgis in the forest. Seeing this chance to fill his stomach, the Buñgisñgis went up to the carabao, and said, "Well, friend, I see that you have prepared food for me."

For an answer, the carabao made a furious attack on him. The Buñgisñgis was angered by the carabao's lack of hospitality,

[1] Narrated by José M. Hilario, a Tagalog from Batangas, Batangas.

and, seizing him by the horn, threw him knee-deep into the earth. Then the Buñgisñgis ate up all the food and disappeared.

When the monkey and the dog came home, they saw that everything was in disorder, and found their friend sunk knee-deep in the ground. The carabao informed them that a big strong man had come and beaten him in a fight. The three then cooked their food. The Buñgisñgis saw them cooking, but he did not dare attack all three of them at once, for in union there is strength.

The next day the dog was left behind as cook. As soon as the food was ready, the Buñgisñgis came and spoke to him in the same way he had spoken to the carabao. The dog began to snarl; and the Buñgisñgis, taking offence, threw him down. The dog could not cry to his companions for help; for, if he did, the Buñgisñgis would certainly kill him. So he retired to a corner of the room and watched his unwelcome guest eat all of the food. Soon after the Buñgisñgis's departure, the monkey and the carabao returned. They were angry to learn that the Buñgisñgis had been there again.

The next day the monkey was cook; but, before cooking, he made a pitfall in front of the stove. After putting away enough food for his companions and himself, he put the rice on the stove. When the Buñgisñgis came, the monkey said very politely, "Sir, you have come just in time. The food is ready, and I hope you'll compliment me by accepting it."

The Buñgisñgis gladly accepted the offer, and, after sitting down in a chair, began to devour the food. The monkey took hold of a leg of the chair, gave a jerk, and sent his guest tumbling into the pit. He then filled the pit with earth, so that the Buñgisñgis was buried with no solemnity.

When the monkey's companions arrived, they asked about the Buñgisñgis. At first the monkey was not inclined to tell them what had happened; but, on being urged and urged by them, he finally said that the Buñgisñgis was buried "there in front of the stove." His foolish companions, curious, began to dig up the grave. Unfortunately the Buñgisñgis was still alive. He jumped out, and killed the dog and lamed the carabao; but the monkey climbed up a tree, and so escaped.

One day while the monkey was wandering in the forest, he saw a beehive on top of a vine.

"Now I'll certainly kill you," said some one coming towards the monkey.

Turning around, the monkey saw the Buñgisñgis. "Spare me," he said, "and I will give up my place to you. The king has appointed me to ring each hour of the day that bell up there," pointing to the top of the vine.

"All right! I accept the position," said the Buñgisñgis.

"Stay here while I find out what time it is," said the monkey.

The monkey had been gone a long time, and the Buñgisñgis, becoming impatient, pulled the vine. The bees immediately buzzed about him, and punished him for his curiosity.

Maddened with pain, the Buñgisñgis went in search of the monkey, and found him playing with a boa-constrictor. "You villain! I'll not hear any excuses from you. You shall certainly die," he said.

"Don't kill me, and I will give you this belt which the king has given me," pleaded the monkey.

Now, the Buñgisñgis was pleased with the beautiful colors of the belt, and wanted to possess it: so he said to the monkey, "Put the belt around me, then, and we shall be friends."

The monkey placed the boa-constrictor around the body of the Buñgisñgis. Then he pinched the boa, which soon made an end of his enemy.

NOTES.

The *pugut*, among the Ilocanos and Pampangos, is a nocturnal spirit, usually in the form of a gigantic Negro, terrifying, but not particularly harmful. It corresponds to the Tagalog *cafre*.[1] Its power of rapid transformation, however, makes it a more or less formidable opponent. Sometimes it takes the form of a cat with fiery eyes, a minute later appearing as a large dog. Then it will turn into an enormous Negro smoking a large cigar, and finally disappear as a ball of fire. It lives either in large trees or in abandoned houses and ruined buildings.

Buñgisñgis is defined by the narrator as meaning "a large strong man that is always laughing." The word is derived from the root

[1] The root *pugut* is found in many of the dialects, and has two distinct meanings: (1) "a Negro or Negrito of the mountains;" (2) "decapitated, or with the hands or feet cut off." Among the Tagalogs, Bicols, and Visayans, the word is not used to designate a night-appearing demon or monster. Tag. *cafre*, which is equivalent to Iloc. *pugut*, is Spanish for Kaffir. Blumentritt defines *cafre* thus: "Nombre árabe (kafir), importado por los Españoles ó Portugueses; lo dan los campesinos Tagalos de la provincia de Tayabas á un duende antropófago, al que no gusta la sal. En las provincias Ilocanas denominan así los Españoles al *Pugot*."

Speaking of the demons and spirits of northern India, W. Crooke writes (1 : 138) that "some of the Bhût [= *pugut* ?], like the Kâfari [= *cafre* ?], the ghost of a murdered Negro, are black, and are particularly dreaded."

ñgisi, "to show the teeth" (Tag.).   This giant has been described to me as being of herculean size and strength, sly, and possessing an upper lip so large that when it is thrown back it completely covers the demon's face.   The Buñgisñgis can lift a huge animal as easily as if it were a feather.

Obviously these two superhuman demons have to be overcome with strategy, not muscle.   The heroes, consequently, are beings endowed with cleverness.   After Suac has killed Pugut and has come into posses-sion of his victim's magic club, he easily slays a man-eating giant (see F⁴ in notes to preceding tale).   The tricks played on the Buñgisñgis by the monkey ("ringing the bell" and the "king's belt") are found in the Ilocano story "Kakarangkang" and in "The Monkey and the Turtle," but in the latter tale the monkey is the victim.   It would thus seem that a precedent for the mixture of two old formulas by the narrator of "Kakarangkang" already existed among the Tagalogs (cf. the end of the notes to No. 3).

We have not a large enough number of variants to enable us to de-termine the original form of the separate incidents combined to form the cycles represented by stories Nos. 3, 4, and 55; but the evidence we have leads to the supposition that Carancal *motifs* ABCDF¹ are very old in the Islands, and that these taken together probably constituted the prototype of the "Carancal" group.   I cannot but believe that the "interrupted-cooking" episode, as found in the Philippines, owes nothing to European forms of "John the Bear;" for nowhere in the Islands have I found it associated with the subsequent adventures comprising the "John the Bear" norm, — the underground pursuit of the demon, the rescue of the princesses by the hero, the treachery of the companions, the miraculous escape of the hero from the under-world, and the final triumph of justice and the punishment of the traitors (see No. 17 and notes).

For a Borneo story of a "Deer, Pig, and Plandok (Mouse-Deer)," see Roth, 1 : 346.   In this tale, as well as in another from British North Borneo (Evans, 471–473, "The Plandok and the Gergasi"), it is the clever plandok who alone is able to outwit the giant.   In the latter story there are seven animals, — carabao, ox, dog, stag, horse, mouse-deer, and barking-deer.   The carabao and horse in turn try in vain to guard fish from the *gergasi* (a mythical giant who carries a spear over his shoulder).   The plandok takes his turn now, after his two companions have been badly mishandled, and tricks the giant into letting himself be bound and pushed into a well, because the "sky is falling."   There he is killed by the other animals when they return.   With this last incident compare the trick of the fox in the Mongolian story in our notes to No. 48.   In two other stories of the cunning of the plandok, "The Plandok and the Tiger" (Evans, 474) and "The Plandok and the Bear" (*ibid.*), we meet with the "king's belt" trick and the "king's gong" trick respectively. For an additional record from Borneo, see Edwin H. Gomes, "Seventeen Years among the Sea Dyaks of Borneo" (Lond., 1911), 255–261.

5. (a) HOW SUAN BECAME RICH.[1]

Pedro and Suan were friends. Pedro inherited a great fortune from his parents, who had recently died; but Suan was as poor as the poorest of beggars that ever lived. Early one morning Suan went to his friend, and said, "I wonder if you have a post that you do not need."

"Yes, I have one," said Pedro. "Why? Do you need it?"

"Yes, I need one badly, to build my house."

"Very well, take it," said Pedro. "Do not worry about paying for it."

Suan, who had not thought evil of his friend, took the post and built his house. When it was finished, his house was found to surpass that of his friend. This fact made Pedro so envious of Suan, that at last he went to him and asked Suan for the post back again.

"Why, if I take it from its place, my house will be destroyed. So let me pay you for it, or let me look for another post in the town and get it for you!"

"No," said Pedro, "I must have my own post, for I wish to use it."

Finally Suan became so greatly annoyed by his friend's insistence, that he exclaimed, "I will not give you back your post."

"Take heed, Suan! for I will accuse you before the king."

"All right! do as you please."

"We will then go to the king Monday," said Pedro.

"Very well; I am always ready."

When Monday came, both prepared to go to the palace. Pedro, who cared for his money more than for anything else, took some silver coins along with him for the journey. Suan took cooked rice and fish instead. Noon came while they were still on the road. Suan opened his package of food and began to eat. Pedro was also very hungry at this time, but no food could be bought on the way. So Suan generously invited Pedro to eat with him, and they dined together.

[1] Narrated by Bonifacio Ynares, a Tagalog living in Pasig, Rizal.

After eating, the two resumed their journey. At last they came to a river. The bridge over it was broken in the middle, and one had to jump in order to get to the other side. Pedro jumped. Suan followed him, but unfortunately fell. It so happened that an old man was bathing in the river below, and Suan accidentally fell right on him. The old man was knocked silly, and as a consequence was drowned. When Isidro, the son, who dearly loved his father, heard of the old man's death, he at once made up his mind to accuse Suan before the king. He therefore joined the two travellers.

After a while the three came to a place where they saw Barbekin having a hard time getting his carabao out of the mire. Suan offered to help. He seized the carabao by the tail, and pulled with great force. The carabao was rescued, but its tail was broken off short by a sudden pull of Suan. Barbekin was filled with rage because of the injury done to his animal: so he, too, resolved to accuse Suan before the king.

When they came to the palace, the king said, "Why have you come here?"

Pedro spoke first. "I have come," he said, " to accuse Suan to you. He has one of my posts, and he won't return it to me."

On being asked if the accusation was true, Suan responded with a nod, and said in addition, "But Pedro ate a part of my rice and fish on the way here."

"My decision, then," said the king, "is that Suan shall give Pedro his post, and that Pedro shall give Suan his rice and fish."

Isidro was the next to speak. "I have come here to accuse Suan. While my father was bathing in the river, Suan jumped on him and killed him."

"Suan, then, must bathe in the river," said the king, "and you may jump on him."

When Barbekin was asked why he had come, he replied, "I wish to accuse Suan. He pulled my carabao by the tail, and it was broken off short."

"Give Suan your carabao, then," said the king. "He shall not return it to you until he has made its tail grow to its full length."

The accused and the accusers now took their leave of the king.

"Give me the carabao now," said Suan to Barbekin when *they* had gone some distance from the palace.

The carabao was young and strong, and Barbekin hated to give it up. So he said, "Don't take the carabao, and I will give you fifty pesos."

"No; the decision of the king must be fulfilled," said Suan.

Barbekin then raised the sum to ninety pesos, and Suan consented to accept the offer. Thus Suan was rewarded for his work in helping Barbekin.

When they came to the bridge, Suan went down into the river, and told Isidro to jump on him. But the bridge was high, and Isidro was afraid to jump. Moreover, he did not know how to swim, and he feared that he would but drown himself if he jumped. So he asked Suan to pardon him.

"No, you must fulfil the decision of the king," answered Suan.

"Let me off from jumping on you, and I will give you five hundred pesos," said Isidro.

The amount appealed to Suan as being a good offer, so he accepted it and let Isidro go.

As soon as Suan reached home, he took Pedro's post from his house, and started for Pedro's house, taking a razor along with him. "Here is your post," he said; "but you must lie down, for I am going to get my rice and fish from you."

In great fright Pedro said, "You need not return the post any more."

"No," said Suan, "we must fulfil the decision of the king."

"If you do not insist on your demand," said Pedro, "I will give you half of my riches."

"No, I must have my rice and fish." Suan now held Pedro by the shoulder, and began to cut Pedro's abdomen with the razor. He had no sooner done that, than Pedro, in great terror, cried out, —

"Don't cut me, and you shall have all my riches!"

Thus Suan became the richest man in town by using his tact and knowledge in outwitting his enemies.

(b) THE KING'S DECISIONS.[1]

Once a poor man named Juan was without relatives or friends. Life to him was a series of misfortunes. A day often passed without his tasting even a mouthful of food.

[1] Narrated by José M. Hilario, a Tagalog from Batangas, who heard the story from his father.

One day, weakened with hunger and fatigue, as he was walking along the road, he passed a rich man's house. It so happened that at this time the rich man's food was being cooked. The food smelled so good, that Juan's hunger was satisfied merely with the fragrance. When the rich man learned that the smell of his food had satisfied Juan, he demanded money of Juan. Juan refused to give money, however, because he had none, and because he had neither tasted nor touched the rich man's food. "Let's go to the king, then," said Pedro, the rich man, "and have this matter settled!" Juan had no objection to the proposal, and the two set out for the palace.

Soon they came to a place where the mire was knee-deep. There they saw a young man who was trying to help his horse out of a mud-hole. "Hey, you lazy fellows! help me to get my horse out of this hole," said Manuel. The three tried with all their might to release the horse. They finally succeeded; but unfortunately Juan had taken hold of the horse's tail, and it was broken off when Juan gave a sudden hard pull.

"You have got to pay me for injuring my horse," said Manuel.

"No, I will not give you any money, because I had no intention of helping you until you asked me to," said Juan.

"Well, the king will have to settle the quarrel." Juan, who was not to be frightened by threats, went with Pedro and Manuel.

Night overtook the three on their way. They had to lodge themselves in the house of one of Pedro's friends. Juan was not allowed to come up, but was made to sleep downstairs.

At midnight the pregnant wife of the host had to make water. She went to the place under which Juan was sleeping. Juan, being suddenly awakened and frightened, uttered a loud shriek; and the woman, also frightened because she thought there were robbers or ghosts about, miscarried. The next morning the husband asked Juan why he had cried out so loud in the night. Juan said that he was frightened.

"You won't fool me! Come with us to the king," said the husband.

When the four reached the palace, they easily gained access to the royal presence. Then each one explained why he had come there.

"I'll settle the first case," said the king. He commanded the servant to fetch two silver coins and place them on the table.

"Now, Pedro, come here and smell the coins. As Juan became satisfied with the smell of your food, so now satisfy yourself with the smell of the money." Pedro could not say a word, though he was displeased at the unfavorable decision.

"Now I'll give my decisions on the next two cases. Manuel, you must give your horse to Juan, and let him have it until another tail grows. — And you, married man, must let Juan have your wife until she gives birth to another child."

Pedro, Manuel, and the married man went home discontented with the decisions of the king, — Pedro without having received pay, Manuel without his horse, and the other man without his wife.

NOTES.

These two Tagalog stories, together with another, "How Piro became Rich," which is almost identical with No. 5(*a*), may possibly be descended directly from an old Buddhist birth-story ("Gāmani-canda-jātaka," No. 257), — a tale in which W. A. Clouston (see Academy, No. 796, for Aug. 6, 1887) sees the germ of the "pound-of-flesh" incident. An abstract of the first part of this Jātaka will set forth the striking resemblance between our stories and this old Hindoo apologue.[1] The part of the Jātaka that interests us is briefly the account of how a man was haled to the king's tribunal for injuries done unwittingly, and how the king passed judgment thereupon. The abstract follows: —

Gāmani, a certain old courtier of the ruling king's dead father, decided to earn his living by farming, as he thought that the new king should be surrounded with advisers of his own age. He took up his abode in a village three leagues from the city, and, after the rainy season was over, one day borrowed two oxen from a friend, with which to help him do his ploughing. In the evening he returned the oxen; but the friend being at dinner, and not inviting Gāmani to eat, Gāmani put the oxen in the stall, and got no formal release from his creditor. That night thieves stole the cattle. Next day the owner of the oxen discovered the theft, and decided to make Gāmani pay for the beasts. So the two set out to lay the case before the king. On the way they stopped for food at the house of a friend of Gāmani's. The woman of the house, while climbing a ladder to the store-room for rice for Gāmani, fell and miscarried. The husband, returning that instant, accused Gāmani of hitting his wife and bringing on untimely labor: so the husband set off with Gāmani's first accuser to get justice from the king. On their way they met a horse that would not go with its groom. The owner of the horse shouted to G. to hit the horse with something and head it back. G. threw a stone at the animal, but broke its leg. "Here's a king's officer for you," shouted the man; "you've broken my horse's leg."

---

[1] For full translation, see Jātaka, ed. by E. B. Cowell (Cambridge University Press, 1895), 2 : 207–215; and FLJ 3 : 337 f. See also C. H. Tawney's discussion of the story in the Journal of Philology, 12 : 112–119.

G. was thus three men's prisoner. By this time G. was in despair, and decided to kill himself. As soon as opportunity came, he rushed up a hill near the road, and threw himself from a precipice. But he fell on the back of an old basket-maker and killed him on the spot. The son of the basket-maker accused G. of murder and went along with the three other plaintiffs to the king. (I omit here the various questions that persons whom G. meets along the road beg him to take to the king for an answer.)

All five appearing in the presence of the king, the owner of the oxen demanded justice. In answer to the king's question, he at first denied having seen G. return the oxen, but later admitted that he saw them in the stall. G. was ordered to pay twenty-four pieces of money for the oxen; but the plaintiff, for lying, was condemned to have his eyes plucked out by G. Terrified at the prospect, he threw money to G. and rushed away. The judgment in the case of the second false accuser was this: G. was to take his friend's wife and live with her until she should bear another son to take the place of the child that miscarried. Again G. was bought off by the plaintiff. In the third case the owner of the horse at first denied having requested G. to hit the beast, but later admitted the truth. Judgment: G. was to pay a thousand pieces (which the king gave him) for the injured animal, but was also to tear out his false accuser's tongue. The fellow gave G. a sum of money and departed. The fourth decision was as follows: inasmuch as G. could not restore the dead father to life, he was to take the dead man's widow to his home and be a father to the young basket-maker; but he, rather than have his old home broken up, gave G. a sum of money and hurried away.

It is to be regretted that this Buddhistic birth-story was not known to Theodor Benfey, who, in his exhaustive discussion of our present cycle, particularly from the point of view of the "pound-of-flesh" incident (1 : 393–410), writes, "I may remark that this recital [i.e., of the decisions], which here borders on the comic, is based upon serious traditional legends which have to do with Buddhistic casuistry" (p. 397). Benfey's fragmentary citations are not very convincing; but this Jātaka proves that his reasoning, as usual, was entirely sound.

An Indo-Persian version called the "Kāzí of Emessa," cited by Clouston (*op. cit.*), might be mentioned here, as it too has close resemblances to our stories.

While a merchant is being taken by a Jew before the king because the merchant will not pay his bond of a pound of flesh, he meets with the following accidents: (1) In attempting to stop a runaway mule, he knocks out one of the animal's eyes with a stone; (2) while sleeping on a flat roof, he is aroused suddenly by an uproar in the street, and, jumping from the roof, he kills an old man below; (3) in trying to pull an ass out of the mud, he pulls its tail off. The owner of the mule, the sons of the dead man, and the owner of the ass, go along with the Jew to present their cases before the king, whose decisions are as follows: (1') The owner of the mule, valued at 1000 dínárs, is to saw the animal in two lengthwise, and is to give the blind half to the merchant, who must pay 500 dínárs for it. As the owner refuses, he is obliged to pay the merchant 100 dínárs for bringing in a troublesome suit. (2') Merchant must stand below a roof and allow himself to be jumped on by the sons of the dead man; but they refuse to take the risk, and are obliged to pay the merchant 100 dínárs for troubling him. (3') The owner of the tailless ass is compelled to try to pull out the tail of the Kází's mule. Naturally the animal resents such treatment, and the accuser is terribly bruised. Finally, to avoid further punishment, he says that his own animal never had a tail. Hence he is forced to give the merchant 100 dínárs for bringing in a false suit.

In the "Kathā-sarit-sāgara" (translated by C. H. Tawney, 2 : 180–181) occurs this story: —

One day, when Bráhman Devabhúti had gone to bathe, his wife went into the garden to get vegetables, and saw a donkey belonging to a washerman eating them. She took up a stick and ran after the donkey; the animal, trying to escape, fell into a pit and broke its hoof. When the master heard of that, he came in a passion, and beat and kicked the Bráhman woman. Accordingly she, being pregnant, had a miscarriage; but the washerman returned home with his donkey. Her husband, hearing of it, went, in his distress, and complained to the chief magistrate of the town. The foolish man, after hearing both sides of the case, delivered this judgment: "Since the donkey's hoof is broken, let the Bráhman carry the donkey's load for the washerman until the donkey is again fit for work; and let the washerman make the Bráhman's wife pregnant again, since he made her miscarry." When the Bráhman and his wife heard this decision, they, in their despair, took poison and died; and when the king heard of it, he put to death that inconsiderate judge.

The Tagalog story of "How Piro became Rich," which I have not printed here, is identical with "How Suan became Rich," with this exception, that a horse's tail, instead of a carabao's, is pulled off by the hero. And there is this addition: while travelling to the king's court, Piro hears cries for help coming from the woods. He rushes to the spot, and sees a young lady fighting a swarm of bees. Piro helps kill the bees with his stick, but, in doing so, injures the woman somewhat severely. Her father, angered, joins the accusers, and requests the king that he order Piro to cure his daughter. The king rules that if Piro is to do this, and if the young woman is to get the best care, she must become Piro's wife. For relinquishing his right to the girl, Piro receives a hundred *alfonsos* from the father.

All in all, the close agreement between our stories and the three Eastern versions cited above makes it reasonably certain that the "Wonderful Decisions" group in the Philippines derives directly from India.

6. (a) THE FOUR BLIND BROTHERS.[1]

There was once a man who had eight sons. Four of them were blind. He thought of sending the children away, simply because he could not afford to keep them in the house any longer. Accordingly one night he called his eight children together, and said, "He who does not provide for the future shall want in the present. You are big enough and are able to support yourselves. To-morrow I shall send you away to seek your fortunes."

When morning came, the boys bade their father good-by. The blind sons went together in one party, and the rest in another. Now begins the pathetic story of the four blind brothers.

They groped along the road, each holding the hand of the other. After a day of continuous walking, the four brothers were very far away from their town. They had not tasted food during all that time. In the evening they came to a cocoanut-grove.

"Here are some cocoanut-trees," said one of them. "Let us get a bunch of cocoanuts and have something to eat!"

So the eldest brother took off his *camisa china* [2] and climbed up one of the trees. When he reached the top, the tree broke. "Bung!" Down came the poor fellow.

"One!" cried the youngest brother.

"Three more!" shouted the rest.

"Don't come down until you have dropped four!" they all cried at once. Who would answer them? Their brother lay dead on the ground.

While they were waiting for the second "Bung!" the second brother climbed up the same tree. What had happened to the first happened also to him, and so to the third in turn. As soon as the youngest brother heard the third fall, he thought of looking for his share. He crept about to find the cocoanuts. Alas! he discovered that his three brothers lay dead on the ground. He went away from the place crying very loud.

Now, his crying happened to disturb the *patianac*,[3] who were trying to sleep. They went out to see what was the matter.

---

[1] Narrated by Eutiqiano Garcia, a Pampangan, who said he heard the story from a boy from Misamis, Mindanao.

[2] *Camisa china*, a thin native coat-shirt worn outside the trousers.

[3] *Patianac*, mischievous birth-spirits that live in the woods and fields, and lead travellers astray at night.

When they found the poor helpless blind man, they were very much moved, and they gave him food and shelter for the night. They also gave him the tail of a *pagui*,[4] which would help him find his fortune, they said. At daybreak they showed him the way out of the grove.

The blind man walked on and on, until he was hailed by a lame man resting under a shady tree. "Friend, carry me on your shoulders, and let us travel together!" said the lame man to the blind.

"Willingly," replied the blind man.

They travelled for many hours, and at last came to a big, lonely house. They knocked at the open door, but nobody answered. At last they entered, and found the place empty. While they were searching through the house, the owner came. He was a two-headed giant. The blind man and the lame man were upstairs.

The giant was afraid to enter the house, but he called in a voice of thunder, "Who's there?"

"We are big men," answered the two companions.

"How big are you?" asked the giant.

"We are so big that the foundation of the house shakes when we walk," the two replied.

"Give me a proof that you are really big men!" cried the giant again.

"We will show you one of our hairs," they answered, and they dropped from the window the tail of the *pagui*.

The giant looked at it in wonder. He was immediately convinced that they were more powerful than he was. So, picking up the "hair," the giant went away, afraid to face such antagonists in single combat.

So the prediction of the *patianac* came true. The house and all the property of the giant fell into the hands of the blind man and the lame man. They lived there happily all the rest of their lives.

(*b*) JUAN THE BLIND MAN.[2]

Many years ago there lived in a little village near a thick forest eight blind men who were close friends. In spite of their

---

[1] *Pagui*, the sting-ray, or skate-fish. Its tail is very efficacious against evil spirits and witches, according to native belief.

[2] Narrated by Pedro D. L. Sorreta, a Bicol from Virac, Catanduanes, where the story is common.

physical defects, they were always happy, — perhaps much happier than their fellow-villagers, for at night they would always go secretly to one of the neighboring cocoanut-groves, where they would spend their time drinking *tuba* [1] or eating young cocoanuts.

One evening a severe typhoon[2] struck the little village, and most of the cocoanut-trees were broken off at the top. The next afternoon the joyous party went to the cocoanut-grove to steal fruits. As soon as they arrived there, seven of them climbed trees. Juan, the youngest of all, was ordered to remain below so as to count and gather in the cocoanuts his friends threw down to him. While his companions were climbing the trees, Juan was singing, —

> "Eight friends, good friends,
> One fruit each eats;
> Good Juan here bends,
> Young nuts he takes."

He had no sooner repeated his verse three times than he heard a fall.

"One," he counted; and he began to sing the second verse: —

> "Believe me, that everything
> Which man can use he must bring,
> No matter at all of what it's made;
> So, friends, a counter you need."

Crrapup! he heard another fall, which was followed by three in close succession. "Good!" he said, "five in all. Three more, friends," and he raised his head as if he could see his companions. After a few minutes he heard two more falls.

"Six, seven — well, only seven," he said, as he began searching for the cocoanuts on the ground. "One more for me, friends — one more, and every one is satisfied." But it was his friends who had fallen; for, as the trees were only stumps, the climbers fell off when they reached the tops.

Juan, however, did not guess what had happened until he found one of the dead bodies. Then he ran away as fast as he could. At last he struck Justo, a lame man. After hearing Juan's story, Justo advised Juan not to return to his village, lest he be accused of murder by the relatives of the other men.

---

[1] *Tuba*, a wine distilled from the coco and other palm trees.

[2] Typhoon (Ar. *tûfân*), a wind of cyclonic force and extraordinary violence.

After a long talk, the two agreed to travel together and seek a place of refuge, for the blind man's proposal seemed a good one to the lame man: —

> "Blind man, strong legs;
> Lame man, good eyes;
> Four-footed are pigs;
> Four-handed are monkeys.
> But we'll walk on two,
> And we'll see with two."

So when morning dawned, they started on their journey.

They had not travelled far when Justo saw a horn in the road, and told Juan about it. Juan said, —

> "Believe me, that everything
> Which man can use he must bring,
> No matter at all of what it's made;
> So, friend, a horn too we need."

The next thing that Justo saw was a rusted axe; and after being told about it, Juan repeated his little verse again, ending it with, "So, friend, an axe too we need." A few hours later the lame man saw a piece of rope; and when the blind man knew of it, he said, —

> "Bring one, bring two, bring all, —
> The horn, the axe, the rope as well."

And last of all they found an old drum, which they took along with them too.

Soon Justo saw a very big house. They were glad, for they thought that they could get something to eat there. When they came near it, they found that the door was open; but when they entered it, Justo saw nothing but bolos, spears, and shields hanging on the walls. After a warm discussion as to what they should do, they decided to hide in the ceiling of the house, and remain there until the owner returned.

They had no sooner made themselves comfortable than they heard some persons coming. When Justo saw the bloody bolos and spears of the men, and the big sack of money they carried, he was terrified, for he suspected that they were outlaws. He trembled; his hair stood on end; he could not control himself. At last he shouted, "Ay, here!"

The blind man, who could not see the danger they were in, stopped the lame man, but not before the owners of the house had heard them.

"Ho, you mosquitoes! what are you doing there?" asked the chief of the outlaws as he looked up at the ceiling.

"Aha, you rascals! we are going to eat you all," answered the blind man in the loudest voice he could muster.

"What's that you say?" returned the chief.

"Why, we have been looking for you, for we intend to eat you all up," replied Juan; "and to show you what kind of animals we are, here is one of my teeth," and Juan threw down the rusted axe. "Look at one of my hairs!" continued Juan, as he threw down the rope.

The outlaws were so frightened that they were almost ready to run away. The chief could not say a single word.

"Now listen, you ants, to my whistle!" said Juan, and he blew the horn. "And to show you how big our stomachs are, hear us beat them!" and he beat the drum. The outlaws were so frightened that they ran away. Some of them even jumped out of the windows.

When the robbers were all gone, Juan and Justo went down to divide the money; but the lame man tried to cheat the blind man, and they had a quarrel over the division. Justo struck Juan in the eyes with the palm of his hand, and the blind man's eyes were opened so that he could see. Juan kicked Justo so hard, that the lame man rolled toward one corner of the house and struck a post. His lameness was cured, so that he could stand and walk.

When they saw that each had done the other a great service, they divided the money fairly, and lived ever after together as close friends.

(c) TEOFILO THE HUNCHBACK, AND THE GIANT.[1]

Once there lived a hunchback whose name was Teofilo. He was an orphan, and used to get his food by wandering through the woods. He had no fixed home. Sometimes he even slept under large trees in the forest. His one blind eye, as well as his crooked body, would make almost any one pity his miserable condition.

One day, while he was wandering through the woods looking

[1] Narrated by Loreta Benavides, a Bicol student, who heard the story from her aunt.

for something to eat, he found a piece of large rope. He was very glad; for he could sell the rope, and in that way get money to buy food. Walking a little farther, he found a gun leaning against a fence. This gun, he supposed, had been left there by a hunter. He was glad to have it, too, for protection. Finally, while crossing a swampy place, he saw a duck drinking in the brook. He ran after the duck, and at last succeeded in catching it. Now he was sure of a good meal.

But it had taken him a long time to capture the duck. Night soon came on, and he had to look for a resting-place. Fortunately he came to a field, and his eye caught a glimpse of light on the other side. He went towards the light, and found it to come from a house, all the windows of which were open. He knocked at the door, but nobody answered; so he just pushed it open and entered. He then began to feel very comfortable. He prepared his bed, and then went to sleep. He did not know that he was in a giant's house.

At midnight Teofilo was awakened by a loud voice. He made a hole in the wall and looked out. There in the dark he saw a very tall man, taller even than the house itself. It was the giant. The giant said, "I smell some one here." He tried to open the door, but Teofilo had locked it.

"If you are really a strong man and braver than I," said the giant, "let me see your hair!"

Teofilo then threw out the piece of rope. The giant was surprised at its size. He then asked to see Teofilo's louse, and Teofilo threw out the duck. The giant was terrified, for he had never seen such a large louse before. Finally the giant said, "Well, you seem to be larger than I. Let me hear your voice!"

Teofilo fired his gun. When the giant heard the gun and saw it spitting fire, he trembled, for he thought that the man's saliva was burning coals. Afraid to challenge his strange guest any more, the giant ran away and disappeared forever.

And so Teofilo the hunchback lived happily all the rest of his days in the giant's house without being troubled by any one.

(*d*) JUAN AND THE BURINGCANTADA.[1]

A long time ago, when the Bicols had not yet been welded into one tribe, there lived a couple in the mountains of Albay who had one son, named Juan. Before the boy was five years

---

[1] Narrated by Pacifico Buenconsejo, a Bicol, who heard the story from his grandmother.

old, his father died. As Juan grew up, he became very lazy: he did not like to work, nor would he help his mother earn their daily bread. Despite his laziness, Juan was dearly loved by his mother. She did not want him to work in the field under the hot sun. Because of his mother's indulgence, he grew lazier and lazier.

Every afternoon Juan used to take a walk while his mother was working. She was a kind-hearted woman, and often told her son to help anybody he met that needed help. One afternoon, while he was walking in a field, he saw two carabaos fighting. One was gored by the other, and was about to die. Juan, mindful of what his mother told him, went between the two animals to help the wounded one. Suddenly the two animals gored him in the back, and he fell to the ground. A man, passing by, found him, and took him to his home. When Juan's mother learned why her son had been gored, she was greatly distressed that her son was so foolish.

Juan soon recovered, and one day he invited his mother to go with him to look for money. He insisted so hard, that finally she agreed to accompany him. On their way they found an axe, which Juan picked up and took along with him. They had not gone much farther, when they saw a long rope stretching across the road. Juan's mother did not want him to take it, but he said that it would be of some use to them later. By and by they came to a river, on the bank of which they found a large drum. Juan took this with him, too.

When they had been travelling about a week, they came upon a big house. Juan said that he wanted to go see what was in the house, but his mother told him that he should not go. However, he kept urging and urging, until at last his mother consented, and went with him. When they reached the hall, they found it well decorated with flowers and leaves. They visited all the apartments of the house; and when they came to the dining-room, they saw a large hole in the ceiling. Juan told his mother that they had better hide in the ceiling until they found out who the owner of the house was. The mother thought that the plan was a wise one; so they went to the ceiling, taking with them the axe, the rope, and the drum.

They had not been hiding many minutes, when the Buringcantada, a giant with one eye in the middle of his forehead and with two long tusks that projected from the sides of his mouth, came in with his friends and servants. When the dinner was ready, the servant called his master and his guests into the dining-room. While they were eating, Juan said in a loud voice, —

"Tawi cami
Sa quisami
Qui masiram
Na ulaman." [1]

The Buringcantada was very angry to hear the voice of a man in the ceiling, and he said in a thundering voice, "If you are a big man like me, let me see one of your hairs!"

Juan showed the rope from the hole in the ceiling.

Astonished at the size of the hair, the Buringcantada said again, "Let me see one of your teeth!" Juan showed the axe.

By this time Juan's mother was almost dead with fear, and she told her son not to move.

After a few minutes the Buringcantada said again, "Beat your stomach, and let me hear the sound of it!" When Juan beat the drum, the Buringcantada and all the guests and servants ran away in fright, for they had never heard such a sound before.

Then Juan and his mother came down from the ceiling. In this house they lived like a rich family, for they found much money in one of the rooms. As for the Buringcantada, he never came back to his house after he left it.

(e) THE MANGLALABAS.[2]

Once upon a time, in the small town of Balubad, there was a big house. It was inhabited by a rich family. When the head of the family died, the house was gloomy and dark. The family wore black clothes, and was sad.

Three days after the death of the father, the family began to be troubled at night by a manglalabas.[3] He threw stones at the house, broke the water-jars, and moved the beds. Some pillows were even found in the kitchen the next day. The second night, Manglalabas visited the house again. He pinched the widow; but when she woke up, she could not see anything. Manglalabas also emptied all the water-jars. Accordingly the family decided to abandon the house.

---

[1] Literally, "Give us here in the ceiling some good food."

[2] Narrated by Arsenio Bonifacio, a Tagalog, who heard the story from his father.

[3] *Manglalabas*, literally, "the one who appears;" i.e., apparition.

A band of brave men in that town assembled, and went to the house. At midnight the spirit came again, but the brave men said they were ready to fight it. Manglalabas made a great deal of noise in the house. He poured out all the water, kicked the doors, and asked the men who they were. They answered, "We are fellows who are going to kill you." But when the spirit approached them, and they saw that it was a ghost, they fled away. From that time on, nobody was willing to pass a night in that house.

In a certain *barrio* [1] of Balubad there lived two queer men. One was called Bulag, because he was blind; and the other, Cuba, because he was hunchbacked. One day these two arranged to go to Balubad to beg. Before they set out, they agreed that the blind man should carry the hunchback on his shoulder to the town. So they set out. After they had crossed the Balubad River, Cuba said, "Stop a minute, Bulag! here is a hatchet." Cuba got down and picked it up. Then they proceeded again. A second time Cuba got off the blind man's shoulder, for he saw an old gun by the roadside. He picked this up also, and took it along with him.

When they reached the town, they begged at many of the houses, and finally they came to the large abandoned house. They did not know that this place was haunted by a spirit. Cuba said, "Maybe no one is living in this house;" and Bulag replied, "I think we had better stay here for the night."

As they were afraid that somebody might come, they went up into the ceiling. At midnight they were awakened by Manglalabas making a great noise and shouting, "I believe that there are some new persons in my house!" Cuba, frightened, fired the gun. The ghost thought that the noise of the gun was some one crying. So he said, "If you are truly a big man, give me some proofs."

Then Cuba took the handle out of the hatchet and threw the head down at the ghost. Manglalabas thought that this was one of the teeth of his visitor, and, convinced that the intruder was a powerful person, he said, "I have a buried treasure near the barn. I wish you to dig it up. The reason I come here every night is on account of this treasure. If you will only dig it up, I will not come here any more."

The next night Bulag and Cuba dug in the ground near the

---

[1] *Barrio*, a small collection of houses forming a kind of suburb to a town.

barn. There they found many gold and silver pieces. When they were dividing the riches, Cuba kept three-fourths of the treasure for himself. Bulag said, "Let me see if you have divided fairly," and, placing his hands on the two piles, he found that Cuba's was much larger.

Angry at the discovery, Cuba struck Bulag in the eyes, and they were opened. When Bulag could see, he kicked Cuba in the back, and straightway his deformity disappeared. Therefore they became friends again, divided the money equally, and owned the big house between them.

NOTES.

A Pampango version, "The Cripple and the Blind Man" (I have it only in abstract), is almost identical with the second part of "The Four Blind Brothers." A blind man and a cripple travel together, blind man carrying, cripple guiding. Rope, drum, hatchet, etc. But these two companions do not quarrel over the distribution of the wealth: they live peacefully together.

I have printed in full five of the versions, because, while they are members of a very widespread family of tales in which a poor but valiant hero deceives and outwits a giant, ogre, ghost, or band of robbers, they form a more restricted brotherhood of that large family, and the deception is of a very definite special sort. The hero and the outwitted do not meet face to face, nor is there a contest of prowess between them. Merely by displaying as tokens of his size and strength certain seemingly useless articles which he has picked up and carried along with him on his travels, the hero frightens forever from their rich home a band of robbers or a giant or a ghost, and remains in possession of the treasures of the deceived one.

Trolls, ogres, giants, robbers, dragons, are proverbially stupid, and a clever hero with more wits than brawn has no difficulty in thoroughly frightening them. Grimm's story of "The Brave Little Tailor" (No. 20), with its incidents of "cheese-squeezing," "bird-throwing," "pretended carrying of the oak-tree," "springing over the cherry-tree," and "escape from the bed," and opening with the "seven-at-a-blow" episode, is typical of one large group of tales about a giant outwitted. (For an enumeration of the analogues, see Bolte-Polívka, I : 148–165; for a fuller discussion of some of them, see Cosquin, I : 96–102.) In another group the hero takes service with the giant, dragon, etc., keeps up the deception of being superhumanly strong, but gets the monster to do all the work, and finally wins his way to wealth and release (see Grimm, No. 183; Von Hahn, No. 18 and notes; Crane, 345, note 34; Dasent, Nos. v and xxxii). Then there is the

group of stories in which the cannibal witch is popped into her own
oven, which she had been heating for her victim (cf. Grimm, No. 15;
and Bolte-Polívka, 1 : 123).

Our particular group of stories, however, seems to owe little or
nothing to the types just mentioned. It appears to belong peculiarly
to the Orient. In fact, I do not know of its occurrence outside of
India and the Philippines. That the tale is well known in the Islands
at least as far north as central Luzon, our five variants attest; and that
it is fairly widespread in India, — I refer particularly to the method
of the deception, for on this the whole story turns, — three Hindoo
versions may be cited as evidence.

(1) "The Blind Man, the Deaf Man, and the Donkey" (Frere, No. 18)
presents many close correspondences to "Juan the Blind Man." In the
Indian tale a blind man and a deaf man enter into partnership. One day,
while on a long walk with his friend, the deaf man sees a donkey with a
large water-jar on its back. Thinking the animal will be useful to them,
they take it and the jar with them. Farther along they collect some large
black ants in a snuff-box. Overtaken by storm, they seek shelter in a
large, apparently deserted house, and lock the door; but the owner, a terrible
Rakshas, returns, and loudly demands entrance. The deaf man, looking
through a chink in the wall, is greatly frightened by the appearance of the
monster; but the blind man boldly says that he is Bakshas, Rakshas's
father. Incredulous, the Rakshas wishes to see his father's face. Donkey's
head shown. On his desiring to see his father's body, the huge jar is rolled
with a thundering noise past the chink in the door. Rakshas asks to hear
Bakshas scream. Deaf man puts ants into the donkey's ear: the animal,
bit by the insects, brays horribly, and the Rakshas flees in fright . . .
(Rakshas returns the next morning, and seeing the blind man, deaf man,
and donkey, laden with treasures, leaving his house, he determines to be
avenged; but by a lucky series of accidents the travellers succeed in dis-
comfiting and thoroughly terrifying the Rakshas and his six companions
summoned to help him, and travel on). In the division of the spoils, the
deaf man attempts to cheat the blind man, who in a rage gives him so
tremendous a box on the ear, that his hearing is restored! In return, the
deaf man gives his neighbor so hard a blow in the face, that the blind
man's eyes are opened. They are both so astonished, that they become
good friends at once, and divide the wealth equally.

(2) "The Brahmin Girl that married a Tiger" (Kingscote, No. x). In this
story, three brothers, on their way to rescue their sister who had been
married to a tiger, take along with them an ass, an ant, a palmyra-tree,
and a big iron washing-tub. The sister hides her brothers and their possessions in a loft. The tiger comes home, and frightens the brothers into
making a noise and thus betraying their presence. He asks to hear their
voice. Youngest brother puts his ant into the ear of the ass, which, when
bit, begins to bawl out horribly. Asking to see their legs, tiger is shown the
trunk of the palmyra-tree, and, on asking to see their bellies, is shown the
iron tub. Frightened, he runs away, and the sister is rescued.

(3) "Learning and Motherwit" (McCulloch, No. xxvi). Here Motherwit,

as in the other stories, deceives a Raghoshi by means of a thick rope (shown for hair), spades (shown for finger-nails), and wet lime (shown for spittle). At last with sharp-pointed hot iron rods, Ulysses fashion, he puts out the monster's eyes.

In another Bengal story, "The Ghost who was afraid of being Bagged" (Lal Behari Day, No. xx), a barber frightens a ghost with a looking-glass and becomes rich.

An interesting parallel to the incident of the death of the blind brothers by climbing up too high on palm-trees the tops of which have been broken off, is to be found in the Arabian story of "The Blind Thief" (JRASB 3 : 645–660, No. iii). A thief who used to steal dates from off the trees became blind, but he still went on thieving. The people planned to get rid of him. In the presence of the blind man, some one praised the dates of So-and-so. (Now, this tree was withered, and no longer had any leaves.) The covetous thief, with his rope, started to climb the tree that night; but his rope slipped off over the naked top of the palm, and he fell to the ground and was killed.

The situation of a blind man and a lame man joining forces and travelling together, the blind man carrying the lame man, who directs the way, is found in the Gesta Romanorum, tale LXXI.

Certain of the false proofs in the Filipino stories have no parallel in the Indian tales; viz., duck for louse, gun or horn for voice, tail of sting-ray (*pagui*) for hair. The suggestion for this last comparison may have come from the belief among the Filipinos that the tail of the sting-ray is a very efficacious charm against demons and witches. It is a "specific" against the *mangkukulam*.[1] On the other hand, there are certain details of the Indian versions lacking in the Filipino, — the donkey, the palmyra-tree, the wash-tub. Nevertheless the close agreement, not only of *motifs*, but of *motifs in the same sequence*, makes it certain beyond all reasonable doubt that the story as we find it in the Islands (most fully represented by the Bicol "Juan the Blind Man") goes back directly to southern India, possibly to the parent story of Miss Frere's old Deccan narrative.

7. (a) SAGACIOUS MARCELA.[2]

Long, long before the Spaniards came, there lived a man who had a beautiful, virtuous, and, above all, clever daughter. He was a servant of the king. Marcela, the daughter, loved her father devotedly, and always helped him with his work. From childhood she had manifested a keen wit and undaunted spirit. She would even refuse to obey unjust orders from the king.

[1] *Mangkukulam*, an old woman endowed with the powers of a witch.
[2] Narrated by Lorenzo Licup, a Pampangan.

No question was too hard for her to answer, and the king was constantly being surprised at her sagacity.

One day the king conceived a plan by which he might test the ingenious Marcela. He bade his servants procure a tiny bird and carry it to her house. "Tell her," said the king, "to make twelve dishes out of that one bird."

The servants found Marcela sewing. They told her of the order of the king. After thinking for five minutes, she took one of her pins, and said to the servants, "If the king can make twelve spoons out of this pin, I can also make twelve dishes out of that bird." On receiving the answer, the king realized that the wise Marcela had gotten the better of him; and he began to think of another plan to puzzle her.

Again he bade his servants carry a sheep to Marcela's house. "Tell her," he said, "to sell the sheep for six *reales*, and with the money this very same sheep must come back to me alive."

At first Marcela could not make out what the king meant for her to do. Then she thought of selling the wool only, and not the whole sheep. So she cut off the wool and sold it for six *reales*, and sent the money with the live sheep back to the king. Thus she was again relieved from a difficulty.

The king by this time realized that he could not beat Marcela in points of subtlety. However, to amuse himself, he finally thought of one more scheme to test her sagacity. It took him two weeks to think it out. Summoning a messenger, he said to him, "Go to Marcela, and tell her that I am not well, and that my physician has advised me to drink a cup of bull's milk. Therefore she must get me this medicine, or her father will lose his place in the palace." The king also issued an order that no one was to bathe or to wash anything in the river, for he was going to take a bath the next morning.

As soon as Marcela had received the command of the king and had heard of his second order, she said, "How easy it will be for me to answer this silly order of the king!" That night she and her father killed a pig, and smeared its blood over the sleeping-mat, blanket, and pillows. When morning came, Marcela took the stained bed-clothing to the source of the river, where the king was bathing. As soon as the king caught sight of her, he said in a voice of thunder, "Why do you wash your stuff in the river when you know I ordered that nobody should use the river to-day but me?"

Marcela replied, "It is the custom, my lord, in our country, to wash the mat, pillows, and other things stained with blood, immediately after a person has given birth to a child. As my father gave birth to a child last night, custom forces me to disobey your order, although I do it much against my will."

"Nonsense!" said the king. "The idea of a man giving birth to a child! Absurd! Ridiculous!"

"My lord," said Marcela, "it would be just as absurd to think of getting milk from a bull."

Then the king, recollecting his order, said, "Marcela, as you are so witty, clever, and virtuous, I will give you my son for your husband."

(b) KING TASIO.[1]

Juan was a servant in the palace of King Tasio. One day King Tasio heard Juan discussing with the other servants in the kitchen the management of the kingdom. Juan said that he knew more than anybody else in the palace. The king called Juan, and told him to go down to the seashore and catch the rolling waves.

"You said that you are the wisest man in the palace," said the king. "Go and catch the waves of the sea for me."

"That's very easy, O king!" said Juan, "if you will only provide me with a rope made of sand taken from the seashore."

The king did not know what to answer. He left Juan without saying anything, went into his room, and began to think of some more difficult work.

The next day he called Juan. "Juan, take this small bird and make fifty kinds of food out of it," said the king.

"Yes, sir!" said Juan, "if you will only provide me with a stove, a pan, and a knife made out of this needle," handing a needle to the king, "with which to cook the bird." Again the king did not know what to do. He was very angry at Juan.

"Juan, get out of my palace! Don't you let me see you walking on my ground around this palace without my consent!" said the king.

"Very well, sir!" said Juan, and he left the palace immediately.

The next day King Tasio saw Juan in front of the palace, riding on his *paragos* [2] drawn by a carabao.

---

[1] Narrated by Leopoldo Faustino, a Tagalog, who says that the story is popular and common among the people of La Laguna province.

[2] *Paragos,* a kind of rude, low sledge drawn by carabaos and used by farmers.

"Did I not tell you not to stand or walk on my ground around this palace? Why are you here now? Do you mean to mock me?" shouted the king.

"Well," said Juan, "will your Majesty's eyes please see whether I am standing on your ground or not? This is my ground." And he pointed to the earth he had on his *paragos.* "I took this from my orchard."

"That's enough, Juan," said King Tasio. "I can have no more foolishness." The king felt very uncomfortable, because many of his courtiers and servants were standing there listening to his talk with Juan.

"Juan, put this squash into this jar. Be careful! See that you do not break either the squash or the jar," said the king, as he handed a squash and a jar to Juan. Now, the neck of the jar was small, and the squash was as big as the jar. So Juan had indeed a difficult task.

Juan went home. He put a very small squash, which he had growing in his garden, inside the jar. He did not, however, cut it from the vine. After a few weeks the squash had grown big enough to fill the jar. Juan then picked off the squash enclosed in the jar, and went to the king. He presented the jar to the king when all the servants, courtiers, and visitors from other towns were present. As soon as the king saw the jar with the squash in it, he fainted. It was many hours before he recovered.

NOTES.

A third version (*c*), a Bicol story entitled "Marcela outwits the King," narrated by Gregorio Frondoso of Camarines, resembles closely the Pampango story of Marcela, with these minor differences: —

The heroine is the daughter of the king's adviser Bernardo. To test the girl's wit, the king sends her a mosquito he has killed, and tells her to cook it in such a way that it will serve twelve persons. She sends back a pin to him, with word that if he can make twelve forks from the pin, the mosquito will serve twelve persons. The second and third tasks are identical with those in the Pampango version. At last, satisfied with her sagacity, the king makes her his chief counsellor.

In addition to the three popular tales of the "Clever Lass" cycle, two chap-book versions of the story, containing incidents lacking in the folk-tales, may be mentioned here: —

A Buhay nang isang pastorang tubo sa villa na naguing asaua nang hari sa isang calabasa. ("LIFE OF A SHEPHERDESS WHO WAS BORN IN A

TOWN, AND WHO BECAME THE WIFE OF A KING BECAUSE OF A PUMP-
KIN.") Manila, 1908. This story is in verse, and comprises sixty-
six quatrains of 12-syllable assonanced lines. It is known only
in Tagalog, I believe.

B Buhay na pinagdaanan ni Rodolfo na anac ni Felizardo at ni Prisca
sa cahariang Valencia. ("LIFE OF RODOLFO, SON OF FELIZARDO AND
PRISCA, IN THE KINGDOM OF VALENCIA.") Maynila, 1910. Like the
preceding, this *corrido* is known only in Tagalog, and is written in
12-syllable assonanced lines.

Of these two printed versions, I give below a literal translation of the
first (A), not only because it is short (264 lines), but also because it will
be seen to be closely connected with the folk-tales. For help in making
this translation I am under obligation to Mr. Salvador Unson, which I
gratefully acknowledge. The second story (B) I give only in partial
summary. It is much too long to be printed in full, and, besides,
contains many incidents that have nothing to do with our cycle. It
will be noticed that "Rodolfo" (B) resembles rather the European
forms of the story; while A and the three folk-tales are more Oriental,
despite the conventional historical setting of A.

A. "CAY CALABASA: THE LIFE OF A SHEPHERDESS BORN IN A TOWN, WHO
BECAME THE WIFE OF A KING BECAUSE OF A PUMPKIN."

1. Ye holy angels in the heavens, help my tongue to express and to relate
the story I will tell.

2. In early times, when Adoveneis, King of Borgona, was still alive, he
went out into the plains to hunt for deer, and accidentally became
separated from his companions.

3. In his wandering about, he saw a hut, which had a garden surrounding it.
A beautiful young maiden took care of the garden, in which were
growing melons and pumpkins.

4. The king spoke to the maiden, and asked, "What plants are you growing
here?" The girl replied, "I am raising pumpkins and melons."

5. Now, the king happened to be thirsty, and asked her for but a drink.
"We were hunting in the heat of the day, and I felt this thirst come
on me."

6. The maiden replied, "O illustrious king! we have water in a mean jar,
but it is surely not fitting that your Majesty should drink from a
jar!

7. "If we had a jar of pure gold, in which we could put water from a blest
fountain, then it would be proper for your Majesty. It is not right
or worthy that you should drink from a base jar."

8. The king replied to the girl, "Never mind the jar, provided the water is
cool." The maiden went into the house, and presently the king
drank his fill.

9. After he had drunk, he handed her back the jar; but when the maiden
had received it (in her hands), she suddenly struck it against the
staircase. The jar was shattered to bits.

10. The king saw the act and wondered at it, and in his heart he thought
that the maiden had no manners. For the impudence of her action,
he decided to punish her.

11. (He said) "You see in me, the traveller, a noble king, and (you know) that I hold the crown. Why did you shatter that jar of yours, received from my hands?"

12. The maiden replied, "The reason I broke the jar, long kept for many years by my mother, O king! is that I should not like to have it used by another."

13. After hearing that, the king made no reply, but returned (back) towards the city, believing in his heart that the woman to whom he had spoken was virtuous.

14. After some time the king one day ordered a soldier to carry to the maiden a new narrow-necked jar, into which she was to put a pumpkin entire.

15. He also ordered the soldier to tell the girl that she should not break the jar, but that the jar and pumpkin should remain entire.

16. Inasmuch as the maiden was clever, her perception good, and her understanding bold, she answered with another problem: she sent him back a jar that already had a pumpkin in it.

17. She delivered it to the soldier, and the upshot of her reply was this: "The pumpkin and the jar are whole. The king must remove the pumpkin without breaking the jar."

18. The soldier shouldered it and went back to the king, and told him that her answer was that he should take the pumpkin out of the jar, and leave both whole.

19. When the king saw the jar, he said nothing; but he thought in his heart that he would send her another puzzle.

20. Again by the soldier he sent her a bottle, and requested that it be filled with the milk of a bull. (He further added,) that, if the order was not complied with, she should be punished.

21. The girl's answer to the king was this: "Last night my father gave birth to a child; and even though you order it, it is impossible for me to get (you?) any bull's milk (to-day?)."

22. Who would not wonder, when he comes to hear of it, at the language back and forth between the king and the girl! For what man can give birth to a child, and what bull can give milk?

23. At a great festival which the king gave, attended by knights and counts, he sent a pipit [1] to the girl, and ordered her to cook seven dishes of it.

24. The maiden (in reply) sent the king a needle, and asked him to make a steel frying-pan, knife, and spit out of it, which she might use in cooking the pipit.

25. The king again sent to her with this word: "If you are really very intelligent and if you are truly wise, you will catch the waves and bind them."

26. The soldier returned at once to the maiden, and told her that the orders of the king were that she should catch and bind the waves.

27. The maiden sent back word by the soldier that it is not proper to disobey a king. "Tell the king to make me a rope out of the loam I am sending."

28. Again the soldier returned to the palace, and, taking the black earth to the king, he said, "Make her a rope out of this loam, with which she will catch and bind the waves."

[1] *Pipit*, a tiny bird.

29. After the soldier had delivered his message, the king was almost shaking with rage. "Who under heaven can make a rope out of loam?"

30. Now he ordered the soldier to fetch the maiden. "And for her impudence," he said, "I will punish her."

31. He ordered the soldier to make haste and to return at once. The maiden did not resist her punishment, and was placed in a well.

32. Now, this well into which she was cast lay in front of the window of the king, so that whenever he should look out of the window he might see her.

33. One morning, as he looked out and saw her there below him, she asked him to give her fire.

34. The king said to her, "I am a world-famed king, and it is not my desire to descend just because of your request. Go ask fire from the mountain."

35. The girl made no answer to his jesting reply. Some time later the king held some games, and ordered that the maiden be taken out of the well.

36. The king told her that she was pardoned for all her offences. "But as long as I have visitors (?)," he said, "you are to be my cook."

37. Then this order was given to the girl: "You are to cook the food. Everything must be well prepared. All the food must be palatable and tasty."

38. The maiden, however, deliberately left all the food unsalted; but she fastened to the bottom of the plate the necessary salt.

39. When at the table the king and his council were not satisfied with the food, because there was no salt in it, the maiden was again summoned.

40. "I ordered you to cook because you were clever; but you took no care of the cooking. Why am I thus insulted and my honor destroyed before my guests?"

41. The maiden at once returned answer to the council and to his Majesty: "Look underneath the plates; and if there is not the necessary salt, my lord, condemn me as you see fit."

42. She had those near the king lift their plates, and she had him look under. The salt was found not lacking, and the king ceased from his contention and thought about the matter.

43. Then he said, "If you had mixed in a little with the food, then it would have been good and palatable. Explain to me the significance of your act."

44. "O great king!" answered the maiden, "I can easily reply to your question. By leaving the salt out, I meant me, and no one else [i.e., she meant to suggest her own case when she was in the well].

45. "You instructed me to get fire from the mountain. Why can you not taste this salt, which is just under the plate?

46. "Because I am an unfortunate person, an unworthy shepherdess from the woods. If I were a city-bred person, even though most ordinary, I should be honored in your presence."

47. To the reply of the girl the king shook his head, and pressed his forehead (in thought). He had fallen in love, and his heart was oppressed. He determined to marry her.

48. They were married at once, and at once she was clothed as a queen;

although she was only a lowly shepherdess, she was loved because of the sweetness of her voice.

49. After living together a long time, they had a quarrel: the king had conceived a dislike for her cleverness.

50. "Return at once to your father and mother," he said. "Go back to the mountains and live there.

51. "I will allow you to take with you whatever you want, — gold, silver, dresses. Take with you also two maids."

52. The queen could not utter a word; silently she let her tears fall. She thought that bad fortune had come upon her.

53. To be brief, the king got up from his chair and lay down in his bed. He pretended to go to sleep in order that he might not see the queen depart.

54. When the queen saw that the king was really sleeping, she covered him up (in her sorrow), and summoned the servants.

55. She ordered them to lift him up and carry him to the mountains. "In carrying him, be careful not to wake him until the mountains are reached."

56. They lifted the bed and took him downstairs; but when they were carrying it out of the palace, the bed struck against the front door. The king awoke in surprise.

57. He said, "What is the reason for carrying away a sleeping man?" He asked them whether they intended to throw away their sovereign.

58. At once he summoned the guards of the palace and ordered the arrest of the servants; but they protested that they were merely obeying the orders of the queen.

59. Then the king asked where the queen was who had ordered that. He had her brought before him, and demanded of her why she wished to cast him away.

60. The queen answered, reminding him thus: "My husband, my beloved, what did you tell me some time ago when you were driving me away?

61. "Did you not tell me to select whatever I might desire, including gold and silver, and take it with me? You are my choice.

62. "Even if I should become very good and very rich, I should still be without honor before God and the people.

63. "It would be shameful to the Divine Word for us married people to separate. You would be taunted by your counsellors for having married some one beneath you."

64. Her reply reminded the king that whatever might happen, they were married, and should remain together all their lives.

65. "Forgive me, my wife, light of my eyes! Forgive the wrongs I have done! I am to blame for the mistake [i.e., for my thoughtlessness]."

66. From then on, they loved each other the more, and were happy because they never quarrelled further.

B. The Story of Rodolfo.

Rodolfo was the only son of Felizardo and Prisca, who lived in Valencia. When Rodolfo was seven years old, he was sent to school, and proved to be an apt scholar; but his father died within a few years, and the boy was obliged to abandon his studies because of poverty. At the suggestion of his mother, Rodolfo one day set out for the capital, where he sought a place in the palace as servant. In time he was appointed head steward (*mayor-domo*) in the royal household. The king became so fond of this trusty servant, whose bravery, executive ability, and cleverness he could not help noticing, that finally he determined to make him his son-in-law by marrying him to the princess Leocadia. When Rodolfo was offered Leocadio's hand by her father, however, he respectfully declined the honor, saying that though he admired the beauty of the princess, he did not admire her character, and could not take her as his wife. The king was so angry that he ordered Rodolfo cast into prison; but after a few days' consideration, he had him released, and promised to pardon him for the insult if within a month he could bring before the king as his wife just such a virtuous woman as he had stipulated his wife should be.

Rodolfo left the palace, taking with him only a pair of shoes and an umbrella. On his way he saw an old man, whom he invited to go along with him. Shortly afterwards they saw a funeral procession, and Rodolfo asked his companion whether the man that was to be buried was still alive. The old man did not reply, because he thought that his companion was a fool. Outside the city they met many persons planting highland rice on a mountain-clearing (*kaingin*). Again Rodolfo spoke, and asked if the rice that the farmers were planting was already eaten; but the old man remained silent. In the course of their journey they reached a shallow river. Rodolfo put on his shoes and waded across. When he reached the other bank, he removed his shoes again and carried them in his hand. Next they passed a great plain. When they became tired from the heat, they rested by the side of the road under a big tree. Here Rodolfo opened his umbrella, which he had not used when they were crossing the hot plain. Once more the old man believed that his companion was crazy.

At last the travellers reached the old man's house, but the old man did not invite Rodolfo to spend the night with him. Rodolfo went into the house, however, for he saw that a young woman lived in the house. This was Estela, the old man's daughter, who received the stranger very kindly. That night, when Estela set the table for supper, she gave to her father the head and neck of the chicken, the wings to her mother, the body to Rodolfo, and the legs to herself. After eating their meal, the old man and his wife left Estela and Rodolfo together in the dining-room. Rodolfo expressed his love for her, for he had already recognized her worth. When she found that he was in earnest, she said that she would accept him if her parents consented to the marriage. Then they joined the old couple in the main room; but there the father scolded her for showing hospitality to a visitor whom he considered a fool. He also felt insulted for having been given only the head and neck of the chicken. Accordingly the old man told his daughter how Rodolfo had foolishly asked him if the person to be buried was still alive, and whether the rice that the farmers were planting on the mountain-clearing had already been eaten. He also mentioned the fact that Rodolfo wore his shoes only when crossing the river, and that he had opened his umbrella only when they were in the shade of the tree. Estela, in reply, cleverly explained to her father the meaning of all Rodolfo had said and done. "The memory of a man who has done good during his lifetime will never be forgotten. Rodolfo wished to know whether the man to be buried was kind to his fellow-men. If he was, he will always be remembered, and he is not dead. When Rodolfo asked you whether the rice which the farmers were planting was already eaten, he wished to know if those farmers had borrowed so much rice from their landlords that the next harvest would only be enough to pay it back. In a river it is impossible to see the thorns which may hurt one's feet, so it is wise to wear shoes while crossing a river. The idea of opening an umbrella under a tree is a very good one, because it forms a protection against falling branches and fruits. I will tell you why I divided the chicken as I did. I gave you the head and neck because you are the head of the family; the wings I gave my mother because she took care of me in my childhood; the body I gave to Rodolfo, because it is courteous to please a visitor; the legs I kept myself, because I am your feet and hands."

The anger of Estela's father was pacified by her explanation. He was now convinced that Rodolfo was not a fool, but a wise man, and he invited Rodolfo to live with them. Rodolfo staid and helped with all the work about the house and in the field. At last, when the old man realized that Rodolfo loved Estela, he gave his consent to their marriage; and the next day they became husband and wife.

After his marriage, Rodolfo returned to Valencia, leaving Estela at her home in Babilonia, and reported to the king that he had found and taken as his wife a virtuous woman. — The rest of the story turns on the "chastity-wager" *motif*, and ends with the establishment of the purity of Rodolfo's wife. (For this *motif*, constituting a whole story, see "The Golden Lock," No. 30.)

An examination of the five representatives of this cycle of the "Clever Lass" in the Philippines reveals at least nine distinct problems (tasks or riddles) to be solved. For most of these, parallels may be found in other Oriental and in Occidental stories.

(1) Problem: catching waves of the sea. Solution: demanding rope of sand for the work. This identical problem and solution are found in a North Borneo story, "Ginas and the Rajah" (Evans, 468–469). In the "Mahā-ummagga-jātaka," No. 546, a series of nineteen tasks is set the young sage Mahosadha. One of these is to make a rope of sand. The wise youth cleverly sent some spokesmen to ask the king for a sample of the old rope, so that the new would not vary from the old. See also Child, I : 10–11, for a South Siberian story containing the counter-demand for thread of sand to make shoes from stone.

(2) Problem: making many kinds of food from one small bird, or twelve portions from mosquito. Solution: requiring king to make stove, pan, and bolo (or twelve forks) from needle (pin). Analogous to this task is Bolte and Polívka's *motif* B² (2 : 349), the challenge to weave a cloth out of two threads. Bolte and Polívka enumerate thirty-five European folk-tales containing their *motif* B².

(3) Problem: putting large squash whole into narrow-necked jar. Solution: hero *grows* squash in the jar (and sometimes demands that

king remove the squash without breaking either it or the jar). I know of no other folk-tale occurrences of this task; it is not found in any of the European stories of this cycle, and may be an addition of the Tagalog narrators. It is a common enough trick, however, to grow a squash or cucumber in a small-necked bottle.

(4) Problem: getting milk from bull. Solution: hero tells king that his father has given birth to a child. Compare "Jātaka," No. 546 (tr. by Cowell and Rouse, 6 : 167–168), in which the king sends his fattened bull to East Market-town with this message: "Here is the king's royal bull, in calf. Deliver him, and send him back with the calf, or else there is a fine of a thousand pieces." The solution of this difficulty is the same as above. See also Child, I : 10–11, for almost identical situation. This problem and No. 1 are to be found in a Tibetan tale (Ralston 2, 138, 140–141).

(5) Problem: selling lamb for a specified sum of money, and returning both animal and coin. Solution: heroine sells only the wool.

Two of these problems, (3) and (5), are soluble, and belong in kind with the "*kalb-geritten*" *motif*, where the heroine is ordered to come to the king not clothed and not naked, not walking and not riding, not in the road and not out of the road, etc. The other three problems are not solved at all, strictly speaking: the heroine gets out of her difficulties by demanding of her task-master the completion of counter-tasks equally hard, or by showing him the absurdity of his demands. (See Bolte-Polívka, 2 : 362–370, for a full discussion of these sub-groups.) "In all stories of the kind," writes Child, "the person upon whom a task is imposed stands acquitted if another of no less difficulty is devised which must be performed first. This preliminary may be something that is essential for the execution of the other, as in the German ballads, or equally well something that has no kind of relation to the original requisition, as in the English ballads." It will be seen that in the nature of the counter-demands the Filipino stories agree rather with the German than the English.

(6) Hero is forbidden to walk on the king's ground. To circumvent the king, hero fills a sledge with earth taken from his own orchard, and has himself drawn into the presence of his Majesty. When challenged, the hero protests that he is not on the king's ground, but his own. This same episode is found in "Juan the Fool," No. 49 (*q. v.*).

(7) The stealing of the sleeping king by the banished wife, who has permission to take with her from the palace what she loves best, is found only in A. This episode, however, is very common elsewhere, and forms the conclusion of more than seventy Occidental stories of this cycle. (See Bolte-Polívka, 2 : 349–355.)

(8) The division of the hen, found in B and also at the end of "Juan the Fool" (No. 49), is fully discussed by Bolte and Polívka (2 : 360). See also R. Köhler's notes to Gonzenbach, 2 : 205–206. The combination of this *motif* with the "chastity-wager" *motif* found in "Rodolfo" (B), is also met with in a Mentonais story, "La femme avisée" (Romania, II : 415–416).

(9) For wearing of shoes only when crossing rivers, and raising umbrella
    only when sleeping under a tree, see again "Juan the Fool." A
    rather close parallel to this incident, as well as to the seemingly
    foolish questions Rodolfo asks Estela's father, and the daughter's
    wise interpretation of them, may be found in the Kashmir story,
    "Why the Fish laughed" (Knowles, 484–490 = Jacob 1, No. xxiv).
    See also a Tibetan story in Ralston 2:111; Benfey in "Ausland,"
    1859, p. 487; Spence Hardy, "Manual of Buddhism," pp. 220–227,
    364. Compare especially Bompas, No. lxxxix, "The Bridegroom
    who spoke in Riddles."

Finally mention may be made of two Arabian stories overlooked by
Bolte and Polívka, in one of which a woman sends supper to a stranger,
and along with the food an enigmatical message describing what she has
sent. The Negress porter eats a part of the food, but delivers the message. The stranger shrewdly guesses its meaning, and sends back a reply
that convicts the Negress of theft of a part of the gift. The other
story opens with the "bride-wager" riddle, and later enumerates
many instances of the ingenuity of the clever young wife. See Phil-
lott and Azoo, "Some Arab Folk-Tales from Haẓramaut," Nos. 1
and xvii (in JRASB 2 [1906] : 399–439).

Benfey (Ausland, 1859, *passim*) traces the story of the "Clever
Lass" back to India. The original situation consisted of the testing
of the sagacity of a minister who had fallen into disgrace. This
minister aids his royal master in a riddle-contest with a neighboring
hostile king. Later in the development of the cycle these sagacity
tests were transferred to a wife who helps her husband, or to a maiden
who helps her father, out of similar difficulties. (Compare the last
part of my note to No. 1 in this collection.) Bolte and Polívka, however (2 : 373) seem to think it probable that the last part of the story
— the marriage of the heroine, her expulsion, and her theft of the sleeping king — was native to Europe.

The Filipino folk-tales belonging to this cycle appear to go back
directly to India as a source. Incident 4 (see above) seems to me con-
clusive evidence, as this is a purely Oriental conception, being recorded
only in India, Tibet, and South Siberia. The chap-book version (A)
doubtless owes much to popular tradition in the Islands, although the
anonymous author, in his "Preface to the Reader," says that he has
derived his story from a book (unnamed), — *hañgo sa novela*. I have
not been able to trace his original; there is no Spanish form of the
tale, so far as I know.

Compare with this whole cycle No. 38, "A Negrito Slave," and the
notes.

8. (*a*) THE STORY OF ZARAGOZA.[1]

Years and years ago there lived in a village a poor couple,
Luis and Maria. Luis was lazy and selfish, while Maria was

---

[1] Narrated by Teodato P. Macabulos, a Tagalog from Manila.

hard-working and dutiful. Three children had been born to this pair, but none had lived long enough to be baptized. The wife was once more about to be blessed with a child, and Luis made up his mind what he should do to save its life. Soon the day came when Maria bore her second son. Luis, fearing that this child, like the others, would die unchristened, decided to have it baptized the very next morning. Maria was very glad to know of her husband's determination, for she believed that the early deaths of their other children were probably due to delay in baptizing them.

The next morning Luis, with the infant in his arms, hastened to the church; but in his haste he forgot to ask his wife who should stand as godfather. As he was considering this oversight, a strange man passed by, whom he asked, "Will you be so kind as to act as my child's godfather?"

"With all my heart," was the stranger's reply.

They then entered the church, and the child was named Luis, after his father. When the services were over, Luis entreated Zaragoza — such was the name of the godfather — to dine at his house. As Zaragoza had just arrived in that village for the first time, he was but too ready to accept the invitation. Now, Zaragoza was a kind-hearted man, and soon won the confidence of his host and hostess, who invited him to remain with them for several days. Luis and Zaragoza became close friends, and often consulted each other on matters of importance.

One evening, as the two friends were conversing, their talk turned upon the affairs of the kingdom. Luis told his friend how the king oppressed the people by levying heavy taxes on all sorts of property, and for that reason was very rich. Zaragoza, moved by the news, decided to avenge the wrongs of the people. Luis hesitated, for he could think of no sure means of punishing the tyrannical monarch. Then Zaragoza suggested that they should try to steal the king's treasure, which was hidden in a cellar of the palace. Luis was much pleased with the project, for he thought that it was Zaragoza's plan for them to enrich themselves and live in comfort and luxury.

Accordingly, one evening the two friends, with a pick-axe, a hoe, and a shovel, directed their way towards the palace. They approached the cellar by a small door, and then began to dig in the ground at the foot of the cellar wall. After a few hours of steady work, they succeeded in making an excavation leading into the interior. Zaragoza entered, and gathered up as many bags of money as he and Luis could carry. During the night they made several trips to the cellar, each time taking back to their house as much money as they could manage. For a long time the secret way was not discovered, and the two friends lost no opportunity of increasing their already great hoard. Zaragoza gave away freely much of his share to the poor; but his friend was selfish, and kept constantly admonishing him not to be too liberal.

In time the king observed that the bulk of his treasure was considerably reduced, and he ordered his soldiers to find out what had caused the disappearance of so much money. Upon close examination, the soldiers discovered the secret passage; and the king, enraged, summoned his counsellors to discuss what should be done to punish the thief.

In the mean time the two friends were earnestly discussing whether they should get more bags of money, or should refrain from making further thefts. Zaragoza suggested that they would better first get in touch with the secret deliberations of the court before making another attempt. Luis, however, as if called by fate, insisted that they should make one more visit to the king's cellar, and then inquire about the unrest at court. Persuaded against his better judgment, Zaragoza followed his friend to the palace, and saw that their secret passage was in the same condition as they had lately left it. Luis lowered himself into the hole; but lo! the whiz of an arrow was heard, and then a faint cry from Luis.

"What is the matter? Are you hurt?" asked Zaragoza.

"I am dying! Take care of my son!" These were Luis's last words.

Zaragoza knew not what to do. He tried to pull up the dead body of his friend; but in vain, for it was firmly caught between two heavy blocks of wood, and was pierced by many arrows. But Zaragoza was shrewd; and, fearing the consequences of the discovery of Luis's corpse, he cut off the dead man's head and hurried home with it, leaving the body behind. He broke the fatal news to Maria, whose grief was boundless. She asked him why he had mutilated her husband's body, and he satisfied her by telling her that they would be betrayed if Luis were recognized. Taking young Luis in her arms, Maria said, —

"For the sake of your godson, see that his father's body is properly buried."

"Upon my word of honor, I promise to do as you wish," was Zaragoza's reply.

Meantime the king was discussing the theft with his advisers. Finally, wishing to identify the criminal, the king decreed that the body should be carried through the principal streets of the city and neighboring villages, followed by a train of soldiers, who were instructed to arrest any person who should show sympathy for the dead man. Early one morning the military procession started out, and passed through the main streets of the city. When the procession arrived before Zaragoza's house, it happened that Maria was at the window, and, seeing the body of her husband, she cried, "O my husband!"

Seeing the soldiers entering their house, Zaragoza asked, "What is your pleasure?"

"We want to arrest that woman," was the answer of the chief of the guard.

"Why? She has not committed any crime."

"She is the widow of that dead man. Her words betrayed her, for she exclaimed that the dead man was her husband."

"Who is her husband? That remark was meant for me, because I had unintentionally hurt our young son," said Zaragoza smiling.

The soldiers believed his words, and went on their way. Reaching a public place when it was almost night, they decided to stay there until the next morning. Zaragoza saw his opportunity. He disguised himself as a priest and went to the place, taking with him a bottle of wine mixed with a strong narcotic. When he arrived, he said that he was a priest, and, being afraid of robbers, wished to pass the night with some soldiers. The soldiers were glad to have with them, as they thought, a pious man, whose stories would inspire them to do good. After they had talked a while, Zaragoza offered his bottle of wine to the soldiers, who freely drank from it. As was expected, they soon all fell asleep, and Zaragoza succeeded in stealing the corpse of Luis. He took it home and buried it in that same place where he had buried the head.

The following morning the soldiers woke up, and were surprised to see that the priest and the corpse were gone. The king soon knew how his scheme had failed. Then he thought of another plan. He ordered that a sheep covered with precious metal should be let loose in the streets, and that it should be followed by a spy, whose duty it was to watch from a distance, and, in case any one attempted to catch the sheep, to ascertain the house of that person, and then report to the palace.

Having received his orders, the spy let loose the sheep, and followed it at a distance. Nobody else dared even to make a remark about the animal; but when Zaragoza saw it, he drove it into his yard. The spy, following instructions, marked the door of Zaragoza's house with a cross, and hastened to the palace. The spy assured the soldiers that they would be able to capture the criminal; but when they began to look for the house, they found that all the houses were similarly marked with crosses.

For the third time the king had failed; and, giving up all hopes of catching the thief, he issued a proclamation pardoning the man who had committed the theft, provided he would present himself to the king within three days. Hearing the royal proclamation, Zaragoza went before the king, and confessed that he was the perpetrator of all the thefts that had caused so much trouble in the court. True to his word, the king did not punish him. Instead, the king promised to give Zaragoza a title of nobility if he could trick Don Juan, the richest merchant in the city, out of his most valuable goods.

When he knew of the desire of the king, Zaragoza looked for a fool, whom he could use as his instrument. He soon found one, whom he managed to teach to say "*Si*" (Spanish for "yes") whenever asked a question. Dressing the fool in the guise of a bishop, Zaragoza took a carriage and drove to the store of D. Juan. There he began to ask the fool such questions as these: "Does your grace wish to have this? Does not your grace think that this is cheap?" to all of which the fool's answer was "*Si*." At last, when the carriage was well loaded, Zaragoza said, "I will first take these things home, and then return with the money for them;" to which the fool replied, "*Si*." When Zaragoza reached the palace with the rich goods, he was praised by the king for his sagacity.

After a while D. Juan the merchant found out that what he thought was a bishop was really a fool. So he went to the king and asked that he be given justice. Moved by pity, the king restored all the goods that had been stolen, and D. Juan wondered how his Majesty had come into possession of his lost *property.*

Once more the king wanted to test Zaragoza's ability. Accordingly he told him to bring to the palace an old hermit who lived in a cave in the neighboring mountains. At first Zaragoza tried to persuade Tubal to pay the visit to the king, but in vain. Having failed in his first attempt, Zaragoza determined to play a trick on the old hermit. He secretly placed an iron cage near the mouth of Tubal's cave, and then in the guise of an angel he stood on a high cliff and shouted, —

"Tubal, Tubal, hear ye me!"

Tubal, hearing the call, came out of his cave, and, seeing what he thought was an angel, knelt down. Then Zaragoza shouted,—

"I know that you are very religious, and have come to reward your piety. The gates of heaven are open, and I will lead you thither. Go enter that cage, and you will see the way to heaven."

Tubal meekly obeyed; but when he was in the cage, he did not see the miracle he expected. Instead, he was placed in a carriage and brought before the king. Thoroughly satisfied now, the king released Tubal, and fulfilled his promise toward Zaragoza. Zaragoza was knighted, and placed among the chief advisers of the kingdom. After he had been raised to this high rank, he called to his side Maria and his godson, and they lived happily under the protection of one who became the most upright and generous man of the realm.

(b) JUAN THE PEERLESS ROBBER.[1]

Not many centuries after Charlemagne died, there lived in Europe a famous brigand named Juan. From childhood he had been known as "the deceitful Juan," "the unrivalled pilferer," "the treacherous Juan." When he was twenty, he was forced to flee from his native land, to which he never returned.

He visited Africa, where he became acquainted with a famous Ethiopian robber named Pedro. Not long after they had met, a dispute arose between them as to which was the more skilful pickpocket. They decided to have a test. They stood face to face, and the Ethiopian was first to try his skill.

"Hey!" exclaimed Juan to Pedro, "don't take my handkerchief out of my pocket!"

It was now Juan's turn. He unbuckled Pedro's belt and slipped it into his own pocket. "What's the matter with you,

---

[1] Narrated by Vicente M. Hilario, a Tagalog from Batangas, who heard the story from a Batangas student.

Juan?" said Pedro after a few minutes. "Why don't you go ahead and steal something?"

"Ha, ha, ha!" said Juan. "Whose belt is this?"

Pedro generously admitted that he had been defeated.

Although these two thieves were united by strong ties of common interest, nevertheless their diverse characteristics and traits produced trouble at times. Pedro was dull, honorable, and frank; Juan was hawk-eyed and double-faced. Pedro had so large a body and so awkward and shambling a gait, that Juan could not help laughing at him and saying sarcastic things to him. Juan was good-looking and graceful.

While they were travelling about in northern Africa, they heard the heralds of the King of Tunis make the following proclamation: "A big bag of money will be given to the captor of the greatest robber in the country." The two friends, particularly Juan, were struck by this announcement.

That night Juan secretly stole out of his room. Taking with him a long rope, he climbed up to the roof of the palace. After making a hole as large as a peso [1] in the roof, he lowered himself into the building by means of the rope. He found the room filled with bags of gold and silver, pearls, carbuncles, diamonds, and other precious stones. He took the smallest bag he could find, and, after climbing out of the hole, went home quickly.

When Pedro heard Juan's thrilling report of the untold riches, he decided to visit the palace the following night. Early in the morning Juan went again to the palace, taking with him a large tub. After lowering it into the room, he departed without delay. At nightfall he returned to the palace and filled the tub with boiling water. He had no sooner done this than Pedro arrived. Pedro was so eager to get the wealth, that he made no use of the rope, but jumped immediately into the room when he reached the small opening his treacherous friend had made in the roof. Alas! instead of falling on bags of money, Pedro fell into the fatal tub of water, and perished.

An hour later Juan went to look for his friend, whom he found dead. The next day he notified the king of the capture and death of the greatest of African robbers. "You have done well," said the king to Juan. "This man was the chief of all the African highwaymen. Take your bag of money."

[1] Why *peso*, I cannot say. A hole the size of a peso would accommodate a rope, but hardly a man or a large tub. The story is clearly imperfect in many respects.

After putting his gold in a safe place, Juan went out in search of further adventures. On one of his walks, he heard that a certain wealthy and devout abbot had been praying for two days and nights that the angel of the lord might come and take him to heaven. Juan provided himself with two strong wings. On the third night he made a hole as large as a peso through the dome of the church.

Calling the abbot, Juan said, "I have been sent by the Lord to take you to heaven. Come with me, and bring all your wealth."

The abbot put all his money into the bag. "Now get into the bag," said Juan, "and we will go."

The old man promptly obeyed. "Where are we now?" said he, after an hour's "flight."

"We are within one thousand miles of the abode of the blessed," was Juan's reply.

Twenty minutes later, and they were in Juan's cave. "Come out of the bag, and behold my rude abode!" said Juan to the old man. The abbot was astounded at the sight. When he heard Juan's story, he advised him to abandon his evil ways. Juan listened to the counsels of his new friend. He became a good man, and he and the abbot lived together until their death.

NOTES.

The story of "Zaragoza" is of particular interest, because it definitely combines an old form of the "Rhampsinitus" story with the "Master Thief" cycle. In his notes to No. 11, " The Two Thieves," of his collection of "Gypsy Folk Tales," F. H. Groome observes, "(The) 'Two Thieves' is so curious a combination of the 'Rhampsinitus' story in Herodotus and of Grimm's 'Master Thief,' that I am more than inclined to regard it as the lost original, which, according to Campbell of Islay, 'it were vain to look for in any modern work or in any modern age.'" By "lost original" Mr. Groome doubtless meant the common ancestor of these two very widespread and for the most part quite distinct cycles, "Rhampsinitus" and the "Master Thief."

Both of these groups of stories about clever thieves have been made the subjects of investigation. The fullest bibliographical study of the "Rhampsinitus" saga is that by Killis Campbell, "The Seven Sages of Rome" (Boston, 1907), pp. lxxxv–xc. Others have treated the cycle more or less discursively: R. Köhler, "Ueber J. F. Campbell's Sammlung gälischer Märchen," No. XVII (*d*) (in Orient und Occident, 2 [1864] : 303–313); Sir George Cox, "The Migration of Popular

Stories " (in Fraser's Magazine, July, 1880, pp. 96–111); W. A. Clouston, "Popular Tales and Fictions" (London, 1887), 2 : 115–165. See also F. H. Groome, 48–53; McCulloch, 161, note 9; and Campbell's bibliography. The "Master Thief" cycle has been examined in great detail as to the component elements of the story by Cosquin (2 : 274–281, 364–365). See also Grimm's notes to the "Master Thief," No. 192 (2 : 464); and J. G. von Hähn, 2 : 178–183.

F. Max Müller believed that the story of the "Master Thief" had its origin in the Sanscrit droll of "The Brahman and the Goat" (Hitopadesa, IV, 10 = Panchatantra, III, 3), which was brought to Europe through the Arabic translation of the "Hitopadesa." Further, he did not believe that the "Master Thief" story had anything to do with Herodotus's account of the theft of Rhampsinitus's treasure (see Chips from a German Workshop [New York, 1869], 2 : 228). Wilhelm Grimm, however, in his notes to No. 192 of the "Kinder- und Hausmärchen," says, "The well-known story in Herodotus (ii, 121) . . . is nearly related to this." As Sir G. W. Cox remarks (*op. cit.*, p. 98), it is not easy to discern any real affinity either between the Hitopadesa tale and the European traditions of the "Master Thief," or between the latter and the "Rhampsinitus" story. M. Cosquin seems to see at least one point of contact between the two cycles: "The idea of the episode of the theft of the horse, or at least of the means which the thief uses to steal the horse away, . . . might well have been borrowed from Herodotus's story . . . of Rhampsinitus" (Contes de Lorraine, 2 : 277).

A brief analysis of the characteristic incidents of these two "thieving" cycles will be of some assistance, perhaps, in determining whether or not there were originally any definite points of contact between the two. The elements of the "Rhampsinitus" story follow : —

A Two sons of king's late architect plan to rob the royal treasure-house.
(A¹ In some variants of the story the robbers are a town thief and a country thief.)
A² They gain an entrance by removing a secret stone, a knowledge of which their father had bequeathed them before he died.
B The king discovers the theft, and sets a snare for the robbers.
C Robbers return; eldest caught inextricably. To prevent discovery, the younger brother cuts off the head of the older, takes it away, and buries it.
D The king attempts to find the confederate by exposing the headless corpse on the outer wall of the palace.
D¹ The younger thief steals the body by making the guards drunk. He also shaves the right side of the sleeping guards' beards.
E King makes second attempt to discover confederate. He sends his daughter as a common courtesan, hoping that he can find the thief; for she is to require all her lovers to tell the story of their lives before enjoying her favors.

E¹ The younger thief visits her and tells his story; when she tries to detain him, however, he escapes by leaving in her hand the hand of a dead man he had taken along with him for just such a contingency.

F The king, baffled, now offers to pardon and reward the thief if he will discover himself. The thief gives himself up, and is married to the princess.

In some of the later forms of the story the king makes various other attempts to discover the culprit before acknowledging himself defeated, and is met with more subtle counter-moves on the part of the thief: (D²) King orders that any one found showing sympathy for the corpse as it hangs up shall be arrested; (D³) by the trick of the broken water-jar or milk-jar, the widow of the dead robber is able to mourn him unsuspected. (D⁴) The widow involuntarily wails as the corpse is being dragged through the street past her house; but the thief quickly cuts himself with a knife, and thus explains her cry when the guards come to arrest her. They are satisfied with the explanation. (E²) The king scatters gold-pieces in the street, and gives orders to arrest any one seen picking them up; (E³) the thief, with pitch or wax on the soles of his shoes, walks up and down the road, and, unobserved, gathers in the money. (E⁴) The king turns loose in the city a gold-adorned animal, and orders the arrest of any person seen capturing it. The thief steals it as in D¹, or is observed and his house-door marked. Then as in E². (E⁵) Old woman begging for "hind's flesh" or "camel-grease" finds his house; but the thief suspects her and kills her; or (E⁶) she gets away, after marking the house-door so that it may be recognized again. But the thief sees the mark, and proceeds to mark similarly all the other doors in the street. (E⁷) The king puts a pro-hibitive price on meat, thinking that only the thief will be able to buy; but the thief *steals* a joint.

However many the changes and additions of this sort (king's move followed by thief's move) rung in, almost all of the stories dealing with the robbery of the king's treasury end with the pardon of the thief and his exaltation to high rank in the royal household. In none of the score of versions of the "Rhampsinitus" story cited by Clouston is the thief subjected to any further tests of his prowess after he has been pardoned by the king. We shall return to this point.

The "Master Thief" cycle has much less to do with our stories than has the "Rhampsinitus" cycle: hence we shall merely enumerate the incidents to be found in it. (For bibliography of stories containing these situations, see Cosquin.)

A Hero, the youngest of three brothers, becomes a thief. For various reasons (the motives are different in Grimm 192, and Dasent xxxv) he displays his skill: —

B¹ Theft of the purse (conducted as a droll: the young apprentice-thief, noodle-like, brings back purse to robber-gang after throwing away the money).

B^2 Theft of cattle being driven to the fair. This trick is usually conducted in one of four ways: (*a*) two shoes in road; (*b*) hanging self; (*c*) bawling in the wood like a strayed ox; (*d*) exciting peasant's curiosity, — "comedy of comedies," "wonder of wonders."

B^3 Theft of the horse. This is usually accomplished by the disguised thief making the grooms drunk.

B^4 Stealing of a live person and carrying him in a sack to the one who gave the order. (The thief disguises himself as an angel, and promises to conduct his victim to heaven.)

Other instances of the "Master Thief's" cleverness, not found in Cosquin, are —

B^5 Stealing sheet or coverlet from sleeping person (Grimm, Dasent).

B^6 Stealing roast from spit while whole family is guarding it (Dasent).

We may now examine the members of the "Rhampsinitus" group that contain situations clearly belonging to the "Master Thief" formula. These are as follows: —

Groome, No. 11, "The Two Thieves," $B^3(d)$, B^4.
F. Liebrecht in a Cyprus story (Jahrb. f. rom. und eng. lit., 13 : 367–
    374 = Legrand, Contes grecs, p. 205), "The Master Thief," $B^3(a, c, d)$.
Wardrop, No. xiv, "The Two Thieves," B^4.
Radloff, in a Tartar story (iv, p. 193), B^4.
Prym and Socin, in a Syriac story (ii, No. 42), B^4.

It seems very likely that the Georgian, Tartar, and Syriac stories are nearly related to one another. The Roumanian gypsy tale, too, it will be noted, adds to the "Rhampsinitus" formula the incident of the theft of a person in a sack. This latter story, again, is connected with the Georgian tale, in that the opening is identical in both. One thief meets another, and challenges him to steal the eggs (feathers) from a bird without disturbing it. While he is doing so, he is in turn robbed unawares of his drawers by the first thief. (Compare Grimm, No. 129; a Kashmir story in Knowles, 110–112; and a Kabylie story, Rivière, 13.)

The number of tales combining the two cycles of the "Master Thief" and "Rhampsinitus's Treasure-House" is so small compared with the number of "pure" versions of each cycle, that we are led to think it very unlikely that there ever was a "lost original." There seems to be no evidence whatsoever that these two cycles had a common ancestor. Besides the fact that the number of stories in which the contamination is found is relatively very small, there is also to be considered the fact that these few examples are recent. No one is known to have existed more than seventy-five years ago. Hence the "snowball" theory will better explain the composite nature of the gypsy version and our story of "Zaragoza" than a "missing-link" theory. These two cycles, consisting as they do of a series of tests of skill, are peculiarly fitted to be interlocked. The wonder is, not that they have become combined in a few cases, but that they have remained separate in so many more, particularly as both stories are very widespread; and, given the ingredients, this is a combination that could have been made independently by many story-tellers. Could not the idea occur to more than one narrator that it is a greater feat to steal a living person (B^4) than a corpse (D^1), a piece of roast meat guarded by a person who knows that the thief is coming (B^6) than a piece of raw meat from an unsuspecting butcher (E^7)? All in all, it appears to me much more likely that the droll and certainly later cycle of the "Master Thief" grew out of the more serious and earlier cycle of "Rhampsinitus's Treasure-House" (by the same process as is suggested in the notes to No. 1 of this present collection) than that the two are branches from the same trunk.

In any case, our two stories make the combination. When or whence these Tagalog versions arose I cannot say. Nor need they be analyzed in detail, as the texts are before us in full. I will merely call attention to the fact that in "Zaragoza" the king sets a snare (cf. Herodotus) for the thief, instead of the more common barrel of pitch. There is something decidedly primitive about this trap which shoots arrows into its victim. Zaragoza's trick whereby he fools the rich merchant has an analogue in Knowles's Kashmir story of "The Day-Thief and the Night-Thief" (p. 298).

"Juan the Peerless Robber," garbled and unsatisfactory as it is in detail and perverted in *dénouement*, presents the interesting combination of the skill-contest between the two thieves (see above), the treachery of one (cf. the Persian Bahar-i-Danush, 2 : 225–248), and the stealing of the abbot in a sack.

9. THE SEVEN CRAZY FELLOWS.[1]

Once there were living in the country in the northern part of Luzon seven crazy fellows, named Juan, Felipe, Mateo, Pedro, Francisco, Eulalio, and Jacinto. They were happy all the day long.

One morning Felipe asked his friends to go fishing. They staid at the Cagayan River a long time. About two o'clock in the afternoon Mateo said to his companions, "We are hungry; let us go home!"

"Before we go," said Juan, "let us count ourselves, to see that we are all here!" He counted; but because he forgot to count himself, he found that they were only six, and said that one of them had been drowned. Thereupon they all dived into

---

[1] Narrated by Cipriano Seráfica, from Mangaldan, Pangasinan.

the river to look for their lost companion; and when they came out, Francisco counted to see if he had been found; but he, too, left himself out, so in they dived again. Jacinto said that they should not go home until they had found the one who was lost. While they were diving, an old man passed by. He asked the fools what they were diving for. They said that one of them had been drowned.

"How many were you at first?" said the old man.

They said that they were seven.

"All right," said the old man. "Dive in, and I will count you." They dived, and he found that they were seven. Since he had found their lost companion, he asked them to come with him.

When they reached the old man's house, he selected Mateo and Francisco to look after his old wife; Eulalio he chose to be water-carrier; Pedro, cook; Jacinto, wood-carrier; and Juan and Felipe, his companions in hunting.

When the next day came, the old man said that he was going hunting, and he told Juan and Felipe to bring along rice with them. In a little while they reached the mountains, and he told the two fools to cook the rice at ten o'clock. He then went up the mountain with his dogs to catch a deer. Now, his two companions, who had been left at the foot of the mountain, had never seen a deer. When Felipe saw a deer standing under a tree, he thought that the antlers of the deer were the branches of a small tree without leaves: so he hung his hat and bag of rice on them, but the deer immediately ran away. When the old man came back, he asked if the rice was ready. Felipe told him that he had hung his hat and the rice on a tree that ran away. The old man was angry, and said, "That tree you saw was the antlers of a deer. We'll have to go home now, for we have nothing to eat."

Meanwhile the five crazy fellows who had been left at home were not idle. Eulalio went to get a pail of water. When he reached the well and saw his image in the water, he nodded, and the reflection nodded back at him. He did this over and over again; until finally, becoming tired, he jumped into the water, and was drowned. Jacinto was sent to gather small sticks, but he only destroyed the fence around the garden. Pedro cooked a chicken without removing the feathers. He also let the chicken burn until it was as black as coal. Mateo and Francisco tried to keep the flies off the face of their old mistress. They soon became tired, because the flies kept coming back; so they took big sticks to kill them with. When a fly lighted on the nose of the old woman, they struck at it so hard that they killed her. She died with seemingly a smile on her face. The two fools said to each other that the old woman was very much pleased that they had killed the fly.

When the old man and his two companions reached home, the old man asked Pedro if there was any food to eat. Pedro said that it was in the pot. The old man looked in and saw the charred chicken and feathers. He was very angry at the cook. Then he went in to see his wife, and found her dead. He asked Mateo and Francisco what they had done to the old woman. They said that they had only been killing flies that tried to trouble her, and that she was very much pleased by their work.

The next thing the crazy fellows had to do was to make a coffin for the dead woman; but they made it flat, and in such a way that there was nothing to prevent the corpse from falling off. The old man told them to carry the body to the church; but on their way they ran, and the body rolled off the flat coffin. They said to each other that running was a good thing, for it made their burden lighter.

When the priest found that the corpse was missing, he told the six crazy fellows to go back and get the body. While they were walking toward the house, they saw an old woman picking up sticks by the roadside.

"Old woman, what are you doing here?" they said. "The priest wants to see you."

While they were binding her, she cried out to her husband, "Ah! here are some bad boys trying to take me to the church." But her husband said that the crazy fellows were only trying to tease her. When they reached the church with this old woman, the priest, who was also crazy, performed the burial-ceremony over her. She cried out that she was alive; but the priest answered that since he had her burial-fee, he did not care whether she was alive or not. So they buried this old woman in the ground.

When they were returning home, they saw the corpse that had fallen from the coffin on their way to the church. Francisco cried that it was the ghost of the old woman. Terribly frightened, they ran away in different directions, and became scattered all over Luzon.

NOTES.

I have a Bicol variant, "Juan and his Six Friends," narrated by Maximina Navarro, which is much like the story of "The Seven Crazy Fellows."

In the Bicol form, Juan and his six crazy companions go bathing in the river. Episode of the miscounting. On the way home, the seven, sad because of the loss of one of their number, meet another sad young man, who says that his mother is dying and that he is on his way to fetch a priest. He begs the seven to hurry to his home and stay with his mother until he returns. They go and sit by her. Juan mistakes a large mole on her forehead for a fly, and tries in vain to brush it away. Finally he "kills it" with a big piece of bamboo. The son, returning and finding his mother dead, asks the seven to take her and bury her. They wrap the body in a mat, but on the way to the cemetery the body falls out. They return to look for the corpse, but take the wrong road. They see an old woman cutting ferns; and, thinking that she is the first old woman trying to deceive them, they throw stones at her. The story ends with the burial of this second old woman, whom the seven admonish, as they put her into the ground, "never to deceive any one again."

These two noodle stories are obviously drawn from a common source. The main incidents to be found in them are (1) the miscounting of the swimmers and the subsequent correct reckoning by a stranger (this second part lacking in the Bicol variant); (2) the killing of the fly on the old woman's face; (3) the loss of the corpse and the burial of the old fagot-gathering woman by mistake.

(1) The incident of *not counting one's self* is found in a number of Eastern stories (see Clouston 1, 28–33; Grimm, 2 : 441). For a Kashmir droll recording a similar situation, where a townsman finds ten peasants weeping because they cannot account for the loss of one of their companions, see Knowles, 322–323.

(2) *Killing of fly on face* is a very old incident, and assumes various forms. In a Buddhist birth-story (Jātaka, 44), a mosquito lights on a man's head. The foolish son attempts to kill it with an axe. In another (Jātaka, 45) the son uses a pestle. Italian stories containing this episode will be found in Crane, 293–294 (see also Crane, 380, notes 13–15). In a Bicol fable relating a war between the monkeys and the dragon-flies, the dragon-flies easily defeat the monkeys, who kill one another in their attempts to slay their enemies, that have, at the order of their king, alighted on the monkeys' heads (see No. 57). Full bibliography for this incident may be found in Bolte-Polívka, 1 : 519.

(3) The killing of a living person thought to be a corpse come to life occurs in "The Three Humpbacks" (see No. 33 and notes).

Our story as a whole seems to owe nothing to European forms, though it has some faint general resemblances to the "Seven Swabians" (Grimm, No. 119). All three incidents of our story are found separately in India. Their combination may have taken place in the Islands, or even before the Malay migration.

10. (*a*) JUAN MANALAKSAN.[1]

Once upon a time there lived in a certain village a brave and powerful datu who had only one son. The son was called Pedro. In the same place lived a poor wood-cutter whose name was Juan Manalaksan. Pedro was rich, and had no work to do. He often diverted himself by hunting deer and wild boars in the forests and mountains. Juan got his living by cutting trees in the forests.

One day the datu and his son went to the mountain to hunt. They took with them many dogs and guns. They did not take any food, however, for they felt sure of catching something to eat for their dinner. When they reached the mountain, Pedro killed a deer. By noon they had become tired and hungry, so they went to a shady place to cook their game. While he was eating, Pedro choked on a piece of meat. The father cried out loudly, for he did not know what to do for his dying son. Juan, who was cutting wood near by, heard the shout. He ran quickly to help Pedro, and by pulling the piece of meat out of his throat he saved Pedro's life. Pedro was grateful, and said to Juan, "To-morrow come to my palace, and I will give you a reward for helping me."

The next morning Juan set out for the palace. On his way he met an old woman, who asked him where he was going.

"I am going to Pedro's house to get my reward," said Juan.

"Do not accept any reward of money or wealth," said the old woman, "but ask Pedro to give you the glass which he keeps in his right armpit. The glass is magical. It is as large as a peso, and has a small hole in the centre. If you push a small stick through the hole, giants who can give you anything you want will surround you." Then the old woman left Juan, and went on her way.

As soon as Juan reached the palace, Pedro said to him, "Go to that room and get all the money you want."

[1] Narrated by Aniclo Pascual of Arayat, Pampanga, who heard the story from an old Pampangan woman.

But Juan answered, "I do not want you to give me any money. All I want is the glass which you keep in your right armpit."

"Very well," said Pedro, "here it is." When Juan had received the glass, he hurried back home.

Juan reached his hut in the woods, and found his mother starving. He quickly thought of his magic glass, and, punching a small stick through the hole in the glass, he found himself surrounded by giants.

"Be quick, and get me some food for my mother!" he said to them. For a few minutes the giants were gone, but soon they came again with their hands full of food. Juan took it and gave it to his mother; but she ate so much, that she became sick, and died.

In a neighboring village ruled another powerful datu, who had a beautiful daughter. One day the datu fell very ill. As no doctor could cure him, he sent his soldiers around the country to say that the man who could cure him should have his daughter for a wife. Juan heard the news, and, relying on his charm, went to cure the datu. On his way, he asked the giants for medicine to cure the sick ruler. When he reached the palace, the datu said to him, "If I am not cured, you shall be killed." Juan agreed to the conditions, and told the datu to swallow the medicine which he gave him. The datu did so, and at once became well again.

The next morning Juan was married to the datu's daughter. Juan took his wife to live with him in his small hut in the woods.

One day he went to the forest to cut trees, leaving his wife and magic glass at home. While Juan was away in the forest, Pedro ordered some of his soldiers to go get the wood-cutter's wife and magic glass. When Juan returned in the evening, he found wife and glass gone. One of his neighbors told him that his wife had been taken away by some soldiers. Juan was very angry, but he could not avenge himself without his magical glass.

At last he decided to go to his father-in-law and tell him all that had happened to his wife. On his way there, he met an old *mankukulam*,[1] who asked him where he was going. Juan did not tell her, but related to her all that had happened to his wife and glass while he was in the forest cutting trees. The

---

[1] *Mankukulam*, see note 1, p. 53.

mankukulam said that she could help him. She told him to go to a certain tree and catch the king of the cats. She furthermore advised him, "Always keep the cat with you." Juan followed her advice.

One day Pedro's father commanded his soldiers to cut off the ears of all the men in the village, and said that if any one refused to have his ears cut off, he should be placed in a room full of rats. The soldiers did as they were ordered, and in time came to Juan's house; but, as Juan was unwilling to lose his ears, he was seized and placed in a room full of rats. But he had his cat with him all the time. As soon as he was shut up in the room, he turned his cat loose. When the rats saw that they would all be killed, they said to Juan, "If you will tie your cat up there in the corner, we will help you get whatever you want."

Juan tied his cat up, and then said to the rats, "Bring me all the glasses in this village." The rats immediately scampered away to obey him. Soon each of them returned with a glass in its mouth. One of them was carrying the magical glass. When Juan had his charm in his hands again, he pushed a small stick through the hole in the glass, and ordered the giants to kill Pedro and his father, and bring him his wife again.

Thus Juan got his wife back. They lived happily together till they died.

(b) JUAN THE POOR, WHO BECAME JUAN THE KING.[1]

Once upon a time there lived in a small hut at the edge of a forest a father and son. The poverty of that family gave the son his name, — Juan the Poor. As the father was old and feeble, Juan had to take care of the household affairs; but there were times when he did not want to work.

One day, while Juan was lying behind their fireplace, his father called him, and told him to go to the forest and get some fire-wood. "Very well," said Juan, but he did not move from his place.

After a while the father came to see if his son had gone, but he found him still lying on the floor. "When will you go get that fire-wood, Juan?"

"Right now, father," answered the boy. The old man returned to his room. As he wanted to make sure, however,

---

[1] Narrated by Amando Clemente, a Tagalog, who heard the story from his aunt.

whether his son had gone or not, he again went to see. When he found Juan in the same position as before, he became very angry, and said, —

"Juan, if I come out again and find you still here, I shall surely give you a whipping." Juan knew well that his father would punish him if he did not go; so he rose up suddenly, took his axe, and went to the forest.

When he came to the forest, he marked every tree that he thought would be good for fuel, and then he began cutting. While he was chopping at one of the trees, he saw that it had a hole in the trunk, and in the hole he saw something glistening. Thinking that there might be gold inside the hole, he hastened to cut the tree down; but a monster came out of the hole as soon as the tree fell.

When Juan saw the unexpected being, he raised his axe to kill the monster. Before giving the blow, he exclaimed, "Aha! Now is the time for you to die."

The monster moved backward when it saw the blow ready to fall, and said, —

> "Good sir, forbear,
> And my life spare,
> If you wish a happy life
> And, besides, a pretty wife."

Juan lowered his axe, and said, "Oho! is that so?"

"Yes, I swear," answered the monster.

"But what is it, and where is it?" said Juan, raising his axe, and feigning to be angry, for he was anxious to get what the monster promised him. The monster told Juan to take from the middle of his tongue a white oval stone. From it he could ask for and get whatever he wanted to have. Juan opened the monster's mouth and took the valuable stone. Immediately the monster disappeared.

The young man then tested the virtues of his charm by asking it for some men to help him work. As soon as he had spoken the last word of his command, there appeared many persons, some of whom cut down trees, while others carried the wood to his house. When Juan was sure that his house was surrounded by piles of fire-wood, he dismissed the men, hurried home, and lay down again behind the fireplace. He had not been there long, when his father came to see if he had done his work. When the old man saw his son stretched out on the floor, he said, "Juan, have we fire-wood now?"

"Just look out of the window and see, father!" said Juan. Great was the surprise of the old man when he saw the large piles of wood about his house.

The next day Juan, remembering the pretty wife of which the monster had spoken, went to the king's palace, and told the king that he wanted to marry his daughter. The king smiled scornfully when he saw the rustic appearance of the suitor, and said, "If you will do what I shall ask you to do, I will let you marry my daughter."

"What are your Majesty's commands for me?" said Juan.

"Build me a castle in the middle of the bay; but know, that, if it is not finished in three days' time, you lose your head," said the king sternly. Juan promised to do the work.

Two days had gone by, yet Juan had not yet commenced his work. For that reason the king believed that Juan did not object to losing his life; but at midnight of the third day, Juan bade his stone build a fort in the middle of the bay.

The next morning, while the king was taking his bath, cannon-shots were heard. After a while Juan appeared before the palace, dressed like a prince. When he saw the king, he said, "The fort is ready for your inspection."

"If that is true, you shall be my son-in-law," said the king. After breakfast the king, with his daughter, visited the fort, which pleased them very much. The following day the ceremonies of Juan's marriage with the princess Maria were held with much pomp and solemnity.

Shortly after Juan's wedding a war broke out. Juan led the army of the king his father-in-law to the battlefield, and with the help of his magical stone he conquered his mighty enemy. The defeated general went home full of sorrow. As he had never been defeated before, he thought that Juan must possess some supernatural power. When he reached home, therefore, he issued a proclamation which stated that any one who could get Juan's power for him should have one-half of his property as a reward.

A certain witch, who knew of Juan's secret, heard of the proclamation. She flew to the general, and told him that she could do what he wanted done. On his agreeing, she flew to Juan's house one hot afternoon, where she found Maria alone, for Juan had gone out hunting. The old woman smiled when she saw Maria, and said, "Do you not recognize me, pretty Maria? I am the one who nursed you when you were a baby."

The princess was surprised at what the witch said, for she thought that the old woman was a beggar. Nevertheless she believed what the witch told her, treated the repulsive woman kindly, and offered her cake and wine; but the witch told Maria not to go to any trouble, and ordered her to rest. So Maria lay down to take a siesta. With great show of kindness, the witch fanned the princess till she fell asleep. While Maria was sleeping, the old woman took from underneath the pillow the magical stone, which Juan had forgotten to take along with him. Then she flew to the general, and gave the charm to him. He, in turn, rewarded the old woman with one-half his riches.

Meanwhile, as Juan was enjoying his hunt in the forest, a huge bird swooped down on him and seized his horse and clothes. When the bird flew away, his inner garments were changed back again into his old wood-cutter's clothes. Full of anxiety at this ill omen, and fearing that some misfortune had befallen his wife, he hastened home on foot as best he could. When he reached his house, he found it vacant. Then he went to the king's palace, but that too he found deserted. For his stone he did not know where to look. After a few minutes of reflection, he came to the conclusion that all his troubles were caused by the general whom he had defeated in battle. He also suspected that the officer had somehow or other got possession of his magical stone.

Poor Juan then began walking toward the country where the general lived. Before he could reach that country, he had to cross three mountains. While he was crossing the first mountain, a cat came running after him, and knocked him down. He was so angry at the animal, that he ran after it, seized it, and dashed its life out against a rock. When he was crossing the second mountain, the same cat appeared and knocked him down a second time. Again Juan seized the animal and killed it, as before; but the same cat that he had killed twice before tumbled him down a third time while he was crossing the third mountain. Filled with curiosity, Juan caught the animal again: but, instead of killing it this time, he put it inside the bag he was carrying, and took it along with him.

After many hours of tiresome walking, Juan arrived at the castle of the general, and knocked at the door. The general asked him what he wanted. Juan answered, "I am a poor beggar, who will be thankful if I can have only a mouthful of rice." The general, however, recognized Juan. He called his servants, and said, "Take this wretched fellow to the cell of rats."

The cell in which Juan was imprisoned was very dark; and as soon as the door was closed, the rats began to bite him. But Juan did not suffer much from them; for, remembering his cat, he let it loose. The cat killed all the rats except their king, which came out of the hole last of all. When the cat saw the king of the rats, it spoke thus: "Now you shall die if you do not promise to get for Juan his magical stone, which your master has stolen."

"Spare my life, and you shall have the stone!" said the king of the rats.

"Go and get it, then!" said the cat. The king of the rats ran quickly to the room of the general, and took Juan's magical stone from the table.

As soon as Juan had obtained his stone, and after he had thanked the king of the rats, he said to his stone, "Pretty stone, destroy this house with the general and his subjects, and release my father-in-law and wife from their prison."

Suddenly the earth trembled and a big noise was heard. Not long afterwards Juan saw the castle destroyed, the general and his subjects dead, and his wife and his father-in-law free.

Taking with him the cat and the king of the rats, Juan went home happily with Maria his wife and the king his father-in-law. After the death of the king, Juan ascended to the throne, and ruled wisely. He lived long happily with his lovely wife.

NOTES.

These two stories belong to the "Magic Ring" cycle, and are connected with the well-known "Aladdin" tale. Antti Aarne (pp. 1–82) reconstructs the original formula of this type, which was about as follows: —

A youth buys the life of a dog and a cat, liberates a serpent, and receives from its parent a wishing-stone, by means of which he builds himself a magnificent castle and wins as his wife a princess. But a thief steals the stone and removes castle and wife over the sea. Then the dog and the cat swim across the ocean, catch a mouse, and compel it to fetch the stone from out of the mouth of the thief. Upon their return journey, cat and dog quarrel, and the stone falls into the sea. After they have obtained it again with the help of a frog, they bring it to their master, who wishes his castle and wife back once more.

In nearly every detail our stories vary from this norm: (1) The hero does not buy the life of any animals, (2) he does not acquire the charm from a grateful serpent that he has unselfishly saved from death, (3) the dog does not appear at all, (4) castle and wife are not transported beyond the sea, (5) the cat does not serve the hero voluntarily out of gratitude, (6) the hero himself journeys to recover his stolen charm. And yet there can be no doubt of the connection of our stories with this cycle. The acquirement of a charm, through the help of which the hero performs a difficult task under penalty of death, and thus wins the hand of a ruler's daughter; the theft of the charm and the disappearance of the wife; the search, which is finally brought to a successful close through the help of a cat and the king of the rats; the recovery of wife and charm, and the death of the hero's enemies, — these details in combination are unmistakable proofs.

Most of the characteristic details, however, of the "Magic Ring" cycle are to be found in the Philippines, although they are lacking in these two stories. For instance, in No. 26 the hero buys the life of a snake for five cents, and is rewarded by the king of the serpents with a magic wishing-cloth (cf. E. Steere, 403). In a Visayan *pourquoi* story, "Why Dogs wag their Tails" (see JAFL 20 : 98–100), we have a variant of the situation of the helpful dog and cat carrying a ring across a body of water, the quarrel in mid-stream, and the loss of the charm. In the same volume (pp. 117–118) is to be found a Tagalog folk-version of the "Aladdin" tale.[1]

Neither "Juan Manalaksan" nor "Juan the Poor, who became Juan the King," can be traced, I believe, to any of the hundred and sixty-three particular forms of the story cited by Aarne. The differences in detail are too many. The last part of Pedroso's Portuguese folk-tale, No. xxx, is like (*b*), in that the hero himself seeks the thief, takes along with him a cat, is recognized by the thief and imprisoned, and by means of the cat threatens the king of the rats, who recovers the charm for him. But the first part is entirely different: the charm is an apple obtained from a hind, and the hero's wife is not stolen along with the charm. No Spanish version has been recorded. It is not

---

[1] As Mr. Gardner notes, a chap-book form of "Aladdin" exists in Tagalog. The full title of my copy runs thus (in translation): "The Wonderful story of Aladin, who got possession of the Marvelous Lamp, and of his Marriage with the Princess of China the Great. Manila, 1901. (Pp. 127.)" W. Retana, in his "Aparato Bibliográfico" (Madrid, 1906), cites an edition before 1898 (see item No. 4161). The story has also been printed in the Pampango, Ilocano, Bicol, and Visayan dialects.

impossible that the story in the Philippines is prehistoric. "Juan Manalaksan," which the narrator took down exactly as it was told to him, clearly dates back to a time when the tribe had its own native datu government, possibly to a time even before the Pampangans migrated to the Philippines. The whole "equipment" of this story is primitive to a degree. Moreover, the nature of the charm in both stories — a piece of glass and an oval stone instead of the more usual ring — points to the primitiveness of our versions, as does likewise the fact that the charm is not stolen from the hero by his wife, but by some other person (see Aarne, pp. 43, 45).

For further discussions of this cycle of folk-tales, and its relation to the Arabian literary version, see Aarne, 61 *et seq.* Compare also Macculloch, 201–202, 237–238; Groome, 218–220; Clouston's "Variants of Burton's Supplemental Arabian Nights," pp. 564–575; Bolte-Polívka, 2 : 451–458; Benfey, I : 211 ff. Add to Aarne's and Bolte's lists Wratislaw, No. 54. See also Dähnhardt, 4 : 147–160.

In conclusion, I may add in the way of an Appendix, as it were, a brief synopsis of a Tagalog romance entitled "Story of Edmundo, Son of Merced in the Kingdom of France; taken from a *novela* and composed by one who enjoys writing the Tagalog language. Manila 1909." This verse-form of a story at bottom the same as our two folk-tales is doubtless much more recent than our folk-tales themselves, and is possibly based on them directly, despite the anonymous author's statement as to the unnamed *novela* that was his source. In the following summary of the "Story of Edmundo," the numbers in parentheses refer to stanzas of the original Tagalog text.

"EDMUNDO."

In Villa Amante there lived a poor widow, Merced by name, who had to work very hard to keep her only son, the infant Edmundo, alive. Her piety and industry were rewarded, however; and by the time the boy was seven years old, she was able to clothe him well and send him to school. Her brother Tonio undertook the instruction of the youth. Edmundo had a good head, and made rapid progress. (7–41)

One day Merced fell sick, and, although she recovered in a short time, Edmundo decided to give up studying and to help his mother earn their living. He became a wood-cutter. (42–53)

At last fortune came to him. In one of his wanderings in the forest in search of dry wood, he happened upon an enormous python. He would have fled in terror had not the snake spoken to him, to his amazement, and requested him to pull from its throat the stag which was choking it. He performed the service for the reptile, and in turn was invited to the cave where it lived. Out of gratitude the python gave Edmundo a magic mirror that would furnish the possessor with whatever he wanted. With the help of this charm, mother and son soon had everything they needed to make them happy. (54–91)

At about this time King Romualdo of France decided to look for a husband for his daughter, the beautiful Leonora. He was unable to pick out a son-in-law from the many suitors who presented themselves; and so he had it proclaimed at a concourse of all the youths of the realm, "Whoever can fill my cellar with money before morning shall have the hand of Leonora." Edmundo was the only one to accept the challenge, for failure to perform the task meant death. At midnight he took his enchanted mirror and commanded it to fill the king's cellar with money. In the morning the king was astonished at the sight, but there was no way of avoiding the marriage. So Leonora became the wife of the lowly-born wood-cutter. The young couple went to Villa Amante to live. There, to astonish his wife, Edmundo had a palace built in one night. She was dumfounded to awake in the morning and find herself in a magnificent home; and when she asked him about it, he confided to her the secret of his wonderful charm. Later, to gratify the humor of the king, who visited him, Edmundo ordered his mirror to transport the palace to a seacoast town. There he and his wife lived very happily together. (92–211)

One day Leonora noticed from her window two vessels sailing towards the town. Her fears and premonitions were so great, that Edmundo, to calm her, sank the ships by means of his magic power. But the sinking of these vessels brought misfortunes. Their owner, the Sultan of Turkey, learned of the magic mirror possessed by Edmundo (how he got this information is not stated), and hired an old woman to go to France in the guise of a beggar and steal the charm. She was successful in getting it, and then returned with it to her master. The Sultan then invaded France, and with the talisman, by which he called to his aid six invincible giants, conquered the country. He took the king, queen, and Leonora as captives back with him to Turkey. Edmundo was left in France to look after the affairs of the country. (212–296)

Edmundo became melancholy, and at last decided to seek his wife. He left his mother and his servant behind, and took with him only a diamond ring of Leonora's, his cat, and his dog. While walking along the seashore, wondering how he could cross the ocean, he saw a huge fish washed up on the sand. The fish requested him to drag it to the water. When Edmundo had done so, the fish told him to get on its back, and promised to carry him to Leonora. So done. The fish swam rapidly through the water, Edmundo holding his dog and cat in his breast. The dog was soon washed "overboard," but the cat clung to him. After a ride of a day and a night, the fish landed him on a strange shore. It happened to be the coast of Turkey. (297–313)

Edmundo stopped at an inn, pretending to be a shipwrecked merchant. There he decided to stay for a while, and there he found out the situation of Leonora in this wise. Now, it happened that the Sultan used to send to this inn for choice dishes for Leonora, whom he was keeping close captive. By inquiry Edmundo learned of the close proximity of his wife, and one day he managed to insert her ring into one of the eggs that were to be taken back to her. She guessed that he was near; and, in order to communicate with him, she requested permission of the king to walk with her maid in the garden that was close by the inn. She saw Edmundo, and smiled on him; but the maid noticed the greeting, and reported it to the Sultan. The

Sultan ordered the man summoned; and when he recognized Edmundo, he had him imprisoned and put in stocks. (314–350)

Edmundo was now in despair, and thought it better to die than live; but his faithful cat, which had followed him unnoticed to the prison, saved him. In the jail there were many rats. That night the cat began to kill these relentlessly, until the captain of the rats, fearing that his whole race would be exterminated, requested Edmundo to tie up his cat and spare them. Edmundo promised to do so on condition that the rat bring him the small gold-rimmed mirror in the possession of the Sultan. At dawn the rat captain arrived with the mirror between its teeth. Out of gratitude Edmundo now had his mirror bring to life all the rats that had been slain. (351–366)

Then he ordered before him his wife, the king, the queen, the crown and sceptre of France. All, including the other prisoners of the Sultan, were transported back to France. At the same time the Sultan's palace and prison were destroyed. Next morning, when the Grand Sultan awoke, he was enraged to find himself outwitted; but what could he do? Even if he were able to jump as high as the sky, he could not bring back Leonora. (367–376)

When the French Court returned to France, Edmundo was crowned successor to the throne: the delight of every one was unbounded. (377–414)

The last six stanzas are occupied with the author's leave-taking. (415–420)

Groome (pp. 219–220) summarizes a Roumanian-Gypsy story, "The Stolen Ox," from Dr. Barbu Constantinescu's collection (Bucharest, 1878), which, while but a fragment, appears to be connected with this cycle of the "Magic Ring," and presents a curious parallel to a situation in "Edmundo :" —

" . . . The lad serves the farmer faithfully, and at the end of his term sets off home. On his way he lights on a dragon, and in the snake's mouth is a stag. Nine years had that snake the stag in its mouth, and been trying to swallow it, but could not because of its horns. Now, that snake was a prince; and seeing the lad, whom God had sent his way, 'Lad,' said the snake, 'relieve me of this stag's horns, for I've been going about nine years with it in my mouth.' So the lad broke off the horns, and the snake swallowed the stag. 'My lad, tie me round your neck and carry me to my father, for he doesn't know where I am.' So he carried him to his father, and his father rewarded him."

It is curious to see this identical situation of the hero winning his magic reward by saving some person or animal from choking appearing in Roumania and the Philippines, and in connection, too, with incidents from the "Magic Ring" cycle. The resemblance can hardly be fortuitous.

11. (a) LUCAS THE STRONG.[1]

Once there was a man who had three sons, — Juan, Pedro, and Lucas. His wife died when his children were young. Un-

---

[1] Narrated by Paulo Macasaet, a Tagalog, who heard the story from a Tagalog farmer.

like most of his countrymen, he did not marry again, but spent his time in taking care of his children. The father could not give his sons a proper education, because he was poor; so the boys grew up in ignorance and superstition. They had no conception of European clothes and shoes. Juan and Pedro were hard workers, but Lucas was lazy. The father loved his youngest son Lucas, nevertheless; but Juan and Pedro had little use for their brother. The lazy boy used to ramble about the forests and along river-banks looking for guavas and birds' nests.

One day, when Lucas was in the woods, he saw a boa-constrictor [Tag. *sawang bitin*]. He knew that this reptile carried the centre of its strength in the horny appendage at the end of its tail. Lucas wished very much to become strong, because the men of strength in his barrio were the most influential. So he decided to rob the boa of its charm. He approached the snake like a cat, and then with his sharp teeth bit off the end of its tail, and ran away with all his might. The boa followed him, but could not overtake him; for Lucas was a fast runner, and, besides, the snake had lost its strength.

Lucas soon became the strongest man in his barrio. He surprised everybody when he defeated the man who used to be the Hercules of the place.

One day the king issued a proclamation: "He who can give the monarch a carriage made of gold shall have the princess for his wife." When Juan and Pedro heard this royal announcement, they were very anxious to get the carriage and receive the reward.

Juan was the first to try his luck. He went to a neighboring mountain and began to dig for gold. While he was eating his lunch at noon, an old leper with her child approached him, and humbly begged him to give her something to eat.

"No, the food I have here is just enough for me. Go away! You are very dirty," said Juan with disgust.

The wretched old woman, with tears in her eyes, left the place. After he had worked for three weeks, Juan became discouraged, gave up his scheme of winning the princess, and returned home.

Pedro followed his brother, but he had no better luck than Juan. He was also unkind to the old leper.

Lucas now tried his fortune. The day after his arrival at the mountain, when he was eating, the old woman appeared, and asked him to give her some food. Lucas gave the woman half of his meat. The leper thanked him, and promised that she would give him not only the carriage made of gold, but also a pair of shoes, a coat, and some trousers. She then bade Lucas good-by.

Nine days passed, and yet the woman had not come. Lucas grew tired of waiting, and in his heart began to accuse the woman of being ungrateful. He repented very much the kindness he had shown the old leper. Finally she appeared to Lucas, and told him what he had been thinking about her. "Do not think that I shall not fulfil my promise," she said. "You shall have them all." To the great astonishment of Lucas, the woman disappeared again. The next day he saw the golden carriage being drawn by a pair of fine fat horses; and in the carriage were the shoes, the coat, and the trousers. The old woman appeared, and showed the young man how to wear the shoes and clothes.

Then he entered the carriage and was driven toward the palace. On his way he met a man.

"Who are you?" said Lucas.

"I am Runner, son of the good runner," was the answer.

"Let us wrestle!" said Lucas. "I want to try your strength. If you defeat me, I will give you a hundred pesos; but if I prove to be the stronger, you must come with me."

"All right, let us wrestle!" said Runner. The struggle lasted for ten minutes, and Lucas was the victor. They drove on.

They met another man. When Lucas asked him who he was, the man said, "I am Sharpshooter, son of the famous shooter." Lucas wrestled with this man too, and overcame him because of his superhuman strength. So Sharpshooter went along with Lucas and Runner.

Soon they came up to another man. "What is your name?" said Lucas.

"My name is Farsight. I am son of the great Sharp-Eyes." Lucas proposed a wrestling-match with Farsight, who was conquered, and so obliged to go along with the other three.

Last of all, the party met Blower, "son of the great blower." He likewise became one of the servants of Lucas.

When Lucas reached the palace, he appeared before the king, and in terms of great submission he told the monarch that he had come for two reasons, — first, to present his Majesty with the golden carriage; second, to receive the reward which his Majesty had promised.

The king said, "I will let you marry my daughter provided that you can more quickly than my messenger bring to me a bottle of the water that gives youth and health to every one. It is found at the foot of the seventh mountain from this one," he said, pointing to the mountain nearest to the imperial city. "But here is another provision," continued the king: "if you accept the challenge and are defeated, you are to lose your head."

"I will try, O king!" responded Lucas sorrowfully.

The king then ordered his messenger, a giant, to fetch a bottle of the precious water. Lucas bade the monarch good-by, and then returned to his four friends. "Runner, son of the good runner, hasten to the seventh mountain and get me a bottle of the water that gives youth and health!"

Runner ran with all his might, and caught up with the giant; but the giant secretly put a gold ring in Runner's bottle to make him sleep. Two days passed, but Runner had not yet arrived. Then Lucas cried, "Farsight, son of the great Sharp-Eyes, see where the giant and Runner are!"

The faithful servant looked, and he saw Runner sleeping, and the giant very near the city. When he had been told the state of affairs, Lucas called Blower, and ordered him to blow the giant back. The king's messenger was carried to the eighth mountain.

Then Lucas said, "Sharpshooter, son of the famous shooter, shoot the head of the bottle so that Runner will wake up!" The man shot skilfully; Runner jumped to his feet, ran and got the precious water, and arrived in the city in twelve hours. Lucas presented the water to the king, and the monarch was obliged to accept the young man as his son-in-law.

The wedding-day was a time of great rejoicing. Everybody was enthusiastic about Lucas except the king. The third day after the nuptials, the giant reached the palace. He said that he was very near the city when a heavy wind blew him back to the eighth mountain.

(b) JUAN AND HIS SIX COMPANIONS.[1]

Not very long after the death of our Saviour on Calvary, there lived in a far-away land a powerful king named Jaime. By judicious usurpations and matrimonial alliances, this wise

[1] Narrated by Vicente M. Hilario, a Tagalog from Batangas, who heard the story from an old woman from Balayan.

monarch extended his already vast dominions to the utmost limits. Instead of ruling his realm as a despot, however, he devoted himself to the task of establishing a strong government based on moderation and justice. By his marvellous diplomacy he won to his side counts, dukes, and lesser princes. To crown his happiness, he had an extremely lovely daughter, whose name was Maria. Neither Venus nor Helen of Troy could compare with her in beauty. Numerous suitors of noble birth from far and near vied with one another in spending fortunes on this pearl of the kingdom; but Maria regarded all suitors with aversion, and her father was perplexed as to how to get her a husband without seeming to show favoritism.

After consulting gravely with his advisers, the monarch gave out this proclamation: "He who shall succeed in getting the golden egg from the moss-grown oak in yonder mountain shall be my son-in-law and heir."

This egg, whose origin nobody knew anything about, rendered its possessor very formidable. When the proclamation had been made public, the whole kingdom was seized with wild enthusiasm; for, though the task was hazardous, yet it seemed performable and easy to the reckless. For five days and five nights crowds of lovers, adventurers, and ruffians set sail for the "Mountain of the Golden Egg," as it was called; but none of the enterprisers ever reached the place. Some were shipwrecked; others were driven by adverse winds and currents to strange lands, where they perished miserably; and the rest were forced to return because of the horrible sights of broken planks and mangled bodies.

Some days after the return of the last set of adventurers, three brothers rose from obscurity to try their fortunes in this dangerous enterprise. They were Pedro, Fernando, and Juan. They had been orphans since they were boys, and had grown up amid much suffering and hardship.

The three brothers agreed that Pedro should try first; Fernando second; and Juan last, provided the others did not succeed. After supplying himself with plenty of food, a good boat, a sword, and a sharp axe, Pedro embraced his brothers and departed, never to return. He took a longer and safer route than that of his predecessors. He had no sooner arrived at the mountain than an old gray-headed man in tattered clothes came limping towards him and asking for help; but the selfish Pedro turned a deaf ear to the supplications of the old man, whom he pushed away with much disrespect. Ignorant of his doom, and regardless of his irreverence, Pedro walked on with hasty steps and high animal spirits. But lo! when his axe struck the oak, a large piece of wood broke off and hit him in the right temple, killing him instantly.

Fernando suffered the same fate as his haughty brother.

Juan alone remained. He was the destined possessor of the egg, and the conqueror of King Jaime. Juan's piety, simplicity, and goodness had won for him the good-will of many persons of distinction. After invoking God's help, he set sail for the mountain, where he safely arrived at noon. He met the same old man, and he bathed, dressed, and fed him. The old man thanked Juan, and said, "You shall be amply requited," and immediately disappeared. With one stroke of his axe Juan broke the oak in two; and in a circular hole lined with down he found the golden egg. In the afternoon he went to King Jaime, to whom he presented the much-coveted egg.

But the shrewd and successful monarch did not want to have a rustic son-in-law. "You shall not marry my daughter," he said, "unless you bring me a golden ship."

The next morning Juan, very disconsolate, went to the mountain again. The old man appeared to him, and said, "Why are you dejected, my son?"

Juan related everything that had happened.

"Dry your eyes and listen to me," said the old man. "Not very far from this place you will find your ship all splendidly equipped. Go there at once!"

The old man disappeared, and Juan ran with all possible speed to where the ship was lying. He went on deck, and a few minutes later the ship began to move smoothly over stumps and stones.

While he was thus travelling along, Juan all of a sudden saw a man running around the mountain in less than a minute. "Corrin Corron,[1] son of the great runner!" shouted Juan, "what are you doing?" The man stopped, and said, "I'm taking my daily exercise."

"Never mind that!" said Juan, "come up here and rest!" And Corrin Corron readily accepted the offer.

Pretty soon Juan saw another man standing on the summit of

[1] From the Spanish *corredor* ("runner").

a high hill and gazing intently at some distant object. "Mirin Miron,[1] son of the great Farsight!" said Juan, "what are you doing?"

"I'm watching a game of *tubigan*[2] seven miles away," answered the other.

"Never mind!" said Juan, "come up here and eat with me!" And Mirin Miron gladly went on deck.

After a while Juan saw a hunter with gun levelled. "Puntin Punton,[3] son of the great Sureshot!" said Juan, "what are you doing?"

"Three miles away there is a bat-fly annoying a sheep. I want to kill that insect."

"Let the creature go," said Juan, "and come with me!" And Puntin Punton, too, joined the party.

Not long after, Juan saw a man carrying a mountain on his shoulders. "Carguin Cargon,[4] son of the great Strong-Back!" shouted Juan, "what are you doing?"

"I'm going to carry this mountain to the other side of the country to build a dam across the river," said the man.

"Don't exert yourself so much," said Juan. "Come up here and take some refreshment!" The brawny carrier threw aside his load; and, as the mountain hit the ground, the whole kingdom was shaken so violently that the inhabitants thought that all the volcanoes had simultaneously burst into eruption.

By and by the ship came to a place where Juan saw young flourishing trees falling to the ground, with branches twisted and broken. "Friends," said Juan, "is a storm blowing?"

"No, sir!" answered the sailors, amazed at the sight.

"Master Juan," shouted Mirin Miron, "sitting on the summit of yonder mountain," pointing to a peak three miles away, "is a man blowing with all his might."

"He is a naughty fellow," muttered Juan to himself; "he will destroy all the lumber-trees in this region if we do not stop him." Pretty soon Juan himself saw the mischievous man, and said, "Soplin Soplon,[5] son of the great Blast-Blower, what are you doing?"

[1] From the Spanish *mirador* ("seer, gazer").
[2] A Tagalog boys' game played in the streets, with lines marked off by water (*tubig*).
[3] From the Spanish *puntador* ("gunner").
[4] From the Spanish *cargador* ("carrier").
[5] From the Spanish *soplador* ("ventilator, blower").

"Oh, I'm just exercising my lungs and trumpeter's muscles," replied the other.

"Come along with us!" After blowing down a long line of trees like grain before a hurricane, Soplin Soplon went on board.

As the ship neared the capital, Juan saw a man lying on a bed of rushes, with his ear to the ground. "What are you doing, friend?" said Juan.

"I'm listening to the plaintive strains of a young man mourning over the grave of his deceased sweetheart, and to the touching love-ditties of a moonstruck lover," answered the man.

"Where are those two men?" asked Juan.

"They are in a city twelve miles away," said the other.

"Never mind, Oirin Oiron,[1] son of the great Hear-All!" said Juan. "Come up and rest on a more comfortable bed! My divans superabound." When Oirin Oiron was on board, Juan said to the helmsman, "To the capital!"

In the evening the magnificent ship, with sails of silk and damask, masts of gold heavily studded with rare gems, and covered with thick plates of gold and silver, arrived at the palace gate.

Early in the morning King Jaime received Juan, but this time more coldly and arrogantly than ever. The princess bathed before break of day. With cheeks suffused with the rosy tint of the morning, golden tresses hanging in beautiful curls over her white shoulders, hands as delicate as those of a new-born babe, eyes merrier than the humming-bird, and dressed in a rich outer garment displaying her lovely figure at its best, she stood beside the throne. Such was the appearance of this lovely mortal, who kindled an inextinguishable flame in the heart of Juan.

After doffing his bonnet and bowing to the king, Juan said, "Will you give me the hand of your daughter?" Everybody present was amazed. The princess's face was successively pale and rosy. Juan immediately understood her heart as he stood gazing at her.

"Never!" said the king after a few minutes. "You shall never have my daughter."

---

[1] From the Spanish *oidor* ("hearer"). These six proper names are given here exactly as they appear in the original narrative. Strictly speaking, they are not derivatives from the Spanish: they merely suggest the Spanish words from which they have been coined as *patronymics*.

"Farewell, then, until we meet again!" said Juan as he departed.

When the ship was beyond the frontier of Jaime's kingdom, Juan said, "Carguin Cargon, overturn the king's realm." Carguin Cargon obeyed. Many houses were destroyed, and hundreds of people were crushed to death. When the ship was within seven miles of the city, Oirin Oiron heard the king say, "I'll give my daughter in marriage to Juan if he will restore my kingdom." Oirin Oiron told Juan what he had heard.

Then Juan ordered Carguin Cargon to rebuild the kingdom; but when the work was done, Jaime again refused to fulfil his promise. Juan went away very angry. Again the kingdom was overturned, and more property and lives were destroyed. Again Oirin Oiron heard the king make a promise, again the kingdom was rebuilt, and again the king was obstinate.

Juan went away again red with anger. After they had been travelling for an hour, Oirin Oiron heard the tramp of horses and the clash of spears and shields. "I can see King Jaime's vast host in hot pursuit of us," said Mirin Miron. "Where is the army?" said Juan. "It is nine miles away," responded Mirin Miron.

"Let the army approach," said Soplin Soplon. When the immense host was within eight hundred yards of the ship, Soplin Soplon blew forcible blasts, which scattered the soldiers and horses in all directions like chaff before a wind. Of this formidable army only a handful of men survived, and these were crippled for life.

Again the king sued for peace, and promised the hand of his daughter to Juan. This time he kept his word, and Juan and Maria were married amidst the most imposing ceremonies. That very day King Jaime abdicated in favor of his more powerful son-in-law. On the site of the destroyed houses were built larger and more handsome ones. The lumber that was needed was obtained by Soplin Soplon and Carguin Cargon from the mountains: Soplin Soplon felled the trees with his mighty blasts, and Carguin Cargon carried the huge logs to the city. Juan made Corrin Corron his royal messenger, and Soplin Soplon commander-in-chief of the raw troops, which later became a powerful army. The other four friends were assigned to high positions in the government.

The royal couple and the six gifted men led a glorious life. They conquered new lands, and ruled their kingdom well.

(c) THE STORY OF KING PALMARIN.[1]

[NOTE. — While the following story is not, strictly speaking, a
folk-tale, since it is a native student's close paraphrase of a Pampango
corrido, or metrical romance, it is typically Filipino in many respects,
and is closely connected with the two foregoing folk-tales. Moreover, it presents significant features lacking in the other stories. As
it is too long to be relegated to the notes, I take the liberty of printing
it here in full. My justification is the fact that, after all, sagas, or
printed folk-tales, are only the crystallized sources — or products, as
the case may be — of folk-tales.]

Long, long ago, the kingdom of Marsella was ruled over by
the worthy King Palmarin and his wife Isberta. They were
attentive to their duty, and kind to their subjects, whose love
they won. All Marsella admired the goodness and generosity
of the king. To whatever he wanted, his counsellors agreed;
and because of his good judgment, his reign was peaceful.

Time came when the queen gave birth to a child. The whole
kingdom rejoiced, and a great feast was prepared. "Let the
feast last six months," said Zetnaen, chief adviser. The new
baby was a girl of peerless beauty. The holy bishop was
summoned to baptize the child. As the Virgin Mary was the
patron saint of the king and queen, they asked the worthy prel-
ate to name the little princess Maria; and so she was named.

One day the king went to hunt in the mountains. There
was no forest or cave that the party did not visit. All the
animals in the mountains were thrown into confusion when they
heard the great noise. Bears, tigers, and lions came out of
their dens. As soon as these wild beasts reached the plain,
they began to pursue the king and his men. The noise and
confusion cannot be imagined. By the help of God, the king
and his men put to flight their savage foes; and when the chase
was ended, nobody had been hurt. After the hunters had been
gathered together by the sound of the trumpet, they all returned
home, thankful that no one had been injured. The king, however, had unwittingly lost his favorite reliquary.

When King Palmarin reached Marsella and discovered that
his locket was missing, he at once sent many of his soldiers back
to look for it. They searched all parts of the mountain and
even the valley. At last they returned to the capital, and said
to the king, "We, whom your Majesty commanded to look for

[1] *Paraphrased from the vernacular by Anastacia Villegas of Arayat, Pampanga.*

the reliquary, have come to tell you that, after a thorough search through the entire forest and valley, we have not been able to find it." The king was very sad to hear this report; but he kept his sorrow to himself, and did not reveal his heart to his counsellors. He grieved, not because of the value of the reliquary, but because it had been handed down to him by his father, whose will and recommendations it contained.

As time went on, the king forgot his lost reliquary. He ceased looking for it. His daughter the princess was now grown up. She was beautiful, happy, good-natured, and modest. Those who saw her said that she was not inferior even to Elsa, Judith, or Anne Boleyn. Now, the king wished his daughter to marry, so that there might be some one to inherit his throne when he died. He made his desire known to his counsellors. He told them that, if they agreed, he would issue proclamations throughout the whole kingdom and the neighboring cities, towns, and villages. While this meeting with his council was going on, the king stood up to powder his face. He took his powder-case out of his pocket; but when he opened it, there inside he found, to his surprise, a *tuma*.[1] He could not imagine how this tiny insect had got into his box to eat the powder. Feeling very much ashamed, he did not powder his face: he merely closed the box. The meeting was adjourned without being finished; for when the king stood up, the counsellors rose from their seats and silently left the room.

The king retired to his room, and opened his powder-case to look at the *tuma* again. He was thoroughly astonished to find that what had been but a tiny insect a moment before now filled the whole box. He was indeed perplexed; so he consulted God. Then it came to his mind to take the *tuma* from the box and place it in the cellar of the palace.

After three days the king found that a miracle had happened. The cellar was filled with the *tuma*. He was not a little surprised. He said to himself, "What a wonderful animal it is! In three days it has grown to such an enormous size! If I let it live, I fear that it will destroy the whole kingdom."

Then he heard a voice saying, "You need not fear, for the *tuma* you nourish shall not produce bad fruit. But if you let it live, it will have a long life, and will fill all of Marsella with its huge body. Listen to me, and obey what I tell you! Let the

---

[1] *Tuma*, Tagalog, Pampangan, and Malayan for "louse."

tuma be killed. Burn all its flesh, but save its skin. Use the skin for the covers of a drum. When you have done all these things, write to all your neighboring kingdoms and bet with them. Let them guess the kind of skin out of which the heads of the drum are made. If you will but obey me, and take care not to let any one know what I have told you, you will become very rich." Then the voice ceased.

The king comprehended well all that the voice had told him: so he called his Negro servant, and led him secretly into his room. The king then said softly, "Let no one know of the secret that I am to disclose to you, and you shall profit by it. I have a *tuma* which accidentally got into my powder-case. One day I put the insect into the cellar, where it has grown to an enormous size. Now, my command to you is to kill the *tuma*, burn all its flesh, and clean its skin. Then have the skin made into a drum. When everything is done perfectly, I will repay you."

Accordingly the Negro servant killed the *tuma*. He followed minutely the king's directions. When the drum was finished, he presented it to the king. Instead of receiving the promised reward, however, the poor Negro was instantly put to death, for the king feared that he might betray the secret.

King Palmarin then summoned all his counsellors. He said to them, "I want you to spread the news of my desire." Taking out the drum and putting it on the table, he continued: "Let all the villages, cities, and kingdoms know of the wager. Any one who can guess of what skin the covers of this drum are made, be he rich or poor, if he is unmarried, he shall be my son-in-law. But if he fails to guess aright, his property shall be forfeited to the crown if he is rich; he shall lose his head if he is poor."

The counsellors proclaimed the edict. Many rich nobles, lords, princes, and knights heard of it. All those who ventured lost their fortune, for they could not guess what the drum was made of. So the king gained much wealth. Among them there was one particularly rich, who declared to the king his great desire to win the princess's hand. King Palmarin said to this knight, "Examine the drum carefully." After looking at it closely, he said, "This drum is made of sheep's hide." — "Your observation has deceived you," said the king. "Now all the wealth you have brought with you shall be mine."

"What can I do if fortune turns against me?" said the knight.

"Let your Majesty send his servants to get all my property from the ship."

The names of the hides of all known animals were given, but no one guessed correctly. At last some of those who had been defeated said to the king, "Of what is the drum made?"

"I cannot tell you yet," replied the king.

In one of the villages where the edict was proclaimed there lived a young man named Juan. He was an orphan. After the death of his parents, the property he had inherited from them he gave to the poor. One day me met the king's messengers, who explained the edict minutely to him, so that he might tell about it to others. Don Juan then went away. He was sad, for he had no wealth to take with him to Marsella. Though he had inherited much property, he had given away most of it, so that now very little was left to him.

One day, while he was looking about his farm, he saw all of a sudden some dead persons lying prostrate in the thicket. They had been murdered by bandits. He hired men to bury these corpses decently in the sacred ground, and paid the priest to celebrate masses for their souls. He then returned home sad, meditating on his bad luck.

At midnight, while he was sleeping soundly, he heard a voice saying to him, "Go to Marsella and take part in the wager of King Palmarin. Do not be troubled because you have no riches. Your horses are enough. Equip them in the best way you can." Then the voice ceased.

Don Juan felt very glad. The next morning he prepared materials for equipping his horses, and hired laborers, whom he paid double so as to hasten the work. The harnesses were of pure gold, decorated with pearls and rubies. The saddle-cloths were embroidered. Two of the horses (they were all very fat, and had long manes) were hazel-colored, two were spotted, two were orange-colored, and one was white. When everything was ready, Don Juan mounted the white one, and loaded on the other six his baggage.

God rewarded Don Juan for what he had done to the dead bodies. He called St. Michael, and said to him, "Go to purgatory and get six of the souls who were benefited by Don Juan, for now is the time for them to repay him. They shall go back to the world to meet Don Juan on his way, follow him to Marsella, and provide him with everything he needs. They must not leave him until you call them back, for there are many serious dangers on his way." The angel went on his errand. He selected six souls, and told them to return to the world to help Don Juan. The spirits were glad to go, for they longed to repay their benefactor.

Don Juan was now on his journey. As he rode along, the birds in the forest sang to cheer him, so that the long journey might not tire him. By and by he saw a man in the middle of the forest, lying on his face. "Grandpa, what are you doing there?" said Juan.

"I am observing the world. Are you not a nobleman? Whither are you bound?"

"To Marsella," replied Don Juan.

"To bet? If that is your purpose, you are sure to lose, for it is certain that you cannot guess of what the drum is made," interrupted the man.

"I entreat you to tell me the right answer, if you know it," said Don Juan.

"I will not only tell it to you, but I will also accompany you. That is why I am here. I was waiting for you to pass," said the man.

"Grandpa, I'm astonished. You must be a prophet."

"You are right. I am the sage prophet Noet Noen,[1] who will go with you to King Palmarin."

"I appreciate your help and am grateful to you, grandpa," said Don Juan. "You had better ride on one of the horses."

Noet Noen and Don Juan rode on together. The prophet then related to Juan the whole story of the *tuma* that had got into the powder-case of the king. While the two travellers were talking, they saw a man sitting under a tree. As it was very hot, they dismounted so that their horses might rest. Don Juan was surprised at the stranger. He was whistling; and every time he whistled, the wind blew strong, so that the trees in the forest were broken off. This man was Supla Supling, a companion and friend of Noet Noen.

"Supla Supling, why are you here?" said Noet Noen.

"To follow you," was the reply.

"If that is your desire," said Don Juan, "you will please mount one of the horses." So the three men went on their

---

[1] Perhaps from the Spanish *conocer* ("to know, understand"). For the names of the other companions, see footnotes to the preceding tale.

journey. They had not gone far when they met a man walking alone. Noet Noen said to him, "What are you here for? Come along with us!" This man was Miran Miron, who had a wonderfully loud voice. When he shouted, his sound was more sonorous than thunder. He also had very keen sight. He could see clearly an object, though it were covered with a cover a hundred yards thick.

When the four travellers had gone a little farther, they saw a man walking swiftly on one leg. They spurred up their horses to overtake him, but in vain. At last Noet Noen said, "I think that is my friend Curan Curing, so there is little hope of our catching him."

"Let me call him!" said Miran Miron, and he shouted.

When Curan Curing heard the voice, he stopped, so they reached him. Miran Miron said to him, "You are in a great hurry. Where are you going?"

"You know that I cannot stop my feet when I walk," said Curan Curing.

"Why do you hold up one of your legs as if it were in pain?" said Don Juan.

"Do not be surprised at my walking on one foot; for, if I should let loose the other one, I should walk straight out of the world."

"Will you join us, Curan Curing?" said Noet Noen.

"Oh, yes! Let me have a horse! If I should walk, you might lose me on account of my speed," replied Curan Curing. So the five adventurers went on together. As it soon grew very warm, they stopped to rest under a tree.

Then they saw a wounded deer coming toward them. As they were hungry, they killed it and cooked it. While they were eating, the hunter Punta Punting came. He said, "Have you seen a wounded deer?"

"Oh, yes! here it is. We are eating it already," said Supla Supling, "for we are very hungry."

"I'm glad that the deer I wounded relieves your hunger," said Punta Punting. "What are you all doing here? Where are you going? Why don't you take me with you?"

"If that is your wish, we are very glad to have you," said Don Juan.

The little party rode on, but suddenly stopped; for a mountain was walking toward them. As it approached, they saw that a man was carrying the mountain. Don Juan was not a little surprised at this astonishing feat of strength. "Where have you been, Carguen Cargon? Where did you get that mountain?" said Noet Noen.

"I took it from behind the church of Candaba, for I want to transfer it here, where the land is level. This mountain is not fitted for Candaba; for the natives, rich or poor, build their houses out of wood, — even the poorest, who cannot afford such luxury. They desolate its forests, for they cut down even the young trees." Then with a great thunder Carguen Cargon dropped his burden on the land of Arayat, just behind the church. On account of its immense size, this mountain reached clear to de la Paz. The slopes reached Calumpit, and its base was in view of Apalit. Thus we see that Mount Alaya (Arayat) has come from Candaba. The original site of this mountain became a river, swamps, and brooks. Now Candaba has many ponds.

"Friend, I entreat you to come with us!" said Noet Noen.

"I shall be glad to go with you, if I shall only have the opportunity of serving you with my strength," replied Carguen Cargon.

Now the little band of seven travelled on. When they came near the gates of Marsella, Noet Noen said, "Let us rest here first!" There they hired a house, where they staid at the expense of Don Juan.

The next morning Don Juan made himself ready to go on alone. Leading his horses, he was about to start for the palace, when Noet Noen called to him, and said, "Be sure not to forget the name of the skin I told you. Put it in the depths of your heart."

"Have no fear that I shall forget," said Don Juan.

"Furthermore, Don Juan, I want you to undertake to do whatever the king may ask of you. Do not refuse. No matter how hard the task the king may impose on you, do not hesitate to undertake it; for God Almighty is ever merciful, and will help you. If the king requires you to do anything, just come back here and let me know of it. Now you may go. Take courage, for God loves a person who suffers," said Noet Noen.

"Good-by to every one of you!" said Don Juan to his companions. Then he went on his journey. When he reached the palace, he asked the soldier who was on guard to announce him to the king. When the king heard of the message, he said to the soldier, "Let him come in, if his purpose is to bet; but assure him that, if he loses, he shall also lose his life."

Then the soldier went back to the gate, and said to the stranger, "The king admits you into his presence."

Don Juan entered the palace. He saluted the king. "What is it that you want? Tell it to me, so that I may know," said the king.

"O king! pardon me for disturbing your Majesty. It is the edict your Highness issued that gives me the right to come here, and that has made me forget my inferiority; for I do rely entirely on the fact that your word in the proclamation will never be broken. So now I hope, that, if fortune goes with me, your Majesty will carry out his promise."

These words made the king laugh, for he was sure that there was no one who could beat him in the wager: so he said, "What property have you with you that you wish to risk?"

Don Juan replied, "Six horses, of which your Highness can make use."

The king looked out the window, and there he saw Don Juan's horses. King Palmarin was much pleased at their beauty, sleekness, and elegance of equipment. Turning to Don Juan, he said, "Do you really wish to bet? I feel as if you were already beaten. Princes and wise kings have taken part in the wager, and all have lost. I tell you about them because I do not want you to repent in the end. Moreover, I have pity for your life and your property."

"What can I do if fortune turns against me? I will never lay the fault on anybody."

"Well," said the king, leading Don Juan to the table where the drum was, "try your skill."

Holding and sounding the drum, and pretending to examine it carefully, Juan said softly to the king, "I think that it is made of the skin of a *tuma*," and he went on relating to the king the whole story of the *tuma* from the time it got into his powder-case, until the king finally interrupted, —

"Enough! You have beaten me."

"I am glad if I have. I hope that the terms of the proclamation will be fulfilled," said Don Juan.

The king remarked, "You are not fitted to join my royal family. Such a low person as you would disgrace me, and humble my dynasty. So take your horses with you and go back to your country."

"O king! I am not at fault in the least. It is your Majesty who issued the edict that any one, rich or poor, who could beat you in the wager, should be wedded to your daughter. Now I only cling to the right your Majesty has given me," returned Don Juan. "I had been thinking that the proclamation your Highness signed would be kept; for it is known far and wide that you are a king."

By this answer King Palmarin was perplexed. He stopped for a moment to consider the matter. Then the thought of getting rid of Don Juan — that is, of killing him — came into his mind: so he said, "Though you are far below my family, if you can do what I shall ask you to do now, I will admit you into the royal line."

"I am always ready to obey your Majesty's command," said Don Juan.

"I had a reliquary, which I inherited from my royal father. I lost it while I was hunting once in the forest twenty years ago. Now I want you to look for it. I will give you three days. If you do not find it in that time, you shall be severely punished," said the king.

Don Juan left the court and returned to his companions. He told them what had passed between him and the king in the palace. Noet Noen encouraged him, and said, "Do not be sad! for by the aid of God the reliquary shall be found. Remember, there is nothing difficult if you call on God. — What do you say, comrades? It is now time for you to help Don Juan, so as to distract him from his sorrow. — Miran Miron, as you have keen eyes, it will not take you long to find it. Try your best, and look everywhere."

"Trust me; I'll be responsible for finding it," said Miran Miron. "To-morrow I will set out in quest of it."

As to the king, he was at ease, for he was sure that Don Juan could not find the reliquary.

The next day Miran Miron set out in search of the reliquary, which he found covered with thirty yards of earth. He dug out the earth until he reached the locket; then he returned to his companions, and delivered it to Don Juan. His comrades, seeing him rejoice at the sight of the reliquary, said, "Again we have beaten the king."

Noet Noen said, "Don Juan, to-morrow take King Palmarin his reliquary."

The next day Don Juan set out for the court. When he reached the palace, he saluted the king, who was astonished. "How! Don Juan, have you given up so soon? How goes the quest?"

"Here, I have found the reliquary," said Don Juan, taking it out and putting it on the table. Then he continued, "Let your Majesty examine to see if it is the right one."

The king looked at it carefully. Indeed, it was his own reliquary. He said to himself, "What a wonder Don Juan is! In two days without any difficulty he has found the reliquary. I did not even tell him the exact place where I lost it, and many people failed to come across it as soon as it was missed. Here in Marsella he has no equal." Then he said to Don Juan, "I am astonished at the ability you have shown. There is no tongue that can express my gratitude to you for bringing me back my reliquary, the delight of my heart."

Don Juan replied, "If there is yet something to be done, let your Highness command his loyal vassal, who is always ready to obey."

"If that is so, in order that you may obtain what you wish," said the king, "go to Rome and take my letter to the Pope. Wait for his answer. I will also send another person to carry the same message. The one who comes after the other shall receive death as a punishment," said the king.

"Your loyal subject will try to obey you," said Don Juan.

So the king wrote two letters to the holy Pope, and gave one to Don Juan, who immediately left the palace and went to his friends. He was sad, meditating on his fate.

The king's messenger, Bruja,[1] set out for Rome that very moment. He was told to use his charm and to hurry up. So he went flying swiftly, like an arrow shot from a bow.

When Don Juan reached his comrades, he said, "I gave the reliquary to the king. Now he wants me to go to Rome to deliver this letter to the Pope and wait for his answer. At the same time the king has sent another messenger. If I come after his arrival in Marsella, I shall lose my life. You see what a hard task the king has given me. I do not know very well the way to Rome, and, besides, the wise Bruja is winged."

[1] In Spanish this word means "witch, sorceress."

"Do not worry," said Noet Noen. "If God will, we shall defeat the king. Even if he has Bruja to send, you have some one also: so pluck up your courage!"

"What do you say, Curan Curing? Show your skill, and go to Rome flying like the wind," said Noet Noen.

"Do not be troubled, Don Juan," said Curan Curing. "I will carry the letter even to the gates of heaven. For me a journey to Rome is not far — in just one leap I shall be there. Give me the letter. To-morrow I will set out. To-day I will rest, so that I can walk fast." Don Juan gave Curan Curing the letter, and they all went to sleep. Perhaps by this time Bruja had already arrived at Rome.

The next morning Curan Curing started on his journey to deliver the letter to the Pope. When he was half way to Rome, he met Bruja walking very swiftly, and already returning to Marsella. "Are you Don Juan?" said Bruja, "and are you just going to Rome now? You are beaten. Do not waste your energy any more. If you walk like that, you cannot reach Rome in two months."

Bruja spoke so, because Curan Curing was walking on only one leg. But when he heard these words, he let loose his other leg and went faster than a bullet. He arrived almost instantly at Rome, and delivered the letter to the holy Pope, who, after reading it, wrote an answer and gave it to the messenger.

Curan Curing then made his way back towards his companions. He went as fast as the wind, and overtook Bruja on the road. "What! Are you still here? What is the matter? How is it that you have not reached Marsella yet? Where is that boast of yours, that I am already beaten? Now I am sure that you will disappoint your king, who relies too much upon your skill," said Curan Curing.

Bruja, fearing that he should be defeated, for Don Juan's messenger was very spry, planned to trick Curan Curing. So Bruja said, "Friend, let us rest here a while! I have a little wine with me. We will drink it, if it pleases you, and take a little rest while the sun is so hot."

"Oh, yes! if you have some wine. It will be a fine thing for us to drink to quench our thirst," replied Curan Curing.

The wine was no sooner handed to him than he fell asleep. Then Bruja put on one of Curan Curing's fingers a ring, so as to insure victory for the king. Whoever had Bruja's ring would sleep soundly and never wake as long as the charmed ring was on his finger. So Bruja, with a light heart, flew away and left the sleeping messenger. Bruja flew so swiftly, that in a moment he was seen by Curan Curing's companions. When they saw the king's messenger coming swiftly near them, they felt very sad. But as soon as Supla Supling was sure that it was Bruja flying through the air toward them, he said, "Let me manage him! I will make his journey longer. I will blow him back, so that he will not win." Supla Supling then breathed deeply and blew. Bruja was carried back beyond Rome. How Don Juan's companions rejoiced! Bruja did not sleep during the whole night: he was trying his best to reach Marsella.

The next morning Noet Noen said, "I never thought that our friend Curan Curing would be so slow. He has not come yet. Bruja has made him drink wine and has put him to sleep. The trickish fellow has placed on one of Curan Curing's fingers a magic ring, which keeps him in a profound sleep."

When Punta Punting heard Noet Noen's words, he shot his arrow, though he could not see the object he was aiming at. But the ring was hit, and the arrow returned to its master with the magic ring on it. Such was the virtue of Punta Punting's arrow. As for Curan Curing, he was awakened. He felt the ring being moved from his finger; but the charm was still working in him, and he fell asleep again.

Noet Noen, knowing that Curan Curing was again asleep, called Miran Miron, and said, "Pray, wake the sleeper under the tree!"

Miran Miron then shouted. Curan Curing awoke suddenly, frightened at the noise. Now, being wide awake, he realized the trick Bruja had played on him. He looked to see if he still had the Pope's letter. Luckily Bruja had not stolen it. Curan Curing then began his journey. Though he went faster than the lightning, he could not overtake Bruja, who was very far ahead of him. In the mean time Bruja was seen by Miran Miron. He was enraged, and cried out loud. When Supla Supling heard his friend shout, he blew strongly. Bruja got stuck in the sky: he was scorched by the glowing sun. Not long afterwards Curan Curing arrived, and gave the letter to Don Juan.

Don Juan at once set out for Marsella. When he reached the palace, he delivered the Pope's letter to the king. The king, realizing that he was beaten, said to Don Juan, "Though you have won, I will not grant your request, for you are too inferior. You may go."

Don Juan replied, "Great King, nobody ordered your Highness to issue the decree to which your hand did sign your name. I trusted your word, and I ventured to take part in the wager. Now, honorable king, my complaint is that your Majesty breaks his word."

The king was meditating as to what to do next to check Don Juan. At last he said, "I want you to show me some more of your wisdom. If you can sail on dry land, and I can see your ship to-morrow morning moored here in front of the palace, I will believe in your power and wisdom. So you may go. My subjects, the queen, and I will be here to see you sail on dry land to-morrow morning."

Don Juan did not complain at all. He rose from his seat, sad and melancholy, and bade the king good-by. When he reached his companions, Noet Noen said, "You need not speak. I know what is the matter. I will manage the business, and all our comrades will help, so that our sailing on dry land to-morrow will not be delayed. — Carguen Cargon, my friend, go to the inn and fetch a large strong ship."

Carguen Cargon went on his errand. It was not long before he found the right ship. So, shouldering it, he brought it back to his companions.

The next day everything was ready for the journey. Noet Noen said, "You will be in charge of the rudder, Carguen Cargon, so that the ship may go smoothly. — Supla Supling, sit at the stern and blow the sails, so that we may go fast. — The rest of us will serve as mariners. Cry 'Happy voyage!' as soon as we enter the city."

Accordingly Supla Supling blew the sails. The wind roared, and many trees fell down. The little band sailed through the kingdom. All the people who saw them were wondering. They said, "Were this deed not by enchantment, they could not sail on dry land. Where do you think this ship came from, if not from the land of enchanters?"

When the sailors reached the city, they found King Palmarin looking out of the window of his palace. Don Juan then disembarked from his ship and went before the king to greet him. Don Juan said, "Your Majesty's servant is here. He is ready to obey your will: so, if there is anything more to be done, let your Highness order him."

The king felt ashamed for being a liar, and did not ask Don Juan to perform any more miracles. "Don Juan, I have now seen your wonderful wisdom. You may return to your country, for I will not give you the hand of my daughter," said King Palmarin.

"Farewell, O king! Your own order has caused all that has happened. Though I have not succeeded in accomplishing my purpose, I have no reason to be ashamed to face anybody. What troubles me is, that, in spite of your widespread reputation for honor, you do not keep even one of your thousand million words. After some one has done you some service, you turn him away. Farewell, king! To my own country I will return," said Don Juan as he left the palace.

The king did not say anything, for he realized the truth of the knight's statement. Don Juan went to the boat. He and his companions sailed back to their station. As they passed out of the city, the people hailed them. His companions cheered him up and encouraged him. When they arrived at their lodging-place, Noet Noen said, "Let us stay a little longer and wait for God's aid, which He always gives to the humble! All that has happened is God's will, so do not worry, Don Juan."

"I will do whatever you wish," said Don Juan.

So they staid in the ship. Several months passed by, but nothing was heard. At last the Moors invaded Marsella. They put to death many of the inhabitants, and shut up the king and the rest of his men in jail. He, the queen, and the princess grieved very much, for they suffered many hardships in their narrow prison. When news of this conquest reached the seven, Noet Noen said to his companions, "Now is our turn to help Marsella. Use all your skill; for in driving away the Moors we serve a double purpose: first, we help the Christians; second, Don Juan."

"Let me be general!" said Curan Curing. "If I rush at the Moors, they will not know what to do."

Supla Supling said, "As for me, no Moor can stay near me, for I will blow him away, and he will be lost in the air."

"Though I have no weapons, no one can face me in battle without tumbling down in fear," said Miran Miron.

Carguen Cargon joined in. "I will pull up a tree and carry

it with me; so that, even if all the Moors unite against me, they shall lie prostrate before me."

"My arrow is enough for me to face Moors with," said Punta Punting.

At the command of Noet Noen they set out. Curan Curing walked with one leg; still he was far ahead of his companions. He then would stop, return to his friends, and say impatiently, "Hurry up!"

At last they told him that he would be overtired. "The general ought to get weary if he commands," said Curan Curing. "But I shall never get tired from walking at this rate!"

When they arrived at Marsella, Noet Noen encouraged his companions. Carguen Cargon pulled up a tree fifteen yards tall and six yards in circumference. He rushed at the Moors, and, by swinging the tree constantly, he swept away the enemy. Curan Curing walked with both his legs. He crushed the enemy, who fell dead as he stepped on them. Miran Miron shouted. His loud voice frightened the Moors. Punta Punting shot with his arrow. Whenever it had killed a Moor, it returned to its master. After many Moors had fallen, the rest could not maintain the fight, and they fled. Noet Noen then gathered together his men, and said, "Let us look for the king!"

They opened all the jails and freed the prisoners. The six victors cried, "Hurrah for Don Juan!" and said to the released persons, "All of you who have been held prisoners must thank Don Juan; for, were it not for him, we should not have come to your aid."

"Who is this benefactor? We wish to know to whom we owe our lives," said the king.

Noet Noen said, "By God's will we gained the victory. It is Don Juan who brought us here to save you from the hands of the infidels. So he is indeed the benefactor."

"Don Juan!" the crowd then shouted. "Our lives we owe to you. — Hurrah for our savior! Hurrah for the whole kingdom!"

The king, queen, princess, counsellors, and the victors went to the palace. They were all happy. When they had taken their seats, the king spoke thus: "What shall we give the victor? As for me, even the whole kingdom is too small a reward for saving us. Lend me your advice."

Noet Noen answered, "Let me make a suggestion, O king!

You already know what Don Juan desires. Do him justice, for he not only beat you in the wager, but also succeeded in accomplishing all your commands. Now he saves you and your kingdom, and restores you to power. Let your issued decree be carried out." The king then consulted the queen, and said that the stranger was right.

The counsellors said, "King, Don Juan deserves the reward named in the edict; for, were it not for him, your people and even you would now be slaves."

So at last the king agreed, and, as a bishop was present, the marriage was performed immediately. After the marriage ceremony, the king said, "Hear me, counsellors! As I am now too old to rule, and can no longer perform the duty of king, I am going to abdicate in favor of my son-in-law. — Don Juan, on your head I lay the crown with its sceptre. Do whatever you will, for you are now full king."

The queen rose from her seat, and, taking off the diadem from her head, she placed it on her daughter, saying, "My darling, receive the diadem of the kingdom, so that all may recognize you as their new queen." All the counsellors then rose, and shouted, "Hurrah for the new couple! May God give them long lives! May they be successful!" The entire kingdom rejoiced, and held banquets.

When Don Juan had become king, he made a trip with his six companions throughout the entire kingdom, giving alms to the needy and sick. When the royal visit was over, he returned with his friends to the palace. Then Noet Noen said to the king, "Our king, Don Juan, do not be astonished at what I am going to tell you. Since you have now got what you wanted, we now bid you farewell."

"Why are you going away? What is there in me that you do not like? Pray do not leave me until I have repaid you!" He then called each of the six, and expressed his great gratitude to him, and begged him not to go away. "I will even abdicate the throne if you want me to," Don Juan said, "for your departure will kill me." The queen also begged the six men not to leave.

At last Noet Noen said, "Don Juan, long have we lived together; yet you know not whence we come, for we have never told you. We cannot be absent from there much longer." The prophet then related minutely to the king who they were, and why they had come to his aid. Then the six men disappeared.

NOTES.

The course of events common to these three stories is this: A king proclaims that he will give the hand of his daughter to the one who can furnish him with a very costly or marvellous conveyance. The poor young hero, because of his kindness to a wretched old man or woman (or corpse), is given the wonderful conveyance. On his way to the palace to present his gift, he meets certain extraordinary men, whom he takes along with him as companions. The king, realizing the low birth of the hero, refuses the hand of his daughter until additional tasks have been performed. With the help of his companions, the hero performs these, and finally weds the princess. This group of stories was almost certainly imported into the Philippines from Europe, where analogues of it abound. I know of no significant Eastern variants. Parallels to certain incidents can be found in Malayan and Filipino lore, but the cycle as a whole is clearly not native to the Islands.

In a broad sense, our stories belong to the "Bride Wager" formula (see Von Hahn, 1 : 54, Nos. 23 and 24). The requirement that a suitor shall guess correctly the kind of skin from which a certain drum-head is made (usually a louse-skin) is to be found in Italian (Basile, 1 : 5; cf. Gonzenbach, No. 22; Schneller, No. 31), Spanish (Caballero, trans. by J. H. Ingram, "The Hunchback"), German (Grimm, 2 : 467, "The Louse," where the princess makes a dress, not a drum, from the skin of the miraculous insect). Only Basile's story combines the louse-skin *motif* with the wonderful companions, — a combination found in our "King Palmarin." There seems to be no close connection, however, between these two tales. Although Oriental *Märchen* turning on this *motif* of the louse-skin drum are lacking, the Filipino *corrido* need not have got the conception from Europe: it is Malayan. In a list of the Jelebu regalia occurs this item: "The royal drums (*gendang naubat*); said to be 'headed' with the skins of lice (*kulit tuma*)" (see Skeat 2, 27).

We have already met with the extraordinary companions (No. 3; see especially variant *d*, "Sandangcal," which relates a contest between the hero's runner and the king's messenger). For the formula, see Bolte-Polívka's notes to Grimm, No. 71. Benfey (Ausland, 1858, pp. 1038 *et seq.*, 1067 *et seq.*) believes the "Skilful Companions" cycle — as represented by Grimm, Nos. 71 and 134; Basile, Nos. 28 and 36; Straparola, 4 : 1, etc. — to be a kind of humorous derivative of the cycle we shall call the "Rival Brothers" (*q.v.*, No. 12 of this collection), and which he shows to have spread into Europe from India. There *are* significant differences, however, between these two groups; and

Benfey's treatment of them together causes confusion. In the "Skilful Companions" cycle, the extraordinary men are in reality servants of the hero, who sets out and wins the hand of a princess. They are picked up by chance. In the "Rival Brothers" cycle, on the other hand, the three (or four) brothers set out to learn trades and to win their fortunes, often wonderful objects of magic; the brothers meet later by appointment, combine their skill to succor a princess, and then quarrel as to which deserves her most. In stories of the "Strong Hans" type (e.g., Grimm, No. 166) or "John the Bear" (Cosquin, No. 1), where the extraordinary companions also appear, they turn out to be rascals, who faithlessly desert the hero. In our stories, however, the specially-endowed men are supplied by a grateful supernatural being, to help the kind-hearted hero win in his contests with the stubborn king. (Compare Gonzenbach's Sicilian story, No. 74, which includes a thankful saint, with characteristics of the "Grateful Dead," a "Land-and-water Ship," and "Skilful Companions.")

The names of the companions in "King Palmarin" and "Juan and his Six Friends" are clearly derived from the Spanish. In Caballero's story of "Lucifer's Ear" we find these names: Carguin ("carrier"), Oidin ("hearer"), Soplin ("sigher or blower"). All three occur in "Juan and his Six Friends." In the three Filipino tales the total number of different strong men is only seven, — Know-All, Blower, Farsight, Runner, Hunter, Carrier, Sharp-Ear. This close conformity, when we consider the wide variety to be found in the European stories (see Bolte-Polívka, 2 : 87–94; Panzer, Beowulf, 66–74), suggests an ultimate common source for our variants. The phrase "Soplin Soplon, son of the great blower" (in "Juan and his Six Friends") is almost an exact translation of "Soplin Soplon, hijo del buen soplador" (Caballero, "Lucifer's Ear"). This same locution in the vernacular is found in the Tagalog folk-tale of "Lucas the Strong."

The ship that will sail on land is often met with in European stories. See R. Köhler, "Orient und Occident," 2 : 296–299; also his notes to Gonzenbach, No. 74. Compare also the Argonaut saga; and Bolte-Polívka, 2 : 87–95 *passim.*

In two of our stories the hero's runner is almost defeated by the king's messenger, who treacherously makes use of a magic sleep-producing ring. One of the other companions, however, discovers the trick, and the skilful hunter awakens the sleeper with a well-aimed shot. For this feat of Sharpshooter's, see Gonzenbach, No. 74; Grimm, No. 71; Meier, No. 8; Ey, Harzmärchenbuch, 116.

Of native beliefs found in our stories, two are deserving of comment. The method by which Lucas becomes possessed of great strength reflects a notion held by certain old Tagalogs. Some of the men around Calamba, Laguna province, make an incision in the wrist and put in it a small white bone taken from the end of the tail of the *sawang bitin* (a species of boa). The cut is then sewed up. Those who have a talisman of this sort believe that at night it travels all over the body and produces extraordinary strength. (For similar Malayan superstitions, see Skeat 2, 303–304.) The legend (in "King Palmarin") about the origin of Mount Arayat and the swamp of Candaba is but one of many still told by old Pampangans. Its insertion into a romance with European setting is an instance of the Filipino romance writers' utter disregard or ignorance of geographical propriety.

In conclusion, attention may be called to the fact that while these three stories have the same basic framework, each has its own peculiar variations. The testimony of the narrator of "Juan and his Six Companions," that his informant, an old Balayan woman, said that the story was very popular in her section of the country, is a bit of evidence that the tale has been known in the Philippines for decades, probably. Whether or not her form of the story was derived from a printed account, I am unable to say; but I suspect that it was; the diction sounds "bookish." Nevertheless I have found no external evidence of a Tagalog *corrido* treating the story we have printed.

12. (a) THE THREE BROTHERS.[1]

There was once an old woman who had three sons. The father died when Tito, the youngest brother, was only five years old; and the mother was left alone to bring up her three boys. The family was very poor; but the good woman worked hard, and her sons grew into sturdy young men.

One day the mother called her sons before her, and said, "Now, my sons, as you see my strength is failing me, I want each of you to go into the world to seek his fortune. After nine years, come back home and show me what you have learned to do." The three brothers consented, and resolved to leave home the very next morning.

Early the following day the three brothers — An-no the oldest, Berto the second, and Tito the youngest — bade their mother good-by, and set out on their travels. They followed a wide road until they came to a place where it branched in three directions. Here they stopped and consulted. It was at last agreed that An-no should take the north branch, Berto the

[1] Narrated by Clodualdo Garcia, an Ilocano, who was told the story by his mother when he was a small boy.

south branch, and Tito the east branch. Before they separated, An-no proposed that at the end of the nine years they should all meet at the cross-roads before presenting themselves to their mother. Then each, wishing the others good luck, proceeded on his way.

Well, to make a long story short, at the end of the nine years the three brothers met again at the place designated. Each of them told what he had learned during that time. An-no had been in the company of glass-makers, and he had learned the art of glass-making. Berto had been employed in a shipyard, and during the nine years had become an expert boat-builder. The youngest brother, unfortunately, had fallen into the company of bad men, some notorious robbers. While he was with this band, he became the best and most skilful robber in the gang. After each had heard of the others' fortunes, they started for their home. Their mother felt very glad to have all her sons with her once more.

Shortly after this family had been re-united, the king issued a proclamation stating that his daughter, the beautiful princess Amelia, had been kidnapped by a brave stranger, and that whoever could give any information about her and restore her to the palace should be allowed to marry her. When the three brothers heard this news, they resolved to use their knowledge and skill to find the missing princess.

An-no had brought home with him a spy-glass in which everything hidden from the eyes of men could be seen. With this instrument, he told his brothers, he could locate the princess. He looked through his glass, and saw her confined in a tower on an island. When An-no had given this information to the king, the next question was how to rescue her. "We'll do the rest," said the two younger brothers.

Accordingly Berto built a ship. When it was finished, the three brothers boarded her and sailed to the island where the princess was confined; but there they found the tower very closely guarded by armed soldiers, so that it seemed impossible to get into it. "Well, that is easy," said Tito. "You stay here and wait for my return. I will bring the princess with me."

The famous young robber then went to work to steal the princess. Through his skill he succeeded in rescuing her and bringing her to the ship. Then the four sailed directly for the king's palace. The beautiful princess was restored to her father. With great joy the king received them, and a great feast was held in the palace in honor of the rescue of his daughter. After the feast the king asked the three brothers to which of them he should give his daughter's hand. Each claimed the reward, and a quarrel arose among them. The king, seeing that all had played important parts in the rescue of the princess, decided not to bestow his daughter on any of them. Instead, he gave half his wealth to be divided equally among An-no, Berto, and Tito.

(b) THREE BROTHERS OF FORTUNE.[1]

In former times there lived in a certain village a wealthy man who had three sons, — Suan, Iloy, and Ambo. As this man was a lover of education, he sent all his boys to another town to school. But these three brothers did not study: they spent their time in idleness and extravagance. When vacation came, they were ashamed to go back to their home town, because they did not know anything; so, instead, they wandered from town to town seeking their fortunes.

In the course of their travels they met an old woman broken with age. "Should you like to buy this book, my grandsons?" asked the old woman as she stopped them.

"What is the virtue of that book, grandmother?" asked Ambo.

"My grandsons," replied she, "if you want to restore a dead person to life, just open this book before him, and in an instant he will be revived." Without questioning her further, Ambo at once bought the book. Then the three continued their journey.

Again they met an old woman selling a mat. Now, Iloy was desirous of possessing a charm, so he asked the old woman what virtue the mat had.

"Why, if you want to travel through the air," she said, "just step on it, and in an instant you will be where you desire to go." Iloy did not hesitate, but bought the mat at once.

Now, Suan was the only one who had no charm. They had not gone far, however, before he saw two stones, which once in a while would meet and unite to form one round black stone,

[1] Narrated by Eugenio Estayo, a Pangasinan, who heard the story from Toribio Serafica, a native of Rosales, Pangasinan.

and then separate again. Believing that these stones possessed some magical power, Suan picked them up; for it occurred to him that with them he would be able to unite things of the same or similar kind. This belief of his came true, as we shall see.

These three brothers, each possessing a charm, were very happy. They went on their way light-hearted. Not long afterward they came upon a crowd of persons weeping over the dead body of a beautiful young lady. Ambo told the parents of the young woman that he would restore her to life if they would pay him a reasonable sum of money. As they gladly agreed, Ambo opened his book, and the dead lady was brought back to life. Ambo was paid all the money he asked; but as soon as he had received his reward, Iloy placed his mat on the ground, and told his two brothers to hold the young woman and step on the mat. They did so, and in an instant all four were transported to the seashore.

From that place they took ship to another country; but when they were in the middle of the sea, a severe storm came, and their boat was wrecked. All on board would have been drowned had not Suan repaired the broken planks with his two magical stones. When they landed, a quarrel arose among the three brothers as to which one was entitled to the young woman.

Ambo said, "I am the one who should have her, for it was I who restored her to life."

"But if it had not been for me, we should not have the lady with us," said Iloy.

"And if it had not been for me," said Suan, "we should all be dead now, and nobody could have her."

As they could not come to any agreement, they took the question before the king. He decided to divide the young woman into three parts to be distributed among the three brothers. His judgment was carried out. When each had received his share, Iloy and Ambo were discontented because their portions were useless, so they threw them away; but Suan picked up the shares of his two brothers and united them with his own. The young woman was brought to life again, and lived happily with Suan. So, after all, Suan was the most fortunate.

(c) PABLO AND THE PRINCESS.[1]

Once upon a time there lived three friends, — Pedro, Juan, and Pablo. One morning they met at the junction of three roads. While they were talking, Pedro said, "Let each of us take one of these roads and set out to find his fortune! there is nothing for us to do in our town." The other two agreed. After they had embraced and wished each other good luck, they went their several ways. Before separating, however, they promised one another to meet again in the same place, with the arrangement that the first who came should wait for the others.

Pedro took the road to the right. After three months' travelling, sometimes over mountains, sometimes through towns, he met an old man. The old man asked him for food, for he was very hungry. Pedro gave him some bread, for that was all he had. The old man thanked the youth very much, and said, "In return for your kindness I will give you this carpet. It looks like an ordinary carpet, but it has great virtue. Whoever sits on it may be transported instantly to any place he desires to be." Pedro received the carpet gladly and thanked the old man. Then the old man went on his way, and Pedro wandered about the town. At last, thinking of his two friends, he seated himself on his carpet and was transported to the cross-roads, where he sat down to wait for Juan and Pablo.

Juan had taken the road to the left. After he had travelled for three months and a half, he, too, met an old man. This old man asked the youth for something to eat, as he was very hungry, he said. So Juan, kind-heartedly, shared with him the bread he was going to eat for his dinner. As a return for his generosity, the old man gave him a book, and said, "This book may seem to you of no value; but when you know of its peculiar properties, you will be astonished. By reading in it you will be able to know everything that is happening in the world at all times." Juan was overjoyed with his present. After thanking the old man and bidding him good-by, the youth returned to the meeting-place at the cross-roads, where he met Pedro. The two waited for Pablo.

Pablo took the road in the middle, and, after travelling four months, he also met an old man, to whom he gave the bread he

[1] Narrated by Dolores Zafra, a Tagalog from La Laguna. She heard the story from her father.

was going to eat for his dinner. "As you have been very kind to me," said the old man, "I will give you this ivory tube as a present. Perhaps you will say that it is worthless, if you look only at the outside; but when you know its value, you will say that the one who possesses it is master of a great treasure. It cures all sick persons of every disease, and, even if the patient is dying, it will restore him instantly to perfect health if you will but blow through one end of the tube into the sick person's nose." Pablo thanked the old man heartily for his gift, and then set out for the meeting-place. He joined his friends without mishap.

The three friends congratulated one another at having met again in safety and good health. Then they told one another about their fortunes. While Pedro was looking in Juan's book, he read that a certain princess in a distant kingdom was very sick, and that the king her father had given orders that any person in the world who could cure his daughter should be her husband and his heir. When Pedro told his companions the news, they at once decided to go to that kingdom. They seated themselves on the carpet, and were transported in a flash to the king's palace. After they had been led into the room of the sick princess, Pablo took his tube and blew through one end of it into her nose. She immediately opened her eyes, sat up, and began to talk. Then, as she wanted to dress, the three friends retired.

While the princess was dressing, Pablo, Juan, and Pedro went before the king, and told him how they had learned that the princess was sick, how they had been transported there, and who had cured her. The king, having heard all each had to say in his own favor, at last spoke thus wisely to them: —

"It is true, Pablo, that you are the one who cured my daughter; but let me ask you whether you could have contrived to cure her if you had not known from Juan's book that she was sick, and if Pedro's carpet had not brought you here without delay. — Your book, Juan, revealed to you that my daughter was sick; but the knowledge of her illness would have been of no service had it not been for Pedro's carpet and Pablo's tube. — And it is just the same way with your carpet, Pedro. — So I cannot grant the princess to any one of you, since each has had an equal share in her cure. As this is the case, I will choose another means of deciding. Go and procure, each one of you, a bow and an arrow. I will hang up the inflorescence of a banana-plant. This will represent the heart of my daughter. The one who shoots it in the middle shall be the husband of my daughter, and the heir of my kingdom."

The first to shoot was Pedro, whose arrow passed directly through the middle of the banana-flower. He was very glad. Juan shot second. His arrow passed through the same hole Pedro's arrow had made. Now came Pablo's turn; but when Pablo's turn came, he refused to shoot, saying that if the banana-flower represented the heart of the princess, he could not shoot it, for he loved her too dearly.

When the king heard this answer, he said, "Since Pablo really loves my daughter, while Pedro and Juan do not, for they shot at the flower that represents her heart, Pablo shall marry the princess."

And so Pablo married the king's daughter, and in time became king of that country.

(d) LEGEND OF PRINCE OSWALDO.[1]

Once upon a time, on a moonlight night, three young men were walking monotonously along a solitary country road. Just where they were going nobody could tell: but when they came to a place where the road branched into three, they stopped there like nails attracted by a powerful magnet. At this crossroads a helpless old man lay groaning as if in mortal pain. At the sight of the travellers he tried to raise his head, but in vain. The three companions then ran to him, helped him up, and fed him a part of the rice they had with them.

The sick old man gradually regained strength, and at last could speak to them. He thanked them, gave each of the companions a hundred pesos, and said, "Each one of you shall take one of these branch-roads. At the end of it is a house where they are selling something. With these hundred pesos that I am giving each of you, you shall buy the first thing that you see there." The three youths accepted the money, and promised to obey the old man's directions.

Pedro, who took the left branch, soon came to the house described by the old man. The owner of the house was selling a rain-coat. "How much does the coat cost?" Pedro asked the landlord.

---

[1] Narrated by Leopoldo Uichanco, a Tagalog from Calamba, La Laguna.

"One hundred pesos, no more, no less."

"Of what value is it?" said Pedro.

"It will take you wherever you wish to go." So Pedro paid the price, took the rain-coat, and returned.

Diego, who took the middle road, arrived at another house. The owner of this house was selling a book. "How much does your book cost?" Diego inquired of the owner.

"One hundred pesos, no more, no less."

"Of what value is it?"

"It will tell you what is going on in all parts of the world." So Diego paid the price, took the book, and returned.

Juan, who took the third road, reached still another house. The owner of the house was selling a bottle that contained some violet-colored liquid. "How much does the bottle cost?" said Juan.

"One hundred pesos, no more, no less."

"Of what value is it?"

"It brings the dead back to life," was the answer. Juan paid the price, took the bottle, and returned.

The three travellers met again in the same place where they had separated; but the old man was now nowhere to be found. The first to tell of his adventure was Diego. "Oh, see what I have!" he shouted as he came in sight of his companions. "It tells everything that is going on in the world. Let me show you!" He opened the book and read what appeared on the page: "'The beautiful princess of Berengena is dead. Her parents, relatives, and friends grieve at her loss.'"

"Good!" answered Juan. "Then there is an occasion for us to test this bottle. It restores the dead back to life. Oh, but the kingdom of Berengena is far away! The princess will be long buried before we get there."

"Then we shall have occasion to use my rain-coat," said Pedro. "It will take us wherever we wish to go. Let us try it! We shall receive a big reward from the king. We shall return home with a *casco* full of money. To Berengena at once!" He wrapped the rain-coat about all three of them, and wished them in Berengena. Within a few minutes they reached that country. The princess was already in the church, where her parents were weeping over her. Everybody in the church wore deep mourning.

When the three strangers boldly entered the church, the

guard at the door arrested them, for they had on red clothes. When Juan protested, and said that the princess was not dead, the guard immediately took him to the king; but the king, when he heard what Juan had said, called him a fool.

"She is only sleeping," said Juan. "Let me wake her up!"

"She is dead," answered the king angrily. "On your life, don't you dare touch her!"

"I will hold my head responsible for the truth of my statement," said Juan. "Let me wake her up, or rather, not to offend your Majesty, restore her to life!"

"Well, I will let you do as you please," said the king; "but if your attempt fails, you will lose your head. On the other hand, should you be successful, I will give you the princess for a wife, and you shall be my heir."

Blinded by his love for the beautiful princess, Juan said that he would restore her to life. "May you be successful!" said the king; and then, raising his voice, he continued, "Everybody here present is to bear witness that I, the King of Berengena, do hereby confirm an agreement with this unknown stranger. I will allow this man to try the knowledge he pretends to possess of restoring the princess to life. But there is this condition to be understood: if he is successful, I will marry him to the princess, and he is to be my heir; but should he fail, his head is forfeit."

The announcement having been made, Juan was conducted to the coffin. He now first realized what he was undertaking. What if the bottle was false! What if he should fail! Would not his head be dangling from the ropes of the scaffold, to be hailed by the multitude as the remains of a blockhead, a dunce, and a fool? The coffin was opened. With these meditations in his mind, Juan tremblingly uncorked his bottle of violet liquid, and held it under the nose of the princess. He held the bottle there for some time, but she gave no signs of life. An hour longer, still no trace of life. After hours of waiting, the people began to grow impatient. The king scratched his head, the guards were ready to seize him; the scaffold was waiting for him. "Nameless stranger!" thundered the king, with indignant eyes, "upon your honor, tell us the truth! Can you do it, or not? Speak. I command it!"

Juan trembled all the more. He did not know what to say, but he continued to hold the bottle under the nose of the princess. Had he not been afraid of the consequences, he would have given up and entreated the king for mercy. He fixed his eyes on the corpse, but did not speak. "Are you trying to joke us?" said the king, his eyes flashing with rage. "Speak! I command!"

Just as Juan was about to reply, he saw the right hand of the princess move. He bade the king wait. Soon the princess moved her other hand and opened her eyes. Her cheeks were fresh and rosy as ever. She stared about, and exclaimed in surprise, "Oh, where am I? Where am I? Am I dreaming? No, there is my father, there is my mother, there is my brother." The king was fully satisfied. He embraced his daughter, and then turned to Juan, saying, "Stranger, can't you favor us now with your name?"

With all the rustic courtesy he knew, Juan replied to the king, told his name, and said that he was a poor laborer in a barrio far away. The king only smiled, and ordered Juan's clothes to be exchanged for prince's garments, so that the celebration of his marriage with the princess might take place at once. "Long live Juan! Long live the princess!" the people shouted.

When Diego and Juan heard the shout, they could not help feeling cheated. They made their way through the crowd, and said to the king, "Great Majesty, pray hear us! In the name of justice, pray hear us!"

"Who calls?" asked the king of a guard near by. "Bring him here!" The guard obeyed, and led the two men before the king.

"What is the matter?" asked the king of the two.

"Your Majesty shall know," responded Diego. "If it had not been for my book, we could not have known that the princess was dead. Our home is far away, and it was only because of my magic book that we knew of the events that were going on here."

"And his Majesty shall be informed," seconded Pedro, "that Juan's good luck is due to my rain-coat. Neither Diego's book nor Juan's bottle could have done anything had not my rain-coat carried us here so quickly. I am the one who should marry the princess."

The king was overwhelmed: he did not know what to do. Each of the three had a good reason, but all three could not marry the princess. Even the counsellors of the king could not decide upon the matter.

While they were puzzling over it, an old man sprang forth from the crowd of spectators, and declared that he would settle the difficulty. "Young men," he said, addressing Juan, Pedro, and Diego, "none of you shall marry the princess. — You, Juan, shall not marry her, because you intended to obtain your fortunes regardless of your companions who have been helping you to get them. — And you, Pedro and Diego, shall not have the princess, because you did not accept your misfortune quietly and thank God for it. — None of you shall have her. I will marry her myself."

The princess wept. How could the fairest maiden of Berengena marry an old man! "What right have you to claim her?" said the king in scorn.

"I am the one who showed these three companions where to get their bottle, rain-coat, and book," said the old man. "I am the one who gave each of them a hundred pesos. I am the capitalist: the interest is mine." The old man was right; the crowd clapped their hands; and the princess could do nothing but yield. Bitterly weeping, she gave her hand to the old man, who seemed to be her grandfather, and they were married by the priest. The king almost fainted.

But just now the sun began to rise, its soft beams filtering through the eastern windows of the church. The newly-married couple were led from the altar to be taken home to the palace; but, just as they were descending the steps that lead down from the altar, the whole church was flooded with light. All present were stupefied. The glorious illumination did not last long. When the people recovered, they found that their princess was walking with her husband, not an old man, however, but a gallant young prince. The king recognized him. He kissed him, for they were old-time acquaintances. The king's new son-in-law was none other than Prince Oswaldo, who had just been set free from the bonds of enchantment by his marriage. He had been a former suitor of the princess, but had been enchanted by a magician.

With magnificent ceremony the king's son-in-law was conducted to the royal residence. He was seated on the throne, the crown and sceptre were transferred to him, and he was hailed as King Oswaldo of Berengena.

NOTES.

I have still a fifth Filipino story (*e*) of three brothers setting out to seek their fortunes, their rich father promising his estate to the son who should show most skill in the profession he had chosen. This Bicol version, which was narrated by Simeon Paz of Nueva Caceres, Camarines, contains a long introduction telling how the youngest brother was cruelly treated by the two older. After the three have left home in search of professions, the older brothers try to kill the youngest, but he escapes. In his wanderings he meets with an old hermit, who, on hearing the boy's story, presents him with a magic booklet and dagger. These articles can furnish their possessor with whatever he wishes. At the appointed time the three brothers meet again at home, and each demonstrates his skill. The oldest, who has become an expert blacksmith, shoes a horse running at full speed. The second brother, a barber, trims the hair of a running man. The youngest causes a beautiful palace to appear instantly. The father, somewhat unfairly, perhaps, bestows his estate on the youngest, who has really displayed no skill at all.

These five Filipino stories belong to a large group of tales to which we may give the name of the "Rival Brothers." This cycle assumes various forms; but the two things that identify the relationship of the members are the rivalry of the brothers and the conundrum or "problem" ending of the stories. Within this cycle we can distinguish at least three simple, distinct types, and a compound fourth made up of parts of two of the others. These four types may be very generally outlined as follows: (1) A number of artisans (usually not brothers), by working cumulatively, as it were, make and bring to life a beautiful woman; they then quarrel as to which one has really produced her and is therefore entitled to have her. (11) Through the combined skill of three suitors (sometimes brothers, oftener not), a maiden is saved from death, and the three quarrel over the possession of her. The difficulty is solved satisfactorily by her father or by some one else appointed to judge. (111) A father promises his wealth to the son that shall become most skilful in his profession; the three sons seek their fortunes, and at an appointed time return, and are tested by their father. He judges which is most worthy of the estate. (1V) A combination of the first part of the third type with the second.

Benfey (in Ausland, 1858 : 969, 995, 1017, 1038, 1067) has made a somewhat exhaustive study of the *Märchen*, which he calls "Das Märchen von den Menschen mit den wunderbaren Eigenschaften." As a matter of fact, he examines particularly the stories of our type 11 (see above), to which he connects the folk-tales of our types 111 and 1V as a later popular development. As has been said in the notes to No. 11, Benfey thinks that the "Skilful Companions" cycle is a droll or comic offshoot of this much older group. Our type I he does not discuss at all, possibly thinking that it is not a part of the "Rival Brothers" cycle. It strikes me, however, as being a part fully as much as is the "Skilful Companions" cycle, which is perhaps more nearly related to the "Bride Wager" group than to the "Rival Brothers." Professor G. L. Kittredge, in his "Arthur and Gorlagon" (Harvard Studies and Notes in Philology and Literature, No. 8), 226, has likewise failed to differentiate clearly the two cycles, and his outline of the "Skilful Companions" is that of our type II of the "Rival Brothers." I am far from wishing to quarrel over nomenclature, — possibly "Rival Brothers" is no better name for the group of tales under discussion than is "Skilful Companions," — but, as G. H. Gerould has remarked ("The Grateful Dead," Folk-Lore Society, 1907 : 126, note 3), Kittredge's analysis would not hold for all variants, even when uncompounded. However, Mr. Gerould does not attempt to explain the cause of the confusion, nor was he called upon to do so in his study of an entirely distinct cycle. Consequently, as no one else has yet done so, for the sake of clearness, I propose a division of the large family of sagas and folk-tales dealing with men endowed with extraordinary powers [1] into at least two cycles, — the "Rival Brothers" and the "Skilful Companions" (see No. 11). The former of these, which is the group discussed here, I subdivide, as has already been indicated, into four types. Of intermixtures of these types with other cycles we shall not concern ourselves here, though they have been many.[2] We now turn to an examination of the four types.[3]

(1) Type I had its origin in India, doubtless. The oldest form seems to be that found in the Sanscrit "Vetâlapancavinçati," No. 22, whence it was incorporated into Somadeva's story collection (twelfth century) called the "Kathâsaritsâgara." An outline of this last version (Tawney's translation, 2 : 348–350) is as follows.

---

[1] Whether or not these powers reside in the men themselves, who have acquired them through practice, or in magic objects which they find or are presented with. Benfey (*loc. cit.*, p. 969) makes two distinct cycles on an entirely different basis from mine, both derived from India: the one telling of the extraordinary endowments of *men;* the other, of extraordinary properties of *objects* (i.e., magic objects). It seems to me a mistake, however, to make a cycle of this second group, for magic articles are only machinery in a story. A family of folk-tales cannot turn merely on *things;* the magic objects are only latently powerful until guided and controlled by the human hero.

[2] For example, "The Grateful Dead," "John the Bear," "The Child and the Hand," "The Ransomed Woman," etc.

[3] The most recent investigation of this cycle that I know of is that of W. E. Farnham in connection with the sources of Chaucer's "Parlement of Foules" (in Publications of the Modern Language Association, 32 : 502–513 [1917]). Dr. Farnham has named the cycle "The Contending Lovers," the stories of which, he says, fall into six clearly marked types. My discussion of the cycle may require some modification in the light of his study; but I have printed it here as I wrote it, some two years before Dr. Farnham's article came *to my notice.*

STORY OF THE FOUR BRÁHMAN BROTHERS WHO RESUSCITATED THE LION.

Four Bráhman brothers, sons of a very poor man, leave home to beg. After their state has become even more miserable, they decide to separate and to search through the earth for some magic power. So, fixing upon a trysting-place, they leave one another, one going east, one west, one north, one south. In the course of time they meet again, and each tells of his accomplishments: the first can immediately produce on a bit of bone the flesh of that animal; the second can produce on that flesh skin and hair appropriate to that animal; the third can create the limbs of the animal after the flesh, skin, and hair have been formed; the fourth can endow the completed carcass with life. The four now go into the forest to find a piece of bone with which to test their skill; they find one, but are ignorant that it is the bone of a lion. The first Bráhman covers the bone with flesh; the second gives it skin and hair; the third completes the animal by supplying appropriate limbs; the fourth endows it with life. The terrible beast, springing up, charges the four brothers and slays them on the spot.

The question which the *vetála* now asks the king is, "Which of these four was guilty in respect of the lion who slew them all?" King Vikramasena answers, "The one that gave life to the lion is guilty. The others produced flesh, skin, hair, and limbs without knowing what kind of animal they were making. Therefore, being ignorant, they were not guilty. But the fourth, seeing the complete lion's shape before him, was guilty of their death, because he gave the creature life."

The "Pancatantra" version (v, 4) varies slightly. Here, as in the preceding, there are four brothers, but only three of them possess all knowledge; the fourth possesses common sense. The first brother joins together the bones of a lion; the second covers them with skin, flesh, and blood; the third is about to give the animal life, when the fourth brother — he who possessed common sense — says, "If you raise him to life, he will kill us all." Finding that the third brother will not desist from his intention, the fourth climbs a tree and saves himself, while his three brothers are torn to pieces. For a modern Indian popular form, see Thornhill, 289.

In the Persian "Tûtî-nâmah" (No. 5) the story assumes a decidedly different form, as may be seen from the following abstract. (I think that there can be no doubt, however, that this tale was inspired by some redaction of "Vetâlapancavinçati," No. 22, not unlikely in combination with "Vetâlapancavinçati," No. 2.)

THE GOLDSMITH, THE CARPENTER, THE TAILOR, AND THE HERMIT WHO QUARRELLED ABOUT A WOODEN WOMAN.

A goldsmith, a carpenter, a tailor, and a hermit, travelling together, come to a desert place where they must spend the night. They decide that each shall take a watch during the night as guard. The carpenter's turn is first: to prevent sleep he carves out a wooden figure. When his turn comes, the goldsmith shows his skill by preparing jewels and adorning the puppet. The tailor's turn is next: he sees the beautiful wooden woman decked with exquisite jewels, but naked; consequently he makes neat clothes becoming a bride, and dresses her. When the hermit's turn to watch comes, he prays to God that the figure may have life; and it begins to speak like a human being.

In the morning all four fall desperately in love with the woman, and each claims her as his. Finally they come to a fifth person, and refer the matter to him. He claims her to be his wife, who has been seduced from his house, and hails the four travellers before the cutwal. But the cutwal falls in love with the woman, says that she is his brother's wife, accuses the five of his brother's murder, and carries them before the cazi. The cazi, no less enamoured, says that the woman is his bondmaid, who had absconded with much money. After the seven have disputed and wrangled a long time, an old man in the crowd that has meantime gathered suggests that the case be laid before the Tree of Decision, which can be found in a certain town. When they have all come before the tree with the woman, the tree divides, the woman runs into the cleft, the tree unites, and she has disappeared forever. A voice from the tree then says, "Everything returns to its first principles." The seven suitors are overwhelmed with shame.

A Mongolian form, to be found in the Ardschi-Bordschi saga (see Busk, 298–304), seems to furnish the link of connection between the "Tûtî-nâmah" version and "Vetâlapancavinçati," Nos. 22 and 2 : —

WHO INVENTED WOMAN?

Four shepherd youths pasture their flocks near one another, and when they have time amuse themselves together. One day one of them there alone, to pass away the time, takes wood and sculptures it until he has fashioned a beautiful female form. When he sees what he has done, he cares no more for his companions, but goes his way. The next day the second youth comes alone to the place, and, finding the image, he paints it fair with the five colors, and goes his way. On the third day the third youth finds the statue, and infuses into it wit and understanding. He, too, cares no more to sport with his companions, and goes his way. On the fourth day the fourth youth finds the figure, and, breathing softly into its lips, behold! he gives it a soul that can be loved, — a beautiful woman.

When the other three see what has happened, they come back and demand possession of her by right of invention. Each urges his claim; but they can come to no decision, and so they lay the matter before the king. The question is, Who has invented the woman, and to whom does she belong by right? The answer of the king is as follows: "The first youth stands in the place of a father to her; the second youth, who has tinted her fairly, stands in the place of a mother; the third, is he not Lama (Buddhist priest, hence instructor)? The fourth has given her a soul that can be loved, and it is he alone who has really made her. She belongs to him, and therefore he is her husband."

I cannot refrain from giving a *résumé* of "Vetâlapancavinçati," No. 2, because it has been overlooked by Benfey, and seems to be of no little significance in connection with our cycle: it establishes the connection between types I and II. This abstract is taken from Tawney's translation of Somadeva's redaction, 2 : 242–244 : —

Bráhman Agnisvámin has a beautiful daughter, Mandáravatí. Three young Bráhmans, equally matched in accomplishments, come to Agnisvámin, and demand the daughter, each for himself. Her father refuses, fearing to cause the death of any one of them. Mandáravatí remains unmarried. The three suitors stay at her house day and night, living on the sight of her. Then Mandáravatí suddenly dies of a fever. The three Bráhmans take her body to the cemetery and burn it. One builds a hut there, and makes her ashes his bed; the second takes her bones, and goes with them to the sacred river Ganges; the third becomes an ascetic, and sets out travelling.

While roaming about, the third suitor reaches a village, where he is entertained by a Bráhman. From him the ascetic steals a magic book that will restore life to dead ashes. (He has seen its power proved after his hostess, in a fit of anger, throws her crying child into the fire.) With his magic book he returns to the cemetery before the second suitor has thrown the maiden's bones into the river. After having the first Bráhman remove the hut he had erected, the ascetic, reading the charm and throwing some dust on the ashes of Mandáravatí, causes the maiden to rise up alive, more beautiful than ever. Then the three quarrel about her, each claiming her as his own. The first says, "She is mine, for I preserved her ashes and resuscitated her by asceticism." The second says, "She belongs to me, for she was produced by the efficacy of sacred bathing-places." The third says, "She is my wife, for she was won by the power of my charm."

The *vetála*, who has been telling the story, now puts the question to King Vikramasena. The king rules as follows: "The third Bráhman must be considered as her father; the second, as her son; and the first, as her husband, for he lay in the cemetery embracing her ashes, which was an act of deep affection."

A modern link is the Georgian folk-tale of "The King and the Apple" (Wardrop, No. XVI), in which the king's magic apple tells three riddle-stories to the wonderful boy : —

(1) A woman is travelling with her husband and brother. The party meets brigands, and the two men are decapitated. Their heads are restored to them by the woman through the help of a magic herb revealed to her by a mouse. However, she gets her husband's head on her brother's body. Q. — Which man is the right husband? A. — The one with the husband's head.

(2) A joiner, a tailor, and a priest are travelling. When night comes, they appoint three watches. The joiner, for amusement, cuts down a tree and carves out a man. The tailor, in his turn, takes off his clothes and dresses the figure. The priest, when his turn comes, prays for a soul for the image, and the figure becomes alive. Q. — Who made the man? A. — He who gave him the soul.

(3) A diviner, a physician, and a swift runner are met together. The diviner says, "There is a certain prince ill with such and such a disease." The physician says, "I know a cure." The swift runner says, "I will run with it." The physician prepares the medicine, the runner runs with it, and the prince is cured. Q. — Who cured the king's son? A. — He who made the medicine.

These three stories, with their framework, appear to be descended in part from the Ardschi-Bordschi saga. A connection between the third and our type ii is obvious.

A Bohemian form of this type is No. 4 of Wratislaw's collection.

(ii) Type ii, according to Benfey, also originated in India. The oldest known form of the story is the "Vetâlapancavinçati," No. 5. A brief summary of Somadeva's version, "The Story of Somaprabhá and her Three Suitors" (Tawney, 2 : 258–260), may be given here: —

In Ujjayiní there lived a Bráhman who had an excellent son and a beautiful proud daughter. When the time for her to be married came, she told her mother to give the following message to her father and her brother: "I am to be given in marriage only to a person possessed of heroism, knowledge, or magic power."

A noble Bráhman (No. 1) in time came to the father and asked for his daughter's hand. When told of the conditions, he said, "I am possessed of magic power," and to demonstrate, he made a chariot and took the father for a ride in the clouds. Then Harisvámin, the father, promised his daughter to the Bráhman possessed of magic power, and set the marriage day seven days hence.

Another Bráhman (No. 2) came and asked the son for his sister's hand. When told the conditions, he said that he was a hero, and he displayed his skill in the use of weapons. The brother, ignorant of what his father had done, promised his sister's hand to this man, and by the advice of an astrologer he selected the same day for the wedding as his father had selected.

A third Bráhman (No. 3) on that same day asked the mother for her daughter's hand, saying that he was possessed of wisdom. Ignorant of what her husband and her son had done, she questioned this Bráhman about the past and the future, and at length promised him her daughter's hand on the same seventh day.

On the same day, then, three bridegrooms appeared, and, strange to say, on that very day the bride disappeared. No. 3, with his knowledge, discovered that she had been carried off by a Rákshasa. No. 1 made a chariot equipped with weapons, and the three suitors and Harisvámin were carried to the Rákshasa's abode. There No. 2 fought and killed the demon, and all returned with the maiden. A dispute then arose among the Bráhmans as to which was entitled to the maiden's hand. Each set forth his claim.

The *vetâla*, who has been telling the story, now makes King Vikramasena decide which deserves the girl. The king says that the girl ought to be given to No. 2, who risked his life in battle to save her. Nos. 1 and 3 were only instruments; calculators and artificers are always subordinate to others.

The story next passed over into Mongolia, growing by the way. The version in the "Siddhi-kür," No. 13, is interesting, because it shows our story already linked up with another cycle, the "True Brothers." Only the last part, which begins approximately where the companions miss the rich youth, corresponds to the Sanscrit above. (This Mongolian version may be found in English in Busk, 105–114.) The story then moved westward, and we next meet it in the Persian and the Turkish "Tûtî-nâmah," "The Story of the Beautiful Zehra." (For an English rendering from the Persian, see "The Tootinameh; or, Tales of a Parrot," Persian text with English translation [Calcutta, 1792], pp. 111–114.)

W. A. Clouston (Clouston 3, 2 : 277–288) has discussed this group of stories, and gives abstracts of a number of variants that Benfey does not mention: Dozon, "Albanian Tales," No. 4; a Persian manuscript text of the "Sindibád Náma;" a Japanese legend known as early as the tenth century; the "1001 Nights" story of "Prince Ahmed and the Peri Bánú;" Powell and Magnussen's "Icelandic Legends," pp. 348–354, "The Story of the Three Princes;" Von Hahn, "Contes Populaires Grecs" (Athens and Copenhagen, 1879), No. 11, p. 98. Of these he says (p. 285), "We have probably the original of all these different versions in the fifth of the 'Vetálapanchaviṇsati,'" — but hardly from No. 5 alone, probably in combination with Nos. 2 and 22 (*cf.* above). At least, the Arabian, Icelandic, and Greek forms cited by Clouston include the search for trades or magic objects by rival brothers, a detail not found in No. 5, but occurring in Nos. 22 and 2. Clouston calls attention to the fact that in No. 5 and in the "Tûtî-nâmah" version the damsel is not represented as being ill, while in the "Sindibád-Námá" and in the Arabian version she *is* so represented.

(III) The third type seems to be of European origin. It is perhaps best represented by Grimm, No. 124, "The Three Brothers." In his notes, Grimm calls this story an old lying and jesting tale, and says that it is apparently very widespread. He cites few analogues of it, however. He does mention an old one (sixteenth century) which seems to be the parent of the German story. It is Philippe d'Alcripe's "Trois frères, excellens ouvriers de leurs mestiers" (No. 1 in the 1853 Paris edition, Biblioth. Elzevirien). As in Grimm, the three skilled brothers in the French tale are a barber, a horse-shoer, and a swordsman; and the performances of skill are identical in the two stories. The French version, however, ends with the display of skill: no decision is made as to which is entitled to receive the "*petite maison,*" the property that the father wishes to leave to the son who proves himself to be the best craftsman. Our fifth story, the Bicol variant, clearly belongs to this type, although it has undergone some modifications, and has been influenced by contact with other cycles.

(IV) The fourth type represents the form to which our four printed stories most closely approximate. As remarked above, it is a combination of the third and the second types. This combination appears to have been developed in Europe, although, as may be seen from the analysis of "Vetâlapancavinçati," No. 2, it might easily have been suggested by the Sanscrit. Compare also the "Siddhi-Kûr" form of type II, where, although not brothers, and six in number instead of three, the six comrades set out to seek their fortunes. But here there is no suggestion of the six acquiring skill: they have that before they separate.

The earliest known European version of this type is Morlini's, Nov. 30 (about 1520). His Latin was translated by Straparola (about 1553) in the "Tredici piacevoli Notti," VII, 5. In outline his version runs about as follows: —

Three brothers, sons of a poor man, voluntarily leave home to seek their fortunes, promising to return in ten years. After determining on a meeting-place, they separate. The first takes service with soldiers, and becomes expert in the art of war: he can scale walls, dagger in hand. The second becomes a master shipwright. The third spends his time in the woods, and becomes skilled in the tongues of birds. After ten years they meet again, as appointed. While they are sitting in an inn, the youngest hears a bird say that there is a great treasure hidden by the corner-stone of the inn. This they dig up, and return as wealthy men to their father's house.

Another bird announces the imprisonment of the beautiful Aglea in a tower on an island in the Ægean Sea. She is guarded by a serpent. The second brother builds a swift ship, in which all three sail to the island. There the first brother climbs the tower, rescues Aglea, and plunders all the serpent's treasure. With the wealth and the lady the three return. A dispute now arises as to which brother has the best claim over her. The matter is left undecided by the story-teller.

At the beginning of the seventeenth century, Basile, working very likely on oral tradition, and independent of Straparola (with whose work he does not appear to have been acquainted), gives another version, "Pentamerone," V, 7: —

Pacione, a poor father, sends his five good-for-nothing sons out into the world for one year to learn a craft. They return at the appointed time. During the year the eldest son has learned thieving; the second has learned boat-building; the third, how to shoot with the cross-bow; the fourth has learned of an herb that will cause the dead to rise; the fifth has learned the language of birds. While the five sons are eating with their father, the youngest son hears sparrows saying that a ghoul has stolen the princess, daughter of the King of Autogolfo. The father suggests that his five sons go to her rescue. So a boat is built, the princess is stolen from the ghoul, the ghoul pursues and is blinded by a shot from the bow, the princess falls in a dead faint and is restored by the life-giving herb. After *the five* brothers have returned the princess to her father, they dispute as to who did the greatest deed of prowess, so as to be worthy of being her husband. Her father the king decides the dispute by giving his daughter to Pacione, because he is the parent-stem of all these branches.

Benfey thinks that the brother who knows of the life-restoring herb is an original addition of Basile's or of his immediate source; but this character is to be found in the cycle from earliest times (see "Vetâlapancavinçati," No. 2; and "Siddhi-Kür," No. 13).

The story is next found as a *Märchen* pretty well scattered throughout Europe. German, Russian, Bohemian, Italian, Greek, and Serbian forms are known (see Benfey's article, and Grimm's notes to No. 129). We may examine briefly six interesting versions not mentioned by Benfey or Grimm: —

Greek (Von Hahn, No. 47). — A king with three sons wishes to marry off the eldest. He seeks a suitable wife for the prince; but when she is found and brought to the court, she is so beautiful, that all three brothers want her. To decide their dispute, the king, on advice, sends them abroad, promising the hand of the princess to the one who shall bring back the most valuable article. The three brothers set out; they separate at Adrianople, agreeing to meet there again at an appointed time. On his travels, the eldest buys a telescope through which he can see anything he wishes to see. The second buys an orange that will restore to life the dying if the sick person but smells of the fruit. The third buys a magic transportation-carpet. They all meet as agreed. By means of the telescope one of the brothers learns that the princess is dying. The magic carpet carries them all home instantaneously, and the orange cures the maiden. A quarrel arises as to which brother deserves her hand. The king, unable to decide, marries her himself.

Bohemian (Waldau [Prag, 1860], "Das Weise Urteil"). — In this there are three rival brothers. One has a magic mirror; another, a magic chariot; and the third, three magic apples. The first finds out that the lady is desperately ill; the second takes himself and his rivals to her; and the third restores her to health. A dispute arising, an old man decides that the third brother should have her, as his apples were consumed as medicine, while the other two still have their chariot and mirror respectively. (Compare the decision in the Georgian folk-tale under type II.)

Serbian (Mme. Mijatovies, 230 ff., "The Three Suitors"). — Three noblemen seek the hand of a princess. As the king cannot make a choice, he says to the three, "Go travel about the world. The one who brings home the most remarkable thing shall be my son-in-law." As in the Greek story, one gets a transportation-carpet; another, a magic telescope; and the third, a wonder-working ointment that will cure all diseases and even bring the dead to life. The three noblemen meet, learn through the telescope of the princess's mortal illness, and, hastening to her side with the help of the magic carpet, cure her with the ointment. A dispute arises as to which suitor shall have her. The king decides that each has as good a claim as the others, and persuades all to give up the idea of marrying the princess. They do so, go to a far-off desert, and become hermits, while the king marries his daughter to another noble. The story does not end here, but thus much is all we are interested *in.*

Italian Tyrolese (Schneller, No. 14, "Die Drei Liebhaber"). — This story is like Von Hahn, No. 47. The magic objects are an apple, a chair, and a mirror. In the magic mirror the three suitors see the bride on the point of death. They are carried to her in the magic chair, and she is saved by means of the apple. The story ends as a riddle: Who married the maiden?

Icelandic (Rittershaus, No. XLIII, "Die drei Freier um eine Braut"). — This story, which closely follows the "1001 Nights" version and is probably derived from it, agrees in the first part with Von Hahn, No. 47. When a folk-tribunal is called to decide which brother most deserves the princess and is unable to agree, the king proposes another test, — a shooting-match. The princess is to be given to the one who can shoot his arrow the farthest. The youngest really wins; but, as his arrow goes out of sight and cannot be found, the princess is given to the second brother. From this point on, the adventures of the hero are derived from another cycle that does not belong with our group.

Icelandic (Rittershaus, No. XLII, "Die Kunstreichen Brüder"). — Although this story is very different from any of ours, I call attention to it here because Dr. Rittershaus says (p. 181) that in it we have, "in allerdings verwischter Form, das Märchen von 'der Menschen mit den wunderbaren Eigenschaften,'" and she refers to Benfey's "Ausland" article. The collector states, however, that the story is so different from the other *Märchen* belonging to this family, that no further parallels can be adduced. As a matter of fact, this Icelandic story is a combination of the "Skilful Companions" cycle with the "Child and the Hand" cycle. For this combined *Märchen*, see Kittredge, "Arthur and Gorlagon," 222–227.

It might be noted, in passing, that a connection between this type of the "Rival Brothers" and the "Skilful Companions" cycle is established through Gonzenbach's Sicilian story of "The Seven Brothers who had Magic Articles," No. 45. (See Köhler's notes to this tale and also to No. 74; to Widter-Wolf, No. 6 [Jahrb. f. rom. und eng. lit., VII]; and to V. Tagić, No. 46 [Köhler-Bolte, 438–440].)

I have not attempted to give an exhaustive bibliographical account of this cycle of the "Rival Brothers," but have merely suggested points that seem to me particularly significant in its history and development. So far as our four Filipino examples are concerned, I think that it is perfectly clear that in their present form, at least, they have been derived from Europe. There is so much divergence among them, however, and they are so widely separated from one another geographically, that it would be fruitless to search for a common ancestor of the four.

The Ilocano story is the best in outline, and is fairly close to Grimm, No. 129, though there are only three brothers in the Filipino tale, and there is no skill contest held by the mother before the youths set out to rescue the princess. The all-seeing telescope and the clever thief, however, are found in both. The solution at the end is the same: the king keeps his daughter, and divides half a kingdom among her rescuers.

The Pangasinan tale has obviously been garbled. The use of two magic articles with properties so nearly the same, the taking ship by the three brothers when they had a transportation-mat at their service, and finally the inhuman decision of the king,[1] — all suggest either a confusion of stories, or a contamination of old native analogies, or crude manufacture on the part of some narrator. It may be remarked, however, that the life-restoring book is analogous to the magic book in "Vetâlapancaviņçati," No. 2, while the repairing of the shattered ship by means of the magic stones suggests the stitching-together of the planks in Grimm, No. 129. The setting appears to be modern.

In the first Tagalog story (c) the three men are not brothers. They are given the magic objects as a reward for kindness. The sentimental *dénouement* reads somewhat smug and strained after all three men have been represented as equally kind-hearted. The shooting-contest with arrows to decide the question, however, may be reminiscent of the "1001 Nights" version. For the resuscitating flute in droll stories, see Bolte-Polívka's notes to Grimm, No. 61 (episode G[1]). The book of knowledge suggests the magic book in the Pangasinan version.

13. (a) THE RICH AND THE POOR.[2]

Once upon a time there lived in the town of Pasig two honest men who were intimate friends. They were called Mayaman[3] and Mahirap,[4] because one was much richer than the other.

One pleasant afternoon these two men made up their minds to take a long walk into the neighboring woods. Here, while they were talking happily about their respective fortunes, they saw in the distance a poor wood-cutter, who was very busy cutting and collecting fagots for sale. This wood-cutter lived in a mean cottage on the outskirts of a little town on the opposite shore of the lake, and he maintained his family by selling pieces of wood gathered from this forest.

When they saw the poor man, Mayaman said to his friend, "Now, which one of us can make that wood-cutter rich?"

"Well, even though I am much poorer than you," said Mahirap, "I can make him rich with just the few cents I have in my pocket."

They agreed, however, that Mayaman should be the first

[1] For practically this identical judgment, see the Dsanglun (St. Petersburg, 1843), p. 94 (cited by Benfey, 1 : 396, note 2).
[2] Narrated by José L. Gomez, a Tagalog from Rizal province.
[3] Tag. for "rich."
[4] Tag. for "poor."

to try to make the poor man rich. So Mayaman called out to the wood-cutter, and said, "Do you want to be rich, my good man?"

"Certainly, master, I should like to be rich, so that my family might not want anything," said the wood-cutter.

Pointing to his large house in the distance, Mayaman said, "All right. Come to my house this evening on your way home, and I will give you four bags of my money. If you don't become rich on them, come back, and I will give you some more."

The wood-cutter was overjoyed at his good luck, and in the evening went to Mayaman's house, where he received the money. He placed the bags in the bottom of his banca,[1] and sailed home. When he reached his little cottage, he spread out all the gold and silver money on the floor. He was delighted at possessing such wealth, and determined first of all to buy household articles with it; but some dishonest neighbors, soon finding out that the wood-cutter had much money in the house, secretly stole the bags.

Then the wood-cutter, remembering the rich man's promise, hastily prepared his banca and sailed across to Pasig. When Mayaman saw the wood-cutter, he said, "Are you rich now, my good man?"

"O kind master!" said the wood-cutter, "I am not yet rich, for some one stole my bags of money."

"Well, here are four more bags. See that you take better care of them."

The wood-cutter reached home safely with this new wealth; but unfortunately it was stolen, too, during the night.

Three more times he went to Mayaman, and every time received four bags of money; but every time was it stolen from him by his neighbors.

Finally, on his sixth application, Mayaman did not give the wood-cutter money, but presented him with a beautiful ring. "This ring will preserve you from harm," he said, "and will give you everything you ask for. With it you can become the richest man in town; but be careful not to lose it!"

While the wood-cutter was sailing home that evening, he thought he would try the ring by asking it for some food. So he said, "Beautiful ring, give me food! for I am hungry." In an instant twelve different kinds of food appeared in his banca,

---

[1] A native dug-out or canoe.

and he ate heartily. But after he had eaten, the wind calmed down: so he said to the ring, "O beautiful ring! blow my banca very hard, so that I may reach home quickly." He had no sooner spoken than the wind rose suddenly. The sail and mast of his little boat were blown away, and the banca itself sank. Forgetting all about his ring, the unfortunate man had to swim for his life. He reached the shore safely, but was greatly distressed to find that he had lost his valuable ring. So he decided to go back to Mayaman and tell him all about his loss.

The next day he borrowed a banca and sailed to Pasig; but when Mayaman had heard his story, he said, "My good man, I have nothing more to give you." Then Mayaman turned to his friend Mahirap, and said, "It is your turn now, Mahirap. See what you can do for this poor man to enrich him." Mahirap gave the poor wood-cutter five centavos, — all he had in his pocket, — and told him to go to the market and buy a fish with it for his supper.

The wood-cutter was disappointed at receiving so small an amount, and sailed homeward in a very downcast mood; but when he arrived at his town, he went straight to the market. As he was walking around the fish-stalls, he saw a very fine fat fish. So he said to the *tendera*,[1] "How much must I pay for that fat fish?"

"Well, five centavos is all I'll ask you for it," said she.

"Oh, I have only five centavos; and if I give them all to you, I shall have no money to buy rice with. So please let me have the fish for three!" said the wood-cutter. But the *tendera* refused to sell the fish for three centavos; and the wood-cutter was obliged to give all his money for it, for the fish was so fine and fat that he could not leave it.

When he went home and opened the fish to clean it, what do you suppose he found inside? Why, no other thing than the precious ring he had lost in the lake! He was so rejoiced at getting back his treasure, that he walked up and down the streets, talking out loud to his ring: —

> "Ha, ha, ha, ha!
> I have found you now;
> You are here, and nowhere else."

When his neighbors who had stolen his bags of money from him heard these words, they thought that the wood-cutter had found

---

[1] A Spanish word meaning "a woman who keeps a little shop or store [*tienda*]."

out that they were the thieves, and was addressing these words
to them. They ran up to him with all the bags of money, and
said, "O wood-cutter! pardon us for our misdoings! Here
are all the bags of money that we stole from you."

With his money and the ring, the wood-cutter soon became
the richest man in his town. He lived happily with his wife
the rest of his days, and left a large heritage to his children.

So Mahirap, with five centavos only, succeeded in making
the wood-cutter rich.

(b) LUCAS THE ROPE-MAKER.[1]

Luis and Isco were intimate friends. They lived in a country
called Bagdad. Though these two friends had been brought
up together in the same school, their ideas were different. Luis
believed that gentleness and kindness were the second heaven,
while Isco's belief was that wealth was the source of happiness
and peace in life.

One day, while they were eating, Isco said, "Don't you believe, my friend, that a rich man, however cruel he may be, is
known everywhere and has great power over all his people?
A poor man may be gentle and kind, but then he is disdainfully
looked upon by his neighbors."

"Oh," answered Luis, "I know it, but to me everybody is
the same. I love them all, and I am not enchanted by anything
that glisters."

"My friend," said Isco, "our conversation is becoming serious.
Let us take a walk this afternoon and see how these theories
work out in the lives of men."

That afternoon Luis and Isco went to a town called Cohija.
On their way they saw a rope-maker, Lucas by name, who by
his condition showed his great suffering from poverty. He
approached Lucas and gave him a roll of paper money, saying,
"Now, Lucas, take this money and spend it judiciously."

Lucas was overjoyed: he hardly knew what to do. When
he reached home, he related to his wife Zelima what had happened to him. As has been said, Lucas was very poor and was
a rope-maker. He had six little children to support; but he
had no money with which to feed them, nor could he get anything from his rope-making. Some days he could not sell

[1] Narrated by Elisa Cordero, a Tagalog from Pagsanjan, Laguna. Miss Cordero
says that the story is well known and is old.

even a yard of rope. When Lucas received the money from Luis, and had gone home and told his wife, he immediately went out again to buy food. He had one hundred pesos in paper money. He bought two pounds of meat, and a roll of *cañamo;*[1] and as there was some more money left, he put it in one of the corners of his hat. Unfortunately, as he was walking home, an eagle was attracted by the smell of the meat, and began flying about his head. He frightened the bird away; but it flew so fast that its claws became entangled in his hat, which was snatched off his head and carried away some distance. When he searched for the money, it was gone. He could not find it anywhere.

Lucas went home very sad. When his wife learned the cause of his sorrow, she became very angry. She scolded her husband roundly. As soon as the family had eaten the meat Lucas bought, they were as poor as before. They were even pale because of hunger.

One day Luis and Isco decided to visit Lucas and see how he was getting along. It happened that while they were passing in the same street as before, they saw Lucas weeping under a mango-tree near his small house. "What is the matter?" said Luis. "Why are you crying?"

Poor Lucas told them all that had happened to him, — how the money was lost, and how his wife had scolded him. At first Luis did not believe the rope-maker's story, and became angry at him. At last, however, when he perceived that Lucas was telling the truth, he pardoned him and gave him a thousand pesos.

Lucas returned home with delight, but his wife and children were not in the house. They were out asking alms from their neighbors. Lucas then hid the bulk of the money in an empty jar in the corner of the room, and then went out to buy food for his wife and children. While he was gone, his wife and children returned. They had not yet eaten anything.

Not long afterward a man came along selling rice. Zelima said to him, "Sir, can't you give us a little something to appease our hunger? I'll give you some *darak*[2] in exchange."

"Oh, yes!" said the man, "I'll give you some rice, but you do not need to give me anything."

Zelima took the rice gladly; and as she was looking for some-

---

[1] *Cañamo,* ordinarily a kind of coarse cloth made from hemp. Here the word probably means the thread from which hempen ropes are made.

[2] *Darak,* "bran, shorts, chaff."

thing with which to repay the man, she happened to see the empty jar in which her husband had secretly put his money. She filled the jar with *darak* and gave it to the rice-seller.

When Lucas came home, he was very happy. He told his wife about the money he had hidden. But when he found out that the money was gone, he was in despair: he did not know what to do. He scolded his wife for her carelessness. As he could not endure to see the suffering of his children, he tried to kill himself, but his children prevented him. At last he concluded to be quiet; for he thought, "If I hurt my wife, and she becomes sick, I can't stand it. I must take care of her."

Two months passed by, and Luis and Isco again visited their friend Lucas. While they were walking in the street, Luis found a big piece of lead. He picked it up and put it in his pocket. When they reached Lucas's house, they were astonished to see him in a more wretched condition than before. Luis asked what was the matter. Lucas related to him all that had occurred; but Luis just said, "Oh, no! you are fooling us. We will not believe you." Lucas was very sad. He asked pardon of Luis for his carelessness, and said, "Don't increase the burden of my suffering by your scolding!"

Now, Luis was by nature gentle and pitiful. He could not endure to see his friend suffering. So he gave him the lead he had found in the street, saying, "Now, take care of that! Maybe your wealth will come from it." Luis accepted the lead unwillingly, for he thought that Luis was mocking him.

When Lucas went into the house, he threw the lead away in the corner, and went to sleep. During the night a neighbor knocked at their door, asking for a piece of lead for her husband. The neighbor said, "My husband is going fishing early in the morning, and he asked me to buy him some lead for his line, but I forgot it. I know he will scold me if I don't have some ready for him." Lucas, who was wakened by the talk, told his wife to get the lead he had thrown in the corner. When Zelima found it, she gave it to their neighbor, who went away happy, promising that she would bring them the first fish her husband should catch.

The next morning Lucas woke very late. The neighbor was already there with a big fish, and Zelima was happy at having so much to eat. While she was cleaning the fish, she found a bright stone inside it. As she did not know of the value of the stone, she gave it to her youngest son to play with; but when the other children saw it, they quarrelled with their brother, and tried to take it away from him. Lucas, too, was ignorant of the fact that the stone was worth anything.

In front of their house lived a rich man named Don Juan. When he heard the noise of his neighbor's children quarrelling, he sent his wife to see what was the matter. Don Juan's wife saw the stone, and wanted to have it very much. She asked Zelima to sell it to her, but Zelima said that she would wait and ask her husband. The rich man's wife went home and told her husband about the jewel. He went to Lucas's house, and offered the rope-maker a thousand pesos for the stone; but Lucas refused, for now he suspected that it was worth more than that. At last he sold it for twenty thousand pesos.

Lucas was now a rich man. He bought clothes for his wife and children, renewed his house, which was falling to pieces, and bought a machine for making rope. As his business increased, he bought another machine. But although Lucas was the richest man in town, he was very kind. His house was open to every comer. He supported crippled persons, and gave alms to the poor.

When Luis and Isco visited Lucas the last time, they were surprised and at the same time delighted to see him so rich. Lucas did not know how to thank them. He gave a banquet in honor of these two men. After the feast was over, Lucas told his friends every detail of all that had happened to him, — how he had lent the lead, how his wife had found the stone in the fish, and how a rich man had bought it for twenty thousand pesos.

Luis was now convinced that Lucas was honest, and had told the truth on former occasions. Lucas lived in his big house happily and in peace with his wife and children.

NOTES.

These two Tagalog stories are probably derived from the same ultimate source; the second, "Lucas the Rope-Maker," being very much closer to the original. That source is the "History of Khevajah Hasan al-Habbal" in the "Arabian Nights Entertainments" (see Burton's translation, Supplemental Nights, III : 341–366). There is also a Tagalog literary version of this story, — "Life of a Rope-maker in the Kingdom of Bagdad," by Franz Molteni. I have at present no copy of this chap-book; but the work may safely be dated 1902–05, as those were the years in which Molteni published. This story follows faithfully the "Arabian Nights" tale. The two rich friends are Saadi and Saad, and the name of the rope-maker is Cojia Hasan.

Our second folk-tale (*b*) seems to stand half way between this literary version and "The Rich and the Poor," — not chronologically, to be sure, but so far as fidelity to the Arabian story is concerned. Although the events are practically the same in (*b*) and in Molteni, the proper names differ throughout. It is possible that (*b*) derives from an earlier Tagalog literary version that is no longer extant. (*a*) is definitely localized on Laguna de Bay, and the story as a whole seems thoroughly native. It is likely much older than either of the other two forms.

A Bengal tale somewhat similar to these is to be found in McCulloch's "Bengali Household Tales," No. III; it is also connected with the Dr. Knowall cycle (our No. 1). Caballero has a Spanish story (see Ingram, "Dame Fortune and Don Money"). For a discussion of the continuously unlucky hero, see Clouston 2, 489–493. In Ralston 1, 195 f., may be found a group of stories dealing with luck. Compare also Thorpe's "Yule-tide Stories," 460 f., for the North German story of "The Three Gifts."

For the "ejaculation guess" in No. 13(*a*), see notes to No. 1 (pp. 7–8).

14. (*a*) THE KING AND THE DERVISH.[1]

Once there lived a young and brave king with his gentle and loving wife. Both had enjoyed an easy, comfortable, and, best of all, happy life. The king ruled his people well. The queen was a good wife as well as a good sovereign: she always cheered her husband when he was sad.

One day a dervish came to the palace. He told the king that he possessed magical power, and straightway they became friends. This dervish had the power to leave his body and enter that of a dead animal or person. Now, the king was fond of hunting, and once he took his new friend with him to shoot deer. After a few hours of hard chasing, they succeeded in killing a buck. To show his power, the dervish left his body and entered that of the dead deer. Then he resumed his former shape. The king was very anxious to be able to do the same thing; whereupon the dervish gave him minute instructions, and taught him the necessary charms. Then the king

[1] Narrated by José M. Hilario of Batangas, Batangas, who heard the story from his father, a Tagalog.

left his body, and took possession of that of the deer. In an instant the dervish entered the king's body and went home as the monarch. He gave orders that a deer with certain marks should be hunted out and killed. The true king was very unhappy, especially when he saw his own men chasing him to take his life.

In his wanderings through the forest, he saw a dead nightingale. He left the deer's body and entered the bird's. Now he was safe, so he flew to his palace. He sang so sweetly, that the queen ordered her attendants to catch him. He gladly allowed himself to be caught, and to be cared for by the queen. Whenever the dervish took the bird in his hands, the bird pecked him; but the beautiful singer always showed signs of satisfaction when the queen smoothed his plumage.

Not long after the bird's capture, a dog died in the palace. The king underwent another change: he left the bird's body and entered that of the dog. On waking up in the morning, the queen found that her pet was dead. She began to weep. Unable to see her so sad, the dervish comforted her, and told her that he would give the bird life again. Consequently he left the king's body and entered the bird's. Seeing his chance, the real king left the dog's body and resumed his original form. He then went at once to the cage and killed the ungrateful bird, the dervish.

The tender queen protested against the king's act of cruelty; but when she heard that she had been deceived by the dervish, she died of grief.

(*b*) THE MYSTERIOUS BOOK.[1]

Once upon a time there lived a poor father and a poor son. The father was very old, and was named Pedro. The son's name was Juan. Although they were very poor, Juan was afraid of work.

One day the two did not have a single grain of rice in the house to eat. Juan now realized that he would have to find some work, or he and his father would starve. So he went to a neighboring town to seek a master. He at last found one in the person of Don Luzano, a fine gentleman of fortune.

Don Luzano treated Juan like a son. As time went on, Don Luzano became so confident in Juan's honesty, that he began to intrust him with the most precious valuables in the house.

---

[1] Narrated by Leopoldo Uichanco, a Tagalog from Calamba, La Laguna.

One morning Don Luzano went out hunting. He left Juan alone in the house, as usual. While Juan was sweeping and cleaning his master's room, he caught sight of a highly polished box lying behind the post in the corner. Curious to find out what was inside, he opened the box. There appeared another box. He opened this box, and another box still was disclosed. One box appeared after another until Juan came to the seventh. This last one contained a small triangular-shaped book bound in gold and decorated with diamonds and other precious gems. Disregarding the consequences that might follow, Juan picked up the book and opened it. Lo! at once Juan was carried by the book up into the air. And when he looked back, whom did he see? No other than Don Luzano pursuing him, with eyes full of rage. He had an enormous deadly-looking bolo in his hand.

As Don Luzano was a big man, he could fly faster than little Juan. Soon the boy was but a few yards in front of his antagonist. It should also be known that the book had the wonderful power of changing anybody who had laid his hands on it, or who had learned by heart one of its chapters, into whatever form that person wished to assume. Juan soon found this fact out. In an instant Juan had disappeared, and in his place was a little steed galloping as fast as he could down the street. Again, there was Don Luzano after him in the form of a big fast mule, with bubbling and foaming mouth, and eyes flashing with hate. The mule ran so fast, that every minute seemed to be bringing Juan nearer his grave.

Seeing his danger, Juan changed himself into a bird, — a pretty little bird. No sooner had he done so than he saw Don Luzano in the form of a big hawk about to swoop down on him. Then Juan suddenly leaped into a well he was flying over, and there became a little fish. Don Luzano assumed the form of a big fish, and kept up the chase; but the little fish entered a small crack in the wall of the well, where the big fish could not pursue him farther. So Don Luzano had to give up and go home in great disappointment.

The well in which Juan found himself belonged to three beautiful princesses. One morning, while they were looking into the water, they saw the little fish with its seven-colored scales, moving gracefully through the water. The eldest of the maidens lowered her bait, but the fish would not see it. The second sister tried her skill. The fish bit the bait; but, just as it was being drawn out of the water, it suddenly released its hold. Now the youngest sister's turn came. The fish allowed itself to be caught and held in the tender hands of this beautiful girl. She placed the little fish in a golden basin of water and took it to her room, where she cared for it very tenderly.

Several months later the king issued a proclamation throughout his realm and other neighboring kingdoms, saying that the youngest princess was sick. "To any one who can cure her," he said, "I promise to give one-half of my kingdom." The most skilful doctors had already done the best they could, but all their efforts were in vain. The princess seemed to grow worse and worse every day. "Ay, what foolishness!" exclaimed Don Luzano when he heard the news of the sick princess. "The sickness! Pshaw! That's no sickness, never in the wide world!"

The following morning there was Don Luzano speaking with the king. "I promise to cure her," said Don Luzano. "I have already cured many similar cases."

"And your remedy will do her no harm?" asked the king after some hesitation.

"No harm, sir, no harm. Rely on my honor."

"Very well. And you shall have half of my kingdom if you are successful."

"No, I thank you, your Majesty. I, being a faithful subject, need no payment whatever for any of my poor services. As a token from you, however, I should like to have the fish that the princess keeps in her room."

"O my faithful subject!" exclaimed the king in joy. "How good you are! Will you have nothing except a poor worthless fish?"

"No more: that's enough."

"Well, then," returned the king, "prepare your remedy, and on the third day we shall apply it to the princess. You can go home now, and you may be sure that you shall have the fish."

Don Luzano took his leave of the king, and then went home. On the third day this daring magician came back to the palace to apply his remedy to the princess. Before he began any part of the treatment, however, he requested that the fish be given to him. The king consented to his request: but as he was about to dip his hand into the basin, the princess boldly stopped him. She pretended to be angry on the ground that Don Luzano would soil with his hands the golden basin of the monarch. She told him to hold out his hands, and she would pour the fish into them. Don Luzano did as he was told: but, before the fish could reach his hands, the pretty creature jumped out. No fish now could be seen, but in its stead was a beautiful gold ring adorning the finger of the princess. Don Luzano tried to snatch the ring, but, as the princess jerked her hand back, the ring fell to the floor, and in its place were countless little *mungo* [1] seeds scattered about the room. Don Luzano instantly took the form of a greedy crow, devouring the seeds with extraordinary speed. Juan, who was contained in one of the seeds that had rolled beneath the feet of the princess, suddenly became a cat, and, rushing out, attacked the bird. As soon as you could wink your eyes or snap your fingers, the crow was dead, miserably torn to pieces. In place of the cat stood Juan in an embroidered suit, looking like a gay young prince.

"This is my beloved," confessed the princess to her father as she pointed to Juan. The king forgave his daughter for concealing from him the real condition of her life, and he gladly welcomed his new son-in-law. Prince Juan, as we shall now call our friend, was destined to a life of peace and joy. He was rid of his formidable antagonist; he had a beautiful princess (who was no longer sick) for a wife; and he had an excellent chance of inheriting the throne. There is no more.

NOTES.

A third form (c) I have only in abstract; it is entitled "The Priest and his Pupil:" —

A boy learns a number of magic tricks from the priest, his master. He changes himself into a hog, and is sold to the priest; then he runs away, transforms himself into a horse, and is again sold to his master for much money. The horse breaks loose and runs off. The priest now realizes the truth, and, transforming himself into a horse, pursues the first horse. When they come to a river, the first horse becomes a small fish, and the second a large fish, and the chase continues. Then the two fish become birds wheeling aloft, the larger chasing the smaller. As he flies over the palace of the King of Persia, the boy becomes a small cocoanut-ring, and drops on to the finger of the princess. The defeated priest returns home, and threatens the King of Persia with war if he will not give up the ring. When the priest calls at the court, the boy has changed himself from a ring into a dog. The priest is told that he shall have the ring provided he

[1] *Mungo*, a small legume about the size and shape of a lentil. Same as *mongo*.

becomes a duck. Immediately when he has complied, the dog seizes him and kills him. The hero later weds the princess.

A fourth form (*d*) is the Tagalog story "The Battle of the Enchanters," printed in JAFL 20 : 309–310.

Both of these variants (*c* and *d*) bear a close resemblance to our second story of "The Mysterious Book," and all three probably go back to a common source; but that source is not the "Arabian Nights" (as Gardner hints, JAFL 20 : 309, note), although the second calendar's tale in that collection represents one form of the "Transformation Combat" cycle. These three Filipino variants are members of the large family of Oriental and European folk-tales of which the Norse "Farmer Weathersky" (Dasent, No. XLI) or the German "The Thief and his Master" (Grimm, No. 68) may be taken as representatives. The essential elements of this form of the "Transformation Combat" cycle have been noted by Bolte-Polívka (2 : 61) as follows:—

A A father gives his son up to a magician to be taught, the condition being that the father at the end of a year must be able to recognize his son in animal form.

B The son secretly learns magic and thieving.

C In the form of a dog, ox, horse, he allows his father to sell him, finally to the magician himself, to whom the father, contrary to directions, also hands over the bridle.

D¹ The son, however, succeeds in slipping off the bridle, and (D²) overcomes the magician in a transformation combat (hare, fish, bird, etc.).

D³ Usually, after the hero has flown in the guise of a bird to a princess and is concealed by her in the form of a ring, the magician appears to the king her father, who has become sick, and demands the ring as payment for a cure. The princess drops the ring, and there lies in its place a pile of millet-seed, which the magician as a hen starts to pick up; but the hero quickly turns himself into a fox, and bites off the hen's head.

With slight variations from the formula as given above, these elements are distributed thus in our stories:—

(*b*) . . . . BD²D³
(*c*) . . . . BCD²D³
(*d*) . . . . BCD¹D³

Bolte and Polívka (2 : 66) cite a number of Oriental versions of the story (Hindoo and Arabian) which in their main outlines are practically identical with our variants. In the absence of the story in any Spanish version, it seems most reasonable to look to India as the source of our tales; unless, as is possible, they were introduced into the Islands from Straparola (viii, 5), whose collection of stories might have found their way there through the Spaniards. For further discussions of this cycle, see Macculloch, 164–166; Clouston 3, I : 413 ff.; Köhler-Bolte, I : 138 ff., 556 f.; Benfey, I : 410–413.

Our first story, "The King who became a Deer, a Nightingale, and a Dog," while containing the "transformation combat" between magician and pupil, differs from the other members of this group in one important respect: the transformation cannot take place unless there is a dead body for the transformer's spirit to enter. It is also to be noted that, as soon as a spirit leaves a body, that body becomes dead. There can be no doubt that this story of ours is derived from the 57th to the 60th "Days" in the "1001 Days" (Persian Tales, 1 : 212 ff.; Cabinet des Fées, XIV, p. 326 f.), the story of Prince Fadlallah. For other variants of this cycle, see Benfey, 1 : 122 f., especially 126. The Persian story might have reached the Philippines through the medium of the French translation, of which our tale appears to be little more than the baldest abstract.

Benfey explains the "transformation combat" as originating in the disputes between Buddhists and Brahmans. Doubtless the story first grew up in India. A very ancient Oriental analogue, which has not hitherto been pointed out, I believe, is the Hebrew account of Aaron's magical contest with the Egyptian sorcerers (see Exodus, vii, 9–12). Compare also the betting-contest between the two kings in No. 1 of this collection, and see the notes.

15. THE MIRACULOUS COW.[1]

There was once a farmer driving home from his farm in his carreton.[2] He had tied his cow to the back of his cart, as he was accustomed to do every evening on his way home. While he was going along the road, two boys saw him. They were Felipe and Ambrosio. Felipe whispered to Ambrosio, "Do you see the cow tied to the back of that carreton? Well, if you will untie it, I will take it to our house."

Ambrosio approached the carreton slowly, and untied the cow. He handed the rope to Felipe, and then tied himself in the place of the animal.

"Come on, Ambrosio! Don't be foolish! Come on with me!" whispered Felipe impatiently.

"No, leave me alone! Go home, and I will soon be there!" answered the cunning Ambrosio.

After a while the farmer happened to look back. What a surprise for him! He was frightened to find a boy instead of his cow tied to the carreton. "Why are you there? Where is my cow?" he shouted furiously. "Rascal, give me my cow!"

---

[1] Narrated by Adela Hidalgo, a Tagalog from Manila, who heard the story from another Tagalog student.

[2] *Carreton*, a heavy two-wheeled springless cart drawn by a carabao.

"Oh, don't be angry with me!" said Ambrosio. "Wait a minute, and I will tell you my story. Once, when I was a small boy, my mother became very angry with me. She cursed me, and suddenly I was transformed into a cow; and now I am changed back into my own shape. It is not my fault that you bought me: I could not tell you not to do so, for I could not speak at the time. Now, generous farmer, please give me my freedom! for I am very anxious to see my old home again."

The farmer did not know what to do, for he was very sorry to lose his cow. When he reached home, he told his wife the story. Now, his wife was a kind-hearted woman; so, after thinking a few minutes, she said, "Husband, what can we do? We ought to set him free. It is by the great mercy of God that he has been restored to his former self."

So the wily boy got off. He rejoined his friend, and they had a good laugh over the two simple folks.

NOTES.

Like the preceding, this story is of Oriental origin. It must have grown up among a people to whom the idea of metempsychosis was well known, but who at the same time held a skeptical view of that doctrine. Whether or not this droll reached the Philippines by way of the Iberian Peninsula, is hard to say definitely. A Spanish folk-tale narrating practically the same incident is to be found in C. Sellers, pp. 1 ff.: "The Ingenious Student." There the shrewd but poverty-stricken Juan Rivas steals a mule from the pack-train of a simple-minded muleteer; and while the companions escape with the animal and sell it, Juan puts on the saddle and bridle, and takes the place of the stolen beast. His explanation that he has just fulfilled a long period of punishment imposed on him by Mother Church satisfies the astonished mule-owner, and Juan escapes with only the admonition never again to incur the wrath of his spiritual Mother.

The oldest version with which I am familiar is the "Arabian Nights" anecdote of "The Simpleton and the Sharper" (Burton's translation, v : 83). This story is practically identical with ours, except that the Filipino version lacks the additional final comical touch of the Arabian. The owner of the ass, after the adventure with the sharper, went to the market to buy another beast, "and, lo! he beheld his own ass for sale. And when he recognized it, he advanced to it, and, putting his mouth to its ear, said, 'Wo to thee, O unlucky! Doubtless thou hast returned to intoxication and beaten thy mother again. By Allah, I will never again buy thee!'" The sharper had previously given as the reason of his transformation the fact that his mother had cursed him when he, in a fit of drunkenness, had beaten her. Clouston tells this story in his "Book of Noodles" (81–83).

Stories of the transformation of a child into an animal because of a parent's curse are found all over Europe. This *motif* is also widespread in the Philippines among both the Christian and the Pagan tribes. It is usually incorporated in an origin story, such as "The Origin of Monkeys." For this belief among a non-Christian people in northern Luzon, see Cole, Nos. 65–67. None of these tales, however, assume the droll form: they are told as serious etiological myths.

16. THE CLEVER HUSBAND AND WIFE.[1]

Pedro had been living as a servant in a doctor's house for more than nine years. He wanted very much to have a wife, but he had no business of any kind on which to support one.

One day he felt very sad. His look of dejection did not escape the notice of his master, who said, "What is the matter, my boy? Why do you look so sad? Is there anything I can do to comfort you?"

"Oh, yes!" said Pedro.

"What do you want me to do?" asked the doctor.

"Master," the man replied, "I want a wife, but I have no money to support one."

"Oh, don't worry about money!" replied his master. "Be ready to-morrow, and I will let you marry the woman you love."

The next day the wedding was held. The doctor let the couple live in a cottage not far from his hacienda,[2] and he gave them two hundred pieces of gold. When they received the money, they hardly knew what to do with it, as Pedro had never had any business of any sort. "What shall we do after we have spent all our money?" asked the wife. "Oh, we can ask the doctor for more," answered Pedro.

Years passed by, and one day the couple had not even a cent with which to buy food. So Pedro went to the doctor and asked him for some money. The doctor, who had always been kind to them, gave him twenty pieces of gold; but these did not last very long, and it was not many days before the money was all spent. The husband and wife now thought of another way by which they could get money from the doctor.

---

[1] Narrated by Elisa Cordero, a Tagalog from Pagsanjan, La Laguna. She heard the story from her servant.

[2] *Hacienda*, a ranch of considerable extent. The fact of Pedro's living at some distance from the doctor might account for the success of the ruse.

Early one day Pedro went to the doctor's house weeping. He said that his wife had died, and that he had nothing with which to pay for her burial. (He had rubbed onion-juice on his eyes, so that he looked as if he were really crying.) When the doctor heard Pedro's story, he pitied the man, and said to him, "What was the matter with your wife? How long was she sick?"

"For two days," answered Pedro.

"Two days!" exclaimed the doctor, "why did you not call me, then? We should have been able to save her. Well, take this money and see that she gets a decent burial."

Pedro returned home in good spirits. He found his wife Marta waiting for him at the door, and they were happy once more; but in a month the money was all used up, and they were on the point of starving again.

Now, the doctor had a married sister whom Pedro and his wife had worked for off and on after their marriage. Pedro told his wife to go to the doctor's sister, and tell her that he was dead and that she had no money to pay for the burial. Marta set out, as she was told; and when she arrived at the sister's house, the woman said to her, "Marta, why are you crying?"

"My husband is dead, and I have no money to pay for his burial," said Marta, weeping.

"You have served us well, so take this money and see that masses are said for your husband's soul," said the kind-hearted mistress.

That evening the doctor visited his sister to see her son who was sick. The sister told him that Marta's husband had died. "No," answered the doctor, "it was Marta who died." They argued and argued, but could not agree; so they finally decided to send one of the doctor's servants to see which one was dead. When Pedro saw the servant coming, he told his wife to lie flat and stiff in the bed as if she were dead; and when the servant entered, Pedro showed him his dead wife.

The servant returned, and told the doctor and his sister that it was Marta who was dead; but the sister would not believe him, for she said that perhaps he was joking. So they sent another servant. This time Marta made Pedro lie down stiff and flat in the bed; and when the servant entered the house, he saw the man lying as if dead. So he hurried back and told the doctor and his sister what he had seen. Now neither knew

what to believe. The next morning, therefore, the doctor and
his sister together visited the cottage of Pedro. They found
the couple both lying as if dead. After examining them,
however, the doctor realized that they were merely feigning
death. He was so pleased by the joke, and so glad to find his
old servants alive, that he took them home with him and made
them stay at his house.

NOTES.

This droll seems to be derived from the "1001 Nights" (271st to
290th nights of the Breslau edition, "The Story of Abu-l-hasan the
Wag, or the Sleeper Awakened"). The Arabian story is not only
more detailed, but contains much preliminary matter that is altogether lacking in our story. In fact, the two are so dissimilar, except for the trick the husband and wife play on their benefactor to
get more money, that it is hard to demonstrate an historical connection
between the two.

I have in text and translation (the latter unpublished) a Tagalog
metrical version of the Arabian story. This metrical version, which is
told in 1240 lines, is entitled (in translation) "The Story of Abu-
Hasan, Who dreamed when he was Awake. Poem by Franz Molteni.
First edition, Manila." Although this work is not dated, it probably
appeared after 1900. In general, the Tagalog poem agrees with the
"1001 Nights" story, though it differs in details. An analysis of the
differences in the first part of the narratives need not concern us
here, as our folk-tale is connected with only the last third of the
romance.

In the metrical version, after Abu, through the favor of the sultan, has
been married to Nuzhat, one of the ladies-in-waiting, the new couple begin to live extravagantly, and soon exhaust the dowry and wedding gifts.
Then after much deliberation Abu decides to go to the sultan, tell him
that Nuzhat his wife is dead, and ask for money for her burial. The ruse
succeeds; Abu returns home with a thousand ounces of gold. He at once
counsels his wife to go to the sultana with a similar story that he is dead
and that money is needed for his funeral. Nuzhat, too, receives a thousand
ounces from the sultana. The sultan now visits his wife, and tells her
of the death of Nuzhat. She insists that it is Abu who is dead, and they
argue violently about the matter. Finally the sultan decides to send
one of his servants to report the truth. When Abu sees the servant coming,
he bids his wife lie on the bier, and the servant is shown her corpse. He
reports that it is Nuzhat who is dead. The sultana is enraged at the servant's statement, and sends her nurse for the truth. This time Abu lies
on the bier, and Nuzhat shows his body to the nurse. When the old woman
returns with her contradictory story, the sultan's servant calls her a black
falsifying witch. At last the sultan and sultana themselves go to see.
Both Abu and Nuzhat are found lying as if dead. The sultan and his

wife now argue so violently as to which of their favorites died first, that the deceitful couple, fearful of the outcome, kneel before their rulers, confess the trick, and beg forgiveness. The royal pair laugh at the joke, and give Abu and his wife enough to support them the rest of their days.

The last part of the Arabian story is substantially as given above, only Nuzhat goes first to the sultana with the account of Abu's death, after which Abu visits the sultan and tells him of Nuzhat's death. Then follows the quarrel between the sultan and his wife over the contradictory reports brought back by the two messengers. All four go in person to discover the truth. Both Nuzhat and Abu are found dead. Sultan: "I would give a thousand pieces of gold to know which died first." Abu jumps up, says that he died first, and claims the reward. Ending as above.

This story of Abu is also told as a folk-tale in Simla, northern India (Dracott, 166–173), where it retains the Arabic title, "Abul Hussain," and is almost identical with the "1001 Nights" version. In the Simla tale, however, the despatching of servants to learn which one is really dead is lacking. The sultan and his wife together go to Abul's house, and find both dead. "If we could only find out which died first!" etc.

Our story, the Tagalog folk-tale, is told almost as an anecdote. The sultan has been transformed into a doctor; the sultana, into the doctor's sister; Abu, into a poor servant, Pedro; and Nuzhat, into Marta. The glitter of the Oriental harem has vanished, as indeed has also the first two-thirds of the story. The descent in setting and language has been so great, that I am inclined to suspect that this droll has existed — at least, in one family — for a long time. It could hardly have been derived from Molteni's poetic version. For the same sort of relationship between another folk-tale and an "Arabian Nights" story, see No. 13 and the notes.

17. THE THREE BROTHERS.[1]

Once upon a time, when wishing was having, there dwelt in the joyous village of Delight a poor farmer, Tetong, with his loving wife Maria. His earning for a day's toil was just enough to sustain them; yet they were peaceful and happy. Nevertheless they thought that their happiness could not be complete unless they had at least one child. So morning and night they would kneel before their rustic altar and pray God to grant them their desire. As they were faithful in their purpose, their wish was fulfilled. A son was born to them, and joy filled their

[1] Narrated by Gregorio Frondoso, a Bicol from Tigaon, Camarines. The narrator says, "This story was told to me by an old man who happened to stay at our house one night. He was a traveller. I was then a little boy."

hearts. The couple's love for their child grew so intense, that they craved for another, and then for still another. The Lord was mindful of their prayers; and so, as time went on, two more sons were born to them. The second son they named Felipe; and the youngest, Juan. The name of the oldest was Pedro. All three boys were lovely and handsome, and they greatly delighted their parents.

In the course of time, however, when they were about eight, seven, and six years old, Pedro, Felipe, and Juan became monstrously great eaters. Each would eat at a single meal six or seven *chupas* [1] of rice: consequently their father was obliged to work very hard, for he had five mouths to feed. In this state of affairs, Tetong felt that, although these children had been born to him and his wife as an increase of their happiness, they would finally exhaust what little he had. Nor was Maria any the less aware of the gluttony of her sons. By degrees their love for their sons ripened into hatred, and at last Tetong resolved to do away with his children.

One night, while he and his wife were sitting before their dim light and their three sons were asleep, Tetong said to his wife, "Do you not think it would be better to get rid of our sons? As you see, we are daily becoming poorer and poorer because of them. I have decided to cast them away into some distant wild forest, where they may feed themselves on fruits or roots."

On hearing these words of her husband, Maria turned pale: her blood ran cold in her veins. But what could she do? She felt the same distress as her husband. After a few moments of silence, she replied in a faltering voice, "My husband, you may do as you wish." Accordingly Tetong made ready the necessary provisions for the journey, which consisted of a sack of rice and some preserved fish.

The next morning, on the pretext of planting camotes [2] and corn on the hill some thirty miles away from the village, he ordered his sons to accompany him. When they came to a forest, their father led them through a circuitous path, and at last took them to the hill. As soon as they arrived there, each set to work: one cut down trees, another built a shed, and the others cleared a piece of land in which to plant the camotes and corn.

[1] *Chupa*, a measure, equal roughly to about four handfuls of raw rice.
[2] *Camotes*, sweet potatoes.

After two weeks their provisions were almost used up. Tetong then called his sons together, and said to them, "My sons, we have very little to eat now. I am going to leave you for some days. I am going back to our village to get rice and fish. Be very good to one another, and continue working, for our camotes will soon have roots, and our corn ears." Having said these words, he blessed them and left.

Days, weeks, and months elapsed, but Tetong did not re-appear. The corn bore ears, and the camotes produced big sound roots; but these were not sufficient to support the three brothers. Nor did they know the way back to their home. At last, realizing that their father and mother did not care for them any more, they agreed to wander about and look for food. They roved through woods, thickets, and jungles. At last, fatigued and with bodies tired and bruised, they came to a wide river, on the bank of which they stopped to rest. While they were bewailing their unhappy lot, they caught sight, on the other side of the river, of banana-trees with bunches of ripe fruit. They determined to get those fruits; but, as they knew nothing about swimming, they had to cut down bamboos and join them together to bridge the stream. So great was their hunger, that each ate three bunches of the ripe bananas. After they had satisfied their hunger, they continued on their way refreshed.

Soon they came upon a dark abyss. Curious to know what it might contain, the three brothers looked down into it, but they could not see the bottom. Not contented, however, with only seeing into the well, they decided to go to the very bottom: so they gathered vines and connected them into a rope.

Pedro was the first to make the attempt, but he could not stand the darkness. Then Felipe tried; but he too became frightened, and could not stay long in the dark. At last Juan's turn came. He went down to the very bottom of the abyss, where he found a vast plain covered with trees and bushes and shrubs. On one side he saw at a short distance a green house. He approached the house, and saw a most beautiful lady sitting at the door. When she saw him, she said to him in friendly tones, "Hail, Juan! I wonder at your coming, for no earthly creature has ever before been here. However, you are welcome to my house." With words of compliment Juan accepted her invitation, and entered the house. He was kindly received by that lady, Maria. They fell in love with each other, and she agreed to go with Juan to his home.

They had talked together but a short while, when Maria suddenly told Juan to hide, for her guardian, the giant, was coming. Soon the monster appeared, and said to Maria in a terrible voice, "You are concealing some one. I smell human flesh." She denied that she was, but the giant searched all corners of the house. At last Juan was found, and he boldly fought with the monster. He received many wounds, but they were easily healed by Maria's magic medicine. After a terrific struggle, the giant was killed. Maria applauded Juan's valor. She gave him food, and related stories to him while he was eating. She also told him of her neighbor Isabella, none the less beautiful than she. Juan, in turn, told her of many things in his own home that were not found in that subterranean plain.

When he had finished eating and had recovered his strength, Juan said that they had better take Isabella along with them too. Maria agreed to this. Accordingly Juan set out to get Isabella. When he came to her house, she was looking out the window. As soon as she saw him, she exclaimed in a friendly manner, "O Juan! what have you come here for? Since my birth I have never seen an earthly creature like you!"

"Madam," returned Juan in a low voice, "my appearance before you is due to some Invisible Being I cannot describe to you." The moment Isabella heard these words, she blushed. "Juan," she said, "come up!"

Juan entered, and related to her his unfortunate lot, and how he had found the abyss. Finally, struck with Isabella's fascinating beauty, Juan expressed his love for her. They had not been talking long together, when footsteps were heard approaching nearer and nearer. It was her guardian, the seven-headed monster. "Isabella," it growled, with an angry look about, "some human creature must be somewhere in the house."

"There is nobody in the house but me," she exclaimed. The monster, however, insisted. Seeking all about the house, it at last discovered Juan, who at once attacked with his sword. In this encounter he was also successful, cutting off all the seven heads of the monster.

With great joy Juan and Isabella returned to Maria's house. Then the three went to the foot of the well. There Juan found vine still suspended. He tied one end of it around Isabella's waist, and then she was pulled up by the two brothers waiting above. When they saw her, Pedro and Felipe each claimed her, saying almost at the same time, "What a beauty! She is mine." Isabella assured them that there were other ladies below prettier than she. When he heard these words, Felipe dropped one end of the vine again. When Maria reached the top of the well, Felipe felt glad, and claimed her for himself. As the two brothers each had a maiden now, they would not drop the vine a third time; but finally Maria persuaded them to do so. On seeing only their brother's figure, however, the two unfeeling brothers let go of the vine, and Juan plunged back into the darkness. "O my friends!" said Maria, weeping, "this is not the way to treat a brother. Had it not been for him, we should not be here now." Then she took her magic comb, saying to it, "Comb, if you find Juan dead, revive him; if his legs and arms are broken, restore them." Then she dropped it down the well.

By means of this magic comb, Juan was brought back to life. The moment he was able to move his limbs, he groped his way in the dark, and finally he found himself in the same subterranean plain again. As he knew of no way to get back to earth, he made up his mind to accept his fate.

As he was lazily strolling about, he came to a leafy tree with spreading branches. He climbed up to take a siesta among its fresh branches. Just as he closed his eyes, he heard a voice calling, "Juan, Juan! Wake up! Go to the Land of the Pilgrims, for there your lot awaits you." He opened his eyes and looked about him, but he saw nothing. "It is only a bird," he said, "that is disturbing my sleep." So he shut his eyes again. After some moments the same voice was heard again from the top of the tree. He looked up, but he could not see any one. However, the voice continued calling to him so loudly, that he could not sleep. So he descended from the tree to find that land.

In his wanderings he met an old man wearing very ragged, worn-out clothes. Juan asked him about the Land of the Pilgrims. The old man said to him, "Here, take this piece of cloth, which, as you see, I have torn off my garment, and show it to a hermit you will find living at a little distance from here. Then tell him your wish." Juan took the cloth and went to the hermit. When the hermit saw Juan entering his courtyard without permission, he was very angry. "Hermit," said Juan, "I have come here on a very important mission. While I was sleeping among the branches of a tree, a bird sang to me repeatedly that I must go to the Land of the Pilgrims, where my lot awaits me. I resolved to look for this land. On my way I met an old man, who gave me this piece of cloth and told me to show it to you and ask you about this place I have mentioned." When the hermit saw the cloth, his anger was turned into sorrow and kindness. "Juan," he said, "I have been here a long time, but I have never seen that old man."

Now, this hermit had in his care all species of animals. He summoned them all into his courtyard, and asked each about the Land of the Pilgrims; but none could give any information. When he had asked them all in vain, the hermit told Juan to go to another hermit living some distance away.

Accordingly Juan left to find this hermit. At first, like the other, this hermit was angry on seeing Juan; but when he saw the piece of cloth, his anger was turned into pity and sorrow. Juan told him what he was looking for, and the hermit sounded a loud trumpet. In a moment there was an instantaneous rushing of birds of every description. He asked every one about the Land of the Pilgrims, but not one knew of the place. But just as Juan was about to leave, suddenly there came an eagle swooping down into the courtyard. When asked if it knew of the Land of the Pilgrims, it nodded its head. The hermit then ordered it to bear Juan to the Land of the Pilgrims. It willingly obeyed, and flew across seas and over mountains with Juan on its back. After Juan had been carried to the wished-for land, the eagle returned to its master.

Here Juan lived with a poor couple, who cared for him as if he were their own child, and he served them in turn. He asked them about the land they were living in. They told him that it was governed by a tyrannical king who had a beautiful daughter. They said that many princes who courted her had been put to death because they had failed to fulfil the tasks required of them. When Juan heard of this beautiful princess, he said to himself, "This is the lot that awaits me. She is to be my wife." So, in spite of the dangers he ran the risk of, he resolved to woo her.

One day, when her tutors were away, he made a kite, to which he fastened a letter addressed to the princess, and flew it. While she was strolling about in her garden, the kite suddenly swooped down before her. She was surprised, and wondered. "What impudent knave," she said, "ventures to let fall his kite in my garden?" She stepped towards the kite, looked at it, and saw the letter written in bold hand. She read it. After a few moments' hesitation, she replaced it with a letter of her own in which she told him to come under the window of her tower.

When he came there, the princess spoke to him in this manner: "Juan, if you really love me, you must undergo hardships. Show yourself to my father to-morrow, and agree to do all that he commands you to do. Then come back to me." Juan willingly promised to undertake any difficulties for her sake.

The next morning Juan waited at the stairway of the king's palace. The king said to him, "Who are you, and what do you come here for?"

"O king! I am Juan, and I have come here to marry your daughter."

"Very well, Juan, you can have your wish if you perform the task I set you. Take these grains of wheat and plant them in that hill, and to-morrow morning bring me, out of these same grains, newly baked bread for my breakfast. Then you shall be married immediately to my daughter. But if you fail to accomplish this task, you shall be beheaded."

Juan bowed his head low, and left. Sorrowful he appeared before the princess.

"What's the matter, Juan?" she said.

"O my dear princess! your father has imposed on me a task impossible to perform. He gave me these grains of wheat to be planted in that hill, and to-morrow he expects a newly baked loaf of bread from them."

"Don't worry, Juan. Go home now, and to-morrow show yourself to my father. The bread will be ready when he awakes."

The next morning Juan repaired to the palace, and was glad to find the bread already on the table. When the king woke up, he was astonished to see that Juan had performed the task.

"Now, Juan," said the king, "one more task for you. Under my window I have two big jars, — one full of mongo,[1] the other of very fine sand. I will mix them, and you have to assort them so that each kind is in its proper jar again." Juan

---

[1] *Mongo,* a variety of legume slightly smaller than the lentil (same as *mungo*).

promised to fulfil this task. He passed by the window of the princess, and told her what the king had said. "Go home and come back here to-morrow," she said to him. "The king will find the mongo and sand in their proper jars."

The next morning Juan went back to the palace. The king, just arisen from bed, looked out of the window, and was astounded to see the mongo and sand perfectly assorted. "Well, Juan," said the king, "you have successfully performed the tasks I required of you. But I have one thing more to ask of you. Yesterday afternoon, while my wife and I were walking along the seashore, my gold ring fell into the water. I want you to find it, and bring it to me to-morrow morning."

"Your desire shall be fulfilled, O king!" replied Juan.

He told the princess of the king's wish. "Come here to-morrow just before dawn," she said, "and bring a big basin and a bolo. We will go together to find the ring."

Just before dawn the next day he went to her tower, where she was waiting for him in the disguise of a village maid. They went to the seashore where the ring was supposed to have been lost. There the princess Maria — that was her name — said to him, "Now take your basin and bolo and cut me to pieces. Pour out the chopped mass into the water in which my father's ring was dropped, but take care not to let a single piece of the flesh fall to the ground!"

On hearing these words, Juan stood dumfounded, and began to weep. Then in an imploring tone he said, "O my beloved! I would rather have you chop my body than chop yours."

"If you love me," she said, "do as I tell you."

Then Juan reluctantly seized the bolo, and with closed eyes cut her body to pieces and poured the mass into the water where the ring was supposed to be. In five minutes there rose from the water the princess with the ring on her finger. But Juan fell asleep; and before he awoke, the ring fell into the water again.

"Oh, how little you love me!" she exclaimed. "The ring fell because you did not catch it quickly from my finger. Cut up my body as before, and pour the mass of flesh into the water again." Accordingly Juan cut her to pieces a second time, and again poured the mass into the water. Then in a short time Maria rose from the water with the ring on her finger; but Juan fell asleep again, and again the ring fell back into the water.

Now Maria was angry: so she cut a gash on his finger, and told him to cut her body to pieces and pour the mass out as before. At last the ring was found again. This time Juan was awake, and he quickly caught the ring as she rose from the water.

That morning Juan went before the king and presented the ring to him. When the monarch saw it, he was greatly astonished, and said to himself, "How does he accomplish all the tasks I have given him? Surely he must be a man of supernatural powers." Raising his head, he said to Juan, "Juan, you are indeed the man who deserves the hand of my daughter; but I want you to do me one more service. This will be the last. Fetch me my horse, for I want to go out hunting to-day." Now, this horse could run just as fast as the wind. It was a very wild horse, too, and no one could catch it except the king himself and the princess.

Juan promised, however, and repaired to Maria's tower. When she learned her father's wish, she went with Juan and helped him catch the horse. After they had caught it, she caught hers too. Then they returned to the palace. Juan and Maria now agreed to run away. So after Juan had tied the king's horse near the stairway, they mounted Maria's horse and rode off rapidly.

When the king could not find his daughter, he got on his horse and started in pursuit of Juan and Maria, who were now some miles ahead. But the king's horse ran so fast, that in a few minutes he had almost overtaken the fugitives. Maria, seeing her father behind them, dropped her comb, and in the wink of an eye a thick grove of bamboos blocked the king's way. By his order, a road was made through the bamboo in a very short time. Then he continued his chase; but just as he was about to overtake them a second time, Maria flung down her ring, and there rose up seven high hills behind them. The king was thus delayed again; but his horse shot over these hills as fast as the wind, so that in a few minutes he was once more in sight of the fugitives. This time Maria turned around and spat. Immediately a wide sea appeared behind them. The king gave up his pursuit, and only uttered these words: "O ungrateful daughter!" Then he turned back to his palace.

The young lovers continued their journey until they came to a small village. Here they decided to be married, so they at once went to the village priest. He married them that very day. Juan and Maria now determined to live in that place the rest of their lives, so they bought a house and a piece of land. As time went by, Juan thought of his parents.

One day he asked permission from his wife to visit his father and mother. "You may go," she said; "but remember not to let a single drop of your father's or mother's tears fall on your cheeks, for you will forget me if you do." Promising to remember her words, Juan set out.

When his parents saw him, they were so glad that they embraced him and almost bathed him with tears of joy. Juan forgot Maria. It happened that on the day Juan reached home, Felipe, his brother, was married to Maria, the subterranean lady, and a feast was being held in the family circle. The moment Maria recognized Juan, whom she loved most, she annulled her marriage with Felipe, and wanted to marry Juan. Accordingly the village was called to settle the question, and Maria and Juan were married that same day. The merry-making and dancing continued.

In the mean time there came, to the surprise of every one, a beautiful princess riding in a golden carriage drawn by fine horses. She was invited to the dance. While the people were enjoying themselves dancing and singing, they were suddenly drawn together around this princess to see what she was doing. She was sitting in the middle of the hall. Before her she had a dog chained. Then she began to ask the dog these questions: —

"Did you not serve a certain king for his daughter?"

"No!" answered the dog.

"Did he not give you grains of wheat to be planted in a hill, and the morning following you were to give him newly baked bread made from the wheat?"

"No!"

"Did he not mix together two jars of mongo and sand, then order you to assort them so that the mongo was in one jar and the sand in the other?"

"No!"

"Do you not remember when you and a princess went together to the seashore to find the ring of her father, and when you cut her body to pieces and poured the chopped mass into the water?"

When Juan, who was watching, heard this last question, he

rushed from the ring of people that surrounded her and knelt before her, saying, "O my most precious wife! I implore your forgiveness!" Then the new-comer, who was none other than Maria, Juan's true wife, embraced him, and their former love was restored. So the feast went on. To the great joy of Felipe, Maria, the subterranean lady, was given back to him; and the two couples lived happily the rest of their lives.

NOTES.

This story, which is a mixture of well-known *motifs* and incidents, really falls into two parts, though an attempt is made at the end to bind them together. The first part, ending with the treachery of the brothers after the hero has made his underground journey and rescued the two beautiful maidens from their giant captors, has resemblances to parts of the "Bear's Son" cycle. The second half of the story is a well-developed member of the "Forgotten Betrothed" cycle, preserving, in fact, all the characteristic incidents, and also prefacing to this whole section details that form a transition between it and part I. I am unable to point out any European parallels to the story as a whole, but analogues of both parts are very numerous. As the latter half constitutes the major portion of our story, we shall consider it first.

The fundamental and characteristic incidents of the "Forgotten Betrothed," cycle (sometimes called the "True Bride" cycle) are as follows: —

A The performance by the hero of difficult tasks through the help of the loved one, who is usually the daughter of a magician.

B The magic flight of the couple, either with transformations of themselves or with the casting behind them of obstacles to retard the pursuer.

C The forgetting of the bride by the hero because he breaks a taboo (the cause of the forgetting is usually a parental kiss, which the hero should have avoided).

D The re-awakened memory of the hero during his marriage ceremony or wedding feast with a new bride, either through the conversation of the true bride with an animal or through the true bride's kiss. In some forms of the story, the hero's memory is restored on the third of three nights sold to the heroine by the venial second bride.[1]

E The marriage of the hero and heroine.

Andrew Lang (Custom and Myth, 2d ed., 87–102) traces incidents A and B as far back as the myth of Jason, the earliest literary reference

[1] This episode is found in a Tagalog folk-tale collected by Gardner (JAFL 20 : 304). This folk-tale, it might be noted, is based directly on a *corrido*, The Story of the Life of Doña Maria of Murcia, Manila, 1909. The romance has been printed in Pampango and Tagalog. Retana (No. 4166) mentions an edition between 1860 and 1898, and one dated 1901 (No. 4307).

to which is in the Iliad (VII, 467; XXIII, 747). But this story does not contain the last three incidents: clearly they have come from some other source, and have been joined to the first two, — a natural process in the development of a folk-tale. The episode of the magic flight is very widely distributed: Lang mentions Zulu, Gaelic, Norse, Malagasy, Russian, Italian, and Japanese versions. Of the magic flight combined with the performance of difficult tasks set by the girl's father, the stories are no less widely scattered: Greece, Madagascar, Scotland, Russia, Italy, North America (Algonquins), Finland, Samoa (p. 94). The only reasonable explanation of these resemblances, according to Lang, is the theory of transmission; and if Mr. Lang, the champion of the "anthropological theory," must needs explain in this rather business-like way a comparatively simple tale, what but the transmission theory can explain far more complicated stories of five or six distinct incidents in the same sequence?

The "Forgotten Betrothed" cycle was clearly invented but once; when or where, we shall not attempt to say. But that its excellent combination of rapid, marvellous, and pathetic situations has made it a tale of almost universal appeal, is attested to by the scores of variants that have been collected within the last half-century and more. In his notes to Campbell's Gaelic story, "The Battle of the Birds," No. 2, Köhler cites Norwegian, Swedish, Italian, German, and Hungarian versions (Orient und Occident, 2 : 107). Ralston (pp. 132–133), Cosquin (2 : No. 32 and notes), Crane (No. xv and notes, pp. 343–344), Bolte (in his additions to Köhler, 1 : 170–174), and Bolte-Polívka (to Nos. 51, 56, 113) have added very full bibliographies. It is unnecessary here to list all the variants of this story that have been collected, but we will examine some of the analogues to our tale from the point of view of the separate incidents.

After the hero of our present story has been deserted by his treacherous brothers, and has found himself once more in the under-world, he is told by a mysterious voice to go to the Land of the Pilgrims, where he will find his fate. He meets an old man, who directs him to a hermit. The hermit, in turn, directs the youth to another hermit, who learns from an eagle where the Land of the Pilgrims is, and directs the bird to carry the youth thither. While the story does not state that the Land of the Pilgrims is on the "upper-world," we must suppose that it is, and that the eagle is the means whereby the hero escapes from the underground kingdom. In a large number of members of the "Bear's Son" cycle, to which, as has been said, the first part of our story belongs, this is the usual means of escape. The incident is also found in a large number of tales not connected otherwise with this group (see Cosquin, 2 : 141–144). It is sometimes combined with the quest for the water of life, with which in turn is connected the situation of the hero's being referred from one guide to another (giants, sages, hermits, etc.), as in our story (cf. Grimm, No. 97, and notes; also Bolte-Polívka to No. 97, especially 2 : 400; Thorpe, 158; Tawney, 1 : 206; Persian Tales, 2 : 171). This whole section appears to have been introduced as a transition between parts 1 and 2.

The second part of our story opens with the "bride-wager" incident (see Von Hahn, 1 : 54, "Oenomaosformel"), though I can point to no parallel of Juan's method of making love to the princess; that is, by means of a letter conveyed by a kite.

The *tasks* which the hero is obliged to perform vary greatly in the different members of the "Forgotten Betrothed" cycle. Juan has to plant wheat and bake bread from the ripened grain in twenty-four hours, separate a jar of mongo from a jar of sand, and fetch a ring from the sea. The first task imposed by the king has analogies in a number of European tales. In Groome's No. 34 the Devil says to the hero, "Here is one more task for you: drain the marsh, and plough it, and sow it, and to-morrow bring me roasted maize" (p. 106). In Groome's No. 7 the king says to the old man, "See this great forest! Fell it all, and make it a level field; and plough it for me, and break up all the earth; and sow it with millet by to-morrow morning. And mark well what I tell you: you must bring me a cake [made from the ripened millet-seed, clearly; see p. 23] made with sweet milk." Cosquin (2 : 24) cites a Catalan and a Basque story in which the hero has not only to fell a great forest, but to sow grain and harvest it. In kind this is the same sort of impossible task imposed on Truth in a Visayan story (JAFL 19 : 100–102), where the hero has to beget, and the princess his wife to bring forth, in one night, three children. Helpful eagles solve this difficulty for Truth by conveying to him three newly-born babes. The second task is a well-known one, and is found in many members of the "Grateful Animals" cycle. Usually it is ants, which the hero has earlier spared, that perform the service of separating two kinds of seed, etc. (see Tawney, 1 : 361 and note). The mixture of sand and mongo, in our story, is not a very happy conception. Originally it must have been either gravel and mongo, or else mongo and some other kind of lentil nearly resembling it in size. The third task, with the method of accomplishing it, is perhaps the most interesting of all. In a Samoan story of the "Forgotten Betrothed" cycle (Lang, *op. cit.*, p. 98), the heroine bids the hero cut her body into pieces and cast them into the sea. There she becomes a fish and recovers the ring. In a Catalan tale (Rondallayre, 1 : 41) the hero is also required to fetch a ring from the bottom of the sea. His loved one tells him to cut her to pieces, taking care not to let any part drop to the ground, and to throw all into the water. In spite of all his care, he lets fall to earth one drop of blood. The heroine recovers the ring, but lacks the first joint of her little finger when she resumes her original shape.

The "magic flight" is discussed by Cosquin (1 : 152–154) and Macculloch (167 ff.). Two kinds of transformation are to be noted in connection with this escape: the pursued either transform themselves, and thus escape detection by the pursuer, or else cast behind them magic objects, which turn into retarding and finally insurmountable obstacles in the path of the pursuer. In our story the transformations are of the second type, as they are in the story of "Pedro and the Witch" (No. 36). So far as I know, the first type does not occur in Filipino folk-tales. Both types are found frequently in Occidental *Märchen*, but in Oriental stories the second seems to predominate over the first (see Cosquin's citations of Oriental occurrences of this incident). In Somadeva (Tawney, 1 : 355 ff.) we have two flights and both types of escape. As to the details of the flight itself in our story, we may note that the comb becoming a thicket of thorns has many analogues. The ring becoming seven mountains suggests with its magic number an Oriental origin. With spittle turning into a lake or sea, compare similar transformations of drops of water and a bladder full of water (Macculloch, 171–172).

The incident of the "forgetting of the betrothed" is usually motivated with some sort of broken taboo. When the hero desires to visit his parents, and leaves his sweetheart outside the city, she usually warns him not to allow himself to be kissed. In a Gaelic *Märchen* he is forbidden to speak; sometimes he is warned by his wife not to eat, etc. (Köhler-Bolte, 172). In our story the taboo is somewhat unusual: the hero is to allow no tears of joy shed by his parents to fall on his cheeks. The idea behind this charge, however, is the same as that behind the forbidden kiss. With the taboo forbidding the partaking of food, compare the episode of the "Lotus-Eaters" in the Odyssey.

In most of the *Märchen* of this group the re-awakening of the memory of the hero is accomplished through the conversation of two birds (doves or hens) which the forgotten betrothed manages to introduce into the presence of her lover just before he is married to another (Köhler-Bolte, 172; Rittershaus, 150). In our story the heroine asks a dog questions about the tasks she had helped the hero perform. I can point to no exact parallel of this situation, though it agrees in general with the methods used in the other members of the group.

For the first part of our story (with the exception of the introduction), compare Köhler-Bolte, 292–296, 537–543; Gonzenbach, No. 58 and notes; F. Panzer's "Beowulf," *passim*. See also the notes to *Nos. 3* and 4 of this collection.

In connection with our story as a whole, I will cite in conclusion two native metrical romances that preserve many of the incidents we have been discussing. The first is a Pangasinan romance (of which I have not the text) entitled "Don Agustin, Don Pedro, and Don Juan." This story contains the pursuit by the three princes of a snake to cure the sick king their father (the "quest" *motif*), the descent into the well by the youngest brother, his fight with monsters in the underworld and his rescue of three princesses, the treachery of the older brothers, the final rescue of the hero by the youngest princess. While this story lacks the "forgotten-betrothed" *motif*, it is unquestionably related with the first part of our folk-tale.[1]

The second romance, which is one of the most popular and widespread in the Islands, having been printed in at least five of the dialects, — Tagalog, Pampango, Visayan, Ilocano, and Bicol, — I will synopsize briefly, because it is either the source of our folk-tale or has been derived from it. The fact that not all the literary versions agree entirely, and that the story as a folk-tale seems to be so universally known, makes it seem more likely that the second alternative expresses the truth; i.e., that the romance has been derived from the folk-tale. In the Tagalog version the title runs thus: "The Story of Three Princes, sons of King Fernando and Queen Valeriana in the Kingdom of Berbania. The Adarna Bird." The poem is long, containing 4136 octosyllabic lines. The date of my copy is 1906; but Retana mentions an edition before 1898 (No. 4169). Briefly the story runs as follows: —

King Fernando of Berbania has three sons, — Diego, Pedro, and Juan. One night the king dreams that Juan was killed by robbers. He immediately becomes sick, and a skilful physician tells him that the magic Adarna bird is the only thing that can cure his illness. Diego sets out to find the bird, but is unsuccessful; he is turned to stone. A year later Pedro sets out — meets the same fate. At last Juan goes, seeing that his brothers do not return. Because of his charity a leper directs the youth to a hermit's house. The hermit tells Juan how to avoid the enchantment, secure the bird, and liberate his brothers. Juan successful. On the return, however, the envious brothers beat Juan senseless, and, taking the bird from him, make their way back to their father's kingdom alone. But the bird be-

[1] I have the text and a complete English paraphrase of a Tagalog metrical romance which combines incidents from this story with incidents from "The Adarna Bird" (*supra*). The romance is entitled "The Story of the Life of King Don Luis, his Three Sons, and Queen Mora. Manila 1906." Retana (Nos. 4190, 4362) cites editions 1860-98 and 1902. This story contains the quest for the water of healing, the two hermits, the flight on the eagle's back, the sleeping enchanted queen, the stolen favor and the theft of the slipper, the ransoming of the two older brothers, their treachery, the hero disguised as servant in his father's palace, the invasion by the magic queen and her recovery of her lover the hero. This story is closely related to Groome No. 55. Compare also Groome's summary of Vernaleken's Austrian story of the "Accursed Garden" (p. 232), which in some respects resembles this Filipino romance more closely than does the Gypsy tale.

comes very ugly in appearance, refuses to sing, and the king grows worse. Juan, meantime, is restored by an angel sent from heaven. He finally reaches home; and the Adarna bird immediately becomes beautiful again, and sings of the treachery of Diego and Pedro. The king, recovered, wishes to banish his two older sons; but Juan pleads for them, and they are restored to favor. The king now charges his three sons with the safe-keeping of the bird, threatening with death the one who lets it fly away.

One night, while Juan is on watch, he falls asleep. His envious brothers open the cage, and the bird escapes. When Juan awakens and sees the mischief done, he leaves home to look for the Adarna. Next day the king, missing both Juan and the bird, sends Pedro and Diego in search of their brother. They find him in the mountains of Armenia. In their joint search for the bird, the three come to a deep well. Diego and Pedro try in turn to go down, but fear to make the descent to the bottom. Juan is then lowered. At the foot of the well he finds beautiful fields. In his wanderings he comes to a large house where a princess is looking out of the window. She tells Juan that she is in the power of a giant; and so, when the monster returns, Juan kills it. He likewise liberates her sister Leonora, who is in the power of a seven-headed snake. All three — Juan and the two princesses — are hoisted to the top of the well; but when Juan starts back for a ring that Leonora has forgotten, his cruel brothers cut the rope. Leonora sends her pet wolf to cure Juan, and the two brothers with the two princesses return to Berbania. Juana is married to Diego; but Leonora refuses to marry Pedro, asking for a seven-year respite to wait for Juan's return.

Meantime Juan has been restored. One day the Adarna bird appears, and sings over his head that there are three beautiful princesses in the kingdom "de los Cristales." Juan sets out to find that place. He meets an old man, who gives him a piece of his shirt and tells him to go to a certain hermit for directions. The hermit receives Juan on presentation of the token, and summons all the animals to question them about the kingdom "de los Cristales;" but none of the animals knows where the kingdom is. This hermit now directs Juan to another hermitage. There the holy man summons all the birds. One eagle knows where it is; and after Juan gets on its back, the eagle flies for a month, and finally reaches the kingdom sought. There, in accordance with the bird's directions, while the princesses are bathing, Juan steals the clothes of the youngest, and will not return them until she promises to marry him. She agrees, and later helps him perform the difficult tasks set him by her enchanter father (levelling mountain, planting wheat, newly-baked bread — recovering flask from sea — removing mountain — recovering ring from sea [same method as in our folk-tale] — catching king's horse). Then the two escape, pursued by the magician. Transformation flight (needle, thorns; piece of soap, mountain; withe [? *coje*], lake). The baffled magician curses his daughter, and says that she will be forgotten by Juan. When Juan reaches home and sees Leonora, he forgets Maria. On his wedding day with Leonora, an unknown princess comes to attend the festivities. From a small bottle which she has she produces a small Negress and Negro, who dance before the young bridal couple. After each dance the Negress addresses Juan, and recounts to him what Maria has done for him. Then she beats the Negro, but Juan feels the blows. Finally, since Juan remains inflexible, Maria threatens to dash to pieces the bottle, which contains Juan's life. Juan consents to marry her; but Leonora protests, saying that her wolf saved Juan's life. Archbishop called to arbitrate the matter, decides in favor of Leonora. When Maria now floods the country and threatens the whole kingdom with destruction, King Fernando persuades Leonora to take his oldest son Pedro. Juan and Maria are married, and return to the kingdom "de los Cristales."

The Visayan version of the "Adarna Bird" is practically identical with the Tagalog up to the point where Juan rescues the two princesses from the underworld. When he and they have been drawn to the top of the well by the two older brothers, Juan tells Pedro and Diego to return home with the two maidens, but says that he will continue the search for the magic bird. He later learns that it is in the possession of Maria, daughter of the King of Salermo. He directs his steps thither, falls in love with the princess, and, together with the bird, they return to Berbania. The three brothers are married at the same time. It will be noticed that here the "forgotten-betrothed" *motif* is lacking altogether.

For a Tagalog folk-tale connected with this romance, but changed so that it is hardly recognizable as a relative, see the story of "The Aderna (*sic*) Bird" (JAFL 20 : 107–108).

It is interesting to note that the Tagalog romance is definitely reminiscent of the "Swan Maidens" cycle in the method Juan uses to win the affections of Maria, the enchanter's daughter. For parallels to Juan's trick of stealing Maria's clothes while she and her sisters are bathing, see Macculloch, 342 f. For a large collection of "Swan Maiden" stories in abstract, see Hartland, chapters x and xi.

Considering the fact that both parts of our story are practically world-wide in their distribution, it is almost impossible to say where and when the two in combination first existed. I am inclined to think, on the whole, that our Filipino folk-tale is an importation, and is not native. As to the relationship between the popular and the literary versions of the story, I believe that in general the literary has been derived from the popular.

18. JUAN AND HIS ADVENTURES.[1]

Once in a certain village there lived a couple who had three daughters. This family was very poor at first. Near the foot of a mountain was growing a tree with large white leaves.[2] Pedro the father earned their living by selling the leaves of that tree. In time he got so much money from them that he

[1] Narrated by José Ma. Katigbak, a Tagalog from Lipa, Batangas. He heard the story from Angel Reyes, another Batangueño.

[2] These were the leaves of a plant which the Tagalogs call *Colis* (see note 2, p. 285).

ordered a large house to be built. Then they left their old home, and went to live in the new house. The father kept on selling the leaves. After a year he decided to cut down the tree, so that he could sell it all at once and get much money. So he went to the foot of the mountain one day, and cut the tree down. As soon as the trunk had crashed to the ground, a large snake came out from the stump. Now, this snake was an enchanter, and was the friend of the kings of the lions, eagles, and fishes, as we shall see.

The snake said to Pedro, "I gave you the leaves of this tree to sell; and now, after you have gotten much money from it, you cut it down. There is but one suitable punishment for you: within three days you must bring all your daughters here and give them to me." The man was so astonished at first, that he did not know what to do. He made no reply, and after a few minutes went home. His sadness was so great that he could not even eat. His wife and daughters, noticing his depression, asked him what he was thinking about. At first he did not want to tell them; but they urged and begged so incessantly, that finally he was forced to do so.

He said to them, "To-day I cut down the tree where I got the leaves which I sold. A snake came out from the stump, and told me that I should bring you three girls to him or we should all die."

"Don't worry, father! we will go there with you," said the three daughters.

The next day they prepared to go to the snake. Their parents wept very much. Each of the three girls gave her mother a handkerchief as a remembrance. After they had bidden good-by, they set out on their journey with their father.

As soon as they reached the foot of the mountain, the three daughters disappeared at once, and the poor father returned home cheerless. A year had not passed by before a son was born to the old couple. They named him Juan. When the boy was about eighteen years old, his mother showed him the handkerchiefs of his sisters.

"Have I any sister?" said Juan to his mother.

"Yes, you have three; but they were taken away by a snake," she told him. Juan was so angry, that he asked his parents to give him permission to go in search of his sisters. At first they hesitated, but at last they gave him leave. So, taking the three handkerchiefs with him, Juan set out, and went to the mountain.

After travelling for more than ten days, Juan came across three boys quarrelling over the possession of a cap, a pair of sandals, and a key. He went near them, and asked them why they all wanted those three things. The boys told him that the cap would make the person who wore it invisible, the sandals would give their owner the power to fly, and that the key would open any door it touched.

Juan told the three boys that it would be better for them to give him those articles than to quarrel about them; and the boys agreed, because they did not want either of the others to have them. So Juan put the key in his pocket, the cap on his head, and the sandals on his feet, and flew away. After he had passed over many mountains, he descended. Near the place where he alighted he saw a cave. He approached its mouth, and opened the door with his key. Inside he saw a girl sitting near a window. He went up to her and took off his cap.

"Who are you?" said the girl, startled.

"Aren't you my sister?" said Juan.

"I have no brother," said the lady, but she was surprised to see the handkerchiefs which Juan showed her. After he had told her his story, she believed that he was really her brother.

"You had better hide," said the lady, holding Juan's hand, "for my husband is the king of the lions, and he may kill you if he finds you here."

Not long afterwards the lion appeared. She met him at the door. "You must have some visitors here," said the lion, sniffing the air with wide-open nostrils.

"Yes," answered the lady, "my brother is here, and I hid him, for I feared that you might kill him."

"No, I will not kill him," said the lion. "Where is he?"

Juan came out and shook hands with the lion. After they had talked for a few hours, Juan said that he would go to look for his other sisters. The lion told him that they lived on the next two mountains.

Juan did not have much trouble in finding his other two sisters. Their husbands were the kings of the fishes and the eagles, and they received him kindly. Juan's three brothers-in-law loved him very much, and promised to aid him whenever he needed their help.

Juan now decided to return home and tell his parents where his three sisters were; but he took another way back. He came to a town where all the people were dressed in black, and the decorations of the houses were of the same color. He asked some people what had happened in that town. They told him that a princess was lost, and that he who could bring her back to the king should receive her hand in marriage and also half the property of the king. Juan then went to the king and promised to restore his daughter to him. The king agreed to reward him as the townspeople had said, if he should prove successful.

Early the next morning Juan, with his cap, sandals, and key, set out to look for the princess. After a two-days' journey he came to a mountain. Here he descended and began to look around. Finally he saw a huge rock, in which he found a small hole. He put the key in it, and the rock flew open. With his cap of invisibility on his head, he entered. There within he saw many ladies, who were confined in separate rooms. In the very last apartment he found the princess with a giant beside her. He went near the room of the princess, and opened the door with his key. The walls of all the rooms were like those of a prison, and were made of iron bars. Juan approached the princess, and remained near her until the giant went away.

As soon as the monster was out of sight, Juan took off his cap. The princess was surprised to see him, but he told her that he had come to take her away. She was very glad, but said that they had better wait for the giant to go away before they started. After a few minutes the giant went out to take a walk. When they saw that he had passed through the main door, they went out also. Juan put on his sandals and flew away with the princess. But when they were very near the king's palace, the princess disappeared: she was taken back by the giant's powerful magic. Juan was very angry, and he returned at once to the giant's cave. He succeeded in opening the main door, but he could not enter. After struggling in vain for about an hour, he at last determined to go to his brothers-in-law for help.

When he had explained what he wanted, the king of the eagles said to him, "Juan, the life and power of the giant are in a little box at the heart of the ocean. No one can get that *box except* the king of the fishes, and no one can open it except the king of the lions. The life of the giant is in a little bird which is inside the box. This bird flies very swiftly, and I am the only one who can catch it. The strength of the giant is in a little egg which is in the box with the bird."

When the king of the eagles had finished his story, Juan went to the king of the fishes. "Will you fetch me the box which contains the life and strength of the giant?" said Juan to the king of the fishes. After asking him many questions, his brother-in-law swam away, and soon returned with the box. When Juan had received it from him, he thanked him and went to the king of the lions.

The king of the lions willingly opened the box for him. As soon as the box was opened, the little bird inside flew swiftly away. Juan took the egg, however, and went back to the king of the eagles, and asked him to catch the bird. After the little bird had been caught, Juan pushed on to the cave of the giant. When he came there, he opened the door and entered, holding the bird in one hand and the egg in the other. Enraged at the sight of Juan, the giant rushed at him; and Juan was so startled, that he crushed the egg and killed the bird. At once the giant fell on his back, and stretched out his legs to rise no more.

Juan now went through the cave, opening all the prison doors, and releasing the ladies. He carried the princess with him back to the palace. As soon as he arrived, a great celebration was held, and he was married to the princess. After the death of the king, Juan became ruler. He later visited his parents, and told them of all his adventures. Then he took them to his own kingdom, where they lived happily together.

NOTES.

A Tagalog variant of this story, entitled "Pedro and the Giants," and narrated by José Hilario from Batangas, runs thus in abstract: —

Two orphan sisters living with their brother Pedro are stolen by two powerful giants. Pedro goes in search of his sisters, and finds them. Contrary to the expectations of all, the two grim brothers-in-law welcome Pedro, and offer to serve him. Pedro later wishes to marry a princess, and the giants demand her of the king her father. He refuses to give her up, although she falls in love with Pedro. To punish his daughter, the king exposes her to the hot sun; but one of the giants shades her with his eagle-like wings. Then the other giant threatens the king; but the monarch says he is safe, for his life is contained in two eggs in an iron box guarded by two clashing rocks. With great personal risk the giant obtains the eggs; and, upon the king's still refusing to give his daughter to Pedro, the giant dashes the eggs to the ground, and the king falls dead. Pedro and the princess are then married.

This analogue of our story is not very close in details, yet there are enough general resemblances between the two to make it pretty certain that they are distantly related.

Our story of "Juan and his Adventures" belongs to the "Animal Brothers-in-Law" cycle, a formula for which Von Hahn (1 : 53) enumerates the following incidents: —

A Three princes who have been transformed into animals marry the sisters of the hero.
B The hero visits his three brothers-in-law.
C They help him perform tasks.
D They are disenchanted by him.

As Crane says (p. 60), this formula varies, of course. Sometimes there are but two sisters (cf. our variant), and the brothers-in-law are freed from their enchantment in some other way than by the hero. For a bibliography of this group, see Crane, 342–343, note 23, to No. 13.

Perhaps the best version of this story is that found in Basile, 4 : 3, the argument of which, as given in Burton's translation (2 : 372), runs thus: —

Ciancola, son of the King of Verde-colle, fareth to seek his three sisters, married one with a falcon, another with a stag, and the other with a dolphin; after long journeying he findeth them, and on his return homewards he cometh upon the daughter of a king, who is held prisoner by a dragon within a tower, and calling by signs which had been given him by the falcon, stag, and dolphin, all three came before him ready to help him, and with their aid he slayeth the dragon, and setteth free the princess, whom he weddeth, and together they return to his realm.

This argument does not quite do justice to the similarities between Basile's story and ours. For instance, in the Italian story, when the daughters leave, they give their mother three identical rings as tokens. Then a son is born to the queen. When he is fifteen years old, he sets out to look for his sisters, taking the rings with him. Nor, again, does this argument mention the fact that in the end the animal brothers-in-law are transformed into men, — a feature which is found in Basile, but not in our story. In the main, however, it will be seen that the two are very close. In Von Hahn, No. 25, the brothers-in-law are a lion, a tiger, and an eagle.

The opening of our story, so far as I know, is not found in any of the other members of this cycle. Usually the sisters are married to the animals in consequence of a king's decision to give his daughters to the first three persons who pass by his palace after a certain hour (Crane, No. XIII); or else the animals present themselves as suitors after the death of the king, who has charged his sons to see that their sisters are married (Von Hahn, No. 25; compare the opening of Wratislaw No. XLI = Wuk, No. 17). In our story, however, Pedro is deprived of his daughters in consequence of his greed. With this situation compare the "Mahā-vānija-jātaka," No. 493, which tells how some merchants find a magic banyan-tree. From this tree the merchants receive wonderful gifts; but they are insatiable, and finally plan to cut it down to see if there is not large treasure at the roots. The guardian-spirit of the tree, the *serpent-king*, punishes them. It is not impossible that some such parable as this lies behind the introduction to our story. There is abundant testimony from early travellers in the Islands that the natives in certain sections regarded trees as sacred, and could not be hired to cut them down for fear of offending the resident-spirit. The three handkerchiefs which the sisters leave with their mother as mementos are to be compared with the three rings in Basile's version. In a Serbian story belonging to this cycle (Wuk, No. 5), the three sisters are blown away by a strong wind (cf. our story of "Alberto and the Monsters," No. 39), and fall into the power of three dragons. When the brother, yet unborn at the time of their disappearance, reaches his eighteenth year, he sets out to seek his sisters, taking with him a handkerchief of each.

The obtaining of magic articles by a trick of the hero is found in many folk-tales. In Grimm, No. 197, which is distantly related to our story, the hero cheats two giants out of a wishing-cap over which they are quarrelling. In Grimm, No. 92, where we find the same situation, the magic articles are three, — a sword which will make heads fly off, a cloak of invisibility, a pair of transportation-boots (see Bolte-Polívka, 2 : 320 f., especially 331–335). In Grimm, No. 193, a flying saddle is similarly obtained. In Crane, No. XXXVI (p. 136 f.), Lionbruno acquires a pair of transportation-boots, an inexhaustible purse, and a cloak of invisibility. This incident is also found in Somadeva (Tawney, 1 : 14), where the articles are a pair of flying-shoes, a magic staff which writes what is going to happen, and a vessel which can supply any food the owner asks for. In another Oriental collection (Sagas from the Far East, pp. 23–24), the prince and his follower secure a cap of invisibility from a band of quarrelling boys, and a pair of transportation-boots from some disputing demons. Compare Tawney's note for other instances. This incident is also found in an Indian story by Stokes, No. XXII, "How the Raja's Son won the Princess Labam." In this the hero meets four fakirs, whose teacher (and master) has died, and has left four things, — "a bed which carried whosoever sat on it whithersoever he wished to go; a bag that gave its owner whatever he wanted, — jewels, food, or clothes; a stone bowl which gave its owner as much water as he wanted; and a stick that would beat enemies, and a rope that would tie them up." Compare also the "Dadhi-vāhana-jātaka," No. 186, which is connected with our No. 27. In the Filipino story of "Alberto and the Monsters" (No. 39) the hero acquires a transportation-boot from two quarrelling boys; from two young men, a magic key that will unlock any stone; and from two old men wrangling over it, a hat of invisibility. In another Tagalog story, "Ricardo and his Adventures" (notes to No. 49), appears a flying saddle, but this is not obtained by trickery.

For the "Fee-fi-fo-fum" formula hinted at in our story, see Bolte-Polívka, 1 : 289–292.

In many of the members of this cycle, when the hero takes his leave of his brothers-in-law, he is given feathers, hair, scales, etc., with which he can summon them in time of need. In our story, however, Juan has no such labor-saving device: he has to visit his brothers a second time when he desires aid against the giant.

The last part of our story turns on the idea of the "separable soul or strength" of the dragon, snake, demon, giant, or other monster. This idea has been fully discussed by Macculloch (chapter v). As this conception is widespread in the Orient and is found in Malayan literature (e.g., in "Bidasari"), there is no need of tracing its occurrence in the Philippines to Europe. In the norm of this cycle, the animal brothers-in-law help the hero perform tasks which the king requires all suitors for his daughter's hand to perform. Here the beasts help the hero secure the life and strength of the giant who is holding the princess captive.

Taken as a whole, our story seems to have been imported into the Philippines from the Occident, for the reason that no Oriental analogues of it appear to exist, while not a few are known from southern Europe. Our two variants are from the Tagalog province of Batangas, and, so far as I know, the story is not found elsewhere in the Islands. As suggested above, however, the introduction is probably native, or at least very old, and the conclusion has been modified by the influence of another cycle well known in the Orient.

19. JUAN WEARING A MONKEY'S SKIN.[1]

Once upon a time there was a couple which was at first childless. The father was very anxious to have a son to inherit his property: so he went to the church daily, and prayed God to give him a child, but in vain. One day, in his great disappointment, the man exclaimed without thinking, "O great God! let me have a son, even if it is in the form of a monkey!" and

[1] Narrated by Lorenzo Licup, a Pampango from Angeles, Pampanga.

only a few days later his wife gave birth to a monkey. The father was so much mortified that he wanted to kill his son; but finally his better reason prevailed, and he spared the child. He said to himself, "It is my fault, I know; but I uttered that invocation without thinking." So, instead of putting the monkey to death, the couple just hid it from visitors; and whenever any one asked for the child, they merely answered, "Oh, he died long ago."

The time came when the monkey grew to be old enough to marry. He went to his father, and said, "Give me your blessing, father! for I am going away to look for a wife." The father was only too glad to be freed from this obnoxious son, so he immediately gave him his blessing. Before letting him go, however, the father said to the monkey, "You must never come back again to our house."

"Very well, I will not," said the monkey.

The monkey then left his father's house, and went to find his fortune. One night he dreamed that there was a castle in the midst of the sea, and that in this castle dwelt a princess of unspeakable beauty. The princess had been put there so that no one might discover her existence. The monkey, who had been baptized two days after his birth and was named Juan, immediately repaired to the palace of the king. There he posted a letter which read as follows: "I, Juan, know that your Majesty has a daughter."

Naturally the king was very angry to have his secret discovered. He immediately sent soldiers to look for Juan. Juan was soon found, and brought to the palace. The king said to him, "How do you know that I have a daughter? If you can bring her here, I will give her to you for a wife. If not, however, your head shall be cut off from your body."

"O your Majesty!" said Juan, "I am sure that I can find her and bring her here. I am willing to lose my head if within three days I fail to fulfil my promise." After he had said this, Juan withdrew, and sadly went out to look for the hidden princess.

As he was walking along the road, he heard the cry of a bird. He looked up, and saw a bird caught between two boughs so that it could not escape. The bird said to him, "O monkey! if you will but release me, I will give you all I have."

"Oh, no!" said the monkey. "I am very hungry, and would much rather eat you."

"If you will but spare my life," said the bird, "I will give you anything you want."

"On one condition only will I set you free," said the monkey. "You must procure for me the ring of the princess who lives in the midst of the sea."

"Oh, that's an easy thing to do," said the bird. So the monkey climbed the tree and set the bird free.

The bird immediately flew to the island in the sea, where fortunately it found the princess refreshing herself in her garden. The princess was so charmed with the song of the bird, that she looked up, and said, "O little bird! if you will only promise to live with me, I will give you anything you want."

"All right," said the bird. "Give me your ring, and I will forever live with you." The princess held up the ring; and the bird suddenly snatched it and flew away with it. It gave the ring to the monkey, who was, of course, delighted to get it.

Now the monkey jogged along the road until finally he saw three witches. He approached them, and said to them, "You are the very beings for whom I have spent the whole day looking. God has sent me here from heaven to punish you for your evil doings toward innocent persons. So I must eat you up."

Now, witches are said to be afraid of ill-looking persons, although they themselves are the ugliest beings in all the world. So these three were terribly frightened by the monkey's threat, and said, "O sir! spare our lives, and we will do anything for you!"

"Very well, I will spare you if you can execute my order. From this shore you must build a bridge which leads to the middle of the sea, where the castle of the princess is situated."

"That shall be speedily done," replied the witches; and they at once gathered leaves, which they put on their backs. Then they plunged into the water. Immediately after them a bridge was built. Thus the monkey was now able to go to the castle. Here he found the princess. She was very much surprised to see this evil-looking animal before her; but she was much more frightened when the monkey showed her the ring which the bird had given him, and claimed her for his wife. "It is the will of God that you should go with me," said the monkey, after the princess had shown great repugnance towards him. "You either have to go with me or perish." Thinking it was useless to attempt to resist such a mighty foe, the princess finally yielded.

The monkey led her to the king's palace, and presented her before her parents; but no sooner had the king and queen seen their daughter in the power of the beast, than they swooned. When they had recovered, they said simultaneously, "Go away at once, and never come back here again, you girl of infamous taste! Who are you? You are not the princess we left in the castle. You are of villain's blood, and the very air which you exhale does suffocate us. So with no more ado depart at once!"

The princess implored her father to have pity, saying that it was the will of God that she should be the monkey's wife. "Perhaps I have been enchanted by him, for I am powerless to oppose him." But all her remonstrance was in vain. The king shut his ears against any deceitful or flattering words that might fall from the lips of his faithless and disobedient daughter. Seeing that the king was obstinate, the couple turned their backs on the palace, and decided to find a more hospitable home. So the monkey now took his wife to a neighboring mountain, and here they settled.

One day the monkey noticed that the princess was very sad and pale. He said to her, "Why are you so sad and unhappy, my darling? What is the matter?"

"Nothing. I am just sorry to have only a monkey for my husband. I become sad when I think of my past happiness."

"I am not a monkey, my dear. I am a real man, born of human parents. Didn't you know that I was baptized by the priest, and that my name is Juan?" As the princess would not believe him, the monkey went to a neighboring hut and there cast off his disguise (*balit cayu*). He at once returned to the princess. She was amazed to see a sparkling youth of not more than twenty years of age — nay, a prince — kneeling before her. "I can no longer keep you in ignorance," he said. "I am your husband, Juan."

"Oh, no! I cannot believe you. Don't try to deceive me! My husband is a monkey; but, with all his defects, I still cling to him and love him. Please go away at once, lest my husband find you here! He will be jealous, and may kill us both."

"Oh, no! my darling, I am your husband, Juan. I only disguised myself as a monkey."

But still the princess would not believe him. At last she said to him, "If you are my real husband, you must give me a proof of the fact." So Juan [we shall hereafter call him by this name] took her to the place where he had cast off his monkey-skin. The princess was now convinced, and said to herself, "After all, I was not wrong in the belief I have entertained from the beginning, — that it was the will of God that I should marry this monkey, this man."

Juan and the princess now agreed to go back to the palace and tell the story. So they went. As soon as the king and queen saw the couple, they were very much surprised; but to remove their doubt, Juan immediately related to the king all that had happened. Thus the king and queen were finally reconciled to the at first hated couple. Juan and his wife succeeded to the throne on the death of the king, and lived peacefully and happily during their reign.

The story is now ended. Thus we see that God compensated the father and mother of Juan for their religious zeal by giving them a son, but punished them for not being content with what He gave them by taking the son away from them again, for Juan never recognized his parents.

NOTES.

A Bicol version, "The Monkey becomes King," narrated by Gregorio Frondoso, who heard the story from an old man of his province, is almost identical with this Pampango tale. There are a few slight differences, however. "In the Bicol, the rich parents give their monkey-offspring away to a man, who keeps the animal in a cage. Finally the monkey manages to escape, and sets out on his travels. Now the king of that country builds a high tower in the middle of the sea, imprisons his daughter there, and promises her hand to the one who can take her from the tower. The monkey succeeds, as in the Pampango. The rest of the story is practically as given in the text, except that the narrator mentions the fact that the monkey's parents fall into poverty, and in their distress seek aid from their son, now become king. However, he refuses to recognize them, because of their former harshness to him, and drives them away." With both these stories may be compared two other Filipino tales already in print, — "The Enchanted Shell" (JAFL 20 : 90–91) and "The Living Head" (*ibid.*, 19 : 106).

The "Animal Child" cycle, of which our story and its variants are members, is widely spread throughout Europe. The main incidents of this group are the following.

A In accordance with the wish of the parents, a child in the form of an animal is brought into the world. This phenomenon usually takes place in consequence of a too vehement prayer for children, or an inconsiderate wish for a son even if he should prove to be only an animal.

B The animal offspring grows up, is married usually through his own ingenuity, and is finally disenchanted through the burning of his animal disguise either with or without his consent.

European representatives of this type are Grimm, Nos. 108, 144; Von Hahn, Nos. 14, 31, 43, 57, 100; Wuk, No. 9; Pröhle, No. 13; Straparola 2 : i; Basile, No. 15; Schott, No. 9; Pitrè, No. 56 (see also his notes); Comparetti, Nos. 9, 66. Compare also Köhler-Bolte, 318–319. Related Oriental forms of this story are discussed by Benfey, 1 : 254 ff. (section 92).

Although our stories are related to this large family of "Animal Child" tales, it appears to be the Oriental branch rather than the Occidental with which they are the more closely connected. The monkey-child, the castle in the midst of the sea, the building of the bridge from the mainland to the island, the retirement of the monkey and his royal wife to live in the forest, — all suggest vaguely but unmistakably Indian material. I am unable to point to any particular story as source, and our tale appears to have incorporated in it other *Märchen motifs;* but it seems to be faintly reminiscent of the "Rāmāyana." The imprisoning or hiding of a princess, and the promise of her hand to the one who can discover her, are found in our No. 21 (*q.v.*). No. 29, too, should be compared.

Among the Santals, the theme of a girl's marrying a monkey is common in *Märchen* (see Bompas, No. xv, "The Monkey Boy;" No. xxxii, "The Monkey and the Girl;" and No. lxx, "The Monkey Husband"). In none of these stories, however, is there a transformation of the animal into a human being.

20. (*a*) HOW SALAKSAK BECAME RICH.[1]

Once upon a time there lived two brothers. The elder was named Cucunu, and the younger Salaksak. Their parents were dead, so they divided the property that had been left to them. In accordance with this division, each received a cow and a piece of land. Salaksak separated from his brother, and built a small house of his own.

Now, the rice of Cucunu grew faster than that of his brother: so his brother became jealous of him. One night Salaksak turned his cow loose in his brother's field. When Cucunu heard of this, he went to his brother, and said to him, "If you let

---

[1] Narrated by Lorenzo Licup, a Pampango from Angeles, Pampanga.

your cow come into my field again, I shall whip you." But Salaksak paid no attention to his brother's threat, and again he let his cow go into the field of Cucunu. At last his brother grew so impatient that he killed the cow. When Salaksak went to look for his animal, all he found was its skin. As he was ashamed of his deed and afraid of his brother, he dared not accuse him: so he took the skin and put it into a basket.

Not long afterward several hundred cows passed him along the road. He followed them. While the herdsmen were eating their dinner, Salaksak threw his skin among the cows. Then he went up to the hut where the herdsmen were, and said to the chief of the herdsmen, "Friend, it is now a week since I lost my cow, and I am afraid that she has become mixed up with your herd. Please be so kind, therefore, as to count them." The chief immediately went over to where the cows were. As he was counting them, Salaksak picked up the skin, and, shaking his head, he said, "Alas! here is the mark of my cow, and this must be my cow's skin. You must pay me a thousand pesos, or else you shall be imprisoned. My cow was easily worth a thousand pesos; for when she was alive, she used to drop money every day." In their great fear, the herdsmen paid Salaksak the money at once.

Salaksak now went home and told his brother of his good fortune. Hoping to become as rich as his brother, Cucunu immediately killed his cow. He took the skin with him, and left the flesh to Salaksak. As he was in the street calling out, "Who wants to buy a hide?" he was summoned by the ruler of the town, and was accused of having stolen the hide, and he was whipped so badly that he could hardly walk home.

Maddened by the disgrace he had suffered, Cucunu burned the house of his brother one day while he was away. When Salaksak came home, he found nothing but ashes. These he put into a sack, however, and set out to seek his fortune again. On his way he overtook an old man who was carrying a bag of money on his back. Salaksak asked him, "Are you going to the ruler's house?"

"Yes," replied the old man, "I have to give this money to him."

"I am sorry for you, old man. I, too, am going to the palace. What do you say to exchanging loads? Mine is very light in comparison with yours."

"With all my heart, kind boy!" said the old man; and so they exchanged sacks.

After they had travelled together a short distance, Salaksak said, "Old man, you seem to be stronger when you have a light load. Let me see how fast you can run." The old man, having no suspicion of his companion, walked ahead as fast as he could. As soon as Salaksak came to a safe place along the road to hide, he deserted his companion. He went to his brother's house, and told him that he had gotten a sack of silver for a sack of ashes.

"Why," said his brother, "my house is bigger than yours! I ought to get two sacks of ashes if I burn it. I think that would be a good bargain." So he burned his house, too. Then he went through the town, crying, "Who wants to buy ashes?"

"What a foolish man!" said the housewives. "Why should we buy ashes when we don't know what to do with those that come from our own stoves?" When Cucunu came near the house of the ruler, the ruler said to his servants, "I think that fellow is the same one I bade you whip before. Call him in and give him a good thrashing, for he is only making a fool of himself." So Cucunu was summoned and lashed again.

Thoroughly enraged, Cucunu determined that his brother should not deceive him a third time. He thought and thought of what he should do to get rid of him. At last he decided to throw his brother into the river. For this purpose he made a strong cage. One day he caught his brother and confined him in it.

"I will give you three days to repent," said Cucunu. "Now you cannot deceive me any more." He then left his brother in the cage by the bank of the river.

As a young man was passing by, Salaksak began to cry out, "They have put me into this cage because I do not want to marry the ruler's daughter." The young man, who had vainly striven for the hand of the girl, immediately approached Salaksak, and said, "If you will let me take your place, so that I may marry her, I will give you all the cows I have with me."

So by this trick Salaksak escaped. Cucunu, thinking that the man in the cage was his brother, would not listen to what he said, but unmercifully threw him into the river. A few days later, Salaksak went to his brother's house, and told him that it was quite beautiful under the water. "There," he said, "I

saw our father and mother. They told me I was not old enough
to stay with them, so they sent me back here with a large
number of cows."

"Well, well!" said Cucunu, "I too must go see our parents."
He then hastened to the river, and threw himself in and was
drowned. Thus Salaksak grew rich because of his craftiness.

(b) CLEVER JUAN AND ENVIOUS DIEGO.[1]

There were once two brothers named Diego and Juan. Their
father had died a long time before, so they lived only with their
good mother. In character these two brothers were very different. Diego, the older, was envious and foolish; Juan was
clever.

One morning, while Diego was away, Juan called his mother,
and said, "Mother, help me fool Diego! Please lie down
as if you were dead; and when he arrives, I will blow air through
your nose through a bamboo tube. As soon as you feel me
blowing, get up and try to look like a woman that has risen from
the dead." His mother agreed to do all that she had been told.
Then Juan watched and waited for Diego. When he saw him
coming, he called to his mother and told her to lie down. Then
he pretended to be crying.

When Diego came in and saw his brother, he said, "Juan,
why are you crying?"

"Don't you see? Our mother is dead," said Juan. Then
Diego felt very sorry, and he too began to weep. Juan then
said, "O brother! I remember that I have a magic instrument
that resuscitates dead persons." He opened his trunk and took
out a short bamboo tube, and began to blow through it into his
mother's nose. His mother then pretended to revive, as she
had been told. Diego rejoiced; he too was very much surprised at his brother's possession.

The next day the envious Diego stole the bamboo tube and
went to the churchyard. There he waited for a funeral to pass
by. After a short time the funeral procession of a small boy
came along. Diego stopped it, and called to the mother of the
boy, "Don't cry! your son is only sleeping. Lay him down
here, and you will soon see that he is alive." The mother then
ordered the carriers to lay the coffin on the ground. Diego

---

[1] Narrated by Pablo Anzures, a Tagalog from Manila, who heard the story from
another Tagalog from Santa Maria, Bulakan.

took out his bamboo tube, and, after he had opened the coffin, he began to blow air into the boy's nose; but the boy did not move. He blew harder and harder, but the boy remained as stiff and lifeless as ever. Then the mother of the dead boy became angry; she kicked Diego, and said, "You are only trying to fool us!" Diego was very much ashamed, so he threw away the bamboo tube and ran home.

Some days later the mother of Diego and Juan became ill and died. She left her sons two carabaos for an inheritance. As Diego was the older, he took the fat carabao for himself, and gave the thin one to Juan. Juan was angry: so he killed his carabao, and decided to sell the hide. He tried to sell it in the neighboring villages, but he could not find a buyer. He then walked on and on until he came to a forest. Not very far off, and coming towards him, he saw a band of Tulisanes.[1] They were on horseback, and had a large amount of treasure with them. Juan was afraid: so he climbed a tree, and hid himself with his hide among the branches and leaves. He had no more than concealed himself when the Tulisanes came up and stopped to eat under that very tree. Juan watched them closely. He unintentionally moved the hide which was on the branch beside him, and it fell crashing down on the Tulisanes. Frightened by this most unexpected noise, they ran away as fast as they could, not stopping to take anything with them. Juan descended quickly, mounted a horse, and made off with as much as he could carry.

When he reached home, his brother said to him, "Where did you get all those riches?" Juan replied that he had been given them by the neighboring villages in return for his carabao-hide. Again Diego envied his brother. He went out and killed his fat carabao and dried its hide. Next he went to the neighboring villages and tried to sell it; but many days passed, and still no one would buy.

Now Diego was very angry. He took a wooden box and put his brother inside. He bound the box and carried it to the seashore. He was about to throw it into the water when he remembered that it was not locked: so he left it, and went back to the house to get the key. Meanwhile a Chinese peddler selling gold rings came along. Juan heard him, and shouted, "Chino, Chino, come and see these beautiful and precious

---

[1] *Tulisanes*, highway robbers or bandits.

things inside!" The Chinaman approached, and opened the box. Juan came out, and said, "I will put you inside, and you will see many beautiful things in the bottom." The Chinaman was willing, so Juan put him in and closed the box. He then took the Chino's gold rings and ran away. Not many minutes later Diego came up, and, after locking the box, he threw it into the ocean.

That same day, while Diego was eating his dinner, Juan came along with some fine gold rings. Diego was astonished to see his brother, and said, "How did you manage to get out of the box, and where did you get those rings?" Juan answered that he sank to the bottom of the ocean, where he saw his mother, and that she had given him all those rings. The foolish Diego believed everything that Juan told him, so he asked his brother to put him into a box and throw him into the ocean. Juan lost no time in obeying. He got a box, put Diego inside, took it to the seashore, and there cast it into the deep water. After that Juan lived happily for many years.

(c) RUINED BECAUSE OF INVIDIOUSNESS.[1]

In time out of memory there lived two brothers, Pedro and Juan. Pedro was rich, for he had a large herd of cattle: consequently he did not have much use for his younger brother, who was very poor. Juan had nothing that he could call his own but a cow. One day, disappointed over his life of poverty, he killed his cow, and some days afterward he set out to find his fortune. He took nothing with him but the hide of his cow. When he reached the next town, he saw large piles of cattle-hides in front of a butcher's shop. Late that night he stole out secretly and put the skin of his cow in one of the piles. The next morning he went to the shop to talk with the butcher.

"Mr. Butcher," he said, "I have come here to look for my lost cow. Have you not killed a cow with a mark J on the right hip?"

"No," answered the honest man, "all the cows which were killed here came from my herd out there in the mountains."

Juan stood musing for a few moments, and then said, "Let us look through these piles of hide to see whether you killed my cow or not!"

---

[1] Narrated by Facundo Esquivel, a Tagalog from Jaen, Nueva Ecija, who was told the story when he was a boy.

"All right," answered the butcher, and so they began the investigation.

When they found the hide which Juan had put there, he began to quarrel with the man. "You must pay me five hundred pesos for my cow, or else I shall bring a law-suit before the court against you," he said angrily.

"I wonder how this could have happened!" the butcher exclaimed.

"There is no use of wondering," said Juan impatiently. "You stole my cow, and now you have to pay for it." The man, who was very much afraid of being brought before the court, gave Juan the five hundred pesos; and Juan went away with the money in his pocket, and the hide on his head.

On his way home he came to a tree standing at a cross-roads. He was very tired and thirsty, but he could not find a house where to ask for water. He climbed the tree to look for a place to go to, but, instead of a house, he saw a company of armed men coming down the road. The men stopped under the tree to rest. Juan was so terrified that he hardly knew what to do. As he was trembling with fright, the hide fell down from the tree and frightened the men away. They thought that it was a curse from heaven because of their misdeeds. When Juan realized that the men were gone, he recovered from his fright and quickly descended. There on the ground he saw a number of sacks full of money, and, loading a horse with two of the sacks, he started for his home town.

As soon as he reached his house, he went to his brother's to borrow a *salop*.[1] Then he inserted several pesetas and ten-centavo pieces in the cracks of the *salop*, and returned the measure. When Pedro saw the coins sticking in the cracks of his measure, he said, "What did you do with the *salop?*"

"I measured money," said Juan.

"Where did you get the money?" Pedro demanded.

"Where did I get the money?" retorted Juan. "Don't you know that I went to the neighboring town to sell my cow-hide?"

"Yes," said Pedro. Then he added, "The price of hides there must be very high, I suppose."

"There is no supposing about it," said Juan. "Just think! one hide is worth two sacks of money."

[1] *Salop*, a dry measure of about fifteen centimetres cube.

Pedro, who was envious of his brother's good fortune, killed all his cattle, old and young, and threw the meat into the river. The he started with several carretons [1] full of hides; but he was disappointed when he came to the town, for nobody would buy hides. Discouraged and tired out, he returned. He found Juan living comfortably in a fine new home. Thus Pedro lost all his property because of his invidiousness.

(d) THE TWO FRIENDS.[2]

Once there lived in a certain village two friends, Juan and Andres. Juan, a very rich man, was tall, big, and strong; while Andres, a very poor man, was small, weak, and short. Andres worked very hard to earn his living, while Juan spent most of his time on pleasure.

One morning Andres went to his friend Juan, and asked to borrow one of his mules. Juan consented, but told Andres that, if any one should ask who the owner of the mule was, he should tell the truth. Andres promised, and went off with the mule. He set to work immediately to plough his small farm. Very soon two neighbors of Andres passed by, and, seeing him with a mule, asked him where he got it. Andres said that he had bought it. The men wondered how a poor man like Andres could buy a mule, and they spread the news about the village. When this news reached Juan, he was very angry, and he ordered his servant to go bring back the mule. The animal was brought back, and Juan was determined not to lend it to his friend any more.

A week later two of Juan's mules, including that which Andres had borrowed, died. Juan threw the carcasses away, but Andres took the skins of those dead mules and dried them to sell in the next town.

The next day Andres set out for the town, resting now and then on account of his heavy load. He was overtaken by night near a solitary house between his village and the town where he was going to sell the hides. He knocked at the house, and asked a woman he found there for a night's lodging. She told him that she could not do anything for him until her husband arrived. So Andres had to wait on the road near the house. Not long afterwards a man came towards the house. Andres went up to

---

[1] *Carreton*, a heavy two-wheeled springless cart.
[2] Narrated by Tomas V. Vargas (of Iloilo?).

him, and asked him if he was the master of the house; but the man said he was not, so Andres had to go back to the road. From where he was sitting, Andres could see that the woman inside was preparing a good supper for the stranger, who meanwhile had entered. While she and the stranger were sitting at the table, Andres saw another man approaching in the distance. The woman hastily opened a big empty trunk and hid the man inside, then she put all the cooked fish in the cupboard.

When the other man, who was the husband, arrived, Andres asked for a night's lodging, and was received kindly. While the husband and Andres were talking, the wife told them that supper was ready, and they went to the table to eat: but there they found nothing for them but rice; so Andres told the husband that he had an enchanted hide, and that they could have fish if he wished. The husband wished to see the skin tested. Andres ordered the skin to bring a man into the trunk; and when the trunk was opened, there was the man. Next he ordered the skin to bring cooked fish to the cupboard; and when the cupboard was opened, there was the cooked fish. The husband then offered Andres a very high price for the enchanted skin, and Andres willingly sold it.

Early the next morning Andres left the house before the others were up. It was not long, however, before the husband found out that the skin was not magic, and he was determined to punish the skin-seller if he should catch him again. Meanwhile Andres had returned to the village. There he met Juan, who, noticing the money in his pocket, asked him where he had gotten it. Andres told him that it was the price of the skins of his dead mules, which he had sold in the neighboring town. On hearing this, Juan went directly home, killed all his mules, and flayed them. As he was passing by the solitary house on his way to the town, he cried out that he had skins for sale. The husband in the house thought that it must be the same man who had sold him the enchanted skin, so he went down and whipped Juan nearly to death.

After this experience, Juan returned home, determined to kill his friend. But Andres was very cunning, and avoided him. Finally Juan, angry beyond all measure, killed the mother of Andres. When Andres found that his mother was dead, he dressed her very well and took her to town. Then he went directly to the town doctor, to whom he explained definitely the sickness of his mother. The doctor immediately prepared medicine for the patient; but just after she had been given the medicine, he noticed that the woman was dead. Andres then accused him of having poisoned his mother; and the doctor, fearing the consequences if Andres should seek justice, agreed to pay him a large sum of money.

Andres returned to his village richer than ever. Juan became friendly again, and asked him where he had gotten his money. Andres told him that it was the price of his mother's corpse, which he had sold in the town. When Juan heard this, he went home and killed his mother. Then he took the corpse to town to sell it; but, as he was passing along the street, a crowd of men began to abuse him, and he narrowly escaped with his life.

Now, Juan was determined not to let Andres escape him. He was after him all the time. Finally one day he caught Andres. He put him inside a sack and carried it down to the seashore. On the way to the sea, he saw a house, and, wishing to have a smoke, he left Andres on the road, and went to the house to get a light. Meanwhile Andres, who was bound in the sack, was crying out that he did not wish to marry the daughter of the king, and that he was being forced against his will. At this instant a cowboy with his herd of cows passed by. He heard Andres, and said that he was willing to marry the king's daughter. Andres told him to unbind the sack, then. He did so, and Andres put the cowherd in his stead. Then Andres hurried away with the cows. Juan came back, picked up the sack, and threw it into the sea. When he returned home, he found Andres there with a fine herd of cows. He asked Andres where he had found them, and Andres said that he had gotten them from under the sea. So Juan, envious as ever, ordered Andres to put him in a sack and throw him into the sea. Andres gladly did so.

(e) JUAN THE ORPHAN.[1]

There once lived a boy whose name was Juan. His parents had died, leaving Juan nothing but a horse. As he did not have a place at home in which to keep the animal, he begged his Uncle Diego to let the horse stay in his stable. From time to time Juan went to the stable to feed his horse. He loved the animal, and took as great care of it as a father would of a son.

[1] Narrated by Leopoldo Uichanco, a Tagalog from Calamba, La Laguna.

One day Uncle Diego noticed that Juan's horse was growing fatter and more beautiful than any of his own animals. In his envy he killed the horse of his nephew, and said to the innocent boy that the animal had been stricken by "bad air." Being thus deprived of his sole wealth, Juan cut off the best meat from the dead horse, and with this food for his only provision he set out to seek his fortune in another country. On his way through a forest he came across an old man dying of starvation; but the old man had with him a bag full of money.

"Pray," said the old man, talking with difficulty in his pain and weakness, "what have you in your sack, my son?"

"Some dried horse-meat," said Juan.

"Let me see!" The old man looked into the sack, and saw with watering mouth the sweet-smelling meat. "Will you exchange your sack of meat for my sack of money?" he said to Juan. "I have money here, but I cannot eat it. Nor can I go to the town to buy food, because I am too weak. Since you are stronger, my son, pray take this sack of money in exchange, and go to the town and buy meat with it for yourself. For God's sake, leave this meat to me! I am starving to death."

Juan accepted the money in exchange for his meat, and pretended to feel great pity for the old man. He put the heavy bag of money on his shoulder, and with difficulty carried it home. "Uncle Diego!" Juan called out from the foot of his uncle's ladder, "come here! Please come here and help me carry this bag upstairs!"

"Tremendous sum of money," Uncle Diego remarked to his nephew. "Where did you get it?"

"I sold the meat of my dead horse. This is what I got for it," said Juan.

The uncle once more became jealous of Juan. "If with only one horse," he muttered to himself, "he could gain so much money, how much should I get for my fifteen horses!" So he killed all the horses he had in his stable and cut the meat from them. Then he placed the meat in bags, and, carrying two on his shoulders, he cried as he went along the street, "Meat, meat! Horse-meat! Who wishes to buy fresh horse-meat?"

"How much?" asked a gray-headed old woman who was looking out of the window.

"Three hundred ninety-nine thousand pesos, ninety-nine pesetas, six and one half centavos a pound," said Uncle Diego.

The people who heard him only laughed, and thought that something was the matter with his head. Nobody would buy his meat. Nobody cared to deal with him in earnest, and all his meat decayed.

He went home in despair, and planned to take vengeance on his nephew for the mischief he had done him. He cast the little orphan into a big sack, and sewed the mouth of the little prison all up. Then he said that at night he would take the sack and throw it into the river. However, Juan managed to get out of the bag, and in his place he put a muzzled dog. When night came, the uncle shouldered the bag, took it to the river, and hurled it into the deep water. He hoped that Juan would perish there, and that he himself could gain full possession of his nephew's money.

But when morning came, Uncle Diego saw Juan smilingly enter the door of his house. "Juan," said the uncle, "I am surprised to see you again. Tell me all about how you managed to escape from the sack."

"Oh, no, Uncle!" returned Juan, "I haven't time; there is not a moment to lose. I have only come here to bid you good-by."

"And where are you going?"

"Back to the bottom of the river. My love, the Sirena,[1] is waiting for me."

"O Juan!" pleaded the uncle, "if I could only go with you!"

"No, no, no!" protested the boy. "Only one can go at a time. The Sirena would be angry, and she would consequently refuse to admit to her glorious habitation any being from this outside world."

"Then let me go first!"

"No, no, no!" said the boy.

But the uncle pleaded so earnestly, that finally the boy yielded with pretended reluctance. The uncle then covered himself with a rice-sack, and Juan tied the mouth of the bag securely. "I will fool him," Uncle Diego said to himself. "When I am under the water and the Sirena takes me to her house to become her husband, I shall never come back to Juan. Ha, ha, ha!"

[1] Sirena, a beautiful enchantress, half woman and half fish, who was supposed to dwell in certain rivers. This belief is fairly common in La Laguna province, especially in the town of Pagsanjan.

"I will fool him," Juan said to himself. "There is no such thing as the Sirena in the river. Thank God, my dreadful uncle will soon be disposed of!" At midnight Juan hurled his happy uncle into the river, saying, "There is no one who owes that must not pay his debt.[1] May my act be justified!"

The heavy sack sank to the bottom of the river, and nothing more was heard of Uncle Diego.

NOTES.

Two other variants, which were collected by Mr. Rusk, and which I have only in abstract, run about as follows: —

JUAN THE ASHES-TRADER. — Juan, a poor dealer in ashes, was in the woods when he heard some robbers coming, and climbed a tree for safety. While they were busy at the foot of the tree, counting their money, he dropped the sack of ashes among them. They ran away in fright, and he acquired all their gold. When the people of the town heard Juan tell how valuable ashes had become, they all burned their houses and took the ashes to the forest, where they arrived just in time to suffer from the wrath of the robbers. Only two escaped to accuse Juan; but Juan was already on a journey, doing good with his money. A dying woman, whom he helped, gave him a magic cane; and when the angry villagers at last found him, he summoned a legion of soldiers by means of his cane, and all of his assailants were killed. [With the second half of this story, cf. No. 28 and notes.]

COLASSIT AND COLASKEL. — Colassit was good but poor; Colaskel, rich but bad. Colaskel, quarrelling with Colassit, killed the latter's only carabao. Colassit skinned his dead animal, and took the hide to Laoag to sell it, but could find no purchaser. At night he asked for shelter at a house, but was refused on the ground that the husband was away from home; yet he boldly staid under the house. At midnight he heard the clatter of dishes above, looked up through a hole in the floor, and saw the woman dining merrily with a man. Just then the husband arrived home and knocked at the door. Colassit saw the woman put her paramour into a box in the corner, and the food in another box. Colassit now appeared at the door, and was invited in by the hospitable husband. On being asked what was in his bag, Colassit replied that it was a miraculous thing, which, when it made a noise, as it had a moment before when he had stepped on it, desired to say something. On being asked to interpret, Colassit said that the skin told him that there was delicious food in one of the boxes. Thereupon the food was produced. Now, it was said in the neighborhood that this house was haunted by the Devil, and the owner thought this a good opportunity to find out by magic where the Devil was. Colassit interpreted for the carabao-hide. The Devil was in the other box, he said. After tying the box with heavy ropes, Colassit started toward the river with it. He repeated a jingle which informed the man inside of his imminent fate. The latter replied (also in verse) that he would give a thousand pesos ransom. Colassit accepted, and so became rich. [The narrator says that this is only one of ten adventures belonging to the complete story. It is a pity that the other nine are missing.]

[1] One of the most common Tagalog proverbs.

The cycle of tales to which all our variants belong, and which may appropriately be called the "Master Cheat" cycle, is one of the most popular known. It occurs in many different forms; indeed, the very nature of the story — merely a succession of incidents in which a poor but shrewd knave outwits his rich friend or enemy (the distinction matters little to the narrator), and finally brings about his enemy's death while he himself becomes rich — is such as to admit of indefinite expansion, so far as the number and variety of the episodes are concerned. There have been at least four comprehensive descriptive or bibliographical studies of this cycle made, — Köhler's (on Campbell's Gaelic story, No. 39), Cosquin's (notes to Nos. 10 and 20), Clouston's (2 : 229–288), and Bolte-Polívka's (on Grimm, No. 61). Of these, the last, inasmuch as it is the latest (1914) and made use of all the preceding, is the most complete. From it (2 : 10) we learn that the characteristic incidents of this family of drolls are as follows: —

A^1 A rabbit (goat, bird) as carrier of messages. A^2 A wolf sold for a ram.
B A gold-dropping ass (or horse).
C A self-cooking vessel.
D A hat which pays the landlord.
E^1 Dirt (ashes) given (sold, substituted) for gold. E^2 Money which was alleged to be in a chest, demanded from the storer of the chest.
F^1 Cowhide (or "talking" bird) sold to adulteress, or (F^2) sold to her husband, or (F^3) exchanged for the chest in which the paramour is concealed, or (F^4) elsewhere exchanged for money.
G^1 A flute (fiddle, staff, knife) which apparently brings to life again the dead woman. G^2 The dead mother killed a second time, and paid for by the supposed murderer.
H Escape of the hero from the sack (chest) by exchanging places with a shepherd.
J Death of the envious one, who wishes to secure some "marine cattle."

The opponents in this group of stories, says Bolte, "are either village companions, or unacquainted marketers, or a rich and an avaricious brother." In addition to the episodes enumerated above, might be mentioned two others not uncommonly found in this cycle: —

F^5 Frightening robbers under tree by dropping hide or table on them.
F^6 Borrowed measure returned with coins adhering to it.

As these last two occur in other stories, both droll and serious (e.g., Grimm, No. 59; and "1001 Nights," "Ali Baba"), they may not originally have belonged to our present group. However, see Cosquin's notes on his No. xx, "Richedeau" (1 : 225 f.). It is hard to say with certainty just what was originally the one basic *motif* to which all the others have at one time or another become attached; but it seems to me likely that it was incident H, the sack-by-the-sea episode, for it is this which is the *sine qua non* of the cycle. To be sure, our third story (c) lacks it, but proves its membership in the family by means of other close resemblances.

Of the elements mentioned by Bolte-Polívka, our five stories and two variants have the following: "How Salaksak became Rich," F^4BE^1HJ; "Clever Juan and Envious Diego," G^1F^4HJ; "Ruined because of Invidiousness," $F^4F^5F^6$; "The Two Friends," F^2G^3HJ; "Juan the Orphan," F^4H (modified) J; "Juan the Ashes-Trader," E^1F^5; "Colassit and Colaskel," F^3. In a Visayan tale (JAFL 19 : 107–109) we find a combination of HJ with a variant of our No. 1. Incident D (hat paying landlord) forms a separate story, which we give below, — No. 50, "Juan and his Painted Hat." Incident B is also narrated as a droll by the Tagalogs; the sharper of the story scattering silver coins about the manure of his cow, and subsequently selling the "magic" animal for a large sum. An examination of the incidents distributed among the Filipino members of this cycle reveals the fact that episode A^1 (hare as messenger) is altogether lacking. I have not met with it in any native story, and am inclined to believe that it is not known in the Islands. It is found widespread in Europe, but does not appear to be common in India: among fifteen Indian variants cited by Bolte it is found only twice (i.e., Indian Antiquary, 3 : 11 f.; Bompas, No. 80, p. 242). These Indian versions show, however, that the story in one form or another is found quite generally throughout that country, the Santali furnishing the largest number of variants (six, in all). It would seem reasonable to conclude, therefore, considering the fact that at least seven forms of the tale are known in the Philippines, extending from the Visayas to the northernmost part of Luzon, that the source of the incidents common to these and the Indian versions need not be sought outside the Orient. The case of incidents $F^1F^2F^3$ seems different. They are lacking in the Far-Eastern representatives of this cycle; and their appearance in the Philippines may be safely traced, I think, to European influence. However, an Indian source for these incidents may yet be discovered, just as sources already have been for so many Italian *novella* and French *fabliaux* of a similar flavor. The fact that the earliest form of the "Master Cheat" cycle known is a Latin poem of the eleventh, possibly tenth, century (Köhler-Bolte, 233–234), is of course no proof that elements F^4G^1HJ, found in that poem, were introduced into India from Europe, though it might be an indication.

21. IS HE THE CRAFTY ULYSSES?[1]

Balbino and Alaga had only one child, a son named Suguid, who was at first greatly beloved by them. The couple was very rich, and therefore the boy wanted nothing that was not granted

[1] Narrated by Lorenzo Licup, a Pampango from Angeles, Pampanga.

by his parents. Now, the son was a voracious eater. While still a baby, he used to pull up the nails from the floor and eat them, when his mother had no more milk to give him. When all the nails were exhausted, he ate the cotton with which the pillows were stuffed. Thus his parents used to compare him to a mill which consumes sugarcane incessantly. It was not many years before the wealth of the couple had become greatly diminished by the lavish expenditure they had to make for Suguid's food. So Suguid became more and more intolerable every day. At last his parents decided to cast him away into a place from which he might not be able to find his way home again.

One day they led him to a dense forest, and there abandoned him. Luckily for Suguid, a merchant soon passed by that place. The merchant heard him crying, and looked for him. He found the boy, and, being a good-natured man, he took the boy home with him. It was not long before the merchant realized that Suguid was a youth of talent, and he put him in school. In a few weeks the boy showed his superiority over his classmates. In time he beat even the master in points of learning. And so it was that after only five months of studying he left the school, because he found it too small for his expanding intellect.

By some mathematical calculation, so the tradition says, or by certain mysterious combinations of characters that he wrote on paper, Suguid discovered one day that a certain princess was hidden somewhere. She had been concealed in such a way that her existence might not be known other than by her parents and the courtiers. Suguid immediately went to the palace of the king, and posted a paper on the palace-door. The paper read as follows: "Your Majesty cannot deny me the fact that he has a daughter secluded somewhere. Your humble servant, Suguid Bociu."

When the king read this note, he became very angry, as he could now no longer keep the secret of his daughter's existence. He immediately despatched his soldiers to look for the presumptuous Suguid. The soldiers found the boy without much difficulty, and brought him before the king. Bursting with anger, the king said, "Are you the one who was bold enough to post this paper?"

"Yes, your Majesty."

"Can you prove what you have stated?"

"Yes, your Majesty."

"Very well," said the king; "if you can, I will give you my daughter for your bride. If within three days you fail to produce her before me, however, you shall be unconditionally executed."

"I will not fail to fulfil my promise, your Majesty," said Suguid.

After this brief interview, Suguid went directly home. He told the merchant all about his plan to marry the princess.

"Why did you dare tell the king that you know where his daughter is," said the merchant, "when there is no certainty at all of your finding her or of gaining her consent?"

"Oh, do not be afraid, father!" said Suguid. "If you will but provide me with twelve of the best goldsmiths that can be found in the whole city, I have no doubt of finding and captivating the fair princess." As the merchant was a rich man, and influential too, he summoned in an hour all the good goldsmiths that could be found in the city. When all the goldsmiths were assembled, Suguid ordered them to make a *purlon*. This *purlon* was made of gold, silver, and precious stones. It was oblong in shape, and hollow inside, being five feet high, three feet deep, and four feet long. Inside it were placed a chair and a lamp. By means of a certain device a person inside the *purlon* could breathe. Altogether its construction was so beautiful, that it seemed as if it were intended for the sight of the gods alone.

When all was ready, Suguid entered the *purlon*, taking with him all the necessary provisions, — food, fine clothes, a poniard, and a guitar. Every part of the *purlon* was so well joined, that no opening whatever could be detected. Before going into the *purlon*, Suguid told the merchant to take the goldsmiths home, and not to allow them to leave the house for three days, lest they should reveal the secret. Suguid then ordered five men to carry the *purlon* towards the king's palace. In the mean time he was playing the sweetest piece of music that mortal ears had ever heard. When the *purlon* was near the palace, the king was so charmed by the melodious music, that he asked the master of the carriers to halt for a moment. "Pray," he said, "are you the owner of that thing?"

"No, sir! a certain man in our district owns it," said the carrier.

"Who gave him this divine gift?"

"Your Majesty, this *purlon*, as it is called, is of a rather mysterious origin. The owner of this (pointing to the *purlon*) was a religious man. He was formerly very wealthy; but because he gave much alms to the poor and the needy, his riches soon came to an end. He is now so poor, that his silken clothes have all been exchanged for ragged cotton ones. Early one morning, when he was about to go to the church, he was surprised to find this *purlon* at his door, giving out music as you hear it now."

The king turned to the queen, who was sitting beside him, and said, "Oh, how happy our daughter would be if she should hear this enchanting piece of music! — Sir, if you will lend me this *purlon*, you may ask of me as a compensation any favor that you may want."

"Your Majesty, I will lend it to you with all my heart, but on condition that it be returned within two days, lest the owner scold me for having given it up."

"Yes," answered the king, "I will give it back as soon as my daughter has seen it." The king and queen then immediately ordered that the *purlon* be carried before the princess. The princess's joy need not be described if we only think how happy we should be if we were in the same situation as she. She was so bewitched by the music, that she told her father never to take it away from her.

"O daughter!" said the king, "we have just borrowed this *purlon*, and we promised to return it as soon as you had seen it. However, you may have it the whole night."

The king and the queen, convinced that their daughter was quite happy, soon bade her good-by. Before leaving, the king said, "You must not spend the whole night in listening to the sweet music."

"Have no fear, father! I will go to sleep early."

Suguid, who was inside the *purlon*, listened very carefully to the retreating footsteps of the king and queen. As soon as he thought they were too far away to hear their daughter in case she should cry out, he came out from the *purlon*, poniard in hand. The princess, of course, was very much frightened when she saw Suguid kneeling before her, and saying, "Fair princess, let not my presence cause any fear! In coming here, I had no other purpose than to reveal to you a secret that I have long cherished in my heart. It is universally acknowledged that you are the most beautiful, the most virtuous, the most accomplished living mortal on earth, and as such you have awakened in me an intense love. So, taking no heed of the danger that I might encounter on the way, I ventured to search for you, Lily of the Valley and Rose of the Town — to love you, to adore you as a living saint. Your ring, my adored princess, will give me life or death, — life, because I shall be spared from being beheaded; death, for I have promised your father to present your ring to him within three days as a token of your acceptance of my suit. Therefore, Queen of Beauty, choose, — your ring, or my death. I have my poniard ready, and I prefer a hundred times to die — nay, die smiling — at your hands."

The princess was so moved by this passionate speech, that she was mute for some time. After a difficult struggle within herself, she said, "Seeing your intense love and devotion for me, I cannot but consent to your proposal. Were not the matter pressing, however, I should not give my consent in so short a time. Here is the ring, if pleasure it will give you."

Suguid took the ring courteously, and said, "How can I paint in words my pleasure and gratitude! As it were, you have snatched me from the cold hands of Death. You have saved me from the fury of your father. You have given me a heaven of joy. Oh, how shall I describe it! I thank you very much. But now I must leave you and go into the *purlon*, — the blessed *purlon*, — as it is almost morning. Your father will soon come and take this *purlon* away. But I must let you know this one fact: as soon as I have presented this ring to the king, you will be taken away from here. You will be made my beloved wife."

"Yes, I have no objection to that," said the princess. Suguid, being thus assured of his success, entered the *purlon* again.

Morning came, and the king and queen went to the princess's palace at ten o'clock. They talked a while with their daughter, who assured them of her great satisfaction with the *purlon*. Then they bade her good-by, as there was important business to be transacted that day. They took the *purlon* with them, and returned it to the agent.

On the appointed day Suguid appeared at the king's palace, carrying with him the emblem of his victory, — the ring. On seeing Suguid approaching so cheerfully, the king knew that he was lost. He therefore swooned, but on recovering he realized that he had to abide by his promise. He reluctantly caused the princess to be summoned from her palace, and she and Suguid were married together; and it was not long before the king and queen began to appreciate the talent of their humble and lowly son-in-law. By Suguid's wise policy the kingdom prospered, and for the first time learned what peace really meant.

NOTES.

I have a variant of this story, "Juan the Poor," told more briefly, narrated by Andrea Mariano, a Tagalog, who heard it from her little brother. It runs thus in outline: —

Juan is the son of a beggar. The beggar dies, and the son sells himself to a merchant for money to bury his father properly. After Juan has been educated, he posts this sign in front of the merchant's house: "I can trace everything that is lost. — Juan." The king sees the sign, and requires the boy to discover his hidden daughter. Method: Golden carriage with Juan playing music inside; old man hired to push it. The king borrows the carriage and takes it to his daughter. When alone with the princess, Juan declares his love, and she gives him her ring. Next day the carriage is returned to the old man. Juan takes the ring to the king, and is given the princess's hand in marriage because he is so wise.

For another Tagalog variant see "The King, the Princess, and the Poor Boy" (JAFL 20 : 307). This is almost identical with the variant above, except that the hero is advised by two statues how to discover where the princess is. Furthermore, the hero is discovered *with* the princess after he has gained access to her by means of the gilt carriage and music-box.

The fullest form of the story, however, is the Tagalog metrical romance popularly known under the title "Juan Bachiller." The full title runs as follows: "The Sad Life of a Father and of his Son named Juan, in the Kingdom of Spain. The son sold himself to a merchant on condition that he would bury the corpse of his father." My copy bears the date 1907, but this is merely a reprint of an older edition. Retana cites an edition dated 1902 (No. 4337) and one before 1898 (No. 4156). The poem is in 12-syllable lines, and contains 350 quatrains. It is still very popular among the Tagalogs, but does not appear to have been printed in any of the other Philippine languages. Inasmuch as there is a close connection between our variants and the verse form of the story, I give a prose paraphrase of the latter: —

There was once a poor beggar, Serbando, who had an only son named Juan. They lived in the kingdom of Spain. They had a little hut outside the city in which Serbando used to go to beg their living. One morning, when Juan returned home from school and was playing around their little hovel, he heard many kinds of birds speaking to him thus: "Juan, be patient and toil in poverty. The time will come when God will reward you." Then a large bird flew to him, and said, "Juan, leave your little miserable hut; go and seek your fortune." When his father returned home, Juan told him all about the advice of the birds. Serbando did not believe that birds could talk, and doubted, of course, the truth of what his son said.

Now, it happened that Serbando became sick, and after a short time died, leaving his son alone in the world. Poor Juan wept bitterly over the dead body. He did not know what to do. He covered the corpse of his father, and then went crying out through the streets of the city, "Who wants to buy a slave?" A merchant heard him. "I will serve you as long as I live if you will only see to the burial of my dead father," said Juan to the merchant. Without hesitation the merchant assented, and together they went to the little hut. The merchant ordered and paid for a funeral; there was a procession, a mass, and after the burial a banquet. Then the merchant took the boy to live with him in the city where the king and queen lived. Moreover, this kind merchant sent Juan to school, and treated him as a son. In time Juan took his bachelor's degree, and was greatly admired and respected by his teachers.

One afternoon Juan put a notice on the door of the merchant's house, which read thus: "If we use money, there is nothing we cannot discover." It happened that on that same afternoon the king and queen were driving through the streets of the city. The king chanced to fix his eyes on the sign which Juan had put up. He did not believe that the notice was true; and so, when he arrived at the palace, he ordered the merchant to appear before him. The merchant was very much frightened at the summons, so Juan himself went and presented himself before the king.

"Is the notice on your door true?" asked the king.

"It is true, your Majesty," said Juan.

"Then go and find my daughter. If you can find her, she shall be your wife; if not, you shall lose your head three days from now," said the king, who hid his daughter in a secret room in the palace.

Juan went home and called all the best goldsmiths in the kingdom. He told them to make a little wagon of pure gold, with a secret cell inside in which a man could sit with a musical instrument and play it. The goldsmiths finished the wagon in two days and were paid off. Then Juan called a man and told him to drag this little wagon along the street toward the palace, and then to the plaza. After entering the secret cell with his musical instrument, he told the driver to do as he had been directed. The man began to drag the wagon along the street toward the palace. Men, women, and children crowded both sides of the street to see this wagon of pure gold, which gave out such sweet music. When the wagon passed in front of the palace, the queen was amazed at it. She asked the king to summon the driver before him. So the king called the driver, and asked him to bring the golden wagon into the hall where the queen was.

"How much will you sell this for?" asked the queen.

"I will not sell it," answered the driver.

"Can you not lend it to me until this afternoon?" said the king; and at last the driver agreed to lend the wagon for a few hours.

The queen then dragged the wagon along the hall, and took it to her daughter in the secret room. The princess was delighted. As she pushed it forwards and backwards, sweet music charmed her ears. At last Juan came out of the secret cell in the wagon and knelt before the princess. He told her why he had been led to play this trick, and last of all he told her that he would have lost his life on the morrow if he had not been able to find her. He also began to express his love for her. At first she hesitated to accept his protestations of affection; but at last she accepted him, and gave him one of her rings as a sign that she would marry him. Fearing that he might be caught in the room by some one else, Juan now entered the secret cell of the wagon again.

At last the king came, and started to drag the wagon out of the palace to the place where the driver was waiting. Juan suddenly opened the door of the secret cell and stood before the king. "O king!" he said, "now I have accomplished your command. I have found and seen your daughter in the secret room, and she has given me this ring."

The king was amazed, and said to himself that, had he known that the wagon contained any one inside, he would not have allowed it to be brought to his hidden daughter. He said to Juan, "You have told the truth, that anything can be discovered if money is used; but you shall not marry my daughter."

"Remember your promise," said Juan.

"Wait, and I will ask the princess," said the king. "She might refuse."

"Whether she refuses or not, she is to be my wife, for I have seen her and found her," replied Juan.

"Then you shall have her," said the king.

So Juan was married to the princess, and there was great rejoicing in the kingdom. The king, however, was very sorry that his daughter had married Juan, who had now the right to inherit the throne from him. He could not endure the idea, so he pondered night and day how to kill Juan under some pretext or other. Juan learned of the king's plot, and decided to leave the city for a while. He asked his wife for permission to go and visit the little hut in which he was born, and at last she consented.

One day Juan left the palace and went to the country. While he was walking in the woods near his old home, two birds flew to him. "Juan, take this ring with you; it has magic power, and will furnish you whatever you ask of it," said the male bird.

"Here, take this pen-point, and use it whenever the king asks you to write for him," said the female bird. "Remember, Juan, you do not need to have any ink; you can use your saliva," it continued. "Now go back to the kingdom, and do not be afraid of the king's plots," said the two birds together. So Juan went back to the palace, and lived there with his wife.

One day the king called Juan, and ordered him to write something. The king thought that if Juan should make any mistakes in the writing, he would order him to be executed. Juan used the pen-point which the second bird had given him. The king furnished him only paper, but no ink, so Juan used his saliva. "Write this, Juan," said the king: "'It is not right that you should be heir to my crown, and successor to the throne.'"

Juan wrote the words just as the king had given them, and they appeared on the paper in letters of pure gold. The king was very much surprised by this demonstration of Juan's ability.

Then the king continued, "Write this: 'You ought not to inherit the crown, you who were born in a little village, and whose ancestors are un- known.'" Juan wrote this dictation, and, as before, the letters were of pure gold. Again the king said, "Write now what I shall say: 'You cannot cheat a king like me; you saw my daughter the princess because you were hiding in the wagon of gold.'"

Juan wrote these words, and they were in pure gold too. The king was now sad, for he could think of no other way in which to detect a fault in Juan. So he dismissed his son-in-law, and showed the queen the golden letters that Juan had written. Juan returned to his apartments.

When night came, Juan decided to ask his magic ring for a tower which should stand beside the palace of the king. During the night the tower was erected; it was garrisoned with field-marshals, colonels, and soldiers. Early in the morning the king was surprised to see this tall tower standing beside his palace. He said to himself, "I rule the kingdom, and the king- dom is mine; this tower is in my kingdom, therefore the tower is mine." So the king went out of the palace and entered the tower. No one saluted him. Then he called Juan, and asked him about the tower. Juan answered that its presence there was due to the will and power of God. When Juan and the king together entered the tower, all the soldiers lined up and saluted Juan, and music was heard everywhere. Everything inside was made of solid silver and gold. The king was astounded at the magic power of his son-in-law, whom he was trying to kill.

"Juan," said the king, "wipe away this tower and erect at this moment a palace in its place. If you can do this, you shall be the king of the whole of Spain." By the magic power of the ring, Juan was able to fulfil the command, and the tower was changed into a beautiful palace. The council of the kingdom, at the order of the king, agreed to crown Juan and his wife king and queen. There was great rejoicing throughout the realm. The old king and his wife abandoned the palace, and went to live in an abbey, where they died.

Juan now called the merchant, his former master, to the palace. The merchant was afraid, for he feared that the king wished to do him mis- chief; he did not know that Juan was now king. But Juan received him affectionately, and from that time on the merchant, Juan, and the beautiful princess lived together happily in the palace.

It will be noticed that the Tagalog poem differs from the three oral versions, in that after Juan has won the first wager from the king, his skill is subjected to further tests, which he comes out of successfully through the aid of magic objects given him by birds. In other words, the poem carries on the folk-tale by adding some additional episodes. The fact that the folk-tales, both Pampango and Tagalog, preserve the simple structure, while only the printed Tagalog verse-form seeks to elaborate and extend the tale, suggests that the simpler form is the older, and that the anonymous author of the romance added to the oral material for mere purposes of length. As it is, the poem is very short compared with the other popular metrical stories, which average well over 2000 lines. The localization of the events in Spain signifies nothing.

The story is known also in southern Europe: e.g., in Greece (Von Hahn, No. 13), in Sicily (Gonzenbach, No. 68; Pitrè, Nos. 95, 96). In the Greek version, after the hero has decided to risk his neck for the hand of the hidden princess, he goes to a shepherd and has himself covered with the hide of a lamb with golden fleece. In this disguise he is taken to the princess. In the night he throws off his fleece covering and makes love to the princess, who finally accepts him, and tells him how he may be able to recognize her among her maidens, all of whom, herself included, her father will change into ducks, and then will require the youth to pick out the duck which is the princess. He succeeds, and wins her hand in marriage. In Gonzenbach, No. 68, the hero is one of three brothers who set out to seek their fortunes. They each come in succession to the beautiful city where the king has issued the proclamation that whoever can find his hidden daughter within eight days shall receive her hand in marriage; whoever tries and fails, loses his head. The first two brothers fail and are killed. The youngest, arriving in the city and reading the proclamation, determines to take the risk. He is advised by an old beggar-woman how to find the princess. He has goldsmiths make a golden lion with crystal eyes. The animal is so contrived that it plays continually beautiful music. The hero hides inside, and the old woman takes the lion to the king, to whom she lends it. Then follow the discovery of the princess, her acceptance of the hero's love, the token given to the hero, etc. The hero is obliged to pick the princess out from among her eleven maids who look exactly like her. In Pitrè, No. 95, we find practically the same incidents recorded: two older sons of a merchant go off to seek their fortunes, and lose their heads because they cannot discover the princess "within a year, a month, and a day." The youngest comes in turn to the same country, wagers his head, and searches a year and fifteen days in vain. On the advice of an old woman, he has built a golden *àcula* (just what this word means I have been unable to determine) large enough to contain a person playing a musical instrument. Four men carry the *àcula* to the palace; discovery of the princess follows. Second test: to pick the princess out from twenty-four maidens dressed exactly alike.

In none of these three stories (nor in Pitrè, No. 96, which is a shorter variant of No. 95) does the opening resemble our forms of the tale. Nor in any of the three, either, does the hero bring the wager on himself because of the announcement he makes that he who has gold can discover anything. With this detail, however, compare the couplet which the hero displays in Pitrè, No. 96: —

"Cu' havi dinari fa chiddu chi voli,
Cu' havi bon cavallu va unni voli."

The line "He who has gold can do whatever he wishes" is almost *identical with the* corresponding line in the Tagalog verse story.

It is to be noted that the bride-wager incident in this group of stories resembles closely the same episode in our No. 19. The opening of our No. 21 has been influenced by the setting of the stories of the Carancal group (No. 3).

22. THE REWARD OF KINDNESS.[1]

In a certain town there once lived a couple who had never had a child. They had been married for nearly five years, and were very anxious for a son. The name of the wife was Clara; and of the man, Philip.

One cloudy night in December, while they were talking by the window of their house, Clara said to her husband that she was going to pray the *novena*,[2] so that Heaven would give them a child. "I would even let my son serve the Devil, if he would but give us a son!" As her husband was willing that she should pray the *novena*, Clara began the next day her fervent devotions to the Virgin Mary. She went to church every afternoon for nine days. She carried a small prayer-book with her, and prayed until six o'clock every evening. At last she finished her *novenario*;[3] but no child was born to them, and the couple was disappointed.

A month had passed, when, to their great happiness, Clara gave birth to a son. The child they nicknamed Idó. Idó was greatly cherished by his parents, for he was their only child; but he did not care much to stay at home. He early began to show a fondness for travelling abroad, and was always to be found in the dense woods on the outskirts of the town.

One afternoon, when the family was gathered together around a small table, talking, a knock was heard at the door. "Come in!" said Philip.

"No, I just want to talk with your wife," answered a hoarse voice from without.

Clara, trembling, opened the door, and, to her great surprise, she saw standing there a man who looked like a bear. "A devil, a devil!" she exclaimed; but the Devil pacified her, and said, "Clara, I have come here to get your son you promised me a long time ago. Now that the day has come when your son can be of some service to me, will you deny your promise?"

---

[1] Narrated by Elisa Cordero, a Tagalog from Pagsanjan, La Laguna, who heard the story from a Tagalog friend.

[2] *Novena*, a devotion consisting of prayers held for nine consecutive days and asking for some special favor.

[3] *Novenario*, the act of performing or holding a *novena*.

Clara could make no reply at first. She merely called her son; and when he came, she said to the Devil, "Here is my son. Take him, since he is yours." Idó, who was at this time about seventeen years old, was not frightened by the Devil.

"Come," said the Devil, "and be my follower!" At first Idó refused; but he finally consented to go, because of his mother's promise.

The Devil now took Idó to his cave, far away outside the town. He tried in many ways to tempt Idó, but was unable to do so, because Idó was a youth of strong character. Finally the Devil decided to exchange clothes with him. Idó was obliged to put on the bear-like clothes of the Devil and to give him his own soldier-suit. Then the Devil produced a large bag full of money, and said to Idó, "Take this money and go travelling about the world for seven years. If you live to the end of that time, and spend this money only in doing good, I will set you free. If, however, you spend the money extravagantly, you will have to go to hell with me." When he had said these words, he disappeared.

Idó now began his wanderings from town to town. Whenever people saw him, they were afraid of him, and would refuse to give him shelter; but Idó would give them money from his bag, and then they would gather about him and be kind to him.

After many years he happened to come to a town where he saw an old woman summoned before a court of justice. She was accused of owing a sum of money, but was unable to pay her debt and the fine imposed on her. When Idó paid her fine for her and thus released her from prison, the woman could hardly express her gratitude. As most of the other people about were afraid of Idó and he had no place to sleep, this woman decided to take him home with her.

Now, this old woman had three daughters. When she reached home with the bear-like man, she called her eldest daughter, and said, "Now, my daughter, here is a man who delivered me from prison. As I can do nothing to reward him for his great kindness, I want you to take him for your husband."

The daughter replied, "Mother, why have you brought this ugly man here? No, I cannot marry him. I can find a better husband."

On hearing this harsh reply, the mother could not say a

word. She called her second daughter, and explained her wishes to her; but the younger daughter refused, just as her sister had refused, and she made fun of the man.

The mother was very much disappointed, but she was unable to persuade her daughters to marry her benefactor. Finally she determined to try her youngest daughter. When the daughter heard her mother's request, she said, "Mother, if to have me marry this man is the only way by which you can repay him for his kindness, I'll gladly marry him." The mother was very much pleased, but the two older daughters were very angry with their sister. The mother told the man of the decision of her youngest daughter, and a contract was signed between them. But before they were married, the bear-like man asked permission from the girl to be absent for one more year to finish his duty. She consented to his going, and gave him half her ring as a memento.

At the end of the year, which was the last of his seven years' wandering, the bear-like man went to the Devil, and told him that he had finished his duty. The Devil said, "You have beaten me. Now that you have performed your seven years' wandering, and have spent the money honestly, let us exchange clothes again!" So the man received back his soldier-like suit, which made him look like a knight, and the Devil took back his bear-skin.

Then the man returned to Clara's [1] house. When his arrival was announced to the family, the two older daughters dressed themselves in their best, for they thought that he was a suitor come to see them; but when the man showed the ring and asked for the hand of Clara's youngest daughter, the two nearly died with vexation, while the youngest daughter was very happy.

NOTES.

This story is a variant of Grimm, No. 101, "Bear-Skin," which it follows fairly closely from the point where the hero makes his pact with the Devil. The bibliography of this cycle is fully given in Bolte-Polívka, 2 : 427–435, to which I have nothing to add except this story itself! Our version is the only one so far recorded from the Orient, and there can be no doubt that it is derived directly from Europe. Ralston and Moe seem to detect a relationship between this cycle and

[1] There seems to be an inconsistency here, — Clara was the mother of Idó, — or, if not an inconsistency (there might be two Claras), at least a useless and confusing repetition of names.

a Hindoo saga translated into Chinese in the seventh century, and from the Chinese into French in the middle of the nineteenth century, by the French orientalist Stanislas Julien; but Bolte is of the opinion (p. 435) that there is probably no connection between the two. In any case, to judge from recorded variants, the Tagalog story is an importation from the Occident.

And yet there are not a few deviations in our version from the norm, if Grimm's tale may be considered representative of the cycle. The most important of these is the opening, which is one form of the "Promised Child" opening (see Macculloch, 415 ff.). This formula of a childless couple finally promising in despair to let their child serve even the Devil if they are granted offspring, or to be satisfied with an animal-child or some other monstrosity, is a favorite one in Filipino *Märchen* (cf. Nos. 3 and variants, 19 and variant, and 23), and its use here may have been influenced by the beginning of the next tale.

Other differences may be noted briefly: (1) The compact made between the hero and the Devil does not include the characteristic prohibitions in the European versions; namely, that the hero is not to comb his hair, wash himself, trim his beard, etc., during his seven years of wandering. The Devil seems to rely merely on his bear-suit, which he makes the hero wear, to produce insurmountable difficulties. It may be that the prohibitions mentioned above were omitted because they involved conditions wholly foreign to Filipino conception. The natives take great pride in their hair, and always dress it carefully, are scrupulously clean personally, and are beardless! I can cite no parallel in folk-tales for the condition substituted; i.e., if the wanderer does good with his money, the Devil will have no power over him at the end of the seven years, while, if he spends it extravagantly and foolishly, he goes to hell. Perhaps none need be sought outside of actual experience. (2) The hero is supplied with money from a large bag which the Devil gives him, not from the inexhaustible pockets of a magic green coat, as in Grimm. The mention of the hero's *soldier-suit*, by the way, since nothing has been said earlier in the story of his having followed the profession of arms, is likely a reminiscence of the characteristic opening of the European versions, where it is a poor *soldier* who has the experience with the Devil. (3) The person ransomed by the hero in our story is an old woman instead of an old man. (4) The two disappointed sisters do not kill themselves, and hence the Devil does not reappear at the end of the story, — as he does in Grimm, — and say, "I have now got two souls in the place of thy one!"

The broken-ring recognition on the return home is a feature which I believe occurs in no other Filipino folk-tale, but is met with not infrequently in European saga and story (cf. Köhler-Bolte, 117, 584; *see also* Bolte-Polívka, 1 : 234; 2 : 348).

23. PEDRO AND SATAN.[1]

Once upon a time there lived a very rich man, whose wife had never given birth to a child. The couple had already made several pilgrimages, and had spent great sums of money for religious services, in the hope that God might give them a child, even though a sickly one, to inherit their money; but all their efforts were in vain. Disappointed, the man resolved to rely upon Satan for the performance of his wish.

One dark night, when he was thinking hard about the matter, he heard a voice say, "Your wish will be quickly fulfilled if you but ask me for it." The rich man was so filled with joy, that he turned towards the voice and knelt before the invisible speaker: "I will give you my life, and even my wife's, in return for a son who will be the heir to my riches," said the man. Meanwhile he perceived in front of him a figure which in an instant assumed the form of Satan. At first he was frightened; but his fear was only momentary, and he was eager to hurry up the agreement with Satan, so that he might receive the child. They therefore made a golden document which provided that the first child of the heir was to be given to the Devil at the age of ten, and that the man and his wife were no longer God's subjects, but Satan's.

After the agreement had been made, the Devil promised the rich man that his wife would give birth to the longed-for son early the next morning. Then he disappeared. The child was born at the appointed time, and grew wonderfully fast, for in five days he was a full-grown youth. But the parents could not but blame themselves for their impious act. They intended to keep the secret from their son; but they could not do so, for the boy was always asking about the nature of his existence. So when Pedro — they called him by this name — knew of his pitiful lot, he decided not to marry until he had succeeded in wresting the golden document from the hands of Satan.

Now, Pedro knew that devils do not like crosses, and cannot even stay where they have to look at them. So one day he asked his mother to make for him two gowns, one having little crosses hanging from it. When these had been finished, Pedro asked his father to give him over to Satan, so that he might work with the demons in hell. No sooner had he expressed

[1] Narrated by Pedro D. L. Sorreta, a Bicol from Catanduanes, who heard the story when he was a little boy.

his desire to his father than the Devil appeared and took the young man off to his kingdom. There Pedro was assigned the task of directing the demons in hauling the logs that were to be used for fuel.

Pedro ordered the demons to tie a strong piece of rope to one end of a log, and ordered them to pull it while he stood on the other end. Every time he counted "One, two, three!" he would hold up his outer gown; and the demons, seeing the crosses, would run away in confusion. As the devils could not endure Pedro's conduct, they ran to their master Satan, and asked him to send the young man away, for he could not do any work. The demons could not say anything about Pedro's trick, however, for they did not dare even speak the word "cross." Satan then summoned Pedro to his office, and had him work there.

Now, the young man had put a strong piece of rope under his gown. One day, when Satan was taking his siesta in a rocking-chair, Pedro tied him fast to the chair. Then he removed his outer gown and woke Satan. The Devil with closed eyes struggled hard to escape; but he could not get loose. So he humbly requested Pedro to go away and leave him alone; but Pedro would neither leave him nor let him go. He demanded the document, but Satan would not give it up. So Pedro kept on frightening the Devil until at last Satan said that he would give up the document if Pedro would release him. Pedro put on his outer robe, and the Devil called his secretary and told him to give the golden document to the young man. Pedro threw the bond into the fire; and when he saw that it was completely melted, he took off his outer robe again, and turned Satan loose. The Devil ran away exceedingly terrified.

Then Pedro went home, where his parents received him with great joy. Thus by his cleverness he saved his parents and his future child from a terrible fate.

NOTES.

Like the preceding, this story is doubtless also an importation into the Islands from Europe. It belongs to the general family of tales known as the "Promised Child," but the narrative takes a turn which leads into a special group of this family. The members of this group are usually not long; and the stories, on the whole, are simple. A parent promises, wittingly or unwittingly, his child to the Devil in return for some service, and gives his signature to the bond. The child grows up, and, noticing the dejection of his parents, forces from them the secret of the pact. After equipping himself for the struggle, he sets out for hell to recover the contract. In hell he frightens or annoys the devils in various ways, and becomes such a nuisance that finally the arch-fiend is glad to get rid of him by surrendering the bond.

In a Lorraine story (Cosquin, No. LXIV, "Saint Etienne") "a woman in confinement is visited by a grand gentleman, who persuades her to sell her child to him for a large sum of money. He is to come for the child in six or seven years. One day after a visit of the stranger, the mother begins to suspect him of being the Devil. Her son notices her sadness, and learns the secret that is troubling her. 'I'm not afraid of the Devil,' he says boldly, and tells her to provide him with a sheep-skin filled with holy water. Thus equipped, he sets off with the stranger when the time comes, and, reaching hell, so frightens the devils by sprinkling them with the holy water, that they are glad to leave him in peace to return to his mother." In this story nothing is said of a contract; but in a variant mentioned by Cosquin (2 : 232) a poor man signs in blood a bond according to which he agrees to give up his son at the age of twenty to the rich stranger (Devil in disguise) who has consented to be godfather to the infant. The demon is finally put to flight with the aid of an image of the cross and with the liberal use of holy water.

In a Wallachian story (Schott, No. 15) we find a close parallel of incident to our story: the hero, acting on the advice of his schoolmaster, makes some ecclesiastical garments decorated with crosses, and, dressed in these, he goes to hell and knocks on the door. The demons, frightened by the sight, want to drive him away; but he will not go until they surrender the parchment signed by his father. This story differs from ours in the opening, however; for the father is a poor fisherman, and promises unwittingly "that which he loves most at home" in exchange for great riches. At the end of the story, too, is added an episode of the conversion by the hero of a band of robbers. With the beginning of this Wallachian story compare the Italian "Lionbruno" (Crane, No. XXXVI). In a Lithuanian tale (Chodzko, Contes des paysans et des pâtres slaves [Paris 1864], p. 107), the hero, before setting out to meet the Devil, arms himself with holy water and a piece of chalk blessed by the priest. With the chalk he draws a magic circle about him, from which he throws water on the demons until they give up the contract. For other variants, see Cosquin, No. LXXV and notes.

Our story, while somewhat crude in style, is well motivated throughout, and has one amusing episode for which I know no parallel, — the tying of Satan in his rocking-chair while he is taking his siesta, and then frightening him into compliance, when he wakes, by dis-

playing before him the cross-embroidered gown. The first task the
hero is put to when he enters hell — directing the hauling of logs for
fuel — seems more appropriate than that of draining two ponds, which
the hero is obliged to perform in Cosquin's "La Baguette Merveil-
leuse," No. LXXV.

The testimony of the narrator that he heard the story from one of his
playmates when he was a little boy, throws an interesting ray of light
on the way in which popular stories circulate in the Philippines.

24. THE DEVIL AND THE GUACHINANGO.[1]

There once lived in a suburb of a town a very religious old
widow who had a beautiful daughter, Piriang by name. Young
men from different parts of the town came to court Piriang,
and the mother always preferred the rich to the poor. Whenever
Piriang's friends told her that the man whom she rejected would
have been a good match for her, she always answered that she
would rather have a devil for a husband than such a man.

One day a devil heard Piriang giving this answer to one of
her friends. Thus encouraged, he disguised himself as a young
man of noble blood, and went to Piriang's house to offer her
his love. The mother and daughter received this stranger with
great civility, for he appeared to them to be the son of a nobleman. In the richness of his dress he was unexcelled by his
rivals. After he had been going to Piriang's house for a few
weeks, the old widow told him one day to come prepared to be
married on the following Tuesday. On the Sunday before the
wedding-day he had a long conversation with Piriang. He
calmly asked her to take off the cross that she had about her
neck, for it made her look ugly, he said. She refused to do so,
however, because she had worn this cross ever since she was a
child. After he had departed, Piriang told her mother what he
had asked her to do.

The next day the mother went to the church. She told the
priest that Piriang's bridegroom had ordered her to take off her
cross from her neck. The priest said that that man was a
devil; for no man, as a son of God, would say that a cross made
the one who wore it look ugly. The priest gave the mother a
small image of the Virgin Mary. He instructed her to show the
image to the bridegroom. If when he beheld it he turned his
back on her as she was holding it, she was to tie him around the

---

[1] Narrated by José Laki of Guagua, Pampanga. He got the story from his uncle,
who heard it from an old Pampango story-teller.

neck with her *cintas*.[1] Then she was to put him in a large jar, and bury him at least twenty-one feet under the ground.

The mother went home very much distressed because she had allowed her daughter to become engaged to a devil. She told Piriang not to talk with her bridegroom, because she feared that he was a devil. That night he came with his friend dressed like him. The mother was very gracious to them. They talked about the wedding. When the old woman held up the image of the Virgin Mary, the two men turned their backs on her. She immediately wound her *cintas* around the neck of her daughter's bridegroom, and Piriang came in with the dried tail of a sting-ray in her right hand. She whipped him with this as hard as she could.[2] Then the two together forced him to get into a large jar. After warning him not to come back to earth again, the old woman covered the jar with a piece of cloth wet with holy water. The other devil suddenly disappeared.

The next morning a guachinango[3] happened to pass by the house of the old woman. She called him in, showed him the jar, and told him to bury it at least twenty-one feet deep. When he asked how much she would pay him, she promised to give him ten pesos. He agreed: so, putting the jar on his right shoulder, he set out. When he reached a quiet place, he heard whispers behind him. He stopped and looked around, but could see nothing. Then he put the jar on the ground to rest a few minutes. Now he discovered that the whispers were coming from inside the jar. He was very much surprised.

"What are you?" asked the guachinango. "Are you a man, or a devil?"

"I am a devil, my friend," answered the voice. "The old woman forced me to go into this jar. Be kind to me, my friend, and liberate me!"

"I shall obey the old woman in order to get my pay," said the guachinango. "I will bury you even deeper than twenty-one feet."

"If you will bury me just three feet deep," said the devil, "I will give you a large sum of money."

"I will bury you just one and a half feet deep, if you can give me much money," said the guachinango.

---

[1] *Cintas*, a holy belt worn by women.

[2] See note 1 on *pagui* ("sting-ray"), p. 43.

[3] *Guachinango*, defined by the narrator as "vagabond." The word is used in Cuba as a nickname for the natives of Mexico.

"I will give you five hundred pesos," said the devil. "Dig the ground near the stump of that mabolo-tree. There you will find the money in a dirty black purse."

After the guachinango had buried the devil, he went to the mabolo-tree and took the money. Then he went to the nearest village and played casino. As soon as he lost all his money, he returned to the devil. "I have lost all the money you gave me," he said. "I will now bury you twenty-one feet deep."

"No, do not bury me so deep as that, my friend!" said the devil calmly. "I can give you twice as much money as I gave you before. You will find it in the same place that you found the other."

The guachinango took the money and went to the village again to gamble. Again he lost. He returned to the devil, and asked him angrily why he always lost the money he gave him. "I don't know," answered the devil. "I have given you fifteen hundred pesos, but you haven't even a cent now. You ought to set me free at once."

"Aha! I won't let you go," said the guachinango. "I will bury you thirty-nine feet now."

"I have a plan in mind," said the devil, "which will benefit you extremely; but before I explain my plan, let me ask you if you would like to marry the daughter of the king."

"I have a great desire to be king some day," said the guachinango; "but how can you make me the husband of a princess, when you are only a devil, and I am nothing but a poor guachinango?"

"As soon as you set me free," said the devil, "I will enter the mouth of the princess and go into her brains. Then I will give her a very painful headache which no physician can cure. The king will make an announcement saying that he who can cure his daughter of her disease shall marry her. When you hear this announcement, go to the palace at once, and offer your services to the king. As soon as you reach the princess, tell me that you have come, and I will leave her immediately. The princess will then recover her former health, and you will be married to her. Do not fail to go to the palace, for I am determined to reward you for your kindness to me."

After the guachinango had liberated the devil, he immediately set out for the city. He had not been there three days when he met a group of soldiers crying that "he who could cure the princess should have her to wife." The guachinango stopped the soldiers, and said that he could cure the princess. They took him before the king, where a written agreement was made. If he could not cure the princess in three days, he should lose his life; but if he cured her by the end of the third day, he should marry her. The guachinango was then conducted to the room of the princess. When he approached her, he said to the devil that he had come. "You must leave the princess now; for, if you don't, I shall be executed." But the devil refused to leave, because he wanted to get revenge. He further told the guachinango that he wanted him to die, for then his soul would go to hell.

The guachinango became more and more hopeless. On the morning of the third day he thought of a good plan to get rid of his enemy. He asked the king to order all the bells of the neighboring churches to be tolled, while every one in the palace was to cry out loud, "Here she comes!" While all this noise was going on, the guachinango approached the princess, and told the devil that the old woman was coming with her *cintas*. When the devil heard this, he was terribly frightened, and left the princess and disappeared. The next day the guachinango was married to the princess.

NOTES.

From the testimony of the narrator, this capital story appears to have been known in Pampanga for some time. The incident of the demon entering the body of the princess, and then leaving at the request of one who has befriended him, occurs in a Tagalog story also, which I will give for the purpose of comparison. While the story is more of a fairy-tale than a *Märchen* proper, it appears to be a variant of our No. 24. Significant differences between the two will be noted, however. The Tagalog story was collected and written down for me by Manuel Reyes, a native of Manila. It runs as follows: —

MABAIT AND THE DUENDE.

Menguita, a king of Cebu, had two slaves, — Mabait and Masama. Mabait was honest and industrious, while Masama was envious and lazy. Mabait did nearly all of the hard work in the palace, so he was admired very much by the king. Masama, who was addicted to gambling, envied Mabait.

One night, while Mabait was asleep, a duende [1] awakened him, and said, "I have seen how you labor here patiently and honestly. I want to be your friend."

---

[1] While the term *duende* is Spanish, the other three spirits mentioned — *tigbalang, iki, mananangal* — are good old native demons.

Mabait was amazed and frightened. He looked at the duende carefully, and saw that it resembled a very small man with long hair and a white beard. It was about a foot high. It had on a red shirt, a pair of green trousers, a golden cap, and a pair of black shoes. At last Mabait answered in a trembling voice, "I don't want to be a friend of an evil spirit."

"I am not evil, I am a duende."

"I don't know what duendes are, so I don't want to be your friend."

"Duendes are wealthy and powerful spirits. They can perform magic. If you are the friend of one of them, you will be a most fortunate man."

"How did you come into the world?" said Mabait.

"Listen! When Lucifer was an angel, a contest in creating animals arose between him and God. He and his followers were defeated and thrown into hell. Many angels in that contest belonged neither to God's side nor to Lucifer's. They were dropped on the earth. Those that fell in the forests became tigbalangs,[1] ikis,[1] and mananangals;[1] those in the seas became mermaids and mermen; and those in the cities became duendes."

"Ah, yes! I know now what duendes are."

"Now let our friendship last forever," said the duende. "I am ready at any time to help you in your undertakings."

From that time on Mabait and the duende were good friends. The duende gave Mabait two or three isabels[2] every day, and by the end of the month he had saved much money. He bought a fine hat and a pair of wooden shoes.

Masama wondered how Mabait, who was very poor, could buy so many things. At last he asked, "Where do you get money? Do you steal it?"

"No, my friend gives it to me."

"Who is your friend?"

"A duende."

Masama, in great envy, went to the king, and said, "Master, Mabait, your favorite slave, has a friend. This friend is a duende, which will be injurious to us if you let it live here. As Mabait said, it will be the means of his acquiring all of your wealth and taking your daughter for his wife."

The king, in great rage, summoned Mabait, and punished him severely by beating his palms with a piece of leather. Then he ordered his servants to find the duende and kill it. The duende hid in a small jar. Masama saw it, and covered the mouth of the jar with a saint's dress. The duende was a-fraid of the dress, and dared not come out. "Open the jar, and I will give you ten isabels," said the little man.

"Give me the money first."

After Masama received the money, he went away to the cock-pit without opening the jar. On his way there he lost his money. He went back to the duende, and said, "Friend, give me ten isabels more, and I will open the jar."

"I know that you will cheat me," answered the duende. "Just let me come out of the jar, and I promise that you shall have the princess here for your wife."

"What! Will the princess be my wife?"

"Yes."

"How can you make her love me?"

---

[1] See footnote 1, p. 217.   [2] Same as the Cuban isabelina.

"I will enter the princess's abdomen. I will talk, laugh, and do everything to make her afraid. I will not leave her for anybody but you."

"Good, good!" Masama opened the jar, and the duende flew away to the princess's tower.

Only a few weeks after that time a proclamation of the king was read in public. It was as follows: "The princess, my daughter, has something in her abdomen. It speaks and laughs. No one knows what it is, and no one can force it to come out. Whoever can cure my daughter shall be my heir and son-in-law; but he who tries and fails shall lose his head."

When Masama heard this, he said to Mabait, "Why don't you cure the princess? You are the only one who can cure her."

"Don't flatter me!" answered Mabait.

"I'm not flattering you. It is the duende, your friend, who is in her abdomen, and no one can persuade it to come out but you. So go now, for fortune is waiting for you."

Mabait was at last persuaded, and so he departed. Before going to the king, he first went to a church, and there he prayed Bathala that he might be successful in his undertakings. When Mabait was gone, Masama said to himself, "It is not fortune, but it is death, that is waiting for him. When he is dead, I shall not have anybody to envy."

After sitting for about a half-hour, Masama also set out for the princess's tower, but he reached the palace before Mabait. There he told the king that he could cure his daughter. He was conducted into the princess's room. He touched her abdomen, and said, "Who are you?"

"I am the duende."

"Why are you there?"

"Because I want to be here."

"Go away!"

"No, I won't."

"Don't you know me?"

"Yes, I know you. You are Masama, who cheated me once. Give your head to the king." So the executioner cut Masama's head off.

Then Mabait came, and told the king that he could cure the princess. After he was given permission to try, he said to the duende, "Who are you?"

"I am the duende, your friend."

"Will you please come out of the princess's abdomen?"

"Yes, I will, for the sake of our friendship."

Mabait was married to the princess, was crowned king, and lived happily with his friend the duende.

Before attempting to decide anything concerning the provenience of these two tales, we shall first examine versions of the story from other parts of the world. The nearest European analogue that I am familiar with is an Andalusian story printed by Caballero in 1866 (Ingram, 107, "The Demon's Mother-in-Law"). An outline of the chief elements of this tale follows: —

Mother Holofernes, while very neat and industrious, was a terrible termagant and shrew. Her daughter Panfila, on the contrary, was so lazy and thoughtless, that once, when the old woman burnt herself badly because her daughter was listening to some lads singing outside, instead of helping her mother with the boiling lye for washing, the enraged Mother Holofernes shouted to her offspring, "Heaven grant that you may marry the Evil One himself!" Not long afterward a rich little man presented himself as a suitor for Panfila's hand. He was accepted by the mother, and preparations for the marriage went forward. The old woman, however, began to dislike the suitor, and, recalling her curse, suspected that he was none other than the Devil himself. Accordingly, on the night of the wedding, she bade Panfila lock all the windows and doors of the room, and then beat her husband with a branch of consecrated olive. So done. The husband tried to escape from his wife by slipping through the key-hole; but his mother-in-law anticipated this move. She caught him in a glass bottle, which she immediately sealed hermetically. Then the old lady climbed to the summit of a mountain, and there deposited the bottle in an out-of-the-way place. Ten years the imp remained there a prisoner, suffering cold, heat, hunger, thirst. One day a soldier, returning to his native town on leave, took a short cut over the mountain, and spied the bottle. When he picked it up, the imp begged to be released, and told him of all he had suffered; but the soldier made a number of conditions, — his release from the army, a four-dollar daily pension, etc., — and finally the imp promised to enter the body of the daughter of the King of Naples. The soldier was to present himself at court as a physician, and demand any reward he wished to, in return for a cure. So done. The king accepted the services of the soldier, but stipulated that if in three days he had not cured the princess, he should be hanged. The soldier accepted the conditions; but the demon, seeing that he had his arrogant enemy's life in his hands, and bent on revenge, refused to leave the body of the princess. On the last day, however, the soldier ordered all the bells rung. On the demon's asking what all the noise was about, the soldier said, "I have ordered your mother-in-law summoned, and she has just arrived." In great terror the Devil at once quitted the princess, and the soldier was left "in victorious possession of the field."

It will be noticed that the last episode is almost identical with the ending of our story "The Devil and the Guachinango," while there is a considerable amount of divergence between the two elsewhere.

For versions collected before 1860 I am indebted to Benfey's treatment of this cycle. It is found in his "Pantschatantra," 1 : 519 ff. I take the liberty of summarizing it in this place, first, because it is the only exhaustive handling of the story I know of; and, second, because Benfey's brilliant work, while constantly referred to and quoted, has long been out of print, and has never been accessible in English.

The occasion for Benfey's dissertation on this particular tale is the relationship he sees between it and the large family of stories turning on the motive of a marvellous cure, a representative of which is "Pantschatantra," 5 : 12, "The Miraculous Cure of a Blind Man, a Humpback, and a Three-breasted Princess."[1] While the story we

[1] The episode of a mutual cure being effected by a blind man and a lame man, we *have already met* with in two of the versions of our No. 6.

are discussing cannot be considered in any sense an offshoot of the Pantschatantra tale, it can scarcely be denied, says Benfey, that between the two there is a definite internal relationship, which is further manifested by the fact that in its later development the latter is actually joined to the former (p. 519).

The earliest form of our story is found in the "Cukasaptati," where it is told as the story for the 45th and 46th nights. In this version, —

A Brahman, driven away from home by the malice of his wife, is be-friended by a demon who had formerly lived in the Brahman's house, but who had also fled in fear from her shrewish tongue. The demon enters the body of a princess; and the Brahman, appearing as a conjurer, forces him to leave, in accordance with their pact, and wins half a kingdom and the hand of the princess. The demon now goes to another city where he possesses the queen, an aunt of the Brahman's new father-in-law. The Brahman, whose reputation as an enchanter has become great, is summoned to cure this queen. When he arrives, the demon threatens and insults him, refusing to leave the queen because they are now quits. The Brahman, however, whispers in the woman's ear, "My wife is coming here close on my heels, I have come only to warn you;" whereupon the demon, terror-stricken, at once leaves the queen. The Brahman is highly honored.

Benfey conjectures that this story must have passed over into the Persian redaction of the "Cukasaptati" (i.e., the "Tūtī-nāmeh"), but what changes it underwent in the transmission cannot yet be determined. The earliest European form of the tale is that found in the Turkish "Forty Vezirs" (trans. by Behrnauer, p. 277).

Here a young wood-cutter saves money to buy a rope; but his shrewish wife, thinking that he is going to spend it on a sweetheart, insists on ac-companying him to his work in the mountains, so that she can keep him under her eye. In the mountains the husband decides to abandon his wife in a well. He tells her to hold a rope while he descends to fetch a treasure which he pretends is concealed at the bottom; but she is so avaricious, that she insists on being let down first. Then he drops the rope, and re-turns home free. A few days later, conscience-smitten, he goes back to rescue his wife, and, lowering another rope, he calls to her that he will draw her up; but he hauls a demon to the surface instead. The demon thanks the wood-cutter for rescuing him from a malicious woman "who some days ago descended, and has made my life unbearable ever since." As in the Cukasaptati story, the demon enters a princess and makes her insane, and the wood-cutter cures her and marries her. Then the demon enters another princess. The wood-cutter is summoned; he has to resort to the well-known trick to force the imp to leave this second maiden.

In the Persian form of this story, in the "1001 Days" (Prenzlau ed.), 11 : 247, is added the death-penalty in case the hero fails to perform the second cure, which consists in persuading the spirit, in the form of a snake, to unwind itself from the body of the vezir's daughter. The hero had already cured the sultan's daughter and married her.

A Serbian story (Wuk, No. 37) is closer to the "Forty Vezirs" version than is the "1001 Days." The only essential difference is that the opening of the Serbian tale is the well-known *fabliau* of the "Meadow that was mowed."

Here the wife falls into a pit. When the husband attempts to draw her out again, a devil appears. The devil is thankful; and, to reward the man, it enters the body of the emperor's daughter. Here the hero appears, not as an enchanter, but as a physician.

Practically identical is the story of "The Bad Wife and the Devil," in Vogl, "Slowenische Volksmärchen" (Wien, 1837).

In a Finnish version of the story (Benfey, 524–525) the hero, as in the preceding, assumes the rôle of a physician.

The husband pushes his bad wife into an abyss. When he attempts to draw her out again, another woman appears. She is the Plague.[1] Out of gratitude for her liberation from that other wicked woman, she proposes to him that they travel together through the world: she, the pest, will make people ill; he, as physician, will cure them. So done. As a result the man becomes rich. But at last he grows weary of his excessive work: so he procures a snappish dog, and puts it in a sack. The next time he is called to the side of a person made sick by the pest, he says to her, "Enter human beings no more: if you do, I will liberate from this sack the woman that tormented you in the abyss," at the same time irritating the dog so that it growls. The Plague, full of terror, begs him for God's sake not to set the woman free, and promises to reform.

It will be seen that in its method of the "sickness and the cure," this story is related to Grimm, No. 44, "Godfather Death," where Death takes the place of the Plague, and where, instead of gratitude, the motive is the godfather relationship of Death toward the hero.

This folk-tale, says Benfey (p. 525), was early put into literary form in Europe. Among others, he cites Machiavelli's excellent version in his story of "Belfagor" (early sixteenth century): —

Belfagor, a devil, is sent to earth by his master to live as a married man for ten years, to see whether certain accusations made against women by souls in hell are true or slanderous. Belfagor marries in Florence; but his imperious wife causes him so much bad fortune, that he is compelled to flee from his creditors. A peasant conceals him, and out of gratitude Belfagor tells his rescuer his story, and promises to make him rich by possessing women and allowing himself to be driven out only by the peasant himself. So done. The peasant wins great renown; and at last Belfagor says that his obligations have been fulfilled, and that the peasant must look out for himself if they meet again. The devil now enters the daughter of Ludwig II, King of France. The peasant is summoned to cure her, but is

---

[1] It may be noted, in passing, that among certain of the Tagalogs the pestilence (cholera particularly) is personified as an old woman dressed in black, who goes about the town at night knocking for admittance. If any one pays attention to her summons, the result is fatal to him. This evil spirit is known as *salut.*

afraid, and refuses. At last he is compelled to go, like the physician, against his will (see Benfey, 515 ff.). Belfagor rages when he sees the peasant, and threatens him vehemently. At last the peasant employs the usual trick: "Your wife is coming!" and the devil flees in consternation, choosing rather to rush back to hell than into the arms of his wife.

Benfey considers a Bohemian story in Wenzig's collection (West-slawische Märchen, Leipzig, 1857, p. 167) to be the best of all the popular versions belonging to this group, and he reproduces it in full (pp. 527–534). This long story we may pass over, since it contains no new features that are found in our story. In fact, it little resembles ours or any of the others, except in general in two or three episodes. Benfey concludes his discussion of this cycle by stating that there have been many other imitations of this tale, and he mentions some of these (p. 534). It may be added that further references will be found in Wilson's note in his edition of Dunlop, 2 : 188–190.

The question of the origin of the Pampango version of this story is not easy to answer definitely, for the reason that it presents details not found in any of the other variants. However, since nearly all the machinery of our story turns on the teachings of the Roman Church, and since the *denouement* is practically identical with the ending of Caballero's Andalusian story, I conclude that in its main outlines our version was derived from Spain. At the same time, I think it likely that the fairy-tale of "Mabait and the Duende" was already existent earlier in the Islands (though this, too, may have been imported), and that the motivation of the spirit's desire to revenge himself on his tormentor for his avarice and greed was incorporated into the *Märchen* from the fairy-tale. My reasons for thinking the fairy-tale the older are: (1) its crudeness (the good and the bad hero are a very awkward device compared with the combination of qualities in the guachinango); (2) its local references and its native names; (3) its use of native superstitions and beliefs.

25. JUAN SADUT.[1]

Many years ago there lived a certain old couple who had an only son. Juan, for that was the boy's name, was known throughout the village as an idler, and for this reason he was called Juan Sadut. He had no liking for any kind of work; in fact, his contempt for all work was so great, that he never even helped his father or mother.

One day his father took him to the fields to have him help harvest their crops; but, instead of going to work, Juan betook himself to a shady spot on the edge of the field, and fell asleep.

[1] Narrated by Nicolas Zafra, an Ilocano from San Fernando, La Union. The story is very popular among the country people about San Fernando, he reports.

His father, who was very much enraged by this conduct of his son, determined then and there to dispose of him. He carried the sleeping boy to another part of the field, and laid him down just beside a large snake-hole. He expected that the snake, when it came out of its hole, would sting the sleeping idler, who would thus be disposed of quietly.

When Juan awoke, he found a large snake coiled near him. In his fright, he sprang to his feet to run away; but the snake looked up at him sympathetically, and then began to speak: "Why do you fear me? Don't you know that I am the king of the snakes? I am going to give you a wonderful gift that will make you happy forever;" and having said this, it dropped a gold ring on the ground, and bade Juan pick it up and wear it on his finger. The ring was of pure gold, and it had on it initials that Juan could not understand. "Keep that ring carefully, for it will be of great use to you," said the snake. "Consult it for anything you want, and it will advise you how to proceed to obtain the object of your desire."

After thanking the snake for its gift, Juan set out on his travels. He never worried about his food from day to day, for from his magic ring he could get anything he needed.

In his wanderings, word reached Juan's ears that the king of that country would give his beautiful daughter to any one who could fulfil three conditions. Juan was thrilled with joy on hearing this news, for he was sure that he would be the successful competitor for the hand of the princess. When he presented himself before the court, his slovenly appearance and awkward movements only excited laughter and mirth among the nobles. "What chance have you of winning the prize?" they asked him in derision.

"Let me know the conditions, and time will show," said Juan.

"You must fulfil three conditions before I give my daughter to you," said the king. "First, you must fight with my tiger, and kill it if you can; second, you must go get and bring back to me the burning stone that the dragon in the mountains has in its possession; third, you must answer correctly a question that I shall ask you."

"Very well," said Juan as he turned to go, "I will do all you require of me." Now, many a young man had risked his life for the hand of the beautiful princess; but no one had yet succeeded in winning even the first contest. The king's tiger was ferocious and strong, and as agile as a mouse. Then there was the formidable dragon in the mountains, whose breath alone was deadly poisonous. This dragon lived in a cave the entrance to which was guarded by poisonous serpents. Every morning it would come out of its cave to play with its wonderful stone by tossing it up into the air and catching it in its mouth when it fell. Hence it was difficult, if not impossible, to succeed in these undertakings. The young men who had been stirred by their intense love for the princess had bartered away their lives for her hand.

When Juan arrived home, he took up his little ring, and said to it, "Advise me as to how I may overcome the king's tiger."

"Get a handful of sand," replied the ring, "and mix with it an equal quantity of red pepper. Take the mixture with you into the arena, and when the tiger comes near you, fling the sand into its eyes."

Juan prepared the sand and pepper as he had been advised. The next day he stepped into the arena amid the shouts and cheers of the spectators. He looked, as usual, to be an idle, slow-moving fellow, who would have no chance at all against the wild beast. The tiger soon appeared at the opposite end of the arena, and advanced rapidly towards Juan. When the animal was about three yards from him, he flung the mixture of sand and pepper into its eyes. The tiger was blinded. Juan then drew his dagger and buried it deep into the animal's heart.

The next task he had to perform was to obtain the dragon's fiery stone. The ring advised him thus: "Go to the cave, and, in order to gain admittance, show me to the serpents. I am sacred to them, and they will fulfil whatever commands my possessor gives them." Juan proceeded to the cave in the mountains. He had no sooner entered it than hissing serpents came towards him in threatening attitudes. Juan, however, showed them the signet ring; and they at once became tame, and showed him that they were glad to obey whatever he should command them to do. "Go and get the dragon's stone," he ordered, and soon they came back with the much-coveted treasure.

When the king saw that Juan had fulfilled two of the hardest conditions, he became alarmed because the new bridegroom was to be a person of very low birth: so he devised the most difficult question possible, with the view of preventing Juan from winning his daughter the princess.

Juan now presented himself before the king and his court to perform the third and last task. "What am I thinking about now?" asked the king.

Juan appeared to hesitate a moment, but he was really consulting his ring. The ring said to him, "The king has in mind the assurance that you will not be able to answer his question." Then looking up, Juan answered the king's question in the precise words of the ring, and thus answered it correctly.

Astonished at the wonderful power of Juan, the king gave his daughter to him; and when he died, the young couple inherited the crown of the kingdom.

NOTES.

I know of no parallels to this story as a whole. In its separate incidents it is reminiscent of other tales; and in its main outline, from the point where the hero sets out to seek adventures with the help of his magic ring, the narrative belongs to the "Bride Wager" group. In this group Von Hahn distinguishes at least two types (1 : 54, Nos. 23 and 24): in the one, the hero bets his head against the bride, and wins by performing difficult tasks; in the other, he wins by answering riddles. In our story there is no formal staking of his head by the hero, but undertaking the first two tasks amounts to the same thing. The third task, it will be noticed, is the answering of a difficult question, which in a way connects our story with Von Hahn's second type.

The two distinctive features in our story are the introduction and the first task. The cruelty displayed by the hero's father is not unusual in folk-tales, but his method of getting rid of his son is. The benevolence of the snake, which is not motivated at all, may be at bottom connected with some such moralizing tradition as is found in Somadeva, "The Story of the Three Brahmin Brothers" (Tawney, 1 : 293), where two older brothers, in order to get rid of the youngest, who has been slandered by their wives ("Potiphar's wife" situation), order him to dig up an ant-hill in which lives a venomous snake. Because of his virtue, however, he finds a pitcher filled with gold! There is nothing else in this story which even in the remotest way suggests ours. While Benfey (1 : 214–215, note) has shown that the conception of the snake-jewel is essentially Indian, — and the belief in one form or another is widespread in the Philippines, — he also shows that it was held in Europe even in classical times; and, as every one knows, the idea is a commonplace in folk-lore. Obviously nothing can be concluded as to the origin of our story from this detail alone. The first task, which is performed without supernatural aid, though the hero asks his ring for advice, may be a remnant of tradition; if so, it is of Indian or Malayan tradition, not Philippine, for the tiger is not found *in the Islands.*

26. AN ACT OF KINDNESS.[1]

Early one morning Andres went out to buy five cents' worth of rice. On his way he came across a man who was about to kill a small snake. "Please don't kill the poor creature!" said Andres. "Did it harm you?"

"No," answered the man, "but it may bite us or some other passer-by," and he again drew out his bolo; but Andres restrained him. "What do you want this snake for?" said the merciless man.

"Leave it alone, for pity's sake!" cried Andres. "Here are five cents! Don't injure the harmless creature!"

The man, very glad to get the money, did not say a word, and went away. After the man was gone, the snake said to Andres, "Kind friend, come home with me. There you will find our huge chief snake, and many others like myself. But don't fear anything! Trust me, for I will never lead you into danger. When we reach our dwelling, I will recommend you to our chief. He will be harsh to you at first, since you are a stranger; but never mind that! When he asks you what you want, ask him to give you his red cloth. This enchanted cloth can supply you with whatever you want." So the two friends started for the horrible snake-cave.

"Who is that stranger with you, — a murderer, or a robber?" hissed the chief as soon as the snake and Andres entered.

"He is neither of the two," replied the snake. "Please don't do a bit of harm to him! Had it not been for him, my life would have been lost. He rescued me from the hands of a cruel person who found me creeping through the grass."

"Well," said the chief to Andres, "what reward do you want me to give you?"

"Only your red cloth, and nothing else," answered Andres.

The chief hesitated for a moment. Then he went into a very dark cell, and got out the red cloth. He returned with it, and said to Andres, "Since you have saved the life of one of our number, I give you this cloth as a reward. You can ask of it anything you want."

Andres thanked the chief, and went away. It was now ten o'clock, and he had not yet bought rice for breakfast. "Poor mother! she must be very hungry." Andres himself felt hungry, so he asked the red cloth to bring him food. Soon a

---

[1] Narrated by Pacita Cordero, a Tagalog from Pagsanjan, La Laguna.

breakfast, richer than the ordinary ones he was accustomed to, was spread before him. Having eaten his hearty meal under the shade of a tree, he resumed his journey homeward. He had yet several miles to go.

After a few hours' walk he again became hungry. He went to a hut and asked the old woman there if he might eat in her house. He said that he had brought his own food with him. The old woman invited him in, and Andres asked his red cloth for food. In an instant a fine luncheon was before them. Andres invited the old woman to eat with him, which she willingly did. She liked the food so very much, that she asked Andres to let her have his wonderful red cloth. She said, "Give me this cloth, and I will let you have my two stones in exchange. When you want to get rid of persons who annoy you, just tell these two stones where to go, and they will inflict heavy blows on the evil-doers." Andres agreed to the exchange.

He proceeded on his way, taking with him the two stones. Tired and exhausted from his long journey, Andres again began to feel hungry. Now what would become of him? His red cloth was gone, and he had nothing to eat. Fortunately he saw another hut by the roadside. He went to it, and easily gained admittance. The witch, the only person in the cottage, had just finished her dinner. She had nothing left to give the starving boy. Andres then said to his stones, "Go to your former mistress, the old woman, and tell her that I take back my red cloth. If she refuses to give it to you, do what you think it best to do."

The two stones went back to the hut. There they found the old woman eating. "We have come here," they said, "to take the red cloth away from you. Our master, the boy who was here this afternoon, wants it back again." The old woman refused to give up the cloth, so the stones struck her with heavy blows until she fell down senseless on the floor. Then the stones rolled themselves in the red cloth and hastened back to their master with it. Andres spread it out and ate his dinner. He asked for an extraordinary breakfast besides. Then he said to the witch, "You need not prepare anything for your breakfast to-morrow. Here is a good meal that I have asked my red cloth to give to you, you have been so kind in letting me come to your hut." The witch was very glad, and thanked the *boy. She* said to him, "Boy, I have here two magic canes which

I want to dispose of. I am very old now, and don't need them
any more. They have served me well. These canes can kill
your enemies, or any bad persons whom you want to be put to
death. Just give them directions, and they will obey you."

Andres now had three enchanted possessions. It was very
late when he reached home, and his mother was very hungry
and very angry. He had no more than reached the foot of
the stairs when she met him with a loud scolding. But Andres
just laughed. He asked his red cloth to bring his mother a good
dinner; and while she was eating, he related to her the occurrences of the day.

Andres and his mother were not rich, and their wealthy
neighbors were greatly surprised to see them become rich so
soon. One particularly selfish neighbor, already rich, who was
eager to deprive Andres and his mother of their wealth, sent a
band of robbers to the cottage one night. At midnight Andres
heard his dogs barking, and he knew that there was some one
lurking about. When he saw the robbers coming, he took out
his magic stones and canes, and commanded them to get rid
of the thieves. In a few minutes all the robbers lay dead.

Andres and his mother remained rich.

NOTES.

Through its main incidents and situations, this story is connected
with a number of tales, although, as in the case of the preceding narrative, I can point to no complete analogue for it. The introduction
has some points of close resemblance to the introduction of the "Language of Animals" cycle, where the hero saves the life of a snake,
usually from fire, and is consequently rewarded by the king of snakes
with the gift of understanding the tongues of birds and beasts. This
cycle has been fully discussed by Benfey (Orient und Occident, 2 :
133–171, "Ein Märchen von der Thiersprache, Quelle und Verbrei-
tung"). Additional bibliographical details may be found in Bolte-
Polívka, 1 : 132–133, note 1. The invitation of the rescued snake to
its savior to visit the king of snakes, and its advice that he ask for one
particular magic reward only, are found in many versions of the
"Language of Animals" group, as well as in our story; but this is
as far as the similarity between the two extends. From this point on,
our story deviates altogether, except for the vaguest reminiscences.

Again, in the fact that Andres does not save the snake from an
accidental death, but buys its life from a cruel person about to kill it,
our story appears to be connected with the "Magic Ring" cycle. We

have already discussed two variants of this cycle in No. 10; but, as has been pointed out in the notes to those stories, the most characteristic beginning is lacking there. In most of the members of the "Magic Ring" group, the kind-hearted hero spends all his money to ransom from death certain animals, including a snake which invites him to the home of its father, and then tells him what to ask for. But in our present story, only the snake is saved; the recompense is a magic wishing-cloth that can do only one thing, not a stone or ring that fulfils any command; and as in the case above of the "Language of Animals" cycle, so here, from this point on, our story is entirely different from the "Magic Ring" group, and attaches itself to still another family of tales. This, for want of a better title, may be called the "Knapsack, Hat, and Horn" cycle. I use this name merely because the most familiar member of that family (Grimm, No. 54) bears it.

In Grimm, No. 54, the youngest of three poverty-stricken brothers who set out to seek their fortunes finds a little table-cloth, which, when spread out and told to cover itself, instantly becomes covered with choice food. Not yet satisfied with his luck, he takes the cloth and continues his wandering. One night he meets a charcoal-burner who is about to make his meal off potatoes. The youth invites the man to eat with him. The charcoal-burner, thinking the cloth just what he needs in his solitude, offers to trade for it an old knapsack, from which, whenever it is tapped, out jump a corporal and six soldiers to do whatever they are ordered to do. The exchange is made. The youth travels on, taps the knapsack, and orders the soldiers to bring him the wishing-cloth that the charcoal-burner has. In this same way the youth acquires from two other charcoal-burners successively a magic hat which shoots off artillery and destroys the owner's enemies, and a magic horn a blast from which throws down walls, fortifications, and houses. By means of these articles the hero finally wins the king's daughter to wife, and becomes ruler. Further adventures follow when the wife tries, but without ultimate success, to steal his treasures from him.

The magic articles are not at all constant in this cycle, as may be seen from an examination of Bolte-Polívka's variants (1 : 467–470), but most of the lists include the wishing-cloth and articles in the nature of weapons or soldiers for offensive purposes. A comparison of our story with this formula discloses an undoubted relationship between the two. The hero trades his wishing-cloth for two fighting stones, which he later sends back to fetch the cloth. He then acquires two magic canes (but not by trickery this time). Later, when he becomes an object of envy, and an attempt is made by a rich neighbor to steal his wealth (corresponding to the envy of the king), the magic stones and canes kill all his opponents. Compare the Tagalog variant in the notes to the following tale (No. 27).

The extraordinary articles are found as machinery in other Philippine stories, though not in the above sequence: a "table, spread yourself" and a magic cane occur in No. 27; a magic guitar, in No. 28; a magic *buyo*, cane, purse, and guitar, in No. 35. Compare also the magic articles in the various forms of No. 12. I know of no other occurrence in folk-tales of two fighting stones. This detail sounds very primitive. It might be compared with the magic "healing stones" in No. 12 (*b*), "Three Brothers of Fortune," though the two objects are wholly dissimilar in power.

As a whole, while our story is reminiscent of at least three different cycles of tales, it nevertheless does not sound like a modern bit of patchwork, but appears to be old; how old, I am unable to say. The most unreasonable part of our narrative is the fact that the hero should find himself so many miles from home when going to buy five cents' worth of rice. It must be supposed that the trip to the snake-cave occupied much more time than it appears in the story to have taken.

27. THE INDOLENT HUSBAND.[1]

Many hundreds of years ago there lived in the isolated village of Hignaroy a poor couple who had many children to care for. Barbara, the wife, was an industrious but shrewish woman. She worked all day in a factory to support her many children. The husband, Alejo, on the other hand, idled away his time. He either ate, or drank, or slept all the time his wife was away at work. In the course of time Barbara naturally became disgusted with her husband's indolence; and every time she came home, she would rail at him and assail him with hot, insolent words, taxing him with not doing anything, and with caring nothing about what was going on in the house: for, on her return home in the evening, she would always find him asleep; while the floor would always be strewn with chairs, benches, and pictures, which the children had left in a disorderly way after playing.

Alejo seemed to take no heed of what she said; he became more sluggish, and had no mind for anything but sleeping all day. What was worse, was that he would eat such big meals, that he left but little food for his wife and children. Barbara's anger and impatience grew so strong, that she no longer used words as a means to reform her husband. She would kick him as he lay lazily on his bed, and would even whip him like a

[1] Narrated by Gregorio Frondoso, a Bicol from Tigaon, Camarines, who heard the story when he was a small boy. One of the servants told it to him.

child.   Finally the thought of leaving home came into his head;
he determined to travel to some distant land, partly with the
purpose of getting away from his wife, who was always inter-
fering with his ease, and partly with the purpose of seeking his
fortune.

One day he set out on a long journey, wandering through
woods, over hills, and along the banks of rivers, where no human
creature could be seen.   After roaming about a long time, he
became tired, and lay down to rest in the shade of a tree near
the bank of a river.   While he was listening to the melodious
sounds of the birds and the sweet murmur of the water, and
was meditating on his wretched condition, an old humpback
came upon him, and addressed him in this manner: "What is
the matter, my friend?   Why do you look so sad?"

"I am in great trouble," said Alejo.   "I will tell you all about
it.   I am married, and have many children to support; but I
am poor.   I have been idling away my time, and my wife has
been kicking and whipping me like a child for not doing anything all day.   So I have finally left home to seek my fortune."

"Don't be worried, my son!" said the old man.   "Here,
take this purse!   It has nothing in it; but, if you need money
at any time, just say these words, — 'Sopot, ua-ua sopot!' [1] —
and it will give you money."

Alejo was very glad to have found his fortune so quickly.   He
took the purse from the old man, and, after thanking him for
it, started for his home with lively spirits.   Soon he reached the
village.   Before going home, however, he went to the house of
his *compadre* and *comadre*,[2] and related to them what he had
found.   They entertained him well; they drank and sang.
While they all were feeling in good spirits, Alejo took out his
magic purse to test it before his friends.

"Friends," said Alejo, now somewhat drunk, "watch my
purse!" at the same time pronouncing the words "Sopot, ua-ua
sopot!"   Then showers of silver coins dropped on the floor.
When the couple saw this wonder, they thought at once that
their friend was a magician.   They coveted the purse.   So they
amused Alejo, gave him glass after glass of wine, — for he was a
great drinker, — until finally he was dead-drunk.   At last he
was overcome by drowsiness, and the couple promptly provided

---

[1] That is, "Purse, spit money from your throat!"
[2] *Compadre* and *comadre*, the godfather and godmother of one's child.

him with a bed. Just as he fell asleep, the wife stealthily untied the purse from Alejo's waist, and put in its place one of
their own.

After a good nap of an hour or two, Alejo awoke. He thanked
his friends for their kind reception and entertainment, and,
after bidding them good-by, went to his own home. There he
found his wife busy sewing by the fireside. He surprised her
with his affectionate greeting. "My dear, lovely wife, be
cheerful! Here I have found something useful, — a magic
purse which will furnish us with money."

"O you rogue!" she replied, "don't bother me with your
foolishness! How could you ever get anything useful? You
are lying to me."

"Believe me, my dear, I am telling the truth."

"All right; prove it to me at once."

"Call all our children, so that they may also see what I have
found." When all the children were called together, Alejo
asked the purse for money, just as the old man had showed him
how to ask; but no shower of coins dropped to the floor, for,
as you know, it was not the magic purse. Barbara was so
enraged, that she stormed at him with all the bitter words
that can be imagined, and drove him from the house. Alejo
was a tender-hearted, if lazy, husband, and it never occurred to
him to beat his wife in turn. In fact, he loved her and his
children very much.

He wandered away again in the direction of the place where
he had met the old humpback. Here he found the old man,
who said to him, "Where are you going, Alejo?"

"Guiloy, your purse did not prove to be any good."

"Well, take this goat home with you. It will give you
money if you ask for it. Whenever you want any money, just
say these words: 'Canding, pag coroquinanding!'" [1]

Alejo gladly accepted the goat, and set out for home again.
Again he passed by his friends' house. There he stopped, and
they entertained him as before: they drank, danced, and sang.
Alejo told them about the virtues of his magic goat when he
was feeling in a jovial mood; and when he fell asleep, they exchanged his beast for one of their own. After his nap, Alejo
started home, his goat flung over his shoulder; but again, when
he tried to demonstrate to his wife the magic powers of the

---

[1] That is, "Goat, leap about!"

goat, the animal did nothing, but stood looking as foolish as before Alejo spoke the words the old man had taught him. Barbara was more angry than ever, and, after railing at her husband, would have nothing more to do with him.

Alejo immediately left home to find the old man again. In a short time he met him. "How now, Alejo? What's the matter?"

"Your magic goat would not obey my command," said Alejo.

"Try this table, then," said the old man. "It will provide you with all kinds of delicious food and drink. Just say, 'Tende la mesa!' [1] and all kinds of foods will be served you."

Thanking the old man and bidding him good-by, Alejo shouldered the magic table and left. He was invited into his friends' house as before, and was entertained by the deceitful couple. Alejo imparted to them the secret of his table. "Tende la mesa!" he said, and in the wink of an eye every kind of food you could wish for appeared on the table. They ate, and drank wine. Again Alejo drank so much, that soon he was asleep, and again the false couple played a trick on him: they exchanged his magic table for a common one of their own. When Alejo woke up, he hastened to his own home, carrying the table on his shoulder. He called his wife, and assured her that the table would provide them with every variety of food. Now, this was indeed good news to Barbara, so she called all their children about them. When every one was seated about the table, Alejo exclaimed, "Tende la mesa!" . . . You cannot imagine what blows, what pinches, what whips, Alejo received from his wife's hands when not even a single grain of rice appeared on the table!

Alejo now felt greatly ashamed before his wife. He wondered why it was that when before his friends' eyes the purse, the goat, and the table displayed their magic properties, they failed to display them before his wife. However, he did not give up hope. He immediately set out to seek the old man again. After a long wandering through the same woods and hills and along river-banks, he came to the place where he usually met him.

"Did the table prove good?" said the old man.

"No, guiloy; so I have come here again."

"Well, Alejo," said the old man, "I pity you, indeed. Take

[1] That is, "Table, spread yourself!"

this cane as my last gift. Be very careful in using it, for I have no other object to give you. The secret of this cane is this: if somebody has done you wrong, say to the cane, 'Baston, pamordon!' [1] and then it will lash that person. There are no princes, kings, or emperors that it will not punish."

Taking the cane and thanking the old man, Alejo hastily returned home. This time, when he reached the village, he did not pass by his friends' house, but went directly home. He told his wife to go call in all their friends, relatives, and neighbors, for they were going to have a sort of banquet. At first Barbara was unwilling to do so, because she remembered how she had been deceived before; but at last Alejo persuaded her to do as he wished.

When all their friends, relatives, and neighbors were gathered in his house, Alejo shut all the doors and even the windows. Then he shouted to his magic cane, "Baston, pamordon!" and it at once began to lash all the people in the house, throwing them into great confusion. At last Alejo's two friends, the deceitful couple, exclaimed almost in one voice, "*Compadre*, please stop, and we will give you back your magic purse, goat, and table." When Alejo heard them say this, he was filled with joy, and commanded the cane to cease.

That very day the magic purse, goat, and table were returned to him by his *compadre* and *comadre*, and now Barbara realized that her husband's wanderings had been profitable. The husband and wife became rich, and they lived many happy years together.

NOTES.

A Tagalog story resembling the Bicol tale in some respects is "The Adventures of Juan" (JAFL 20 : 106–107), in which —

A magic tree furnishes the lad who spares it a goat that shakes silver money from its whiskers, a net which will catch fish even on dry ground, a magic pot always full of rice, and spoons full of whatever vegetables the owner wishes, and finally a stick that will beat and kill. The first three articles a false friend steals from Juan by making him drunk. With the help of his magic cane, however, he gets them back, and becomes rich and respected. One night a hundred robbers come to break into the house, to take all his goods and kill him; but he says to the stick, "Boombye, boomba!" and with the swiftness of lightning the stick flies around, and all those struck fall dead, until there is not one left. Juan is never troubled again by robbers, and in the end marries a princess and lives happily ever after.

[1] That is, "Cane, whip!"

The last part of this story I have given in full, because it is almost identical with the episode at the end of the preceding tale (No. 26, *q.v.*), and consequently connects that story with our present cycle. In a "Carancal" variant (III, *e*) the hero finds a magic money-producing goat.

The hero of our tale is a lazy, good-natured man, whose industrious wife's reproaches finally drive him from home. Analogous to this beginning, but not furnishing a complete parallel, is Caballero's "Tio Curro el de la porra" (Ingram, 174–180).

Uncle Curro is pleasure-loving and improvident, and soon finds himself and his family in the direst need. Unable finally to bear the reproaches of his wife, he goes out in the field to hang himself, when a little fairy dressed like a friar appears, and blames him for his Judas-like thought. The fairy then gives him an inexhaustible purse, but this is stolen from him by a rascally public-house keeper. Again he goes to hang himself; but the fairy restrains him, and gives him a cloak that will furnish him with all kinds of cooked food. This is likewise stolen. The third time he is given a cudgel. While on his way home, he is met by his wife and children, who begin to insult him. "Cudgel, beat them!" Magistrates and officers are summoned. These are put to rout; and finally Uncle Curro and his stick make such havoc among all sent to restrain him, that the king promises him a large estate in America.

This version differs from the usual form, in that the inn-keeper is not punished, nor are the first two magic objects recovered.

The "Ass-Table-Stick" cycle, of which the "Indolent Husband" is clearly a member, is one of the most widespread *Märchen* in the world. For a full bibliography of this group, see Bolte-Polívka, I : 346–361 (on Grimm, No. 36). The usual formula for this cycle is as follows: —

A young servant (or a poor man) is presented by his master (or by some powerful personage — in some of the versions, God himself) on two different occasions with a magic object, usually a gold-giving animal, and a table or cloth which miraculously supplies food. When in an inn, he is robbed of the magic object and magic animal by the inn-keeper or his wife, and worthless objects resembling those that are stolen are substituted while the hero sleeps (or is drunk). The third magic article, which he gets possession of in the same way as he acquired the other two, is a magic cudgel or cane, through the aid of which he recovers his stolen property.

This is the form of the story as it is found in Basile (I : i), Gonzenbach (No. 52), Cosquin (Nos. IV and LVI), Schott (No. 20), Schneller (No. 15), Jacobs (English Fairy Tales, "The Ass, the Table, and the Stick"), Dasent (No. XXXIV, "The Lad Who Went to the North Wind" = Asbjörnsen og Moe, 1868, No. 7), Crane (No. XXXII, "The Ass that Lays Money"); and it is this formula that our story follows. Grimm, No. 36, however, differs from these stories in two respects: (1) it has a framework-story of the deceitful goat on whose account the father drives from home his three sons; (2) the story proper concerns *three* brothers, one of whom acquires the little wishing-table, another the gold-ass, and the third the cudgel. However, as in the other tales, the possessor of the stick compels the thieving inn-keeper to return the property stolen from his brothers.

In their details we notice a large number of variations, even among the European forms. The personage from whom the poor man receives the magic objects is sometimes God, Fortune, a fairy, a statue, a magician, a dwarf, a priest, a lord, a lady, etc. (Cosquin, 1 : 52). The old humpback in our story may be some saint in disguise, though the narrator does not say so. The gold-producing animal is not always an ass, either: it may be a ram (as in the Norse and Czech versions), a sheep (Magyar, Polish, Lithuanian), a horse (Venetian), a mule (Breton), a he-goat (Lithuanian, Norwegian), a she-goat (Austrian), a cock (Oldenburg), or a hen (Tyrolese, Irish). For references see Macculloch, 215.

The Indian members of this cycle are Lal Behari Day, No. 3, "The Indigent Brahman;" Minajev, "Indiiskia Skaski y Legendy" (1877), No. 12; Stokes, No. 7, "The Foolish Sakhouni;" Frere, No. 12, "The Jackal, the Barber, and the Brahmin who had Seven Daughters." Of these versions, Day's most closely resembles the European form (Cosquin, 1 : 57).

Numerous as are the Indian and other Oriental variants, it seems to me very likely that our story was not derived directly from them, but from Europe. However, I shall not undertake to name the parent version.

28. CECILIO, THE SERVANT OF EMILIO.[1]

Once upon a time there lived a witty orphan whose name was Cecilio. His parents had died when he was six years old. After that time he became a servant of Emilio, a man of wealth living in a very lonely and desolate barrio. The boy was faithful and kind-hearted, but his master was cruel. Cecilio had no wages at all. In short, he served Emilio for four years, and at the end of that time he was given five hundred centavos as a payment for his services. Cecilio thought that he had been given too much: he was so simple-minded, that he did not know he had been cheated by his master, who should have given him ten times five hundred centavos.

Cecilio put his money in a new purse, and rushed out into the main road of the barrio to find his companions and tell

[1] Narrated by Sancho B. de Leon, a Tagalog from Santa Cruz, Laguna. He heard the story from his grandfather.

them of the reward he had received. He was so very happy, that before he knew it, and without feeling at all tired, he had reached another barrio. Suddenly on his way he met two men with drawn bolos. They stopped him, and said, "Boy, your money, or your life!" Cecilio was much amazed at these words, but was also so frightened that he gave up the money at once. He only said to himself, "Well, since I am not strong enough to defend myself, I either have to surrender my money or die." He sat under a tree lamenting his fortune. But the two robbers were in trouble, because one of them wanted a greater share than the other. The second robber said that their shares should be the same, for they had stolen the money together; but the former answered, "I am in all respects better than you are." — "Oh, no! for we have not yet had a trial," said the second. At this they began to fight; and soon both fell so severely wounded, that they died before Cecilio, who had heard the noise of the struggle, could reach the place where they were disputing.

Now the boy was very happy again, for he had gotten his money back. As he had already travelled very far, he did not know where he was: he was lost. But he proceeded along the road until he met another man, who said roughly to him, "Give me your money, or else you will die!" Cecilio, thinking that he would rather live than try to defend his wealth, which he would lose in any case, gave his purse to the man. Then the boy went away and wept. While he was crying over his bad luck, a very old woman came near him, and said, "Why are you weeping, my boy?"

The boy replied, "I am weeping because somebody took my money."

"Well, why did you give it up?" said the old woman.

"I gave it up because he said that he would kill me if I didn't."

Then the old woman said, "Take this cane with you, and whenever you see him, let it loose and pronounce these words: —

"'*Sigue garrote, sigue garrote,*[1]
Strike that fellow over there!'

When you want the cane to stop, all you need to say is —

[1] (Spanish) "At him, cudgel!"

> "'Stop, stop,
> For that is enough!'"

The boy then said, "Is that all?"

"After you have recovered your money," said the old woman, "you must turn back here; but you had better hurry up now."

Cecilio then bade the old woman good-by, and at once ran away to overtake the man who had robbed him. When he saw the man, he said, "Give me back my money, or else you now shall die, and not I!"

The man laughed at him, and said, "Of course I shall not give you back your money."

When he heard these words, the boy said, "Is that so?" and, letting go of his cane, he uttered the formula that the old woman had told him to pronounce. The cane at once began to rain blows on the stranger's head and body. When he could no longer endure the blows, and saw that he could not catch the stick, the man said, "If you will call off your cane, I will return your purse."

"Very well, I will pardon you," said Cecilio; "but if you had treated me as you should have treated me and others, you would not have been harmed." Then he said to the cane, —

> "Stop, stop,
> For that is enough!"

At once the magic stick stopped, and returned to its owner. The money was given back, and the man promised Cecilio that he would not rob any poor boy again.

On his way back toward the old woman, Cecilio met another man who wanted to rob him; but the boy said, "Don't you dare attempt to take my purse, or you will get yourself into trouble!" The man became angry, and rushed at Cecilio to knock him down; but the boy pronounced the words which the old woman had taught him, and let the cane loose. The cane at once began to rain blows on the man's head and body. When he could no longer endure the pain, the man asked Cecilio's pardon. As the youth was kind-hearted, he forgave the man.

When he reached the old woman's house, Cecilio told her that the cane had been very useful to him, for it had saved both his life and his money. Then he returned the stick to the old woman, and thanked her very much. She now offered to sell him a guitar which she had, the price of which was five hundred centavos. Since she had been so good to him, Cecilio at once agreed to the exchange; and after he had once more bade her good-by, he set out for his master's house.

When he came near his old home, Cecilio saw his master Emilio shooting at a very handsome bird on the top of a bamboo-tree. The bird fell down, and the man ran to pick it up. As Emilio was making his way up to the bird through the thorny bamboo undergrowth, Cecilio sat down to wait for him, and, having nothing else to do, began to play his guitar. The master at once began to dance among the bamboo-trees, and he received many wounds because of the sharp spines. Now, in reality, the boy was playing his guitar unintentionally, and did not know of its magic power; but Emilio thought that Cecilio had discovered the deceit that had been practised on him, and was playing for revenge. Now, it happened that Emilio had a purse of money with him to give to the laborers working in his hacienda, so he promised to give all this money to Cecilio if he would only stop playing. The boy, who had by this time learned of the magic power of his guitar, stopped his music and received the money.

The crafty Emilio, however, at once hastened to the town, and asked the magistrate to apprehend Cecilio, a young robber. Cecilio set out for the old woman's house again; but the policemen soon overtook him, arrested him, and took him before the magistrate. There the boy was sentenced to death the next morning. Emilio's money was given back to him. The following day, when he was about to be shot, Cecilio asked permission to play his guitar once more, and he was not refused it. As soon as he began to play, all began to dance, even his master, who was still sore from the previous day's exercise. Finally Emilio could endure no more. He begged Cecilio to stop playing, and promised to give him all his wealth. He then told the soldiers to set the boy free, for it was all his own fault. Cecilio stopped playing, and was liberated by the magistrate. Emilio kept his word, and bestowed on the boy all his wealth. When the old man died, Cecilio was the richest man in the town. He became a capitan,[1] and was greatly honored by the inhabitants of his barrio.

[1] *Capitan.* In the Philippines this word is used as a title of address to a justice of the peace (*gobernadorcillo*). It is also used to designate the office itself.

NOTES.

A Tagalog variant of this story by the same narrator may be given here in abstract. While this briefer form seems to bear evidence of some contamination with the tale of "Cecilio," each, nevertheless, preserves characteristics lacking in the other; and again, while the two seem to be more or less distinct versions, there can be no doubt that they go back to the same original. The title of the variant is "The Fortunes of Andoy, an Orphan." In abstract it runs thus: —

Once a poor orphan named Andoy, while taking a walk, found a purse. On his way home he met a man who, without a word, took the purse from him. The boy beginning to cry, the man had pity on him, and returned the purse, keeping only a few coins for himself. Andoy next met two hunters, who robbed him; but these men had not gone far when two genuine robbers met them, and a fight ensued in which all four were killed. When Andoy heard the noise of the struggle, he ran to see what was happening. He found hunters and robbers dead; so he recovered his purse and went on. Not long afterward he met a hermit, who sold him a magic cane. The next man he encountered was looking for a purse he had lost in the road, and, when he saw Andoy's, took it without a word; but the money did not really belong to this man. The boy immediately turned his cane loose on his assailant, who, after being badly beaten, confessed that the purse was not his, and promised Andoy half his wealth if he would call off his stick. The rich man kept his word; and when he died, Andoy received his entire fortune.

Another variant, which was collected by Mr. R. L. Rusk of Indiana University, and which I have only in abstract, is called "Peter the Violinist." It runs thus: —

Peter, a lazy ne'er-do-well, ran away from home, leaving his parents to die of grief. For being kind to a sick "old woman" he was given a magic violin. Soon after, he was arrested for climbing into a house at night. When he was about to be hanged for a thief, he was granted a last request. He asked to be allowed to play his favorite piece on his violin. As soon as he began, every one commenced to dance. He continued, and all cried out for him to stop; but he would not cease until they pardoned him and promised to make him king besides.

The history of the cycle of tales to which our story and the two variants belong has been traced briefly in Bolte-Polívka, 2 : 491–503. The earliest forms of the *Märchen* are the Middle-English poems of the fifteenth century entitled "Jack and his Step-Dame" and "The Frere and the Boye."

Here the hero is Jack, who is hated by his step-mother. Since his father is not willing to turn him out of the house altogether, the step-mother manages to bring it about that Jack is set to watch the cattle, and she allows him only rotten food. An old man with whom he shares his victuals grants him three wishes in return for his kindness. He asks for a bow and a fife; and the old man gives him a bow that never misses its aim, and a fife that compels every one to dance. He also grants Jack's third wish, that every time his step-mother hurls a bad word at him or about him, she shall give forth another noise not permitted in polite society. When this happens that evening at home to the amusement of all, the step-mother plans to send the monk Tobias into the field the next day to punish Jack. However, Jack asks the monk to fetch from the brambles a bird which he has shot, and then he begins to play dance-music for the monk. All scratched and bloody, Tobias returns home. That night the father calls his son to account; but he is so pleased at the effects of the magic fife, that he decides not to punish the boy. The official, too, the bishop's agent, at whose court the next Friday step-mother and monk bring charges of witch-craft against Jack, has to hear the fife, and is obliged to dance until he promises to let Jack go unpunished.

The English story seems to have passed over into Holland, where in 1528 a Dutch form appeared, with some additions. A most significant modification appears in a German handling of the Dutch form, by Dieterich Albrecht in 1599: —

Here the hero is not a cowherd plagued by his malicious step-mother, but a simple-minded servant who serves an avaricious master for three years and receives as pay three *pfennigs* for the whole time. Pleased with his earnings, however, he goes away singing. When he meets two beggars who ask him for alms, he gives them his three coins. They grant him three wishes in return for his goodness; and he gets a "never-miss" crossbow, a magic fiddle that makes all dance, and the promise that no one shall ever be able to deny him a request. By a lake he meets a monk, who jeers at his shooting-ability, and undertakes, if the youth can bring down a raven there on the island, to swim over naked and fetch the bird. Soon, however, the monk regrets his bargain, for the crossbow does not miss. While the monk stands naked in the bushes on the island, the boy begins to fiddle. Wailing and moaning, the ecclesiastic promises the youth the hundred ducats that he has stolen from the monastery, and he is now per-mitted to return and get his clothes. But he treacherously follows the youth, lodges a complaint against him with the council of the nearest city, and succeeds in getting him condemned. When the youth is already on the gallows ladder, he requests the judge to allow him to play just one more song; and he makes all those present dance so violently, that the judge agrees to pardon him if he will only cease playing. Then the monk confesses his own theft and deceit, and receives his deserved punishment.

In this version, as Bolte and Polívka note (2 : 493), the chief deviations from the English-Dutch form of the story are the omission of the step-mother rôle, the nature of the third wish, and the modifi-cation of the character of the monk, who, from a mere tool of the step-mother, has here developed into a thieving rascal. A Czech redaction (1604) of the German poem substitutes for the runaway monk a Jew. This substitution is also found in the German prose tale "Von Knecht Treurecht" (about 1690).

Of the modern oral folk-versions of the story, some are based on the Middle-English droll; but by far the larger number omit the hostile step-mother, and retain only the dance of the monk or the Jew and the scene at the gallows. For a complete list of stories of this second type, see Bolte-Polívka, 2 : 495–501. All the variants, both literary and popular, cited in this bibliography, are Occidental; and we must inevitably conclude that the story was imported into the Philippines some time during the Spanish occupation of the Islands. Some rather important differences are presented by our versions, however; and these we shall call attention to briefly, first mentioning the details that definitely connect our forms with the European.

The opening of the story of "Cecilio" is like that of Albrecht's, given above. Our hero works four years for a cruel master, and receives five hundred centavos as pay, — a sum with which he is more than satisfied. At this point our story digresses. After two adventures with robbers, in the first of which he recovers his money by a lucky accident (this incident is considerably elaborated in the variant), he meets an old woman who lends him a magic cane, and with its help he is able to regain his money from a second robber. This feature of the magic beating-stick seems to be borrowed from the preceding story. He now returns the cane to the old woman, and she sells him a magic guitar. The next adventure — with his former master, who is substituted for the knavish monk — contains a distorted reminiscence of the shooting of the bird, and ends with the dance among the thorns (here bamboo-spines). The hero is bought off by his master, who immediately rushes to town and accuses him of theft. The rest is practically as in Albrecht.

While our version introduces two magic articles, it can be seen that the first does not properly belong to the story. The "three-wishes" incident, and accordingly the third wish itself, is lacking altogether. A rather artistic attempt to unify the story as a whole is the substitution of the rascally master introduced in the beginning of the story, for the knavish monk or Jew later on; though it is to be noticed that the narrator fails to motivate the hero's return to the house that he had apparently left for good when he was paid off. The episode of the shooting is obscure, and appears to be only a vague echo of the detail definitely connected with one of the three gifts in some of the European literary forms. Again, in "Cecilio" the musical instrument is a guitar instead of the usual violin or fife; while in the variant "Andoy" the magic cane is the only enchanted object, no musical instrument appearing at all. The episode of the two robbers killing each other over the treasure (paralleled in "Andoy," where two robbers fight with two hunters, and all four are killed) is an interesting addition, the source of which I am unable to point out. It may be derived from some moral tale related in kind to the "Vedabbha-jātaka," No. 48; "Cento Novelle Antiche," No. 82; Morlini, No. 42; Chaucer's "Pardoner's Tale," etc.; although the characteristic treachery emphasized in those stories is lacking here. The incident is not found in other versions of our tale that I know of.

I am unable to name the immediate source of our story of "Cecilio" and of the two variants; though, as has been remarked above, it was pretty certainly European. None of the three seems to owe anything in particular to the Spanish ballad printed in the "Romancero General," No. 1265, which Bolte and Polívka think is based directly on Grimm, No. 110. The local modifications in our story, and the definite native atmosphere maintained throughout, suggest that it is not a recent importation.

An interesting animal version from South Africa, containing the magic bow and magic fiddle, is given by Honeÿ (p. 14), "The Monkey's Fiddle." This story was doubtless taken over by the natives from the Dutch.

29. CHONGUITA.[1]

There was a king who had three sons, named Pedro, Diego, and Juan. One day the king ordered these three gentlemen to set out from the kingdom and seek their fortunes. The three brothers took different directions, but before they separated they agreed to meet in a certain place in the forest.

After walking for many days, Don Juan met an old man on the road. This old man gave Don Juan bread, and told him to go to a palace which was a mile away. "But as you enter the gate," said the old man, "you must divide the bread which I have given you among the monkeys which are guarding the gate to the palace; otherwise you will not be able to enter."

Don Juan took the bread; and when he reached the palace, he did as the old man had advised him. After entering the gate, he saw a big monkey. Frightened at the sight of the animal, Don Juan was about to run away, when the animal called to him, and said, "Don Juan, I know that your purpose in coming here was to find your fortune; and at this very moment my daughter Chonguita will marry you." The archbishop of the monkeys was called, and Don Juan and Chonguita were married without delay.

A few days afterwards Don Juan asked permission from his wife to go to the place where he and his brothers had agreed

[1] Narrated by Pilar Ejercito, a Tagalog from Pagsanjan, Laguna. She heard the story from her aunt, who had heard it when she was still a little girl.

to meet. When Chonguita's mother heard that Don Juan was going away, she said to him, "If you are going away, take Chonguita with you." Although Don Juan was ashamed to go with Chonguita because she was a monkey, he was forced to take her, and they set out together. When Don Juan met his two brothers and their beautiful wives at the appointed place, he could not say a word. Don Diego, noticing the gloomy appearance of his brother, said, "What is the matter with you? Where is your wife, Don Juan?"

Don Juan sadly replied, "Here she is."

"Where?" asked Don Pedro.

"Behind me," replied Don Juan.

When Don Pedro and Don Diego saw the monkey, they were very much surprised. "Oh!" exclaimed Don Pedro, "what happened to you? Did you lose your head?"

Don Juan could say nothing to this question. At last, however, he broke out, "Let us go home! Our father must be waiting for us." So saying, Don Juan turned around and began the journey. Don Pedro and Don Diego, together with their wives, followed Don Juan. Chonguita walked by her husband's side.

When the return of the three brothers was announced to the king, the monarch hastened to meet them on the stairs. Upon learning that one of his sons had married a monkey, the king fainted; but after he had recovered his senses, he said to himself, "This misfortune is God's will. I must therefore bear it with patience." The king then assigned a house to each couple to live in.

But the more the king thought of it, the greater appeared to be the disgrace that his youngest son had brought on the family. So one day he called his three sons together, and said to them, "Tell your wives that I want each one of them to make me an embroidered coat. The one who fails to do this within three days will be put to death." Now, the king issued this order in the hope that Chonguita would be put to death, because he thought that she would not be able to make the coat; but his hope was disappointed. On the third day his daughters-in-law presented to him the coats that they had made, and the one embroidered by Chonguita was the prettiest of all.

Still anxious to get rid of the monkey-wife, the king next ordered his daughters-in-law to embroider a cap for him in two days, under penalty of death in case of failure.   The caps were all done on time.

At last, thinking of no other way by which he could accomplish his end, the king summoned his three daughters-in-law, and said, "The husband of the one who shall be able to draw the prettiest picture on the walls of my chamber within three days shall succeed me on the throne."   At the end of the three days the pictures were finished.   When the king went to inspect them, he found that Chonguita's was by far the prettiest, and so Don Juan was crowned king.

A great feast was held in the palace in honor of the new king. In the midst of the festivities Don Juan became very angry with his wife for insisting that he dance with her, and he hurled her against the wall.   At this brutal action the hall suddenly became dark; but after a while it became bright again, and Chonguita had been transformed into a beautiful woman.

NOTES.

A Visayan variant of this story, though differing from it in many details, is the story of the "Three Brothers," printed in JAFL 20 : 91–93.

A number of Indian *Märchen* seem to be related more or less closely to our story.   Benfey cites one (1 : 261) which appears in the "Asiatic Journal" for 1833.

Some princes are to obtain their wives by this device: each is to shoot an arrow; and where the arrow strikes, there will each find his bride.   The arrow of the youngest hits a tamarind-tree; he is married to it, but his bride turns out to be a female monkey.   However, he lives happily with her, but she never appears at his father's court.   The sisters-in-law are curious to know what kind of wife he has.   They persuade the father-in-law to give a feast for all his sons' wives.   The prince is grieved over the fact that the secret will out.   Then his wife comforts him; she lays off her monkey covering, and appears as a marvellously beautiful maiden.   She enjoins him to preserve the monkey-skin carefully, since otherwise great danger threatens her; but he, in order to keep her in her present beautiful human form, burns the hide while she is at the feast.   She disappears instantly. The prince seeks her again, and at last discovers her in heaven as the queen of the monkeys.   There he remains with her.

In a Simla tale, "The Story of Ghose" (Dracott, 40 f.), the animal is a squirrel, which is finally changed by the god Mahadeo into a human being, after the little creature has performed many services for her husband.   Somewhat analogous, also, is Maive Stokes, "The Monkey

Prince" (No. x, p. 41 ff.). Compare also the notes to our No. 19 and Benfey's entire discussion of "The Enchanted Son of the Brahman" (1 : 254–269).

These forms are not close enough to our version, however, to justify our tracing it directly to any one of them. Both it and the Visayan variant are members of the European cycle of tales represented by Grimm's "Three Feathers" (No. 63). The skeleton outline of this family group Bolte and Polívka construct as follows (2 : 37): —

A father wishes to test the skill of his three sons (or their wives), and requests that they produce extraordinary or costly articles. The despised youngest son wins the reward with the help of an enchanted princess in the form of a cat, rat, frog, lizard, monkey, or as a doll, or night-cap, or stocking. At last she regains her human form. The disenchantment is sometimes accomplished by a kiss, or by beheading, or by the hero's enduring for three nights in silence the blows of spirits.

In only two of the variants cited by Bolte-Polívka (to Grimm, No. 63) is the animal wife a monkey, — Comparetti, No. 58, "Le Scimmie;" and Von Hahn, No. 67, "Die Aeffin." Of these, only the Greek story resembles our tale; but here the similarities are so many, that I will summarize briefly the main points of Von Hahn's version: —

An old king once called his three sons to him, and said, "My sons, I am old; I should like to have you married, so that I may celebrate your wedding with you before I die. Therefore each of you are to shoot an arrow into the air, and to follow its course, for there each will find what is appointed for him." The eldest shot first: his arrow carried him to a king's daughter, whom he married. The second obtained a prince's daughter. But the arrow of the third stuck in a dung-hill. He dug a hole in it, and came to a marble slab, which, when raised, disclosed a flight of stairs leading down. Courageously he descended, and came to a cellar in which a lot of monkeys were sitting in a circle. The mother of the monkeys approached him, and asked him what he wanted. He answered, that, according to the flight of his arrow, he was destined to have a monkey-wife. "Choose one for yourself," she said. "Here sit my maids; there, my daughters." He selected one, and took her back to his father. His brothers, however, ridiculed him.

After a time the eldest son asked the king to divide up his kingdom, as he was already old and was likely to die. "I'll give you three tasks," said the king to his sons. "The one who performs them best shall be king." The first count was to be won by the son whose house forty days thence was cleanest and most beautifully adorned. The youngest son was very sad when inspection-time approached. "Why so sad?" said his wife. He told her; and she said to him on the morning of the last day, "Go to my mother, and ask her for a hazel-nut and an almond." He did so. When the time for inspection arrived, the monkey-wife cracked the hazel-nut and drew from it a diamond covering for the whole house. From the almond she drew a very beautiful carpet for the king to walk on. Youngest son won the first count, naturally. The second task was to furnish the king with fresh fruits in the winter-time. The two oldest sons were unable to get any, but the youngest son got a fine supply from the monkeys' garden under the dung-hill. The third count was to be won by the son whose wife should be declared the most beautiful at a feast to be given ten days thence. The monkey-wife sent her husband again for an almond, a hazel-nut, two stallions, and five servants. When he returned with them, she cracked the almond and drew from it a magnificent dress for herself. From the hazel-nut she drew *her own beauty*, and handsome equipment for her husband. When she was arrayed, she rode into the courtyard of the king, and tried to escape without being recognized; but the king was too quick for her: she was caught, and her husband was declared the final winner. He became king when his father died.

This Greek story can hardly have any immediate relationship with "Chonguita," though it does appear in its first half to be connected with the 1833 Indian *Märchen* given above. Our story, it will be noticed, lacks the shooting of arrows, so characteristic of the European forms; it mentions the monkey-kingdom to which the youngest prince was directed by an old man, and where Chonguita is forced on him; it represents the king as requiring his daughters-in-law to perform difficult tasks because he wishes to find an excuse for putting to death the animal-wife. Moreover, the three tasks themselves are different, although the first two are reminiscent of some found in the Occidental versions. For the third I know of no folk-tale parallel. On the whole, I am prone to believe that our story was not imported from Europe, but that it belongs to an Oriental branch of the family.

The disenchantment of the monkey-wife by hurling her in anger against the wall is exactly like the disenchantment of the frog-prince in Grimm, No. 1. This conceit is most unusual, and, it might be added, unreasonable. Hence this identity of detail in two stories so far removed in every other way is particularly striking. I know of no further occurrences of the incident.

30. THE GOLDEN LOCK.[1]

Long ago there lived in a distant kingdom an influential noble named Ludovico, who vastly increased his wealth by his marriage to a rich heiress called Clotilde. During the first ten years of their union she had never peeped out of her window or stirred out of her room: she only walked to the door of her chamber to bid farewell to her husband or to receive his parting kiss when he was off to attend to his official business, and to meet him with a

---

[1] Narrated by Vicente Hilario of Batangas, Batangas, who heard the story from an old man (now deceased) from the barrio of Balayan.

tender embrace when he returned. Nobody else but Ludovico and her chaperon could see or talk with her: to these two persons only did Clotilde reveal her secrets and convey the thoughts of her spotless soul. She spent her time in voluntary seclusion, not in the luxuries of the court or the gaieties of society, but in embroidery, knitting, and in the unnecessary embellishment of her extremely lovely person.

But an incident now happened that seriously threatened to destroy the foundations of their blissful union, for there may be eddies and counter-currents in the steady and swift flow of a stream. The king invited all the nobles in the land to a sumptuous banquet to be given in one of the principal frontier cities. Ludovico was among the first persons to accept the king's invitation. When the luxurious repast was over, the guests gathered in groups around small tables in the adjoining grounds to while away the sultry hours and to discuss the questions of the day. One of these groups was composed of Ludovico and six other nobles, among whom was a bold, sharp-tongued rich youth named Pio. The conversation touched on topics concerning the fair sex, especially of women historically famous for their personal charms, virtues, and vices. The garrulous Pio ridiculed the noble constancy and other excellent traits of the fair Clotilde.

"I will bet you anything you want to bet, that you cannot learn the secrets of my wife in fifteen days," said Ludovico, his face flushed with wrath.

"All right," said Pio, exasperated by Ludovico's boast. "The loser shall be hanged. I will bet my life that I'll know the secrets of your wife within fifteen days."

The terms of the contract were carefully written down, solemnly ratified by the king, and signed by the two contestants and by the other high-born gentlemen.

Pio set out the next day for Ludovico's home town. The inexperienced youth looked in vain for Ludovico's residence. Finally he asked a jolly fellow, who showed him the house after a long roundabout conversation. Pio went upstairs, where he saw the gray-haired chaperon sitting alone in the spacious hall, which was decorated to vie in magnificence with the most gorgeously furnished apartment of the king. The accomplished Pio doffed his bonnet to the old woman, and politely asked for her mistress.

"Nobody but her husband and me is allowed to see her," said the ugly old hag.

Pio then sat down and began to talk to her. By his persuasive language and the magnetic touch of his hands he easily insinuated himself into her confidence. Then, dropping a piece of gold on her palm, he said, "Will you tell me the secrets of your mistress?"

The old woman looked at him suspiciously, but the brilliant coin proved too great a temptation for her. "Clotilde," she said, "has three golden [1] locks of hair under her left armpit. I know this fact, because I bathe her every day."

Pio heaved a deep groan and turned his face aside. After recovering himself, he dropped another gold-piece into the hand of the chaperon, and said, "Will you get one of those locks for me?"

She hesitated, but his eloquence was irresistible. "I'll give you the lock to-morrow," she said. Pio then departed, and she returned to her mistress.

Early the next morning, while the old woman was bathing Clotilde as usual, she pulled out one of Clotilde's golden locks. "Aray!" exclaimed Clotilde, "what's the matter with you?"

"Never mind, never mind!" said the old woman with many caresses. "This is the only reward I want for my many faithful services to you."

Ignorant of the treasonable intrigues of her chaperon, Clotilde said nothing more. Before noon Pio arrived. With trembling hands and pale cheeks, the old woman gave him the golden lock. She was amply rewarded with a purse of gold. Ignorant of the fatal consequences of her treacherous act, she gayly went back to Clotilde's private chamber.

Pio left the town late in the afternoon, and soon arrived at the capital. Ludovico was struck aghast at the sight of the golden lock. He at once wrote a letter to his wife which ran in part as follows: —

"I have spent ten years of my life in perfect happiness with you. I expected to enjoy such blissful days for a much longer period. But now everything is hopeless. My life shall be ended by violence, because of your faithlessness. We shall see each other no more. Receive the sad farewell of your Ludovico."

---

[1] "Golden," in this story, does not mean merely "of the color of gold," but also "made of gold."

When Clotilde read this letter, she swooned. When she came
to her senses, she awoke as from a trance. But when she beheld the letter again, she read again the opprobrious word
"faithlessness" in her husband's handwriting. She did not
know what act of disloyalty she had committed. She moved
about in her room by fits and starts. At last a thought came to
her mind: she sent for the best goldsmith in town, and told him
to make her a gold slipper adorned with precious stones. Under
her strict supervision the work was completed in a marvellously
short time. Then she put on her best clothes and the precious
slipper, and with all possible expedition set out for Ludovico.

Clotilde arrived in the city just a few minutes before the
execution. She drove directly to the king's pavilion. Her
only companion was the same old woman who had caused all
this trouble. The turbulent persons who had gathered in
the public square to witness the horrible spectacle were awed by
the loveliness and magnificent attire of Clotilde. When she
reached the king, and asked him for all the details concerning
Ludovico's case, and when the king had given her all the information he could, she turned and pointed toward Pio, and said,
"That man has stolen my other slipper which looks like this
one I am wearing."

The king called Pio from the place where he was standing,
and told him all about the fair lady's accusation. "I have not
committed any crime against her," said Pio angrily. "I don't
even know her. This is the first time I have ever seen her."

"Sir," said Clotilde sneeringly, "why, then, did you tell his
Majesty and other persons that you have discovered my secrets?
I am the wife of Ludovico, whose life you have threatened to
end by your deceit. I know now by what means you got possession of my golden lock."

Clotilde's statement sealed Pio's fate. He was hanged in
place of Ludovico, who deeply regretted having doubted his
faithful wife. And what happened to the old woman, who
preferred the gold of an impostor to the kindness of a virtuous
woman? The hag was sentenced to spend the remainder of
her life in a damp, dreary dungeon.

NOTES.

A close Tagalog parallel is to be found in the last part of the metrical
romance entitled (in English translation) "The Life of Duke Almanzor

and the Kind and Clever Maria, in the Kingdom of Toledo when it was under the Moors." My copy bears no date, but Retana mentions an edition before 1898 (No. 4159). The poem is in 402 quatrains of 12-syllable lines. The section which resembles our story begins at line 1260, and may be paraphrased in prose as follows: —

Soon after this, Almanzor was baptized (he had been a Moor), and was married to Maria. After a few months of happy life, the duke was called away to Cordova on important business. When Duke Almanzor arrived at the court of the Governor of Cordova, he found that all the noblemen were present. As he arrived somewhat late, he excused himself by saying that he was newly married, and that he could not leave his wife any sooner. Among the nobles was a proud, self-confident man named Abdala, who, when Almanzor had finished speaking, remarked that he (Abdala) did not mean to marry, as he could very easily seduce any woman, be she unmarried or a wife. Almanzor was angered by this remark. He said to Abdala, "I have my wife in Toledo: go and see if you can seduce her." Abdala said that there was no doubt of his being able to do so. A wager of death for the loser was agreed upon.

Abdala immediately set out for Toledo. He tried to gain access to the duke's palace; but ever since her husband's departure, Maria had ordered the servants to keep all the windows and doors closed. Moreover, nobody but women were allowed to enter the palace. Abdala was about to give up in despair, when he met a sorceress, who offered to help him. This witch gained admittance into the palace, and was allowed to pass the night there. At midnight the hag secretly went to Maria's bedroom and jotted down a brief description of it. Then she cut off a lock of Maria's hair. The next morning the witch left the palace. She went to Abdala, and gave him the lock of hair, together with the description of the bedroom.

Abdala hurriedly returned to Cordova. When he reached the palace, the governor at once assembled the nobles. Abdala then showed the lock of hair, and described minutely Maria's bedroom. Almanzor was asked what he had to say. The noble duke said that he acknowledged to be true everything that Abdala had said. Then the governor ordered his guards to take the duke to prison. The duke was to be beheaded on the third day. While in prison, Duke Almanzor wrote to his wife, telling her of his coming death. Maria resolved at once to save her husband. She went to Cordova, carrying with her all her wealth. She had a famous jeweller make for her a large, beautiful ear-ring.

The third day came, and the soldiers took Duke Almanzor out of prison. The governor and all the nobles accompanied the duke to the plaza where he was to be executed. Maria stopped the procession, and addressed the governor thus: "My lord, do you see this ear-ring?" The governor nodded. "Then I ask you to give me justice. My other ear-ring was stolen by that gentleman who is standing near you," and she pointed at Abdala as she made the accusation. Abdala became very angry. He said, "I don't know you; I have never seen you before. How could I steal your ear-ring?" — "Do you say that you have never seen me before?" Maria asked. "I do say so," said Abdala emphatically. "Why, then, do you claim that you have been in my room, and that I gave you a lock of my hair?" Maria demanded. Abdala could not answer. "Answer, Abdala," the governor said. But Abdala could not utter a single word. At last he confessed that he had never seen Maria, and that the description of the room and the lock of hair had been furnished him by a sorceress. The governor then ordered him to be seized. Duke Almanzor was set free. His wife gently reprimanded him for risking his life so foolishly. As for Abdala, he was beheaded, and the sorceress who helped him was burned at the stake.

In our notes to No. 7 we have already summarized the first part of the "Story of Rodolfo." The last episode of this romance is an analogue of our present story, and runs briefly thus: —

After his marriage, Rodolfo went back to Valencia, and informed the king that he had found a virtuous woman and had married her. She was then in Babilonia. The king detained him for a few days in the palace. At the same time he sent Fortunato, a gallant, to court Rodolfo's wife, to test whether or not she was true to her husband. Fortunato went to Babilonia and declared his love to Estela; but she would have nothing to do with him. Ashamed to return to the palace without having won her affection, Fortunato stole her underskirt and took it to the king, stating that Estela had given it to him as a remembrance. Rodolfo was summoned; and when he saw the skirt with Adela's name on it, he was thunderstruck. The king then said, "You see, your wife is no more virtuous than my daughter Leocadia. Remember your boast; your life is forfeit." Rodolfo, however, asked for a complete investigation of his wife's alleged treachery. Estela was accordingly summoned to Valencia; and when asked how her underskirt happened to be there in the palace, she asked in turn who had brought it. "Fortunato," she was told. Then she said, "The underskirt is mine. The knight Fortunato declared his love to me, but I rejected it because I am married. He stole the underskirt while I was taking a bath, and ought to be punished." When confronted with the charge, Fortunato denied the theft, and maintained that he had been given the garment by Estela as a token of her love for him. When Rodolfo heard this denial, he begged the king to assemble all the dignitaries and judges in the kingdom. Before the court Rodolfo asked Fortunato for definite proof to back up his assertions. He was unable to give any, and was consequently sentenced to be deported for ten years to a lonely island. Rodolfo and his wife were now honored by the king, and Rodolfo was finally made a knight.

Although this portion of the romance is only a distant analogue of our story, inasmuch as it lacks both the wager and the clever trick of the wife to get her maligner to convict himself, I give it, because this same combination of the "chastity-wager" motive with the "hen-divided" motive (see first part of "Rodolfo," notes to No. 7) occurs in a Mentonese story, "La Femme Avisée" (Romania, 11 : 415–416). The tale may be briefly summarized: —

A prince benighted in a forest is entertained for the night at a countryman's house. At dinner the prince carves the fowl, and gives the head to the father, the stomach to the mother, and the heart to the daughter.

On the old man's complaining later of his guest's strange division of the bird, the girl explains to her father just why the prince acted as he did. The prince overhears her, admires her wit, falls in love with her, and marries her. Some time afterward the prince is called to Egypt on business. He leaves his wife behind at home, and she promises to be very discreet. The prince communicates her promise to a friend, who wagers that he will be able to tell the prince of any defects on her body. The friend goes to the home of the prince and bribes the lady-in-waiting. She informs him, that, beautiful as the young wife is, she has a strawberry-mark on her shoulder. When the prince, on his return, is told this intimate detail by his friend, he is very angry, and, going home, accuses his wife of faithlessness. She proves her innocence by going before the king and swearing that her maligner has stolen one of her golden slippers. He denies the charge, and swears that he has never seen his accuser before. Thus self-convicted, he is imprisoned for many years.

The Mentonese folk-tale and "Rodolfo" emphasize not only the virtue of the wife, but her cleverness as well, and definitely connect the "Chastity Wager" cycle with our No. 7. While it would be difficult to maintain successfully that the "Chastity Wager" cycle and the "Clever Lass" group are descended from the same parent, — I really believe the latter to be much the older, — it seems that we have a sort of combination of the two as early as the time of the "Tūtī-nāmeh" collection. In the following story taken from that compilation, traces of both cycles may be discerned, though clearly the tale is more nearly related as a whole to the "Chastity Wager" group. This Persian story is entitled "The Nobleman and the Soldier's Wife, whose Virtue he put to the Proof" (No. 4, pp. 42 ff., of "The Tootinameh; or, Tales of a Parrot: in the Persian Language, with an English Translation; Calcutta, 1792"). An abridged version of it follows: —

In a certain city dwelt a military man who had a very beautiful wife. He was always under apprehension on her account; and one day, after he had been idle a long time, she asked him why he had quitted his profession. He answered, "I have no confidence in you, and therefore I do not go anywhere in quest of employment." The wife told him that he was perverse; for no one could seduce a virtuous woman, and a vicious woman no husband could guard successfully. Then she told him a story to illustrate the second type of wife. When he asked if she had anything more to say to him, she replied, "It is right for you to travel and seek service. I will give you a fresh nosegay: as long as the nosegay continues in this state, you may be assured that I have not committed any bad action; if the nosegay should wither, you will then know that I have been guilty of some fault." The soldier heeded her words, and set out on a journey, taking the nosegay with him. When he arrived at a certain city, he entered the service of a nobleman of that place. Winter came on, and the nobleman was astonished to see the soldier wearing a fresh nosegay every day, though flowers were practically unattainable, and he asked him about it. The soldier told him that his wife had given the nosegay to him as an emblem of her chastity; that as long as it continued fresh, he was sure that her honor was unspotted.

Now, the nobleman had two cooks remarkable for their cunning and adroitness. To one of these he said, "Repair to the soldier's country, where, through artifice and deceit, contrive to form an intimacy with his wife, *and return quickly with a particular account of her*. Then we shall see whether this nosegay continues fresh or not." The cook, in accordance with his master's command, went to the soldier's city, and sent a procuress to the wife with his message. The wife did not assent directly, but told the procuress to send the man to her, so that she might see whether he was agreeable or not. The wife made a secret assignation with the cook, but trapped him in a dry well; and when he found that he could not get out, he confessed the nobleman's plot. When the cook did not return, the nobleman sent the second cook; but he fared no better: he too was captured in the same way by the clever wife. Now the nobleman resolved to go himself. He set out under the pretext of hunting, accompanied by the soldier. When they arrived at the soldier's city, the soldier went to his own home and presented the fresh nosegay to his wife, who told him all that had happened. So the next day the soldier conducted the nobleman to his home, where a hospitable entertainment was given him. The two cooks, under promise of subsequent liberty, consented to dress as women and wait on the guests. When the nobleman saw them, he failed to recognize them, for their long confinement and bad air had made them thin and pale. He asked the soldier about the "girls," but the soldier told the cooks to tell their own story. Then the nobleman recognized them; and when they testified to the woman's chastity, he was abashed, and asked forgiveness for his offences.

Another Oriental form of this story is given by Somadeva, chapter XIII (Tawney, 1 : 85 f.), "The Story of Devasmita." It runs in part as follows: —

Here, on the departure of the husband, the divinity Siva says to the couple, "Take each of you one of these red lotuses; and, if either of you shall be unfaithful during your separation, the lotus in the hand of the other shall fade, but not otherwise." Then the husband set out for another city, where he began to buy and sell jewels. Four merchants of that country, astonished at the never-fading lotus in his hand, wormed the secret out of the husband by making him drunk, and then planned the seduction of the wife out of mere curiosity. To aid them in their plan, they had recourse to a female ascetic. She went to the wife, and attempted to move her to pity by showing her a weeping bitch, which she said was once a woman, but was transformed into a dog because of her hard-heartedness [for this device worked with better success; see Gesta Romanorum, chap. XXVIII]. The wife divined the plot and the motive of the young merchants, and appeared to be glad to receive them; but when they came at appointed times, she drugged them, and branded them on the forehead with an iron dog's foot. Then she cast them out naked in a dung-heap. The procuress was later served even worse: her nose and ears were cut off. The young wife, fearing that for revenge the four merchants might go slay her husband, told her whole story to her mother-in-law. The mother-in-law praised her for her conduct, and devised a plan to save her son. The wise wife disguised herself as a merchant, and embarked in a ship to the country where her husband was. When she arrived there, she saw him in the midst of a circle of merchants. He, seeing her afar off in the dress of a man, thought to himself, "Who may this merchant be that looks so like my beloved wife?" But she went to the king, said that she had a petition to present, and asked him to assemble all his subjects. He did so, and asked her what her petition was. She replied, "There are residing here four escaped slaves of mine; let the king give them back to me." She was told to pick out her slaves, which she did, choosing the four merchants who had their heads tied up. When asked how these distinguished merchants' sons could be her slaves, she said, "Examine their foreheads, which I marked with a dog's foot." So done. The truth came out; the other merchants paid the wife a large sum of money to ransom the four, and also a fine to the king's treasury.

There can be no doubt of a rather close relationship between the Persian and the Indian stories; nor can there be any doubt, it seems to me, of the relationship of these two with the "Chastity Wager" cycle. The additional details in Somadeva's narrative connect it with European *Märchen;* e.g., J. F. Campbell, No. 18, and Groome, No. 33.

Our story of the "Golden Lock," as well as the variants, is unquestionably an importation from Europe; but what the immediate source of the tale is, I am unable to say. For the convenience of any, however, who are interested in this group of stories, and care to make a further study of it, I give here a list of the occurrences of the tale in literature and in popular form. In literature, this story in Europe dates from the end of the twelfth century.

Roman de Guillaume de Dole (c. 1200). Ed. by G. Servois for the Soc. des Anc. Textes français. Paris, 1893.

Roman de la Violette (13th century). Ed. by Michel. 1834.

Roman du Comte de Poitiers (13th century). Ed. by Michel. 1831.

Le roi Flore et la belle Jehanne (a 13th century prose story). Published by L. Moland et C. d'Hericault in Nouvelles françaises en prose du xiii° siècle, 1856 : 87–157; also in Monmerqué et Michel, Théâtre français au Moyen Age, 1842 : 417.

Miracle de Othon, roy d'Espaigne (a 14th century miracle), in the Miracles de Nostre Dame. Published by G. Paris and U. Robert for the Soc. des Anc. Textes français, 4 : 315–388; and in Monmerqué et Michel, *op. cit.*, p. 431 f.

Perceforest, bk. iv, ch. 16, 17 (an episode, where the chastity token is a rose), retold by Bandello, part I, nov. 21 (cf. R. Köhler, in Jahrb. für rom. u. eng. lit., 8 : 51 f.).

Boccaccio's Decameron, 2 : 9 (cf. Landau, Die Quellen des Dekameron, 1884 : 135 ff.).

Two important treatments of the story in dramatic form are sixteenth-century Spanish, Lope de Rueda's "Eufemia," where the heroine tricks her maligner by accusing him of having spent many nights with her and of finally having stolen a jewel from under her bed; he denies all knowledge of her (cf. J. L. Klein, Geschichte des Dramas, 9 [1872]: 144–156); and English, Shakespeare's "Cymbeline." For modern dramas and operas dealing with this theme, see G. Servois, *op. cit.*, p. xvi, note 5. In ballad form the'story occurs in "The Twa Knights" (Child, 5 : 21 ff., No. 268).

Popular stories belonging to this cycle and containing the wager are the following: —

J. F. Campbell, No. 18.
J. W. Wolf, p. 355.
Simrock, Deutsche Märchen, No. 51 (1864 ed., p. 235).
H. Pröhle, No. 61, p. 179 (cf. also p. xlii).
Ausland, 1856 : 1053, for a Roumanian story.
F. Miklosisch, Märchen und Lieder der Zigeuner der Bukowina, No. 14.
D. G. Bernoni, Fiabe popolari veneziane, No. 1.
Gonzenbach, No. 7.
G. Pitrè, Nos. 73, 75.
V. Imbriani, La Novellaja Fiorentina, p. 483.

Other folk-tales somewhat more distantly related are, —

Comparetti, Nos. 36 and 60.
Webster, Basque Legends, p. 132.
F. Kreutzwald, Estnische Märchen (übersetzt von F. Löwe), 2d Hälfte, No. 6.
H. Bergh, Sogur m. m. fraa Valdris og Hallingdal, p. 16.

For the story in general, see the following: —

Landau on the Dekameron, *op. cit.*
A. Rochs, Ueber den Veilchen Roman und die Wanderung der Euriant saga. Halle, 1882. (Reviewed as a worthless piece of work by R. Köhler in Literaturblatt für germ. und rom. Philologie, 1883 : No. 7.)
R. Ohle, Shakespeares Cymbeline und seine Romanischen Vorläufer. Berlin, 1890. (This does not discuss the popular versions at all.)
H. A. Todd, Guillaume de Dole, in Transactions and Proceedings of the Modern Language Association of America, 2 (1887): 107 ff.
Von der Hagen, Gesammtabenteuer, 3 : LXXXIII.
G. Servois, *op. cit.*, Introduction.

For some additional bibliographical items in connection with this cycle, see Köhler, "Literaturblatt," etc., p. 274. To the list above should be added finally, of course, the stories given in more detail earlier in this note.

31. WHO IS THE NEAREST RELATIVE?[1]

"On my life!" exclaimed old Julian one day to his grandson Antonio, who was clinging fast to his elbows and bothering him,

---

[1] Narrated by Leopoldo Uichanco, a Tagalog of Calamba, Laguna.

as usual, "you will soon become insane with stories. Now, I
will tell you a story on this condition: you must answer the
question I shall put at the end of the narrative. If you give
the correct answer, then I will tell you some more tales; if not,
why, you must be unfortunate." Antonio nodded, and said,
"Very well!" as he leaned on the table to listen to his grandfather. Then the old man began: —

"There was once a young man who had completed his course of
study and was to be ordained a priest. Now, whenever a man was
about to be entrusted with the duty of being a minister of God, and
Christ's representative on earth, it was the custom to trace his an-
cestry back as far as possible, to see that there was no bad member
on any branch of his family tree. Inquiries were made and information was sought regarding the young man's relatives. Unfortunately
his mother's brother was an insurrecto. But the boy wanted very
much to become a priest, so he set out for Mount Banahaw to look for
his uncle.

"As he was walking along the mountain road, he came across his
uncle, but neither knew the other. The uncle had a long bolo in his
hand. 'Hold!' shouted the old man as the boy came in sight. 'Hands
up!'

"'Mercy!' entreated the young man. 'I am a friend, not an
enemy.'

"'What are you doing in this part of the country, then? Have
you come to spy?'

"'No,' said the youth. 'I have come in search of my uncle named
Paulino, general of the Patriots of Banahaw.'

"'And who are you to seek for him? What is your name?'

"'Federico.'

"The uncle stared at him. 'If that is so,' he said, 'I am the man
you are looking for. I am your uncle.' Federico was amazed, but
was very glad to have found his uncle so easily. Then the old man
took his nephew to the cave where he dwelt with his soldiers.

"Weeks passed by, months elapsed, but Federico never thought of
going back to his mother. So one day Federico's father went out to
seek for his son, and soon found him and his uncle. The father, too,
remained there with the soldiers, and never thought of going back
home.

"One day Josefa received news that the bandits of Banahaw had
been caught by the government authorities. Among the prisoners
were her brother Paulino, her son Federico, and her husband. The
captives were to be executed at sunrise without any trial. Josefa
hurried to the *capitan general*, and pleaded with him to release her

husband, her son, and her brother. Besides, the woman presented the officer with some gifts. She pleaded so hard, that finally the *capitan general* was moved with pity. He consented to release one of the prisoners, but one only. Josefa did not know what to do. Whom should she select of the three, — her husband, the other half of her life; her son, the fruit of her love; or her brother, that brother who came from the same womb and sucked the same milk from the same mother? To take one would mean to condemn the other two to death. She wished to save them all, but she was allowed to select only one."

"If you, Antonio, were in her place, whom would you select?"

Antonio did not speak for some moments, but with knitted eyebrows looked up to the ceiling and tried to think of the answer.

"Nonsense!" exclaimed the grandfather; "you cannot find the answer in the ceiling! You really do not know, do you? Very well. I will give you until next Tuesday to get your answer. You have one week in which to think it out. Tell me the correct answer before you go to school on that day."

When Tuesday came, Antonio had gotten the answer to his grandfather's puzzle-tale; but the rascally little boy deceived the old man: he had sought the information from his uncle.

"If you were in the place of the woman," asked the playful grandfather with a smile on his face, "whom would you select?"

Antonio timidly said that he would select the brother.

"You are only guessing, aren't you?" said old Julian doubtfully.

"Bah! No, sir!" said the boy. "I can give you a reason for my selection."

"Very well, give your reason, then."

"The woman would be right in selecting her brother" —

"Because" —

"Because, what to a woman is a husband? She can marry again; she can find another."

"That is true," said the old man.

"And what to a woman is her son? Is it not possible to bear another one after she marries again?"

"To be sure," said old Julian.

"But," continued the boy, raising his voice, "is it possible for her to bring into the world another brother? Is it possible? The woman's parents were dead. Therefore she would be right in selecting her brother instead of her husband or her son."

"Exactly so, my boy," returned the satisfied old man, nodding his gray head. "Since you have answered correctly, to-morrow I will tell you another story."

NOTES.

This saga-like story is of peculiar literary interest because of its ancient connections. I know of no modern analogues; but there are two very old parallels, as well as two unmistakable references to the identical situation in our story which date from before the Christian era, and also a Persian *Märchen* that goes back as far as the twelfth century.

Herodotus (III, 119) first tells the story of a Persian woman who chooses rather to save the life of her brother than of her husband and children.

"When all the conspirators against Darius had been seized [i.e., Intaphernes, his children, and his family], and had been put in chains as malefactors condemned to death, the wife of Intaphernes came and stood continually at the palace-gates, weeping and wailing. So Darius after a while, seeing that she never ceased to stand and weep, was touched with pity for her, and bade a messenger go to her and say, 'Lady, King Darius gives thee as a boon the life of one of thy kinsmen; choose which thou wilt of the prisoners.' Then she pondered a while before she answered, 'If the king grants the life of one alone, I make choice of my brother.' Darius, when he heard the reply, was astonished, and sent again, saying, 'Lady, the king bids thee tell him why it is that thou passest by thy husband and thy children, and preferrest to have the life of thy brother spared. He is not so near to thee as thy children, nor so dear as thy husband.' She answered, 'O king! if the gods will, I may have another husband and other children when these are gone; but, as my father and mother are no more, it is impossible that I should have another brother. That was my thought when I asked to have my brother spared.' The woman appeared to Darius to have spoken well, and he granted to her the one that she asked and her eldest son, he was so pleased with her. All the rest he put to death."

This story from the Greek historian clearly supplied not merely the thought but also the form of the reference in lines 909–912 of Sophocles' "Antigone." In Campbell's English translation of the Greek play, the passage, which is put into the mouth of the heroine, runs thus: —

> "A husband lost might be replaced; a son,
> If son were lost to me, might yet be born;
> But with both parents hidden in the tomb,
> No brother may arise to comfort me."

Chronologically, the next two occurrences of the story are Indian. In the "Ucchanga-jataka" (Fausböll, No. 67, of uncertain date, but possibly going back to the third century B.C.) we are told —

"Three husbandmen were by mistake arrested on a charge of robbery, and imprisoned. The wife of one came to the King of Kosala, in whose realm the event took place, and entreated him to set her husband at liberty. The king asked her what relation each of the three was to her. She answered, 'One is my husband, another my brother, and the third is my son.' The king said, 'I am pleased with you, and I will give you one of the three; which do you choose?' The woman answered, 'Sire, if I live, I can get another husband and another son; but, as my parents are dead, I can never get another brother. So give me my brother, sire.' Pleased with the woman, the king set all three men at liberty."

In the Cambridge translation of this " Jātaka," the verse reply of the woman is rendered thus : —

> "A son's an easy find; of husbands too
> An ample choice throngs public ways. But where
> With all my pains another brother find?"

In the "Rāmāyana," the most celebrated art epic of India, we are told how, in the battle about Lankā, Lakshmana, the favorite brother and inseparable companion of the hero Rāma, is to all appearances killed. Rāma laments over him in these words: "Anywhere at all I could get a wife, a son, and all other relatives; but I know of no place where I might be able to acquire a brother. The teaching of the Veda is true, that Parjanya rains down everything; but also is the proverb true that he does not rain down brothers." (Ed. Gorresio, 6 : 24, 7–8.) This parallel was pointed out by R. Pischel in "Hermes," 28 (1893) : 465.

The Persian *Märchen* alluded to above is cited by Th. Nöldeke in "Hermes," 29 : 155.

In this story the wife, when she is given the opportunity to choose which she will save of her three nearest relatives, — i.e., her husband, her son, and her brother, who have been selected to be the food for the man-eating snake that grows from the devil-prince Dahāk's shoulder, — says, "I am still a young woman. I can get another husband, and it may happen that I might have another child by him: so that the fire of separation I can quench somewhat with the water of hope, and for the poison of the death of a husband find a cure in the antidote of the survival of a son; but it is not possible, since my father and mother are dead, for me to get another brother; therefore I bestow my love on him [i.e., she chooses the brother]." The Dahāk is moved to pity, and spares her the lives of all three.

The riddle form in which our story is cast is possibly an invention of the narrator; but folk-tales ending thus are common (see notes to No. 12). Again, our story fails to state whether or not all three men were pardoned. The implication is that they were not. The localization of the events seems to point either to a long existence of the story in La Laguna province or to exceptional adaptive skill on the part of the narrator.

32. WITH ONE CENTAVO JUAN MARRIES A PRINCESS.[1]

In ancient times, in the age of foolishness and nonsense, there lived a poor gambler. He was all alone in the world: he had no parents, relatives, wife, or children. What little money he had he spent on cards or cock-fighting. Every time he played, he lost. So he would often pass whole days without eating. He would then go around the town begging like a tramp. At last he determined to leave the village to find his fortune.

One day, without a single cent in his pockets, he set out on his journey. As he was lazily wandering along the road, he found a centavo, and picked it up. When he came to the next village, he bought with his coin a small native cake. He ate only a part of the cake; the rest he wrapped in a piece of paper and put in his pocket. Then he took a walk around the village; but, soon becoming tired, he sat down by a little shop to rest. While resting, he fell asleep. As he was lying on the bench asleep, a chicken came along, and, seeing the cake projecting from his pocket, the chicken pecked at it and ate it up. Tickled by the bird's beak, the tramp woke up and immediately seized the poor creature. The owner claimed the chicken; but Juan would not give it up, on the ground that it had eaten his cake. Indeed, he argued so well, that he was allowed to walk away, taking the chicken with him.

Scarcely had he gone a mile when he came to another village. There he took a rest in a barber-shop. He fell asleep again, and soon a dog came in and began to devour his chicken. Awakened by the poor bird's squawking, Juan jumped up and caught the dog still munching its prey. In spite of the barber's protest and his refusal to give up his dog, Juan seized it and carried it away with him. He proceeded on his journey until he came to another village. As he was passing by a small house, he felt thirsty: so he decided to go in and ask for a drink. He tied his dog to the gate and went in. When he came out again, he found his dog lying dead, the iron gate on top of him. Evidently, in its struggles to get loose, the animal had pulled the gate over. Without a word Juan pulled off one of the iron bars from the gate and took it away with him. When the owner shouted after him, Juan said, "The bar belongs to me, for your gate killed my dog."

---

[1] Narrated by Gregorio Frondoso, a Bicol, who heard the story from another Bicol student. The latter said that the story was traditional among the Bicols, and that he had heard it from his grandfather.

When Juan came to a wide river, he sat down on the bank to rest. While he was sitting there, he began to play with his iron bar, tossing it up into the air, and catching it as it fell. Once he missed, and the bar fell into the river and was lost. "Now, river," said Juan, "since you have taken my iron bar, you belong to me. You will have to pay for it." So he sat there all day, watching for people to come along and bathe.

It happened by chance that not long after, the princess came to take her bath. When she came out of the water, Juan approached her, and said, "Princess, don't you know that this river is mine? And, since you have touched the water, I have the right to claim you."

"How does it happen that you own this river?" said the astonished princess.

"Well, princess, it would tire you out to hear the story of how I acquired this river; but I insist that you are mine."

Juan persisted so strongly, that at last the princess said that she was willing to leave the matter to her father's decision. On hearing Juan's story, and after having asked him question after question, the king was greatly impressed with his wonderful reasoning and wit; and, as he was unable to offer any refutation for Juan's argument, he willingly married his daughter to Juan.

NOTES.

I know of no complete analogues of this droll; but partial variants, both serious and comic, are numerous. In our story a penniless, unscrupulous hero finds a centavo, and by means of sophistical arguments with foolish persons makes more and more profitable exchanges until he wins the hand of a princess. A serious tale of a clever person starting with no greater capital than a dead mouse, and finally succeeding in making a fortune, is the "Cullaka-setthi-jātaka," No. 4. This story subsequently made its way into Somadeva's great collection (Tawney, 1 : 33–34), "The Story of the Mouse Merchant" (ch. VI). Here it runs approximately as follows: —

A poor youth, whose mother managed to give him some education in writing and ciphering, was advised by her to go to a certain rich merchant who was in the habit of lending capital to poor men of good family. The youth went; and, just as he entered the house, that rich man was angrily talking to another merchant's son: "You see this dead mouse here upon the floor; even that is a commodity by which a capable man would acquire wealth; but I gave you, you good-for-nothing fellow, many *dinars*, and, so far from increasing them, you have not even been able to preserve what you got." The poor stranger-youth at once said to the merchant that he would

take the dead mouse as capital advanced, and he wrote a receipt for it. He
sold the mouse as cat-meat to a certain merchant for two handfuls of *gram*.
Next he made meal of the *gram*, and, taking his stand by the road, civilly
offered food and drink to a band of wood-cutters that came by. Each, out
of gratitude, gave him two pieces of wood. This wood he sold, bought more
gram with a part of the price, and obtained more wood from the wood-
cutters the next day, etc., until he was able in time to buy all their wood for
three days. Heavy rains made a dearth of wood, and he sold his stock for a
large sum. Then he set up a shop, began to traffic, and became wealthy by
his own ability. Now he had a golden mouse made, which he sent to the
rich merchant from whom he had gotten his start, and that merchant bestowed the hand of his daughter on the once poor youth.

The comic atmosphere, it will be seen, is altogether absent from this
Buddhistic parable.

A slight resemblance to our story may be traced in Bompas, No.
XLIX, "The Foolish Sons," where the clever youngest (of six brothers)
manages to acquire ten *rupees*, starting with one *anna*. He proceeds by "borrowing," and paying interest in advance. The trick
used here is the same as that practised on the foolish wife in "Wise
Folks" (Grimm, No. 104), where a sharper buys three cows, and
leaves one with the seller as a pledge for the price of the three (see
Bolte-Polívka, 2 : 440 f.).

Much closer parallels than the preceding, to the incidents of our
story, are to be found in a cycle of tales discussed by Bolte-Polívka
(2 : 201–202) in connection with "Hans in Luck" (Grimm, No. 83).
It will be recalled that in the Grimm story the foolish Hans exchanges
successively gold for horse, horse for cow, cow for pig, pig for goose,
goose for grindstone, which he is finally glad to get rid of by throwing it
into the water. "A counterpart of this story," say Bolte and Polívka,
"is the *Märchen* of the 'profitable exchange,' in which a poor man
acquires from another a hen because it has eaten up a pea or millet-seed
that belonged to him; for the hen he gets a pig which has killed it; for
the pig, a cow; for the cow, a horse. But when he finally levies his claim
for damages upon a girl, and places her in a sack, his luck changes:
strangers liberate the maiden without the knowledge of her captor,
and put in her place a big dog, which falls upon him when he opens
the sack." It is to be noted that the cycle as here outlined consists
really of two parts, — the "biter biting" and the "biter bit." Cosquin (2 : 209) believes that the last two episodes — the maiden gained
by chicanery, and the substitution of an animal for her in the sack —
form a separate theme not originally a part of the cumulative motive;
and, to prove his belief, he cites a number of Oriental tales containing
the former, but lacking the cumulative motive (*ibid.*, 209–212). Cosquin seems to be correct in this; although, on the other hand, he is
able to cite only one story (Rivière, p. 95) in which there is not some

trace of the "biter-bit" idea. Moreover, even in the animal stories belonging to this group, — and he analyzes Stokes, No. 17, and Rivière, p. 79, — the animal-rogue meets with an unlucky end. The same is true of Steel-Temple, No. 2, "The Rat's Wedding." In another Indian story, however, "The Monkey with the Tom-Tom" (Kingscote, No. xiv, a rather pointless tale), the monkey, whose last exchange is puddings for a tom-tom, is left at the top of a tree lustily beating his drum and enumerating his clever tricks. A very similar story is to be found in Rouse, p. 132, "The Monkey's Bargains." It will thus be seen that Bolte and Polívka's analysis holds for the larger number of human hero tales of this cycle, as well as for the animal tales; but that the first half of the sequence of events, where the hero's good luck is continually on the increase, is also to be found as a separate story, — Kingscote's, Rouse's, and our own.

The Filipino version appears to be old, and I am inclined to think that it is native; that is, if any stories may be called native. Several facts point to the primitiveness of the tale: (1) the local color and realistic touches, slight though they are; (2) the non-emphasis of the comic possibilities of the situations; (3) the somewhat unsystematic arrangement of incidents, the third demand and exchange (iron rod for dead dog) not appearing to be an upward progression; (4) the crudity of invention displayed in this same third exchange (though an iron-picketed fence seems modern). My reasons for thinking our story not imported from the Occident are the differences in beginning, middle, and end between it and the European versions cited by Bolte-Polívka (*loc. cit.*). The good luck coming to the hero from the exchange of *dead* animals suggests a distant basic connection between our story and the "Jātaka," although it must be admitted that the idea could occur independently to many different peoples.

33. (*a*) THE THREE HUMPBACKS.[1]

Pablo was badly treated by his older brothers Pedro and Juan. The coarsest food was given to him. His clothes were ragged. He slept on the floor, while his two brothers had very comfortable beds. In fact, he was deprived of every comfort and pleasure.

In the course of time this unfortunate youth fell in love with a well-to-do girl, and after a four-years engagement they were married. Thus Pablo was separated from his brothers, to their great joy. Pedro and Juan now began spending their money lavishly on trifles. They learned how to gamble. Pablo, however, was now living happily and out of want with his wife.

[1] Narrated by Pacita Cordero, a Tagalog from Pagsanjan, Laguna, who heard the story from her *lavandera*, or washer-woman.

Every morning he went to fish, for his wife owned a large fishery.

One day, as Pablo was just leaving the house at the usual hour to go fishing, he said to his wife, "Wife, if two humpbacks like myself ever come here, do not admit them. As you know, they are my brothers, and they used to treat me very badly." Then he went away. That very afternoon Pedro and Juan came to pay their brother a visit. They begged Marta, Pablo's wife, to give them some food, for they were starving. They had squandered all their money, they said. Marta was so impressed by the wretched appearance of her brothers-in-law, that she admitted them despite her husband's prohibition. She gave them a dinner. When they had finished eating, she said to them, "It is now time for my husband to come home. He may take vengeance on you for your past unkindness to him, if he finds you here, so I'll hide you in two separate trunks. You stay there till to-morrow morning, and I'll let you out when my husband is gone again."

She had scarcely locked the trunks when Pablo entered. He did not find out that his brothers had been there, however. The next morning Pablo went to his work, as usual. Marta had so much to do about the house that day, that she forgot all about Pedro and Juan. The poor boys, deprived of air and food, died inside the trunks. Not until two days later did Marta think of the two humpbacks. She ran and opened the trunks, and found their dead bodies inside. Her next thought was how to dispose of them. At last a plan occurred to her. She called to her neighbor, and asked him to come bury one of her brothers-in-law who had just died in her house. She promised to pay him five pesos when he came back from his work.

The neighbor lifted the heavy body of Pedro, and, putting it on his shoulder, carried it away to a far place. There he dug a hole that was waist deep, put the corpse into it, and covered it up. Then he hastened back to Marta, and said, "Madam, I have buried the dead man in a very deep grave."

"No, you have not," said Marta. "What is that lying over there?" and she pointed to the corpse of Juan.

"That's very strange!" exclaimed the neighbor, scratching his head. "You are very artful," he said to the dead body of Juan. He was very angry with the corpse now, for he had not yet received his pay. So he bore the corpse of Juan to the seashore. He got a *banca* [1] and dug a very deep grave beneath the water. Then he said to the corpse, "If you can come out of this place, you are the wisest person in the world." He then returned to Marta's house.

On his way back he happened to look behind him, when he saw, to his great surprise, the humpback following him, carrying some fish. The gambler gazed at him; and when he saw that he resembled exactly the corpse that he had just buried, he said, "So you have come out of the grave again, have you, you naughty humpback!" And with these words he killed the humpback that very instant. This humpback was Marta's husband returning home from the fishery.

Thus Marta tried to deceive, but she was the one who was deceived.

(*b*) THE SEVEN HUMPBACKS. [2]

Once there lived seven brothers who were all humpbacks, and who looked very much alike. Ugly as these humpbacks were, still there was a lady who fell in love with one of them and married him. This lady, however, though she loved her husband well, was a very stingy woman. Finally the time came when the unmarried humpbacks had to depend on the other one for food. Naturally this arrangement was very displeasing to the wife; and in time her hate grew so intense, that she planned to kill all her brothers-in-law.

One day, when her husband was away on business, she murdered the six brothers. Next she hired a man to come and bury a corpse. She told him of only one corpse, because she wanted to deceive the man. When he had buried one of the bodies, he came back to get paid for his work. The woman, however, before he had time to speak, began to reproach him for not burying the man in the right place. "See here!" she said, showing him the corpse of the second brother, "you did not do your work well. Go and bury the body again. Remember that I will not pay you until you have buried the man so that he stays under the earth."

The man took the second corpse and buried it; but when he returned, there it was again. And so on: he repeated the operation until he thought that he had buried the same corpse six times. But after the sixth, the last humpback, had been

[1] *Banca,* a native dug-out.
[2] Narrated by Teofilo Reyes, a Tagalog from Manila.

buried, the married humpback came home from his work. When the grave-digger saw this other humpback, he immediately seized and killed him, thinking he was the same man he had buried so many times before.

When the wicked woman knew that her very husband had been killed, she died of a broken heart.

NOTES.

A Pampango variant (*c*), which I have only in abstract, is entitled "The Seven Hunchbacked Brothers." It was collected by Wenceslao Vitug of Lubao, Pampanga. It runs thus: —

There were seven hunchbacked brothers that looked just alike. One of them married, and maintained the other six in his house. The wife, however, grew tired of them, and locked them up in the cellar, where they starved to death. In order to save burial-expenses, the woman fooled the grave-digger. When he had buried one man and returned for his money, she had another body lying where the first had lain, and told him that he could not have his money until the man was buried to stay. Thus the poor grave-digger buried all six corpses under the impression that he was working with the same one over and over again. On his way back from burying the sixth, he met the husband riding home on horseback. Thinking him to be the corpse, which he exactly resembled, the grave-digger cried out, "Ah! so this is the way you get ahead of me!" and he struck the living hunchback with his hoe and killed him.

This Pampango variant, although it is a little more specific than the Tagalog, is identical with our second version.

Our two stories and the variant represent a family of tales found scattered all over Europe. They are also connected distantly with one of the stories in the "1001 Nights," and thus with the Orient again. For a discussion of this cycle, see Clouston, "Popular Tales and Fictions," 2 : 332 ff., where are cited and abstracted versions from the Old-English prose form of the "Seven Wise Masters," from the Gesta Romanorum, also the *fabliau* "Destourmi;" then five other *fabliaux* from Legrand's and Barbasan's collections, especially the *trouvère* Dutant's "Les Trois Bossus;" and the second tale of the seventh sage in the "Mishlé Sandabar," the Hebrew version of the book of Sindibad. On pp. 344–357 Clouston gives variants of the related story in which the same corpse is disposed of many times. For further bibliography, see Wilson's Dunlop, 2 : 42, note.

The nearest parallel I know of to our first story is Straparola, 5 : 3, from which it was probably derived.

There were three humpbacked brothers who looked very much alike. The wife of one of them, disobeying the order of her husband, secretly received her two brothers-in-law. When her husband returned unexpectedly, she hid the brothers in the kitchen, in a trough used for scalding pigs. There the two humpbacks smothered before the wife could release them. In order to rid herself of their corpses, she hired a body-carrier to cast one of them into the Tiber; and when he returned for his pay, she informed him that the corpse had come back. After the man had removed the second corpse, he met the humpbacked husband, whom he now likewise cast into the river.

The identity of this story with ours makes a direct connection between the two practically certain. The two stories differ in this respect, however: the Italian has a long introduction telling of the enmity between the hunchback brothers, and of the knavish tricks of Zambo, the oldest, who goes out to seek his fortune, and is finally married in Rome. All this detail is lacking in the Filipino version, as is likewise the statement (found in Straparola) that the wife rejoiced when she learned that she had been rid of her husband as well as of the corpses of her brothers-in-law.

In our other story and the Pampango variant we note some divergences from the preceding tale. Here the one married brother charitably supports his six indigent brothers, whom the wife subsequently murders. In the majority of the European versions the deaths are either accidental or are contrived by the husband and wife together (e.g., Gesta Romanorum; and Von der Hagen, No. 62). While I am inclined to think these two stories of ours imported, they do not appear to be derived immediately from the same source (Straparola). However, the facts that the seven men are brothers and are humpbacks, and that the husband is killed by mistake, make an Occidental source for our second story and for the Pampango variant most probable.

I know of no Oriental analogues to the story as a whole, though the trick of getting a number of corpses buried for one appears in several stories from Cochin-China, Siam, and the Malay Archipelago: —

(1) Landes, No. 180, which I summarize here from Cosquin (2 : 337):

In the course of some adventures more or less grotesque, four monks are killed at one time near an inn. The old woman who keeps this hostelry, fearful of being implicated in a murder, wishes to get rid of the corpses. She hides three of the bodies, and has one buried by a monk who is passing by. She pretends that the dead man is her nephew. The monk, returning to the inn after his task, is stupefied to see the corpse back there again. The old woman tells him not to be astonished, for her nephew loved her so much that he could not bear to leave her; he would have to be buried deeper. The monk carries this corpse away, and on his return has the same experience with the third and fourth corpses. After the last time, he meets, while crossing a bridge, another, live monk resembling those he has interred. "Halloo!" he says, "I have been burying you all day, and now you come back to be buried again!" With that he pushes the fifth monk into the river.

(2) Skeat, 1 : 36–37, "Father Follow-My-Nose and the Four Priests:"

Father Follow-My-Nose would walk straight, would climb over a house rather than turn aside. One day he had climbed up one side of a *Jerai*-tree and was preparing to descend, when four yellow-robed priests, lest he should fall, held a cloak for him. But he jumped without warning, and the four cracked their heads together and died. Old Father Follow-My-Nose travelled on till he came to the hut of a crone. The crone went back and got the bodies of the four priests. An opium-eater passed by; and the crone said, "Mr. Opium-Eater, if you'll bury me this yellow-robe here, I'll give you a dollar." The opium-eater agreed, and took the body away to bury it; but when he came back for his money, there was a second body waiting for him. "The fellow must have come to life again," he said; but he took the body and buried it too. After he had buried the fourth in like manner, it was broad daylight, and he was afraid to go collect his money.

(3) A story communicated to me by a Chinese student, Mr. Jut L. Fan of Canton, who says that he saw the tale acted at a popular theatre in Canton in 1913. The story I give is but the synopsis of the play:

In Canton, the capital of Kwong Tung, a mile's walk from the market-place, stood a prehistoric abbey, away from the busy streets, and deep in the silent woods. In this old monastery an aged abbot ruled over five hundred young monks; but they were far from being like their venerable master. Men and women, rich and poor, for fear of the dread consequences if they should incur the displeasure of the gods, went in great numbers to worship in the ancient buildings, kneeling in long rows before the sacred figures and incense.

These gatherings made it possible for the young monks and the young girls to become intimately acquainted, — so intimate, that sometimes shame and disgrace followed. One young girl who had been seduced, on an appropriate occasion and after great consideration, persuaded seven of the disciples who had been engaged in her ruin to enter her house. Then she invited them into her private chamber. As if by chance, there came a sharp rap on the locked door; so she hid her unusual visitors in a big ward-robe. What this young lady next did might seem unnatural; but, with the help of her servants, she poured boiling oil into the wardrobe, and killed the miscreants.

She next hired a porter to convey one body to the river near by and bury it. This porter was not informed as to the number of corpses he would have to bury; but every time he came back for his pay, there was another body for him. So one after another he dropped the bodies of the young monks into the swift-flowing stream, wondering all the while by what magic the lifeless body managed to return to the original spot.

Just after he had disposed of the seventh, up came the old abbot himself, with dignified mien. "Ah! I see now how you return," said the drudger, and he laid hold of the priest and ended his natural days. The old abbot thus suffered the fate of his seven unworthy disciples.

34. (a) RESPECT OLD AGE.[1]

Once there lived a poor man who had to support his family, the members of which were a hot-headed wife who predominated over the will of her husband; a small boy of ten; and an old man of eighty, the boy's grandfather. This old man could no longer work, because of his feebleness. He was the cause of many quarrels between the husband and wife, but was loved by their son.

One rainy morning the husband was forced by his wife to send his father away. He called his son, and ordered him to carry a basket full of food and also a blanket. He told the boy that they were to leave the old man in a hut on their farm some distance away. The boy wept, and protested against this harsh treatment of his grandfather, but in vain. He then cut the blanket into two parts. When he was asked to explain his action, he said to his father, "When you grow old, I will leave you in a hut, and give you this half of the blanket." The man was astonished, hurriedly recalled his order concerning his father, and thereafter took good care of him.

(b) THE GOLDEN RULE.[2]

A long time ago there lived in a town a couple who had a son. The father of the husband lived with his son and daughter-in-law happily for many years. But when he grew very old, he became very feeble. Every time he ate at the table, he always broke a plate, because his hands trembled so. The old man's awkwardness soon made his son angry, and one day he made a wooden plate for his father to eat out of. The poor old man had to eat all his food from this wooden plate.

When the grandson noticed what his father had done, he took some tools and went down under the house. There he took a piece of board and began to carve it. When his father saw him and said to him, "What are you doing, son?" the boy replied to him, "Father, I am making wooden plates for you and my mother when you are old."

As the son uttered these words, tears gushed from the father's eyes. From that time on, the old man was always allowed to eat at the table with the rest of the family, nor was he made to eat from a wooden plate.

MORAL: Do unto others as you want them to do unto you.

[1] Narrated by José Ignacio, a Tagalog from Malabon, Rizal.
[2] Narrated by Cipriano Seráfica, a Pangasinan from Mangaldan, Pangasinan.

NOTES.

A Pampango variant of these stories, entitled "The Old Man, his Son, and his Grandson," and narrated by Eutiquiano Garcia of Mexico, Pampanga, has been printed by H. E. Fansler (p. 100). Mr. Garcia says that he heard the story told by his father at a gathering of a number of old story-tellers at his home during the Christmas vacation in 1908. The tale has every appearance of having long been naturalized in the Islands, if not of being native. It is brief, and may be reprinted here: —

In olden times, when men lived to be two or three hundred years old, there dwelt a very poor family near a big forest. The household had but three members, — a grandfather, a father, and a son. The grandfather was an old man of one hundred and twenty-five years. He was so old, that the help of his housemates was needed to feed him. Many a time, and especially after meals, he related to his son and his grandson his brave deeds while serving in the king's army, the responsible positions he filled after leaving a soldier's life; and he told entertaining stories of hundreds of years gone by. The father was not satisfied with the arrangement, however, and planned to get rid of the old man.

One day he said to his son, "At present I am receiving a peso daily, but half of it is spent to feed your worthless grandfather. We do not get any real benefit from him. To-morrow let us bind him and take him to the woods, and leave him there to die."

"Yes, father," said the boy.

When the morning came, they bound the old man and took him to the forest. On their way back home the boy said to his father, "Wait! I will go back and get the rope." — "What for?" asked his father, raising his voice. "To have it ready when your turn comes," replied the boy, believing that to cast every old man into the forest was the usual custom. "Ah! if that is likely to be the case with me, back we go and get your grandfather again."

This *exemplum* is known in many countries and in many forms. For the bibliography, see Clouston, "Popular Tales and Fictions," 2 : 372–378; T. F. Crane, "Exempla of Jacques de Vitry" (FLS, 1890 : No. 288 and p. 260); Bolte-Polívka (on Grimm, No. 78), 2 : 135–140. The most complete of these studies is the last, in which are cited German, Latin, Dutch, English, French, Spanish, Greek, Croatian, Albanian, Bulgarian, Polish, Russian, Lettish, Turkish, and Indian versions. Full as Bolte-Polívka's list is, however, an old important Buddhistic variant has been overlooked by them, — the "Takkaḷa-jātaka," No. 446. This Indian form of the story, it seems to me, has some close resemblances to our Pampango variant; and I give it here briefly, summarizing from Mr. Rouse's excellent English translation: —

In a certain village of Kāsi there lived a man who supported his old father. The father regretted seeing his son toil so hard for him, and against the son's will sent for a woman to be his daughter-in-law. Soon the son began to be pleased with his new wife, who took good care of his father. As time went on, however, she became tired of the old man, and planned to set his son against him. She accused her father-in-law of being not only very untidy, but also fierce and violent, and forever picking quarrels with her, and at last, by constant dinning her complaints in his ear, persuaded her husband to agree to take the old man into a cemetery, kill him, and bury him in a pit. Her small son, a wise lad of seven, overheard the plot, and decided to prevent his father from committing murder. The next day he insisted on accompanying his father and grandfather. When they reached the cemetery, and the father began to dig the pit, the small boy asked what it was for. The father replied, —

> "Thy grandsire, son, is very weak and old,
> Opprest by pain and ailments manifold;
> Him will I bury in a pit to-day;
> In such a life I could not wish him stay."

The boy caught the spade from his father's hands, and at no great distance began to dig another pit. His father asked why he dug that pit; and he answered, —

> "I too, when thou art aged, father mine,
> Will treat my father as thou treatest thine;
> Following the custom of the family,
> Deep in a pit I too will bury thee."

By repeating a few more stanzas the son convinced his father that he was about to commit a great crime. The father, penitent, seated himself in the cart with his son and the old man, and they returned home. There the husband gave the wicked wife a sound drubbing, bundled her heels over head out of the house, and bade her never darken his doors again. [The rest of the story, which has no connection with ours, tells how the little son by a trick made his mother repent and become a good woman, and brought about a reconciliation between her and his father.]

The chief difference between our Pampango variant and the "Jātaka," it will be seen, is in the prominent rôle played by the wife in the latter. She is lacking altogether in the Filipino story. The resemblances are strong, on the other hand. The father plans to *kill* the grandfather, — a turn seldom found in the Occidental versions, — and, accompanied by his son, he goes out to the forest (in the Indian, cemetery) to despatch the old man. The small boy's thinking (or pretending to think) it a family custom to put old men out of the way is found in both stories. Our Pampango variant appears to me to represent a form even older than the "Jātaka," but at the same time a form that is historically connected with that Indian tale.

Of our two main stories, — "Respect Old Age" and "The Golden Rule," — the second is very likely derived from Europe. Compare it, for instance, with Grimm, No. 78. The "machinery" of the wooden plates establishes the relationship, I believe. This form of the story, however, is not unlike an Oriental *Märchen* cited by Clouston (*op. cit.*, 2 : 377). It is from a Canarese collection of tales called the "Kathâ Manjarí," and runs thus: —

A rich man used to feed his father with *congi* from an old broken dish. His son saw this, and hid the dish. Afterwards the rich man, having asked his father where it was, beat him [because he could not tell]. The boy exclaimed, "Don't beat grandfather! I hid the dish, because, when I become a man, I may be unable to buy another one for you." When the rich man heard this, he was ashamed, and afterwards treated his father kindly.

The Pangasinanes may have got this story of "The Golden Rule" through the Church, from some priest's sermon.

Our first example, "Respect Old Age," is the only one of the three which turns on the "*housse partie*" idea. This is the form found in the thirteenth-century French *fabliau* "La Housse Partie;" and a variant of it is given by Ortensio Lando, an Italian novelist of the sixteenth century (Dunlop, 2 : 206). The only Spanish example I know of is found in the fourteenth-century "El Libro de los Enxemplos" (printed in Bibliotéca de Autores Españoles, vol. 51 [Madrid, 1884]), No. CCLXXII. It runs in the original as follows: —

Patri qualis fueris, tibi filius talis erit.

Cual fueres á tu padre que trabajó por tí,
El fijo que engendrares tal será á tí.

Cuentan que un viejo dió á un fijo que lo sirvió mucho bien todos sus bienes; mas despues que gelos hobo dado, echólo de la cámara onde dormia é tomóla para él é para su mujer, é fizo facer á su padre el lecho tras la puerta. É de que vino el invierno el viejo habia frio, ca el fijo le habia tomado la buena ropa con que se cobria, é rogó á un su nieto, fijo de su fijo, que rogase á su padre que le diese alguna ropa para se cobrir; é el mozo apenas pudo alcanzar de su padre dos varas de sayal para su abuelo, é quedábanle al fijo otros dos. É el mozo llorando rogó al padre que le diese las otros dos, é tanto lloró, que gelas hobo de dar, é demandóle que para qué las queria, é respondióle: "Quiérolas guardar fasta que tú seas tal commo es agora tu padre, é estonce non te daré mas, así commo tú non quieres dar á tu padre."

Finally may be given another Indian story, No. 16 in the "Antarakathāsamgraha" of Rājaśekhara (Bolte-Polívka, 2 : 139), which connects the "divided-blanket" *motif* with the old "Jātaka." Rājaśekhara flourished about A.D. 900. This story runs thus: —

In Haripura lived a merchant named Sankha, who had four sons. When he became old, he handed over his business and all his wealth to them. But they would no longer obey him; their wives mistreated him; and the old man crept into a corner of the house, wasted by hunger and oppressed with years. Once in the cold time of the year he asked his oldest son, Kumuda, for a cloth to protect him from the night frost. Kumuda spoke this verse: —

"For an old man whose wife is dead, who is dependent on his sons for money, who is cut by the words of his step-daughters, death is better than life."

But at the same time he said to his son Kuntala, "Give him that curtain there!" Kuntala, however, gave the old man only half of the small curtain. When the old man showed the piece to Kumuda, Kumuda angrily asked his son why he had not given his grandfather the whole curtain. Respectfully placing his hands together, Kuntala replied, "Father, when old age also overtakes you, there will be ready for you the half-curtain which corresponds to the one here." Then Kumuda was shamed; and he said, "Son, we have been instructed by you; you have become a support for us whose senses have been stupefied by the delirium of power and wealth." And from that time on he began to show his father love, and so did the whole family.

In conclusion, and by way of additional illustrative material, I give in full another brief Tagalog moral tale which seems to be distantly related to our stories. It was collected by Felix Guzman, a Tagalog from Gapan, Nueva Ecija, who got it from his uncle. It is entitled "Juan and his Father."

Five hundred years ago there lived in Pagao an old man, and his son named Juan. The latter had a wife. As Juan's father was very weak on account of old age, and could not do any work in the house, Juana, his daughter-in-law, became discontented. One day the old man became sick. He moaned day and night so constantly, that Juana could get no sleep at all. So she said to her husband, "If you do not drive your father away from the house immediately, I shall go away myself. I cannot sleep, because he is always moaning." Juan then drove his poor father away for the sake of his wife.

The poor old man went begging about the neighborhood. After a long walk, he found at last a cave where he could live. After he had recovered his health, he found in the cave a bag of ashes. He further discovered, that, whenever he took some of the ashes and exposed them to the light, they became money. Now the old man went back to his son with the magic bag. On his arrival, he was welcomed, for the couple saw that he was carrying a bag that might contain something useful for them.

The old man next gave his son a certain sum of money, and said, "Juan, with this you may find another wife." So Juan gladly took the money and went and bought him another wife. When he returned, the old man gave his son some more money, and said, "Go over there, Juan, and buy an old man in that house to serve us as our servant." When Juan reached the house where the other old man was, he said, "I want to buy your father, the old man." Juan had scarcely got the sentence out of his mouth when the son of the old man fell on him with a whip and drove him away. Juan went running to his father, and said, "Father, I only said that I wanted to buy their father, but they began to whip me. Why did they do that?"

"You see," said the old man, "you can buy a wife with money, but not a single father can you buy."

Compare this last story with No. 31.

35. COCHINANGO.[1]

Once upon a time there lived in a small village on the border of a powerful kingdom a poor farmer, who had a son. This son was called a fool by many; but a palmer predicted that Cochinango would some day dine with the king, kiss the princess, marry her, and finally would himself be king.

Cochinango wondered how he could ever marry the princess and himself be king, for he was very poor. One day he heard that the king had summoned all those who would like to attempt to answer the questions of the princess. It was announced that the person who could answer them all without fail should marry her. Cochinango thought that the time had now come for him to try his fortune, so he mounted his ass and rode towards the king's palace.

On his way Cochinango had to pass through a wide forest. Just at the edge of the wood he met a weary traveller. Cochinango had forgotten to bring *buyo* with him, so he asked the traveller for some. The traveller said, "I have with me a magic *buyo* that will answer any question you put to it. If you give me some food, I will give you my *buyo*." Cochinango willingly exchanged a part of his provisions for it. Then he rode on.

He came to a stream, where he met an old man leaning on his cane. Seeing that the old man wanted to get on the other side, but was too weak to swim, Cochinango offered to carry him across. In return for his kindness, the old man gave him his cane. "You are very kind, young man," said he. "Take this cane, which will furnish you with food at any time." Cochinango thanked the old man, took the cane, and rode on. It is to be known that this old man was the same one who had given him the magic *buyo*. It was God himself, who had come down on earth to test Cochinango and to reward him for his kindness.

Cochinango had not ridden far when he met a wretched old woman. Out of pity he gave her a centavo, and in return she gave him an empty purse from which he could ask any sum of money he wanted. Cochinango rode on, delighted with his good fortune, when he met God again, this time in the form of a jolly young fellow with a small guitar. He asked Cochinango

[1] Narrated by Felix Y. Velasco, who heard the story from his grandmother, a native of Laoag, Ilocos Norte.

to exchange his ass for the guitar. At first Cochinango hesitated; but, when he was told that he could make anybody dance by plucking its strings, he readily agreed to exchange.

Cochinango now had to proceed on foot, and it took him two days to reach the gates of the palace. Luckily he arrived on the very day of the guessing-contest. In spite of his mean dress, he was admitted. The princess was much astonished at Cochinango's appearance, and disgusted by his boldness; but she was even more chagrined when he rightly answered her first question. Yet she denied that his answer was correct. She asked him two more questions, the most difficult that she could think of; but Cochinango, with the help of his magic *buyo,* answered both. The princess, however, could not admit that his answers were right. She shrunk from the idea of being married to a poor, foolish, lowly-born man. So she asked her father the king to imprison the insolent peasant, which was instantly done.

In the prison Cochinango found many nobles who, like himself, were victims of the guessing-match. Night came, and they were not given any food. The princess wanted to starve them to death. Cochinango told them not to worry; he struck a table with his cane, and instantly choice food appeared. When this was reported to the princess by the guards, she went to the prison and begged Cochinango to give her the cane; but he would not give it up unless she allowed him to kiss her. At last she consented, and went away with the cane, thinking that this was the only way by which she could starve her prisoners. The next day Cochinango asked for a large sum of money from his magic purse. He distributed it among his companions and among the guards, and they had no difficulty in getting food. Again the princess went to the prison, and asked Cochinango for the purse; but he would give it up only on condition that he be allowed to dine with the king. Accordingly he was taken to the king's table, where he ate with the king and the princess; but he was put in prison again as soon as the dinner was over.

At last Cochinango began to be tired of prison life, so he took up his wonderful guitar and began to play it. No sooner had he touched the strings than his fellow-prisoners and the guards began to dance. As he played his guitar louder and louder, the inmates of the palace heard it, and they too began to dance. He kept on playing throughout the night; and the king, princess, and all got no rest whatsoever. By morning most of them were tired to death. At last the king ordered the guards to open the prison doors and let the prisoners go free; but Cochinango would not stop playing until the king consented to give him the princess in marriage. The princess also at last had to agree to accept Cochinango as her husband, so he stopped playing. The next day they were married with great pomp and ceremony.

Thus the poor, foolish boy was married to a princess. More than once he saved the kingdom from the raiding Moros by playing his guitar; for all his enemies were obliged to dance when they heard the music, and thus they were easily captured or killed. When the king died, Cochinango became his successor, and he and the princess ruled happily for many years.

NOTES.

I know of no parallel to this story as a whole; the separate incidents found in it, however, are widespread.

The first part of the story — the prophecy concerning the hero — recalls the opening of many *Märchen;* but our narrative is so condensed, that it is impossible to say just what material was drawn on to furnish this section. The riddle-contest for the hand of a princess forms a separate cycle, to which we have already referred (notes to No. 25); but the turn the motive takes here is altogether different from the norm. Our hero, provided with his magic *buyo*, has really won the wager before the contest is begun. As for the magic objects, the last three — cane, purse, guitar — we have met with before, with properties either identical with or analogous to those attributed in this story. The method of the hero's acquiring them, too, is not new (cf. No. 27). The magic *buyo*, however, is unusual: it is very likely native Ilocano belief, or else a detail borrowed from the Ilocanos' near neighbors, the Tinguian (see Cole, 18–19, Introduction, for betel-nuts with magic powers). In No. 25, it will be recalled, the hero's magic ring furnishes the answer to the king's question, just as the *buyo* does in this tale. Indeed, there may be some association of idea between a *buyo* and a ring suggested here. The last part of the story — the imprisonment of the hero, and his success in thwarting the evil designs of the obstinate princess — is reminiscent of various cycles of tales, but I know of no exact analogue.

With the general outline of the story of "Cochinango" might be compared a Tagalog tale, — "The Shepherd who became King" (H. E. Fansler, 78 ff.), though the resemblances between the two are only vague. The Tagalog story, it might be noted in passing, is connected with the second half of Grimm, No. 17, and with Grimm,

No. 165. For the "sack full of words" in the Tagalog tale, see Rittershaus, 419–421 (No. cxviii, and notes).

The reference at the end to raiding Moros appears to be a remnant of very old native tradition.

36. PEDRO AND THE WITCH.[1]

Pedro was the son of a poor man. He lived with his father and mother by the seashore. Early one morning his parents went to look for food, leaving him alone in the house. He staid there all day waiting for them to return. Evening came, but his father and mother did not appear; some misfortune had overtaken them. Pedro felt very hungry, but he could find no food in the house. In the middle of the night he heard some one tapping at the door. Thinking that it was his mother, he arose and went to meet her. When he opened the door, however, he saw that it was not his mother who had rapped, but Boroka,[2] whom children are very much afraid of. Now, Boroka was a witch. She had wings like a bird, four feet like a horse, but a head like that of a woman. She devoured boys and girls, and was especially fond of their liver. As soon as Pedro opened the door, she seized him and carried him off to her home in the mountains.

Pedro was not afraid of the witch; he was obedient to her, and soon she made him her housekeeper. Whenever she went out at night to look for food, he was sure to have flesh and liver for breakfast the next day. Whenever the witch was away, Pedro used to amuse himself riding on the back of a horse that would often come to see him. It taught him how to ride well, and the two became great friends.

One day when children began to get scarce, and Boroka was unable to find any to eat, she made up her mind to kill Pedro. She left the house and went to invite the other witches, so that they might have a great feast. While she was gone, the horse came and told Pedro of his danger, and advised him what to do. It gave him two handkerchiefs, — one red and the other white. Then Pedro jumped on the horse's back, and the horse ran away as fast as it could. Not long afterward he noticed that the witches were pursuing them. When they came nearer, Pedro dropped the red handkerchief, which was immediately

[1] Narrated by Santiago Dumlao of San Narciso, Zambales.
[2] *Boroka*, apparently a corruption of the Spanish *bruja* ("witch").

changed into a large fire. The wings of the witches were all burnt off. However, the witches tried to pursue the horse on foot, for they could run very fast. When they were almost upon him again, Pedro dropped the white handkerchief, which became a wide sea through which the witches could not pass. Pedro was now safe, and he thanked the horse for its great help.

NOTES.

While this story is not much more than a fragment, I have given it because of its interesting connections. The chief elements appear to be three: (1) the kidnapping of the hero by a cannibal witch, (2) the friendly horse, (3) the transformation-flight and the escape of the hero. Clearly much is missing. What becomes of the hero is not stated, except that he escapes from the witches. The story is in the form rather of a fairy-tale than of a *Märchen* proper, since it deals primarily with an ogress fond of the flesh of children. On its surface it might be mistaken for a native demon-story told as an *exemplum* to children not to answer strange knocks at the door at night. But a glance below the surface reveals the fact that the details of the story must have been imported, as they are not indigenous, — Boroka, horse, transformation-flight; and a little search for possible sources reveals the fact that this tale represents the detritus of a literary tradition from Europe. To demonstrate, I will cite a Pampangan metrical romance and a Tagalog romance, the former probably the parent of our folk-tale. These two romances, in turn, will be shown to be a borrowing from the Occident.

The Pampangan romance is a long story in 954 quatrains of 12-syllable lines, and is entitled "Story of the Life of King Don Octavio and Queen Teodora, together with that of their son Don Fernando, in the Kingdom of Spain [no date]." The inside of the cover bears the statement that the work is the property of Doña Modesta Lanuza. Señora Lanuza was doubtless the redactor of this version; her name appears on other *corridos* (see JAFL 29 : 213). Although a consideration of this literary form takes us somewhat out of the realm of popular stories, strictly speaking, we may give as our excuse for summarizing it the fact that the related Tagalog romance, "Juan Tiñoso," is one of the most widely-known stories in the Islands, and is told as a folk-tale in many of the provinces where no printed translations of it exist. The story of "Don Octavio" — or "Pugut Negro," as it is popularly known among the Pampangans — runs as follows: —

In Spain there lived a king whose queen, in the ninth month of pregnancy, longed greatly for some *pau* (a species of mango). As it was the custom then to procure any kind of fruit a pregnant woman might desire to eat, the whole kingdom was stirred up in search of some *pau*, but in vain.

At last a general and a company of soldiers who had been sent out to scour the kingdom found a *pau*-tree in the mountain of Silva; but the owner, a giant, Legaspe by name, would not give up any of the fruit except to the king himself. When the king was informed of this, he went to the giant, and was obliged to agree that the giant should be the godfather of the expected child. Then he was given the fruit.

Not long after this event the queen gave birth to a son. While the baby was being carried to the church to be baptized, the giant appeared and claimed his right. After the baptism, the giant snatched the boy from the nurse's hands and carried him off to his cave. He found an old woman to take care of the infant, which grew to be a fine youth.

Now, this giant fed on human flesh. One day, when the boy was about fifteen, the giant gave this horrible command to the old woman: "If I fail to catch any human beings for dinner to-day, you will have to cook my godchild, for I am intolerably hungry." No sooner had the giant disappeared than the old woman woke up the youth, and said to him, "My master wants me to cook you for his dinner, but I cannot do such a thing. I will save you. Yonder you see a horse. Fetch it to me, so that we can depart at once." The boy got the horse, and he and the old woman mounted it and rode off as fast as they could.

They had not gone very far, however, when they heard the giant roaring after them. The old woman immediately dropped her comb to the ground, and it became a big mountain. Thus they gained some time; but the giant was soon after them again. The old woman dropped her pin, which became a dense underbrush of thorns; but the giant got through this too. Now the old woman poured out the contents of a small bottle, and all at once there was a large sea, in which the giant was drowned. By this time the two companions were a great distance from Spain. Then the old woman said to the young prince, "Take this whip. On your way home you will see a dead Negro. Flay him, and put on his skin so that you will be disguised. Cultivate humility, be kind to others, and look to the whip in time of need." Having given these directions, the old woman, who was none other than the Virgin Mary in disguise, disappeared.

Pugut-Negru ("disguised Negro") went on his way, and soon found the dead Negro. When he had flayed him and put on the black skin, he mounted his horse and rode facing its tail. When he reached the capital of Albania, he was greatly ridiculed by every one. However, he went to the king and applied for work. The king said that he might take care of his sheep which were in a certain meadow. When he had been conducted to the meadow where the sheep were, he saw the bones of many men. It was said that every shepherd in that place had been killed by "spirits" (*multos*). That night the spirits threw bones at Pugut-Negru; but he chastised them with his whip, and was left in peace.

This Negro disguise of Prince Fernando, however, was only for Albania. Leaving Albania for a time, he went in his princely garments to visit his parents. He found them in the power of the Moors, who had conquered the kingdom of Spain. With his whip he drove all the Moors out of the country, and freed his family. Later he went to Navarre, and won a tournament and the hand of the princess. Instead of marrying her, however, — for he had already fallen in love with the youngest daughter of the King of Albania,

— he went back and resumed his old work as shepherd, disguised as a Negro.

Some time afterwards it was proclaimed that whoever could cure the king's illness would be amply rewarded. The king had an eye-disease, but none of the learned doctors could help him. Finally it was said that Pugut-Negru knew how to cure eye-diseases, and so the king summoned him. "If you can cure my disease," said the afflicted king, "I will marry one of my daughters to you. If you cannot, you shall be hung." — "I'll do my best, your Majesty," said Pugut-Negru humbly. Then he gathered certain herbs, and applied them to the king's eyes. The king soon got well, and asked his three daughters which of them wanted to marry his savior. "I won't!" said the eldest. "Neither will I," rejoined the second. But the youngest and prettiest one said, "I am at your disposal, father." So Pugut-Negru took the youngest for his wife. After the ceremony he went back to his sheep, but he did not live with his wife; he left her at the palace.

It was not many months after the king had been cured when the queen fell ill. As before, it was proclaimed that any one who could cure her would receive one of her daughters in marriage. Two princes presented themselves, and promised to get the lion's milk that was needed to make the queen well. After they had started on their search, they came to the dwelling of Pugut-Negru, whom they forced to accompany them. Pugut-Negru pretended to be lame, and so he could not keep up with them. As he was so slow, they mercilessly threw him into a bush of thorns and left him there. But he said to his magical whip, "Build me at once, along the road in which the two princes will pass, a splendid palace; and let lions, leopards, and other animals be about it." No sooner was the order given than the palace was built, and Pugut-Negru was in it, attired like a king. When the two princes came up, they said to him, "May we have some of your lion's milk?" — "Yes, on one condition I will give you the milk: you must let me brand you with my name." Although this condition was very bitter to them, they agreed. Then they hastened back to present the milk to the queen, who at once married them to her two older daughters. Pugut-Negru went back to his old life as shepherd.

Not long after this event the Moors declared war on the Christians. The king's country was invaded, and the Christians were about to be disastrously defeated, when a strange knight with a magic whip (Pugut-Negru) appeared on the field and put the Saracens to flight. This knight wounded himself in his left arm so that he might receive the attention of the princess. The king's youngest daughter (Pugut-Negru's own wife) dressed his wound without recognizing her husband. After the battle was over, the knight said to the king, "Do you know where my brother Pugut-Negru lives?" But the king was ashamed at the way he had treated Pugut-Negru, so he denied all knowledge of him. Although the king pressed the strange knight to come to the palace, he refused. He hastened back to his sheep, and donned his disguise once more.

One day the youngest princess, the wife of Don Fernando, went stealthily to the hut of Pugut-Negru. She found him undisguised, and at once recognized her handkerchief with which she had tied the strange knight's wound. She embraced her husband with joy, and hastened back to the palace to tell the king of her discovery. The king immediately despatched his prime-minister to the hut in the fields, and Don Fernando was brought back in state. When he had been welcomed to the palace, he told all about his treatment by the two cruel princes, who he said were his slaves. When the king was convinced of their imposture, — they said they had got the lion's milk by their own bravery, — he drove them and their heartless wives from his kingdom. After many other adventures, in which he was always successful, Don Fernando took his wife Maria to Spain, where they lived with his father, King Octavio.

While it is not absolutely certain that our folk-tale of "Pedro and the Witch" was derived from the first part of this romance, I think it most likely. The problem here is the same as that we have met with in the notes to Nos. 13, 16, and 21: Which are earlier, — the more elaborate literary forms, or the simpler popular forms? Obviously no general rule can be made that will hold: each particular case must be examined. In the present instance, as I have shown at the beginning of the note, the evidence seems to point to the folk-tale as being the derivative, not necessarily of this particular form of the story, but at any rate of the *source* of the romance.

The romance of "Prince Don Juan Tiñoso, Son of King Artos and Queen Blanca of the Kingdom of Valencia, and the Four Princesses, the Daughters of Don Diego of Hungary," which we have spoken of above as a Tagalog romance, has been printed also in the Pampangan, Visayan, Ilocano, Bicol, and Pangasinan dialects. As to the date of the Tagalog version, Retana mentions an edition between 1860 and 1898 (No. 4176). This romance is not directly connected with our folk-tale, it will be seen, but is related closely (in the second half, at least) with "Pugut-Negru." Briefly the life of Juan Tiñoso runs thus: —

King Artos and Queen Blanca of Valencia had one son, Don Juan Tiñoso, — handsome, brave, strong, kind. One day, while passing the prison, Don Juan heard sounds of great lamentation. On being admitted, he saw the giant Mauleon, a captive of his father's. Moved by the giant's entreaties, Juan freed him; and the monster, grateful in return, gave him a magic handkerchief that would furnish him with everything he wanted, and would, if displayed, subdue all wild animals. Then the giant departed. King Artos, extremely wroth with his son for freeing one of his captives, drove Juan out of his kingdom. Juan went to the mountains, and there became king of the animals.

One night Juan dreamed of the beautiful Flocerpida, the youngest and most beautiful of the four daughters of Diego, King of Hungary. But, determined to do penance for the liberty he had taken in freeing Mauleon, Juan asked his magic handkerchief for the disguise of an old leper, which he vowed he would wear for seven years. He went to Hungary and entered the service of King Diego as a gardener. The princess Flocerpida was very compassionate toward the old leper, and Juan's love grew stronger. One night, when Juan was bathing, Flocerpida saw him without his dis-

guise, and immediately fell in love with him. One day King Diego summoned all the knights of his kingdom, so that his daughters might choose
husbands. The three older princesses threw their golden granadas, which
were caught by men of rank; but Flocerpida refused to throw hers. Angry,
the king next day ordered all his subjects to be present, and required his
daughter to throw her golden apple. She threw it to the old leprous
gardener, and the two were married; but the king drove his daughter from
the palace.

Soon King Diego grew sick. The doctors prescribed lion's milk, and
the three noble sons-in-law set out to get it. They forced the gardener,
their brother-in-law, to go with them, reviling him all the way; but, as he was
on foot, they soon left him behind. By means of his magic handkerchief,
Juan procured a prince's armor and mount, and, riding fast, he anticipated
his brothers-in-law at the cave of the lioness. They soon came up and
asked for milk. Juan, king of the animals, would give it to them only on
condition that they allowed themselves to be branded on the back with an
inscription saying that they were the servants of Don Juan Tiñoso. They
agreed, and received the milk. On the return Don Juan again outstripped
them, resumed his old disguise, and was reviled by the brothers when they
came up. King Diego drank the milk and recovered his health.

Later King Diego received an embassy from the Moors saying that they
were coming to fight him. He appointed his three sons-in-law generals.
While they were at the war, Juan Tiñoso summoned three giants, and told
them to go fight the Moors too, to get the Moorish flag, and to exchange it
with the generals for their three golden granadas. On the return of the
Christian army, a big fiesta was prepared to honor the successful princes.
King Artos and Queen Blanca of Valencia were invited. On the first day
some of the guests asked about Flocerpida, and the king gave orders that
she should appear on the morrow in an old beggar's gown that he was sending her; but Juan Tiñoso supplied her with beautiful clothes and a coach,
and he himself was dressed as a prince. They went to the fiesta, where,
in the presence of the king, he demanded his three servants, pointing to his
three brothers-in-law. They were made to undress, and the brands on
their backs became clear. Then Juan Tiñoso told his story: he said that
it was he who obtained the lion's milk, who won against the Moors, (and
showed the golden granadas exchanged for the enemy's standard.) King
Diego and King Artos were then reconciled to him and Flocerpida, and the
other three princes and their wives were driven out of Hungary.

Next to "Doce Pares" and "Bernardo Carpio," this romance is
the most popular of the metrical romances circulating in the Philippines. It is read, told as a folk-tale, and acted as a *moro-moro* (see
JAFL 29 : 205 [note], 206). It belongs to the same cycle of stories as
Grimm, No. 136, "Iron John," which has many members. (For
bibliography, see Köhler-Bolte, 330–334; Cosquin, 1 : 138–154.)
These members vary greatly, and some of them (e.g., Cosquin, No.
XII) establish definitely the connection between the "Pugut-Negru"
type — kidnapping of hero, friendly horse, transformation-flight,
disguise of hero, etc. — and the "Juan Tiñoso" type, although it

will be seen that our second romance lacks the first three incidents mentioned.

This whole family of stories is one well worth studying in detail. Unfortunately the war has held up the appearance of Bolte-Polívka's "Anmerkungen," Volume III, which is to contain the notes to the Grimm story; but, with the references furnished by Köhler-Bolte and Cosquin, a good beginning towards such a study might be made. Compare also Rittershaus, No. xxiv and notes; Von Hahn, No. 6 and notes; Macculloch, 173.

It might be added as an item of some interest that "Juan Tiñoso" is written as a sequel to another story of widespread popularity, "The Story of Prince Oliveros and Princess Armenia in the Kingdom of England, and that of Prince Artos and Princess Blanca, who were the Father and Mother of Don Juan Tiñoso in the Kingdom of Valencia." This tale of Oliveros and Artos is directly derived from a Spanish romance of chivalry, and is one form of the "Grateful Dead" type (see Gerould, "The Grateful Dead," FLS 1907).

37. THE WOMAN AND HER *COLES* PLANT.[1]

One summer afternoon I saw several men talking to one another. They seemed to be lively and enjoying themselves, for they had finished their work for the day. I went towards them; and, upon coming within earshot, I found out that they were telling tales to one another. The following was one of the stories I heard that afternoon: —

Once there lived a very poor woman. She lived practically by begging, but sometimes she got money with which to buy rice by selling small vegetables in the market. She had a little garden, and one day planted some seeds. Out of one of these seeds there grew up a plant which we call *coles*.[2] This plant grew very fast, and in a few months it reached the sky.

Out of curiosity, one day the woman began to climb the plant. When she was assured that it was strong, she kept on climbing, and did not stop until she reached the sky. There she called to St. Peter, and asked him to give her a magic wand from which she could ask anything she wished. St. Peter gave her what she asked for, but told her not to disturb him again. Then she descended, and went down so quickly that she almost hurt

[1] Narrated by José Hilario of Batangas, who says that the tale is common among the Tagalogs, especially among the people living in the city of Batangas.

[2] *Coles.* — *Memecylon edule* Roxb. (*Melastomata taceæ*), a common and widely distributed shrub in the forests, with small purple flowers and small black or purple berries. It is found in the Indo-Malayan region generally.

herself. When she reached her little hut, she at once asked the wand for food. Immediately there appeared a table on which was the best food in the world. When she had finished eating, she commanded the table to disappear, and it disappeared instantly. Now she became very proud on account of her wonderful possession. She did not recognize her friends any more.

One day an archbishop arrived in the town in which she was living, and all the bells were rung in his honor. She then became very angry, and wondered why the bells were not rung for her whenever she passed in front of the church. So she went to the tower where the bells were, and commanded them to toll for her. They began to ring, but she was struck on the head and was knocked senseless. When she recovered, she hastened home, and began to climb the plant to ask St. Peter for another gift; but, before she had covered one-half the distance to the sky, the plant broke, and she was killed by her fall. Thus she was punished for her vanity.

NOTES.

This story is a sort of *exemplum* of the sin of pride and avarice. In this respect it is connected in idea with Grimm's story of "The Fisherman and his Wife" (No. 19). In its method and machinery, again, it belongs to the "Jack and the Beanstalk" cycle, the main feature of which is a magic plant which grows rapidly until it reaches the sky and enables its owner to climb to the upper regions and secure magic articles. Macculloch devotes a whole chapter (XVI) to the discussion of this cycle, and cites many folk-tales turning on the incident of the magic plant reaching from earth to heaven (see especially pp. 434–435). Brief, and lacking in detail though our story is, it is nevertheless interesting as a combination of incidents from the two cycles just mentioned; and in its combination it shows, I believe, that it has been derived from some southern European *Märchen*, — such a one, perhaps, as the following from Normandy (given in Köhler-Bolte, 102–103), the story of poor Misère and his ever-dissatisfied wife: —

Misère meets Christ and St. Peter, and begs from them. Christ gives him a bean, and tells him to be satisfied with it. Misère goes home with his gift, and sticks the bean in the hearth inside his hut. Straightway a plant grows out of the bean, and rapidly pushes its way up through the chimney. The next day its top is entirely out of sight. The wife now orders Misère to find out if there are any beans on it ready to be picked. He climbs up the plant, and, since he finds no pods, continues higher and higher, until he finds himself before a large golden house. This house is Paradise. St. Peter opens the door for him, and in answer to his request promises him that he will find at home food and drink. The next day Misère's wife gives her husband no rest until he again climbs up to Paradise and asks St. Peter for a new house. Some days later Misère is again forced to visit St. Peter and ask him to make him and his wife king and queen. The saint fulfils this wish likewise, but warns Misère against coming any more. In brief, however, Misère's wife is still unsatisfied, and even wishes to become the Holy Virgin and her husband to be made God himself. When Misère, with this request, comes again to Paradise, St. Peter angrily sends him away; and the poor man finds on earth his old hut and everything else just as it was in the first place.

Köhler (*ibid.*, p. 103) says that probably the heaven-reaching plant did not originally belong to this story of the poor man's proud wife, and that it was probably taken over from the English folk-tale of " Jack and the Beanstalk." Bolte and Polívka, in their notes to Grimm, No. 19 (1 : 147), observe: "It can easily be seen that these stories (i.e., the variants of the 'Fisherman and his Wife') fall into two groups. In the one, which is particularly widespread among the Germanic and Slavic peoples, but is also found in France and Spain, a captive goblin in the form of a fish grants his captor three or more wishes; among the French and Italians, on the other hand, it is usually God or the door-keeper of heaven who grants the same wishes to a poor man who reaches Paradise by means of a bean-stalk. This bean-stalk here may have originated from the story of 'Jack and the Bean-stalk' or from the 'lying-story,' Grimm No. 112." In a French folk-tale given by Carnoy (Romania, 8 : 250), "La Tige de Fève," the husband plants a bean which he has received from a beggar, and climbs up the stalk to heaven. When he asks for his last wish, he plunges down to earth. This story, it will be seen, resembles ours in its tragic conclusion, although the protagonist, as in the Normandy version, is a man instead of a woman. The fact that in our story no husband is mentioned counts for little, as practically all the *exempla* of this type are directed against woman's vanity; and the woman's case in our story illustrates the punishment for that vanity, or pride. There appears to be recorded no Spanish story containing the insatiable wife and the heaven-reaching plant. It seems reasonable to conclude, therefore, that our folk-tale was derived from the French or Italian, and probably through the medium of the clergy.

38. A NEGRITO SLAVE.[1]

Once upon a time there were three princes who owned a Negrito slave. Although he was called a slave, he was not really one: he was only nominally a slave; for the princes, especially the youngest, whom he loved most, treated him

[1] Narrated by Jesus de la Rama, a Visayan from Valladolid, Occidental Negros.

kindly. One striking characteristic of this Negrito was that his grinning was like that of a monkey; and he often grinned, and grinned without cause. He would often follow his young master when he went out for a walk; and he had a suit similar to the prince's, so that, when they were out on the street, they looked very much alike. The only difference between them was that he was black, and the prince was white. Yet he owned a ring, a charm which had been given him by a woman for saving her from the hands of a robber. This ring gave him power to call for anything he wanted; and this was the reason, doubtless, why he was treated with kindness by his masters.

In a neighboring land there was a king who had a beautiful daughter. This princess wanted to marry. She was so desirous of having a companion, that she could not sleep day or night, meditating on how she could have a husband that would suit both herself and her father. At last, won over by her many entreaties, the king proclaimed to all the world that his daughter would marry any one who had a handsome appearance, and who could answer his three difficult questions. Those who came to the court and were unable to answer the questions of the king were to lose their lives.

The three princes were all handsome. The two elder brothers tried to answer the king's questions, but lost their lives. The youngest remained, and, although he wanted to try, he was sure that he would fail too. The Negrito determined to help him. By means of his ring he was able to make his skin white. He also got a mask that was exactly like the face of his young master. Then he dressed himself to resemble the prince, and went to the court of the king. The king said to him, "Will you have your head cut off, too?" He answered, "Yes, if I cannot answer your questions; but let us see!"

"All right," said the king. Then he asked, "Who owns this kingdom?"

The prince answered, "God owns this kingdom." The king was surprised at his bold reply. However, he could not say that it was not God's, for that would be untrue: therefore he could not compel the prince to answer that it was his, the king's.

The next question was this: "How much am I worth?"

The prince answered, "You are not worth more than thirty pieces of silver." The king was furious when he heard this, and said that, if the prince could not give a good reason for his *insulting* words, he would be put to death instantly.

"Yes, yes!" said the Negrito. "Our Saviour was sold for that much: therefore you, who are inferior to the Saviour, cannot be worth more than he was sold for." The people at the court were astounded by this bold answer; and they murmured to one another, "The prince is wise. He is wise, indeed!"

"Well," said the king, "answer this third question, and you shall be married to my daughter: Can you drink all the fresh water in the world?"

"Yes," said the prince.

"Well, then," said the king, "drink it."

"But here," answered the prince, "in many parts of the world the water of the ocean mixes with the fresh water: so, before I drink, you must separate the fresh water from the salt." As the king was unable to do this, he acknowledged himself vanquished.

"All right," said the king. "To-morrow come here for the wedding." The Negrito hastened home, and told his young master all that had happened. The prince gave him five thousand pesetas, and promised him that he would urge the princess to give her consent to the marriage of the Negrito with her maid of honor. The next morning the prince and the princess were married, and the following day the Negrito received the maid of honor for his wife.

NOTES.

Like the preceding, this story was doubtless imported from Europe, and probably through the medium of the religious. The occasion for the three questions, as well as the questions themselves, varies widely in the many different forms of the story; but the relationship among the members of the cycle is unmistakable. A general outline that would embrace most of the variants is this: A certain person, on penalty of losing his head if he fails, is required to give satisfactory answers to three (or four) difficult questions; a friend of the contestant, who resembles him, wears the other's clothes, and answers the questions ingeniously, thus saving his friend's life and winning a considerable reward for him and himself. The fullest bibliography of this cycle is that given by Oesterley in his edition of Pauli's "Schimpf und Ernst" (Stuttgart, 1866), p. 479. For other references to the group of stories, see Grimm, No. 152, and his notes; Rittershaus, 404-408 (No. cxv, "Der König und der Bischof"); Köhler-Bolte, 82 (on Moncaut's French story "Le Meunier et le Marquis"), 267

(on J. F. Campbell's No. 50), and 492 (on the Turkish Nasr-eddin's
70th jest).

The opening of our story is like that of many of the tales in the
"Bride Wager" group, in which the youngest of three brothers, after
the two older have lost their lives, risks his. Compare, for instance,
the European variants cited in our notes to No. 21. This opening,
which does not belong to our present cycle, was doubtless attached
to the story of the three questions in the Islands themselves. The
combination does not appear to have been very happily effected,
although it is easy to see the basis for the association (cf. Von Hahn's
formula 24 and bibliography). Very little distinction is made between the good qualities of the three brothers, and the Negrito's
determination to help the last only is not motivated. The Negrito
himself, however, is necessary to the story, — he takes the place of
the miller in most of the European forms, — and he had to be fitted
in as best he could. The magic ring of the slave, with the aid of which
he is able to make himself look exactly like his master, does not
appear in any of the other variants that I know of. In many of the
European forms the occasion of the questions is this: A king or a
nobleman becomes angry with a priest or bishop, and threatens him
with death if he cannot answer within a definite time three questions
that are put to him. As the chief interest of the story is in the solving
of the riddles or problems, it is easy to see how there might be a wide
variation in setting if the story passed around much by word of mouth.

The questions themselves are curious. Here are some of those
found in the European versions: (1) How much water is there in the
sea? (2) How many days have passed since Adam lived? (3) Where
is the centre of the earth? (4) How far is it from earth to heaven?
(5) What is the breadth of heaven? (6) What is the exact value of the
king and his golden crown? (7) How long a time would it take to
ride around the whole world? (8) What is the king thinking of this
very moment? (9) How far is fortune removed from misfortune?
(10) How far is it from East to West? (11) How heavy is the moon?
(12) How deep is water?

Some of the answers to these questions are clever; others are only
less stupid than the persons who asked the questions. The solutions
to the twelve just given are: (1) "A tun." — "How can you prove
that?" — "Just order all the streams which flow into the sea to
stand still." This reply is not unlike the counter-demand to the
third question in our story. (2) "Seven; and when they come to an
end, they begin again." (3) "Where my church stands: let your servants measure with a cord, and if there is the breadth of a blade of grass
more on one side than on the other, I have lost my church." (4)
"Just so far as a man's voice can easily be heard." (5) "A thousand

fathoms and a thousand ells: then take away the sun and moon and all the stars, and press all together, and it will be no broader." (6) This question is answered exactly as the second in our story. (7) "If you set out with the Sun and ride with him, you will get around the earth in twenty-four hours." (8) "The king thinks I'm an abbot, and I'm only a shepherd (or miller)." With this question and answer compare the last task in our No. 25. (9) "Only one night, for yesterday I was a shepherd, and to-day I am an abbot." (10) "A day's journey." (11) "A quarter (of a pound): if the king doesn't believe it, let him weigh the moon himself." (12) "A stone's throw."

The method of answering the questions asked in this cycle of stories, and the obscure origin of the clever substitute, form a direct connection, I believe, between this group and the "Clever Lass" cycle. Not only do we find in both the situation of a person out of favor required to answer difficult riddles, and the task assumed voluntarily by some one humbler but more clever than he, but even some of the questions themselves, and the same style of answers, are found in both cycles. For example, compare questions and answers 1, 3, 5, 7, above, with tasks 1, 2, 4, in the notes to our No. 7. In Grimm, No. 152, "The Shepherd Boy," the hero is asked three questions impossible to answer, — How many drops of water are there in the sea? How many stars are in the heavens? How many seconds has eternity? He gets out of his difficulty just as the "Clever Lass" gets out of hers, — by making equally impossible counter-demands, or else giving answers that cannot be proved incorrect.

39. ALBERTO AND THE MONSTERS.[1]

Once there was a king in Casiguran named Luis. King Luis had three beautiful daughters, but the youngest was the fairest of all. One day the three princesses went to the orchard to amuse themselves. It happened that on that day the wind blew very hard, and they were swept away. The king felt very sad over the loss of his daughters; and he issued proclamations in all parts of his kingdom, saying that any one who could find his daughters within three days would be allowed to choose one of the three for his wife.

At that time there was also in the neighboring kingdom of Sinucuan a king who had a brave son named Alberto. When Alberto heard of the matter, he went to the king, and said that he would look for his lost daughters. King Luis accepted his offer. Prince Alberto now began his search. He walked and

---

[1] Narrated by Pacita Cordero of Pagsanjan, Laguna. She says, "This story is common among the Tagalogs. It was told to me by my nurse when I was a little girl."

walked until he came to a large forest where he found two boys fighting. "What are you fighting about?" he said. The one answered that the other boy was taking his boot away from him. Alberto then said to the other boy, "Why don't you give the boy his boot? The boot is old." The boy said that the boot, if worn by any one, would carry him to whatever place he wanted to go, provided he kicked the ground. To settle the contest between the two, Prince Alberto took the boot from them, and said, "Go over by that large tree, and the one who can run here first shall have the boot." While the boys were walking towards the tree, the prince put on the boot and kicked the ground. He was at once carried far away. When the boys got back to the original place, Alberto had disappeared.

' At the place where the boot carried him Alberto found two young men fighting over a rusty key. He said to them, "Why do you fight for such an old rusty key? You are not children: you are young men. You ought to be ashamed of yourselves." The elder of them answered that the key, if it were knocked against a stone, would open the stone, however hard it might be. The prince took the key from them, and said, "Go to a certain place, and race back here. The one to reach here first shall have the key." The two agreed, and started away. While they were gone, Alberto kicked the ground, and the boot carried him to another place. When the young men came back, the prince was no longer there.

This time Prince Alberto found two old men fighting. He asked them the same question as he had asked the others; and one of them answered, "If that hat is worn by any one, his body will be invisible; he will not be seen." The prince secured the hat from these old men by telling them the same thing he had told the others. While they were running their race, he put the hat on and kicked the ground.

The boot now brought him before a huge rock which had a small hole in it. Alberto put the key in the hole, and the rock suddenly opened. When he entered it, he found a street leading to a palace. He went up to the palace; and when he entered the door, a beautiful princess met him. Before Alberto could say a word, the princess told him to go away; for she said that a seven-headed monster was living with her. "If that is the case," said the prince, "show me his sword, and I will kill *him.*" The princess pointed to the sword, which was hanging on the wall. The prince went to get it, but it was too heavy for him: he could not even move it. Then the princess gave him a pail of water to drink. She said that that was the water the monster always drank before touching his sword. The prince drank the water, and then sat down on an iron chair, and the chair broke. The princess now told him that he was strong. Soon steps were heard on the stairs. Prince Alberto put on his hat, and stood by the door, sword in hand. When the monster came up, he thrust one of his heads through a window near the door, and said, "I smell something human!" The prince cut off that head. "Somebody must be here!" cried the monster; but the princess answered that there was no one there with her. The prince then cut off the monster's heads one after another until only the main one was left. The monster waved his arms, but he could not grasp anything. At last he entered the door. The prince cut off his last head, and he fell dead.

Inexpressible was the joy of the princess when she saw the monster lying dead on the floor. She embraced the prince, and thanked him for her deliverance. Then she told him how she happened to be there. When the prince knew that she was one of the daughters of King Luis, he said to her that she was the very one for whom he was looking. The princess then told the prince about her two sisters, who were kept prisoners in the same way. So Prince Alberto left her, saying that he would go save her two sisters and then return.

He went outside and kicked the ground, and was brought before another huge rock. He entered it, and another princess met him. After asking him a few questions, she told him to go away, for the ten-headed monster who was living with her would soon return. But the prince said that he did not fear anything, and he told her to give him the monster's sword. Before he could lift the sword he had to drink two pails of water, which the princess gave him. Then he sat down on an iron bed, and the bed broke in two, so he thought he was strong enough. When the ten-headed monster came home, Alberto killed him in the same way he had killed the other. The princess rejoiced, and told the prince that he had saved her life. Then she embraced him and thanked him. Her joy was increased when Alberto told her that he had saved her younger sister. She begged him to save her eldest sister, who was in the next rock.

The prince answered that that was what he had come for. So he left her without further talk, for it was already the night of the second day.

He then kicked the ground, and found himself in front of another huge rock, which he opened. Here the third princess greeted him. After asking him several questions as to how he had come there, she begged him to go away, for she said that it was time for the twelve-headed monster to come home. But he did not go away. He asked for the sword of the monster, but of course he could not move it. So the princess gave him three pails of water to drink. When the monster came home, the prince cut his heads off one after another, as he had done to the other two. The main head was now the only one left. Then the prince removed his hat, and presented himself before the monster, who thought that he could easily kill him, now that he could see him. He said, "Wait, I'll go and get my sword." But he could not find it, for the prince had already taken it. When he returned, he said to the prince, "You have my sword." He had scarcely spoken these words when Alberto cut off his remaining head. When Alberto told the princess that he had already saved her two sisters, she jumped with joy and embraced him.

Alberto now took the princess in his arms, kicked the ground, and they were brought to the palace of the second sister. Then the prince kicked the ground again, and all three were carried to the palace of the youngest sister. But there was no time for delay, as the third day was nearly gone. So he quickly brought all three princesses back to their father's kingdom. When they arrived at the palace, King Luis was overjoyed to see his daughters again. He told the prince to decide which one he wanted for a wife. While the three princesses were talking about their life with the monsters, Alberto managed, without being noticed, to give his handkerchief to the youngest.

The next day Alberto called at the palace. "Have you decided whom you are going to take for a wife?" said the king. The prince answered, "The one who has a handkerchief just like mine shall be my wife." Now, all three were anxious to have the brave prince for their husband, so they hastened to their rooms to get their handkerchiefs. The two older sisters first presented theirs, but neither resembled Alberto's. Then the youngest showed the one which Alberto had given her the day before, and so she was married to him. For three days banquets of thanksgiving were held, and the marriage festivities lasted for two days. The other two princesses were also married to kings' sons.

There is a striking analogy between the opening of our story and that of a Servian tale (Wuk, No. 5), where a Kaiser has three daughters whom he rears in close confinement, but whom he permits one day, after they have become of marriageable age, to dance the *kolo*. While they are dancing, a storm blows up, and carries them all away. The rest of the story is a variant of our No. 18, with which our present story, too, has some points of contact.

For the magic articles secured by the hero from certain persons quarrelling over them, and for the "Fee-fi-fo-fum" formula, see notes to No. 18.

The hero's drinking a pail of magic water, and becoming so strong that when he sits in an iron chair it breaks down under him, recalls the similar feat of Strong Hans (Grimm, No. 166).

The three monsters of increasingly greater formidability — Seven-Heads, Ten-Heads, Twelve-Heads — which are slain by the hero, who uses their own weapons on them, recall the underworld monsters killed by the hero in the "Bear's Son" cycle (cf. our notes to No. 17).

Although the events of our story are located in the Philippines, the Casiguran mentioned probably being the town in Tayabas on the west coast of Luzon, the tale as a whole appears to have been imported. The Sinucuan referred to is probably the famous legendary King of Pampanga, of whom the Pampangans have a rich oral literature. He is said to have lived on Mount Arayat. He figures in our No. 79 (*b*).

40. JUAN AND MARIA.[1]

Once there lived in a barrio an old beggar couple. They had a son named Juan, and a daughter Maria. The proceeds from their begging were hardly enough to support the family. One day, after the old man had returned home from town, he ordered his wife to cook the rice that had been given him. The old woman obeyed him. When he saw that the rice was not enough for him and his wife and children, he angrily said to her, "From now on, don't let me see our children in this house. Chase them as far as you can, and let them find their own food." The old mother wept when she heard the words of her cruel

[1] Narrated by Aniclo Pascual of Arayat, Pampanga, who says, "This story is often told by Pampangan grandmothers to their grandchildren. I have heard it many times. Lately it was told to me again by an old woman."

husband. She did not want to be separated from her children; but she feared that she would be whipped if she kept them, so she obeyed the cruel order. At first the poor children did not want to go away; but, when they saw that their bad father was going to kick them, they ran off crying.

Soon the children came to a wild forest. "Maria, what will become of us here?" said Juan. "I am very hungry," said the little girl. "I don't think that I can get you any food in this wilderness," said the kind brother, "but let me see!" He then looked around. By good luck he found a guava-tree with one small fruit on it. He immediately climbed up for the guava, and gave it to his hungry sister. Then the two children resumed their journey.

As they were walking along, Maria found a hen's egg on the grass. She picked it up and carried it along with her in her dirty ragged skirt. At last they saw a very small hut roofed with dry *talahib* (coarse, long grass). An old woman in the hut welcomed them, and asked them where they were going. After Juan had told her their story, she invited the tired children to stay in the hut with her. She promised that she would treat them as her little son and daughter. From that time on, Juan and Maria lived with the kind old woman. Juan grew to be a strong fine man, and Maria became a beautiful young woman. Juan spent almost all his time hunting in the mountains and woods.

One morning he caught a black deer. While he was taking the animal home, the deer said to him, "Juan, as soon as you reach your home, kill me, eat my flesh, and put my hide in your trunk. After three days open your trunk, and you will see something astonishing." When Juan reached home, he did as the deer had told him to do. On the third day he found in the trunk golden armor. He was greatly delighted by the precious gift.

Maria had not been living long with the old woman when she found that the egg had hatched into a chick, which soon grew into a fine fighting cock. One morning the cock crowed, "Tok-to-ko-kok! Take me to the cockpit. I'll surely win!" Maria told the old woman what the cock had said, and the next Sunday Juan took the fighting cock to the cockpit. There the rooster was victorious, and won much money for Juan.

One day Juan heard that a tournament would be held in

front of the king's palace. The winner of the contest was to become the husband of the princess, and would inherit the throne. Juan quickly put on his golden armor, and hastened to the palace to try his skill. He defeated all his opponents. The next day his bridal ceremony was celebrated, and the crown was placed on his head. That very day he ascended the throne to rule over the kingdom. Although Juan was now king, he was not proud. He and the queen visited Maria to get her to live in the palace; but the old woman would not allow her to go with her brother, as she had no other companion in the hut.

One day a prince was lost in the forest. He happened to come across the hut in which Maria was living. He fell in love with her, and wanted to marry her. As the old woman offered no objections to the proposal of the prince, the following day Maria became a queen, just as her brother had become king. Although the parents of Juan and Maria had been very cruel, yet the king and queen did not forget them. The brother and sister visited their father and mother, whom they found in the most wretched condition. When the father saw that his children had become king and queen, he wept greatly for his former cruelty to them.

NOTES.

A Tagalog folk-tale printed in the "Journal of American Folk-Lore" (20 : 306), "Tagalog Babes in the Woods," is related to our story. "There the twins Juan and Maria are driven to the forest by their cruel father. After days of wandering, Juan climbs a tree, and sees in the distance a house. They approach it, and, having asked permission to enter, are invited in; but there is no one to be seen in this magic house, although food and drink and clothing are supplied the two wanderers in abundance." The story is evidently incomplete. It is based on a metrical romance, "The Life of the Brother and Sister, Juan and Maria, in the Kingdom of Spain," of which I will give a brief synopsis, since the chap-book version contains details which are lacking in the fragment cited above.

This metrical romance is printed in both Tagalog and Pampangan. My Tagalog copy, which contains 1836 lines, bears the date 1910, but is clearly a reprint. The Pampangan text is slightly shorter, with 1812 lines. Retana (No. 4164) cites a Pampangan version some time between the years 1860 and 1898, and a later reprint of 1902 (No. 4349). The summary that follows is based on the Tagalog.

JUAN AND MARIA.

During the reign of King Charles the Fifth there lived in Spain a poor couple, Fernando and Juana. They had a son Juan, ten years old, and a daughter Maria, but eight months in age. Fernando was very cruel to his wife and children. He was also very selfish. During meal-times he ate alone, without inviting the rest of his family to eat with him.

One day Fernando said to his wife, "You must send our two children away. If my command is not executed, your life shall answer for your disobedience." The broken-hearted mother summoned her children, and with tears in her eyes told them of the cruel order of their father. The children had to obey their father, for they feared him, and so set off for the mountains. For many days they wandered around, living on wild fruits, and sleeping under trees.

One day Juan was greatly surprised to hear Maria ask for some water to drink, for she had never spoken before. They were far from any stream, and Juan did not know what to do to satisfy his sister. At last he climbed a tree to see whether there was any water near by, and he saw in a valley not far off a beautiful house surrounded with flowers. Juan quickly came down the tree, and the two children set out for the house. When they reached it, they knocked at the door, but no one answered. After knocking again in vain, the boy decided to enter. He pushed open the door, and found himself in a golden *salon*, luxuriously furnished with gold and silver chairs. On the silver wall hung an image of the Immaculate Conception. The two children knelt down in front of the image and prayed. Then they went to the dining-room, where they found a golden table with exquisite dishes of all kinds.

Several years passed by. Under the care of the Virgin, Maria grew to be a beautiful young woman. One day, as Maria was praying, the Virgin spoke to her through the image. She said that the gallant prince of Borgoña would come to the mountains to hunt deer, and that he would lose his way in the woods. He would come to their house to ask for some water, and would fall in love with Maria. Everything turned out as had been predicted. The gallant prince was so attracted by the beauty and grace of Maria, that he could not help saying to her, "I love you." With the consent of her guardian the Virgin, Maria accepted the Prince of Borgoña, and the day for their wedding was set. The king, his son, and all the nobility of Borgoña, set out for the mountains to get Maria, and on their arrival were surprised at the magnificence of her house. The bishop who was with the company married the couple, and all the retinue went back to the capital.

When Juan now found himself left all alone in the house, he knelt before the image and complained to the Virgin of his situation. The Virgin said to him, "Don't worry! To-morrow mount the horse which is in the stable, clothe yourself in iron, and go to the kingdom of Moscobia to help the king drive the Moors away." Juan did so, and upon his arrival in Moscobia he found thousands of Moors threatening the king. With his sword he killed half the enemy: the rest were routed. Because of his great services, the king married his daughter to Juan, and the new couple were proclaimed king and queen.

Some time afterwards, Juan wrote to his sister, suggesting that they visit their parents. The two couples, accompanied by many of the nobles of their kingdoms, set out for Spain. Their cruel father was astounded to see his children raised to such a lofty position, and he begged their pardon for his former harsh treatment of them. They forgave him, and then returned to their respective kingdoms, where they lived peacefully for many years.

The connection between our folk-tale and the romance is not very clear. In both we have the abandoned children, the discovery of the house in the woods where the children are reared to manhood and womanhood, and the marriage of Maria with a prince who loses his way in the forest. In both Juan becomes a king, and in both the two children seek again their cruel parents and forgive them. On the other hand, there is much in the folk-tale that is lacking in the romance; e.g., the incident of the egg that hatches into a fighting cock, and the incident of the black deer with the miraculous hide. In the folk-tale Juan becomes king because of his skill in a tournament; in the romance, because, with the help of the Virgin, he defeats a large Moorish army. In the one, the shelter in the woods is but a thatch-roofed hut inhabited by a kindly old woman; in the other, it is a magnificent house occupied by no one except the image of the Virgin. The correspondences as well as the differences between the two versions, neither of which appears to be new, suggest that the source of the folk-tale and the romance is one and the same, but that the folk-tale went its own way, the way of the people, and thus acquired its more native appearance. That the common source was some European story, can hardly be doubted, I think.

The opening of our story is not unlike that of the German "Hänsel und Gretel" (Grimm, No. 15). Bolte and Polívka (1:123) note that various different *Märchen* have this beginning "of children whom their father, either because of bitter necessity or because he is forced by their step-mother, takes to the woods and there abandons." One of the most widespread cycles in which it occurs is "Hop o' my Thumb," a version of which is told among the Tagalogs. I will give this Tagalog version here in the notes, by way of compromise, as it were: for while the story is a *bona fide* Tagalog tale, in that it is told in the dialect, it must have been received directly from Europe; and it appears to have retained the form in which it was received, with but few modifications. No other Oriental form whatsoever of this story has been recorded (see Bolte-Polívka, 1 : 124–126). The Tagalog story was narrated by Pacita Cordero of Pagsanjan, Laguna, and runs thus: —

PITONG.

Melanio and Petrona had seven sons. The father was a woodman. They were so poor, that sometimes the whole family went without dinner. One day Melanio said to his wife, "Petrona, our children are growing, and I don't see how we shall be able to support them all. At present they cannot help us earn a living, because they are too small. Don't you think we should get along better without them?" — "Yes," answered Petrona, "if we could only get rid of them some way!" — "Well, to-morrow I will take them to the forest to gather fuel," said the husband. "While they are busy, I will leave them on the pretext of looking for better kinds of wood, and will hurry home. They will not be able to get home, for they won't know the way."

The wife agreed to this cruel plan. But the youngest son overheard the conversation, and told his brothers about it. At last Pitong (seventh), for that was the name of the youngest, and he was the wisest of all, made this suggestion: "Before we go to the forest to-morrow, I will pick up white stones. I will carry them with me, and as we go along I will drop them one by one. I'll walk behind, so that father will not notice what I am doing. Then, if he leaves us, we can easily follow the track of stones back home." While the six brothers consented to the plan, their minds were troubled, for they doubted the ability of so small a boy to save them.

The next day the children marched straight into the forest with their father as if they were going on a picnic. Pitong dropped his stones one by one. When they reached the woods, their father commanded them to get together what sticks they could find. He left them there, promising that he would meet them in a certain place; but really he hurried home and told his wife. "We are now rid of a heavy burden," he said, and the two were very happy. When the poor boys had finished their work, they looked in vain for their father. Of course they could not find him; but Pitong led the company, and they followed the track of stones. The boys reached home safely, and the parents were mute with astonishment.

The next morning Melanio took his sons out with him again. This time all the boys took white stones with them, besides bread, which they intended to eat if they should get hungry; but the part of the forest to which they went was so far, that all the stones were used up before they got there. Pitong did not eat his bread; he broke it into pieces, and dropped them on the ground as they went along. They now reached the nook where their father proposed to leave them. This place was grown up with wild shrubs, so that there were plenty of twigs to keep the boys busy. Melanio slipped away from them without their noticing it. After the seven brothers had worked a long time, they thought of returning home. But they could not find the track: the pieces of bread had been eaten by the ants. They cried out, "Father, father! where are you?" When they were so hungry and tired that they could not shout any more, they sat down on the ground and began to weep.

It began to grow dark. Pitong advised his brothers to pluck up courage, and said to them, "Follow me." So they went on without taking any particular course, and in about a half-hour they came to a tall tree. Pitong climbed it to see if there was a road near by. When he reached the top, he said, "Brothers, I see a lighted house from here. Let us go look for the house! Maybe we can get something to eat there."

When they came near the house, they saw that it was well lighted and richly adorned, as if there were a banquet going on; only it was very quiet. Pitong, followed by his brothers, knocked at the door. A woman kindly admitted them, and the boys begged for some food. They told her how they had been deserted by their selfish father. The woman said to them, "I have a giant husband who is a great eater of human beings. If he finds you here, you will surely be devoured; but I can give you something to eat. I will hide you before he comes, and you must remain perfectly still." The boys had hardly finished dinner when a loud sound was heard from without. The woman said to them, "Here comes my husband! Boys, follow me into that room! You all get into this big trunk and stay here."

The door was suddenly flung open. As soon as the giant entered, he said in a fierce voice, "I smell something human: somebody must be here." He said this many times; and although the wife did not want to show him the boys, she finally did so, for she feared that she would be punished. She beckoned to them to come out of the trunk. "Welcome, my young friends!" said the giant. "I am very glad to have you here." Pitong gazed fearlessly at him, but the others trembled with fright. "Give these boys some food, and prepare them a comfortable bed," said the giant to his wife. "To-morrow early in the morning they will all be killed."

These words increased the terror of the six older brothers. They could not swallow a morsel more of food when the old woman set it before them. Pitong, however, kept trying to think of a plan by which he could save them all. Now, the room in which they were to sleep was also the room of the giant's seven sons, who were about the same height as the woodman's sons. But the giant's sons had on rich garments. At midnight Pitong awoke his brothers. They quietly and carefully exchanged clothes with the giant's sons, and then pretended to sleep. At four o'clock in the morning the giant came in. He paused before the two beds, but at last turned to the one his sons were in. When he felt their rough clothes, he thought them the strangers, and with his axe he cut off the heads of all seven. Then he went away and slept again.

Now Pitong and his six brothers stealthily hurried away into the forest. When morning came, and the giant found that he had killed his own children, he was enraged. He at once took his magic cane, and put on his magic boots and cap. When the boys heard the giant coming after them, they went down into a big hole they had dug. There they hid. But the giant had a keen sense of smell, and he walked around and around, looking for them. At last he became tired; he leaned against a tree and fell asleep. Pitong peeped through a small opening from under the ground. When he saw that the giant was asleep, he called out to his brothers. They quickly stole the magic boot, cap, and cane of the giant, and were soon carried home. Their parents were very much surprised to see them back; but they welcomed their children when they knew of the magic objects. By means of these the family became rich.

As for the giant, when he awoke, he was deprived of all his power. He was so weak that he could not even get up from the ground, so he died there in the woods.

41. THE ENCHANTED PRINCE.[1]

Many years ago there lived a very rich king in a beautiful city near a wild forest, the home of many wicked witches.

[1] Narrated by Pedro D. L. Sorreta, a Bicol from Virac, Albay, who heard the story from his grandfather.

The king had a gallant son named Ucay, who fell in love with a beautiful young witch, the daughter of the most bitter enemy of his father. When Ucay became old enough to marry, his father requested him to select the most beautiful lady in the city for his wife; but the prince would neither select one, nor would he tell his father about his love for the witch. So the rich king ordered his soldiers to bring to the palace all the beautiful women that could be found in the kingdom. His order was soon obeyed, but none of the girls suited the prince. So the king took the matter of selection into his own hands; and, after choosing a very handsome girl, he forced his son to marry her. Out of fear, Ucay consented to do as his father bade him. But the beautiful young witch to whom he had already pledged his love became angry with him for his timidity, and so she resolved to change the city into a forest of beautiful trees. Her fickle lover she transformed into a monkey, who should live in the tallest tree, and who should not be able to recover his human shape till five centuries had passed, when a charming girl would live with him and love him more than anything else. Moreover, she changed the king's subjects into other animals as she pleased. No sooner had the marriage of the prince been proclaimed, then, than the desire of the witch was accomplished, to the great surprise of the neighboring cities.

Four centuries had already passed. The wonderful disappearance of the city was already forgotten, and people from other places began to build houses in the enchanted city. The monkey-prince was always watching for an opportunity to catch a beautiful girl who should break the spell that kept him in his miserable condition. Soon a church was built near the foot of the tree in which he lived. He had already succeeded in capturing two ladies, but they had died of fear. After incalculable suffering and extraordinary patience, the time for his recovery came at last.

One Sunday morning before the mass was over, a very beautiful girl, the daughter of a poor man, came out of the church and sat at the foot of the tree. She had been disappointed in her love with a rich man's son, who had forsaken her in order to marry the daughter of a rich man. So she wished to die. When the monkey-prince saw her sitting there alone, he noiselessly went down, carefully took her by the right hand, and carried her to the top of the tree. She would have died of fright, as was the fate of the two former women, had she not seen in the monkey's eyes a noble look that filled her with wonder and sympathy. As days went by, she lived on delicious fruits which were entirely strange to her; and her love for the poor creature grew greater and greater, until at last she loved him more than anything else.

On the evening of the tenth day she was surprised to find herself beside a gallant prince in a richly-decorated room. At first she thought that she was dreaming; but when the prince woke up, kissed her, and then told her the history of his life, she knew that it was real. She was so astonished, that she exclaimed, "Ah, me! God is wise!" The next morning she was crowned queen of her husband's happy subjects, whom she had restored from the enchantment of the wicked witch. Every one in the kingdom loved his new queen as long as he lived.

NOTES.

I know of no parallels to this interesting story, which appears to be old native tradition. The hero transformed by enchantment into a beast, and saved by the devotion of the human lover, suggests the "Beauty and Beast" cycle (Macculloch, ch. IX; Crane, 7, 324 [notes 5 and 6]; Ralston, Tibetan Tales, p. XXXVII f.); only it is to be noted that those stories are, after all, heroine tales, not hero tales, for the interest in them is centred on the disenchantment brought about by the maiden who comes to love the prince in his beast form. The curse by a disappointed witch, and the prophecy that only after five hundred years will the curse be removed, suggest in a way the "Sleeping Beauty" cycle (Grimm, No. 50; and Bolte-Polívka's exhaustive notes); only here, too, the resemblance is but vague. There is no magic sleep in our story, but a Circe-like transformation of the prince and all his subjects into animals, the city itself being changed into a forest of trees. We have already met with stories in the Philippines based on the idea of animal-marriages (e.g., Nos. 18, 19, 29); but, even were it demonstrable that all those tales were imported, it would not necessarily follow that the savage idea behind them, too, was imported. Their adoption by the natives might indicate, on the contrary, that the basic idea was already well known.

I might call attention to the fact that the number *500* and the *monkey*-prince suggest vaguely Buddhistic lore.

42. THE PRINCE'S DREAM.[1]

Once there lived a young prince who, after his father's death, succeeded to the throne as the sole heir of a vast, rich kingdom. He indulged himself in all worldly pleasures. He gave dances, and all sorts of merry-making surrounded his court to attract the most beautiful ladies of the kingdom. Meanwhile the royal treasury was being drained, and his subjects were becoming disloyal to him; for, his time being chiefly absorbed in personal cares, he often neglected his duties as king. Disappointed by his conduct, his counsellors plotted against him: they resolved to dismiss him from the realm. The prince's mother, the widowed queen, learned of their plot. So, when he returned to the palace from his evening walk one day, she said to him, "My son, I wish you would turn from your foolish trifling, and govern your people as you ought to do; for your advisers are planning to dethrone you." The prince, who was not bad at heart, followed his mother's sensible advice: he now began to devote himself to the welfare of his subjects. His ministers, too, gave up their plan, and aided the young king in his royal tasks.

One noon, when the prince was taking his siesta, he had a dream. A ghost appeared to him, and spoke in this manner: "Your father left a hidden treasure of gold and diamonds, which he forgot to mention in his will. Should you care to have that treasure, go to the city of Black. There you will find a Negro, the richest in that city, who will tell you all about the treasure." On hearing these words, the prince woke up, and hurriedly acquainted his mother with his dream. "Undeceive yourself," she said. "Never believe in dreams. I don't believe in them myself." In spite of his mother's words, he decided to look for the Negro.

The next day, disguising himself as a poor traveller, the prince set out for the city of Black. He arrived there at ten o'clock at night, and the gate of the city was closed; for there was a law there, that, after the bell had rung ten, no person could enter the city. So he had to sleep outside the walls. Then the very same ghost that had spoken to him in his palace appeared to him, and said, "Go back to your palace, prince, and there in the cellar you will find the treasure I spoke of." The moment he

---

[1] Narrated by Gregorio Frondoso, a Bicol of Tigaon, Camarines. The narrator says, "This story was told to me by my guardian while I was in Nueva Caceres. He told it to me in the Bicol dialect, and said that this must be a Bicol story."

heard the voice, the prince got up and returned to his own city. When his mother saw him, she said to him, "Did you find what you were looking for?" — "Mother, the very same ghost told me that the treasure is buried in the cellar of the palace."

"I have told you that dreams are never true," she said. "The ghost must be joking you. You see, you have gone to a far-away land in vain. Banish all thoughts of that treasure, and continue ruling your kingdom well, and you will be very much better off."

At first the prince followed his mother's counsel, and tried to rid his mind of the thought of the treasure; but the ghost haunted him in his sleep, day and night, reminding him of the gold and diamonds. Early one morning, without the knowledge of his mother, he took a pointed iron bar and went down into the cellar of the palace. There he dug where the treasure was supposed to be. He dug and dug to find the coveted gold and diamonds. He remained there several hours, and had excavated a hole some three metres deep, but had found no sign of the hidden wealth. Just as he was about to give up, his bar struck something hard which produced a metallic sound. He went on digging until finally he uncovered an iron platform in the form of a square. It was locked with a padlock, and the key was in the lock. He lifted the platform, and to his great surprise and wonder found a low ladder made of diamond bars, leading down into a small apartment all shining bright as if it were day. Here he found two columns of diamond bars, each a foot in thickness and a metre in height, whose brightness shot through all the corners like sunbeams. This subterranean chamber immediately led to another in which there was a big safe about five feet in height and three feet wide. He opened the safe, and from out of it flowed gold coins like water in torrents from a cliff. His eyes were dazzled by their brightness; and he was so startled at the inexhaustible flow of money, that he said to himself, "Are these gold coins and diamonds real, or am I simply dreaming?" To assure himself, he filled his cap with the gold coins and went up into the sunlight. He rubbed his eyes and examined the coins: they were of pure gold. Greatly delighted by his discovery, he hastened to his mother, and said, "I have found the treasure, I have found the treasure!" When the queen saw the gold glittering in her son's hand, she was very glad. Now both mother and son hurried down to the cellar.   There the prince continued his search for the hidden treasure, while his mother contemplated in awe the columns of diamonds she saw in those underground apartments.   Now the prince came to a third chamber, in which he found two more columns of diamonds like those in the first room; and finally he came to a fourth apartment, in which he saw a wide curtain of silk hanging on the wall.   Back of this wall was another apartment, but it was securely locked.   On the curtain were embroidered the following words in big golden letters: "Inside this chamber is another column of diamonds twice as large and twice as high as those in the other two; none can unlock this apartment but the wealthiest Negro in the city of Black."

Anxious to have this last column of diamonds, the prince determined to find the Negro.   Disguising himself again as a poor traveller, he set out for the city of Black.   There he found the Negro, who received him very kindly.   In the course of their talk the prince spoke of his dream, and told how he found the gold coins and the diamond columns, and finally gave the reason for his coming there as a poor traveller.   Furthermore, the prince mentioned his father's name.   On hearing the prince's story, the Negro knelt down before him, saying, "My prince, I was the most beloved servant of your father.   I acknowledge you as my master, and am disposed and ready to do anything for your sake.   As to the chamber you spoke of, I have not the power to unlock it.   There is but one man who can unlock it, who knows very well your dead father, and who was his friend.   He knows me, too, very well.   This man is the king of the demons.   And to him we will go together; but before we go, we should eat our dinner."   Then the Negro ordered all kinds of delicious dishes, and the two feasted together.

After they had dined, they set out on their journey to the palace of the king of the demons.   Soon they came to a river. There the Negro instructed the prince not to say anything if he should see any extraordinary sights, lest some terrible danger befall them.   The Negro waved his hand, and in a moment there came a sphinx paddling a small banca towards them.   They got into it, and the sphinx rowed back to the other side.   Then they walked on till they came to the palace of the king of the demons, which was protected by two circular walls.   They knocked at the gate of the first.   The moment they knocked, it became dark all around them; lightnings flashed before their eyes, and it thundered. Then the gate opened. After passing through the first gate, they came to the second. They knocked, and the gate flung open. At once two lions ran out towards them with eyes glowing like balls of fire, and were ready to spring upon them and devour them; but on coming nearer the strangers, and recognizing the Negro, these two kings of beasts wagged their tails as a sign of welcome.

The Negro and the prince were conducted to the king's throne. The king of the demons asked them what they wanted. The prince spoke: "King of the demons, I have found in the cellar of my palace a store of gold coins and several diamond columns, my father's hidden treasure which he forgot to mention in his will. The last column is locked up in a separate apartment, and there is none who has the power to unlock it but yourself."

"Young king," replied the king of the demons, "it is true that I am the only one who can unlock it. I gave that diamond column to your father as a gift which he might bequeath to his son; and if you are his son, you shall have it. But, before giving it to you, I should like to have you do me a favor in return for that rich gift. If you will bring me a very beautiful woman to be my companion, one whose heart is untainted by any worldly passion, I will unlock for you your wished-for treasure, the diamond room."

At this request the young man stood speechless for some time. At last, perplexed, he replied, "O king of the demons! it seems to me impossible to fulfil your wish. I am not a man of super-human power to read into a woman's heart."

"Well," returned the king of the demons, taking out of his pocket a small oval mirror, "if you see a beautiful woman, hold this mirror before her face. If the surface of the mirror becomes clouded, leave her; but if the surface of the mirror remains as clear as before, bring her to me, for she is the one I want for my comfort."

The prince took the mirror, and with his Negro companion left the palace to look for the desired girl for the king of the demons. They visited cities and villages. In three days they had searched through three cities and three villages, but every girl that looked on the magic mirror clouded its surface. Then, discouraged by their failure, the travellers decided to go back

to the palace of the king of the demons. On their return they
felt very tired, and so stopped in a small village to rest. There
they found a most beautiful girl, the daughter of a poor farmer.
It was the very girl desired by the king of the demons; for, after
she had looked on the magic mirror, its surface remained as
clear as before. Then with joyful hearts the Negro and the
prince set out with the lady for the abode of the king of the
demons.

On their way, the prince, fascinated by her beauty, fell in
love with the girl. He did not want to give her up to the king
of the demons, and so proposed to the Negro that they take
her to his palace. But the Negro would not consent, for the
king of the demons knew all about their doings, he said. So
the prince gave up his plan on condition that the girl's face be
veiled.

When they arrived at the palace, the king of the demons
gladly met them, and said to the prince, "Now you have fulfilled my wish. You may go back to your palace, and there
you will find the diamond apartment unlocked for you." The
sorrowing prince turned his back and left the palace with heavy
heart; for he no longer thought of the treasure of gold and
diamonds, but had his whole soul centred in that beautiful
maiden that he had given up to the king of the demons. He
reached his own palace sad and dejected. Yet, to divert his
mind from the thought of her, he went to the subterranean
apartment; and there he found the last chamber unlocked.

After some hesitation, he went into the apartment. There
he found two veiled figures, — the one in the form of a king with
his sceptre and crown; the other, a maiden. He unveiled the
one with the crown, and was astounded to find the very same
king of the demons. "Prince, unveil that figure," said the
king of the demons to him. The young king did so, and to his
great joy saw the beautiful maiden he had lost his heart to.
At once his sadness disappeared. Then the king of the demons
said to the prince, "Young king, since on your way to my
palace you fell in love with this maiden, I deem it fit that you
should have her for your companion; but do not expect the
diamond column any more." Then the king of the demons
disappeared. The prince at once embraced the maiden, and
conducted her up to his palace. That same day their marriage
was celebrated with pomp and luxury.

NOTE.

Dr. Franz Boas informs me that this story is from the "Arabian Nights," "The Tale of Zayn Al-Asnam" (see Burton, Supplemental Nights," iii, 3–38; for Clouston's discussion of variants and analogues, *ibid.*, 553–563).

43. THE WICKED WOMAN'S REWARD.[1]

Once there lived a certain king. He had concubines, five in number. Two of them he loved more than the others, for they were to bear him children. He said that the one who should give birth to a male baby he would marry. Soon one of them bore a child, but it was a girl, and shortly afterward the other bore a handsome boy. The one which had given birth to the baby girl was restless: she wished that she might have the boy. In order to satisfy her wish, she thought of an ingenious plan whereby she might get possession of the boy.

One midnight, when all were sound asleep, she killed her own baby and secretly buried it. Then she quietly crept to her rival's bed and stole her boy, putting in his place a new-born cat. Early in the morning the king went to the room of his concubine who had borne the boy, and was surprised to find a cat by her side instead of a human child. He was so enraged, that he immediately ordered her to be drowned in the river. His order was at once executed. Then he went into the room of the wicked woman. The moment he saw the boy-baby, he was filled with great joy, and he smothered the child with kisses. As he had promised, he married the woman. After the marriage the king sent away all his other concubines, and he harbored a deep love for his deceitful wife.

Soon afterwards there was a great confusion throughout the kingdom. Everybody wondered why it was that the river smelled so fragrant, and the people were very anxious to find out the cause of the sweet odor. It was not many days before the townspeople along the river-bank found the corpse of the drowned woman floating in the water; and this was the source of the sweetness that was causing their restlessness. It was full of many different kinds of flowers which had been gathered by the birds. When the people attempted to remove the corpse from the water, the birds pecked them, and would not let the body be taken away.

[1] Narrated by Gregorio Frondoso, a Bicol from Camarines. The story was told by a father to one of his sons.

At last the news of the miracle was brought to the ears of the king. He himself went to the river to see the wonderful corpse. As soon as he saw the figure of the drowned woman, he was tortured with remorse. Then, to his great surprise and fear, the corpse suddenly stood up out of the water, and said to him in sorrowful tones, "O king! as you see, my body has been floating on the water. The birds would have buried me, but I wanted you to know that you ordered me to be killed without any investigation of my fault. Your wife stole my boy, and, as you saw, she put a cat by my side." The ghost vanished, and the king saw the body float away again down the river. The king at once ordered the body of his favorite to be taken out of the water and brought to the palace; and he himself was driven back to the town, violent with rage and remorse. There he seized his treacherous wife and hurled her out of the window of the palace, and he even ordered her body to be hanged.

Having gotten rid of this evil woman, the king ordered the body of the innocent woman to be buried among the noble dead. The corpse was placed in a mganificent tomb, and was borne in a procession with pompous funeral ceremonies. He himself dressed entirely in black as a sign of his genuine grief for her; yet, in spite of his sorrow for his true wife, he took comfort in her son, who grew to be a handsome boy. As time went on, the prince developed into a brave youth, who was able to perform the duties of his father the king: so, as his father became old, no longer able to bear the responsibilities of regal power, the prince succeeded to the throne, and ruled the kingdom well. He proved himself to be the son of the good woman by his wise and just rule over his subjects.

NOTE.

I know of no other versions of this story. The incident of the animal substitution for child is a commonplace in folk-tales, though it is usually ascribed to an envious step-mother rather than an envious co-wife. For abstracts of Filipino stories containing this incident see JAFL 29 : 226 *et seq.*, 228, 229; 19 : 265–272.

44. THE MAGIC RING [1] ("ANG SINGSING NGA TANTANAN").

In the town of X, not far from the kingdom of Don Fernando, there lived an old religious woman named Carmen. She had a son named Carlos. She had been a widow since Carlos was

---

[1] Narrated by Encarnacion Gonzaga, a Visayan from Jaro, Iloilo. The story, she says, is very popular among the Visayans.

nine months old. She was poor — poor even to raggedness. One day she said to her son, "I have named you Carlos because I love you. For me, no name is prettier than yours. Every letter in it means something." Carlos asked his mother to tell him the meaning of his name; but she said to him, "I'll tell it to you later. First go to the king's palace, and there beg something for us to eat. O my son! if you only knew the miseries I have had to endure to bring you up, you would not refuse this request of your poor mother," she said, weeping.

Carlos pitied his mother very much, so he ran towards the king's palace to beg some food; but when he reached the gate, he hesitated to enter. He was ashamed to beg, so he went and stood silently under the orange-tree which was not far from the princess's window. "If I should obey my mother's request," he said to himself, "what would the princess say? She would probably say to me, 'You are too young to beg.' What a disgrace then would it be for me!" As Carlos was looking at the declining sun with tears in his eyes, the princess raised her window and unintentionally spit on his head. Carlos's eyes flashed. He looked at the princess sternly, and said, "If the Goddess of the Sea, who has a star on her forehead [1] and a moon on her throat, does not dare to spit on me, how can you — you who are but the shadow of her power and beauty?"

At these harsh words the princess fainted. When she came to herself, she cried. Her tears were like drops of dew falling from the leaves in the morning. Her father entered her room, and found her in her sorrow. "Why do you weep, Florentina?" asked Don Fernando.

"O Father!" answered Florentina, "my heart is broken. I have been disgraced."

"Why should you say so?" replied her father. "Who broke your heart, and who disgraced you?"

"There's a man under the orange-tree," answered the princess, "who said to me these words " — and she repeated what Carlos had said to her.

The king instantly ordered Carlos to be seized and brought into his presence. Carlos stood fearless before him, and answered all his questions. Don Fernando at last said, "If within a week you cannot show me that what you said to my daughter is true, you'll be hanged without mercy."

[1] For this very old symbol of beauty and noble lineage, see Prato, Zeitschrift für Volkskunde, 5 : 376; 6 : 28.

These words frightened Carlos. With tears in his eyes and with his thoughts devoted to God, who alone could give him consolation, he walked down the shore of the Golden River. He sat down to rest under a pagatpat-tree. An eagle which had a nest at the very top of the tree saw him crying, and said to him, "Why do you weep, Carlos?"

"O Eagle, queen of the birds! I'd be very thankful to you if you'd only tell me where the home of the Goddess of the Sea is," said Carlos.

"Why do you want her house?" asked the eagle. "Don't you know that no human being is able to see her?"

"I didn't know that; but if I cannot see her, my life is lost," said Carlos sadly.

The eagle pitied Carlos very much: so she said, "Come, Carlos, come! and I'll lead you to the right path." Carlos followed her until they came to the mouth of the river. There they stopped. The eagle shouted, "O king of the fishes! come and help me, for I am in great need of assistance." The king of the fishes appeared, and asked what the eagle needed. The eagle told him the story of Carlos, and asked him if he could take Carlos to the home of the Goddess of the Sea. As the fish could not refuse the request of the queen of the birds, he said to Carlos, "Carlos, lie on my back and close your eyes: within five minutes you'll be in the home of the goddess."

Carlos obeyed the fish. When he opened his eyes, he found that he was in a very beautiful house. He was lying on a golden bed, and beside him was standing a beautiful woman with a star on her forehead and a moon on her throat. Carlos could not believe that the vision was true. By and by he heard a sweet voice saying, "What has brought you to this place?"

Carlos trembled, and answered, "I have come here to ask for your help."

"What help do you desire?" asked the goddess. Carlos related his story. The goddess could not refuse help to one who had spoken so well of her beauty, so she took her diamond ring off her finger and gave it to Carlos, saying, "Take this ring with you. Whenever you want or need my help, touch the ring thrice, and say, 'O God, help me!' If the king wants my presence, touch the ring six times, and I'll appear before you."

Carlos received the ring, and, humbly kneeling before the goddess, said, "I can find no words in which to express to you *my gratitude.* I thank you with all my heart."

The goddess then called to the king of the fishes, and ordered him to take Carlos back to land. When Carlos arrived at the shore of the river, he met the eagle, who showed him the way to the king's palace.

The king Don Fernando, on seeing Carlos once more before him, said, "You wretch! one day more is all you have to live."

"To-morrow," replied Carlos, "I'll come before your Highness, and I'll show to you that what I said to the princess is true." When morning came the next day, Carlos was ordered into the king's presence. All the lords and nobles of the kingdom were in the palace, anxious to see the Goddess of the Sea. It was already eight o'clock, and the goddess had not yet appeared. The king asked, "Where is she, Carlos?"

"She cannot come," replied Carlos; "but, if your Highness wants me to, I'll give you a trunk filled with gold in exchange for my life."

"No," said the king angrily: "what we want is the Goddess of the Sea. If you cannot show her to us, prepare to be hanged."

Carlos touched the ring six times, and the beautiful Goddess of the Sea appeared. All were amazed to see a woman with curly hair, a star on her forehead, a moon on her throat, and wearing a white dress glistening with diamonds. "Carlos is an enchanter!" cried the king, and he ran to embrace the goddess. In five minutes she disappeared, and Carlos's life was saved.

Don Fernando now proposed to marry his daughter Florentina to Carlos. At first the princess hesitated to say yes, but at last she consented. Carlos was glad to marry the beautiful princess; but, before the marriage took place, he went to get his poor mother, who was anxiously awaiting his return home.

Carlos with his diamond ring could now have everything he needed. In fact, he made the chapel in which he was married all of gold. The wedding-dress of the princess was adorned with diamonds. Immediately after the wedding, poor Carmen died of happiness. Carlos continued to live in the palace with his wife Florentina, but he never came to know the meaning of his name.

NOTE.

I know of no variants of this story. The detail of the helpful animals is common in Filipino *Märchen;* here, however, the kindness of the eagle and the fish lack the usual motivation.

45. (a) MARIA AND THE GOLDEN SLIPPER.[1]

Once there lived a couple who had an only daughter, Maria. When Maria was a little girl, her mother died. A few years later Maria's father fell in love with a widow named Juana, who had two daughters. The elder of these daughters was Rosa, and the younger was Damiana. When Maria was grown to be a young woman, her father married the woman Juana. Maria continued to live with her father and step-mother. But Juana and her two daughters treated Maria as a servant. She had to do all the work in the house, — cook the food, wash the clothes, clean the floors. The only clothes she herself had to wear were ragged and dirty.

One day Prince Malecadel wanted to get married: so he gave a ball, to which he invited all the ladies in his kingdom. He said that the most beautiful of all was to be his wife. When Damiana and Rosa knew that all the ladies were invited, they began to discuss what clothes they would wear to the ball; but poor Maria was in the river, washing the clothes. Maria was very sad and was weeping, for she had no clothes at all in which she could appear at the prince's fête. While she was washing, a crab approached her, and said, "Why are you crying, Maria? Tell me the reason, for I am your mother."

Then Maria said to the crab, "I am treated by my aunt (*sic!*) and sisters as a servant; and there will be a ball to-night, but I have no clothes to wear." While she was talking to the crab, Juana came up. The step-mother was very angry with Maria, and ordered her to catch the crab and cook it for their dinner. Maria seized the crab and carried it to the house. At first she did not want to cook it, for she knew that it was her mother; but Juana whipped her so hard, that at last she was forced to obey. Before it was put in the earthen pot to be cooked, the crab said to Maria, "Maria, don't eat my flesh, but collect all my shell after I am eaten, and bury the pieces in the garden near the house. They will grow into a tree, and you can have what you want if you will only ask the tree for it." After her parents had eaten the flesh of the crab, Maria collected all its shell and buried it in the garden. At twilight she saw a tree standing on the very spot where she had buried the shell.

[1] Narrated by Dolores Zafra, a Tagalog from Pagsanjan, Laguna. She says that this is a Tagalog story, and was told to her when she was a little girl.

When night came, Rosa and Damiana went to the ball, and Juana retired for the night as soon as her daughters were gone. When Maria saw that her aunt was sleeping, she went into the garden and asked the tree for what she wanted. The tree changed her clothes into very beautiful ones, and furnished her with a fine coach drawn by four fine horses, and a pair of golden slippers. Before she left, the tree said to her, "You must be in your house before twelve o'clock. If you are not, your clothes will be changed into ragged, dirty ones again, and your coach will disappear."

After promising to remember the warning of the tree, Maria went to the ball, where she was received by the prince very graciously. All the ladies were astonished when they saw her: she was the most beautiful of all. Then she sat between her two sisters, but neither Rosa nor Damiana recognized her. The prince danced with her all the time. When Maria saw that it was half-past eleven, she bade farewell to the prince and all the ladies present, and went home. When she reached the garden, the tree changed her beautiful clothes back into her old ones, and the coach disappeared. Then she went to bed and to sleep. When her sisters came home, they told her of everything that had happened at the ball.

The next night the prince gave another ball. After Rosa and Damiana had dressed themselves in their best clothes and gone, Maria again went to the garden to ask for beautiful clothes. This time she was given a coach drawn by five (?) horses, and again the tree warned her to return before twelve. The prince was delighted to see her, and danced with her the whole evening. Maria was so enchanted that she forgot to notice the time. While she was dancing, she heard the clock striking twelve. She ran as fast as she could down stairs and out the palace-door, but in her haste she dropped one of her golden slippers. This night she had to walk home, and in her old ragged clothes, too. One of her golden slippers she had with her; but the other, which she had dropped at the door, was found by one of the guards, who gave it to the prince. The guard said that the slipper had been lost by the beautiful lady who ran out of the palace when the clock was striking twelve. Then the prince said to all the people present, "The lady whom this slipper fits is to be my wife."

The next morning the prince ordered one of his guards to

carry the slipper to every house in the city to see if its owner could be found. The first house visited was the one in which Maria lived. Rosa tried to put the slipper on her foot, but her foot was much too big. Then Damiana put it on her foot, but her foot was too small. The two sisters tried and tried again to make the slipper fit, but in vain. Then Maria told them that she would try, and see if the slipper would fit her foot; but her sisters said to her, "Your feet are very dirty. This golden slipper will not go on your foot, for your feet are larger than ours." And they laughed at her. But the guard who had brought the slipper said, "Let her try. It is the prince's order that all shall try." So he gave it to Maria. Then Maria put it on, and it fitted her foot exactly. She then drew the other slipper from underneath her dress, and put it on her other foot. When the two sisters saw the two slippers on Maria's feet, they almost fainted with astonishment.

So Maria became the wife of the prince, and from that time on she was very dear to her sisters and aunt.

(b) ABADEJA.[1]

Once upon a time there lived in the town of Baybay a man whose name was Abac. The name of his wife was Abadesa. They had a beautiful daughter named Abadeja. The mother died when her daughter was about thirteen years old; and in a year her father married again, a widow who had three daughters. The second wife envied her step-daughter because Abadeja was much more beautiful than her own children: consequently she treated the poor girl very badly, and made her do all the hard work. When Abadeja could not do the work, her step-mother punished her severely.

One evening the step-mother said to Abadeja, "Take these two handkerchiefs to the river and wash them. The white one must be black, and the black one white, when you bring them back to me. If they are not, I shall beat you." Abadeja went to the river, where she sat down on a rock and began to cry. In a little while she heard a noise that made her look up. There in front of her stood a beautiful woman. The woman asked Abadeja why she was crying. Abadeja replied, "I am crying because my step-mother has commanded me to do the

---

[1] This is a Visayan story from Leyte. Unfortunately I have no record of the name of narrator.

impossible. She told me that I must change this white hand-kerchief into black, and the black one into white." The woman took the handkerchiefs, and in an instant they were transformed. Then she gave them back to Abadeja, and invited the girl to come see her any time she needed help. After she had spoken thus, she disappeared. Abadeja went home and gave the handkerchiefs to her cruel step-mother, who now had no excuse to punish her.

The next morning Abadeja was ordered to put some rice on a mat in the sun to dry. While she was in the house doing other work, a pig came, ate up the rice, and tore the mat to pieces. When the step-mother knew what had happened, she whipped Abadeja severely for having lost the rice, and told her that she would have to repair the mat so that it was as good as new. Abadeja took the mat and went across the river, crying. The beautiful woman met her again, and, taking her by the hand, led her to her home among the high trees. Then she asked Abadeja what she wanted. Abadeja told her friend that her step-mother had ordered her to repair the mat so that it would be as good as new. The woman took the mat from the girl and waved it in the air. Immediately it became a whole mat again. Then she gave Abadeja a beautifully-colored chicken. Abadeja thanked her for her help and her gift, and hurried home, for she knew that her step-mother would be waiting to scold her if she were late.

The next day when Abadeja was away from the house, her cruel step-mother took the chicken, killed it, and cooked it. When the girl returned, only the feet of her chicken were left. She cried over her loss, and ran to the river to ask the beautiful woman what she should do. The beautiful woman, when she heard what had happened, told the girl to take the chicken's feet and plant them in the forest. Abadeja went home, took the feet, and carried them with her to the forest. There she made a little garden, in which she planted the right foot toward the east, and the left foot toward the west.

A month later she visited her garden in the woods, and was astonished to see that the feet had grown up into the air, and that they bore pearls, diamonds, gold dresses, rings, bracelets, shoes, necklaces, and ear-rings. She was delighted, but she did not tell her step-mother about her garden.

One day the son of the richest man in Baybay came across

this little garden in the forest.   He picked off a ring and put
it on his finger.   When he reached home, his finger began to
swell.   His father called in all the best physicians, but they
could not remove the ring.   Then he called in all the girls
of the town, and said that the one who could take the ring from
the finger of his son should be his son's wife.   All the girls of
the town tried except Abadeja.   She did not try, because her
mother would not allow her to go.   At last some one told the
rich man that there was still a girl who had not tried, and
that it was Abadeja: so he sent for her.   Now, her step-mother
did not dare refuse to let her go.   Abadeja ran to her little
garden, put on one of the gold dresses, and went to the rich
man's house.   As soon as she touched the ring, it slid off.

The next day Abadeja was married to the son of the rich
man.   The beautiful woman attended the wedding unseen by
every one except Abadeja.   The young couple lived happily
for many years.

NOTES.

In another variant (*c*), "The Wonderful Tree," which was collected
by Mr. Rusk, and of which I have only an abstract, —

Maria's mother was drowned by the cruel husband, a fisherman, who desired to marry another woman.   The daughter was now ill-treated by her
step-mother, and often went to the seashore to talk with the spirit of her
dead mother.   When the mother could no longer continue the meetings with
Maria, she told her to plant in a certain place all the fins of all the fish the
family should eat on a certain day.   From these fins there grew up a magic
tree of gold and precious stones.   One day a prince, hearing the music
made by the wind in the magic tree, approached the tree and found the
beautiful Maria.   Later he married her.

For still other Philippine variants of the Cinderella story, see
JAFL 19:265–272, where Fletcher Gardner gives two oral Tagalog
versions.   In the same journal (29:226 f.) I have given synopses
of two Tagalog metrical romances which open with the Cinderella
setting.

The Cinderella story is perhaps the most widespread *Märchen* in
the world.   See M. R. Cox's bibliographical study of it: "Cinderella,
345 Variants of Cinderella, Catskin, and Cap o' Rushes, abstracted
and tabulated, with a discussion of medieval analogues, and notes.
London, 1893."   Bolte-Polívka's notes to Grimm, No. 21, examine
Miss Cox's material from a somewhat new angle, and are very useful
for reference.   It seems hardly necessary to attempt to add here to
those two exhaustive monographs.   Attention may be called to the
fact, however, that our story of "Abadeja," which comes from Leyte,

presents a number of interesting items not found in the other Filipino variants: e.g., (1) the task of washing a black handkerchief white, and *vice-versâ;* (2) the magic tree growing up from the feet of a wonderful chicken given the heroine by the mysterious woman; (3) the unusual device for providing a rich husband for the heroine. There are some slight resemblances between these last two details and corresponding incidents in Mr. Rusk's variant "The Wonderful Tree."

46. JUAN THE POOR.[1]

Many years ago there lived a king who was always sad. He used to go to a mountain and climb the highest tree that was growing there. One day when he was in the top of the tree, he saw on another high mountain a beautiful princess, Doña Maria. When he returned home to his palace, he sent a proclamation all over his kingdom, saying that the one who could take Doña Maria from her mountain and bring her before him should have one-half of his kingdom.

Juan was a beggar; and it was his custom, whenever he saw a beggar like himself, to share with that beggar the alms which had been given him. One day he saw a wretched old woman, and out of pity for her he gave her all the food he had begged that day. Then the old woman, who knew of the proclamation of the king, said to Juan, "You must tell the king, my boy, that you will fetch Doña Maria for him." Juan did not want to, because he said that he did not know where and how he might get Doña Maria; but the old woman at last persuaded Juan to go by telling him that she would accompany him, and promising her help. After Juan had visited the palace and told the king that he would bring the princess Doña Maria to him, the poor boy and the old woman set out on their journey to the distant mountain. When they reached the gates of the city, the old woman said to Juan, "Juan, I am very tired, and I cannot go any farther, but I will give you this handkerchief. When you come to the first mountain, you must spread the handkerchief on the ground, and many fat horses will approach you; but I advise you not to choose any of them. You must choose the very last one, which will be lean and weak-looking. That is the horse which can endure hardships, and which will be able to carry you to the princess's palace."

Juan followed the advice of the old woman, when the time

[1] Narrated by Dolores Zafra, a Tagalog from Pagsanjan, who heard this story from her grandfather.

came, and chose the thin horse. He mounted on its back, and rode on towards the mountain of Doña Maria. When he had ridden very far, he saw before him a hill full of ants. He was afraid to try to pass over this hill, lest the ants should devour him and his animal. The horse said to him, "You must ask the handkerchief for food, and we will feed the ants." Juan spread out the handkerchief, and asked it to bring him much food. After he had scattered it on the ground for the ants, the leader of the ants approached Juan, and said, "Since you have been very kind to us, I will give you one of my legs; and at any time you want aid from us, you must burn the leg, and let the ashes be carried by the wind. Then we will come to help you."

When Juan had again gone a long distance from the hill, he saw the sky full of birds flying around and looking for food. Again the horse told Juan to ask for food from the handkerchief; so that they might feed the birds, and not be killed by them and eaten. Juan did so, and gave the birds all they wanted to eat. Then the king of the birds, the eagle, flew up to Juan, and said, "To repay you for your kindness, I will give you some feathers from my wings. Any time you want aid from us, just burn some of the feathers, and let the ashes be carried by the wind. Then we will come to you." Juan thanked the bird, and put the feathers in his pocket where he kept the leg of the ant.

Then he continued his journey. When they came near the palace of Doña Maria, the horse told Juan to hide, and said that he alone would enter her garden; but before he should hide, Juan should ask his handkerchief for a complete equipment of saddle and bridle, so that the horse could be mounted by a lady. Juan did so, hid himself, and the horse wandered into the garden of Doña Maria. When the princess saw the horse, she became very angry, and said, "Who is the one who is so bold as to let his horse enter my garden?" She looked all about, but could see no one: so she said to herself, "I will mount this horse and find out who its owner is." She mounted the horse, which immediately ran to the place where Juan was hiding, and told him to get up on its back. Then the horse carried them swiftly back to the small house of Juan. When he reached home, Juan sent word to the king that the princess Doña Maria was in his home. The king, accompanied by all his retinue, went in great state to Juan's house, made over to him one-half of his dominion, and took Doña Maria back to his palace.

Now, Doña Maria was very beautiful, and the king fell deeply in love with her. When he was alone with her in the palace, he began to court her. He asked her to be his wife; but Doña Maria said, "Only the one who can do what I wish him to do shall be my husband. I will mix one hundred *cavans* of husked rice with one hundred *cavans* of unhusked rice (*palay*). He who in one night can separate the two kinds of rice, and also bring my palace here to your kingdom, shall be married to me." The king said that no one could accomplish those things; but Doña Maria told him that there was one who could accomplish the tasks, and that was Juan.

The king then sent for Juan, and said to him, "Juan, here are one hundred *cavans* of husked rice mixed with one hundred *cavans* of unhusked rice. To-night you must separate the grain into two piles, and also transport the palace of Doña Maria to my kingdom. If you have not done both by to-morrow morning, you shall lose your head." Juan went away very sad toward the mountain. As he was walking along, he met the thin horse which had helped him before. The horse said to him, "Why are you so sad, Juan?" Juan told the horse what the king had ordered him to do. Then the horse said, "Don't be sad, Juan! you can accomplish both those difficult tasks. Don't you remember the leg of the ant and the feathers of the eagle which were given to you, and the promise of the ant and eagle?" So Juan took the ant's leg and the feathers from his pocket, burned them, and threw the ashes into the air. In a short time thousands of birds and ants came to him and asked him what he wanted. Then Juan said, "I want the palace of Doña Maria brought here before daybreak, and the two hundred *cavans* of mixed rice separated." When they heard Juan's order, the birds flew to the mountain to get the palace, and the ants hastened to the king's grounds to separate the unhusked from the husked rice.

By morning both tasks were completed: so Juan was married to Doña Maria, for she would have no other husband.

NOTES.

Although this story is clearly derived from the Tagalog romance of the "Life of King Asuero," nevertheless it is also told as a folk-tale, and for that reason I have included it in this collection. As has been intimated already so many times, it is often hard to draw the line between folk-tales and literary tales, especially when the latter are widely told and read.   Since our object in this collection is to present to Occidental readers a comprehensive account of what *is* in Philippine popular literature, it has seemed unwise to exclude this story.

The full title of the romance is "The Story and Life of King Asuero, Doña Maria, and Juan the Poor, in the City of Jerusalem."   My copy is dated 1905; Retana (No. 4192) mentions an edition between the years 1860 and 1898.   In outline the folk-tale differs little from the romance, hence it is unnecessary to give a detailed summary of the printed version.   The more important variations might be noted, however.   The romance opens thus: —

Once there lived an old man whose name was Asuero.   He was the king of Jerusalem.   One night he dreamed that he should be dethroned, and that a poor young countryman would take his place.   He awoke and became sad and thoughtful.   Unable to go to sleep again, he climbed a tower of his palace, and began to look around with a spy-glass.   When he directed his gaze toward a mountain-region beyond the Nile (!), he saw an enchantress who was looking out of her window.   She was Doña Maria.   He was charmed by her beauty, and became restless.   At length he resolved to relate to his council of chiefs what he had seen, and to ask their advice.   Many suggestions were made, and many objections.   Since the king could not be deterred from his purpose of attempting to get possession of Doña Maria, his chief counsellor proposed an assembly of all the people of the kingdom, where the king's desire might be made known.   At the assembly the king promised money to any one who dared to undertake the adventure, and his appointment as chief counsellor if he were successful.

The folk-tale and the romance are practically identical, except that the romance is more detailed, up to the point where the horse leaves Juan to go to entice Doña Maria from her palace and get her in its power.

The horse told Juan that it would go with the golden bit and saddle and get Doña Maria, while Juan should hide in a bush near by until they should come back.   The horse also told Juan that when it passed by the bush, he should seize its tail and hold on tight.   Then the horse left, and after a time came to the garden of Doña Maria.   When the maiden saw the animal, she became angry at its owner for letting it into her garden. After looking about for the rider in vain, she claimed the horse, and was about to mount it when the animal spoke to her, and told her to put on a better dress, one which would be more appropriate for the golden saddle. When she returned, she had on a magnificent gown, and wore a magic ring. The horse told her that it had been sent by God to be her faithful steed, and then suggested that she visit the abode of the eagles.   She was very anxious to see this wonderful place, and agreed to be taken there.   Before they set out, the horse asked her for her magic ring, saying that he would carry it safely for her in his mouth.   She surrendered the ring, and the horse carried her to the place where Juan was concealed.   Juan seized the tail of the horse, and the animal flew into the air and alighted beyond the sea. Here, by the magic power of the handkerchief, Juan produced food, a table, and two chairs at the request of the horse. Six maids served them. The horse now gave Juan the ring of Doña Maria; and as long as he kept this, he was sure of keeping the maiden. After eating, Doña Maria asked Juan why she had been brought there; but Juan, following the advice of the horse, made no reply. She flattered him and tried to get him to sleep, but he paid no attention to her. At length the horse told them that they must resume their journey. The horse travelled rapidly, and soon reached the royal palace; but the gates were closed, for it was then about midnight. So the riders decided to spend the rest of the night at Juan's house. There the old mother received them all gladly. When the saddle and bit had been taken from the horse, the animal said that it would return the following morning and carry Juan to the palace. It further warned Juan not to sleep if he valued his life. . . .

The romance closes with the inevitable war with the Moors, and the rescue of the kingdom from the hands of the Pagans by the invincible Juan.

The exact source of this romance I am unable to point to; but without question it is Occidental, I believe.

47. THE FATE OF AN ENVIOUS WOMAN.[1]

There lived once upon a time a young couple of the middle class. The man was a reckless scapegrace and spendthrift; but the woman was a pious, faithful, and virtuous housewife. Juan was the husband's name; Maria, the wife's. One of the worst things about Juan was that he spent on another woman the greater part of the money which Maria could with difficulty scrape together. This other woman's name was Flora. It is true that she surpassed Maria in personal charm, but in real worth Flora was greatly Maria's inferior. Hence we should not wonder at the fact that Maria soon grew distasteful to her husband, and that after a year of married life he should seek to be entertained by a more beautiful woman. He spent most of his time in listless indolence by the side of Flora, returning home only to get his meals, which Maria prepared with the greatest care. But her efforts were all to no purpose. In vain did Maria array herself in her best clothes, and scent herself with the most delicate perfumes: her face remained pitted with small-pox scars, as before.

Years came and passed, and Juan became more and more harsh to his wife. At last Maria sought the aid of St. Vicente Ferrer. She knelt before the image, and asked the saint to

[1] Narrated by Vicente M. Hilario, a Tagalog from Batangas, Batangas. He was told the story by his gardener.

rescue her husband from the pit into which he had fallen. Her prayers were soon answered. The image became animated. It touched her face several times, and in a few seconds Maria was converted into an extraordinary beauty. Her once rough skin was now smooth and velvety. She then went to the window to await her husband's return. When he arrived an hour later, he was at first unwilling to come up into the house, for he did not believe that the beautiful woman was his wife; but at last she disclosed her true self to him. A great change now came over Juan. The once despised wife now began to enjoy the caresses of her husband, who pressed her close to his heart.

Days elapsed, and Flora began to get uneasy at her home. She wondered why Juan did not come to see her. At length she went to his house. After asking Maria how she had acquired her beauty, Flora decided to try her fortune also. She too knelt before the image of St. Vicente Ferrer. But, alas! instead of becoming as white and as beautiful as the women of a Turkish harem, she became as black and as ugly as the mistress of a Kaffir household. Her once delicate lips became thick and coarse, and her nose became as long as a monkey's tail. Filled with shame at her appearance, and with a consciousness of her own guilt, she went home, where she pined away and died.

The once homely Maria, whose home had rung with laughter by the taunt and ridicule of those who made fun of her ugliness,[1] now graced her house with sweet smiles and engaging features, which drew scores of visitors to her home. Juan confessed his sins, and underwent penance for his wickedness; and the two lived together in peace and happiness the rest of their lives.

NOTES.

A Visayan variant, "The Two Wives and the Witch," may be found in JAFL 19 : 105. In the southern version "Juan puts away his first, plain-looking wife, and takes another, handsomer one. The first wife, weeping by a well, is transformed by a witch into a beautiful woman. She wins her husband's affections back again. The second wife, deserted in turn, weeps by the well, and is transformed by the witch into such a hideous old hag, that, when she looks at herself in

---

[1] The Filipinos have many mocking children's rhymes making fun of personal deformities, such as pock-marks, cross-eyes, very black skin, etc. They always raise a laugh when recited.

the glass and sees her ugliness, she refuses to eat, and in a few days dies."

In a broad way this story and ours belong to the "Toads and Diamonds" group (see Grimm, No. 13 ["The Three Little Men in the Wood "] and No. 24 ["Mother Holle"]; and Bolte-Polívka's notes to the two stories). In these groups, however, the two young women are sisters, — one bad, and the other good. About all there is in common between the norm of the "Toads and Diamonds" cycle and our tales is the situation of the plain-looking but faithful, unselfish, good-hearted woman being granted by some supernatural creature wealth and beauty; while the handsome but selfish and wicked woman, envious of her rival's good luck, becomes loathsome and miserable when she asks a boon from the same supernatural source.

The only other member of this group that narrates the story of *two wives* instead of two sisters is Lal Behari Day's No. 22. This Bengal tale, it appears to me, is related both to our stories and to those of the "Mother Holle" group, thus linking ours with the latter also. Following is Cosquin's summary of Day's story (2 : 123) : —

A man had two wives, — one young, and one old. The latter was treated by the other as if she were a slave. One day her rival, in a fit of anger, snatched from the old woman's head the one tuft of hair she had, and drove her from the door. The old woman went into the forest. Passing by a cotton-tree, she saw that the ground round about the tree needed sweeping, and she swept it. The tree, much pleased, showered its blessings on her. She did the same thing for other trees — a banana and a *tulasi* — and also for a bull, whose stall she swept out. All blessed her. She arrived next at the hut of a venerable *mouni* (a kind of ascetic), and she told him of her misery. The *mouni* told her to go plunge herself once, but only once, in a certain pool. She obeyed, and came up out of the water with the most beautiful hair in the world, and altogether rejuvenated. The *mouni* next told her to enter his hut and to select from among many willow baskets that which pleased her. The woman took one very simple in appearance. The *mouni* bade her open it: it was filled with gold and precious stones, and was never empty. On her way back home she passed in front of the *tulasi*. The tree said to her, "Go home in peace! your husband will love you to madness." Next the bull gave her some shell ornaments which were about its horns, and told her to place them on her wrists: if she would but shake them, she would have all the ornaments she could wish. The banana-tree gave her one of its large leaves, which filled itself of its own accord with excellent dishes. And, last of all, the cotton-tree gave her one of its branches, which would give her, if she shook it, every kind of beautiful garment. When she returned to the house, the other wife could hardly believe her eyes. Having learned of the old woman's adventures, she too went into the forest; but she passed by the trees and the bull without stopping. And instead of dipping herself only once in the pool, as the *mouni* told her to do, she plunged in a second time, hoping to become even more beautiful; and so she came out of the water as ugly as before. The *mouni* did not give her any present, either; and thenceforth, disdained by her husband, she finished her life as a servant in his house.

It is unsafe to attempt to trace a story with only three examples as data: but it appears to me not unreasonable to suppose that our Tagalog story is a refined, pious, Christianized modernization of the Visayan form represented by "The Two Wives and the Witch;" and that the Visayan form, in turn, goes back to some Indian or Malayan moral tale of two wives, rivals for the affection of their husband. The Bengali tale can hardly be the direct source of our Visayan form, but it appears to be fairly closely related to that source.

48. (*a*) THE MONKEY AND JUAN PUSONG TAMBI-TAMBI.[1]

Tiring-tirang was a barrio in the town of Tang-tang, situated at the foot of a hill which was called "La Campana" because of its shape. Around the hill, about a mile from the barrio, flowed the Malogo River, in which the people of the town used to bathe. It so happened that one time an epidemic broke out in the community, killing off all the inhabitants except one couple. This couple had an only son named Juan Pusong Tambi-tambi.

When Juan had reached his twelfth year, his father died: consequently the boy had to go to work to earn money for the support of himself and his mother. At first Juan followed the occupation of his father, that of fisherman; but, seeing that he made little money from this, he decided to become a farmer. His mother had now reached the age of seventy (!), and was often sick. Juan frequently had to neglect his farm in order to take care of her.

One day Juan went to Pit-pit to buy medicine for his mother. On his way to the town he saw a flock of crows eating up his corn. He paid no attention to the birds; but on his way back, when he saw these same birds still eating his corn, he became angry. He picked up a stone about the size of his fist, and crept into a bush near by. He had hardly hidden himself when the birds heard a rustling, and began to fly off. Juan jumped up, and hurled his stone with such accuracy and force that one of the crows fell dead to the ground. He tied the dead crow to a bamboo pole, and planted it in the middle of his corn-field. No sooner was he out of sight than the crows flew back

[1] Narrated by Encarnacion Gonzaga, a Visayan from Jaro, Iloilo. She says that she has often heard this story; that it was very popular among the "inhabitants of yesterday;" and that even now many are fond of it.

to the field again; but when they saw their dead companion, they flew off, and never troubled Juan again.

For six months Juan had no trouble from birds. He did not know, however, that not far from his field there was a monkey (*chongo*) living in a large tree. This monkey used to come to his field every day and steal two or three ears of corn. One day, as Juan was walking across his field, he saw many dead cornstalks. He said to himself, "I wonder who it is that comes here and steals my corn! I am no longer troubled by birds; and yet I find here many husks." He went home and made an image of a crooked old man like himself. This he covered with sticky wax. He placed it in the middle of the field.

The next morning, when the sun was shining very brightly, the monkey felt hungry, so he ran towards the field to steal some corn to eat. There he saw the statue. Thinking that it was Juan, he decided to ask permission before he took any corn. "Good-morning, Juan!" said the monkey in a courteous tone; but the image made no reply. "You are too proud to bend your neck, Juan," continued the monkey. "I have only come to ask you for three or four ears of corn. I have not eaten since yesterday, you know; and if you deny me this request, I shall die before morning." The waxen statue still stood motionless. "Do you hear me, Juan?" said the monkey impatiently. Still the statue made no reply. "Since you are too proud to answer me, I will soon give you some presents. Look out!" he cried, and with his right paw he slapped the statue which he thought was Juan; but his paw stuck to the wax, and he could not get free. "Let my hand loose!" the monkey shouted, "or you will get another present." Then he slapped the statue with his left paw, and, as before, stuck fast. "You are foolish, Juan. If you do not let me go this very moment, I'll kick you." He did so, first with one foot, and then with the other. At last he could no longer move, and he began to curse the statue. Juan, who had been hiding in a bush near by, now presented himself, and said to the monkey, "Now I have caught you, you thief!" He would have killed the monkey at once, had not the monkey begged for mercy, and promised that he would at some future time repay him for his kindness if he would only spare his life. So Juan set the monkey free.

It was now the month of April. The monkey, impatient to

fulfil his word to Juan, went one day to the field, and there he found Juan hard at work. "Good-morning, Master Juan!" he cried. "I see that you are busy."

"Busy indeed!" replied Juan.

"Master Juan, do you want to marry the king's daughter? If you do, I'll arrange everything for you," said the monkey.

Juan replied, "Yes," little thinking that what the monkey promised could be true.

The monkey scampered off towards the market. When he entered the market, he saw a boy counting his money. The monkey pretended to be looking in the other direction, but walked towards the boy. When he saw that the money was fairly within his reach, he seized it and ran back to Juan. After telling his master what he had done, the monkey went to the king's palace, and said, "Sir, my master, Juan, wants to borrow your *ganta*, for he desires to measure his money." The king gave him the *ganta*. In three days the monkey appeared at the palace again to return the measure, in the bottom of which he stuck three centavos. "My master, Juan, thanks you for your kindness," said the monkey. The monkey was about to leave the room when the king perceived the three centavos sticking to the bottom of the measure.

"Here, monkey, here are your three cents!" said the king.

"Oh, oh, oh, oh, oh!" answered the monkey, laughing, "my master cares not for three cents. He has too much money. He is very, very rich." The king was much surprised to hear that there was a man richer than himself.

Two weeks later the monkey returned to the palace again, and said, "Pray, king, my master, Juan, desires to borrow your *ganta* again. He wants to finish measuring his money."

The king was filled with curiosity; and he said, "I'll let you borrow the *ganta*, monkey, but you must tell me first who is this Juan whom you call your master."

"My master, Juan," replied the monkey, "is the richest man in the world."

Before giving the measure to the monkey, the king went to his room and stuck four pieces of gold on the four corners of the *ganta*. "I'll find out who is the richer, Juan or I," he said to himself. The monkey took the measure, and left the hall with a polite bow.

As he was walking towards Juan's farm, the monkey noticed

the four pieces of gold sticking to the corners of the *ganta*. He knew that they had been artfully placed there by the king himself. Two weeks later he went back to the palace to return the measure, not forgetting to stick a gold dollar on each corner. "Good-afternoon, king!" said he, "my master, Juan, returns you your *ganta* with a thousand thanks."

"Very well," replied the king; "but tell me all about this master of yours who measures his money. I am a king; still I only count my money."

The monkey remained silent. Not receiving a prompt reply, the king turned to Cabal, one of his lords, and said in a whisper, "Do you know who this Juan is who measures his money?"

"I have not heard of him," replied the lord, "except from this monkey and yourself."

The king then turned to the monkey, and said, "Monkey, if you don't tell me who your master is, where he lives, and all about him, I'll hang you." Doubtless the king was jealous of Juan because of his great wealth.

Fearing that he would lose his life, the monkey said to the king, "My master, Juan, the richest and best man in the world, lives in the town of XYZ. He goes to church every morning wearing his striped (*tambi-tambi*) clothes. This is why he is known among his people as Juan Pusong Tambi-tambi. If you will just look out of your window to-morrow morning, you will see him pass by your garden."

The king's anger was appeased by this explanation. Early the next morning he was at his window, anxious to get a glimpse of Juan. He had not been there long when his attention was attracted by the appearance of a crooked man dressed in striped clothes. "This must be the man whom the monkey described to me yesterday," he said to himself. Soon his servant entered the room, and said, "The monkey desires to see you."

The king left the window and went to where the monkey was waiting for him. As soon as the monkey saw the king, he bowed politely, and said, "My master, Juan, sends me to tell you frankly that he loves your daughter, and that, if it pleases you, he will marry her." At first the king was angry to hear these words; but, being very desirous to get more money, he at last consented without even asking his daughter.

"If my master does not call on you to-day, he will surely come to-morrow." So saying, the monkey left the palace, and ran about town, trying to think of some way he might escape the great danger he was in. It so happened that an old man who was carrying a bundle of clothes to his son in the mountains passed along the same road where the monkey was. The sun was very hot, so the old man decided to rest under a leafy tree. No sooner was he seated there than the cunning monkey climbed the tree, and shook the branches with such force that twigs and fruits fell all around the old man. Panic-stricken, he ran away as fast as his feet would carry him, leaving everything behind him. When the man was out of sight, the monkey climbed down the tree, picked up the bundle of clothes, and carried it to Juan.

"To-morrow, Juan," said the monkey, "you will marry the princess. I'll arrange everything for you if you will only follow my advice." Half doubting and half believing, Juan asked the monkey if he really meant what he said. "What do you think of me?" asked the monkey.

Without waiting for a reply from Juan, the monkey left the hut, and ran towards the home of the Burincantadas who lived on the summit of the hill. As soon as he entered the gate, he began to scoop up the ground as fast as he could. The Burincantadas, who at that very moment were looking out of the window, saw the monkey. They rushed downstairs, and, half frightened, said to him, "What are you trying to do?"

"Why, our king has been defeated in the war. The enemies have already taken possession of the crown. The princess is dead, and it is said that everybody will be killed before to-morrow noon," replied the monkey, his teeth chattering. "I am resolved to hide myself under the ground to save my life."

The three Burincantadas seized him by the arm, and said, "For mercy's sake, have pity on us! Tell us where we can hide!" They were already trembling with fear.

"Oh, oh, oh, oh, oh! let me loose! The enemy are coming!"

On hearing these words, the Burincantadas all shouted at once, "Tell us where to hide!"

"If you will not let me scoop out a hole here, I'll jump into the well," said the monkey in a hoarse voice.

As soon as the Burincantadas heard the word "well," they all ran as fast as they could, following the monkey. "Let me jump first!" said the monkey.

"No, let us jump first!" shouted the Burincantadas; and so they did. The monkey made a motion as if he were going to follow; but, instead, he lifted up the biggest stone he could find and threw it down the well. "They are dead," he said to himself, laughing. "Ah, I have caught you! Ha, ha!"

The Burincantadas now being dead, the monkey was at leisure to decide what to do next. He entered their palace, and there he found everything magnificent. "This is the very place where my master shall live!" He opened the first room, but there he found nothing but bones. He closed the door and opened the second, where he found many prisoners who were waiting to be eaten. He set them all free, and told them to clean up the palace at once. The prisoners set to work, not forgetting to thank the monkey for his kindness. Before he left the palace, he addressed the crowd as follows: "My brothers and sisters, if any one comes and asks you who your master is, tell him that he is Don Juan Pusong Tambi-tambi."

Then he left the crowd of people busy cleaning the palace, and went to the farm, where he found thousands of horses, cows, and sheep. "My master is indeed rich," he said to himself. He called the shepherd who was lying under the tree, and said to him, "Tell your other companions that, if any one comes and asks whose animals these are, they must answer that they all belong to Don Juan Pusong. Don Juan is your master now."

After seeing that everything was in order, the monkey hastened to his master, who was still ploughing, and said, "Throw away your plough. Let's go to the king's palace, for to-night you will be married to the princess Doña Elena."

Night came. The palace was splendidly adorned. The princess was sitting by her father, when Don Juan, dressed in his striped clothes and accompanied by the monkey, entered the gate of the palace. Soon the priest came, and the princess was called to the reception-hall. When she saw her bridegroom, she ran away in despair, and cried to her father, "Father, how dare you accept as my husband such a base, dirty, crooked man! Look at him! Why, he is the meanest of the mean."

But the king replied, "He is rich. If you don't marry him, I'll punish you very severely." The princess had to obey her father; but, before giving her hand to Juan Pusong, she said, "O God! let me die."

When the marriage ceremony was over, the king called the monkey, and asked, "Where is the couple going to live?"

"In Don Juan's palace," was the reply of the monkey.

The king immediately ordered carriages to be gotten ready. Then they started on their journey. Four hours passed, and still no palace was to be seen. The king became impatient, and said to the monkey, "Monkey, if what you have said to me is not true, your head shall answer for your lie." Hardly had he said these words when he beheld before him a number of men watching a herd of cattle. "I wonder who owns these, monkey!" said the king.

The monkey made some signs, and soon three shepherds came running up to them. "Good-evening, king!" they said.

"Good-evening!" replied the king. "Whose cattle are these?"

"They are all owned by Don Juan Pusong," said the shepherds.

The king nodded, and said to himself, "He is truly rich." The palace was now in sight. The king could hardly express his joy on seeing such a magnificent building. "Why, it is not a palace: it is heaven itself," he said.

They were now upstairs. The king, on seeing still more beauties, said, "I confess, I am not the richest man on earth." Soon he died of joy, and his body was placed in a golden coffin and buried in the church.

The couple inherited his dominion; but Queen Elena could not endure her ugly husband, and two weeks later she died broken-hearted. So Juan was left as sole ruler of two kingdoms. The monkey became his chief minister.

This story shows that a compassionate man oftentimes gets his reward.

(b) ANDRES THE TRAPPER.[1]

Once upon a time there lived in a village a poor widow who had an only son named Andres. They lived in a small hut situated near the Patacbo forest. When Andres was between twelve and thirteen years old, his mother died. From now on he lived alone in his mean little hut, where he had to cook his own food and wash his clothes.

One morning some boys invited Andres to go to the woods with them to trap. When they got to the forest, his companions set their traps in the places where the wild chickens

---

[1] Narrated by Domingo Perez of San Carlos, Pangasinan, who heard the story from his grandfather, now dead. The story is popular among the Pangasinanes.

used to feed. Then they went home. In the afternoon they returned to the woods, where they found that each trap had caught a wild cock. Now Andres became envious of his companions: so when he reached home, he took his knife and made two traps of his own. After he had finished them, he ran to the forest and set them. Early the next morning he went to the woods to see if he had caught anything. There he found two wild cocks snared. He took them home, sold one, and ate the other for his dinner. When he had finished eating, he made many traps, which he set up that afternoon. From now on he made his living by trapping, often catching as many as fifteen birds in a day. From the money he earned he was able to feed himself and buy clothes.

One day, after Andres had been a trapper for many years, he went to the forest, as usual, to see what he had caught. He found that his traps had been moved, and that in one of them was a big monkey caught by the leg. As Andres was about to kill the monkey with a big stick which he picked up, the animal said to him, "My dear Andres, don't harm me! and I will be your helper by and by."

Andres was much astonished to hear the monkey talk. He was moved to pity, and set the animal free. When he started toward his home, the monkey followed him. From now on they lived together. Soon the monkey learned how to sell wild chickens in the market.

Now, in that town there lived a very rich man by the name of Toribio, who had a daughter named Aning. The people considered Aning the most beautiful lady in the province. However, none of the young men of the town courted Aning, for they felt unworthy and ashamed to woo the richest and most beautiful girl. One fine day the monkey went to town and sold wild chickens, as usual. On his way home he stopped at Don Toribio's house. Don Toribio asked what he wanted, and the monkey said that his master had sent him to borrow their money-measure.

"Who is your master?" said Don Toribio.

"Don't you know? Don Andres, a very rich, handsome young gentleman who lives in the valley of Obong," said the monkey.

Don Toribio at once lent the *ganta*-measure to the monkey, who thanked him and hurried home. Before he returned it to the owner the next morning, he put a peso, a fifty-centavo piece, a peseta, and a media-peseta in the cracks of the measure.

When the monkey handed the *ganta* back to Don Toribio, the man said, "Why do you return it? Has your master finished measuring his money?"

"No, sir!" said the monkey, "we have not finished; but this box is too small, and it takes us too long to measure with it."

"Well," said Don Toribio, "we have a bigger one than that; do you want to borrow it?"

"Yes, I do, if you will let me keep it till to-morrow," said the monkey.

Don Toribio then brought a *cavan*, which equals about twenty-five *gantas*. When the monkey reached home carrying the large measure, Andres said to him, "Where did you get that box?" The monkey said that it had been lent to him by the richest man in the town.

"What did you tell the man that you were going to do with it?" said Andres.

"I told him that you wanted to count your money," said the monkey.

"Ah, me!" said Andres, "what money are you going to count? Don't you know that we are very poor?"

"Let me manage things, Andres," said the monkey, "and I promise you that you shall marry the beautiful daughter of the rich man."

The following day Andres caught many wild chickens. When the monkey had sold them all in the market, he went back to their hut, and took the *cavan* which he had borrowed. Before returning it to Don Toribio, he stuck money in the cracks, as he had done to the first measure.

"Good-morning, Don Toribio!" said the monkey. Don Toribio was sitting in a chair by the door of his house.

"Good-morning, monkey! How do you do?" replied the rich man. "Have you come to return the box?"

"Yes, sir!" said the monkey, "we have finished. My master sends his thanks to you." When Don Toribio took the box and saw the money inside, he told the monkey about it; but the monkey said, "Never mind! we have plenty more in our house."

"I am the richest man in town, yet I cannot throw money away like the master of this fellow," said Don Toribio to himself. "Perhaps he is even richer than I am." When the monkey was about to take his leave, the rich man told him to tell his master to come there on the third day. The monkey said that he would, and thanked Don Toribio for the invitation.

On his way home, the monkey stopped at the market to buy a pair of shoes, some ready-made clothes, and a hat for Andres. He took these things home to his master, and in three days had taught Andres how to walk easily with shoes on, how to speak elegantly, how to eat with a spoon and fork and knife, and how to tell Don Toribio that he wanted to marry his daughter.

When the time came, Andres and the monkey set out for the town. They were welcomed by Don Toribio and his daughter Aning. After a short talk, Andres spoke of his purpose in coming there. He said that he wanted to marry Don Toribio's daughter. Don Toribio gladly accepted the offer, and said that the wedding would be held the next morning. Hasty preparations were made for the ceremony. In the morning a priest came, and Andres and Aning were married. Many guests were present, and everybody had a good time.

A few years later Don Toribio died, and Andres inherited all his wealth. He then became a very rich man.

NOTES.

Two other Philippine variants of the "Puss in Boots" cycle have been printed, — one Visayan, "Masoy and the Ape" (JAFL 20 : 311–314); and the other Tagalog, "Juan and the Monkey" (*ibid.*, 108–109). It would thus appear, not only from the fact of its wide distribution, but also from the testimony of the recorders of the stories, that the tale is fairly well known and popular throughout the Archipelago.

The most complete bibliography of this cycle is Bolte-Polívka's notes on Grimm, No. 33 (*a*), "Puss in Boots" (Anmerkungen, 1 : 325–334). See also Köhler's notes to Gonzenbach, No. 65, "Vom Conte Piro" (2 : 242 f.); Macculloch, ch. VIII (p. 225 f.); W. R. S. Ralston in the "Nineteenth Century" (13 [1883] : 88–104). The oldest known version of the story is Straparola's (XI, i), which is translated in full by Crane (pp. 348–350). The second oldest is also Italian, by Basile (2 : iv) ; the third, French, Perrault's "Le Chat Botté." In all three the helpful animal is a cat, as it is without exception in the German, Scandinavian, English, and French forms. In the Italian the animal is usually a cat, though the fox takes its place in a number of Sicilian tales. In the Greek, Roumanian, Bulgarian, Serbian, Russian, and in general all East European forms, the helpful animal is regularly the fox, as it is also in the examples collected from Siberia, Kurdestan, Daghestan, and Mongolia. In the four Indian variants known, the animal is a jackal; in the four from the Philippines, a monkey. In a Swahili tale (Steere, p. 13) it is a gazelle. It is not hard to see how, through a process of transmission, jackal, fox, and cat might become interchanged; but where the Philippine monkey, consistently used in all versions, came from, is more difficult to explain; so the Swahili gazelle. I have, however, attempted an explanation below.

An examination of the four members of the Philippine group reveals some striking family resemblances: (1) The motive of the monkey's gratitude is the same in all the stories: the thieving animal is caught in some sort of trap, and promises to serve the hero for life if he will only spare it. The animal is true to its word. (2) In all the stories occurs the incident of the borrowed measure returned with coins sticking to it. (3) In all the versions occurs the marriage of the poor hero with the chief's daughter, brought about by the ingenious monkey. (4) In three of the versions (all except the Pangasinan) we have as the final episode the destruction of a powerful witch or demon, and the winning of all its fortune by the monkey for the hero. In the Hindoo variants we find that the motive of the jackal's gratitude agrees with the motive in our versions. In other respects they differ (with the exception of the marriage, which is found in nearly all members of the "Puss in Boots" cycle): the Hindoo tales lack the incidents of the borrowed measure and the destruction of the demon. So far as the opening is concerned, then, our variants and the Indian belong to the same family. The separation, however, must have taken place ages ago; for in India the animal is consistently a jackal, and in the Philippines a monkey. The only other form that I know of in which the animal is a monkey is the Arabian, in the "1001 Nights," "Aboo Mohammed the Lazy;" but here the helpful ape later turns out to be a malicious demon, who treacherously abducts the hero's beautiful wife. At last, through the aid of a friendly *jinnee*, the hero recovers her, captures the ape, and encloses it forever in a bottle of brass. He then gains possession of all the demon's enormous wealth. It is difficult to see any immediate connection between the Arabian version and ours.

Our two Visayan forms are of particular interest in that they make use of the "Tar Baby" device to catch the monkey. If Joseph Jacobs is correct in tracing this incident to the Buddhist birth-story, the "Pancāvudha-jātaka," No. 55 (see Indian Fairy Tales, pp. 305 ff.), the Philippines may easily have derived it directly from India along with other Buddhistic fables (e.g., "The Monkey and the Crocodile," No. 56, below). Indeed, Batten's ingenious explanation that the Brer Rabbit of Negro lore is a reminiscence of an incarnation of Buddha may be applied equally well to the monkey in our Visayan tales, for the monkey is a much more common form for the Bodhisatta than is the hare. In the five hundred and forty-seven Jātakas, Buddha is born as a hare only once; whereas in eleven separate stories he appears as a monkey, — oftener, indeed, than as any other animal (lion, ten times; stag, nine; elephant, seven). This same explanation (viz., that "Puss in Boots" is the Bodhisatta) would account for the gazelle (deer) in the Swahili tale. The extreme cleverness of the Bodhisatta in most of his animal manifestations might easily have suggested the "Puss in Boots" cycle. Another point worth noticing in connection with this theory is the consistent faithfulness of the animal. The ingratitude of the human hero, which is found even in some of the Occidental versions, and the gratitude of the animal, form a favorite Buddhistic contrast. Altogether it appears to me wholly reasonable to derive not only the "Tar Baby" incident, but also the whole "Puss in Boots" cycle, from Buddhistic lore. For the appearance of both in the Philippines we do not need to go to Europe as a source. The "Tar Baby" device to catch a thieving *jackal* is found in a Santal story, "The Jackal and the Chickens" (Bompas, No. CXII). See also two South African tales in Honey, — "The Story of a Dam" (p. 73), and "Rabbit's Triumph" (p. 79). For other references, see Dähnhardt, 4 : 26–43 (ch. 2).

There is a connection, however, between some of the Occidental versions and three of ours, — the incident of the destruction of the demon. This detail, as I have pointed out, is hinted at in the "1001 Nights" version.[1] In spite of the fact that it exists in a number of the oldest European literary forms of the story and is not found in modern Indian folk-tales, I believe that this incident is of Oriental origin. In Straparola it has been rationalized, so to speak. A significant version intermediary between the Orient and Occident in this respect, as well as geographically, is the Mongolian tale of "Boroltai Ku" (FLJ 4 : 32 f): —

This story has the Oriental opening: the animal is a fox, which the hero digs out of its hole and spares. Through its cleverness the fox brings about the marriage of Boroltai Ku, the man who spared its life, with the daughter of Gurbushtën Khan. After the wedding the khan sends the new

---

[1] The Arabian story, I believe, is well worth study in connection with the theory of the Buddhistic origin of this cycle. The rôle of the ape; the conflict between the good and bad *jinn*, the ape belonging with the latter group; and the narrator's statement, "All this I have received from the bounty of God, whose name be exalted!" — suggest at the base of this version the struggle between Buddhism and Mohammedanism; with Mohammedanism triumphant, of course.

couple back to their home, and with them an official attendant. On the return journey the fox runs on ahead, and requests every herdsman it meets to say, if he is asked whose cattle he is tending, "It is the cattle of Boroltai Ku, the rich khan." At last the fox comes to the tent of Khan Manguis, and groans. "What's the matter?" says the khan. "A storm is coming," says the fox. "That is a misfortune for me too," says the khan. "How so? You can order a hole ten fathoms deep to be dug, and can hide in it," says the fox. So done. Boroltai Ku and his party now appear, and he occupies the khan's tent as if it were his own. The fox assures the official attendant that the tent is Boroltai Ku's, but that it has one defect. "What is that?" — "Under the tent lives a demon. Won't you bring down lightning to slay him?" The attendant brings down lightning and slays Khan Manguis, who is sitting in the hole. Boroltai Ku becomes khan, and takes all the possessions, cattle, and people of Khan Manguis, and goes to live near his father-in-law.

In this story, it will be noticed, the animal's ruse is the same as ours, — it persuades the rich khan (demons in ours) to hide himself in a pit. There he is subsequently killed.

The borrowed measure returned with coins sticking to it has already been met with in No. 20 (c). The incident occurs elsewhere in Filipino drolls. It is curious to find it so consistently a part of the Filipino "Puss in Boots" stories.

In conclusion may be noted the fact that in "Andres the Trapper" the monkey's solicitude over the appearance his master will make at the rich man's house has a parallel in the jackal's similar concern in the Santal story: —

Before the wedding-feast, the jackal gave Jogeswhar some hints as to his behavior. He warned him that three or four kinds of meats and vegetables would be handed round with the rice, and bade him to be sure to help himself from each dish; and when betel-nut was handed to him after the feast, he was not to take any until he had a handful of money given him; by such behavior he would lead every one to think he was really a prince. — BOMPAS, p. 175.

In Dracott's story the human hero is a weaver also, as in the Santal. His last exploit has been borrowed from another Indian tale not connected with our group, "Valiant Vicky the Weaver" (Steel-Temple, p. 80; cf. Kingscote, No. IX).

49. JUAN THE FOOL.[1]

(NARRATOR'S NOTE. — This story was told to me by a student. He said that he first heard it in one of the informal gatherings which are very common in Bocawe, Bulakan, during the hot season. The young men often assemble at a little shop kept by a young woman,

[1] This story was narrated by Remedios Mendoza of Manila, but the story itself comes from the Tagalog province of Bulakan.

and there the story-teller of the barrio tells stories. This story of Juan was told at one of these gatherings by an old man about fifty years old.)

Juan is twenty years old. At this age he begins to become famous in his little barrio. He is short in stature. His eyes are neither bright nor dull: they are very black, and slowly roll in their sockets. His mouth is narrow. He has a double chin, and a short flat nose. His forehead is broad, and his lips are thick. His hair is black and straight. His body is round like a pumpkin, and his legs are short. He seems to be always tired. In spite of all these physical peculiarities, however, he is invited to every *bayluhan* and *katapusan*,[1] because he is sure·to bring with him laughter and merriment.

Juan lives in a poor barrio, which consists of a few poor *nipa* huts. It has a small chapel of stone, with a turret and bells. In the courtyard in front of the chapel is erected a cross. A few *nipa* cottages are scattered along the lonely streets of the barrio. There is a rivulet just outside the village. Its course is hidden and lost in a thick forest which extends to the foot of a mountain.

At the time the story opens Juan is eating his breakfast with his mother. She is an old widow, whose sole ambition is to establish Juan in a good social position. She is constantly advising her son, when there is any occasion to preach, to be on the lookout for a virtuous wife. She tells him that, since she is an old and experienced woman, he must follow her advice. Her advice is that a good wife is always quiet and tongue-tied, and does not go noisily about the house. As Juan is an obedient son, he soon determines to get him a good wife. After a short time Juan comes home to his mother, and says to her, "Mother, I have found the girl you will like, — the one who shall be my wife. She is speechless and motionless. Her eyes are staring in just one place. Though I have watched her closely for about twelve hours, I have not observed the slightest motion in her lips and eyelids. She remained quiet in her bed, although there were many noisy people in the house."

"And is that all?" says his mother.

"No, mother," says Juan, "her hands were very cold. She was deaf, and she did not answer me. This fact makes her all

---

[1] *Bayluhan* (from the Spanish *baile*), "a dancing-party." *Katapusan* (Tag.; from *tapus*, "end, finish"), a *fiesta* given nine days after the death of an adult, or three days after the death of a child.

the lovelier, and I am sure you will like her. There is only one thing you did not tell me, however."

"I think," says the mother, "that I advised you well."

"Yes, I think so too," says Juan. "The girl had a stinking waxy-like odor."

"O Juan!" exclaims his mother, "I already suspected from your long description that you followed my instructions too literally. The girl you found is a dead one. Now, remember: those who stink are dead."

"Thanks, mother," says Juan quietly, "I will never forget that."

A few days later, when Juan and his mother are eating their breakfast, Juan smells a stinking odor. He looks around the little room. As he does not see any one else there, he thinks that his mother is dead. Then, when his mother is taking her siesta, Juan says to himself, "Surely mother is dead." He goes out quietly and digs a grave for her. Then he buries her in it, and mourns for her nine days. Now Juan is alone in the world.

One morning, when Juan is eating his breakfast by himself, he smells again a stinking odor. He looks around, and, as he does not see any one, he thinks that he himself is dead. There is nobody to bury him. So he goes to the river, takes five or six banana-trunks, and makes a raft of them. He lies down on the raft, and lets the current of the river carry him away. In three hours the current has carried him into the woods. While he is floating through the forest, all of a sudden he is called in a fierce voice by some one on shore. This man was the captain of a band of robbers. Juan does not stir in his place. The second shout is accompanied by a terrible oath. Juan opens his eyes. He sadly looks at the robbers, and tells them that he is a dead man. The robbers laugh; but when Juan insists on remaining on the river, the captain frightens Juan, and says that he will shoot if he does not get up. As Juan does not care for the taste of bullets, he goes to the bank of the river, still thinking that he is a walking dead body.

Juan goes with the robbers into the woods. Their house is in a deserted spot. The captain appoints Juan their housekeeper. He tells him to cook rice, but orders him to keep very still and quiet, for they may be caught by the Spanish soldiers (*cazadores*). Then the robbers go out on an expedition, and Juan is left alone in the house. He shuts the windows, and everything is quiet and undisturbed. He even tries to control his breathing for fear of the noise it may make. He cautiously takes an earthen pot and puts rice and water into it. Then he places the pot on the fire, and sits down near it. Everything is silent. But suddenly a murmuring sound seems to come from the pot. (The water is beginning to boil.) Soon the sound seems to be very loud. Juan thinks that the pot is saying, "Buluk ka." This expression means, "You are decayed." So Juan gets very angry. He whispers to the pot to stop; but the pot does not seem to hear him, for the murmuring sound becomes louder and louder. At last Juan is so exasperated, that he takes a piece of bamboo-bellows (*ihip*) and gives the pot a fatal blow. This puts an end to the pot, the rice, and the flames.

At noon the hungry robbers come home. They find Juan almost breathless in the darkest corner of the house, the pot broken, and the rice scattered over the floor. They ask Juan what is the matter. Juan says that the naughty pot was making too much noise, and was mocking him; and, as the captain bade him be careful about making a noise, he struck the pot and broke it into pieces. The captain cannot help smiling at Juan's foolishness, and he tells Juan to prepare a lunch with anything he can find in the house.

The next day comes, and all the food is eaten. The captain gives Juan some money, and tells him to go to the market to buy some earthen pots and some crabs. When Juan reaches the barrio, he buys all the crabs he can find, and about two dozen large earthen pots. He next finds out that the pots are too bulky for him to carry, although they are not heavy. At last he thinks of a good way to carry them. He has the pots carried to one corner of the market, where he buys a long piece of rattan. He sharpens one end of the rattan and passes it through the bottoms of all the pots, so that they are now very easy to be carried. He slings them over his shoulder, and starts for home with the pots and the crabs. Soon he comes to a large, wide river with a very strong current. He sits down on the bank and wonders what is to be done. He remembers that crabs are good swimmers, so he decides to untie them and let them swim to the other side of the river. As he unties the crabs, he says, "Now, crabs, we have to cross this broad river. I know that you are good swimmers. I am a slow swimmer myself, and especially with these pots to carry. Please swim to the other side of the river as quickly as you can, for I cannot carry you. If you reach the other side before I do, you may go straight home, or wait for me." With this warning, he releases the crabs one by one so that they may go in a straight line. He is very glad to see them swim so fast. Then with the help of a piece of bamboo, and after a long struggle, he himself reaches the opposite shore. He looks around for the crabs; but, seeing none, he says to himself, "Perhaps they have become tired of waiting for me and have gone straight home, as I ordered them to do. What a surprise for the captain!" Juan is very glad at the decision of the crabs, and he sets out for the robbers' house, always hoping to overtake the rear of the long procession of crabs. He soon reaches home. He asks the robbers if the crabs have arrived. When Juan finds out that not one of the naughty crabs obeyed him, he blames himself for his quiet nature, and swears that he will never trust a crab again. The captain asks him about the pots. Juan tells him that they are all safe, and that the captain must thank him for his wit in solving the problem of how to carry two dozen large pots at the same time. All the robbers are eager to see what Juan's scheme was. When they find out what Juan has done, and see the holes in the bottom of all the pots, they cannot help laughing. The captain, however, addresses Juan with all the epithets found in a common slang dictionary. The captain now decides never to let Juan stay in the house alone, and from that time on takes him with them on their expeditions.

Several days later the captain calls Juan one night, and tells him to get ready, for they are going to rob a certain house. They go through the forest, and soon come to a clearing, in the middle of which stands a large *nipa* house. While they are still in the thicket, the captain calls Juan to him, and says, "Juan, go into the *silong*[1] of the house, and see if the people are awake. Now, remember, if you feel something hot, it is a man; but if it is cold, it is a bolo. Do you understand?" Juan answers, "Yes," and obediently goes to the house, repeating to himself the orders of the captain. He cautiously goes under the house, and looks around. After a while something hot falls on his back. He quickly runs away, and begins to cry, "Tao,

[1] *Silong*, the ground floor of a Filipino house. Usually it has only a dirt floor, and is not finished off.

tao!" ("Man, man!") All the robbers get frightened, so they run away too. After a few minutes they come together. Seeing that they are not pursued, the captain calls Juan, and says to him, "Juan, why did you fool us? Nobody is pursuing us."

"Well," says Juan, "I followed your orders. You said that if I felt something hot, it was a man; but if cold, it was a bolo. I went into the *silong*. I looked up. There was a faint light, and I saw a large mat outlined on the floor. As I was looking at it, a hot thing fell on my back. Then I ran away to warn you."

"Let us see," says the captain impatiently, "what *tao* that is which has fallen on your back." One of the robbers lights a match. The robbers examine Juan's back, and they see only a little lizard clinging to his worn-out *camisa* (loose, thin cotton coat).[1] Some of the robbers get angry, and some laugh at Juan's foolishness. The captain tells Juan that he may go away, for he is not worth anything. He also tells Juan not to tell anybody that he has been with them, for, if he does, they will kill him.

Juan leaves the band of robbers, and decides to live up in a tree, because he is all alone, he says. He takes a low bamboo table and goes up into a very large mango-tree. He chooses a well-hidden place, and there he ties his table firmly to the branches. He spends the day in the neighboring towns looking for food, but at night he comes back to the tree and sleeps there.

Early one morning Juan wakes up and hears faint whispers. He looks down, and sees two men talking very earnestly together. One is carrying a bag of money. Juan loosens his table and lets it fall on the men. It makes a loud crash, and they run away. Juan quickly climbs down the tree and makes off with the bag of money. He now decides to live in town. After he has found a barrio that suits him, he buys a house, a carabao, and a cart. He lives peacefully in his new house. Sometimes he works; but he spends most of his time sleeping, for he is a very lazy fellow.

One morning the capitan of the town sends a town crier around to announce an order to the people. The town crier says, "The capitan orders you all to sprinkle with water the

---

[1] The narrator has probably made the original episode a little more delicate here. There are inconsistencies in the present form of the story: a lizard would feel cold, not hot; besides, it would hardly remain clinging to Juan's coat as he rushed through the forest. Clearly, something other than a lizard fell on Juan.

street in front of your houses." Juan takes a small cocoanut-shell full of water, and goes out and sprinkles the street. In the afternoon the capitan of the town goes about the streets to see if the people have obeyed his orders. He sees that every-body has obeyed him except Juan. He goes to Juan's house, and asks him why he has not sprinkled the street; and Juan tells him what he has done. The capitan then tells him that he must use much water. As soon as the capitan has left, Juan begins to pour buckets of water on the street. But when the water all flows away, Juan thinks that his irrigation is not good enough: so he takes his cart and carabao, and with their help he digs a large ditch. All night long Juan works filling the ditch with water. The next morning, when the capitan sees the ditch, he becomes very angry, and summons Juan. Juan ex-cuses himself by saying that the laws of the town are not stated clearly. So the capitan has to let Juan go.

When Sunday comes, Juan goes to church. In the pulpit the priest tells the people to put a little cross on their street doors. When Juan goes home, he takes a piece of *tinting* (the rib of a cocoanut-leaf) and makes a little cross about two inches high. When the priest makes his rounds, he does not see the cross, for it is so small. He asks Juan where his cross is. Juan shows him; and the priest tells him to make a large one, for it is too small, and the evil spirits will not be able to see it. Juan takes his bolo and cuts two long pieces of bamboo. This time his cross is so large, that the priest cannot see it, either. The priest becomes so angry at Juan's stupidity, that he expels him from the town. Juan good-naturedly goes away. He sells his house, and with his cart and carabao he moves on to another town.

He settles in a barrio where the soil is red. Here he lives several weeks, but he is always longing to go back to his old home. He finally says to himself that he is going there in spite of the anger of the priest. He fills his cart with red earth, and hitches his carabao to it. He sits in the middle of his cart, and slowly drives to the town where he had lived before. As he is driving down the main street in the afternoon, whom should he meet but the priest himself! The priest cries, "Juan, so you are here again! Didn't I tell you that you must never tread the soil of this town again? If you do not go away, I shall tell *the* capitan to imprison you."

"Dear priest," says Juan humbly, "before you accuse me, use your eyes. I am not treading on your soil. This earth which I have in my cart is my own." The priest looks in the cart. By this time there are many people around them, and they too look in the cart. They laugh at Juan's wit. The priest wants to laugh too; but he controls himself, for he is afraid that the people will not respect him any more if he laughs. So he angrily threatens Juan, and tells him to leave the town instantly. Poor Juan has nothing to do but go.

He sells his carabao and cart, and spends the money foolishly in the neighboring villages. Soon Juan is reduced to poverty again, so he decides to go back to his native town. There he finds everything changed: the houses are better, and the little chapel is prettier. He looks for relatives or friends, but he finds only his old grandmother, who lives by herself in the field. He goes to her and tells her the history of his family. The old woman recognizes him at last, and asks him if he is not the Juan who buried his mother. Juan answers, "Yes," but excuses himself by saying that he only obediently followed his mother's advice.

Juan now stays with his grandmother. Her hut, which is very small, is surrounded by a small garden of vegetables. Juan does nothing but eat and sleep. He soon develops the bad habit of throwing things out of the window. His grandmother tells him that he must throw them far away. One morning the old woman does not find Juan, and he does not appear until midnight. She asks him where he has been, and he tells her that he went to the other side of the mountain to throw away a banana-skin which was left on his plate. She tells him that he does not need to go so far, that he can throw the banana-skins behind the fence.

One day early in the morning the old woman leaves Juan in charge of the house, for she is going to town. She tells him to cook two small measures (*chupas*) of rice for her, for perhaps she will be very hungry when she gets home. Then she goes away quite happy, thinking that Juan understands her. As soon as she leaves, Juan thinks it is time to begin to cook. He is surprised to find only one measure in the earthen jar. He looks for the other one everywhere; but, as he cannot find it, he thinks his grandmother was mistaken when she told him to cook two measures of rice. So he takes his bolo, goes outside,

cuts a piece of bamboo, and makes a wooden measure just
like the other one. This takes him a long time; but when he
has finished, he fills the two measures with dry rice, and puts
them in the fire. While the measures are burning, the grandmother arrives. She calls Juan, and asks him if the rice is
ready, for she is very hungry. Juan tells her that it is quite
ready. The old woman sees that it is very bright in the house,
and she fears that it is on fire. Juan says that it is the two
measures burning. When the old woman sees what Juan has
done, she becomes angry. However, she controls herself, and
teaches Juan how to cook rice. Under the supervision of the old
woman, Juan takes an earthen pot, cleans it, and puts rice
into it. Then he puts water into the pot, and finally puts
the pot on the fire. The old woman goes to rest, telling him
to watch the rice. After a while she calls to Juan, and says,
"Did you cover the pot [*tinungtungan mo na ang paliok*]?" [1]

"No, I did not," says Juan.

"Cover the pot, then [*tungtungan mo*]!" she cries.

"That is impossible," says Juan.

"Why impossible?" cries the old woman. "The rice will
have a smoky taste if you don't."

"All right," says Juan, getting up. He goes to the fireplace
and thinks for a little while. Then he jumps up to the rafters
of the ceiling, which are but two feet above his head. He goes
just above the pot, adjusts his feet very well, and then lets himself fall. The pot is broken to pieces. The old woman wakes
up at the noise of the crash, and says, "What is that, Juan?
Is the rice cooked?"

"Why do you ask me that?" says Juan impatiently. "You
told me to step on the pot, and now you ask me if the rice is
cooked!"

She goes out to the kitchen; and when she sees her broken
pot, the old woman becomes truly angry. She drives Juan
from the house, telling him that he cannot live with her any
more because he is too troublesome.

Juan now goes off, and wanders from town to town. Sometimes he is obliged to work in order to get anything to eat.
Finally he comes to a large town where the people wear shoes

---

[1] *Tuntung* is the earthen cover of an earthen pot. The verb derived from it, *tuntungan*,
has two meanings: one is "to cover something," the other is "to step on or over something."
Hence Juan's mistake.

and carry umbrellas. He becomes enchanted with the shoes and umbrellas: so he works hard, and saves enough money to buy both. But he surprises every one who sees him; for he carries his shoes dangling at his belt, and his umbrella closed under his arm. Some of the more curious fellows follow after him. They see that, although it rains or the sun is very hot, Juan never opens his umbrella except when he sits to rest under a tree; and also that he never puts his shoes on when he is on dry land, but only when he is crossing a river. At last they ask him why he does such foolish things. Juan says, "Don't you know that there are many worms and loose branches in a tree? If, for example, a snake should fall down, well, it would hit my umbrella. As for the shoes, it is better for one to wear his shoes when he crosses a river, for there he cannot see thê ground." The people leave him alone; but some persons think he is wise, and imitate his example.

Juan goes on with his travels. At last he falls in love. He serves the girl's parents, and becomes their cook. He always keeps the best parts of the chicken for the girl and himself, and gives only the bones to the parents. They ask him why he gives them the worst parts. Juan replies, "I do that because you are our supporters. The bones, compared with a house, are the foundation and framework." The parents find Juan's reasoning so good, that they at once marry their daughter to him. After this Juan is a good and sensible fellow, and does not do foolish things any more.

NOTES.

This long, loosely-constructed droll is not of any fixed length, according to the narrator; adventures are added or omitted at the caprice of the story-teller. It would be useless to attempt to parallel the tale as a whole, because of the very nature of its composition. The separate incidents, however, we may examine, pointing out analogues already in print, and citing others from my own manuscript collection.

(1) "*If it smells bad, it's dead.*" This joke is common among the Tagalogs and Pampangans, and forms the basis of many of their comical stories. As an example I will give the opening of a story entitled "Ricardo and his Adventures" narrated by Paulo Macasaet, a Tagalog from Batangas: —

RICARDO AND HIS ADVENTURES.

Once there was a widow who had a son named Ricardo. One day the mother said to the boy, "Ricardo, I want you to go to school, so that you may learn something about our religion." Ricardo was willing enough, so he took his Catechism and set out. Instead of going to the school, however, he went to a neighboring pond and listened to the merry croaking of the frogs. When eleven o'clock came, he went home and told his mother about the real school. The poor woman was very happy, thinking that her son was spending his time wisely. Ricardo took great delight in joining the chorus of the frogs, for his mother gave him food as a reward for his diligence.

One morning the woman asked her son to read his lesson. The boy opened his Catechism and croaked very loudly. His mother was glad when she heard that her son could croak so well, because she thought that that was the way to read the book.

As Ricardo was playing with his schoolmates one day, he saw a dead cat. It smelled very bad, so he left the pond and went home. He said, "Mother, I saw a cat lying near our school. It had a very bad odor." The mother said, "My son, remember this: whenever a body smells bad, you may be sure that it is dead." Ricardo repeated the words of his mother many times to himself, and learned them by heart.

One day, when he was on his way to the pond, Ricardo smelled something bad. He looked in every direction, but he could not find anybody. So he said, "Since I cannot find any dead body here, I must be the one who is dead." He lay down on the ground, and said, "Ricardo is dead! I cannot eat any more. O how unhappy I am!" While he was lying there, he saw a ripe guava above his head. He exclaimed, "Delicious fruit, you are very fortunate! If I were alive, I would eat you." He wished to get the fruit, but he dared not do so. After a while, when he could no longer smell the stink, he got up and went home, and told his mother his story.

[As the rest of the story is not droll, and is in no way connected with our present tale, it may be given in abstract.]

One day Ricardo learned from his mother how his father had been killed by a giant who had afterwards carried away his sister. The boy set out in search of the giant. An old man along the way, whom he treated kindly, gave him two bottles of magic water, — one that would make invulnerable the man who should drink it, another that would take away all the strength of him on whose head it should be poured. Later a leprous old woman to whom he gave some food presented him with a magic saddle that would carry him through the air. So equipped, he soon arrived at the cave of the giant. He succeeded in killing that seven-headed monster and in freeing his sister and many other prisoners. Ten barrels of money were found in the cave. Of these, Ricardo took two; the rest he gave to the prisoners he had freed. Later Ricardo married a beautiful woman named Lucia.

(2) *Destruction of the singing rice-pot.* Another Tagalog form of this incident, likewise connected with Juan's experiences while cook for a band of robbers, was collected from Singalong, Manila. It was related by Crisanto H. Aragon, and runs as follows: —

JUAN AND THE ROBBERS.

Once there was a young man named Juan, who left his parents to seek his fortune. While he was wandering in the mountains, he reached the cave of some robbers. Juan decided to be a robber, and asked the chief to admit ʰim. The chief accepted Juan.

One night Juan was left alone in the cave, for his companions had gone to town to make a raid. Before leaving, the chief said, "Juan, you will stay here and take care of our property. If you hear a noise, take your bolo and kill whoever makes that noise, for he is our enemy. Cook some rice, so that when we return we may have something to eat."

While Juan was cooking the rice, to his great surprise he heard a noise. Faithful to the command that had been laid upon him, Juan took his bolo and walked around the cave to see where the noise came from. When he reached the kitchen, he noticed that the noise was louder. After a careful observation, he concluded that it was coming from the rice-pot. "The enemies must be here," said Juan, pointing to the rice-pot; and, without a moment's hesitation or fear, Juan smashed the pot into a thousand pieces. The noise stopped at once, and Juan was satisfied.

When the robbers came home and asked Juan for rice, he told them what had happened. The chief realized that the fault was his, so he only laughed at Juan; but, from that time on, Juan was never allowed to stay alone in the cave.

One night the robbers decided to rob the captain of the Municipal Police in a town near by. When they reached the captain's house, they saw that it was empty: so they took everything they could find. Juan entered the captain's bedroom, but, instead of searching for valuables, he took the captain's uniform and put it on. Then Juan went out to join his companions. But as soon as the robbers saw the uniformed man, they thought it was the captain, and ran away as fast as their legs would carry them. Juan ran too, for he thought that the captain must be after them. The robbers were so frightened, that they separated; but Juan decided to follow the chief. Finally the chief became so tired, that he made up his mind to stop and fight his pursuer; but when Juan came up, the chief recognized him, and it was only then that both of them felt that they had gotten rid of the real captain.

For a Santal story of a stupid hero joining a band of thieves, see A. Campbell, "Jhorea and Jhore," pp. 11–12; Bompas, p. 19.

(3) *Adventure with the crabs.* Compare "The Adventures of Juan" (JAFL 20 : 106), in which Juan's mother sends her foolish son to town to buy meat to eat with the boiled rice. He buys a live crab, which he sets down in the road and tells to go to his mother to be cooked for dinner. The crab promises, but, as soon as Juan's back is turned, runs in another direction. Clearly our version of the incident is superior to this.

(4) *Juan as a thief.* With this incident may be compared another Tagalog story, narrated by Adolfo Scheerer. It is entitled —

THE ADVENTURE OF TWO ROBBERS.

There were once two robbers, who, hearing of the trip that a certain family was about to make, decided to rob them during the night. They were encouraged in their purpose by the thought that everything in the house would be in a state of great confusion. During the night the two thieves climbed a tree which grew close by a window of this house. From this place they could easily observe what the people inside were doing. As they sat there waiting, they saw two servants packing something which seemed to be very heavy. They believed that the bundle contained much money, so they decided to steal it.

In the dead of night one of the robbers went up into the house, took the bundle, and passed it to his companion below. When he joined the other, they took to their heels, carrying the bundle between them on their shoulders. When they had gone some way, the one in the rear began to get curious as to what they were carrying, so he cut an opening in the mat that was wrapped around the contents. To his great surprise, he noticed a human toe stick out; and he at once shouted, "Man, man, man!" The one in front took this shout as a warning that some one was chasing them, so he ran faster. The other only continued to shout, "Man, man!" but his companion paid no attention to him. Finally his foot caught in the root of a tree, and he fell down. When he understood the situation, the two villains left the bundle and ran away.

(5) *Frightening robbers under tree.* This incident is widespread, and has made its way into many *Märchen* cycles. It is distinctly comic in its nature. For references to its occurrence, see Köhler-Bolte, 99 and 341 (*sub* "Herabwerfen der Thür"); Crane, 380, note 19; Cosquin, I : 243 f.; and especially Bolte-Polívka, I : 521–525 (on Grimm, No. 59), episode F.

(6) *Walking on his own soil.* This trick of Juan's we have already met with in "King Tasio," No. 7 (*b*).

(7) *Cooking rice-measures.* Juan's misunderstanding about cooking two measures of rice is almost exactly paralleled in a Santal story in Bompas, No. 1. The story is entitled "Bajun and Jhore," and this is the first of a series of noodle-like incidents: —

Once upon a time there were two brothers named Bajun and Jhore. Bajun was married, and one day his wife fell ill of fever. So, as he was going ploughing, Bajun told Jhore to stay at home and cook the dinner, and he bade him put into the pot three measures of rice. Jhore staid at home, and filled the pot with water and put it on to boil; then he went to look for rice-measures. There was only one in the house; and Jhore thought, "My brother told me to put in three measures, and if I only put in one, I shall get into trouble." So he went to a neighbor's house and borrowed two more measures, and put them into the pot, and left them to boil. At noon Bajun came back from ploughing, and found Jhore stirring the pot, and asked him whether the rice was ready. Jhore made no answer: so Bajun took the spoon from him, saying, "Let me feel how it is getting on!" but when he stirred with the spoon, he heard a rattling noise; and when he looked into the pot, he found no rice, but only three wooden measures floating about. Then he turned and abused Jhore for his folly; but Jhore said, "You yourself told me to put in three measures, and I have done so." So Bajun had to set to work and cook the rice himself, and got his dinner very late.

This ludicrous mistake suggests a not dissimilar droll of the Tinguian (Cole, 198, No. 86): —

A man went to the other town. When he got there, the people were eating bamboo sprouts (*labon*). He asked them what they ate, and they said *pangaldanen* (the bamboo ladder is called *aldan*). He went home and had nothing to eat but rice: so he cut his ladder into small pieces, and cooked all day, but the bamboo was still very hard. He could not wait longer, so he called his friends, and asked why he could not make it like the people had in the other town. Then his friends laughed and told him his mistake.

For an almost identical Santal story, see Bompas, No. cxxiv, "The Fool and his Dinner."

(8) The last two episodes — *wearing of shoes only when crossing rivers and raising umbrella under tree*, and *the division of the fowl* — we have discussed in the notes to No. 7 (see pp. 63–64, [9], [8]). Add to the bibliography given there, Bompas, No. cxxviii, "The Father-in-law's Visit," which contains a close parallel to the first episode.

In conclusion I will give two other Filipino noodle stories, which, while not variants of any of those given above, have the same combination of stupidity and success as that found in "Juan the Fool." The first is an Ilocano story narrated by Presentacion Bersamin of Bangued, Abra, and runs thus: —

JUAN SADUT.

Juan Sadut was a very lazy fellow. His mother was a poor old woman, who earned their living by husking rice. What she earned each day was hardly enough to last them until the next. When a boy, Juan was left at home to watch over their hens and chickens. One day, as his mother went to work, she told Juan to take care of the little chicks, lest a hawk should get them. Now, Juan had been told this so many times, that he had grown tired of watching chickens: consequently, when his mother went away, he tied all the chickens and hens together, and hung them on a tree. He did this, because he thought that no bird of prey could see them there. In the evening, when his mother came home, she asked if everything was all right. Juan said, "Nana, I tied all the hens and chickens by their legs, and hung them in that tree, so that they would be safe." The mother asked where they were. Juan showed them to her, but they were all dead. The mother was angry, and whipped Juan very severely.

Time passed on, and Juan grew up to be a man; but he was as lazy as ever. He wanted to get married, but the girl he had picked out was the daughter of a rich man; and his mother told him that he was not a good match for the girl, for they were very poor, and, besides, he was too lazy to support a wife. Still Juan was determined to marry the girl, and he thought out a way to get her. One day Juan went to work in the fields, and earned a peseta. The next day he earned another. Then he said to his mother, "Nana, please go to the father of Ines Cannogan (for such was the name of the girl) and borrow their salup (a half cocoanut-shell used for measuring). The mother went, and Ines asked her who had sent for the

,

salup. The mother told her that her son Juan was a merchant that had just arrived from a successful trip. So the salup was lent. When returning the measure, Juan put the two pesetas in the husk of the cocoanut-shell, and told his mother to take it back to Ines, pesetas and all. When Ines examined the salup, she found the pesetas, and told her father all about them.

Not long afterwards Juan sent his mother again to borrow the measure. Again Juan returned it with money sticking in the husk of the shell. This he did several times, until at last Ines's father believed that Juan was very rich. Juan now had a chance to talk with Ines's father about his daughter, and of course the old man accepted his proposal immediately. So Juan and Ines were married.

After their marriage, when the old man found out that his new son-in-law was not only very poor, but also very lazy, he repented of his rashness. However, he compelled both Juan and his wife to go work on his farm. Once, when Ines was taking her siesta, many wild cocks and hens came to eat the rice which she had put in the sun to dry. Juan was too lazy to get up and drive them away, so he took Ines's gold hairpin and threw it at the birds. When Ines awoke, she missed her hairpin. Juan told her what he had done with it. She scolded him so severely, that he felt hurt, and began to weep bitterly, for even his wife disliked him.

The next day Juan went to look for the hairpin at the place where he had thrown it. To his great surprise, he found a bush with golden branches, and on one of them was the hairpin. Immediately he called his wife. They pulled up the bush, and discovered at its roots a jar full of gold and silver money. Now Ines was very proud of her husband's luck. They went to the town to tell their father of their good fortune. From now on, the old man no longer hated Juan, but loved him, and gave him all his property to supervise.

Thus Juan Sadut became a rich man without any effort. Fortune favors the lazy — sometimes.

The other story comes from the other end of the Archipelago, from the province of Misamis. It was narrated by Antonio Cosin of Tagoloan, Misamis, and is a Visayan tale. As may easily be seen, it is distantly related to Grimm, No. 7, "A Good Bargain." For the "sale to animals" comic episode, see Grimm's notes; Clouston, "Book of Noodles," p. 148; and Bolte-Polívka, I : 60. For the "sale to statue" incident, which is analogous to our third episode below, see Clouston, *ibid.*, p. 146; Crane, 379, note 12; Cosquin, 2 : 178. The story follows: —

JUAN LOCO.

A great many years ago there lived a certain fool that went by the name of Juan Loco. He was the son of a butcher, in so far as the following experiences of his are concerned; he had many other experiences that are not recorded in this story.

Juan could not be intrusted with anything, he was such a dunce; but one day he persuaded his father to let him go out and sell meat. So about eight in the morning Juan left home with about three pesos' worth of pork, full of many a hopeful expectation. After having wandered through many streets, he noticed that a big horse-fly was following him with an imploring murmur. Imagining that the fly wanted to buy meat, this sapient vender said to it, "Do you want to buy meat?" The fly answered with a "buzzzzz." For Juan this was a sufficient answer: so he left one-third of the pork with the fly, saying that he was coming back again for his pay. Next he met a hungry and greatly-abused pig, and he asked it if it wanted to buy meat. The pig merely said, "hack, hack," and gave a few angry nods, but Juan understood it to be saying, "Yes:" so he threw it one-half of the meat he had left, with the same warning as he gave the fly, — that he was coming back to collect the price of the meat. His third customer was himself, or his reflection. Warm, tired, and thirsty from his wanderings, he came to a well, where he thought he would take a drink. On looking down, however, he saw a man in the bottom of the well. When Juan shouted to him and made gestures, the man — or his reflection and the echo of his own voice — returned some sort of inarticulate sound, and made the same gestures as Juan. For the third time this sufficed for a "Yes." So Juan threw the rest of his pork down the well, and said he would come back for his money.

Now comes the collection, which he found to be quite easy. He entered a dry-goods store, where he saw a fly on the hand of the shop-keeper. Juan talked to the fly and demanded his money. It did not answer: so he began chasing it around the room, sometimes striking at it when it was on some customer's hand. At last, tired of the disturbance, the shop-keeper paid him off to get rid of him. Next Juan came to a garden where there was a pig. With the pig he encountered the same obstinate silence. He began to chase the pig, and he beat it whenever he was near enough to hit it. When the owner of the animal saw what he was doing, and realized that he was crazy, he paid him off, too. Now, as to his third customer. The reflection in the pool simply mocked him and made him disgusted. So Juan got a long pole and stirred the bottom of the well. When he found that this treatment simply made his customer disappear, he began shouting at the top of his voice. Finally the owner of the well came; and, to avoid further disturbance, he also paid him off, for every one could easily see that the vender was crazy (*loco*) from the way he talked and acted.

So Juan went home in ecstasy. He received much praise from his father, who promised to let him sell meat every day; and the poor fellow gloried in being thus praised.

For other noodle stories of the Filipinos, see our No. 9 and JAFL 20 : 104–106.

50. JUAN AND HIS PAINTED HAT.[1]

There once lived a man by the name of Juan, who did nothing but fool people all the time. Once, when he had only seventy pesos left in his pockets, he determined to resort to the following scheme: he bought a *balangut* hat (a very cheap straw), and painted it five different colors. In the town where Juan was

[1] Narrated by Adolfo Scheerer, a Tagalog from Manila, who heard the story from their native servant some fifteen years ago.

to operate, there were only three stores. He went to each one of them and deposited twenty pesos, saying to the owner of each, "I will deposit twenty pesos in your store, and to-morrow afternoon I will bring some friends here with me. We will perhaps take some refreshments or buy some goods, but in any case I will see to it that the total amount of the things we take is not over the twenty pesos. Then, when we leave, do not ask me to pay you for the things. I will simply make you a bow with my hat, and your attendants should thank me with much courtesy. That mere bow with my hat is to be the payment. You may keep the twenty pesos, but you must also keep this little plan a secret." The owners of the three stores promised.

The next day Juan was walking in the street with his painted hat on, when one of his friends met him. "Halloo, Juan!" exclaimed his friend, "where did you get that funny hat?"

Juan looked serious, and said, "Don't be foolish! Don't you know that this hat is the only means I have of earning a living?"

"Means of living?" returned the other.

"Why, of course. I can go in any store, take anything I please, and pay for it with a mere bow of my hat."

By this time two other friends of Juan had come along, and they too were surprised to see what Juan had on his head. To convince them of the marvellous character of the hat, Juan took his friends to one of the stores. There they sat down, and Juan ordered some refreshments. They ate much, and of the best that the store could furnish. After they had had enough, Juan stood up, made a bow to the proprietor with his hat, and then they all left. Then they visited another store, where the same thing took place.

The friends of Juan were very much astonished, and each wished to possess the hat. One offered him a thousand pesos for it; another, two thousand; and the third, one-half of all his property, which amounted to about five thousand pesos. Juan, of course, was willing to sell it to the highest bidder; but when the sale was about to be concluded, the buyer began to doubt the power of the hat. So he asked Juan to take him to another store to prove once more the qualities of the hat, after which trial, he said, he would pay him the money. Juan took his friend to the third store, and the friend was now sure that the hat could really work wonders. So he paid Juan the five thousand pesos.

When he had received the money, Juan left his friends, went on board ship, and sailed away to a foreign country. One day the friend who had bought the hat desired to make a showing with it. So he invited several friends, among them some ladies. He took them to one of the stores, and there ordered some refreshments to be served them. When they had finished, the man bowed with his hat, and started to leave.

"Thank you, sir!" said the owner of the store, "but where is my payment for the refreshments you have just eaten?"

The owner of the hat was astonished, and, thinking that perhaps he held the hat in the wrong way, or else his fingers were not on the right color, he turned the hat around. Then he made another bow. The owner of the shop now became angry, and began to swear at the man. The other became excited, twirling the hat around, and holding it in as many different ways as he could think of. Finally the shop-keeper ordered the man arrested.

When the owner of the hat heard how Juan had played his trick by paying twenty pesos in advance, he fainted and became very sick. In the mean time Juan was performing other tricks in some different country.

NOTES.

This droll was without doubt imported from Europe, where it has a fairly wide distribution. It does not appear hitherto to have been found in the Orient. In the European forms we find it both as a separate tale, like our story, and also as a part of the "Master Cheat" cycle, which we have discussed in the notes to No. 20. For a complete list of the known occurrences of the "hat pays" episode, see Bolte-Polívka, 2 : 10–15, incident D (on Grimm, No. 61). According to their classification, versions from Holland, Denmark, Sweden, Rumania, Serbo-Croatia, Poland, Russia, and Lithuania are known. See also Köhler-Bolte, 246, 251 (note 1).

51. JUAN AND CLOTILDE.[1]

In ages vastly remote there lived in a distant land a king of such prowess and renown, that his name was known throughout the four regions of the compass. His name was Ludovico.

[1] Narrated by Vicente Hilario, a Tagalog, who heard the story from an old man living in Batangas.

His power was increased twofold by his attachment to an aged magician, to whom he was tied by strong bonds of friendship.

Ludovico had an extremely lovely daughter by the name of Clotilde. Ever since his arrival at the palace the magician had been passionately in love with her; but his extreme old age and his somewhat haughty bearing were obstacles in his path to success. Whenever he made love to her, she turned aside, and listened instead to the thrilling tales told by some wandering minstrel. The magician finally succumbed to the infirmities of old age, his life made more burdensome by his repeated disappointments. He left to the king three enchanted winged horses; to the princess, two magic necklaces of exactly the same appearance, of inimitable workmanship and of priceless worth. Nor did the magician fail to wreak vengeance on the cause of his death. Before he expired, he locked Clotilde and the three magic horses in a high tower inaccessible to any human being. She was to remain in this enchanted prison until some man succeeded in setting her free.

Naturally, King Ludovico wanted to see his daughter before the hour of his death, which was fast approaching. He offered large sums of money, together with his crown and Clotilde's hand, to anybody who could set her free. Hundreds of princes tried, but in vain. The stone walls of the tower were of such a height, that very few birds, even, could fly over them.

But a deliverer now rose from obscurity and came into prominence. This man was an uneducated but persevering peasant named Juan. He possessed a graceful form, herculean frame, good heart, and unrivalled ingenuity. His two learned older brothers tried to scale the walls of the tower, but fared no better than the others. At last Juan's turn came. His parents and his older brothers expostulated with him not to go, for what could a man unskilled in the fine arts do? But Juan, in the hope of setting the princess free, paid no attention to their advice. He took as many of the biggest nails as he could find, a very long rope, and a strong hammer. As he lived in a town several miles distant from the capital, he had to make the trip on horseback.

One day Juan set out with all his equipment. On the way he met his disappointed second brother returning after a vain attempt. The older brother tried in every way he could to divert Juan from his purpose. Now, Juan's parents, actuated partly by a sense of shame if he should fail, and partly by a deep-seated hatred, had poisoned his food without his knowledge. When he felt hungry, he suspected them of some evil intention: so before eating he gave his horse some of his provisions. The poor creature died on the road amidst terrible sufferings, and Juan was obliged to finish the journey on foot.

When he arrived at the foot of the tower, he drove a nail into the wall. Then he tied one end of his rope to this spike. In this way he succeeded in making a complete ladder of nails and rope to the top of the tower. He looked for Clotilde, who met him with her eyes flooded with tears. As a reward for his great services to her, she gave him one of the magic necklaces. While they were whispering words of love in each other's ears, they heard a deafening noise at the bottom of the tower. "Rush for safety to your ladder!" cried Clotilde. "One of the fiendish friends of the magician is going to kill you."

But, alas! some wanton hand had pulled out the nails; and this person was none other then Juan's second brother. "I am a lost man," said Juan.

"Mount one of the winged horses in the chamber adjoining mine," said Clotilde. So Juan got on one of the animals without knowing where to go. The horse flew from the tower with such velocity, that Juan had to close his eyes. His breath was almost taken away. In a few seconds, however, he was landed in a country entirely strange to his eyes.

After long years of struggle with poverty and starvation, Juan was at last able to make his way back to his native country. He went to live in a town just outside the walls of the capital. A rich old man named Telesforo hired him to work on his farm. Juan's excellent service and irreproachable conduct won the good will of his master, who adopted him as his son. At about this time King Ludovico gave out proclamations stating that any one who could exactly match his daughter's necklace should be his son-in-law. Thousands tried, but they tried in vain. Even the most dextrous and experienced smiths were baffled in their attempts to produce an exact counterfeit. When word of the royal proclamations was brought to Juan, he decided to try. One day he pretended to be sick, and he asked Telesforo to go to the palace to get Clotilde's necklace. The old man, who was all ready to serve his adopted son, went that very afternoon and borrowed the necklace, so that he might try to copy it. When he returned with the magic article, Juan jumped from his bed and kissed his father. After supper Juan went to his room and locked himself in. Then he took from his pocket the necklace which Clotilde had given him in the tower, and compared it carefully with the borrowed one. When he saw that they did not differ in any respect, he took a piece of iron and hammered it until midnight.

Early the next morning Juan wrapped the two magic necklaces in a silk handkerchief, and told the old man to take them to the king. "By the aid of the Lord!" exclaimed Clotilde when her father the king unwrapped the necklaces, "my lover is here again. This necklace," she said, touching the one she had given Juan, "is not a counterfeit: for it is written in the magician's book of black art that no human being shall be able to imitate either of the magic necklaces. — Where is the owner of this necklace, old man?" she said, turning to Telesforo.

"He is at home," said Telesforo with a bow.

"Go and bring him to the palace," said Clotilde.

Within a quarter of an hour Juan arrived. After paying due respect to the king, Juan embraced Clotilde affectionately. They were married in the afternoon, and the festivities continued for nine days and nine nights. Juan was made crown-prince, and on the death of King Ludovico he succeeded to the throne. King Juan and Queen Clotilde lived to extreme old age in peace and perfect happiness.

NOTES.

This Tagalog *Märchen* appears to be closely related to an eighteenth-century Spanish ballad by Alonso de Morales. The ballad is No. 1263 in the "Romancero General," and is entitled, "Las Princesas Encantadas, y Deslealtad de Hermanos." Although in general outline the two stories are very close to each other, there are some significant differences.

In the Spanish, the king's name is Clotaldo, and he rules in Syria. The king builds a very high tower, and puts in it his *three* beautiful daughters; then he calls a powerful magician to cast a spell about the place, so that the tower cannot be scaled until the king wishes it to be. Confined in the tower with the princesses are three winged horses (*o satánicas arpias*). The king then issues a proclamation that whoever can reach the princesses shall be married to them. The three brothers that make the attempt are knights from Denmark. The two older proceed to Syria on horseback, fail, and on their return home meet their youngest brother making his way leisurely in a bullock-cart. He too is going to try, and is taking with him abundant provisions, many nails, and a rope. After they have tried in vain to persuade him to return home, they accompany him. [The episode of the poisoned food is lacking.] Juan gains the top of the tower, lowers the two older princesses, and then, last of all, the youngest, who gives him a necklace before she descends. The treacherous brothers now destroy Juan's means of escape, and make off with the three maidens, leaving him on the tower. He mounts one of the winged horses, and it flies with him to a distant country. Making his way back to Syria on foot, he exchanges clothes with a drover, and appears in Clotaldo's kingdom in disguise, pretending to be simple-minded. The king has already married his two older daughters to Juan's treacherous brothers, and is now trying to persuade his youngest daughter to marry: but she wishes only her rescuer. She paints a necklace in every respect like the one which she gave Juan, and says that she will marry only when a person is found who can make a necklace exactly like the picture. The king sends the painting to an alchemist in the city, and orders him, under penalty of death if he fails, to produce the necklace in two months. He is unable to do so, and becomes downcast. Juan, who has been in service as a porter, and is the one who carried the command of the king to the alchemist, asks him why he is sad. He tells the reason. Juan gives the alchemist his necklace. [The rest is practically as in our story.]

There is a sequel to this ballad, No. 1264, which has a close resemblance to the Tagalog "Juan Tiñoso," already summarized in the notes to No. 36.

The Spanish story, says the editor of the "Romancero General," is one of those founded directly on Oriental material which was transmitted by the Arabs. It is curious that so few of these tales, which have been preserved for generations as oral tradition, have made their way into print. The differences noticeable between our *Märchen* and the ballad may be due to a tradition somewhat divergent from that on which Alonso de Morales's poem is based.

52. THE POOR MAN AND HIS THREE SONS.[1]

Once there lived a poor man who had three sons. When the father was on his death-bed, he called his sons, and said to them, "My sons, I shall die very soon; and I shall not be able to leave you much wealth, for wealth I have not. But I will give each one of you something which, if you will only be able to find a place in which it has no equal, will make you happy men." The father then gave to one a rooster, to another a cat, and to the third a scythe. Then he died.

The owner of the scythe was the first to try his fortune and test his father's advice. He left his brothers, and went on a journey until he came to a town where he saw the people harvesting rice by pulling the stalks out of the ground. He

---

[1] Narrated by Gregorio Velasquez, a Tagalog from Pasig, Rizal. He says, "This is a primitive Tagalog fable, I think. I heard it from old people."

showed the people the convenience of the scythe. They were so delighted and astonished, that they offered to give him a large sum of money in exchange for the tool. Of course he was willing to sell it, and he went home a rich man.

The owner of the rooster, seeing the good luck of his brother, next resolved to try his fortune with the bird. Like his brother, he travelled until he came to a town where there was no rooster. The people were very much interested in the rooster's crowing, and asked the owner why the bird crowed. He said that the bird told the time of day by its crowing. "The first crow in the night announces midnight," he said; "the second, three o'clock in the morning; and the third crow announces five o'clock." The people were very anxious to get the rooster for their town, and offered to buy it. The owner was willing, and he returned to his home as rich as his brother who had sold the scythe.

The last brother now set out to try his luck with his cat. At last he came to a town where the rats were vexing the people very much. He showed them the use of his cat. With wonder the people watched the cat kill the rats, and were astounded to see how the rats fled from this strange animal. The news of the cat reached the king, who summoned its owner to the palace. The king asked the brother to try his cat on the rats in the palace, and so the cat was turned loose. In a short time all the rats had either been killed or driven away. The king wanted the cat, and offered to pay a large sum of money for it. So the owner of the cat, after the king had paid him, went home as rich as his other two brothers.

Thus the three brothers became rich, because they followed their father's wise advice: select the right place in which to trade.

NOTES.

This story, like the preceding, is clearly an importation from the Occident. The bibliography of the cycle to which it belongs may be found in Bolte-Polívka, 2 : 69–71 (on Grimm, No. 70). German, Breton, French, Flemish, Swedish, Catalan, Serbian, Bulgarian, Czech, Polish, Russian, Lithuanian, and Finnish versions have been recorded. The story as a whole does not appear to have been collected from the Far East hitherto, though separate tales turning on the sale of a cat in a catless country (Dick Whittington type) are found among the Jews and in Africa. Bolte and Polívka give the *bibliography* of this latter group of stories on pp. 71–76.

The oldest form of our story known is that found in Nicholas de Troyes' "Grand Parangon des nouvelles Nouvelles," No. x, dating from 1535. The three things here bequeathed by the father are a cock, a cat, and a sickle, as in our version. I think it probable that the tale was introduced into the Philippines through the medium of a French religious. The Catalan form differs from the French in mentioning a fourth "heirloom," a *raven*, and was probably not the parent of our Tagalog version.

53. THE DENIED MOTHER.[1]

(One day little Antonio fell down and· sprained his elbow. His grandfather told him to put on his *camisa* and they would go to Tandang Fruto, an old *manghihilot* (a man who pretends to correct dislocated bones by means of certain prayers). On their way they met a beggar with a guitar. He sat down on a stone in front of a house and began to sing. Antonio wished to hear him, and so did the old grandfather: so they stopped and listened. The beggar sang the story of "The Denied Mother" in Tagalog verse. The story is this: —)

In a certain country there lived a king who had a pet dog. He loved the dog so much and treated it so kindly, that, wherever he went, the dog followed him. In the course of time the dog gave birth to three puppies. The most striking thing about these new-born creatures was that they were real human beings in every particular. So the king ordered them to be baptized. The eldest sister was named Feliza; the second, Juana; and the youngest, Maria. When they grew up into beautiful young women, they married three princes, each of a different kingdom. After the marriage-festivities, each went to live in the country of her husband.

Feliza was very happy: she dressed elegantly, and had all that a woman of her rank could wish for. One day, when her husband was away from home, a lean, dirty, spectre-looking dog came to her. It was Feliza's mother, who, after the death of her master the king, had been cast out of the palace. The poor dog had had nothing to eat for many days. She had been driven away from every house, and had been frightened by mischievous boys with sticks and stones. Although Feliza's kingdom was very far away, she had managed, in spite of difficulty, to reach it. She hoped to gain her daughter's pity.

[1] Narrated by Leopoldo Uichanco, a Tagalog from Calamba, Laguna.

"My daughter," she said, as she ascended the steps of the ladder(!), "have compassion on me! I, your mother, am in a very wretched condition."

"What care I?" returned Feliza. "What business have you to come here? Don't you know that I will never sacrifice anything for your sake? Get out of here!" And she kicked the poor dog until it fell tumbling to the ground. Feliza did not want her husband to find out that her mother was a dog.

Sadly the dog went away, and decided to go to her daughter Juana's kingdom. The country was far away, but what else could she do? As Juana was coming out of the church with her husband, she saw the dog hurrying after her. Like Feliza, she was ashamed of her mother. She whispered to one of the guards to catch the dog and tie it securely in a distant forest, so that it might no longer annoy her.

Not long after this, Maria, the youngest daughter, was riding through the forest with her husband. There they found the poor dog crying and yelping in a pitiful manner. Maria recognized her mother. She got out of the carriage, and with her own hands untied the dog. She wrapped her veil around it, and ordered the carriage to turn back to the palace. "Husband," she said as she ascended the steps of the royal residence, "this dog that I am carrying is my mother, so please your Majesty."

The husband only said, "Thank God!" and not another word. Maria ordered the cook to prepare delicious food for the dog. She assigned the best chamber in the palace to the animal. While the dog was eating with Maria, the prince, and the courtiers, the dining-room was suddenly illuminated with a bright light. The dog disappeared, and in its place stood a beautiful woman in glorious attire. The woman kissed Maria, and said, "I am the dog your mother. God bless you, my good child!"

NOTES.

I can offer no close parallels for this somewhat savage tale, though a few analogies to incidents in our story are to be found in an Indian story in Frere (No. 2, "A Funny Story"), the first part of which may be abstracted here for comparison.

A certain Rajah and Ranee are sad because they have no children and the little dog in the palace has no puppies; but at last the Ranee is confined, and bears two *puppies*, while the little dog at the same time gives birth to two *female infants*. In order to keep her offspring from the Ranee, who wishes to substitute her own for the dog's, the dog carries its two daughters to the forest, and there rears them. When they have become of marriageable age, they are found by two princes, who take them away and make them their wives. For twelve years the poor dog looks in vain for her lost children. One day the *eldest* daughter looks out of her window, and sees a dog running down the street. "That must be my long-lost mother!" she exclaims to herself; and she runs out, gets the animal, bathes it and feeds it. The dog now wants to go visit her younger daughter, although the elder tries in vain to dissuade her mother from going. When the younger daughter sees the dog, she says, "That must be my mother! What will my husband think of me if he learns that this wretched, ugly, miserable-looking dog is my mother?" She orders the servants to throw stones at it and drive it away. Wounded in the head, the dog runs back to her elder daughter, but dies, in spite of the tender care it receives. The daughter now tries to conceal the body until she can bury it. The husband discovers the corpse of the dog, but it has become a statue of gold set with diamonds and other precious stones. He asks where the treasure came from. His wife lies, and says, "Oh, it is only a present my parents sent me!" [The rest of the story has nothing to do with ours: it is a variant of the "Toads and Diamonds" cycle (see notes to No. 47).]

It will be noticed that in the Indian tale the rôles of the daughters are the reverse of what they are in our story.

54. TOMARIND AND THE WICKED DATU.[1]

Before the Spanish occupation there were in the Philippines many petty kingdoms headed by native princes known as *datus*. Luzon, the scene of countless ravages and hard fightings of warlike tribes, was the home of Datu Nebucheba. His kingdom — at first only a few square miles — was greatly extended by the labor of his young brave warrior, Tomarind. Tomarind had a very beautiful wife, with whom Datu Nebucheba fell in love; but the ruler kept his vile desire secret in his heart for many years. Many times he thought of getting rid of his warrior Tomarind, and thus getting possession of his beautiful wife.

One day Tomarind was sent on a dangerous errand. He was ordered to get an enchanted marble ball from one of the caves in a certain mountain. Two monsters of terrible aspect, whose joy was the burning of villages, and whose delight was the killing of human beings, guarded the entrance of that cave. Many persons had entered the door of that death-chamber, but nobody had come from it alive. Suspicious of the coming danger, Tomarind did not go directly to the cave. He sought

[1] Narrated by Eutiquiano Garcia of Mexico, Pampanga. He says that this is an old Pampangan tale.

the famous witch of Tipuca, and told her about his situation. Immediately the witch performed a sort of diabolical ceremony, gave Tomarind a magic cane, and sent him away. When he reached the cave, those that guarded the cave received Tomarind very kindly, and they delivered the enchanted marble ball to him.

"To-morrow," said Nebucheba to himself, "the wife of Tomarind will be mine." Alas for him! very early the next morning Tomarind presented the marble ball to Datu Nebucheba. "How quickly he executed my orders!" exclaimed Nebucheba. "What shall I do to destroy this brave man? The next time he will not escape the danger. I will ask him to take a letter to my parents, who are living under ground, in the realm of the spirits," he said to himself.

The *datu* caused a well to be dug, and big stones to be piled near the mouth of it. When everything was ready, he summoned the brave warrior. He gave him the letter, and told him to start the next morning. Tomarind went again to the witch of Tipuca. "This is a very great task," said the witch; "but never mind! you will get even with Datu Nebucheba." That night the witch, with the help of unseen spirits, made a subterranean passage connecting the bottom of the *datu's* well with that of Tomarind's. "Nebucheba," the witch said to Tomarind, "will ask you to go down into his well; and as soon as you are at the bottom, he will order that the pile of stones be thrown on you. Lose no time, but go into the subterranean passage that I have prepared for you." When morning came, Tomarind went to execute the orders of the *datu*.

Now, Nebucheba firmly believed that Tomarind was dead. There was great rejoicing in the *datu's* house. In the evening, while the revelry was going on, Tomarind appeared with the pretended answer from Nebucheba's parents. The letter read, "We wish you to come and see us here. We have a very beautiful girl for you." Nebucheba was greatly surprised. He made up his mind to go down into the well the next day. He gathered all his subjects together, and said to them, "I am going to see my parents. If the place there is better than the place here, I shall not come back. Tomarind will be my successor."

In the morning Nebucheba's subjects took him to the well and lowered him slowly into it. When he reached the bottom, Tomarind threw big stones down on him, and Nebucheba was crushed to death. The people never saw him again. Tomarind became *datu*, and he ruled his subjects with justice and equity for many years.

NOTE.

I know of no variants of this tale, which pretty evidently represents old tribal Pampangan tradition. The device by which Tomarind lures the wicked *datu* to his death is not unlike incident J in our No. 20 (see notes), but there is clearly no other connection between the two stories.

II. FABLES AND ANIMAL STORIES.

55. (a) THE TURTLE AND THE MONKEY.[1]

It was mid-day. The blinding heat of the sun forced all the water-loving animals — such as pigs, carabaos, and turtles — to go to the river-banks and there seek to cool themselves in the water. On that part of the bank where a big shady tree stood, a monkey and a turtle were having a good time, discussing the past, present, and future. Just then they saw a banana-stalk floating by.

"Don't you think that it would be a wise thing for us to get that banana-stalk and plant it?" said the monkey.

"Can you swim?" replied the turtle.

"No, I can't, but you can," said the monkey.

"I will get the banana-tree," said the turtle, "on condition that we divide it. You must allow me to have the upper part, where the leaves are." The monkey agreed; but when the stalk was brought to shore, the monkey took the leaves himself, and gave the turtle only the roots. As the humble turtle was unable to fight the monkey, all he could do was to pick up his share and take it to the woods and plant it. It was not strange that the monkey's part died, while that of the turtle brought forth clusters of ripe bananas in time.

When the monkey learned that the bananas were ripe, he went to visit his friend the turtle. "I will give you half the bananas," said the turtle, "if you will only climb the stalk and get the fruit for me."

"With great pleasure," replied the monkey. In less than a minute he was at the top of the tree. There he took his time, eating all he could, and stopping now and then to throw a banana-peeling down to his friend below. What could the poor turtle do? It was impossible for him to climb.

"I know what I'll do!" he said to himself. He gathered pointed sticks, and set them all around the base of the tree. Then he cried out to the monkey, saying, "The hunters are coming! The hunters are coming!" The monkey was very much frightened, so he jumped down in the hope of escaping;

[1] Narrated by Eutiquiano Garcia of Mexico, Pampanga.

but he was pierced by the sharp sticks, and in a few hours he died. Thus the turtle got his revenge on the selfish monkey.

When the monkey was dead, the turtle skinned him, dried his meat, and sold it to the other monkeys in the neighborhood. But, in taking off the skin, the turtle was very careless: he left here and there parts of the fur sticking to the meat; and from this fact the monkeys which had bought the meat judged the turtle guilty of murder of one of their brethren. So they took the turtle before their chief, and he was tried.

When the turtle's guilt had been established, the monkey-chief ordered him to be burned.

"Fire does not do me any harm," said the turtle. "Don't you see the red part on my back? My father has burned me many times."

"Well, if fire doesn't harm him, cut him to pieces," said the monkey-chief angrily.

"Neither will this punishment have any effect on me," continued the wise turtle. "My back is full of scars. My father used to cut me over and over again."

"What can we do with him?" said the foolish monkeys. At last the brightest fellow in the group said, "We will drown him in the lake."

As soon as the turtle heard this, he felt happy, for he knew that he would not die in the water. However, he pretended to be very much afraid, and he implored the monkeys not to throw him into the lake. But he said to himself, "I have deceived all these foolish monkeys." Without delay the monkeys took him to the lake and threw him in. The turtle dived; and then he stuck his head above the surface of the water, laughing very loud at them.

Thus the turtle's life was saved, because he had used his brains in devising a means of escape.

(b) THE MONKEY AND THE TURTLE.[1]

Once there lived two friends, — a monkey and a turtle. One day they saw a banana-plant floating on the water. The turtle swam out and brought it to land. Since it was but a single plant and they had to divide it, they cut it across the middle.

"I will have the part with the leaves on," said the monkey,

---

[1] Narrated by Bienvenido Gonzales of Pampanga. He heard the story from his younger brother, who heard it in turn from a farmer. It is common in Pampanga.

thinking that the top was best. The turtle agreed and was very well pleased, but she managed to conceal her joy. The monkey planted his part, the top of the tree; and the turtle planted hers, the roots. The monkey's plant died; but that of the turtle grew, and in time bore much fine fruit.

One day, since the turtle could not get at the bananas, she asked the monkey to climb the tree and bring down the bananas. In return for this service she offered to give him half the fruit. The monkey clambered up the tree, but he ate all the fruit himself: he did not give the turtle any. The turtle became very angry, waiting in vain; so she collected many sharp sticks, and stuck them in the trunk of the tree. Then she went away. When the monkey slid down to the ground, he injured himself very badly on the sharp sticks; so he set off to find the turtle and to revenge himself.

The monkey looked for a long time, but finally found the turtle under a pepper-plant. As the monkey was about to strike her, she said, "Keep quiet! I am guarding the king's fruits."

"Give me some!" said the monkey.

"Well, I will; here are some!" said the turtle. "But you must promise me not to chew them until I am far away; for the king might see you, and then he would punish me." The monkey agreed. When the turtle was a long way off, he began to chew the peppers. They were very hot, and burned his mouth badly. He was now extremely angry, and resolved that it would go hard with the turtle when he should catch her.

He searched all through the woods and fields for her. At last he found her near a large snake-hole. The monkey threatened to kill the turtle; but she said to him, "Friend monkey, do you want to wear the king's belt?"

"Why, surely! Where is it?" said the monkey.

The turtle replied, "It will come out very soon: watch for it!" As soon as the snake came out, the monkey caught it; but the snake rolled itself around his body, and squeezed him nearly to death. He finally managed to get free of the snake; but he was so badly hurt, that he swore he would kill the turtle as soon as he should find her.

The turtle hid herself under a cocoanut-shell. The monkey was by this time very tired, so he sat down on the cocoanut-shell to rest. As he sat there, he began to call loudly, "Turtle, where are you?"

The turtle answered in a low voice, "Here I am!"

The monkey looked all around him, but he saw nobody. He thought that some part of his body was joking him. He called the turtle again, and again the turtle answered him.

The monkey now said to his abdomen, "If you answer again when I don't call you, stomach, I'll punish you." Once more he called the turtle; and once more she said, "I am here!"

This was too much for the monkey. He seized a big stone, and began to hit his belly with it. He injured himself so much, that he finally died.

(c) THE MONKEY AND THE TURTLE.[1]

Once upon a time there was a turtle who was very kind and patient. He had many friends. Among them was a monkey, who was very selfish. He always wanted to have the best part of everything.

One day the monkey went to visit the turtle. The monkey asked his friend to accompany him on a journey to the next village. The turtle agreed, and they started early the next morning. The monkey did not take much food with him, because he did not like to carry a heavy load. The turtle, on the contrary, took a big supply. He advised the monkey to take more, but the monkey only laughed at him. After they had been travelling five days, the monkey's food was all gone, so the turtle had to give him some. The monkey was greedy, and kept asking for more all the time. "Give me some more, friend turtle!" he said.

"Wait a little while," said the turtle. "We have just finished eating."

As the monkey made no reply, they travelled on. After a few minutes the monkey stopped, and said, "Can't you travel a little faster?"

"I can't, for I have a very heavy load," said the turtle.

"Give me the load, and then we shall get along more rapidly," said the monkey. The turtle handed over all his food to the monkey, who ran away as fast as he could, leaving the turtle far behind.

"Wait for me!" said the turtle, doing his best to catch his friend; but the monkey only shouted, "Come on!" and scam-

[1] Narrated by José M. Katigbak of Batangas, Batangas. This is a genuine Tagalog story, he says, which he heard from his friend Angel Reyes.

pered out of sight. The turtle was soon very tired and much out
of breath, but he kept on. The monkey climbed a tree by the
roadside, and looked back. When he saw his friend very far
in the rear, he ate some of the food. At last the turtle came up.
He was very hungry, and asked the monkey for something to
eat.

"Come on a little farther," said the selfish monkey. "We
will eat near a place where we can get water." The turtle did
not say anything, but kept plodding on. The monkey ran
ahead and did the same thing as before, but this time he ate
all the food.

"Why did you come so late?" said the monkey when the
turtle came up panting.

"Because I am so hungry that I cannot walk fast," answered
the turtle. "Will you give me some food?" he continued.

"There is no more," replied the monkey. "You brought
very little. I ate all there was, and I am still hungry."

As the turtle had no breath to waste, he continued on the
road. While they were on their way, they met a hunter. The
monkey saw the hunter and climbed a tree, but the man caught
the turtle and took it home with him. The monkey laughed
at his friend's misfortune. But the hunter was kind to the
turtle: he tied it near a banana-tree, and gave it food every
hour.

One day the monkey happened to pass near the house of the
hunter. When he saw that his friend was tied fast, he sneered
at him; but after he had remained there a few hours, and had
seen how the turtle was fed every hour, he envied the turtle's
situation. So when night came, and the hunter was asleep,
the monkey went up to the turtle, and said, "Let me be in your
place."

"No, I like this place," answered the turtle.

The monkey, however, kept urging and begging the turtle,
so that finally the turtle yielded. Then the monkey set the
turtle free, and tied himself to the tree. The turtle went off
happy; and the monkey was so pleased, that he could hardly
sleep during the night for thinking of the food the hunter would
give him in the morning.

Early the next morning the hunter woke and looked out of
his window. He caught sight of the monkey, and thought that
the animal was stealing his bananas. So he took his gun and

shot him dead. Thus the turtle became free, and the monkey was killed.

MORAL: Do not be selfish.

NOTES.

The story of these two opponents, the monkey and the turtle, is widespread in the Philippines. In the introduction to a collection of Bagobo tales which includes a version of this fable, Laura Watson Benedict says (JAFL 26 [1913] : 14), "The story of 'The Monkey and the Turtle' is clearly modified from a Spanish source." In this note I hope to show not only that the story is native in the sense that it must have existed in the Islands from pre-Spanish times, but also that the Bagobo version represents a connecting link between the other Philippine forms and the original source of the whole cycle, a Buddhistic Jātaka. Merely from the number of Philippine versions already collected, it seems reasonable to suspect that the story is Malayan: it is found from one end of the Archipelago to the other, and the wild tribes have versions as well as the civilized. In addition to our one Tagalog and two Pampangan versions, five other Philippine forms already exist in print, and may be cited for comparison. These are the following: —

(*d*) Bagobo, "The Monkey and the Tortoise" (JAFL 26 : 58).
(*e*) Visayan, "Ca Matsin and Ca Boo-ug" (JAFL 20 : 316).
(*f*) Tagalog, "The Monkey and the Turtle" (JAFL 21 : 46).
(*g*) Tinguian, "The Turtle and the Monkey" (Cole, 195, No. 77).
(*h*) Tagalog, Rizal's "Monkey and the Turtle." [1]

Before discussing the origin of the story, we may examine the different incidents found in the Philippine versions. That they vary considerably may be seen from the following list: —

A The division of the banana-stalk: monkey takes top; and turtle, roots. Monkey's share dies, turtle's grows: or (A[1]) monkey and turtle together find banana-tree growing; turtle unable to climb, but monkey easily gets at the fruit.

B Monkey steals turtle's bananas and will not give him any, or (B[1]) sticks banana up his anus and throws it to turtle, or (B[2]) drops his excrement into turtle's mouth.

C Turtle, in revenge, plants sharp stakes (or thorns) around base of the banana-tree; and when monkey descends, he is severely injured, or (C[1]) he is killed.

D Turtle sells monkey-flesh to other monkeys; either his trick is discovered accidentally by the monkeys, or (D[1]) the turtle jeers them for eating of their kind.

E Turtle is sentenced to death. He says, "You may burn me or pound me, but for pity's sake don't drown me!" The monkeys "drown" the turtle, and he escapes.

[1] Unfortunately this work is inaccessible at present, and I am unable to indicate definitely its episodes. It contains nothing unique, however.

F The monkeys attempt to drink all the water in the lake, so as to reach the turtle: they burst themselves and perish. Or (F¹) they get a fish to drain the pond dry; fish is punctured by a bird, water rushes out, and monkeys are drowned. Or (F²) monkeys summon all the other animals to help them drink the lake dry. The animals put leaves over the ends of their urethras, so that the water will not flow out; but a bird pecks the leaves away, and the monkeys turn to revenge themselves on the bird. (F³) They catch him and pluck out all his feathers; but the bird recovers, and revenges himself as below (G).

G Monkeys and other animals are enticed to a fruit-tree in a meadow, and are burned to death in a jungle fire kindled by the turtle and his friend the bird.

H Episode of guarding king's fruit-tree or bread-tree (Chile peppers).

J Episode of guarding king's belt (boa-constrictor).

K Turtle deceives monkey with his answers, so that the monkey thinks part of his own body is mocking him. Enraged, he strikes himself with a stone until he dies.

L Turtle captured by hunter gets monkey to exchange places with him by pointing out the advantages of the situation. Monkey subsequently shot by the hunter.

These incidents are distributed as follows:—

Version (a).... ABC¹DE
Version (b).... ABCHJK
Version (c).... (Opening different, but monkey greedy as in B) L
Version (d).... A¹B²C¹D¹EF²F³G
Version (e).... ABC¹DEF¹
Version (f).... A¹BC (glass on trunk of tree) EF (monkey in his rage leaps after turtle and is drowned)
Version (g).... AB¹C¹ (sharp shells) DEF (monkeys dive in to catch fish when they see turtle appear with one in his mouth, and are drowned). Incidents K and a form of J are found in the story of "The Turtle and the Lizard" (Cole, 196)

The incidents common to most of these versions are some form of ABCDEF; and these, I think, we must consider as integral parts of the story. It will be seen that one of our versions (c) properly does not belong to this cycle at all, except under a very broad definition of the group. In all these tales the turtle is the injured creature: he is represented as patient and quiet, but clever. The monkey is depicted as selfish, mischievous, insolent, but stupid. In general, although the versions differ in details, they are all the same story, in that they tell how a monkey insults a turtle which has done him no harm, and how he finally pays dearly for his insult.

The oldest account I know of, telling of the contests between the monkey and the turtle, is a Buddhist birth-story, the "Kacchapa-jātaka," No. 273, which narrates how a monkey insulted a tortoise by thrusting his penis down the sleeping tortoise's throat, and how the monkey was punished. Although this particular obscene jest is

not found in any of our versions, I think that there is a trace of it
preserved in the Bagobo story. The passage runs thus (*loc. cit.* pp. 59–
60): "At that all the monkeys were angry [incident D], and ran
screaming to catch the tortoise. But the tortoise hid under the felled
trunk of an old *palma brava* tree. As each monkey passed close by
the trunk where the tortoise lay concealed, the tortoise said, 'Drag
(or lower) your membrum! Here's a felled tree.' Thus every monkey
passed by clear of the trunk, until the last one came by; and he was
both blind and deaf. When he followed the rest, he could not hear
the tortoise call out, and his membrum struck against the fallen trunk.
He stopped, and became aware of the tortoise underneath. Then
he screamed to the rest; and all the monkeys came running back, and
surrounded the tortoise, threatening him." This incident, in its
present form obscure and unreasonable (it is hard to see how following
the tortoise's directions would have saved the monkeys from injury,
and how the *blind and deaf* monkey "became aware" of the tortoise
just because he hit the tree), probably originally represented the
tortoise as seizing the last monkey with his teeth (present form, "his
membrum struck against the fallen trunk"), so that in this way the
monkey became painfully aware of the tortoise's close proximity.
Hence his screams, too, — of pain. With incident B² two other Buddhist stories are to be compared. The "Mahisa-jātaka," No. 278,
tells how an impudent monkey voids his excrement on a patient
buffalo (the Bodhisatta) under a tree. The vile monkey is later
destroyed when he plays the same trick on another bull. In the
"Kapi-jātaka," No. 404, a bad monkey drops his excrement first on
the head and then into the mouth of a priest, who later takes revenge
on the monkey by having him and all his following of five hundred
destroyed. All in all, the agreement in general outline and in some
details between these Hindoo stories and ours justifies us, I believe,
in assuming without hesitation that our stories are descended directly
from Buddhistic fables, possibly these very Jātakas. Compare also
the notes to Nos. 48 and 56.

For a Celebes variant of the story of "The Monkey and the Turtle,"
see Bezemer, p. 287.

The sources of the other incidents, which I have not found in the
Buddhistic stories, I am unable to point out. However, many of
them occur in the beast tales of other Oriental and Occidental countries: for instance, incident E is a commonplace in "Brer Rabbit"
stories both in Africa and America, whence it has made its way into
the tales of the American Indians (see, for example, Honeÿ, 82; Cole,
195, note; Dähnhardt, 4 : 43–45); incident J and another droll episode
found in an Ilocano story — "king's bell" (= beehive) *motif* — occur
in a Milanau tale from Sarawak, Borneo, "The Plandok, Deer, and

the Pig" (Roth, I : 347), and in two other North Borneo stories given by Evans (p. 474), "Plandok and Bear" and "Plandok and Tiger." In Malayan stories in general, the mouse-deer (*plandok*) is represented as the cleverest of animals, taking the rôle of the rabbit in African tales, and of the jackal in Hindoo. In the Ilocano story referred to, both these incidents — "king's belt" and "king's bell" — are found, though the rest of the tale belongs to the "Carancal" group (No. 3; see also No. 4 [b]). Incident L is found among the Negroes of South Africa (Honeÿ, 84, where the two animals are a monkey and a jackal). With incident G compare a Tibetan story (Ralston, No. XLII), where men take counsel as to how to kill a troop of monkeys that are destroying their corn. The plan is to cut down all the trees which stand about the place, one Tinduka-tree only being allowed to remain. A hedge of thorns is drawn about the open space, and the monkeys are to be killed inside the enclosure when they climb the tree in search of food. The monkeys escape, however; for another monkey goes and fires the village, thus distracting the attention of the men. Incident D, the Thyestean banquet, is widespread throughout European saga and *Märchen* literature: but even this incident Cosquin (I : xxxix) connects with India through an Annamite tale. With incident F³ compare a story from British North Borneo (Evans, 429–430), in which the adjutant-bird (*lungun*) and the tortoise revenge themselves on monkeys. The monkeys pull out all of the bird's feathers while it is asleep. In two months the feathers grow in again, and the bird seeks vengeance. It gets the tortoise to help it by placing its body in a large hole in the bottom of a boat, so that the water will not leak in; the bird then sails the boat. The monkeys want a ride, and the bird lets forty-one of them in. When the boat is out in the ocean and begins to roll, the bird advises the monkeys to tie their tails together two and two and sit on the edge of the boat to steady it. Then the bird flies away, the tortoise drops out of the hole, and the boat sinks. All the monkeys are drowned but the odd one.

56. THE MONKEY AND THE CROCODILE.

(a) *Tagalog Version.*[1]

One day, while a clever monkey was searching for his food along the river-bank, he saw a tall *macopa*-tree laden with ripe fruits. The tree was standing just by the shore of a river where a young crocodile lived. After eating all the fruit he wanted, the monkey climbed down the tree. He suddenly conceived the desire of getting on the other side of the wide river, but he found no means by which to cross. At last he saw the crocodile,

---

[1] Narrated by Engracio Abasola of Manila. He heard the story from his nephew.

who had just waked up from his siesta; and the monkey said to him in a friendly way, "My dear crocodile, will you do me a favor?"

The crocodile was greatly surprised by this amicable salutation of the monkey. However, he answered humbly, "Oh, yes! If there is anything I can do for you, I shall be glad to do it." The monkey then told the crocodile that he wanted to reach the other side of the river. Then the crocodile said, "I'll take you over with all my heart. Just sit on my back, and we'll go at once."

When the monkey was firmly seated on the crocodile's back, they began their trip. In a short while they reached the middle of the stream, and the crocodile began to laugh aloud. "Now, you foolish monkey!" it said, "I'll eat your liver and kidneys, for I'm very hungry." The monkey became nervous; but he concealed his anxiety, and said, "To be sure! I thought myself that you might be hungry: so I prepared my liver and kidneys for your dinner; but unfortunately, in our haste to depart, I left them hanging on the macopa-tree. I'm very glad that you mentioned the matter. Let us return, and I'll get you the food."

The foolish crocodile, convinced that the monkey was telling the truth, turned back toward the shore they had just left. When they were near, the monkey nimbly jumped on to the dry land and scampered up the tree. When the crocodile saw how he had been deceived, he said, "I am a fool."

(b) *Zambal Version.*[1]

One stormy day a monkey was standing by the shore of a river, wondering how he could get to the other side. He could not get over by himself; for the water was deep, and he did not know how to swim. He looked about for some logs; but all he saw was a large crocodile with its mouth wide open, ready to seize him. He was very much frightened; but he said, "O Mr. Crocodile! pray, do not kill me! Spare my life, and I will lead you to a place where you can get as many monkeys as will feed you all your life."

The crocodile agreed, and the monkey said that the place was on the other side of the river. So the crocodile told him to get on his back, and he would carry him across. Just before

[1] Narrated by Leopoldo Uichanco, a Tagalog, who heard the story from a native of Zambales.

they reached the bank, the monkey jumped to land, ran as fast as he could, and climbed up a tree where his mate was. The crocodile could not follow, of course: so he returned to the water, saying, "The time will come when you shall pay."

Not long afterwards the monkey found the crocodile lying motionless, as if dead. About the place were some low Chile pepper-bushes loaded with numerous bright-red fruits like ornaments on a Christmas tree. The monkey approached the crocodile, and began playing with his tail; but the crocodile made a sudden spring, and seized the monkey so tightly that he could not escape. "Think first, think first!" said the monkey. "Mark you, Mr. Crocodile! I am now the cook of his Majesty the king. Those bright-red breads have been intrusted to my care," and the monkey pointed to the pepper-shrubs. "The moment you kill me, the king will arrive with thousands of well-armed troops, and will punish you."

The crocodile was frightened by what the monkey said. "Mr. Monkey, I did not mean to harm you," he said. "I will set you free if you will let me eat only as many pieces of bread as will relieve my hunger."

"Eat all you can," responded the monkey kindly. "Take as many as you please. They are free to you."

Without another word, the crocodile let the monkey go, and rushed at the heavily-laden bushes. The monkey slipped away secretly, and climbed up a tree, where he could enjoy the discomfiture of his voracious friend. The crocodile began to cough, sneeze, and scratch his tongue. When he rushed to the river to cool his mouth, the monkey only laughed at him.

MORAL: Use your own judgment; do not rely on the counsel of others, for it is the father of destruction and ruin.

NOTES.

Like the monkey and the turtle, the monkey and the crocodile have been traditional enemies from time immemorial. In our present group of stories, however, the rôles are reversed: the monkey is clever; the water-animal (crocodile), cruel and stupid. Two very early forms of this tale are the "Vānarinda-jātaka," No. 57, which tells how the crocodile lay on a rock to catch the monkey, and how the latter outwitted the crocodile; and the "Suṁsumāra-jātaka," No. 208, in which a crocodile wanted the heart of a monkey, and the monkey pretended that it was hanging on a fig-tree. From the Buddhistic writings the story made its way into the famous collection known as the "Kalilah and Dimnah," of which it forms the ninth chapter in De Sacy's edition, and the fifth section in the later Syriac version (English translation by I. G. N. Keith-Falconer, Cambridge, 1885). In the "Pancatantra" this story forms the framework for the fourth book. For a discussion of the variations this tale underwent when it passed over into other collections and spread through Europe, see Benfey, 1 : 421 ff. Apparently Benfey did not know of these two Buddhistic birth-stories; but he has shown very ingeniously that most of the fables in the "Pancatantra" go back to Buddhistic writings. Nor can there be any doubt in this case, either, though it is not to be supposed that the five hundred and forty-seven Jātakas were invented by the Buddhistic scribes who wrote them down. Many of them are far older than Buddhism.

Our Zambal form of the story does not represent the purest version. A variant much closer to the Buddhistic and close to the Tagalog is a tale collected by Wenceslao Vitug of Lubao, Pampanga. He says that the story is very common throughout his province, and is well known in the Visayas. His version follows in abstract form: —

A crocodile goes out to look for a monkey-liver for his wife, who is confined at home. As the crocodile starts to cross a stream, a monkey asks for passage on its back. The crocodile gladly complies, and, on arriving in mid-stream, laughs at the credulous monkey, and tells him that he must have a monkey-liver. The monkey says, "Why didn't you tell me before? There's one on a tree near the bank we just left." The simple crocodile went back to the bank, whereupon the monkey escaped and scrambled up into a tree to laugh at the crocodile. The crocodile then tried to "play dead," but he could not fool the monkey. Next he decided to go to the monkey's house. The monkey, suspecting his design, said aloud, "When no one is in my house, it answers when I call." The crocodile inside was foolish enough to answer when the monkey called to his house, and the monkey ran away laughing.

Our Zambal story has evidently been contaminated with the story of "The Monkey and the Turtle;" for it lacks the characteristic incident of the monkey-heart (or liver), and contains incident H from our No. 55. However, it does preserve an allusion to the principal episode of the cycle, — in the ride the monkey takes on the crocodile's back across the stream. Other Oriental versions of the "heart on tree" incident are the following: Chinese, S. Beal's "Romantic Legend of Sâkya Buddha" (London, 1875), pp. 231–234, where a dragon takes the place of the crocodile; Swahili, Steere, p. i, where, instead of a crocodile, we have a shark (so also Bateman, No. 1); Japanese, W. E. Griffis's "Japanese Fairy World," p. 144, where the sea-animal is a jelly-fish. An interesting Russian variant, in which a fox takes the place of the monkey, is printed in the Cambridge Jātaka, 2 : 110.

Once upon a time the king of the fishes was wanting in wisdom. His advisers told him that, once he could get the heart of a fox, he would become wise. So he sent a deputation consisting of the great magnates of the sea, — whales and others. "Our king wants your advice on some state affairs." The fox, flattered, consented. A whale took him on his back. On the way the waves beat upon him. At last he asked what they really wanted. They said what their king really wanted was to eat his heart, by which he hoped to become clever. He said, "Why didn't you tell me that before? I would gladly sacrifice my life for such a worthy object. But we foxes always leave our hearts at home. Take me back, and I'll fetch it. Otherwise I'm sure your king will be angry." So they took him back. As soon as he got near to the shore, he leaped on land, and cried, "Ah, you fools! Have you ever heard of an animal not carrying his heart with him?" and ran off. The fish had to return empty.

A reminiscence of this incident is also found in Steel-Temple, No. xxi, "The Jackal and the Partridge," where a partridge induces a crocodile to carry her and the jackal across a river, and *en route* suggests that he should upset the jackal, but at last dissuades him by saying that the jackal had left his life behind him on the other shore. Related to our Zambal story are two modern Indian folk-tales in which a jackal is substituted for the monkey (this substitution is analogous to the Indian substitution of the jackal for the Philippines monkey in the "Puss-in-Boots" cycle). In the first of these — Frere, No. xxiv, "The Alligator and the Jackal" — we have the incident of the house answering when the owner calls. In Steel-Temple, No. xxxi, "The Jackal and the Crocodile," the jackal makes love to the crocodile, and induces her, under promise of marriage, to swim him across a stream to some fruit he wants to eat. When she has brought him back, he says that he thinks it may be a long time before he can make arrangements for the wedding. The crocodile, in revenge, watches till he comes to drink, and then seizes him by the leg. The jackal tells her that she has got hold of a root instead of his leg: so she lets go, and he escapes. Next she goes to his den to wait for him, and shams dead. When the jackal sees her, he says that the dead always wag their tails. The crocodile wags hers, and the jackal skips off. Closely connected with this last is a story by Rouse, No. 20, "The Cunning Jackal," only here the jackal's opponent is a turtle. The original, unadapted story runs thus as given in the notes by Mr. Rouse: —

Jackal sees melons on the other side of the river. Sees a tortoise. "How are you and your family?" — "I am well, but I have no wife." — "Why did you not tell me? Some people on the other side have asked me to find a match for their daughter." — "If you mean it, I will take you across." Takes him across on his back. When the melons are over (gone?), the jackal dresses up a *jhan*-tree as a bride. "There is your bride, but she is too modest to speak till I am gone." Tortoise carries him back. Calls to the stump. No answer. — Goes up and touches it. Finds it a tree.

Vows revenge. As jackal drinks, catches his leg. "You fool! you have got hold of a stump by mistake; see, here is my leg!" pointing to stump. Tortoise leaves hold, Jackal escapes. Tortoise goes to jackal's den. Jackal returns, and sees the footprints leading into the den. Piles dry leaves at the mouth, and fires them. Tortoise expires.

Compare also a Borneo tale of a mouse-deer and a crocodile (Evans, 475). In a Santal story (Bompas, No. CXXIII, "The Jackal and the Leopards") a jackal tricks some leopards. In the second half he outwits a crocodile. Crocodile seizes jackal's leg. Jackal: "What a fool of a crocodile to seize a tree instead of my leg!" Crocodile lets go, and jackal escapes. Crocodile hides in a straw-stack to wait for jackal. Jackal comes along wearing a sheep-bell it has found. Crocodile says, "What a bother! Here comes a sheep, and I am waiting for the jackal." Jackal hears the exclamation, burns the straw-stack, and kills the crocodile.

The "Vānarinda-jātaka," No. 57, contains what I believe is the original of the "house-answering owner" droll episode in our Pampangan variant. The monkey suspected the crocodile of lurking on the rock to catch him: so he shouted, "Hi, rock!" three times, but received no answer. Then he said, "How comes it, Friend Rock, that you won't answer me to-day?" The crocodile, thinking that perhaps it was the custom of the rock to return the greeting, answered for the rock; whereupon the monkey knew of his presence, and escaped by a trick. The "house-answering owner" episode is also found in a Zanzibar tale of "The Hare and the Lion" (Bateman, No. 2, pp. 42–43). The hare here suggests a Buddhistic source.

Of all the modern Oriental forms of the story, our Tagalog version and Pampangan variant are closest to the Jātakas, and we may conclude without hesitation that they mark a direct line of descent from India. The fact that the story is popular in many parts of the Islands makes it highly improbable that it was re-introduced to the Orient through a Spanish translation of the "Kalilah and Dimnah."

For further bibliography and discussion of this cycle, see Dähnhardt, 4 : 1–26.

57. THE MONKEYS AND THE DRAGON-FLIES.[1]

One day, when the sun was at the zenith and the air was very hot, a poor dragon-fly, fatigued with her long journey, alighted to rest on a branch of a tree in which a great many monkeys lived. While she was fanning herself with her wings, a monkey approached her, and said, "Aha! What are you doing here, wretched creature?"

---

[1] Narrated by Pedro D. L. Sorreta, a Bicol from Albay, who says that the story is very common in the island of Catanduanes.

"O sir! I wish you would permit me to rest on this branch while the sun is so hot," said the dragon-fly softly. "I have been flying all morning, and I am so hot and tired that I can go no farther," she added.

"Indeed!" exclaimed the monkey in a mocking tone. "We don't allow any weak creature such as you are to stay under our shelter. Go away!" he said angrily, and, taking a dry twig, he threw it at the poor creature.

The dragon-fly, being very quick, had flown away before the cruel monkey could hit her. She hurried to her brother the king, and told him what had happened. The king became very angry, and resolved to make war on the monkeys. So he despatched three of his soldiers to the king of the monkeys with this challenge: —

The King of the Monkeys.

"Sir, — As one of your subjects has treated my sister cruelly, I am resolved to kill you and your subjects with all speed.

DRAGON.

The monkey-king laughed at the challenge. He said to the messengers, "Let your king and his soldiers come to the battle-field, and they will see how well my troops fight."

"You don't mean what you say, cruel king," answered the messengers. "You should not judge before the fight is over."

"What fools, what fools!" exclaimed the king of the monkeys. "Go to your ruler and tell him my answer," and he drove the poor little creatures away.

When the king of the dragon-flies received the reply, he immediately ordered his soldiers to go to the battle-field, but without anything to fight with. Meanwhile the monkeys came, each armed with a heavy stick. Then the monkey-king shouted, "Strike the flying creatures with your clubs!" When King Dragon heard this order, he commanded his soldiers to alight on the foreheads of their enemies. Then the monkeys began to strike at the dragon-flies, which were on the foreheads of their companions. The dragon-flies were very quick, and were not hurt at all: but the monkeys were all killed. Thus the light, quick-witted dragon-flies won the victory over the strong but foolish monkeys.

NOTES.

A Visayan variant, "The Ape and the Firefly" (JAFL 20 : 314) shows the firefly making use of the same ruse the dragon-flies employ to get the monkeys to slay one another. The first part of this variant is connected with our No. 60. The "killing fly on head" incident we have already met with in No. 9, in the notes to which I have pointed out Buddhistic parallels. It also occurs in No. 60 (*d*). In a German story (Grimm, No. 68, "The Dog and the Sparrow") the sparrow employs the same trick to bring ruin and death on a heartless wagoner who has cruelly run over the dog.

A closer analogue is the Celebes fable of "The Butterfly and the Ten Monkeys," given in Bezemer, p. 292.

Our story belongs to the large cycle of tales in which is represented a war between the winged creatures of the air and the four-footed beasts. In these stories, as Grimm says in his notes to No. 102, "The Willow-Wren and the Bear," "the leading idea is the cunning of the small creatures triumphing over the large ones. . . . The willow-wren is the ruler, for the saga accepts the least as king as readily as the greatest." For the bibliography of the cycle and related cycles, see Bolte-Polívka, 1 : 517–519, and 2 : 435–438, to which add the "Latukika-jātaka," No. 357, which tells how a quail brought about the destruction of an elephant that had killed her young ones. I am inclined to think that the Bicol and Visayan stories belonging to this group are native — at least, have not been derived through the Spanish.

I have another Visayan story, however, relating a war between the land and the air creatures, which may possibly have come from the Occident. It was narrated by José R. Cuadra, and runs thus : —

THE BATTLE BETWEEN THE BIRDS AND THE BEASTS.

A great discussion once took place between the lion, king of the land-animals, and the bat, king of the air-animals, over the relative strength of each. The lion claimed to be more powerful than the bat, while the bat claimed to be more powerful than the lion. The final outcome was a declaration of war. The lion then called a general meeting of all his subjects. Among them were tigers, leopards, elephants, carabaos, wolves, and other fierce land-animals. The carabao was appointed leader of the army. Each animal in turn made a speech to the king, promising a sure victory for him. At the same time the bat also called a general meeting of his subjects. There were present all kinds of birds and insects. The leadership of the army was given to the bees and the wasps. Early in the morning the two opposing armies were assembled on the battle-field. At a given signal the battle began. The land-animals tried to chase the air-animals, but in vain, for they could not leave the ground. The bees and wasps were busy stinging the eyes and bodies of their enemy. At last the land-animals retired defeated, because they could not endure longer their severe punishment.

58. THE MONKEY, THE TURTLE, AND THE CROCODILE.[1]

There was once a monkey who used to deceive everybody whom he met. As is the case with most deceivers, he had many enemies who tried to kill him.

One day, while he was walking in the streets of his native town, he met in a by-lane a turtle and a crocodile. They were so tired that they could hardly breathe. "I'll try to deceive these slow creatures of the earth," said the monkey to himself. So said, so done. He approached the crocodile and turtle, and said to them, "My dear sirs, you are so tired that you can hardly move! Where did you come from?"

The two travellers were so much affected by the kind words of the monkey, that they told him all about themselves with the greatest candor imaginable. They said, "We are strangers who have just made a long journey from our native town. We don't know where to get food or where to spend this cold night."

"I'll conduct you to a place where you can spend the night and get all you want to eat," said the monkey.

"All right," said the two travellers. "Lead on! for we are very hungry and at the same time very tired."

"Follow me," said the crafty monkey.

The turtle and the crocodile followed the monkey, and soon he brought them to a field full of ripe pumpkins. "Eat all the pumpkins you want, and then rest here. Meanwhile I'll go home and take my sleep, too."

While the two hungry travellers were enjoying a hearty meal, the owner of the plantation happened to pass by. When he saw the crocodile, he called to his laborers, and told them to bring long poles and their bolos. The turtle clung to the tail of the crocodile, and away they went.

"Don't cling to my tail! Don't cling to my tail!" said the crocodile. "I cannot run fast if you cling to my tail. Let go! for the men will soon overtake us."

"I have to cling to your tail," said the turtle, "or else there will be no one to push you."

But their attempt to escape was unsuccessful. The men overtook them and killed them both. Such was the unhappy end of the turtle and the crocodile.

MORAL: Never trust a new friend or an old enemy.

[1] Narrated by Vicente Hilario, a Tagalog from Batangas. He heard the story from his father, who said that it is common among the country people around Batangas town.

NOTES.

I know of no exact parallels for this story, though the character of the monkey as depicted here is similar to that in No. 55. Compare with it the rôle of the deceitful jackal in some of the South African stories (e.g., Metelerkamp, No. v; Honeÿ, 22, 24, 45, 105, etc.). This may be a sort of "compensation story," manufactured long ago, however, in which the monkey gets even with his two traditional opponents, the crocodile and the turtle.

59. THE IGUANA AND THE TURTLE.[1]

Once upon a time there lived two good friends, — an iguana and a turtle. They always went fishing together. One day the turtle invited the iguana to go catch fish in a certain pond that he knew of. After they had been there about two hours, the old man who owned the pond came along. The iguana escaped, but the turtle was caught. The old man took the turtle home, tied a string around its neck, and fastened it under the house.

Early in the morning the iguana went to look for his friend the turtle. The iguana wandered everywhere looking for him, and finally he found him under the old man's house, tied to a post.

"What are you doing here, my friend?" said the iguana.

"That old man wants me to marry his daughter, but I do not want to marry her," said the turtle.

Now, the iguana very much wanted a wife, and he was delighted at this chance. So he asked the turtle to be allowed to take his place. The turtle consented. So the iguana released the turtle, and was tied up in his place. Then the turtle made off as fast as he could.

When the old man woke up, he heard some one saying over and over again, "I want to marry your daughter." He became angry, and went down under the house to see who was talking. There he found the iguana saying, "I want to marry your daughter." The old man picked up a big stick to beat its head, but the iguana cut the string and ran away.

On his way he came across the turtle again, who was listening to the sound produced by the rubbing of two bamboos when the wind blew. "What! are you here again?" said the iguana.

---

[1] Narrated by Sixto Guico of Binalonan, Pangasinan, who says that the story is fairly common among the Pangasinanes.

"Be quiet!" said the turtle. "I am listening to the pipe of my grandfather up there. Don't you hear it?"

The iguana wanted to see the turtle's grandfather, so he climbed up the tree, and put his mouth between the two bamboos that were rubbing together. His mouth was badly pinched, and he fell down to the ground. The turtle meanwhile had disappeared.

MORAL: This teaches that the one who believes foolishly will be injured.

NOTES.

This story is doubtless native. A Tinguian tale related to ours is given by Cole (No. 78), whose abstract runs thus: —

A turtle and lizard go to steal ginger. The lizard talks so loudly that he attracts the attention of the owner. The turtle hides; but the lizard runs, and is pursued by the man. The turtle enters the house, and hides under a cocoanut-shell. When the man sits on the shell, the turtle calls. He cannot discover source of noise, and thinks it comes from his testicles. He strikes these with a stone, and dies. The turtle and the lizard see a bees' nest. The lizard hastens to get it, and is stung. They see a bird-snare, and turtle claims it as the necklace of his father. Lizard runs to get it, but is caught and killed.

Some of the incidents found in the Tinguian story we have met with in No. 55; e.g., episodes K, J, L, and "king's bell." Indeed, there appears to be a close connection between the "Monkey and Turtle" group and this story. A Borneo tale of the mouse-deer (*plandok*), small turtle (*kikura*), long-tailed monkey (*kra*), and bear contains the "king's necklace" incident, and many other situations worthy of notice. A brief summary of the droll, which may be found in Roth, 1 : 342–346, is here given: —

The Kikura deceives the Plandok with the necklace sell (snare), and the Plandok is caught. When the hunter comes up, the little animal feigns death, and is thrown away. Immediately it jumps up, and is off to revenge itself on the turtle. It entices the turtle into a covered pit by pretending to give it a good place to sleep. Man examining pitfall discovers turtle, and fastens it with a forked stick. Monkey comes along, exchanges places with the turtle, but escapes with his life by feigning dead, as did the Plandok. Monkey, turtle, and Plandok go fishing. Monkey steals ride across stream on back of good-natured fish, which he later treacherously kills. The three friends prepare the fish, and Bruin comes along. Fearing the size of the bear's appetite, they send him to wash the pan; and when he returns, fish, monkey, turtle, and mouse-deer have disappeared.

The escape of snared animals and birds by shamming dead, and then making off when the hunter or fowler throws them aside as worthless, is commonly met with in Buddhistic fables.

60. (a) THE TRIAL AMONG THE ANIMALS.[1]

In ancient times Sinukuan, the judge of the animals, lived in one of the caves of Mount Arayat. He had formerly lived in a neighboring town; but, since he was so brave and strong, the people began to envy him, then to hate him. At last they made so many plots against his life, that he gave up all his property and friends in the town, and went to live in Mount Arayat, where he devoted all his time to gaining the friendship of the animals there.

Now, it was not hard for Sinukuan to win the love of the animals, for he had the power of changing himself into whatever form he pleased; and he always took the form of those animals who came to him. It was not long before all the animals realized the power, wisdom, and justice of their good companion, so they made him their judge.

One day a bird came to Sinukuan's court, and asked Sinukuan to punish the frog for being so noisy during the night, while it was trying to sleep. Sinukuan summoned the troublesome frog, and asked him the reason for his misbehavior. The frog answered respectfully, "Sir, I was only crying for help, because the turtle was carrying his house on his back, and I feared that I might be buried under it."

"That is good enough reason," said Sinukuan; "you are free."

The turtle was the next to be summoned to Sinukuan's court. On his arrival, he humbly replied to the question of the judge, "Honorable Judge, I carried my house with me, because the firefly was playing with fire, and I was afraid he might set fire to my home. Is it not right to protect one's house from fire?"

"A very good reason; you are free," said Sinukuan.

In the same way the firefly was brought to court the next day; and when the judge asked him why he was playing with fire, he said in a soft voice, "It was because I have no other means with which to protect myself from the sharp-pointed dagger of the mosquito." This seemed a reasonable answer, so the firefly was liberated too.

Finally the mosquito was tried; and, since he did not have any good reason to give for carrying his dagger, Sinukuan sentenced him to three days' imprisonment. The mosquito was obliged to submit; and it was during this confinement of the mosquito that he lost his voice. Ever since, the male

[1] Narrated by Domingo Pineda of Pampanga.

mosquito has had no voice; and he has been afraid to carry his dagger, for fear of greater punishment.

(b) THE PUGU'S CASE.[1]

"Why, horse," said the *pugu* (a small bird), "did you touch my eggs, so that now they are broken?"

"Because," said the horse, "the cock crowed, and I was startled."

"Why, cock," said the *pugu*, "did you crow, so that the horse was startled and broke my eggs?"

"Because," said the cock, "I saw the turtle carrying his house; that made me crow."

"Why, turtle," said the *pugu*, "did you carry your house with you, so that the cock crowed, and the horse was startled and broke my eggs?"

"Because," said the turtle, "the firefly was carrying fire, and I was afraid that he would burn my house."

"Why, firefly," said the *pugu*, "did you bring fire, so that the turtle was frightened and carried his house, and the cock crowed when he saw him, and the horse was startled and broke my eggs?"

"Because," said the firefly, "the mosquito will sting me if I have no light."

"Why, mosquito," said the *pugu*, "did you try to sting the firefly, so that he had to carry fire, so that the turtle was frightened and carried his house, so that the cock laughed at the turtle, so that the horse was startled and broke my eggs?"

"Because," said the mosquito, "Juan put up his mosquito-net, and there was nobody for me to sting except the firefly (*alipatpat.*)"

"Why, Juan," said the *pugu*, "did you put up your mosquito-net? The mosquito could not sting you, and tried to harm the firefly; the firefly brought fire; the turtle was frightened, and carried his house with him; the cock crowed when he saw the turtle; the horse was startled when he heard the cock, and broke my eggs."

"Because," said Juan, "I did not care to lose any blood."

[1] Narrated by Bienvenido Tan of Manila, who got the story from Pampanga.

(c) WHY MOSQUITOES HUM AND TRY TO GET INTO THE HOLES
OF OUR EARS.[1]

A long time ago, when the world was much quieter and younger than it is now, people told and believed many strange stories about wonderful things which none of us have ever seen. In those very early times, in the province of Bohol, there lived a creature called Mangla;[2] he was king of the crabs.

One night, as he was very tired and sleepy, Mangla ordered his old sheriff, Cagang,[3] leader of the small land-crabs, to call his followers, Bataktak,[4] before him. Although the sheriff was old, yet he brought them all in in a very short time. Then Mangla said to the Bataktak, "You must all watch my house while I am sleeping; but do not make any noise that will waken me." The Bataktak said, "We are always ready to obey you." So Mangla went to sleep.

While he was snoring, it began to rain so hard that the guards could not help laughing. The king awoke very angry; but, as he was still very tired and sleepy, he did not immediately ask the Bataktak why they laughed. He waited till morning came. So, as soon as the sun shone, he called the Bataktak, and said to them, "Why did you laugh last night? Did I not tell you not to make any noise?"

The Bataktak answered softly, "We could not help laughing, because last night we saw our old friend Hu-man [5] carrying his house on his shoulder." On account of this reasonable reply, the king pardoned the Bataktak. Then he called his sheriff, and told him to summon Hu-man. In a short time he came. The king at once said to him, "What did you do last night?"

"Sir," replied Hu-man humbly, "I was carrying my house, because Aninipot [6] was bringing fire, and I was afraid that my only dwelling would be burned." This answer seemed reasonable to the king, so he pardoned Hu-man. Then he told his sheriff Cagang to summon Aninipot. When Aninipot appeared, the king, with eyes flashing with anger, said to the culprit, "Why were you carrying fire last night?"

[1] Narrated by Fermin Torralba, a Visayan from Tagbilaran, Bohol. He heard the story from an old man of his province.

[2] *Mangla,* big land-crabs.

[3] *Cagang,* small land-crabs.

[4] *Bataktak,* non-edible frogs.

[5] *Hu-man,* land-snails.

[6] *Aninipot,* fireflies.

Aninipot was very much frightened, but he did not lose his wits. In a trembling voice he answered, "Sir, I was carrying fire, because Lamoc[1] was always trying to bite me. To protect myself, I am going to carry fire all the time." The king thought that Aninipot had a good reason, so he pardoned him also.

The king now realized that there was a great deal of trouble brewing in his kingdom, of which he would not have been aware if he had not been awakened by the Bataktak. So he sent his sheriff to get Lamoc. In a short time Cagang appeared with Lamoc. But Lamoc, before he left his own house, had told all his companions to follow him, for he expected trouble. Before Lamoc reached the palace, the king was already shouting with rage, so Lamoc approached the king and bit his face. Then Mangla cried out, "It is true, what I heard from Bataktak, Hu-man, and Aninipot!" The king at once ordered his sheriff to kill Lamoc; but, before Cagang could carry out the order, the companions of Lamoc rushed at him. He killed Lamoc, however, and then ran to his home, followed by Lamoc's friends, who were bent on avenging the murder. As Cagang's house was very deep under the ground, Lamoc's friends could not get in, so they remained and hummed around the door.

Even to-day we can see that at the doors of the houses of Cagang and his followers there are many friends of Lamoc humming and trying to go inside. It is said that the Lamoc mistake the holes of our ears for the house of Cagang, and that that is the reason mosquitoes hum about our ears now.

(d) A TYRANT.[2]

Once there lived a tyrannical king. One of his laws prohibited the people from talking loudly. Even when this law had been put in force, he still was not satisfied: so he ordered the law to be enforced among the animals.

One of his officers once heard a frog croak. The officer caught the frog and carried it before the king. The king began the trial by saying, "Don't you know that there is a law prohibiting men and animals from making a noise?"

"Yes, your Majesty," said the frog, "but I could not help

[1] *Lamoc*, mosquitoes.
[2] Narrated by Facundo Esquivel of Jaen, Nueva Ecija. This is a Tagalog story.

laughing to see the snail carrying his house with him wherever he goes."

The king was satisfied with the frog's answer, so he dismissed him and called the snail. "Why do you always carry your house with you?" asked the king.

"Because," said the snail, "I am always afraid the firefly is going to burn it." The king next ordered the firefly to appear before him. The king then said to the firefly, "Why do you carry fire with you always?"

"Because the mosquitoes will bite me if I do not carry this fire," said the firefly. This answer seemed reasonable to the king, so he summoned the mosquito. When the mosquito was asked why he was always trying to bite some one, he said, "Why, sir, I cannot live without biting somebody."

The king was tired of the long trial, so with the mosquito he determined to end it. After hearing the answer of the mosquito, he said, "From now on you must not bite anybody. You have no right to do so." The mosquito tried to protest the sentence, but the king seized his mallet and determined to crush the mosquito with it. When the mosquito saw what the king was going to do, he alighted on the forehead of the king. The king became very angry at this insult, and hit the mosquito hard. He killed the mosquito, but he also put an end to his own tyranny.

MORAL: It is foolish to carry matters to extremes.

NOTES.

A fifth form (*e*) of this "clock" story is "The Bacuit's Case," narrated by W. Vitug of Lubao, Pampanga. As I have this tale only in abstract, I give it here in that form: —

The *bacuit* (small, light gray bird which haunts marshes and ponds) went to the eagle-king and brought suit against the frog because the latter croaked all night, thus keeping the *bacuit* awake. The frog said he croaked for fear of the turtle, who always carried his house with him. The turtle, being summoned, explained that he carried his house with him for fear that the firefly would set it on fire. The firefly, in turn, showed that it was necessary for him to carry his lamp in order to find his food.

There is a striking agreement of incident in all these stories, as may be seen from the following abstracts of the versions.

Version *a* (Pampango), "Trial among Animals," Bird *vs.* frog; frog *vs.* turtle; turtle *vs.* firefly; firefly *vs.* mosquito.

Version *b* (Pampango), "The Pugu's Case" . . Pugu *vs.* horse; horse *vs.* cock; cock *vs.* turtle; turtle *vs.* firefly; firefly *vs.* mosquito; mosquito *vs.* Juan.

Version *c* (Visayan), "Why Mosquitoes Hum" . Crab *vs.* frogs; frogs *vs.* snail; snail *vs.* firefly; firefly *vs.* mosquito.

Version *d* (Tagalog) "A Tyrant". . . . . . . King's officer *vs.* frog; frog *vs.* snail; snail *vs.* firefly; firefly *vs.* mosquito.

Version *e* (Pampango), "The Bacuit's Case". . Bacuit *vs.* frog; frog *vs.* turtle; turtle *vs.* firefly.

With the exception of the substitution of snail for turtle, and crab for bird, in the Tagalog and Visayan versions, four of these forms (*a, c, d, e*) are practically identical. Pampango *e* lacks the fourth link in the chain (firefly *vs.* mosquito). Pampango *b* adds one link (horse *vs.* cock), and substitutes cock for frog; the method of narration varies somewhat from the others, also. The punishment of the mosquito differs in *a, c,* and *d.* "The Trial among Animals" develops into a "just-so" story, and may be a connecting link between a Tinguian fable (Cole, No. 84) and two Borneo sayings (Evans, 447). In the Tinguian, a mosquito came to bite a man. The man said, "You are very little, and can do nothing to me." The mosquito answered, "If you had no ears, I would eat you." The Bajan (Borneo) saying is, "Mosquitoes do not make their buzzing unless they are near men's ears; and then they say, 'If these were not your ears, I would swallow you.'" The Dusun version (Borneo) is, "The mosquito says, 'If these were not your horns, I would swallow you.'" The "killing fly on face" droll episode, which terminates the Tagalog version (*d*), we have already met with twice, Nos. 9 and 57 (*q.v.*). The link "firefly *vs.* mosquito" is found in the Visayan story "The Ape and the Firefly" (JAFL 20 : 314).

There can be no question but that this cycle is native to the Islands, and was not imported from the Occident. A Malayan story given by Skeat (Fables and Folk-Tales from an Eastern Forest, 9–12), "Who Killed the Otter's Babies?" is clearly related to our tales, at least in idea and method: —

The mouse-deer (*plandok*) is charged with killing the otter's babies by trampling them to death, but excuses himself by saying that he was frightened because the woodpecker sounded his war-gong. In the trial before King Solomon, the above facts come out, and the woodpecker is asked why he sounded the war-gong.

WOODPECKER. Because the great lizard was wearing his sword.
GREAT LIZARD. Because the tortoise had donned his coat of mail.
TORTOISE. Because King Crab was trailing his three-edged pike.
KING CRAB. Because Crayfish was shouldering his lance.
CRAYFISH. Because Otter was coming down to devour my children.

Thus the cause of the death of the otter's children is traced to the otter himself.

Another Far-Eastern story from Laos (French Indo-China), entitled "Right and Might" (Fleeson, 27), is worth notice: —

A deer, frightened by the noise of an owl and a cricket, flees through the forest and into a stream, where it crushes a small fish almost to death. The fish complains to the court; and the deer, owl, cricket, and fish have a lawsuit. In the trial comes out this evidence: As the deer fled, he ran into some dry grass, and the seed fell into the eye of a wild chicken, and the pain caused by the seed made the chicken fly up against a nest of red ants. Alarmed, the red ants flew out to do battle, and in their haste bit a mongoose. The mongoose ran into a vine of wild fruit, and shook several pieces of it on the head of a hermit, who sat thinking under a tree. The hermit then asked the fruit why it fell, and the fruit blamed the mongoose; mongoose blamed ants; ants blamed chicken; chicken blamed seed; seed blamed deer; deer blamed owl. "O Owl!" asked the hermit, "why didst thou frighten the deer?" The owl replied, "I called but as I am accustomed to call; the cricket, too, called." Having heard the evidence, the judge says, "The cricket must replace the crushed parts of the fish and make it well," as he, the cricket, called and frightened the deer. Since the cricket is smaller and weaker than the owl or the deer, he had to bear the penalty.

61. THE GREEDY CROW.[1]

One day a crow found a piece of meat on the ground. He picked it up and flew to the top of a tree. While he was sitting there eating his meat, a *kasaykasay* (a small bird) passed by. She was carrying a dead rat, and was flying very fast. The crow called to her, and said, "Kasaykasay, where did you get that dead rat that you have?" But the small bird did not answer: she flew on her way. When the crow saw that she paid no attention to him, he was very angry; and he called out, "Kasaykasay, Kasaykasay, stop and give me a piece of that rat, or I will follow you and take the whole thing for myself!" Still the small bird paid no attention to him. At last, full of greed and rage, the crow determined to have the rat by any means. He left the meat he was eating, and flew after the small creature. Although she was only a little bird, the Kasaykasay could fly faster than the crow: so he could not catch her.

[1] Narrated by Agapito O. Gaa, from Taal, Batangas. He heard the story from an old Tagalog man who is now dead.

While the crow was chasing the Kasaykasay, a hawk happened to pass by the tree where the crow had left his meat. The hawk saw the meat, and at once seized it in his claws and flew away.

Although the crow pursued the Kasaykasay a long time, he could not overtake her: so at last he gave up his attempt, and flew back to the tree where he had left his meat. But when he came to the spot, and found that the meat was gone, he was almost ready to die of disappointment and hunger. By and by the hawk which had taken the meat passed the tree again. He called to the crow, and said to him, "Mr. Crow, do you know that I am the one who took your meat? If not, I will tell you now, and I am very sorry for you."

The crow did not answer the hawk, for he was so tired and weak that he could hardly breathe.

The moral of this story is this: Do not be greedy. Be contented with what you have, and do not wish for what you do not own.

NOTES.

This fable appears to be distantly related to the European fable of "The Dog and his Shadow." More closely connected, however, is an apologue incorporated in a Buddhistic birth-story, the "Culladhanuggaha-jātaka," No. 374. In this Indian story, —

An unfaithful wife eloping with her lover arrives at the bank of a stream. There the lover persuades her to strip herself, so that he may carry her clothes across the stream, which he proceeds to do, but never returns. Indra, seeing her plight, changes himself into a jackal bearing a piece of meat, and goes down to the bank of the stream. In its waters fish are disporting; and the Indra-jackal, laying aside his meat, plunges in after one of them. A vulture hovering near seizes hold of the meat and bears it aloft; and the jackal, returning unsuccessful from his fishing, is taunted by the woman, who had observed all this, in the first *gātha:* —

> "O jackal so brown! most stupid are you;
> No skill have you got, nor knowledge, nor wit;
> Your fish you have lost, your meat is all gone,
> And now you sit grieving all poor and forlorn."

To which the Indra-jackal repeats the second *gātha:* —

> "The faults of others are easy to see,
> But hard indeed our own are to behold;
> Thy husband thou hast lost, and lover eke,
> And now, I ween, thou grievest o'er thy loss."

The same story is found in the "Pancatantra" (V, viii; see Benfey, 1 : 468), whence it made its way into the "Tūtī-nämeh." It does not appear to be known in the Occident in this form (it is lacking in the "Kalilah and Dimnah").

Although the details of our story differ from those of the Indian fable of "The Jackal and the Faithless Wife," the general outlines of the two are near enough to justify us in supposing a rather close connection between them. I know of no European analogues nearly so close, and am inclined to consider "The Greedy Crow" a native Tagalog tale. From the testimony of the narrator, it appears that the fable is not a recent importation.

62. THE HUMMING-BIRD AND THE CARABAO.[1]

One hot April morning a carabao (water-buffalo) was resting under the shade of a quinine-tree which grew near the mouth of a large river, when a humming-bird alighted on one of the small branches above him.

"How do you do, Friend Carabao?" said the humming-bird.

"I'm very well, little Hum. Do you also feel the heat of this April morning?" replied the carabao.

"Indeed, I do, Friend Carabao! and I am so thirsty, that I have come down to drink."

"I wonder how much you can drink!" said the carabao jestingly. "You are so small, that a drop ought to be more than enough to satisfy you."

"Yes, Friend Carabao?" answered little Hum as if surprised. "I bet you that I can drink more than you can!"

"What, you drink more than I can, you little Hum!"

"Yes, let us try! You drink first, and we shall see."

So old carabao, ignorant of the trick that was being played on him, walked to the bank of the river and began to drink. He drank and drank and drank; but it so happened that the tide was rising, and, no matter how much he swallowed, the water in the river kept getting higher and higher. At last he could drink no more, and the humming-bird began to tease him.

"Why, Friend Carabao, you have not drunk anything. It seems to me that you have added more water to the river instead."

"You fool!" answered the carabao angrily, "can't you see that my stomach is almost bursting?"

"Well, I don't know. I only know that you have added more water than there was before. But it is now my turn to drink."

But the humming-bird only pretended to drink. He knew that the tide would soon be going out, so he just put his bill in

[1] Narrated by Eusebio Lopez, a Tagalog from the province of Cavite.

the water, and waited until the tide did begin to ebb. The water of the river began to fall also. The carabao noticed the change, but he could not comprehend it. He was surprised, and agreed that he had been beaten. Little Hum flew away, leaving poor old Carabao stupefied and hardly able to move, because of the great quantity of water he had drunk.

NOTES.

That this story was not imported from the Occident is pretty clearly established by the existence in North Borneo of a tale almost identical with it. The Borneo fable, which is told as a "just-so" story, and is entitled "The Kandowei [rice-bird] and the Kerbau [carabao]," may be found in Evans (pp. 423–424). It runs about as follows: —

The bird said to the buffalo, "If I were to drink the water of a stream, I could drink it all." — "I also," said the buffalo, "could finish it; for I am very big, while you are very small." — "Very well," said the bird, "to-morrow we will drink." In the morning, when the water was coming down in flood, the bird told the buffalo to drink first. The buffalo drank and drank; but the water only came down the faster, and at length he was forced to stop. So the buffalo said to the bird, "You can take my place and try, for I cannot finish." Now, the bird waited till the flood had gone down; and when it had done so, he put his beak into the water and pretended to drink. Then he waited till all the water had run away out of the stream, and said to the buffalo, "See, I have finished it!" And since the bird outwitted the buffalo in this manner, the buffalo has become his slave, and the bird rides on his back.

I know of no other Philippine versions, but I dare say that many exist between Luzon and Mindanao.

63. THE CAMANCHILE AND THE PASSION.[1]

Once upon a time there grew in a forest a large *camanchile-*tree [2] with spreading branches. Near this tree grew many other trees with beautiful fragrant flowers that attracted travellers. The camanchile had no fragrant flowers; but still its crown was beautifully shaped, for the leaves received as much light as the leaves of the other trees. But the beauty of the crown proved of no attraction to travellers, and they passed the tree by.

One day Camanchile exclaimed aloud, "Oh, what a dreary

[1] Narrated by Fernando M. Maramag of Ilagan, Isabella province. He says that this is an Ilocano story.

[2] *Camanchile, Pithecolobium dulce* Benth. (*Leguminosæ*), a native of tropical America; introduced into the Philippines by the Spaniards probably in the first century of Spanish occupation; now thoroughly naturalized and widely distributed in the Archipelago.

life I lead! I would that I had flowers like the others, so that travellers would visit me often!" A vine by the name of Passion, which grew near by, heard Camanchile's exclamation. Now, this vine grew fairly close to the ground, and consequently received only a small amount of light. Thinking that this was its opportunity to improve its condition, it said, "Camanchile, why is your life dreary?"

"Ah, Passion!" replied Camanchile, "just imagine that you were unappreciated, as I am! Travellers never visit me, for I have no flowers."

"Oh, that's easy!" said Passion. "Just let me climb on you, and I'll display on your crown my beautiful flowers. Then many persons will come to see you." Camanchile consented, and let Passion climb up on him. After a few days Passion reached the top of the tree, and soon covered the crown.

A few months later Camanchile realized that he was being smothered: he could not get light, so he asked Passion to leave him. "O Passion! what pain I am in! I can't get light. Your beauty is of no value. I am being smothered: so leave me, I beg of you!"

Passion would not leave Camanchile, however, and so Camanchile died.

MORAL: Be yourself.

NOTE.

With this story compare the "Palāsa-jātaka," No. 370, which tells how a Judas-tree was destroyed by the parasitic growth of a banyan-shoot. The general idea is the same in both stories, though I hardly suspect that ours is descended from the Indian. The situation of a tree choked to death by a parasite is such a commonplace in every-day experience, that a moral story based on it might arise spontaneously almost anywhere.

64. AUAC AND LAMIRAN.[1]

Once Auac, a hawk, stole a salted fish which was hanging in the sun to dry. He flew with it to a branch of a *camanchile*-tree, where he sat down and began to eat. As he was eating, Lamiran, a squirrel who had his house in a hole at the foot of the tree, saw Auac. Lamiran looked up, and said, "What beautiful shiny black feathers you have, Auac!" When he

---

[1] Narrated by Anastacia Villegas of Arayat, Pampanga. She heard the story from her father, and says that it is well known among the Pampangans.

heard this praise, the hawk looked very dignified. Nevertheless he was much pleased. He fluttered his wings. "You are especially beautiful, Auac, when you walk; for you are very graceful," continued the squirrel. Auac, who did not understand the trick that was being played on him, hopped along the branch with the air of a king. "I heard some one say yesterday that your voice is so soft and sweet, that every one who listens to your song is charmed. Please let me hear some of your notes, you handsome Auac!" said the cunning Lamiran. Auac, feeling more proud and dignified than ever, opened his mouth and sang, "Uac-uac-uac-uac!" As he uttered his notes, the fish in his beak fell to the ground, and Lamiran got it.

A heron which was standing on the back of a water-buffalo near by saw the affair. He said, "Auac, let me give you a piece of advice. Do not always believe what others tell you, but think for yourself; and remember that 'ill-gotten gains never prosper.'"

NOTES.

This is the old story of the "Fox and Crow [and cheese]," the bibliography for which is given by Jacobs (2 : 236). Jacobs sees a connection between this fable and two Buddhistic apologues: —

(1) The "Jambu-khādaka-jātaka," No. 294, in which we find a fox (jackal) and a crow flattering each other. The crow is eating *jambus*, when he is addressed thus by the jackal: —

> "Who may this be, whose rich and pleasant notes
> Proclaim him best of all the singing birds,
> Warbling so sweetly on the *jambu*-branch,
> Where like a peacock he sits firm and grand!"

The crow replies, —

> "'Tis a well-bred young gentleman who knows
> To speak of gentlemen in terms polite!
> Good sir, — whose shape and glossy coat reveal
> The tiger's offspring, — eat of these, I pray!"

Buddha, in the form of the genius of the *jambu*-tree, comments thus on their conversation: —

> "Too long, forsooth, I've borne the sight
> Of these poor chatterers of lies, —
> The refuse-eater and the offal-eater
> Belauding each other."

(2) The "Anta-jātaka," No. 295, in which the rôles are reversed,

the crow wheedling flesh from the jackal; here, too, the Buddha comments as above.

Our Pampangan story is of particular interest because of the moralizing of the heron at the end, making the form close to that of the two Jātakas. Possibly our story goes back to some old Buddhistic fable like these. The squirrel (or "wild-cat," as Bergaño's "Vocabulario," dated 1732, defines *lamiran*) is not a very happy substitution for the original ground-animal, whatever that was; for the squirrel could reach a fish hanging to dry almost as easily as a bird could. Besides, squirrels are not carnivorous. Doubtless the older meaning of "wild-cat" should be adopted for *lamiran*.

III. "JUST–SO" STORIES.

65. WHY THE ANT IS NOT SO VENOMOUS AS THE SNAKE.[1]

God first created the earth. Then he took a rock from the earth and threw it on the terrestrial surface. When the rock was broken into many small pieces, he breathed into them the breath of life, and they became living creatures. At first these creatures, though differing in shapes and sizes, were not given different powers.

Among these creatures of God's were the snake and the ant. One day the snake went to God to ask for power. It said, "I come to thee, O God! to ask for thy favor. The world thou hast just created is wild with confusion. I have come to ask thee to give me the special power to kill all those that are rebellious and troublesome."

"Go back to your fellow-creatures!" answered God. "Hereafter you are endowed with the power to store in your teeth this poison. When you bite the vile and contemptible, inject into the wound some of this poison, and they will be killed; but first of all, observe their actions, and be conscientious and thoughtful." Then God gave the snake the poison. The snake returned to the earth in great joy.

When the ant heard that the snake was endowed with such power, it at once went to God to ask that the same privilege be granted it. The ant found God on his heavenly throne, instructing his host of angels. The ant approached God, and addressed him thus: "O thou almighty God! my brother the snake has been granted a great privilege by thee. Why art thou so unkind to me? Give me the same power, and I will be of great aid to the snake in destroying sinners." God, thinking that the snake might need an assistant, gave the ant the same privilege that he had given the snake.

The ant was so greatly overjoyed, that it ran as fast as it could to the earth. When God saw it running, he called to the ant, but it paid no attention to him. Then God, being very much enraged, took away some of the ant's power, lest the ant might use it unreasonably. And so to-day the ant's bite is not so poisonous as the snake's.

[1] Narrated by Francisco M. Africa of Lipa, Batangas. This is a Tagalog story.

Another form of this story, recorded by Andrea Silva, also of Lipa, Batangas, runs as follows: —

In the olden times, when this great universe was still young, the inhabitants of this Archipelago had a sacred belief in a superior god whom they called Bathala. He was the creator of all things.

One day Bathala called the animals one by one, and bestowed upon each a gift, or the power of doing something. To the bird he gave the power to fly. Next Bathala called the ant, likewise intending to bestow on it more power than on any other animals, because it was so very small; but the ant was the most stupid and lazy of all creatures. It did not pay any attention to the summons of the god, but pretended to be deaf. Whereupon Bathala became so angry that he called the snake and gave to it the wonderful power that he had intended to give the ant. "You, Sir Snake, shall seldom be caught by any person, for you shall have the power of being very nimble. Besides, every one shall be afraid of you."

When finally the ant appeared before the god, asking him for the gift he had promised, Bathala said, "O you poor, tiny, imprudent creature! Since you disobeyed your god, from now on you and your tribe shall meet with death very often, for you shall be pinched by those whom you bite."

And so it is to-day that we pinch to death the ants whenever they bite us.

The narrator testified that she heard the story from an old woman in her town of Lipa. So far as I know, this "just-so" fable of "The Ant and the Snake and God" has not been recorded outside of Lipa, Batangas; and I am inclined to believe that it represents old local tradition.

66. WHY LOCUSTS ARE HARMFUL.[1]

During the dawn of humanity, some angels headed by Satanas revolted against God. They wanted to establish a kingdom for themselves. In a battle against the army of God, in which God himself was present, Satanas threw a handful of sand into God's face; but the heavenly monarch just laughed, and said, "I turn the sand back to thee. The particles shall become the scourge of all ages to thee and to thy followers, O Satanas!"

No sooner had God uttered these words than the particles of sand became a mighty swarm of locusts, that flew in all directions. Such was the beginning of the pest.

A tribal Bicol story narrated by Maximina Navarro of Albay runs thus: —

THE ORIGIN OF LOCUSTS.

Many years ago there lived a head man whose home was situated in a very fertile valley, all the inhabitants of which he governed. He was not a

[1] Narrated by Francisco M. Africa.

good ruler, however; for he was so greedy, that he wanted to hoard up all the rice produced by his people. Every year, therefore, he squeezed from his subjects as much rice as he could get, so that at the end of four years his granaries were full to bursting. It happened that in the fifth year the crop failed, and the people knew that they should starve unless their ruler would let them have rice from his barns. At first they were afraid to go petition the head man, for they feared that he would refuse them; but, when nearly one-half of the children had died from starvation, they agreed to send some representatives to beg for rice.

Seven men were chosen to be the ambassadors. When they reached the house of the datu, for so they called their ruler, they asked for admittance, crying that they wanted rice for their wives and children. When the datu heard their cry, he went to the door and made a motion as if he would knock the petitioners off the ladder leading to the house. He lost his balance and fell, striking his head sharply on the bottom of the ladder. Thinking that he was dead, the seven men made no attempt to help him, but went home, proclaiming that soon there would be rice enough for all.

But the datu was not dead, only badly stunned. The next morning, as he was walking around his granaries, they exploded with a loud noise; and all the rice flew away in the form of insects, and vanished from his sight. This kind of insect which originated from the rice we call *doron* (from the Spanish word *duro*), on account of the toughness of its skin.

A more intelligible version of this story is the following related by Felix de la Llana, who was told it by an old farmer of Candelaria, Zambales. It appears to represent old Pagan tradition modified somewhat by Christianity.

THE ORIGIN OF LOCUSTS.

When all the surface of the earth was yet a wilderness and the people were very few, there lived a farmer who wished to become rich all at once. So he told his wife to pray to Kayamanan, the goddess of riches, to give them fortune.

One night the goddess with arms extended appeared to them in a dream, and advised the ambitious farmer to build six large barns. Then she went to the goddess of plenty, Kainomayan, and asked her to give this farmer abundant crops. When the farmer harvested his rice the next season, he was astounded to find that the crop more than filled his six barns. So delighted was he, and so greedy, that he and his wife thought no more of the source of their good fortune, and they neglected to celebrate a feast in honor of God and his goddesses. He felt like a powerful monarch, and did not wish to work any more. However, his riches did not last long, as we shall see.

One day the goddess Kayamanan disguised herself, and in the form of a beggar came to the house of the rich farmer. She begged him to let her rest for a little while under his roof, for she had been travelling in many countries, she said. When she asked for some remnants of rice to eat, the ungrateful farmer said to her, "Get off my grounds! don't come here to bother me! If you don't leave at once, I shall let this dog loose, and you will be its food." The poor beggar went away without a word, but she begged almighty God to give her the power to change anything to any form or creature she wished. As she was God's favorite, her request was granted. So she assumed her own form, and went again to the farmer's house. To him she said, "You who became rich by my aid, and have denied food and shelter to a beggar, shall be punished. Since you have neglected your duty both to the poor and to me, I therefore, with the consent of the almighty God, punish you thus: your rice shall turn to a swarm of locusts, which will destroy all the crops of the farmers of your own race and those of other countries."

The punishment was carried out, and the farmer was left destitute.

This story is also known in the Tagalog province of Batangas.

In a Rumanian saga (Dähnhardt, 3 : 250) a swarm of locusts is sent by God to punish an emperor who would not invite any priests or nuns to his wedding-banquet. When the guests were about to eat the feast prepared, the insects appeared and devoured everything. *Since that time locusts have appeared whenever mankind has forgotten God.*

67. HOW LANSONES BECAME EDIBLE.[1]

Once upon a time the fruit of the *lansone*-tree was very poisonous. Its very juice could make a man sick with leprosy. One day a very religious old man was passing through a forest to attend the fiesta of the neighboring town. When he reached the middle of the thick wood, he became very hungry and tired, and he felt that he could go no farther. No matter where he looked, he could see nothing but the poisonous *lansone*-trees. So he lay down on the soft grass. Hardly a moment had passed, when a winged being from heaven approached him, and said, "My good Christian pilgrim, take some of these *lansone*-fruits, eat them, and you will be much relieved." At first the old man would not do it, but the angel picked some of the fruits and handed them to the pilgrim. He then ate, and soon his hunger was removed. After thanking Heaven, he continued on his journey. Ever since this time, *lansones* have been good to eat. All the fruits still bear the marks of the angel's fingers.

NOTES.

The *lanson* (*Lansium domesticum*) is a small tree of Malaysia, extensively cultivated for its fruit, which resembles a yellow plum (from E. Ind. *lansa*). It is not native to the Philippines, and was probably introduced into the Islands by the Malays in prehistoric times. Our story, which I think we must consider not imported, is based on a

[1] Narrated by Francisco M. Africa.

fancied etymological connection between *lanson* and *lason* (Tag. for "poison"), and does not appear to be known except to the Tagalogs of La Laguna province, although in Pampango also the word *lason* means "poison." *Lason* itself is derived from the Malay *rachūn*, perhaps through the Sulu *lachūn*.

Two other Tagalog versions, both from Laguna province, also show the influence of Christianity, but vary enough from our story to be worthy of record here. One, related by Manuel Gallego of San Antonio, Nueva Ecija, is entitled "The Adam and Eve of the Tagalogs." Mr. Gallego heard the story from a farmer living in Lubang, La Laguna. It runs as follows: —

Many hundreds of years ago, when Luzon was still uninhabited, Bathala, our supreme god, was envious of Laon, the god of the Visayans, because Laon had many subjects, while Bathala's kingdom was a barren desert. It was within the power of Bathala to create human beings, but not food for them; and so he asked for advice from Diwata, the supreme god of the universe.

Diwata told Bathala that the next day he would send an angel to earth with seeds to be planted. The promise was fulfilled, and Bathala scattered the seeds all over Luzon. Within a short time the island was covered with trees and shrubs, and was then ready for human habitation. Accordingly Bathala created Adam and Eve, the ancestors of the Tagalogs. In spite of the fact that they were forbidden to eat the green fruit of a certain plant, they disobeyed and ate it; so, as a punishment, they were poisoned and made very sick. They did not die, however. As a result of their experience, they gave the name *lason* ("poison") to this plant. Conscious of their fault, Adam and Eve implored forgiveness of Diwata. By order of Diwata, Bathala forgave the criminals; but the *lason* still remained poisonous. In order to rid it of its dangerous properties, an angel was sent to earth. He put the marks of his finger-nails on the surface of the pulp of each *lason*-seed, and these marks may be seen to this day. Afterwards the name of the plant was changed from *lason* to *lanzon*, the name by which it has been known ever since.

In the other Tagalog version, narrated by Eulogio Benitez of Pagsanjan, La Laguna, the incident of the finger-prints is told as a local saint-legend of Paete. The story is entitled "How Lanzones became Edible."

The little town of Paete, on the southern and western shore of Laguna de Bay, produces more *lanzones* than any other town in the province. Steamers call daily at her wharves for the fruits which have made her famous. In the church of this town may still be seen the image of the mother of God, the Virgin Mary, leading her child.

One evening a long time ago it was discovered that the beautiful image was missing from its accustomed place in the church. The news spread like wildfire, and all the people were in great amazement and consternation. While all was confusion in the town, a heavenly sight was being presented in a little place outside the municipality. A beautiful woman dressed in white was walking over the grass with a child in her arms. They were going towards a *lanson*-tree on the other side of the meadow. The boy, who was evidently tired of being carried, asked to be put down. When the child saw the fruits scattered all over the ground, he felt very thirsty, and, picking up one of the tempting fruits, began to open it. The mother told her son that the fruit was poisonous; but the child said that he was very thirsty, and could go no farther if he did not have a drink. Then the mother took the fruit from his hands, and with her delicate white fingers pinched the pulp gently. Turning to her son, she said, "Now you may take this and eat it. You will find it the most delicious and refreshing of all fruits." The child obeyed, and the fruit was indeed sweet.

This is the way by which the *lansones* were transformed from a poisonous, dangerous fruit to a sweet, delicate food. If any one discredits this story, all he needs to do to prove its truth is to open up any *lanson* he finds, and he will see without fail the finger-prints of the Virgin.

68. WHY COCKS FIGHT ONE ANOTHER.[1]

Once upon a time in an unknown country there lived a royal couple endowed with almost all the blessings of God. Their palace was decorated with all kinds of precious stones, — diamonds, sapphires, and emeralds. They were often honored with visits from the celestial beings. There was hardly an hour of the day when some sort of jubilation or festival was not being held in the royal home. But, in spite of all his riches, there was a melancholy in the mind of the king, — a brooding, a cankering thought, that would not give him an hour of rest or contentment. In spite of all the favors lavished on him by God, he felt miserable and uneasy. He had a happy and wealthy kingdom, but — he had no heir. There was nobody to manage the government after his death. Whenever the thought of death came to his mind, he fell on his knees and implored the Almighty to give him a son: "Have mercy on me, O God! Give me a son to manage my kingdom after I am gone!"

One evening an angel from Paradise came to visit him, and, on finding the king at his prayers, said, "Dry thy tears, O king! Thy royal prayer is heard in heaven. Thou shalt be given more than a son, but not in the same shape as thou art. Thy sons shall see the light of day crowned with their own flesh." The king was so greatly overjoyed, that he could not speak a single word of gratitude in reply.

Not long afterward the queen gave birth to a cock that crowed on seeing the light of day. The couple were very glad:

---

[1] Narrated by Francisco M. Africa.

night and day they caressed the royal babe, and they would have made for him a cage of gold had not God forbidden them to do so. Every year a cock was born into the royal family, until the feathered sons numbered thirteen. But these sons were jealous of one another: each thought that the others had no right to wear crowns.

At last the old king and queen died, and no one was left to manage the royal demesne but the dumb sons. Thereafter the feathered orphans began fighting one another, each one trying to wrest the crown from the others.

NOTE.

I know of no variant of this story.

69. WHY BATS FLY AT NIGHT.[1]

Many years ago the earth was inhabited by only one man. His body was composed of minute organisms that were incessantly warring against one another. One day this man became so weak that he could not obtain food for his support. He laid himself down on some soft moss by the bank of a river, and there he remained till night.

The organisms that lived in his body began to fight against one another most fiercely. Each ate his fellow until he became very big. At last the man died, and only one organism remained alive. This organism then flew away, and became the ancestor of the bats. The light of day so dazzled his eyes, that he could not fly very far, so he decided to fly only at night. And ever since, his descendants, too, have hidden themselves in the day-time, and come out only when it is dark.

NOTE.

This somewhat unsatisfactory *pourquoi* story appears to represent at bottom very ancient tradition. I know of no parallels; but tales explaining why the bat flies at night are found among many peoples (e.g., Dähnhardt, 3 : 94, 267, 270; Dayrell, Nos. VII, XII).

70. WHY THE SUN SHINES MORE BRIGHTLY THAN THE MOON.[2]

Long, long ago there lived a fairy with two very beautiful daughters. Araw, the elder daughter, was very amiable, and

[1] Narrator, Francisco M. Africa.
[2] A Tagalog story narrated by Francisco M. Africa.

had a kindly disposition; but Buwan, unlike her sister, was disobedient, cruel, and harsh. She was always finding fault with Araw. One night, when the fairy came home from her nocturnal rambles and saw Buwan badly mistreating her elder sister, she asked God for help against her unruly daughter.

Before this time God had prepared very valuable gifts for the two sisters. These gifts were two enormous diamonds that could light the whole universe. When God heard the prayer of the fairy, he descended to earth disguised as a beggar. On learning for himself how bad-tempered Buwan was, and how sweet and kind-hearted Araw, God gave the older sister her diamond as a reward. Buwan was greatly angered by this favoritism on the part of the Almighty, so she went to the heavenly kingdom and stole one of God's diamonds. Then she returned to earth with the precious stone, but there she found that her jewel was not so brilliant as Araw's.

When God went back to heaven and learned what Buwan had done, he sent two angels to punish her. But the angels abused their commission: they seized both sisters and hurled them into the sea. Then they threw the two stones upward into the sky, and there they stuck. But Araw's diamond was bigger and brighter than the one Buwan stole. Thereafter the bigger jewel was called Araw ("day" or "sun"); and the smaller one, Buwan ("moon").

NOTES.

A Pangasinan myth, narrated by Emilio Bulatao of San Carlos, Pangasinan, tells how the light from the sun and the moon proceeds from two fiery palaces. The story follows: —

THE SUN, THE MOON, AND THE STARS.

There was once a powerful god called Ama ["father"], the father and ruler of all others, and the creator of man. He had a wonderful aerial abode, from which he could see everything. Of all his sons, Agueo ["sun, day"] and Bulan ["moon"] were his two favorites, and to these he gave each a fiery palace. In accordance with the wish of their father, Agueo and Bulan daily passed across the earth side by side, and together they furnished light to mankind. Now, Agueo was of a morose and taciturn disposition, but he was always very obedient to his father; Bulan, on the other hand, was merry and full of mischief.

Once, when they were near the end of their day's labor, they saw thieves on the earth below, wishing that it were night so that they might proceed with their unlawful business. Bulan, who was one of their kind, urged Agueo to be quick, so that the earth might soon be left in darkness. As

Agueo obstinately refused to be hurried, a quarrel ensued between the two brothers. Their father, who had been watching the two boys and had heard all that passed between them, became very angry with the mischievous Bulan; and, in his wrath, he seized an enormous rock and hurled it whistling through the air. The rock struck the palace of Bulan, and was broken into thousands of pieces, which got perpetual light from contact with the fiery palace. These may still be seen in the heavens, and they are called Bituen ["stars"]. Bulan was forbidden to travel with Agueo any more, but was commanded to light the ways of thieves henceforth with his much-dimmed fiery palace.

A somewhat similar Pampango myth may also be given here, as it has never before been printed. It was narrated by Leopoldo Layug of Guagua, Pampanga, and is entitled "The Sun and the Moon."

Long ago the earth was created and ruled by Bathala. He had two children, Apolaqui and Mayari. From the eyes of these two children the earth received its first light. The people, the birds of the air, the animals of the mountains, and even the fishes of the sea, were glad because they had light, and so they were great friends of the two children.

Bathala loved his children tenderly, and never wanted them to be separated from him. So, no matter how tired he was, he always followed them in their daily walks. But as time went on, and Bathala became old and feeble and could no longer keep up with his active son and daughter, he asked them to stay with him at all times; but they were so absorbed in their pleasures, that they paid no heed to their father's wish. One day he became sick, and died suddenly, without leaving any written will as to the disposition of his kingdom. Now Apolaqui wanted to rule the earth without giving any power to his sister Mayari. She refused to consent to her brother's plan, and a bitter conflict arose between them. For a long time they fought with bamboo clubs. At last Mayari had one of her eyes put out. When Apolaqui saw what he had done to his sister, he felt very sorry for her, and said that they should struggle no longer, but that they should exercise equal power on the earth, only at different times. Since that time, Apolaqui, who is now called the Sun, has ruled the earth during the day, and from his eyes we receive bright light. Mayari, who is called the Moon, rules the world at night. Her light, however, is fainter than her brother's, for she has but one eye.

This same struggle between the two great luminaries is reflected in two short cradle-songs that Pampangan mothers sing to their children to still them. These verses were contributed by Lorenzo Licup of Angeles: —

Ing bulan ilaning aldo
Mitatagalan la baho
Pangaras da quetang cuarto
Nipag sundang, mipagpusto.

"The Moon and the Sun chased each other above. When they came into a room, they took their daggers from their sides and were ready to fight each other."

Ing aldo ilaning bulan	"The Sun and the Moon chased
Mitatagalan la lalan	each other below. When they
Pangaras da quetang Pampang	came to a bank, they first made
Mipagpustu,'t, mitabacan.	preparation, and then began to
	fight each other with bolos."

The two stories and the two stanzas just given appear to be genuine old native tradition, unmodified by Christianity.

For Tinguian, Bukidnon, Mandaya, and Visayan myths of the sun, moon, and stars, see M. C. Cole, 65, 124, 145, 201.

71. (a) WHY THE CULING HAS A TONSURE.[1]

In a certain field there lived two birds, — Pogô ("quail") and Culing (a small black bird that has no feathers on the top of its head). One day Pogô, while scratching the ground for food, met Culing. When Culing saw Pogô, he said in a taunting tone, "Where are you going, lazy one? Be more active. Don't be as lazy as a leech!"

Pogô became very angry. "You call me lazy!" he said. "You are much lazier than I. Let us see which can fly higher into the sky!"

Thereupon Culing agreed, and he began to fly upward until he was lost from sight. He flew so high, that his head touched the surface of the sky. As the sky was hot, all the feathers on the top of his head were burned off; and ever since, the culing has had a tonsure.

(b) THE CULETO AND THE CROW.[2]

The culeto is a fine singer, but it is bald-headed. The natives often capture it and train it to talk. Formerly this little black bird was not so bald as it is to-day: its head, in fact, was covered with a thick growth of feathers. And the crow, too: it was not black once, but its feathers were as white as starch.

Once upon a time, shortly after the Deluge, the crow was merrily crowing on the branch of a tree when the culeto came by. The voice of the crow was so harsh, that the culeto made fun of it. "Good-morning, Mr. Crow!" said the culeto, "I am very glad to hear you sing. Your voice is so fine, that I cannot help closing my ears."

[1] Narrated by Francisco M. Africa.

[2] Narrated by Leopoldo Uichanco, a Tagalog from Calamba, La Laguna. He says, "This tradition is a favorite one among Tagalog children. I have often heard the story told by old men while I was waiting my turn at barber-shops in my province."

"Pray, think first of yourself!" answered the crow. "What do I care for a good voice, so long as I have a strong body? Why don't you laugh at yourself? See how weak and tiny you are!"

"Weak!" said the culeto. "Do you call me weak? I would fly a race even with an eagle."

"Ha, ha, ha!" laughed the crow. "The idea of racing the eagle when you do not even dare race me!"

"Race with you! Why, you would only disgrace yourself," retorted the culeto.

"Wait!" answered the crow. "Eat some more rice, drink some more water, fill your body with more air! And wait till you grow bigger before you venture to race with me!"

"The strength of a person," said the culeto, nettled, "is not to be judged by his size. Don't you know that it is the smallest pepper that is the hottest?"

"Well, then," replied the crow, "if you wish to race me now at your own risk, let us begin!"

"One, two, three!" counted the culeto, and up they flew. During their flight the two birds became separated from each other by a dense cloud. The culeto flew at full speed so high upward, that he knocked his head very hard against the door of the sky, — so hard, in fact, that a large piece of skin was scraped from his scalp. The crow, having lost his way, flew so near the sun, that his feathers were burned black.

It is on account of this bet between the culeto and the crow that all the descendants of the former have been bald-headed, while all the descendants of the crow have black feathers to-day.

(c) THE HAWK AND THE COLING.[1]

Early one morning a hawk sallied forth from his nest to find something to eat. He flew so high that he could hardly be seen from the earth. He looked down; but as he could not see anything, he flew lower and lower, until he came to the top of a tree. On one of the branches he saw sitting quietly a coling. The hawk despised the little bird, and at once made up his mind to challenge him to a flight upward.

So the hawk said to the coling, "Do you wish to fly up into the sky with me to see which of us can fly the faster and the higher?"

[1] Narrated by Agapito Gaa of Taal, Batangas. He says that this Tagalog story is well known in every town in Batangas province. He heard the story from his grandfather.

The coling did not answer at once, but he thought of the matter for a while. Then he said to the hawk, "When do you want to have the race?"

"That is for you to decide," said the hawk. "If you wish to have it now, well and good."

"Well," said the coling, "let us have it to-morrow morning before sunrise!"

"All right," said the hawk.

"But," said the coling, "each of us is to carry a load with him to make the flight a little more difficult."

"Well, what do you want to take with you?" said the hawk.

"I will take some salt," said the coling.

"Then I will take some cotton," replied the hawk. "Let us meet here in this tree early to-morrow!" This agreed upon, the two birds separated. The hawk went to the cotton-field and got his load of cotton, while the coling went to the sea and got some salt.

The next morning they met in the tree, each having the object he would carry with him in his flight. They asked the crow, who was present, to be the judge of the contest. The crow accepted the commission, and said that he would give a caw as a signal for them to start. He did so, and the two contestants were off. At first the hawk flew faster and higher than the coling; but very soon it began to rain. The cotton on the hawk's back became soaked with water, and soon was very heavy; but the salt on the coling's back was soon dissolved, and then he had no load at all. Under these conditions, the coling soon overtook the bigger bird. For a time they flew side by side; but after a few minutes the coling had the best of the race, and in a little while longer the hawk could no longer see his rival. But the coling flew so high, that at last his head touched the sun, and all the feathers on the top were burned off. The hawk now flew down to the crow, and said that he had won the race, for the coling had fallen to the ground dead. But by and by the coling himself came. He showed them the top of his head as a proof that he had won the race. The crow gave his decision in favor of the coling, and the hawk flew off disgraced.

From that time all colings have had the tops of their heads bald to show that they are the descendants of the victorious bird.

NOTES.

These three forms of the "flight-contest" incident are all from southern Luzon, — the provinces of La Laguna and Batangas. The tale seems to be definitely localized there. I know of its occurrence nowhere else in the Islands. Nor have I found any Malayan variants.

For other *pourquoi* stories of why certain birds are bald, see Dähnhardt, 3 : 11–14. Dähnhardt (*ibid.*, 142) cites a Ceylon tale of the crow and the *drongo*, who had a bet as to which could fly the higher carrying a load. Crow selected tree-cotton for his burden; but Drongo, noticing the black rain-clouds overhead, carried salt, and thus won; for his load became constantly lighter, while Crow's became heavier.

With the explanation given in the second tale of this group of why the crow is black, compare a Pawnee story (JAFL 6 : 126), in which a crow, which is sent to the sun to get fire, has all his feathers singed.

72. (a) WHY THE COW'S SKIN IS LOOSE ON THE NECK.[1]

There was once a poor farmer who possessed a cow and a carabao. These two animals were his only wealth. Every day he led them to the field to plough. He worked his animals so hard, that they often complained to him; but the cruel master would not even listen to their words. One day the cow, who had grown tired of this kind of life, said to the carabao, "Let us run away from this evil man! Though we are very dirty, he is not willing for us even to take a bath. If we remain here with him, we shall be as ugly and as filthy as pigs. If we run away from him, however, he will have to do his own work, and then we shall be revenged. Hurry up! Let us go!"

The spirit of the carabao was aroused: he jumped with a loud roar, and said, "I too have long been meditating escape, but I hesitated because I was afraid you might not be willing to join me in flight. We are so ill-treated by our cruel master, that God will have pity on us. Come on! Let us go!"

The two animals at once set out, running as fast as they could, always trying to avoid any human beings. When they came to a river, the cow said, "We are very dirty. Let us take a bath before we go on! The water of this river is so clean and clear, that we shall soon be as clean as we were before our contemptible master got hold of us."

The carabao answered, "We would better run a little farther, for perhaps our master is already in pursuit of us. Besides,

---

[1] Narrated by Francisco M. Africa.

we are very tired now, and I have been told that to take a bath when one is tired injures the health."

"Don't believe that!" returned the cow. "Our bodies are so big, that we do not need to fear sickness."

At last the carabao was persuaded by the arguments of the cow; and he said, "All right! Let us take off our clothes before we go into the water!"

The two animals then stripped themselves of all their clothes; then they plunged into the deep, cool river. They had been in the water less than an hour, however, when they saw their master coming after them with a big stick in his hand. They ran up to where their clothes were; but in their haste the carabao put on the cow's clothes, and the cow got the carabao's. As soon as they were dressed, they continued their mad flight; and as their master was very tired, he had to give up the chase and return home disappointed.

Since the carabao was larger than the cow, the skin on the cow's neck has been loose ever since, because the two friends were separated and could never exchange clothes again. And likewise the skin on the carabao's neck has been tight ever since these two animals made their mistake in dressing.

(b) THE FIRST LOOSE-SKINNED COW AND THE FIRST TIGHT-SKINNED CARABAO.[1]

Many years ago, when the people of the world were still few in number and the animals took the place of servants, an old man bought a cow and a carabao from his neighbor. With these animals he travelled until he reached the top of a mountain. There they saw a cave, and the old man told his servants to enter and see if there was any danger inside. With slow and cautious steps the carabao and the cow went in, examining every corner. All at once the cow perceived something moving. In his fright he jumped back, and hid behind his companion; but the slow-going carabao did not see the figure, and suddenly he felt his hind leg seized in a strong grasp. The god of the cave had caught him. Then the god of the cave spoke. His voice was terrifying, but his words were kind. He told them how for many days he had been hungry, and he asked for meat. The cow, whose courage had by this time been somewhat re-

[1] Narrated by Amanda Morente, a Tagalog from Pinamalayan, Mindoro. She heard the story from an old woman of her town.

stored, gladly offered him some of her master's provisions, which she was carrying. In return for this kindness, the god gave each of the animals a dress: to the carabao he gave one of gold; and to the cow, one of bronze. He also invited the two to remain with him and be his servants.

Some time after the two friends had been installed in their new home, the god of the cave sent them one day to gather fruits. The carabao and the cow were delighted at this prospect of a change, and they jumped with joy. They rushed out into the woods; and when they came to a pond, they took off their new clothes and plunged into the soft mud. While they were enjoying their bath, they saw their master coming. He was carrying a big stick. They knew very well that he would beat them, for they had been away the whole morning. In their haste to get their clothes back on, they made a mistake: the carabao got into the cow's dress, and the cow into the carabao's. After that they never exchanged their clothes, which finally became their outer skin. So to-day the carabao has a tight bronze-colored skin; and the cow, a loose golden-colored one.

NOTE.

Like the preceding, this story appears to be a native Tagalog tale. I know of no other variants.

73. WHY THE MONKEY IS WISE.[1]

Once upon a time there lived a poor man who had seven sons. These young men, all except the youngest, helped their aged father with the work; but the family became poorer and poorer. One day, when they had exhausted all their means of support, the father called his sons before him. To every son he assigned a certain kind of work, so that there might be co-operation, and hence efficiency, in the labors of the humble family. To the youngest son was assigned the task of gathering sticks in the forest for fuel.

Not long afterwards a pestilence broke out in the little town where the old man lived, and all his sons but the youngest died. The father was left to starve on his bed, for his only living son was so ungrateful as not to give any help to his father in his last years. When the old man was about to breathe his last, he called his son to give him his final benediction; but the

---

[1] Narrated by Francisco M. Africa.

ungrateful boy, instead of going to his dying father, ran away into the woods, and the old man passed away without anybody to care for him.

But God punished the unfilial son: he cursed him; and the boy lost his power of speech, and was condemned to live in the forests ever after as a monkey. Thus, although monkeys cannot talk, they are wise because they are descended from a human being.

NOTES.

I know of no analogues of this story, but will cite two other Filipino myths accounting for the origin of monkeys. The first was narrated by Antonio Maceda, a Tagalog from Pagsanjan, who heard it from his grandfather. The story follows.

ORIGIN OF THE MONKEY.

A long time ago the world, which was divided into earth and heaven, was very lonesome, for Bathala was the only living being in it. He lived in heaven. One day Bathala felt so lonely, that the thought of creating some living beings for his companions came into his mind. He had never thought of this before, although with his infinite power he could do anything he pleased. So he came down to earth to get some clay; but he found the ground very dry, for there was no such thing as rain on the earth. Immediately he said, "Let there be rain!" and the rain fell down. Then, with a large load of slippery clay, Bathala returned to heaven and began the work of creation. He created men, birds, plants, mountains, and rivers (*sic!*). While he was in the act of creating men, however, an accident occurred. As he was moulding a piece of clay into the shape of a man, the mould slipped from his left hand. Bathala was quick enough to grasp the back of this lifeless mass of clay; but the clay was so soft that it stretched out into a long rope, and the mould fell into a tree. In his anger, Bathala said, "I curse thee! Thou shalt have life, but thou shalt inhabit trees. The part of thy body that has been stretched out into a rope shall become thy tail."

The lifeless mould was at once changed into a monkey, the great-grandfather of all the monkeys.

The following story was written down by Sotero Albano, an Ilocano from Dingras, Ilocos Norte: —

THE FIRST MONKEY.

Long years ago there lived in a thick forest a young girl under the care of the goddess of weaving. Here she lived happily and without care, for everything that she wanted to eat was provided for her by her patroness.

One day the goddess said to the girl, "Take this cotton, clean it, and make out of it a dress for yourself." Now, the girl knew nothing about making cloth and weaving it: so she said to the goddess, "When the cotton is cleaned, is it ready for use?"

"No," answered her guardian; "after it is cleaned, it must be beaten."
"Well, after it is beaten, is it ready for use?" said the lazy girl.

The goddess said that before it could be used, it would have to be spun.
"Well, after it is spun," persisted the saucy maiden, "is it ready for use?"

"No; it must next be woven into cloth, cut, and sewed," answered the patient goddess.

"Oh!" said the girl, "it will take a long time and much hard work to make clothes that way. This leather hide, which you have given me to beat the cotton on, will make me better clothing, because it will wear longer." So she covered herself with the leather. The goddess was so angry at the girl for her laziness, that she determined that the leather should not only be her dress, but also become her very skin. Then the goddess took the stick for beating the cotton, and, thrusting it between the maiden's buttocks, said to her, "This stick will become a part of your body, and you will use it for climbing-purposes. As a penalty for your laziness, henceforth you shall live in trees in the forest, and there you will find your food."

Thus originated the first monkey with a coat of leather and a tail.

Obviously connected with this Ilocano story are three Tinguian myths recorded by Cole, who abstracts them thus: —

(No. 65.) A lazy man, who is planting corn, constantly leans on his planting-stick. It becomes a tail, and he turns into a monkey.

(No. 66.) A boy is too lazy to strip sugarcane for himself. His mother, in anger, tells him to stick it up his anus. He does so, and becomes a monkey.

(No. 67.) A lazy girl pretends she does not know how to spin. Her companions, in disgust, tell her to stick the spinning-stick up her anus. She does so, and at once changes into a monkey.

Compare also a Bagobo story collected by Miss Benedict (JAFL 26 : 21), where a ladle becomes a monkey's tail; also an African saga in Dähnhardt (3 : 488).

The Filipinos have other explanatory myths which credit Lucifer with the creation of monkeys and snakes.

74. (a) THE LOST NECKLACE.[1]

Once a crow bought a fine necklace from a merchant. He was very proud of his purchase, which he immediately put around his neck, so that everybody could see it. Then he flew away, and came to a beautiful little garden, where he met his old friend the hen strutting about, with her chicks following her. The hen said to him, "Oh, what a fine necklace you have! May I borrow it? I will return it to you to-morrow without fail."

[1] Narrated by Facundo Esquivel, a Tagalog, who heard the story from a friend from Cebu. The story is Visayan.

Now, the crow liked the hen: so he willingly lent her the necklace for a day. The next morning, when the crow returned for his property, he found the hen and her chicks scratching the ground near an old wall. "Where is my necklace?" said the crow.

"It is lost," said the hen. "My chicks took it yesterday while I was asleep, and now they do not remember where they put it. We have been looking for it all day, and yet we have not been able to find it."

"You must pay for it at once," said the crow, "or else I shall go to the king and tell him that you stole my necklace."

The hen was frightened at this reply, and she began to wonder how she could raise the necessary money. The crow, who was on his way to a fiesta, at last said impatiently, "I will take one of your chicks every day in payment of what you owe me. As soon as you find the necklace, give it to me, and then I will stop eating your chicks." The hen had to be satisfied with this arrangement, for she feared that the crow would go to the king if she refused.

Unto this day, then, you can find hens and chicks together looking for the lost necklace by scratching the ground; and the crows are still exacting payment for the lost jewel by eating chicks. It is said that the hens and chickens will never cease scratching the ground until the lost necklace is found.

(*b*) THE COCK AND THE SPARROW-HAWK.[1]

Long ago the sparrow-hawk and the cock were very good friends. Once, when the cocks were going to hold a great fiesta in the neighboring village, a proud young rooster, who wished to get the reputation for being rich and consequently win him a wife, went to the sparrow-hawk, and said, "My friend, please lend me your bracelet! I am going to our fiesta; and I wish to make some young hens there believe that I am rich, in order that they may love me."

The sparrow-hawk answered, "With much pleasure, my friend."

So the cock went to the fiesta wearing the borrowed bracelet. While he was dancing, however, he lost the jewel, and could find it nowhere. At last he went back to the sparrow-hawk, and said, "I am very sorry, my friend, but I lost your bracelet

[1] Narrated by Dolores Asuncion of Manila. She heard the story from an old Tagalog.

while I was dancing, and I can find it nowhere.   What do you wish me to give you in payment for it?"

The sparrow-hawk answered, "Since that bracelet was an heirloom, I valued it very highly.   You must go back to the place where you think you lost it, and there look for it until you find it.   In the mean time I reserve the right to take from your flock a chicken whenever I please."

So, ever since that time sparrow-hawks are often seen carrying off young chickens, while the cocks have been busy scratching the ground to find the lost bracelet.   Hens also scratch the soil, for they hate to lose their chicks, and they want to find the bracelet as soon as possible.   They look up into the sky to see if the sparrow-hawk is near; then they scratch the soil vigorously, and cry, "Tac-ta-laoc!" which means, "Come and help me!"

NOTE.

Another Visayan variant of these two stories may be found in the "Journal of American Folk-Lore" (20 : 100), whence it has been reprinted by M. C. Cole (p. 212), "The Hawk and the Hen."   An African analogue may be found in Dayrell (No. xv, p. 62).

75. THE STORY OF OUR FINGERS.[1]

"Why," said Antonio to his grandfather one day, "does our thumb stand separate from the other fingers?"

"That is only so in our days," replied old Julian.   "In the days of long ago the fingers of our ancestors stood together in the same position.   One day one of these fingers, the one we call the little finger, became very hungry, and he asked the finger next to him to give him some food.

"'O brother!' said the Ring-Finger in reply, 'I am hungry also; but where shall we get food?'

"'Heaven is merciful,' put in the Middle-Finger, trying to comfort his two brothers; 'Heaven will give us some.'

"'But, Brother Middle-Finger,' protested the Forefinger, 'what if Heaven gives us no food?'

"'Well, then,' interposed the Thumb, 'let us steal!'

"'Steal!' echoed the Forefinger, not at all pleased by the advice that had just been given.   'Mr. Thumb knows better than to do that, I hope!'

"'That is bad policy, Mr. Thumb,' concluded the other

[1] Narrated by Leopoldo Uichanco, a Tagalog from Calamba, La Laguna.

three unanimously. 'Your idea is against morality, against God, against yourself, against everybody. Our conscience will not permit us to steal.'

"'Oh, no, no!' returned Thumb angrily, 'you are greatly mistaken, my friends! Haven't you sense enough even to know how foolish you are to oppose my plan? Do you call my scheme bad policy, — to save your lives and mine?'

"'Ay, if that be your plan,' said the other four fingers, 'you can go your own way. As for us, we would rather starve and die than steal.' Then the four virtuous brothers drove Thumb in shame out of their community, and would have nothing more to do with him.

"So that is why," concluded old Julian, "we see our thumbs separated from the other four fingers. He was a thief; and the other four, who were honest, did not care to live with him. And it is because Little-Finger did not have enough to eat, that we see him lean and weak these days."

NOTE.

I know of no other Filipino accounts of why the thumb is separated from the rest of the fingers. As an interesting curiosity, however, I might cite a Bicol children's jingle of five lines which characterize briefly the five fingers (the thumb is the last described) : —

Maya-mayang saday	"Pretty little sparrow,
Magayon na singsignan	Beautiful for a ring,
Daculang mangmang	Long but lazy fellow,
Atrevido	Froward, insolent thing,
Hababang tao	Dumpy, dwarfish one."

76. WHY SNAILS CLIMB UP GRASS.[1]

Long ago, when the various kinds of animals dwelt together in a kind of community, a *dalag* (a kind of mud-fish), a dragon-fly, a wasp, and a snail agreed to live together in a common house. They furthermore agreed to divide up the different household duties according to their power and skill. Accordingly, Dalag, since he was the biggest and strongest of all, was made the head of the house. He was also to provide food for his little companions. Dragon-Fly was made the messenger, because he was the swiftest of them all, but was too weak for any other kind of work. Wasp was made the house-guard because of his poisonous sting. Besides being guard, he was also

[1] Narrated by José E. Tomeldan of Binalonan, Pangasinan.

to keep the house in repair, because he could carry bits of earth
and other building-materials. Snail was made the cook, because he was too slow for any other duty except tending the
house.

Early one day Dalag went out to look for food. He swam
slowly here and there among the water-plants, when suddenly
he saw something moving on the surface of the water. When
he approached nearer, he saw that it was a big frog swimming
helplessly among the duck-weeds. "This is a big piece of sweet
food for us," thought Dalag, and without hesitation he seized
the frog. When he had assured himself that it could not get
away from him, he started to swim home. But, alas! he never
reached his companions; for a sharp hook was inside the frog,
and poor Dalag was caught fast. He tried hard to free himself,
but in vain. Soon a fisherman came, and, putting Dalag in his
basket, took him home and ate him.

In the mean time Dalag's three companions were anxiously
waiting for him. When they realized that he was lost, Dragon-
Fly was sent out to look for him. Before he went, Dragon-Fly
spent a long time arranging his neck-tie. Then he flew away,
turning his head in all directions to look for Dalag. At last
he met Bolasi (a kind of fish whose lips always move in and out
on the surface of the water), and he became very angry because
he thought that Bolasi was laughing at his neck-tie. Dragon-
Fly thought that his tie must be too loose, so he tightened it.
Still Bolasi laughed every time he saw Dragon-Fly. Dragon-
Fly kept drawing his tie tighter and tighter, until at last he
cut his own head off, and that was the end of him.

Two days had now passed; still Dalag and Dragon-Fly were
missing from home. By this time Wasp and Snail were very
hungry. But Snail had the advantage over Wasp; for Snail
could eat mud to pass away the time, while Wasp could not
eat mud, but could only draw in his belt a little tighter. At
last Wasp could no longer endure his hunger. His abdomen
by this time had become very slender: so he flew forth in search
of either Dalag or Dragon-Fly. While he was flying about, his
hunger oppressed him so much, that he tightened his belt again
and again, until he finally broke in two; and that was the end
of Wasp.

Now only Snail was left. He set out from his home, and
wandered everywhere in search of his three companions, weep-

ing as he went. His food consisted mostly of mud. Whenever he could find a stalk of grass or the stem of a water-plant, Snail would climb up to look around and to see if any of his old friends were in sight. Even to-day the snails still weep; and whenever they see a stalk of grass projecting above the surface of the water, they climb up and look around, trying to discover their old friends.

77. WHY THE CUTTLE-FISH AND SQUIDS PRODUCE A BLACK LIQUID.[1]

A long time ago, after Bathala[2] had created the fishes, he assigned a certain day for all of them to meet in the Dark Sea. The object of this convention was to appoint some officers. Early in the morning of the day designated, the fishes were to be seen hurrying to the meeting. When they reached the assembly hall, they found Bathala sitting on a beautiful stone, waiting for them. He called the roll when it seemed that all of the fishes were present. It was found that the cuttle-fish and squid were absent, so they waited for them a half-hour; but still they did not come. At last Bathala arose, and said, "The meeting will come to order." After the fishes had taken their proper positions, Bathala continued, "The object of this meeting is to appoint some officers and to issue their appointments."

At once all the fishes became very quiet and respectful, for all were anxious to know what offices each was going to hold. Bathala appointed the sting-ray sergeant-at-arms: hence all sting-rays now have whip-like tails. The crocodile was appointed cadaver-carrier: so now all its children have a coffin-like skin on their backs. The crab was made a soldier: so to-day all its descendants have large and strong fore-legs. Bathala had not finished giving out his appointments when the two missing members came. They at once interrupted the meeting by asking what it was all about. Bathala became very angry at the interruption, so he scolded the sting-ray and the squid severely. The rebuke humiliated them so, that they agreed between themselves to go get mud and throw it on the official appointments. When they had gotten the mud, they came back and asked Bathala to give them something to do; but,

[1] Narrated by Victoria Ciudadano of Batangas. She says she heard the story from an old woman. It is known by both the Tagalogs and the Visayans.

[2] Bathala, the Supreme Being of the ancient Tagalogs.

instead of appointing them to some work, he only scolded them for being late. Angered, they now threw mud on all the appointments that had already been drawn up. This insulting act of the cuttle-fish and the squid so enraged Bathala, that he stood up, and said in thundering tones, "Now I shall punish you. From this time on, you and your descendants shall carry pouches of mud with you all the time. Besides, you shall be very slow in moving because of your heavy loads." The squid tried to make excuses, but Bathala became angrier than ever, and said, "You are the naughtiest creature I ever had. As a punishment, you and your children shall remain the same size as you are now." And all of Bathala's words have turned out to be true.

78. WHY COCKS HAVE COMBS ON THEIR HEADS.[1]

Once upon a time there was a magician named Pablo, who had a son called Juan. Pablo was very industrious, but Juan was lazy and disobedient. Juan cared for nothing but fine clothes and his own appearance; he would not help his father. One day Pablo went into his son's room to find out what he was doing. There he was, standing before a mirror, and combing his hair. Pablo was so angry at his son, that he immediately snatched the comb from his hand. Then he angrily struck the boy's head with the comb, and spoke these harsh words: "Since you always want to use the comb, let it be on your head forever! I prefer to have no son at all. I would rather see you changed into a bird than to remain such a disobedient, worthless boy." The father struck his son's head so hard, that the comb stuck deep into the skull. By Pablo's magic power, Juan was immediately changed into a cock, and the comb on his head was changed into flesh. We can see it to-day on the heads of all the descendants of Juan.

NOTE.

I know of no variants of stories Nos. 76–78.

79. (a) HOW THE CROW BECAME BLACK.[2]

A long time ago, when Bathala, the god of the land, was peacefully ruling his dominions, he had many pets. Among

[1] Narrated by Rosita Nieva, a Tagalog from Boac, Marinduque. She heard the story from her grandmother.

[2] Narrated by Vicente L. Neri, a Visayan from Cagayan, Misamis. He was told the story by his grandmother.

these, his two favorites were the dove and the crow. The crow was noted for its bright, pretty plumage.

One day Bathala had a quarrel with Dumagat, the god of the sea. Bathala's subjects had been stealing fish, which were the subjects of Dumagat. When Dumagat learned of this, and could get no satisfaction from Bathala, he retaliated. He opened the big pipe through which the water of the world passes, and flooded the dominions of Bathala, until nearly all the people were drowned. When the water had abated somewhat, Bathala sent the crow, his favorite messenger, to find out whether all his subjects had been killed. The crow flew out from the palace where the god lived, and soon saw the corpses of many persons floating about. He descended, alighted on one, and began to eat the decaying cadaver. When Bathala saw that it was late and that the crow had not returned, he sent the dove on the same errand, telling the bird also to find out what had become of the first messenger. The dove flew away, looking for any signs of life. At last he saw the crow eating some of the decaying bodies. Immediately he told the crow that the king had sent for him, and together they flew back to Bathala's palace.

When the two birds arrived at the king's court, the dove told Bathala that the crow had been eating some dead bodies, and consequently had not done what he had been sent to do. Bathala was very angry at this disobedience. Without saying a word, he seized his big inkstand filled with black ink and threw it at the crow, which was immediately covered. Bathala then turned to the dove, and said, "You, my dove, because of your faithfulness, shall be my favorite pet, and no longer shall you be a messenger." Then he turned to the crow, and said, "You, foul bird, shall forever remain black; you shall forever be a scavenger, and every one shall hate you."

So that is why to-day the dove is loved by the people, and the crow hated. The crows to-day are all black, because they are descendants of the bird punished by Bathala.

(b) WHY THE CROW IS BLACK.[1]

The first crow that lived on the earth was a beautiful bird with a sweet voice. The universe was ruled over by the god

[1] Narrated by Ricardo Ortega, an Ilocano living in Tarlac. The story, however, is Pampangan.

Sinukuan, and all his subjects were either plants or animals. No human beings were yet in existence. Sinukuan lived in a beautiful palace surrounded with gardens of gold. In these gardens lived two crows who sang sweet songs, and did nothing but fly about among the flowers and trees. Their golden plumage was beautiful to see, and Sinukuan took great delight in them.

Once a terrible pestilence visited the earth, and a great many of Sinukuan's animals began to die. In his distress and sorrow, Sinukuan at once set out and made a tour of his kingdom to give what relief he could to his suffering subjects. After being away three days, he returned to his palace, his mind weighted down by all the death and sickness he had seen. When he reached his garden, he called to his two birds to come sing for him and relieve his mental anguish; but neither of the birds came. Sinukuan went through his gardens, but he called in vain. "O birds! where are you?" he cried. Thinking that perhaps they had flown away and had been attacked by the pestilence, he determined to make another trip through his kingdom and look for them.

He had not walked a mile, when, approaching a number of dead animals, he saw the pair feasting on the decaying flesh. When they saw their master, they bowed their heads in shame. Had not Sinukuan restrained himself, he might have killed them that very moment; but he thought of a better way to punish them. "Now," he said, as he cursed them, "from this time on, you shall be very ugly black birds; you shall lose your beautiful voice, and shall be able to make only a harsh cry."

From that time on, those birds were black, and their offspring are the crows of to-day.

(c) THE DOVE AND THE CROW.[1]

A few days after the inundation of the world, God sent a crow down to earth to see how deep the water was on the land. When the crow flew down to earth, he was surprised to see so many dead animals everywhere. It came to his mind that perhaps they would taste good, so he alighted on one of them and began to eat. He was so very much pleased with the abundance of food about him, that he forgot all about the command God had given him, and he remained on the earth.

---

[1] Narrated by Restituto D. Carpio, a Zambal from Cabangan, Zambales.

On the third day, since the crow had not returned, God sent a dove down to earth to find out the depth of the water, and to make other observations of the things that had taken place on the earth. As the dove was a faithful creature, she did not forget what God told her. When she reached the earth, she did not alight on any dead animal, but alighted directly in the water. Now, the water was red from the blood of so many creatures that had been slain. When the dove stood in the bloody water, she found that it was only an inch deep. She at once flew back to heaven, where, in the presence of God, she related what she had seen on earth, while the crimson color on her feet was evidence of the depth of the water.

After a short time the crow returned. He came before God, who spoke to him thus: "What made you so long? Why did you not return sooner from the earth?" As the crow had no good reason to give for his delay, he said nothing: he simply bent his head.

God punished the crow by putting a chain on his legs. So that to-day the crow cannot walk: all he can do is to hop from place to place. The dove, which was faithful to God, is now the favorite pet bird the world over. The red color on her feet may be seen to-day as evidence that she performed her duty.

NOTES.

None of our stories presents the exact sequence of events found in other folk-tales of the sending-out of the raven and the dove after the Deluge to measure the depth of the water; but there can be no doubt that the Zambal story (c) derives immediately from one of these. The Visayan account mentions a flood, but not the Deluge. In the fact that the cause of the great inundation is a quarrel between two chief Pagan deities, there seems to be preserved an old native tradition. In the Pampangan story not only is the curse of the crow attributed to a Pagan deity, Sinukuan, but the occasion of the bird's downfall is a pestilence. There is no mention whatever of a flood, nor is the dove alluded to.

Dähnhardt (1 : 283–287) has discussed a number of folk-tales and traditions of the punishment of the raven and the rewarding of the dove. These are for the most part associated with popular accounts of events immediately after the Deluge. Two that seem to be nearly related to our versions may be reproduced here in English: —

(Polish story of the dove.) When Noah had despatched a dove from the Ark, the bird alighted on an oak, but soiled its feet in the water of the Flood, which was all red from the blood of the multitudes that had been drowned. Since then, doves have all had red feet. (This detail appears in part word for word in our Zambal story.)

(Arabian tradition recorded by the ninth-century historian Tabarí.) Noah said to the raven, "Go and set foot on the earth and see how deep the water is now." The raven flew forth. But on the way it found a corpse; it began to eat of it, and did not return to Noah. Noah, troubled, cursed the raven: "May God make you despised of mankind, and may your food always be corpses!" Then Noah sent the dove forth. The dove flew away, and without alighting dipped its feet in the water. But the water of the Flood was salty and stinging; it burned the dove's feet so that the feathers did not grow in again, and the skin dropped off. Those doves that have red feet without feathers are the descendants of the dove that Noah sent forth. Then Noah said, "May God make you welcome among mankind!" For this reason the dove is even to-day beloved of mankind. (This version is of especial interest in connection with the Visayan story, which comes from Mindanao, the home of Mohammedanism in the Philippines. Note the close correspondences.)

While it appears to me more than likely that our Filipino stories derive ultimately from Arabian sources through the Moros of the southern islands rather than through the Spaniards, nevertheless to settle the question absolutely more variants are needed for comparison.

Attention might be called to incidents peculiar to the Philippine accounts and not found in any of the versions cited by Dähnhardt: —

(1) A deity, not Noah, sends out the birds.

(2) The crows of Sinukuan (*b*), in addition to becoming black, are condemned forever afterward to have raucous, unpleasant voices.

(3) In the Visayan story Bathala makes the crow black by hurling an inkstand at it. This undignified detail may have been taken over from one of the popular metrical romances ("Baldovinos" or "Doce Pares") in which Charlemagne loses his temper and throws an ink-well at Roland (see JAFL 29 : 208, 214, 215). Or it is just barely possible that this popular bit of machinery became attached to our story of the crow on the analogy of an Annamite tale (Landes, Contes annamites, p. 210 f., cited by Dähnhardt, 3 : 65): —

The raven and the *coq de pagode* were once men in the service of the saint (Confucius), who transformed them into birds as a punishment for disobedience. In order to undo the punishment and to make the saint laugh, the raven smeared itself all over with ink. The *coq de pagode* wished to do the same to itself, but had only enough black ink for half its body; for the rest it was obliged to use red. Therefore the raven is black, and the *coq de pagode* is half red, half black.

(4) In the Zambal story the crow is punished, not by being made black, but by having a chain put on its legs; so that the crows to-day cannot walk, but must hop from place to place.

In conclusion I will cite merely for completeness an American Indian version not found in Dähnhardt. It is referred to by Sir J. G. Frazer (Folk-Lore in the Old Testament [1918], 1 : 297), who writes as follows: —

"The same missionary [i.e., Mgr. Faraud, in Annales de la Propagation de la Foi, xxxvi (1864), 388 *et seq.*] reports a deluge legend current among the Crees, another tribe of the Algonquin stock in Canada; but this Cree story bears clear traces of Christian influence, for in it the man is said to have sent forth from the canoe, first a raven, and second a wood-pigeon. The raven did not return, and as à punishment for his disobedience the bird was changed from white to black; the pigeon returned with his claws full of mud, from which the man inferred that the earth was dried up; so he landed."

For other folk explanations of the black color of the crow or raven, see Dähnhardt, 3 : 59, 65–66, 71, 369. An entirely different account of how the crow's feathers, which were originally as white as starch, became black, is given in our No. 71 (*b*).

80. WHY THE OCEAN IS SALTY.[1]

A few years after the creation of the world there lived a tall giant by the name of Ang-ngalo, the only son of the god of building. Ang-ngalo was a wanderer, and a lover of work. He lived in the mountains, where he dug many caves. These caves he protected from the continual anger of Angin, the goddess of the wind, by precipices and sturdy trees.

One bright morning, while Ang-ngalo was climbing to his loftiest cave, he spied across the ocean — the ocean at the time was pure, its water being the accumulated tears of disappointed goddesses — a beautiful maid. She beckoned to him, and waved her black handkerchief: so Ang-ngalo waded across to her through the water. The deep caverns in the ocean are his footprints.

This beautiful maid was Sipgnet, the goddess of the dark. She said to Ang-ngalo, "I am tired of my dark palace in heaven. You are a great builder. What I want you to do for me is to erect a great mansion on this spot. This mansion must be built of bricks as white as snow."

Ang-ngalo could not find any bricks as white as snow: the only white thing there was then was salt. So he went for help to Asin, the ruler of the kingdom of Salt. Asin gave him pure bricks of salt, as white as snow. Then Ang-ngalo built hundreds

[1] Narrated by José M. Paredes of Bangued, Ilocos Sur. He heard the story from a farmer.

of bamboo bridges across the ocean. Millions of men were
employed day and night transporting the white bricks from one
side of the ocean to the other. At last the patience of Ocean
came to an end: she could not bear to have her deep and quiet
slumber disturbed. One day, while the men were busy carrying the salt bricks across the bridges, she sent forth big waves
and destroyed them. The brick-carriers and their burden were
buried in her deep bosom. In time the salt dissolved, and to-
day the ocean is salty.

NOTE.

I know of no close analogues to this etiological myth.

The hero of the tale, Ang-ngalo, is the same as the Aolo (Angalo)
mentioned in the notes to No. 3 (p. 27, footnote). Blumentritt (*s.v.*)
writes, "Angangalo is the name of the Adam of the Ilocanos. He
was a giant who created the world at the order of the supreme God."

81. (*a*) WHY THE SKY IS CURVED.[1]

Many, many years ago, when people were innocent, as soon
as they died, their souls went directly to heaven. In a short
time heaven was crowded with souls, because nearly every one
went there. One day, while God was sitting on his throne, he
felt it moved by some one. On looking up, he saw that the
souls were pushing towards him, because the sky was about to
fall. At once he summoned five angels, and said to them,
"Go at once to the earth, and hold up the sky with your heads
until I can have it repaired." Then God called together all
his carpenters, and said to them, "Repair the heavens as soon
as possible."

The work was done; but it happened that the tallest angel
was standing in the centre of the group; and so, ever since, the
sky has been curved.

(*b*) WHY THE SKY IS HIGH.[2]

In olden days the sky was low, — so low that it could be
reached by a stick of ordinary length. The people in those
days said that God had created the sky in such a way that he
could hear his people when they called to him. In turn, God

---

[1] Narrated by Aurelia Malvar, a Tagalog from Santo Tomas, Batangas. Her father
told her the story.

[2] Narrated by Deogracias Lutero of Janiuay, Iloilo. He says that the story is often
heard in his barrio.

could send his blessings to earth as soon as men needed them. Because of this close connection between God and his subjects, the people were well-provided for, and they did not need to work. Whenever they wanted to eat, they would simply call God. Before their request was made, almost, the food would be on the table; but after the expulsion of Adam and Eve, God made men work for their own living. With this change in their condition came the custom of holding feasts, when the men would rest from their labors.

One day one of the chiefs, Abing by name, held a feast. Many people came to enjoy it. A *sayao*, or native war-dance, was given in honor of the men belonging to the chief, and it was acted by men brandishing spears. While acting, one of the actors, who was drunk, tried to show his skill, but he forgot that the sky was so low. When he darted his spear, he happened to pierce the sky, and one of the gods was wounded. This angered God the Father: so he raised the sky as we have it to-day, far from the earth.

NOTES.

I have come across no variants of the Tagalog story of why the sky is curved.

Our second story, however, "Why the Sky is High," is without doubt a Malayan tradition, as analogues from the Bagobos and the Pagan tribes of Borneo attest. Miss Benedict (JAFL 26 : 16–17) furnishes two Bagobo myths on "Why the Sky Went Up:" —

(a) "In the beginning the sky lay low over the earth — so low that when the Mona wanted to pound their rice, they had to kneel down on the ground to get a play for the arm. Then the poor woman called Tuglibung said to the sky, 'Go up higher! Don't you see that I cannot pound my rice well?' So the sky began to move upwards. When it had gone up about five fathoms, the woman said again, 'Go up still more!' This made the sun angry at the woman, and he rushed up very high."

(b) "In the beginning the sky hung so low over the earth that the people could not stand upright, could not do their work. For this reason the man in the sky said to the sky, 'Come up!' Then the sky went up to its present place."

With Miss Benedict's first version, compare Hose and McDougall (2 : 142): —

"According to an old man of the Long Kiputs of Borneo, the stars are holes in the sky made by the roots of trees in the world above the sky projecting through the floor of that world. At one time, he explained, the sky was close to the earth, but one day *Usai*, a giant, when working sago with a wooden mallet, accidentally struck his mallet against the sky; since which time the sky has been far up out of the reach of man."

A different explanation of why the sky went up is current in British North Borneo. It is embodied in the story of "The Horned Owl and the Moon" (Evans, JRAI 43 : 433): —

"The moon is male and the Pwak (horned owl) is female.

"Long ago, when the sky was very low down, only a man's height from the ground, the moon and the Pwak fell in love and married. At that time there was a man whose wife was with child. The woman came down from the house, and as the heat of the sun struck her on the stomach, she became ill, for the sky was very low. Then the man was very angry because his wife was ill, and he made seven blow-pipe arrows. Early the next morning he took his blow-pipe with him and went to the place where the sun rises, and waited. Now at that time there were seven suns. When they rose, he shot six of them and left one remaining; then he went home. At the time the man shot the suns the Pwak was sitting on the house-top in the sky combing her hair. The comb fell from the sky to the ground, and the Pwak flew down to get it; but when she found it, she could no longer fly back to the sky; for, while she had been looking for the comb, the sky had risen to its present place; since, when the man had shot the six suns, the remaining sun, being frightened, ran away up into the air and took the sky with it. And so on the present day, whenever the moon comes out, the Pwak cries to it; but the moon says to it, 'What can I do, for you are down there below, while I am up here in the sky?'"

82. AN UNEQUAL MATCH; OR, WHY THE CARABAO'S HOOF IS SPLIT.[1]

Once a carabao and a turtle met on a road. They walked in the woods, and had a fine talk together. The turtle was a sort of humorist, and was constantly giving exhibitions of his dexterity in getting food by trickery. But he was especially anxious to win the friendship of the carabao; for he thought that, if they were friendly, this big fellow would help him whenever he got into trouble. So he said to the carabao, "Let us live together and hunt our food together! thus we shall break the monotony of our solitary lives."

But the carabao snorted when he heard this proposal; and he replied, "You slow thing! you ought to live with the drones, not with a swift and powerful person like me."

The turtle was very much offended, and to get even he challenged the carabao to a race. At first the carabao refused to accept the challenge, for he thought it would be a disgrace for him to run against a turtle. The turtle said to the carabao, "If you will not race with me, I will go to all the forests, woods, and mountains, and tell all your companions and all my friends and all the animal kingdom that you are a coward."

[1] Narrated by Godofredo Rivera, a Tagalog from Pagsanjan, La Laguna.

Now the carabao was persuaded; and he said, "All right, only give me three days to get ready for the race." The turtle was only too glad to have the contest put off for three days, for then he too would have a chance to prepare his plans. The agreement between the turtle and the carabao was that the race should extend over seven hills.

The turtle at once set out to visit seven of his friends; and, by telling them that if he could win this race it would be to the glory of the turtle kingdom, he got them to promise to help him. So the next day he stationed a turtle on the top of each hill, after giving them all instructions.

The third day came. Early the next morning the turtle and the carabao met at the appointed hill. At a given signal the race began, and soon the runners lost sight of each other. When the carabao reached the second hill, he was astonished to see the turtle ahead of him, shouting, "Here I am!" After giving this yell, the turtle at once disappeared. And at every hill the carabao found his enemy ahead of him. When the carabao was convinced at the seventh hill that he had been defeated, he became so angry that he kicked the turtle. On account of the hardness of its shell, the turtle was uninjured; but the hoof of the carabao was split in two, because of the force of the blow. And even to-day, the carabaos still bear the mark which an unjust action on the part of their ancestor against one whom he knew was far inferior to him in strength produced on himself.

NOTES.

A Pampangan story furnished by Wenceslao Vitug of Lubao, Pampanga, runs thus in abstract: —

THE DEER AND THE SNAIL.

Snail challenges deer to race, and stations his friends at intervals along the way. Every time deer stops and calls out to see where his antagonist is, a snail answers from a spot a few yards ahead of deer. At the end of the course the defeated deer falls fainting. His gall is sucked out by the snails near him. To this day snails taste bitter, and the deer has no gall.

For a similar Visayan tale see "The Snail and the Deer" (JAFL 20 : 315). A Tinguian version may be found in Cole (No. 82, p. 198).

This very widespread story is comprehensively discussed by Dähnhardt (4 : 46–97), who gives a large number of variants from all parts of the world. The Philippine forms of it may reasonably be adjudged native, I believe; at any rate, they need not have been derived from Europe.

A Borneo version (Evans, 475–476) not given in Dähnhardt may be mentioned here in conclusion.   In it the *plandok* · (mouse-deer), which has deceived and brought about the deaths of all the larger animals, agrees to run a race with the *omong* (hermit-crab).   The crab stations three companions at corners of the square race-course, and wins.   The mouse-deer runs itself to death.

APPENDIX.

[Additional notes, chiefly in the nature of American Indian, Negro, and Sinhalese (Ceylon) variants.]

SUPPLEMENTARY BIBLIOGRAPHY.

BOLTE (JOHANNES) UND POLÍVKA (GEORG). Anmerkungen zu den Kinder- und Hausmärchen der Brüder Grimm. Vol. 3 (Nos. 121–225). Leipzig, 1918.

Journal of American Folk-Lore. (Cited JAFL.)

— Boas, F. Notes on Mexican Folk-Lore (JAFL 25 : 204–260). 1912.

— Bolduc (E.), Tremblay (M.), and Barbeau (C.-M.). Contes populaires canadiens (troisième série) (JAFL 32 : 90–167). 1919.

— Bundy, R. C. Folk-Tales from Liberia (JAFL 32 : 406–427). 1919.

— Espinosa, A. M. Comparative Notes on New-Mexican and Mexican Spanish Folk-Tales (JAFL 27 : 211–231). 1914.

— — New-Mexican Spanish Folk-Lore (JAFL 27 : 105–147). 1914.

— — New-Mexican Spanish Folk-Lore: Folk-Tales (JAFL 24 : 397–444). 1911.

— Folk-Tales from Alabama (JAFL 32 : 397–401). 1919.

— Folk-Tales from Georgia (JAFL 32 : 402–405). 1919.

— Mason, J. A. Folk-Tales of the Tepecanos (JAFL 27 : 148–210). 1914.

— Mechling, W. H. Stories and Songs from the Southern Atlantic Coastal Region of Mexico (JAFL 29 : 547–558). 1916.

— — Stories from Tuxtepec, Oaxaca (JAFL 25 : 199–203). 1912.

— Parsons, E. C. Pueblo-Indian Folk-Tales, probably of Spanish Provenience (JAFL 31 : 216–255). 1918.

— — Tales from Guilford County, North Carolina (JAFL 30 : 168–200). 1917.

— Recinos, Adrián. Cuentos populares de Guatemala (JAFL 31 : 472–487). 1918.

— Skinner, Alanson. European Tales from the Plains Ojibwa (JAFL 29 : 330–340). 1916.

— — Plains Ojibwa Tales (JAFL 32 : 280–305). 1919.

— Speck, F. G. Malecite Tales (JAFL 30 : 479–485). 1917.

— Stewart, Sadie E. Seven Folk-Tales from the Sea Islands, South Carolina (JAFL 32 : 394–396). 1919.

— Teit, James. European Tales from the Upper Thompson Indians (JAFL 29 : 301–329). 1916.

LAIDLAW, GEORGE E.   Ojibwa Myths and Tales (reprinted from the
      Archæological Report, 1918).
PARKER, H.   Village Folk-Tales of Ceylon.   London: Vol. 1, 1910;
      Vol. 2, 1914; Vol. 3, 1914.
PARSONS, ELSIE CLEWS.   Folk-Tales of Andros Island, Bahamas
      (Memoirs of the American Folk-Lore Society, Vol. 13).   New
      York, 1918.   (Cited MAFLS 13.)   See also under *Journal
      of American Folk-Lore.*
RADIN-ESPINOSA.   El Folklore de Oaxaca, recogido por Paul Radin y
      publicado por Aurelio M. Espinosa (Anales de la Escuela
      Internacional de Arqueología y Etnología Americanas).   New
      York, 1917.
SAUNIÈRE, S. DE.   Cuentos populares araucanos y chilenos (Revista
      de folklore chileno, Vol. 7).   Santiago de Chile, 1918.
THOMPSON, STITH.   European Tales among the North American
      Indians (Colorado College Publication).   Colorado Springs,
      1919.

SUPPLEMENTARY NOTES.

1.[1]

Dr. Boas gives the bibliography of "Dr. Know-All" in America in
JAFL 25 : 151.

A Sinhalese variant may be found in Parker, 1 : 179–185 (No. 23).

2.

Page 11 (footnote).   Dr. Boas informs me that *petate* is a Mexican-
Spanish word borrowed from the Nahuatl.

Full bibliography of Grimm, No. 122 ("Donkey Cabbages") is
given in Bolte-Polívka, 3 : 3–9.

In JAFL 28 : 56 is a Penobscot story containing the loss of three
magic objects, transportation to a distant place, escape of princess
by means of transportation-cap, discovery by hero of magic apples,
punishment of princess, and the recovery of the magic objects (see
Thompson, 401).

3.

Page 25 (A).   For a list of Hindoo stories in which the hero is
only a span high, see Parker, 2 : 256.

Page 25–26 (B[1-5]).   In a Biloxi tale not belonging in other respects
to our group, the hero's uncle puts the hero to some hard tests, hoping
to make away with him (see Thompson, 376).

---

[1] This and the serial numbers following refer to corresponding numbers of tales.

Page 26 (B²). The attempts to kill the hero in a well by throwing huge rocks on him are found in some of the American variants of the "Strong John" cycle. (See Thompson, 435–436, for French-Canadian and Maliseet versions.)

Page 26 (D.) In a Maliseet tale (Thompson, 340) the strong hero sets out on his travels with a giant cane that will hold fifty salted cattle.

Page 27 (E). In ten of the American Indian versions of "John the Bear" are found the extraordinary companions (see Thompson, 336–344).

Page 29. With Kakarangkang's adventure inside the crocodile, compare an Araucano story (Saunière, No. 3), in which the heroine with a knife is swallowed by the big king of fishes. She cuts her way out, saving her brother and others imprisoned.

4.

Interrupted-cooking episode. For a Negro version from Bahamas, see MAFLS 13, No. 93; also bibliography on p. 142 (footnote). In his analysis of " John the Bear " stories among the American Indians, Thompson (336–342) notes this episode in Assiniboin, Tehuano, Shoshone, Thompson River, Maliseet, Loucheux, and Micmac versions.

Bee-hive hoax. Three Mexican variants on this idea may be noted. In one (JAFL 25 : 237), rabbit pretends that the bee-hive is a school, which he permits coyote to keep. In another (*ibid.*, 206) rabbit pretends that a wasp-nest is a cradle, and gets coyote to rock it. The third is a Cora story given in abstract by Dr. Boas (*ibid.*, 260), which is nearest the form of the incident as found in our tales. Opossum pretends that the bee-hive is a bell which coyote is to ring when he hears the sky-rockets. In a New-Mexican Spanish story (JAFL 27 : 134–135) fox tells coyote that the bee-hive is his school humming.

5.

Parker's Sinhalese story "The Elephant-Fool" (3 : 100–111, No. 203) tells of a man who borrowed another's elephant; but the beast died before it could be returned. The borrower offers payment or another animal, but the owner will accept nothing but his own elephant alive. Through the cleverness of his wife, the borrower is able to make the obdurate man break a water-pot, and in turn demands his very water-pot back unbroken. Unable to do anything else, the owner of the elephant says that the two debts cancel each other, and goes away. Parker notes that in another Sinhalese form of this story both persons institute law-suits. He also cites a Chinese variant (p. 111).

6.

Page 51, line 41. For bibliography of Grimm, No. 183, see Bolte-Polívka, 3 : 333–335.

Parker (2 : 247–268, No. 137) gives a Sinhalese story, with three variants, which is definitely connected with our tales, and confirms my belief that the "False-Proofs" cycle is native to southern India. In Parker's main story the false proofs are five, — ass (voice), two winnowing-trays (ears), two bundles of creepers (testicles?), a tom-tom (eye), and two elephant tusks (teeth). In variant *b* the false proofs are drum (roar), deer-hide rope (hair), pair of elephant tusks (teeth).

For another Sinhalese story of how a man and his wife "bluffed" a terrible Yakā hiding under the bed to kill him, see Parker, 1 : 148–149 (No. 17).

7.

Page 62. Analogous to the task cited from Jātaka, No. 546, is one of the problems in the Liberian story "Impossible *vs.* Impossible" (JAFL 32 : 413). Problem: Make a mat from rice-grains. Solution: Old rice-mat demanded as pattern. — For making *rope out of husks*, and analogous tasks, see Bolte-Polívka, 2 : 513.

Page 62 (3). In Parker, No. 79, a king requires a man to put a hundred gourd-fruits in a hundred small-mouthed vessels. His clever daughter *grows* them there. Parker cites a story from Swynnerton's Indian Night's Entertainment, in which a clever girl sends melons in jars to a prince and requires him to remove the melons without injuring them or the jars. This problem is identical with one on our p. 58 (16–17).

In still another Sinhalese story a foolish king requires a Paṇḍitayā, under penalty of death, to teach the royal white horse to speak. The wise man's daughter saves her father's life by telling him what to reply to the king (Parker, 1 : 199–200, No. 27). — In Parker, 3 : 112–113 (No. 204), a country-girl meets a prince, to whose questions she gives enigmatical replies. He is clever enough to interpret them correctly.

Page 63 (4). In Parker, 2 : 7–9 (No. 78), a king requires milk from oxen. The clever village girl's answer is of a kind with Marcela's (our collection, p. 55): she sets out for the washerman's with a bundle of cloths, is met by the king, and tells him her father has come of age in the same manner as women (i.e., he has menstruated).

8.

For *stealing eggs from under bird*, see Bolte-Polívka, 3 : 57–58.

Bolte-Polívka's notes on Grimm, No. 192, include a discussion of both the "Master Thief" cycle (3 : 379–395) and the Rhampsinitus "Treasure-House" saga (3 : 395–406). Two Sinhalese variants of the latter cycle, lacking in Bolte-Polívka's bibliography, are Parker's No. 189 and variant (3 : 41–46). Here the thieves are father and son; son cuts off father's head to prevent identification. The stories end with the exposure of the body and the escape of the son, who falls from a tree when his mother bursts into laments at the sight of her husband's corpse.

Four American Indian versions of the "Master Thief" are analyzed by Thompson (427–429), — Maliseet, Dakota, Thompson River, Wyandot.

A Oaxaca version of the "Master Thief" is given in Radin-Espinosa, 225–227 (No. 116): it preserves a number of features of the Rhampsinitus story. Likewise a New-Mexican Spanish tale (JAFL 24: 423–424), in which, after preliminary skill-tests, the two thieves rob the king. The Mexican thief is caught; the Spanish thief cuts off his head. The corpse, by order of the king, is carried through town, and the house of the mourner is marked with blood. The Spanish thief escapes by marking *all* the houses with blood. (For the bibliography of *marking all the house-doors with chalk* to prevent discovery, see Bolte-Polívka, 3 : 145, note.)

9.

Page 78. *Not counting self.* This incident occurs in a Sinhalese story (Parker, 1 : 258, No. 44). (See *ibid.*, 259, for three variants from India and one from China.) Comparative bibliography of this motif is given in Bolte-Polívka, 3 : 149 (note 1).

Page 78. *Killing fly on face.* Sinhalese (Parker, 1 : 319–321, No. 58): The stupid hero strikes with a rice-pestle at a fly on his mother's head, and kills her. Wyandot (Thompson, 423): The numskull hero hits the head of a sleeping child to kill mosquito, and kills child. Ojibwa (Laidlaw, 63): Flies on baby's head "killed" with rubber boot.

10.

Page 87. Add to the bibliography of the "Magic Ring" cycle three American forms of the story, — French-Canadian, Micmac, and Maliseet (analyzed by Thompson, 398–399).

An interesting Sinhalese version is Parker's No. 208 (3 : 127–131). Here a lazy prince buys a cobra, parrot, and cat. From the snakeking he receives a ring by means of which he can create anything he wants. He creates a palace and a princess. The princess and ring are stolen by an old woman acting as agent for a king who came to know of the beautiful princess (hair floating down-stream). Through the aid of his faithful animals, especially the cat, which coerces the king of the rats, the hero recovers his wife and magic object. (See also Parker's extensive notes [131–135] for other Oriental versions.)

11.

Page 114. See Bolte-Polívka, 3 : 483–486, for notes on Grimm's fragment "The Louse."   Bolte and Polívka (3 : 84–85) give brief notes on Grimm, No. 134, mostly in the nature of *addenda* to their notes on Grimm, No. 71, with which this story is closely related.

Three American Indian variants of Grimm, No. 71, are analyzed by Thompson (346–347).

For a Negro version from the Bahamas, see MAFLS 13, No. 20.

12.

Page 125, line 21.   For "Diego and Juan" read "Diego and Pedro."

Page 128, note 3.   Dr. Farnham presents a fuller and more recent study of the cycle of the "Contending Lovers" in Publications of the Modern Language Association, 28 (1920): 247–323.

Page 128.   Full bibliographical treatment of our Type I, the "Creation of Woman," may be found in Bolte-Polívka, 3 : 53–57.

Page 133.   Bibliography of Grimm, No. 124, will be found in Bolte-Polívka, 3 : 10–12; of Grimm, No. 129, *ibid.*, 45–58.   Bolte and Polívka are of the opinion that Grimm, Nos. 71, 124, and 129, are all related (3 : 45).

A New-Mexican Spanish variant of Grimm, No. 129 (JAFL 24 : 411–414), tells of three brothers sent out to learn trades.   One becomes a carpenter; another, a silversmith; and the third, a thief.   They are tested by the king, who is satisfied that they have learned their trades well.   A Negro version from the Bahamas (MAFLS 13 : 43–44, No. 23) tells of four brothers who went out and became skilled (tailor, robber, thief, archer).   Skill-test with egg (stealing from nest, shooting it into four parts, stitching egg together, replacing under bird). Rescue of princess stolen by dragon (stitching planks of shattered ship together).

Very close to the Bahamas tale, except in the *dénouement*, is a Sinhalese story (Parker, 2 : 33 ff., No. 82).   Four princes set out to learn sciences: the first learns sooth; the second, theft; the third, archery; the fourth, carpentry.   They are tested by their father the king (stealing egg from crow, cutting it with arrow, repairing it, and restoring it to nest).   They then search for and bring back the queen, who had been stolen by a Rākshasa.   They then quarrel as to who should have the sovereignty.   In variant *a* (*ibid.*, 36–39) a nobleman's five sons learn sciences (soothsayer, marksman, thief, runner, physician) and jointly restore a dead princess to life.   In variant *b* (39–42) seven princes become skilled.   In variant *c* four Brahmans learn sciences to win the hand of a princess, and afterwards restore her to life.   As they cannot settle their quarrel, they all give her up.   (For other versions, see Parker, 2 : 43–45, 157–159 [No. 109]).

Page 136, line 31.   For "Tagić" read "Jagić."

13.

In a Oaxaca story (Radin-Espinosa, 249–250, No. 137) a rich compadre tries with no success to advance the fortunes of his poor compadre, and comes to the conclusion that he who is born to be poor will always be poor.

14 *b.*

A Oaxaca version of "The Thief and his Master," with the transformation-combat detail, is given in Radin-Espinosa, 240 (No. 131). An analogous story has also been recorded by F. Boas at Zuñi.

Three Sinhalese versions of "The Magician and his Pupil" may be found in Parker, 3 : 400–407 (No. 266). Many other Oriental variants are given in abstract in the notes to these stories (*ibid.*, 408–410).

15.

In JAFL 31 : 480–481 is given a Guatemala droll which is clearly derived from the Arabian Nights form of our story.

For additional bibliography of the tricky thief who pretends he had been transformed into the ass which he has just stolen from the simple peasant, see Bolte-Polívka, 3 : 9. Related to this motif are two Oriental tales given in abstract by Parker (3 : 205–206).

17.

Page 161. Identical with our first task is one found in a Oaxaca version (Radin-Espinosa, 223, No. 112). No. 109 in this same collection is a variant of "John the Bear." An excellent New-Mexican Spanish version of "John the Bear" is given by Espinosa (JAFL 24 : 437–444). (For American Indian versions of this cycle, see Thompson, 336–344.)

Page 165. For comparative bibliography of the "Forgotten Betrothed" cycle, see Bolte-Polívka, 2 : 516–527 (on Grimm, No. 113); for American versions of the tasks and magic flight, MAFLS 13 : 54 n^2; and for American Indian versions of this cycle as a whole, Thompson, 370–381. In only four of the twenty Indian stories analyzed, however, does the incident of the forgetting of his fiancée by the hero occur.

The first part of the "Forgotten Betrothed" cycle is found in an Araucano story (Saunière, No. 9), in which the hero takes service with a supernatural being, falls in love with his daughter, performs two difficult tasks and answers three questions, and flees with her in a transformation-flight that ends with the death of the pursuer.

In a Negro story from Bahamas (MAFLS 13 : No. 27) are found the tasks, magic-flight, and forgotten-betrothed elements.

18.

Our story is closely related to Grimm, No. 82 *a* (see Bolte-Polívka, 2 : 190–196, for text), a story derived from Musäus.   Grimm, No. 197 (Bolte-Polívka, 3 : 424–443), is also related.   Thompson (410) cites a Micmac version that agrees with ours in its main outlines,—a version which he believes goes back to a French original.   A very brief Kutenai version is given in Boas, "Kutenai Tales" (Bulletin 59, Bureau of American Ethnology), p. 34.

19.

See Bolte-Polívka's notes on Grimm, No. 108 (2 : 234 ff.).

20.

Page 196.   The following American Indian variants of motifs found in our stories are analyzed by Thompson (419–426) : —

Fatal imitation (G^1): Maliseet (wife), Ojibwa, Dakota, Zuñi.

Substitute for execution (H): Maliseet, Ojibwa, Wyandot, Thompson River, Dakota, Tepecano, Creek, Yuchi, Jicarilla Apache, Pochulta, Chalina, Aztec, Tuxtepec.

Marine cattle (J): Micmac, Maliseet, Ojibwa, Thompson River, Dakota, Tepecano.

Frightening robbers under tree (F^5): Micmac, Maliseet, Wyandot, Ojibwa (for Ojibwa see also Laidlaw, 196).

For a Negro (Bahamas) variant of G^1, see MAFLS 13, No. 41; of F^5, *ibid.*, No. 46.   In a Oaxaca story, "Los Dos Compadres" (Radin-Espinosa, 198–199, No. 101), one compadre frightens a band of robbers unwittingly and acquires treasure (*sale-of-ashes* incident).   Then follows the incident of the borrowed measure returned with coins adhering, whereupon the rich compadre tries to "sell ashes," and is killed by the robbers.   For bibliography of the motif *coins sticking to borrowed measure*, see Bolte-Polívka, 1 : 520; 2 : 6; 3 : 143 *n*.

The incident of *frightening robbers under tree* appears to be characteristic of the Pedro di Urdemales group (see JAFL 27 : 119–134, especially 125, 133).   For the *sack-by-sea* episode in the same story, see *ibid.*, 134.

To Bolte-Polívka's bibliography of Grimm, No. 61, should be added a Sinhalese version (Parker, 2 : 116–119, No. 101), which contains the rejuvenating-cudgel, sack-by-sea, and marine-cattle motifs.

21.

Page 206.   In a Oaxaca story (Radin-Espinosa, 246, No. 134) closely related to our No. 21, a king sentences a gentleman to death for having said, "El que tiene dinero hace lo que quiere."   This sentiment is almost identical with that found in the Sicilian story by Pitrè. In both, too, the device by means of which the hero discovers the hidden princess is a golden eagle which gives forth beautiful music.

In a New-Mexican Spanish version (JAFL 27 : 135-137) the hero gains access to the princess by means of a bronze eagle.

23.

Page 213. In a New-Mexican Spanish story (JAFL 27 : 128) one of the adventures of Pedro di Urdemales is to make a pact with the Devil in return for much money. In hell he wins his freedom by sticking the demons to their chairs with varnish and then frightening them with a cross. This version seems nearly related to our story. In a Tepecano tale of the same hero (*ibid.*, 171) Pedro frightens and beats devils with a holy palm-leaf.

24.

Page 221. Add to Benfey's Oriental versions a Sinhalese story by Parker (2 : 288-291, No. 141). Parker analyzes three other Hindoo variants which should be noted.

Page 222. Parker, No. 252 (3 : 339-341), "How Mārayā was put in the Bottle," is a close variant of Grimm, No. 44. Death is finally outwitted by the hero, who persuades him to creep into a bottle to demonstrate that he had been able to enter a closed room through a keyhole. Thereafter all the hero has to do to cure a sick person is to place the bottle at his head! This detail of enclosing a demon in a bottle is found in Caballero's story.

In another Sinhalese story (Parker, 3 : 185-186, No. 222) a water-snake, pleased by a beggar's actions, promises to make him rich by creeping up the trunk of the king's tusk elephant and making the animal mad. The beggar "cures" the elephant when he tells the snake to leave, and becomes wealthy.

27.

Thompson (413-414) cites two American Indian stories, Penobscot and Maliseet, which open with the obtaining of a gold-dropping horse from an old man because of kindness, the loss of it at an inn at the hands of a rascally landlord, and the recovery of the animal through the generous use of a magic cudgel. The remainder of the two stories is connected with the last part of the "Golden Goose" cycle (Grimm, No. 64).

Page 237. To the East Indian variants of this story add Parker, No. 97 (2 : 101-104), in which an indigent man who frightens a Yakā obtains from the demon a magic self-filling plate, a ring which when sold will always return to its owner, and a gold-dropping cow. These are stolen from him on successive days by a Hettiyā, and worthless imitations substituted. Then the Yakā gives the hero a magic cudgel, with which he regains his magic articles. (See Parker, *ibid.*, 104–105, for other Oriental versions.)

29.

Page 247. A Sinhalese story, "The Mouse Maiden" (Parker, I : 308 f., No. 54), tells of a princess in the form of a mouse who was married to a prince. Her permanent disenchantment is brought about by the burning of her mouse-jacket. Similarly in No. 223 (Parker, 3 : 187–188) the youngest of seven princes is married to a female hare, which is permanently disenchanted when her husband burns her hare-skin. This story and another cited by Parker, in which the youngest of seven princes married a female monkey who in the end proved to be a fairy and took off her monkey-skin (Chilli: Folk Tales of Hindustan, 54), appear to be related to the Indian *Märchen* cited by Benfey (1 : 251).

For other tales of animal-marriages with transformation, see Parker, Nos. 151, 207 (turtle), No. 163 (snake), No. 164 (lizard), No. 165 (frog); without transformation, No. 158 (bear), No. 159 (leopard).

30.

A Sinhalese variant of the "Chastity-Wager" story is Parker, No. 149 (2 : 334–336).

33.

In a French-Canadian version (JAFL 32 : 161–163), while a jealous hunchback is away from home, three other hunchbacks (unrelated to the husband) apply to the wife for food. While they are eating, she sees her husband returning. She hides her three guests in a chest, where they are smothered. The remainder of the story is regular.

35.

Page 278. Our story appears to be related to some of the variants of Grimm, No. 22, though there is little resemblance between it and the German story itself. Compare, however, an Ojibwa tale (JAFL 29 : 337), in which a princess is offered in marriage to whoever can propose a riddle she cannot solve (in our story it is the hero who must give the answer to the princess's riddle). On his way to court, the hero receives magic objects. He successfully outriddles his opponent, but is put in prison. He wins release and the princess's hand by means of the magic objects. (See Thompson, 415–416.)

36.

Page 283. A New-Mexican Spanish variant of "Juan Tiñoso" (JAFL 24 : 403–408) combines features from "John the Bear."

Page 284. The "Iron Hans" cycle (Grimm, No. 136) Bolte and Polívka (3 : 97) outline as follows:—

(A¹) A prince sets free a wild man, Iron Hans, whom his father has captured; (A²) the prince flees from the machinations of his hostile or wanton stepmother; (A³) the wild man bestows on a childless couple a son, who, however, after a definite term, must be surrendered to him.

(B) While with Iron Hans, whose orders he disobeys, the boy acquires golden hair, and (B¹) is either forgiven and restored to favor, or (B²) escapes on a talking horse.

(C) After covering his gold hair with a hat or cloth, he takes service as a gardener at a king's palace, where the princess falls in love with him.

(D) At a tournament he appears three times on a magnificent horse that Iron Hans has furnished him with, and he gains the hand of the king's daughter.

(E) He manifests his nobility as victor in a combat, as a dragon-killer, as a bringer of a cure for the sick king (cf. No. 97), or on a hunt, where he disgraces his mocking brothers-in-law.

(F) Iron Hans or the helpful horse is disenchanted.

For American Indian variants of the "Iron Hans" cycle, see Thompson, 350–357.

Page 284, line 3. For *throwing of apples to intended husbands*, see Bolte-Polívka, 2 : 381; 3 : 111.

Line 16. For the *branding of the brothers-in-law*, see Grimm, Nos. 59, 91, 97; also Bolte-Polívka, 3 : 114 (note 1).

Juan Tiñoso means John the Scabby. Two French versions have exactly the same title, "Jean le Teignous" and "Jean le Tigneux" (Bolte-Polívka, 3 : 99). A somewhat distant Sinhalese relative of "Juan Tiñoso," in which the hero is a turtle, is Parker, No. 151 (2 : 345–352).

In an Osage Indian story occurs the release of an imprisoned monster by a boy (Thompson, 331).

38.

Page 288. For bibliography of the question "How much is the king worth?" see Bolte-Polívka, 3 : 232. The Negrito's counter-demand to the king's third task (i.e., drink all the fresh water) is identical with the counter-demand to the task of counting the drops in the sea (*ibid.*, 3 : 231).

Page 291. Bolte and Polívka (3 : 214) emphasize the fact of the mutual borrowing of incidents by this cycle and the "Clever Lass" cycle.

Two Sinhalese stories not unlike our No. 38 are given by Parker,—

"The Three Questions" (1 : 150–152), "The Four Difficult Questions" (153–154).

40.

Page 299, "Pitong." In a Oaxaca story (Radin-Espinosa, 204, No. 104) occur the abandoned-children opening, corn-trail, fruit-trail, ogre's house, advice of rat, ogre pushed in oven. A Chile version of "Le Petit Poucet" is "Piñoncito" (Saunière, 262). The following American Indian versions are noticed by Thompson (361–365): Thompson River (3), Shuswap (2), Ojibwa, Maliseet, Ponka, Bellacoola, Mewan, Uintah Ute.

45.

For a Negro (Bahamas) version of "Cinderella," see MAFLS 13, No. 17; for American Indian versions, Thompson, 384–385.

47.

Compare a Negro story from the Bahamas (MAFLS 13, No. 14); also a Sinhalese tale, "The Roll of Cotton" (Parker, 1 : 364–366, No. 69), in which the two women are sisters.

48.

Two Hindoo (Sinhalese) versions of the "Puss-in-Boots" cycle are Parker, No. 49 (1 : 278–283) and No. 235 (3 : 243–248). These are of extreme importance in trying to establish the provenience of our stories: for in both the helpful animal is a *monkey;* both contain the incident of the borrowed measure, the incident of the killing of the demon by the monkey (obscure but unmistakable in No. 49) and the claiming of the monster's palace as his master's; in both the monkey marries his master to a king's daughter. These two stories differ from ours in the conclusion: the master proves ungrateful, and the faithful monkey runs off into the forest. Again, too, in the opening, these two Sinhalese stories differ from ours: the monkey's gratitude is not motivated; the animal is not a thieving animal, hence there is no tar-baby device.

Page 336, *Tar-Baby.* For the distribution of the "Tar-Baby" story among the American Indians, see Boas (JAFL 25 : 249), supplemented by Thompson (444–446). For Negro versions, see MAFLS 13 : Nos. 10, 11, 12; JAFL 30 : 171, 222; Thompson, 440. Other American versions are Mexico (JAFL 29 : 549); Guatemala (JAFL 31 : 472 f.); Oaxaca (Radin-Espinosa, 120–121, 183, 197; JAFL 25 : 200, 201, 235–236).

49.

In a Sinhalese noodle-story the foolish hero joins a band of thieves and tries to steal a millstone, wakening the owner of the house and asking him for assistance (Parker, 2 : 70–75, No. 90). In another tale in the same collection, No. 57 (1 : 317–318), a gang of robbers steal a devil-dancer's box. While they are sleeping, one of their number, a fool, puts on the costume. They awake, think he is the Devil, and flee, the fool pursuing and calling, "Stay there! stay there!" This story is like our "Juan and the Robbers" (348–349). Compare also the story cited by Parker on p. 318.

50.

Since writing the notes to No. 50, I have found a Sinhalese version of the "Hat-pays-landlord" story which is essentially the same as ours, only a three-cornered hat, not a painted one, is the hoax. The motive of the hero's trick is his desire for revenge on three sharpers who have cozened him out of a bull which they pretend is a goat (Parker, 3 : 200–205, No. 226). For this last situation, compare our No. 15 and notes.

53.

In the Sinhalese "Story of the Bitch" (Parker, 3 : 102–104, No. 201) a bitch gives birth to two princesses, who marry princes. Later the elder daughter drives her dog-mother away when it seeks to visit her, but the younger treats it kindly. The elder daughter is killed by a cobra-bite because of her avariciousness. This version is nearly related to Miss Frere's old Deccan story.

54.

In the latter part of a long Sinhalese story (Parker, No. 145) a king conceives a passion for the hero's wife, and resorts to the same ruse as the wicked datu in our story, — underground tunnel, and letter to parents in the underworld. The hero escapes by means of a cross-tunnel, returns with marvellous raiment (provided by heroine) and news that the king's father and mother are happy. The avaricious king makes the same trip, and is destroyed. Parker, No. 146 (2 : 313–314), contains almost the identical situation.

55.

Page 371 (E). Probably the earliest literary version of the *drowning-turtle* motif (undoubtedly the prototype of the *brier-patch punishment*) is Buddhistic: Jātaka, No. 543. This motif occurs in a Sinhalese story otherwise wholly unrelated to the cycle of which this punishment is usually a part (Parker, No. 150, 2 : 339–340; see also 343–344).

For additional bibliography of the *brier-patch punishment*, in many of the American Indian versions of which the turtle or tortoise is substituted for the rabbit, see Thompson, 446–447; JAFL 31 : 229 (note). Thompson (440) also lists some American Negro variants.

Page 372. With Jātaka, No. 273, compare a Negro story from the Bahamas (MAFLS 13 : 92, No. 45, II). Skinner (JAFL 32 : 295–297) gives an Ojibwa story in which occurs the "drowning" of the turtle and the biting-off of otter's testicles by the turtle. This second detail appears reminiscent of the turtle's revenge discussed on our pp. 372–373.

56.

Page 379. Some American versions of the *house-answering-owner* episode are the following: Oaxaca (Radin-Espinosa, 184–185; 194, rabbit and coyote; JAFL 25 : 208, rabbit and crocodile); Chile (JAFL 25 : 248, a curious modification of the motif); Mexico (JAFL 29 : 552). In another Mexican story we find the episode of the rabbit crossing the river on the crocodile's back (JAFL 29 : 551–552).

In a Sinhalese story of "The Crocodile and the Jackal" (Parker, I : 380–381, No. 75), the crocodile shams dead. Jackal says, "In our country dead crocodiles wag their tails." (This appears to me a variant of the *house-answering-owner* motif.) Later follows the incident of the seizure of the foot of the jackal, who pretends crocodile has hold of a root. (See also Parker, No. 36 [I : 235 f.] for deceptions turtle practises on jackal.)

57.

Page 381. A Oaxaca story (Radin-Espinosa, 190, No. 94) combines an account of a war between the animals and the winged creatures (animals defeated) with a race between the lion and the cricket.

59.

American versions of the *let-me-take-your-place* motif are numerous: Oaxaca (Radin-Espinosa, 121, 153, 183, 185, 197; JAFL 25 : 201, 236); Mexico (JAFL 29 : 550); Tepecano (JAFL 27 : 152); Negro (JAFL 32 : 400, 402; MAFLS 13 : Nos. 12, 33, 39).

60.

The following American forms of the accumulative story may be noted: Guatemala (JAFL 31 : 482–483); Mexico (JAFL 25 : 219 f.); Oaxaca (Radin-Espinosa, 195, No. 99); New-Mexican Spanish (JAFL 27 : 138); Tepecano (JAFL 27 : 175). See also Thompson, 453–454. The stories resemble ours only in general method, not at all in detail. For discussion and abstracts of some South American variants that are closer to our form than are those of Central and North America, see Boas (JAFL 25 : 352–353 and notes).

A curious Sinhalese accumulative story, No. 251 in Parker's collection (3 : 336–338), tells how, when some robbers were apprehended for digging into the king's palace and were sentenced, they replied that the mason who made the walls was at fault, not they. The mason accused his lime-mixer; the lime-mixer, a beautiful woman for having distracted his attention; the woman, a goldsmith. The goldsmith is condemned, but by a ruse succeeds in getting a wholly innocent fat-bellied Mohammedan trader executed in his place. Parker abstracts a similar story from southern India (p. 338). (See also his No. 28 [1 : 201–205] for another kind of "clock-story" nearer the type of "The Old Woman and her Pig.")

61.

Page 392. Parker's No. 107 (2 : 146–149) is an elaboration of Jātaka, No. 374. (For other Oriental variants of this theme, see *ibid.*, 149–150.)

71.

For a Negro version of a *flight-contest* (not etiological) between a crow and a pigeon, see MAFLS 13 : No. 53.

79.

The Upper Thompson Indians have a story of how the raven and the crow were sent out after the Flood to find land. They did not return, but fed on the corpses of the drowned people. For this reason they were transformed into birds of black color, where formerly they were white-skinned (JAFL 29 : 329).

82.

For bibliography of the *relay-race* motif among the American Indians see Boas (JAFL 25 : 249; Thompson, 448–449). Thompson cites fourteen American Indian versions, in all but two of which the winner is the turtle. In one, the clever animal is a gopher; in the other, a frog. For American Negro variants, see Thompson, 441; JAFL 31 : 221 (note 2); JAFL 32 : 394. In a Negro version from Bahamas (MAFLS 13 : No. 54), horse and conch race; horse is defeated, and kicks the little conches to death (cf. the ending of our No. 82). For a Mexican version (rabbit and toad) see JAFL 25 : 214–215; for Oaxaca (toad and deer), Radin-Espinosa, 193.

In an Araucano story (Saunière, No. XI) the race between the fox and the crawfish does not assume the relay form.

INDEX.

Crocodile threatens to eat monkey's liver and kidneys, 375, 377.

Cross, priest orders doors to be marked with, 344.
gown decorated with, 211–213.
used to frighten demons, 212, 213, 439.

Crow chases *kasaykasay*, 391.
eats carrion and is cursed, 424, 445.
flatters jackal, 396.
is black, why, 408, 410, 420–425.
is obliged to hop, 423, 424.
lends necklace to hen, 415.
loses meat, 392.

Crumb-trail, 300.

Cudgel, magic punishing, 236, 439.
— rejuvenating, 438.

"Cukasaptati," 221.

Culing challenges quail to flying-contest, 407.

Cure, marvellous, motif of, 320.

Curse, baffled magician pronounces, on daughter, 170.
of God changes boy to monkey, 413.
— — — clay mould into monkey, 413.

Cutting hair of running man, 127.

Cuttle-fish condemned to carry pouch of mud, 420.

"Cymbeline," 257.

Dähnhardt, O., 87, 337, 373, 379, 401, 404, 410, 414, 424, 425.

Dancing as medical treatment and punishment, 14.
in thorns, 240, 242.

Darak defined, 141 (note).

Dasent, G. W., 51, 73.

Datu defined, 1 (note).

Day, L. B., (No. 3) 237, (No. 20) 53, (No. 22) 325.

Dayrell, E., 404, 416.

Deaf man and blind man, 52.

Deafness cured by blow on ear, 52.

Debt, collecting, from fly, pig, and well, 353.

"Decameron" (ii. 9), 256.

Decisions, king's, 35–40.

Deer blames owl, 391.
miraculous black, 296.
races snail, and loses, 429.

Deer's antlers mistaken for tree, 76.

Demon hauled up from pit, 221.
sealed up in bottle, 439.

"Demon's Mother-in-law," story of, outlined, 219–220.

Demons, cross used to frighten, 212, 213, 439.
king of, 306.

Dervish and king, 144 f.

Devil and old woman, story of, 214 f.
as godfather, 213.
as suitor, 214.
beaten with holy palm-leaf, 439.
buried in large jar, 215.
compact between hero and, 208, 210, 439.
dressed in bear-skin, 207.
enters body of princess, 216.
exchanges clothes with hero, 208.
frightened by sight of crosses, 212, 439. See *Demons*.
son sold to, for money, 213.
tied in rocking-chair, 212, 439.
— with holy belt, 215.
tries to escape through key-hole, 220.

Dick Whittington type, 360.

Dining with king, hero fulfils prophecy by, 277.

Fleece of gold, hero conceals himself in, 206.

Flight, magic, 163, 168, 279–281, 437.

Flight-contest, 407–410, 445.

Flood stories, 421 f., 445.

Flowers, freshness of, indication of chastity, 254.

Fly, meat sold to, 353.
on face, killing, 77, 78, 381, 389.

Food eaten demanded back, 36.
poisoned, 357.
supplied from magic vessel, 177.

Fool buries live mother, 340.
buys crabs and sends them home on foot, 341–342, 349.
destroys singing rice-pot, 341.
frightens man under tree and secures bag of money, 342.
is frightened while robbing house, 342.
joins robber band, 340.
makes holes in bottom of pots to carry them more easily, 341.
thinks himself dead, 340, 348.

Forbidden fruit eaten of, 402.

Forgotten Betrothed cycle analyzed, 165, 168, 437.

Forks. See *Tasks.*

Forty Vezirs, 221.

Fox, 377.
and Crow, 396.
as helpful animal, 335–336, 337.

Frere, M., (No. 2) 362, (No. 12) 237, (No. 18) 52, 53.

"Frere and the Boye," 241.

Friendly animals: ants and birds, 320.

Frightening robbers under tree, 187, 189, 195, 342, 350, 438.

Frog, bird brings suit against, 385 f., 389.
brings suit against turtle, 385 f.

Frog croaks at night, why, 385.

Frogs brought to trial for laughing at snails, 387.

Fruit blames mongoose, 391.

Fruit-trail, 442.

Fruits produce horns, 12.
remove horns, 12.

Gallows, hero saved from, 241–243.

Game, Tagalog boys', 95 (note).

"Gamelyn, Tale of," 26.

Garment, piece of, given as token, 159–160.

Garments decorated with crosses to frighten devils, 211–213.

Gate, iron, demanded by hero for killing his dog, 262.

Gazelle as helpful animal, 336.

Gerould, G. H., 128, 285.

"Gesta Romanorum," 17, (LXXI) 53, 269.

Ghost appears to prince in dream, 304.

Giant as godfather, 281.
devours food of hero, 20.
man-eating, slain, 28, 31.
seven-headed, 28.
two-headed, frightened by blind man and lame man, 43.
— — by hunchback's gun, rope, duck, 47.

Ginger, turtle and lizard steal, 384.

Glass, magic, 79 ff.

Glass-maker, eldest of three brothers becomes expert, 117.

Goat as messenger, 196.
deceitful, 236.
money-producing, 29, 233, 235.

God and the fish, 419–420.
as benefactor, 237.
disguises himself to aid hero, 276.

[1] The numbers in parentheses refer to the tales as numbered in Bolte-Polívka.

Also from Benediction Books ...
Wandering Between Two Worlds: Essays on Faith and Art
Anita Mathias
Benediction Books, 2007
152 pages
ISBN: 0955373700

Available from www.amazon.com, www.amazon.co.uk

In these wide-ranging lyrical essays, Anita Mathias writes, in lush, lovely prose, of her naughty Catholic childhood in Jamshedpur, India; her large, eccentric family in Mangalore, a sea-coast town converted by the Portuguese in the sixteenth century; her rebellion and atheism as a teenager in her Himalayan boarding school, run by German missionary nuns, St. Mary's Convent, Nainital; and her abrupt religious conversion after which she entered Mother Teresa's convent in Calcutta as a novice. Later rich, elegant essays explore the dualities of her life as a writer, mother, and Christian in the United States-- Domesticity and Art, Writing and Prayer, and the experience of being "an alien and stranger" as an immigrant in America, sensing the need for roots.

About the Author

Anita Mathias is the author of *Wandering Between Two Worlds: Essays on Faith and Art.* She has a B.A. and M.A. in English from Somerville College, Oxford University, and an M.A. in Creative Writing from the Ohio State University, USA. Anita won a National Endowment of the Arts fellowship in Creative Nonfiction in 1997. She lives in Oxford, England with her husband, Roy, and her daughters, Zoe and Irene.

Visit Anita at
    http://www.anitamathias.com, and
Anita's blog Dreaming Beneath the Spires at:
    http://theoxfordchristian.blogspot.com, and
Anita's Read Through the Bible blog at:
    http://readthroughthebiblewithanita.blogspot.com/

The Church That Had Too Much
Anita Mathias
Benediction Books, 2010
52 pages
ISBN: 9781849026567

Available from www.amazon.com, www.amazon.co.uk

The Church That Had Too Much was very well-intentioned. She
wanted to love God, she wanted to love people, but she was both
hampered by her muchness and the abundance of her possessions, and beset by ambition, power struggles and snobbery.
Read about the surprising way The Church That Had Too Much
began to resolve her problems in this deceptively simple and
enchanting fable.

About the Author

Anita Mathias is the author of *Wandering Between Two Worlds:
Essays on Faith and Art.* She has a B.A. and M.A. in English
from Somerville College, Oxford University, and an M.A. in
Creative Writing from the Ohio State University, USA. Anita
won a National Endowment of the Arts fellowship in Creative
Nonfiction in 1997. She lives in Oxford, England with her husband, Roy, and her daughters, Zoe and Irene.

Visit Anita at
    http://www.anitamathias.com, and
Anita's blog Dreaming Beneath the Spires at:
    http://theoxfordchristian.blogspot.com, and
Anita's Read Through the Bible blog at:
    http://readthroughthebiblewithanita.blogspot.com/

www.ingramcontent.com/pod-product-compliance
Lightning Source LLC
Chambersburg PA
CBHW030924020726
47498CB00001B/107